BEST SHORT STORIES OF

ALGERNON BLACKWOOD

Best Short Stories of Algernon Blackwood
By Algernon Blackwood

Print ISBN 13: 978-1-4209-6511-7
eBook ISBN 13: 978-1-4209-6512-4

Cover Image: a detail of "Going Home by Moonlight", by John Atkinson Grimshaw (1836-93), c. 19th century / Photo © Christie's Images / Bridgeman Images.

Please visit *www.digireads.com*

CONTENTS

The Empty House

Certain houses, like certain persons, manage somehow to proclaim at once their character for evil. In the case of the latter, no particular feature need betray them; they may boast an open countenance and an ingenuous smile; and yet a little of their company leaves the unalterable conviction that there is something radically amiss with their being: that they are evil. Willy nilly, they seem to communicate an atmosphere of secret and wicked thoughts which makes those in their immediate neighbourhood shrink from them as from a thing diseased.

And, perhaps, with houses the same principle is operative, and it is the aroma of evil deeds committed under a particular roof, long after the actual doers have passed away, that makes the gooseflesh come and the hair rise. Something of the original passion of the evil-doer, and of the horror felt by his victim, enters the heart of the innocent watcher, and he becomes suddenly conscious of tingling nerves, creeping skin, and a chilling of the blood. He is terror-stricken without apparent cause.

There was manifestly nothing in the external appearance of this particular house to bear out the tales of the horror that was said to reign within. It was neither lonely nor unkempt. It stood, crowded into a corner of the square, and looked exactly like the houses on either side of it. It had the same number of windows as its neighbours; the same balcony overlooking the gardens; the same white steps leading up to the heavy black front door; and, in the rear, there was the same narrow strip of green, with neat box borders, running up to the wall that divided it from the backs of the adjoining houses. Apparently, too, the number of chimney pots on the roof was the same; the breadth and angle of the eaves; and even the height of the dirty area railings.

And yet this house in the square, that seemed precisely similar to its fifty ugly neighbours, was as a matter of fact entirely different— horribly different.

Wherein lay this marked, invisible difference is impossible to say. It cannot be ascribed wholly to the imagination, because persons who had spent some time in the house, knowing nothing of the facts, had declared positively that certain rooms were so disagreeable they would rather die than enter them again, and that the atmosphere of the whole house produced in them symptoms of a genuine terror; while the series of innocent tenants who had tried to live in it and been forced to decamp at the shortest possible notice, was indeed little less than a scandal in the town.

When Shorthouse arrived to pay a "week-end" visit to his Aunt Julia in her little house on the sea-front at the other end of the town, he found her charged to the brim with mystery and excitement. He had only received her telegram that morning, and he had come anticipating boredom; but the moment he touched her hand and kissed her apple-skin wrinkled cheek, he caught the first wave of her electrical condition. The impression deepened when he learned that there were to be no other visitors, and that he had been telegraphed for with a very special object.

Something was in the wind, and the "something" would doubtless bear fruit; for this elderly spinster aunt, with a mania for psychical research, had brains as well as will power, and by hook or by crook she usually managed to accomplish her ends. The revelation was made soon after tea, when she sidled close up to him as they paced slowly along the sea-front in the dusk.

"I've got the keys," she announced in a delighted, yet half awesome voice. "Got them till Monday!"

"The keys of the bathing-machine, or—?" he asked innocently, looking from the sea to the town. Nothing brought her so quickly to the point as feigning stupidity.

"Neither," she whispered. "I've got the keys of the haunted house in the square—and I'm going there to-night."

Shorthouse was conscious of the slightest possible tremor down his back. He dropped his teasing tone. Something in her voice and manner thrilled him. She was in earnest.

"But you can't go alone—" he began.

"That's why I wired for you," she said with decision.

He turned to look at her. The ugly, lined, enigmatical face was alive with excitement. There was the glow of genuine enthusiasm round it like a halo. The eyes shone. He caught another wave of her excitement, and a second tremor, more marked than the first, accompanied it.

"Thanks, Aunt Julia," he said politely; "thanks awfully."

"I should not dare to go quite alone," she went on, raising her voice; "but with you I should enjoy it immensely. You're afraid of nothing, I know."

"Thanks *so* much," he said again. "Er—is anything likely to happen?"

"A great deal has happened," she whispered, "though it's been most cleverly hushed up. Three tenants have come and gone in the last few months, and the house is said to be empty for good now."

In spite of himself Shorthouse became interested. His aunt was so very much in earnest.

"The house is very old indeed," she went on, "and the story—an unpleasant one—dates a long way back. It has to do with a murder committed by a jealous stableman who had some affair with a servant in the house. One night he managed to secrete himself in the cellar, and when everyone was asleep, he crept upstairs to the servants' quarters, chased the girl down to the next landing, and before anyone could come to the rescue threw her bodily over the banisters into the hall below."

"And the stableman—?"

"Was caught, I believe, and hanged for murder; but it all happened a century ago, and I've not been able to get more details of the story."

Shorthouse now felt his interest thoroughly aroused; but, though he was not particularly nervous for himself, he hesitated a little on his aunt's account.

"On one condition," he said at length.

"Nothing will prevent my going," she said firmly; "but I may as well hear your condition."

"That you guarantee your power of self-control if anything really horrible happens. I mean—that you are sure you won't get too frightened."

"Jim," she said scornfully, "I'm not young, I know, nor are my nerves; but *with you* I should be afraid of nothing in the world!"

This, of course, settled it, for Shorthouse had no pretensions to being other than a very ordinary young man, and an appeal to his vanity was irresistible. He agreed to go.

Instinctively, by a sort of sub-conscious preparation, he kept himself and his forces well in hand the whole evening, compelling an accumulative reserve of control by that nameless inward process of gradually putting all the emotions away and turning the key upon them—a process difficult to describe, but wonderfully effective, as all men who have lived through severe trials of the inner man well understand. Later, it stood him in good stead.

But it was not until half-past ten, when they stood in the hall, well in the glare of friendly lamps and still surrounded by comforting human influences, that he had to make the first call upon this store of collected strength. For, once the door was closed, and he saw the deserted silent street stretching away white in the moonlight before them, it came to him clearly that the real test that night would be in dealing with *two fears* instead of one. He would have to carry his aunt's fear as well as his own. And, as he glanced down at her sphinx-like countenance and realised that it might assume no pleasant aspect in a rush of real terror, he felt satisfied with only one thing in the whole adventure—that he had confidence in his own will and power to stand against any shock that might come.

Slowly they walked along the empty streets of the town; a bright autumn moon silvered the roofs, casting deep shadows; there was no breath of wind; and the trees in the formal gardens by the sea-front watched them silently as they passed along. To his aunt's occasional remarks Shorthouse made no reply, realizing that she was simply surrounding herself with mental buffers—saying ordinary things to prevent herself thinking of extra-ordinary things. Few windows showed lights, and from scarcely a single chimney came smoke or sparks.

Shorthouse had already begun to notice everything, even the smallest details. Presently they stopped at the street corner and looked up at the name on the side of the house full in the moonlight, and with one accord, but without remark, turned into the square and crossed over to the side of it that lay in shadow.

"The number of the house is thirteen," whispered a voice at his side; and neither of them made the obvious reference, but passed across the broad sheet of moonlight and began to march up the pavement in silence.

It was about half-way up the square that Shorthouse felt an arm slipped quietly but significantly into his own, and knew then that their adventure had begun in earnest, and that his companion was already yielding imperceptibly to the influences against them. She needed support.

A few minutes later they stopped before a tall, narrow house that rose before them into the night, ugly in shape and painted a dingy white. Shutterless windows, without blinds, stared down upon them, shining here and there in the moonlight. There were weather streaks in the wall and cracks in the paint, and the balcony bulged out from the first floor a little unnaturally. But, beyond this generally forlorn appearance of an unoccupied house, there was nothing at first sight to single out this particular mansion for the evil character it had most certainly acquired.

Taking a look over their shoulders to make sure they had not been followed, they went boldly up the steps and stood against the huge black door that fronted them forbiddingly. But the first wave of nervousness was now upon them, and Shorthouse fumbled a long time with the key before he could fit it into the lock at all. For a moment, if truth were told, they both hoped it would not open, for they were a prey to various unpleasant emotions as they stood there on the threshold of their ghostly adventure. Shorthouse, shuffling with the key and hampered by the steady weight on his arm, certainly felt the solemnity of the moment. It was as if the whole world—for all experience seemed at that instant concentrated in his own consciousness—were listening to the grating noise of that key. A stray puff of wind wandering down the empty street woke a momentary rustling in the trees behind them, but otherwise this rattling of the key was the only sound audible; and at last it turned in the lock and the heavy door swung open and revealed a yawning gulf of darkness beyond.

With a last glance at the moonlit square, they passed quickly in, and the door slammed behind them with a roar that echoed prodigiously through empty halls and passages. But, instantly, with the echoes, another sound made itself heard, and Aunt Julia leaned suddenly so heavily upon him that he had to take a step backwards to save himself from falling.

A man had coughed close beside them—so close that it seemed they must have been actually by his side in the darkness.

With the possibility of practical jokes in his mind, Shorthouse at once swung his heavy stick in the direction of the sound; but it met nothing more solid than air. He heard his aunt give a little gasp beside him.

"There's someone here," she whispered; "I heard him."

"Be quiet!" he said sternly. "It was nothing but the noise of the front door."

"Oh! get a light—quick!" she added, as her nephew, fumbling with a box of matches, opened it upside down and let them all fall with a rattle on to the stone floor.

The sound, however, was not repeated; and there was no evidence of retreating footsteps. In another minute they had a candle burning, using an empty end of a cigar case as a holder; and when the first flare had died down he held the impromptu lamp aloft and surveyed the scene. And it was dreary enough in all conscience, for there is nothing more desolate in all the abodes of men than an unfurnished house dimly lit, silent, and forsaken, and yet tenanted by rumour with the memories of evil and violent histories.

They were standing in a wide hall-way; on their left was the open door of a spacious dining-room, and in front the hall ran, ever narrowing, into a long, dark passage that led apparently to the top of the kitchen stairs. The broad uncarpeted staircase rose in a sweep before them, everywhere draped in shadows, except for a single spot about half-way up where the moonlight came in through the window and fell on a bright patch on the boards. This shaft of light shed a faint radiance above and below it, lending to the objects within its reach a misty outline that was infinitely more suggestive and ghostly than complete darkness. Filtered moonlight always seems to paint faces on the surrounding gloom, and as Shorthouse peered up into the well of darkness and thought of the countless empty rooms and passages in the upper part of the old house, he caught himself longing again for the safety of the moonlit square, or the cosy, bright drawing-room they had left an hour before. Then realizing that these thoughts were dangerous, he thrust them away again and summoned all his energy for concentration on the present.

"Aunt Julia," he said aloud, severely, "we must now go through the house from top to bottom and make a thorough search."

The echoes of his voice died away slowly all over the building, and in the intense silence that followed he turned to look at her. In the candle-light he saw that her face was already ghastly pale; but she dropped his arm for a moment and said in a whisper, stepping close in front of him—

"I agree. We must be sure there's no one hiding. That's the first thing."

She spoke with evident effort, and he looked at her with admiration.

"You feel quite sure of yourself? It's not too late—"

"I think so," she whispered, her eyes shifting nervously toward the shadows behind. "Quite sure, only one thing—"

"What's that?"

"You must never leave me alone for an instant."

"As long as you understand that any sound or appearance must be investigated at once, for to hesitate means to admit fear. That is fatal."

"Agreed," she said, a little shakily, after a moment's hesitation. "I'll try—"

Arm in arm, Shorthouse holding the dripping candle and the stick, while his aunt carried the cloak over her shoulders, figures of utter comedy to all but themselves, they began a systematic search.

Stealthily, walking on tip-toe and shading the candle lest it should betray their presence through the shutterless windows, they went first into the big dining-room. There was not a stick of furniture to be seen. Bare walls, ugly mantel-pieces and empty grates stared at them. Everything, they felt, resented their intrusion, watching them, as it were, with veiled eyes; whispers followed them; shadows flitted noiselessly to right and left; something seemed ever at their back, watching, waiting an opportunity to do them injury. There was the inevitable sense that operations which went on when the room was empty had been temporarily suspended till they were well out of the way again. The whole dark interior of the old building seemed to become a malignant Presence that rose up, warning them to desist and mind their own business; every moment the strain on the nerves increased.

Out of the gloomy dining-room they passed through large folding doors into a sort of library or smoking-room, wrapt equally in silence, darkness, and dust; and from this they regained the hall near the top of the back stairs.

Here a pitch black tunnel opened before them into the lower regions, and—it must be confessed—they hesitated. But only for a minute. With the worst of the night still to come it was essential to turn from nothing. Aunt Julia stumbled at the top step of the dark descent, ill lit by the flickering candle, and even Shorthouse felt at least half the decision go out of his legs.

"Come on!" he said peremptorily, and his voice ran on and lost itself in the dark, empty spaces below.

"I'm coming," she faltered, catching his arm with unnecessary violence.

They went a little unsteadily down the stone steps, a cold, damp air meeting them in the face, close and mal-odorous. The kitchen, into which the stairs led along a narrow passage, was large, with a lofty ceiling. Several doors opened out of it—some into cupboards with empty jars still standing on the shelves, and others into horrible little ghostly back offices, each colder and less inviting than the last. Black beetles scurried over the floor, and once, when they knocked against a deal table standing in a corner, something about the size of a cat jumped down with a rush and fled, scampering across the stone floor into the darkness. Everywhere there was a sense of recent occupation, an impression of sadness and gloom.

Leaving the main kitchen, they next went towards the scullery. The door was standing ajar, and as they pushed it open to its full extent Aunt Julia uttered a piercing scream, which she instantly tried to stifle by placing her hand over her mouth. For a second Shorthouse stood stock-still, catching his breath. He felt as if his spine had suddenly become hollow and someone had filled it with particles of ice.

Facing them, directly in their way between the doorposts, stood the figure of a woman. She had disheveled hair and wildly staring eyes, and her face was terrified and white as death.

She stood there motionless for the space of a single second. Then the candle flickered and she was gone—gone utterly—and the door framed nothing but empty darkness.

"Only the beastly jumping candle-light," he said quickly, in a voice that sounded like someone else's and was only half under control. "Come on, aunt. There's nothing there."

He dragged her forward. With a clattering of feet and a great appearance of boldness they went on, but over his body the skin moved as if crawling ants covered it, and he knew by the weight on his arm that he was supplying the force of locomotion for two. The scullery was cold, bare, and empty; more like a large prison cell than anything else. They went round it, tried the door into the yard, and the windows, but found them all fastened securely. His aunt moved beside him like a person in a dream. Her eyes were tightly shut, and she seemed merely to follow the pressure of his arm. Her courage filled him with amazement. At the same time he noticed that a certain odd change had come over her face, a change which somehow evaded his power of analysis.

"There's nothing here, aunty," he repeated aloud quickly. "Let's go upstairs and see the rest of the house. Then we'll choose a room to wait up in."

She followed him obediently, keeping close to his side, and they locked the kitchen door behind them. It was a relief to get up again. In the hall there was more light than before, for the moon had travelled a little further down the stairs. Cautiously they began to go up into the dark vault of the upper house, the boards creaking under their weight.

On the first floor they found the large double drawing-rooms, a search of which revealed nothing. Here also was no sign of furniture or recent occupancy; nothing but dust and neglect and shadows. They opened the big folding doors between front and back drawing-rooms and then came out again to the landing and went on upstairs.

They had not gone up more than a dozen steps when they both simultaneously stopped to listen, looking into each other's eyes with a new apprehension across the flickering candle flame. From the room they had left hardly ten seconds before came the sound of doors quietly closing. It was beyond all question; they heard the booming noise that accompanies the shutting of heavy doors, followed by the sharp catching of the latch.

"We must go back and see," said Shorthouse briefly, in a low tone, and turning to go downstairs again.

Somehow she managed to drag after him, her feet catching in her dress, her face livid.

When they entered the front drawing-room it was plain that the folding doors had been closed—half a minute before. Without hesitation Shorthouse opened them. He almost expected to see someone facing him in the back room; but only darkness and cold air met him. They went through both rooms, finding nothing unusual. They tried in every way to make the doors close of themselves, but there was not wind enough even to set the candle flame flickering. The doors would not move without strong pressure. All was silent as the grave. Undeniably the rooms were utterly empty, and the house utterly still.

"It's beginning," whispered a voice at his elbow which he hardly recognised as his aunt's.

He nodded acquiescence, taking out his watch to note the time. It was fifteen minutes before midnight; he made the entry of exactly what had occurred in his notebook, setting the candle in its case upon the floor in order to do so. It took a moment or two to balance it safely against the wall.

Aunt Julia always declared that at this moment she was not actually watching him, but had turned her head towards the inner room, where she fancied she heard something moving; but, at any rate, both positively agreed that there came a sound of rushing feet, heavy and very swift—and the next instant the candle was out!

But to Shorthouse himself had come more than this, and he has always thanked his fortunate stars that it came to him alone and not to his aunt too. For, as he rose from the stooping position of balancing the candle, and before it was actually extinguished, a face thrust itself forward so close to his own that he could almost have touched it with his lips. It was a face working with passion; a man's face, dark, with thick features, and angry, savage eyes. It belonged to a common man, and it was evil in its ordinary normal expression, no doubt, but as he saw it, alive with intense, aggressive emotion, it was a malignant and terrible human countenance.

There was no movement of the air; nothing but the sound of rushing feet—stockinged or muffled feet; the apparition of the face; and the almost simultaneous extinguishing of the candle.

In spite of himself, Shorthouse uttered a little cry, nearly losing his balance as his aunt clung to him with her whole weight in one moment of real, uncontrollable terror. She made no sound, but simply seized him bodily. Fortunately, however, she had seen nothing, but had only heard the rushing feet, for her control returned almost at once, and he was able to disentangle himself and strike a match.

The shadows ran away on all sides before the glare, and his aunt stooped down and groped for the cigar case with the precious candle. Then they discovered that the candle had not been *blown* out at all; it had been *crushed* out. The wick was pressed down into the wax, which was flattened as if by some smooth, heavy instrument.

How his companion so quickly overcame her terror, Shorthouse never properly understood; but his admiration for her self-control increased tenfold, and at the same time served to feed his own dying flame—for which he was undeniably grateful. Equally inexplicable to him was the evidence of physical force they had just witnessed. He at once suppressed the memory of stories he had heard of "physical mediums" and their dangerous phenomena; for if these were true, and either his aunt or himself was unwittingly a physical medium, it meant that they were simply aiding to focus the forces of a haunted house already charged to the brim. It was like walking with unprotected lamps among uncovered stores of gunpowder.

So, with as little reflection as possible, he simply relit the candle and went up to the next floor. The arm in his trembled, it is true, and his own tread was often uncertain, but they went on with thoroughness, and after a search revealing nothing they climbed the last flight of stairs to the top floor of all.

Here they found a perfect nest of small servants' rooms, with broken pieces of furniture, dirty cane-bottomed chairs, chests of drawers, cracked mirrors, and decrepit bedsteads. The rooms had low sloping ceilings already hung here and there with cobwebs, small windows, and badly plastered walls—a depressing and dismal region which they were glad to leave behind.

It was on the stroke of midnight when they entered a small room on the third floor, close to the top of the stairs, and arranged to make themselves comfortable for the remainder of their adventure. It was absolutely bare, and was said to be the room—then used as a clothes closet—into which the infuriated groom had chased his victim and finally caught her. Outside, across the narrow landing, began the stairs leading up to the floor above, and the servants' quarters where they had just searched.

In spite of the chilliness of the night there was something in the air of this room that cried for an open window. But there was more than this. Shorthouse could only describe it by saying that he felt less master of himself here than in any other part of the house. There was something that acted directly on the nerves, tiring the resolution, enfeebling the will. He was conscious of this result before he had been in the room five minutes, and it was in the short time they stayed there that he suffered the wholesale depletion of his vital forces, which was, for himself, the chief horror of the whole experience.

They put the candle on the floor of the cupboard, leaving the door a few inches ajar, so that there was no glare to confuse the eyes, and no shadow to shift about on walls and ceiling. Then they spread the cloak on the floor and sat down to wait, with their backs against the wall.

Shorthouse was within two feet of the door on to the landing; his position commanded a good view of the main staircase leading down into the darkness, and also of the beginning of the servants' stairs going to the floor above; the heavy stick lay beside him within easy reach.

The moon was now high above the house. Through the open window they could see the comforting stars like friendly eyes watching in the sky. One by one the clocks of the town struck midnight, and when the sounds died away the deep silence of a windless night fell again over everything. Only the boom of the sea, far away and lugubrious, filled the air with hollow murmurs.

Inside the house the silence became awful; awful, he thought, because any minute now it might be broken by sounds portending terror. The strain of waiting told more and more severely on the nerves; they talked in whispers when they talked at all, for their voices aloud sounded queer and unnatural. A chilliness, not altogether due to the night air, invaded the room, and made them cold. The influences against them, whatever these might be, were slowly robbing them of self-confidence, and the power of decisive action; their forces were on the wane, and the possibility of real fear took on a new and terrible meaning. He began to tremble for the elderly woman by his side, whose pluck could hardly save her beyond a certain extent.

He heard the blood singing in his veins. It sometimes seemed so loud that he fancied it prevented his hearing properly certain other sounds that were beginning very faintly to make themselves audible in the depths of the house. Every time he fastened his attention on these sounds, they instantly ceased. They certainly came no nearer. Yet he could not rid himself of the idea that movement was going on somewhere in the lower regions of the house. The drawing-room floor, where the doors had been so strangely closed, seemed too near; the sounds were further off than that. He thought of the great kitchen, with the scurrying black-beetles, and of the dismal little scullery; but, somehow or other, they did not seem to come from there either. Surely they were not *outside* the house!

Then, suddenly, the truth flashed into his mind, and for the space of a minute he felt as if his blood had stopped flowing and turned to ice.

The sounds were not downstairs at all; they were upstairs—upstairs, somewhere among those horrid gloomy little servants' rooms with their bits of broken furniture, low ceilings, and cramped windows—upstairs where the victim had first been disturbed and stalked to her death.

And the moment he discovered where the sounds were, he began to hear them more clearly. It was the sound of feet, moving stealthily along the passage overhead, in and out among the rooms, and past the furniture.

He turned quickly to steal a glance at the motionless figure seated beside him, to note whether she had shared his discovery. The faint candle-light coming through the crack in the cupboard door, threw her strongly-marked face into vivid relief against the white of the wall. But it was something else that made him catch his breath and stare again. An extraordinary something had come into her face and seemed to spread over her features like a mask; it smoothed out the deep lines and drew the skin everywhere a little tighter so that the wrinkles disappeared; it brought into the face—with the sole exception of the old eyes—an appearance of youth and almost of childhood.

He stared in speechless amazement—amazement that was dangerously near to horror. It was his aunt's face indeed, but it was her face of forty years ago, the vacant innocent face of a girl. He had heard stories of that strange effect of terror which could wipe a human countenance clean of other emotions, obliterating all previous expressions; but he had never realised that it could be literally true, or could mean anything so simply horrible as what he now saw. For the dreadful signature of overmastering fear was written plainly in that utter vacancy of the girlish face beside him; and when, feeling his intense gaze, she turned to look at him, he instinctively closed his eyes tightly to shut out the sight.

Yet, when he turned a minute later, his feelings well in hand, he saw to his intense relief another expression; his aunt was smiling, and though the face was deathly white, the awful veil had lifted and the normal look was returning.

"Anything wrong?" was all he could think of to say at the moment. And the answer was eloquent, coming from such a woman.

"I feel cold—and a little frightened," she whispered.

He offered to close the window, but she seized hold of him and begged him not to leave her side even for an instant.

"It's upstairs, I know," she whispered, with an odd half laugh; "but I can't possibly go up."

But Shorthouse thought otherwise, knowing that in action lay their best hope of self-control.

He took the brandy flask and poured out a glass of neat spirit, stiff enough to help anybody over anything. She swallowed it with a little shiver. His only idea now was to get out of the house before her collapse became inevitable; but this could not safely be done by turning tail and running from the enemy. Inaction was no longer possible; every minute he was growing less master of himself, and desperate, aggressive measures were imperative without further delay. Moreover, the action must be taken *towards* the enemy, not away from it; the climax, if necessary and unavoidable, would have to be faced boldly. He could do it now; but in ten minutes he might not have the force left to act for himself, much less for both!

Upstairs, the sounds were meanwhile becoming louder and closer, accompanied by occasional creaking of the boards. Someone was moving stealthily about, stumbling now and then awkwardly against the furniture.

Waiting a few moments to allow the tremendous dose of spirits to produce its effect, and knowing this would last but a short time under the circumstances, Shorthouse then quietly got on his feet, saying in a determined voice—

"Now, Aunt Julia, we'll go upstairs and find out what all this noise is about. You must come too. It's what we agreed."

He picked up his stick and went to the cupboard for the candle. A limp form rose shakily beside him breathing hard, and he heard a voice say very faintly something about being "ready to come." The woman's courage amazed him; it was so much greater than his own; and, as they advanced, holding aloft the dripping candle, some subtle force exhaled from this trembling, white-faced old woman at his side that was the true source of his inspiration. It held something really great that shamed him and gave him the support without which he would have proved far less equal to the occasion.

They crossed the dark landing, avoiding with their eyes the deep black space over the banisters. Then they began to mount the narrow staircase to meet the sounds which, minute by minute, grew louder and nearer. About half-way up the stairs Aunt Julia stumbled and Shorthouse turned to catch her by the arm, and just at that moment there came a terrific crash in the servants' corridor overhead. It was instantly followed by a shrill, agonized scream that was a cry of terror and a cry for help melted into one.

Before they could move aside, or go down a single step, someone came rushing along the passage overhead, blundering horribly, racing madly, at full speed, three steps at a time, down the very staircase where they stood. The steps were light and uncertain; but close behind them sounded the heavier tread of another person, and the staircase seemed to shake.

Shorthouse and his companion just had time to flatten themselves against the wall when the jumble of flying steps was upon them, and two persons, with the slightest possible interval between them, dashed past at full speed. It was a perfect whirlwind of sound breaking in upon the midnight silence of the empty building.

The two runners, pursuer and pursued, had passed clean through them where they stood, and already with a thud the boards below had received first one, then the other. Yet they had seen absolutely nothing—not a hand, or arm, or face, or even a shred of flying clothing.

There came a second's pause. Then the first one, the lighter of the two, obviously the pursued one, ran with uncertain footsteps into the little room which Shorthouse and his aunt had just left. The heavier one followed. There was a sound of scuffling, gasping, and smothered screaming; and then out on to the landing came the step—of a single person *treading weightily*.

A dead silence followed for the space of half a minute, and then was heard a rushing sound through the air. It was followed by a dull, crashing thud in the depths of the house below—on the stone floor of the hall.

Utter silence reigned after. Nothing moved. The flame of the candle was steady. It had been steady the whole time, and the air had been undisturbed by any movement whatsoever. Palsied with terror, Aunt Julia, without waiting for her companion, began fumbling her way downstairs; she was crying gently to herself, and when Shorthouse put his arm round her and half carried her he felt that she was trembling like a leaf. He went into the little room and picked up the cloak from the floor, and, arm in arm, walking very slowly, without speaking a word or looking once behind them, they marched down the three flights into the hall.

In the hall they saw nothing, but the whole way down the stairs they were conscious that someone followed them; step by step; when they went faster IT was left behind, and when they went more slowly IT caught them up. But never once did they look behind to see; and at each turning of the staircase they lowered their eyes for fear of the following horror they might see upon the stairs above.

With trembling hands Shorthouse opened the front door, and they walked out into the moonlight and drew a deep breath of the cool night air blowing in from the sea.

Keeping His Promise

It was eleven o'clock at night, and young Marriott was locked into his room, cramming as hard as he could cram. He was a "Fourth Year Man" at Edinburgh University and he had been ploughed for this particular examination so often that his parents had positively declared they could no longer supply the funds to keep him there.

His rooms were cheap and dingy, but it was the lecture fees that took the money. So Marriott pulled himself together at last and definitely made up his mind that he would pass or die in the attempt, and for some weeks now he had been reading as hard as mortal man can read. He was trying to make up for lost time and money in a way that showed conclusively he did not understand the value of either. For no ordinary man—and Marriott was in every sense an ordinary man— can afford to drive the mind as he had lately been driving his, without sooner or later paying the cost.

Among the students he had few friends or acquaintances, and these few had promised not to disturb him at night, knowing he was at last reading in earnest. It was, therefore, with feelings a good deal stronger than mere surprise that he heard his door-bell ring on this particular night and realised that he was to have a visitor. Some men would simply have muffled the bell and gone on quietly with their work. But Marriott was not this sort. He was nervous. It would have bothered and pecked at his mind all night long not to know who the visitor was and what he wanted. The only thing to do, therefore, was to let him in—and out again—as quickly as possible.

The landlady went to bed at ten o'clock punctually, after which hour nothing would induce her to pretend she heard the bell, so Marriott jumped up from his books with an exclamation that augured ill for the reception of his caller, and prepared to let him in with his own hand.

The streets of Edinburgh town were very still at this late hour—it was late for Edinburgh— and in the quiet neighbourhood of F— Street, where Marriott lived on the third floor, scarcely a sound broke the silence. As he crossed the floor, the bell rang a second time, with unnecessary clamour, and he unlocked the door and passed into the little hallway with considerable wrath and annoyance in his heart at the insolence of the double interruption.

"The fellows all know I'm reading for this exam. Why in the world do they come to bother me at such an unearthly hour?"

The inhabitants of the building, with himself, were medical students, general students, poor Writers to the Signet, and some others whose vocations were perhaps not so obvious. The stone staircase, dimly lighted at each floor by a gas-jet that would not turn above a certain height, wound down to the level of the street with no pretence at carpet or railing. At some levels it was cleaner than at others. It depended on the landlady of the particular level.

The acoustic properties of a spiral staircase seem to be peculiar. Marriott, standing by the open door, book in hand, thought every moment the owner of the footsteps would come into view. The sound of the boots was so close and so loud that they seemed to travel disproportionately in advance of their cause. Wondering who it could be, he stood ready with all manner of sharp greetings for the man who dared thus to disturb his work. But the man did not appear. The steps sounded almost under his nose, yet no one was visible.

A sudden queer sensation of fear passed over him—a faintness and a shiver down the back. It went, however, almost as soon as it came, and he was just debating whether he would call aloud to his invisible visitor, or slam the door and return to his books, when the cause of the disturbance turned the corner very slowly and came into view.

It was a stranger. He saw a youngish man short of figure and very broad. His face was the color of a piece of chalk and the eyes, which were very bright, had heavy lines underneath them. Though the cheeks and chin were unshaven and the general appearance unkempt, the man was evidently a gentleman, for he was well dressed and bore himself with a certain air. But, strangest of all, he wore no hat, and carried none in his hand; and although rain had been falling steadily all the evening, he appeared to have neither overcoat nor umbrella.

A hundred questions sprang up in Marriott's mind and rushed to his lips, chief among which was something like "Who in the world are you?" and "What in the name of heaven do you come to me for?" But none of these questions found time to express themselves in words, for almost at once the caller turned his head a little so that the gas light in the hall fell upon his features from a new angle. Then in a flash Marriott recognised him.

"Field! Man alive! Is it you?" he gasped.

The Fourth Year Man was not lacking in intuition, and he perceived at once that here was a case for delicate treatment. He divined, without any actual process of thought, that the catastrophe often predicted had come at last, and that this man's father had turned him out of the house. They had been at a private school together years before, and though they had hardly met once since, the news had not failed to reach him from time to time with considerable detail, for the family lived near his own and between certain of the sisters there was great intimacy. Young Field had gone wild later, he remembered hearing about it all—drink, a woman, opium, or something of the sort—he could not exactly call to mind.

"Come in," he said at once, his anger vanishing. "There's been something wrong, I can see. Come in, and tell me all about it and perhaps I can help—" He hardly knew what to say, and stammered a lot more besides. The dark side of life, and the horror of it, belonged to a world that lay remote from his own select little atmosphere of books and dreamings. But he had a man's heart for all that.

He led the way across the hall, shutting the front door carefully behind him, and noticed as he did so that the other, though certainly sober, was unsteady on his legs, and, evidently much exhausted. Marriott might not be able to pass his examinations, but he at least knew the symptoms of starvation—acute starvation, unless he was much mistaken—when they stared him in the face.

"Come along," he said cheerfully, and with genuine sympathy in his voice. "I'm glad to see you. I was going to have a bite of something to eat, and you're just in time to join me."

The other made no audible reply, and shuffled so feebly with his feet that Marriott took his arm by way of support. He noticed for the first time that the clothes hung on him with pitiful looseness. The broad frame was literally hardly more than a frame. He was as thin as a skeleton.

But, as he touched him, the sensation of faintness and dread returned. It only lasted a moment, and then passed off and he ascribed it not unnaturally to the distress and shock of seeing a former friend in such a pitiful plight.

"Better let me guide you. It's shamefully dark—this hall. I'm always complaining," he said lightly, recognising by the weight upon his arm that the guidance was sorely needed, "but the old cat never does anything except promise." He led him to the sofa, wondering all the time where he had come from and how he had found out the address. It must be at least seven years since those days at the private school when they used to be such close friends.

"Now, if you'll forgive me for a minute," he said, "I'll get supper ready—such as it is. And don't bother to talk. Just take it easy on the sofa. I see you're dead tired. You can tell me about it afterwards, and we'll make plans."

The other sat down on the edge of the sofa and stared in silence, while Marriott got out the brown bag scones, and huge pot of marmalade that Edinburgh students always keep in their cupboards. His eyes shone with a brightness that suggested drugs, Marriott thought, stealing a glance at him from behind the cupboard door. He did not like yet to take a full square look. The fellow was in a bad way, and it would have been so like an examination to stare and wait for explanations. Besides, he was evidently almost too exhausted to speak. So, for reasons of delicacy—and for another reason as well which he could not exactly formulate to himself—he let his visitor rest apparently unnoticed, while he busied himself with the supper. He lit the spirit lamp to make cocoa, and when the water was boiling he drew up the table with the good things to the sofa, so that Field need not have even the trouble of moving to a chair.

"Now, let's tuck in," he said, "and afterwards we'll have a pipe and a chat. I'm reading for an exam, you know, and I always have something about this time. It's jolly to have a companion."

He looked up and caught his guest's eyes directed straight upon his own. An involuntary shudder ran through him from head to foot. The face opposite him was deadly white and wore a dreadful expression of pain and mental suffering.

"By Gad!" he said, jumping up, "I quite forgot. I've got some whisky somewhere. What an ass I am. I never touch it myself when I'm working like this."

He went to the cupboard and poured out a stiff glass which the other swallowed at a single gulp and without any water. Marriott watched him while he drank it, and at the same time noticed something else as well— Field's coat was all over dust, and on one shoulder was a bit of cobweb. It was perfectly dry; Field arrived on a soaking wet night without hat, umbrella, or overcoat, and yet perfectly dry, even dusty. Therefore he had been under cover. What did it all mean? Had he been hiding in the building . . . ?

It was very strange. Yet he volunteered nothing; and Marriott had pretty well made up his mind by this time that he would not ask any questions until he had eaten and slept. Food and sleep were obviously what the poor devil needed most and first he was pleased with his powers of ready diagnosis and it would not be fair to press him till he had recovered a bit.

They ate their supper together while the host carried on a running one-sided conversation, chiefly about himself and his exams and his "old cat" of a landlady, so that the guest need not utter a single word unless he really wished to—which he evidently did not! But, while he toyed with his food, feeling no desire to eat, the other ate voraciously. To see a hungry man devour cold scones, stale oatcake, and brown bread laden with marmalade was a revelation to this inexperienced student who had never known what it was to be without at least three meals a day. He watched in spite of himself, wondering why the fellow did not choke in the process.

But Field seemed to be as sleepy as he was hungry. More than once his head dropped and he ceased to masticate the food in his mouth. Marriott had positively to shake him before he would go on with his meal. A stronger emotion will overcome a weaker, but this struggle between the sting of real hunger and the magical opiate of overpowering sleep was a curious sight to the student, who watched it with mingled astonishment and alarm. He had heard of the pleasure it was to feed hungry men, and watch them eat, but he had never actually witnessed it and he had no idea it was like this. Field ate like an animal—gobbled, stuffed, gorged. Marriott forgot his reading, and began to feel something very much like a lump in his throat.

"Afraid there's been awfully little to offer you, old man," he managed to blurt out when at length the last scone had disappeared, and the rapid, one-sided meal was at an end. Field still made no reply, for he was almost asleep in his seat. He merely looked up wearily and gratefully.

"Now you must have some sleep, you know," he continued, "or you'll go to pieces. I shall be up all night reading for this blessed exam. You're more than welcome to my bed. To-morrow we'll have a late breakfast and— and see what can be done—and make plans—I'm awfully good at making plans, you know," he added with an attempt at lightness.

Field maintained his "dead sleepy" silence, but appeared to acquiesce, and the other led the way into the bedroom, apologizing as he did so to this half-starved son of a baronet—whose own home was almost a palace—for the size of the room. The weary guest, however, made no pretence of thanks or politeness. He merely steadied himself on his friend's arm as he staggered across the room, and then, with all his clothes on, dropped his exhausted body on the bed. In less than a minute he was to all appearances sound asleep.

For several minutes Marriott stood in the open door and watched him; praying devoutly that he might never find himself in a like predicament, and then fell to wondering what he would do with his unbidden guest on the morrow. But he did not stop long to think, for the call of his books was imperative, and happen what might, he must see to it that he passed that examination.

Having again locked the door into the hall, he sat down to his books and resumed his notes on *materia medica* where he had left off when the bell rang. But it was difficult for some time to concentrate his mind on the subject. His thoughts kept wandering to the picture of that white-faced, strange-eyed fellow, starved and dirty, lying in his clothes and boots on the bed. He recalled their schooldays together before they had drifted apart, and how they had vowed eternal friendship—and all the rest of it. And now! What horrible straits to be in. How could any man let the love of dissipation take such hold upon him?

But one of their vows together Marriott, it seemed, had completely forgotten. Just now, at any rate, it lay too far in the background of his memory to be recalled.

Through the half-open door—the bedroom led out of the sitting-room and had no other door—came the sound of deep, long-drawn breathing, the regular, steady breathing of a tired man, so tired that, even to listen to it made Marriott almost want to go to sleep himself.

"He needed it," reflected the student, "and perhaps it came only just in time!"

Perhaps so; for outside the bitter wind from across the Forth howled cruelly and drove the rain in cold streams against the window-panes, and down the deserted streets. Long before Marriott settled down again properly to his reading, he heard distantly, as it were, through the sentences of the book, the heavy, deep breathing of the sleeper in the next room.

A couple of hours later, when he yawned and changed his books, he still heard the breathing, and went cautiously up to the door to look round.

At first the darkness of the room must have deceived him, or else his eyes were confused and dazzled by the recent glare of the reading lamp. For a minute or two he could make out nothing at all but dark lumps of furniture, the mass of the chest of drawers by the wall, and the white patch where his bath stood in the centre of the floor.

Then the bed came slowly into view. And on it he saw the outline of the sleeping body gradually take shape before his eyes, growing up strangely into the darkness, till it stood out in marked relief—the long black form against the white counterpane.

He could hardly help smiling. Field had not moved an inch. He watched him a moment or two and then returned to his books. The night was full of the singing voices of the wind and rain. There was no sound of traffic; no hansoms clattered over the cobbles, and it was still too early for the milk carts. He worked on steadily and conscientiously, only stopping now and again to change a book, or to sip some of the poisonous stuff that kept him awake and made his brain so active, and on these occasions Field's breathing was always distinctly audible in the room. Outside, the storm continued to howl, but inside the house all was stillness. The shade of the reading lamp threw all the light upon the littered table, leaving the other end of the room in comparative darkness. The bedroom door was exactly opposite him where he sat. There was nothing to disturb the worker, nothing but an occasional rush of wind against the windows, and a slight pain in his arm.

This pain, however, which he was unable to account for, grew once or twice very acute. It bothered him; and he tried to remember how, and when, he could have bruised himself so severely, but without success.

At length the page before him turned from yellow to grey, and there were sounds of wheels in the street below. It was four o'clock. Marriott leaned back and yawned prodigiously. Then he drew back the curtains. The storm had subsided and the Castle Rock was shrouded in mist. With another yawn he turned away from the dreary outlook and prepared to sleep the remaining four hours till breakfast on the sofa. Field was still breathing heavily in the next room, and he first tip-toed across the floor to take another look at him.

Peering cautiously round the half-opened door his first glance fell upon the bed now plainly discernible in the grey light of morning. He stared hard. Then he rubbed his eyes. Then he rubbed his eyes again and thrust his head farther round the edge of the door. With fixed eyes he stared harder still, and harder.

But it made no difference at all. He was staring into an empty room.

The sensation of fear he had felt when Field first appeared upon the scene returned suddenly, but with much greater force. He became conscious, too, that his left arm was throbbing violently and causing him great pain. He stood wondering, and staring, and trying to collect his thoughts.

He was trembling from head to foot.

By a great effort of the will he left the support of the door and walked forward boldly into the room.

There, upon the bed, was the impress of a body, where Field had lain and slept. There was the mark of the head on the pillow, and the slight indentation at the foot of the bed where the boots had rested on the counterpane. And there, plainer than ever—for he was closer to it— was the *breathing*!

Marriott tried to pull himself together. With a great effort he found his voice and called his friend aloud by name!

"Field! Is that you? Where are you?"

There was no reply; but the breathing continued without interruption, coming directly from the bed. His voice had such an unfamiliar sound that Marriott did not care to repeat his questions, but he went down on his knees and examined the bed above and below, pulling the mattress off finally, and taking the coverings away separately one by one. But though the sounds continued there was no visible sign of Field, nor was there any space in which a human being, however small, could have concealed itself. He pulled the bed out from the wall, but the sound *stayed where it was*. It did not move with the bed.

Marriott, finding self-control a little difficult in his weary condition, at once set about a thorough search of the room. He went through the cupboard, the chest of drawers, the little alcove where the clothes hung—everything. But there was no sign of anyone. The small window near the ceiling was closed; and, anyhow, was not large enough to let a cat pass. The sitting-room door was locked on the inside; he could not have got out that way. Curious thoughts began to trouble Marriott's mind, bringing in their train unwelcome sensations. He grew more and more excited; he searched the bed again till it resembled the scene of a pillow fight; he searched both rooms, knowing all the time it was useless,—and then he searched again. A cold perspiration broke out all over his body; and the sound of heavy breathing, all this time, never ceased to come from the corner where Field had lain down to sleep.

Then he tried something else. He pushed the bed back exactly into its original position—and himself lay down upon it just where his guest had lain. But the same instant he sprang up again in a single bound. The breathing was close beside him, almost on his cheek, and between him and the wall! Not even a child could have squeezed into the space.

He went back into his sitting-room, opened the windows, welcoming all the light and air possible, and tried to think the whole matter over quietly and clearly. Men who read too hard, and slept too little, he knew were sometimes troubled with very vivid hallucinations. Again he calmly reviewed every incident of the night; his accurate sensations; the vivid details; the emotions stirred in him; the dreadful feast—no single hallucination could ever combine all these and cover so long a period of time. But with less satisfaction he thought of the recurring faintness, and curious sense of horror that had once or twice come over him, and then of the violent pains in his arm. These were quite unaccountable.

Moreover, now that he began to analyze and examine, there was one other thing that fell upon him like a sudden revelation: *During the whole time Field had not actually uttered a single word*! Yet, as though in mockery upon his reflections, there came ever from that inner room the sound of the breathing, long-drawn, deep, and regular. The thing was incredible. It was absurd.

Haunted by visions of brain fever and insanity, Marriott put on his cap and macintosh and left the house. The morning air on Arthur's Seat would blow the cobwebs from his brain; the scent of the heather, and above all, the sight of the sea. He roamed over the wet slopes above Holyrood for a couple of hours, and did not return until the exercise had shaken some of the horror out of his bones, and given him a ravening appetite into the bargain.

As he entered he saw that there was another man in the room, standing against the window with his back to the light. He recognised his fellow-student Greene, who was reading for the same examination.

"Read hard all night, Marriott," he said, "and thought I'd drop in here to compare notes and have some breakfast. You're out early?" he added, by way of a question. Marriott said he had a headache and a walk had helped it, and Greene nodded and said "Ah!" But when the girl had set the steaming porridge on the table and gone out again, he went on with rather a forced tone, "Didn't know you had any friends who drank, Marriott?"

This was obviously tentative, and Marriott replied drily that he did not know it either.

"Sounds just as if some chap were 'sleeping it off' in there, doesn't it, though?" persisted the other, with a nod in the direction of the bedroom, and looking curiously at his friend. The two men stared steadily at each other for several seconds, and then Marriott said earnestly— "Then you hear it too, thank God!"

"Of course I hear it. The door's open. Sorry if I wasn't meant to."

"Oh, I don't mean that," said Marriott, lowering his voice. "But I'm awfully relieved. Let me explain. Of course, if you hear it too, then it's all right; but really it frightened me more than I can tell you. I thought I was going to have brain fever, or something, and you know what a lot depends on this exam. It always begins with sounds, or visions, or some sort of beastly hallucination, and I—"

"Rot!" ejaculated the other impatiently. "What are you talking about?"

"Now, listen to me, Greene," said Marriott, as calmly as he could, for the breathing was still plainly audible, "and I'll tell you what I mean, only don't interrupt." And thereupon he related exactly what had happened during the night, telling everything, even down to the pain in his arm.

When it was over he got up from the table and crossed the room.

"You hear the breathing now plainly, don't you?" he said. Greene said he did. "Well, come with me, and we'll search the room together." The other, however, did not move from his chair.

"I've been in already," he said sheepishly; "I heard the sounds and thought it was you. The door was ajar—so I went in."

Marriott made no comment, but pushed the door open as wide as it would go. As it opened, the sound of breathing grew more and more distinct.

"*Someone* must be in there," said Greene under his breath.

"*Someone* is in there, but *where*?" said Marriott. Again he urged his friend to go in with him. But Greene refused point-blank: said he had been in once and had searched the room and there was nothing there. He would not go in again for a good deal.

They shut the door and retired into the other room to talk it all over with many pipes. Greene questioned his friend very closely, but without illuminating result, since questions cannot alter facts.

"The only thing that ought to have a proper, a logical, explanation is the pain in my arm," said Marriott, rubbing that member with an attempt at a smile. "It hurts so infernally and aches all the way up. I can't remember bruising it, though."

"Let me examine it for you," said Greene. "I'm awfully good at bones in spite of the examiners' opinion to the contrary." It was a relief to play the fool a bit, and Marriott took his coat off and rolled up his sleeve.

"By George, though, I'm bleeding!" he exclaimed. "Look here! What on earth's this?"

On the forearm, quite close to the wrist, was a thin red line. There was a tiny drop of apparently fresh blood on it. Greene came over and looked closely at it for some minutes. Then he sat back in his chair, looking curiously at his friend's face.

"You've scratched yourself without knowing it," he said presently. "There's no sign of a bruise. It must be something else that made the arm ache."

Marriott sat very still, staring silently at his arm as though the solution of the whole mystery lay there actually written upon the skin.

"What's the matter? I see nothing very strange about a scratch," said Greene, in an unconvincing sort of voice. "It was your cuff links probably. Last night in your excitement——"

But Marriott, white to the very lips, was trying to speak. The sweat stood in great beads on his forehead. At last he leaned forward close to his friend's face.

"Look," he said, in a low voice that shook a little. "Do you see that red mark? I mean *underneath* what you call the scratch?"

Greene admitted he saw something or other, and Marriott wiped the place clean with his handkerchief and told him to look again more closely.

"Yes, I see," returned the other, lifting his head after a moment's careful inspection. "It looks like an old scar."

"It *is* an old scar," whispered Marriott, his lips trembling. "*Now* it all comes back to me."

"All what?" Greene fidgeted on his chair. He tried to laugh, but without success. His friend seemed bordering on collapse.

"Hush! Be quiet, and—I'll tell you," he said. "*Field made that scar.*"

For a whole minute the two men looked each other full in the face without speaking.

"Field made that scar!" repeated Marriott at length in a louder voice.

"Field! You mean—last night?"

"No, not last night. Years ago—at school, with his knife. And I made a scar in his arm with mine." Marriott was talking rapidly now.

"We exchanged drops of blood in each other's cuts. He put a drop into my arm and I put one into his——"

"In the name of heaven, what for?"

"It was a boys' compact. We made a sacred pledge, a bargain. I remember it all perfectly now. We had been reading some dreadful book and we swore to appear to one another—I mean, whoever died first swore to show himself to the other. And we sealed the compact with each other's blood. I remember it all so well—the hot summer afternoon in the playground, seven years ago—and one of the masters caught us and confiscated the knives—and I have never thought of it again to this day——"

"And you mean—" stammered Greene.

But Marriott made no answer. He got up and crossed the room and lay down wearily upon the sofa, hiding his face in his hands.

Greene himself was a bit non-plussed. He left his friend alone for a little while, thinking it all over again. Suddenly an idea seemed to strike him. He went over to where Marriott still lay motionless on the sofa and roused him. In any case it was better to face the matter, whether there was an explanation or not. Giving in was always the silly exit.

"I say, Marriott," he began, as the other turned his white face up to him. "There's no good being so upset about it. I mean—if it's all an hallucination we know what to do. And if it isn't—well, we know what to think, don't we?"

"I suppose so. But it frightens me horribly for some reason," returned his friend in a hushed voice. "And that poor devil—"

"But, after all, if the worst is true and—and that chap *has* kept his promise—well, he has, that's all, isn't it?"

Marriott nodded.

"There's only one thing that occurs to me," Greene went on, "and that is, are you quite sure that—that he really ate like that—I mean that he actually *ate anything at all*?" he finished, blurting out all his thought.

Marriott stared at him for a moment and then said he could easily make certain. He spoke quietly. After the main shock no lesser surprise could affect him.

"I put the things away myself" he said, "after we had finished. They are on the third shelf in that cupboard. No one's touched 'em since."

He pointed without getting up, and Greene took the hint and went over to look.

"Exactly," he said, after a brief examination; "just as I thought. It was partly hallucination, at any rate. The things haven't been touched. Come and see for yourself."

Together they examined the shelf. There was the brown loaf, the plate of stale scones, the oatcake, all untouched. Even the glass of whisky Marriott had poured out stood there with the whisky still in it.

"You were feeding—no one," said Greene. "Field ate and drank nothing. He was not there at all!"

"But the breathing?" urged the other in a low voice, staring with a dazed expression on his face.

Greene did not answer. He walked over to the bedroom, while Marriott followed him with his eyes. He opened the door, and listened. There was no need for words. The sound of deep, regular breathing came floating through the air. There was no hallucination about that, at any rate. Marriott could hear it where he stood on the other side of the room.

Greene closed the door and came back. "There's only one thing to do," he declared with decision. "Write home and find out about him, and meanwhile come and finish your reading in my rooms. I've got an extra bed."

"Agreed," returned the Fourth Year Man; "there's no hallucination about that exam; I must pass that whatever happens."

And this was what they did.

It was about a week later when Marriott got the answer from his sister. Part of it he read out to Greene—

"It is curious," she wrote, "that in your letter you should have enquired after Field. It seems a terrible thing, but you know only a short while ago Sir John's patience became exhausted, and he turned him out of the house, they say without a penny. Well, what do you think? He has killed himself. At least, it looks like suicide. Instead of leaving the house, he went down into the cellar and simply starved himself to death. . . . They're trying to suppress it, of course, but I heard it all from my maid, who got it from their footman. . . . They found the body on the 14th and the doctor said he had died about twelve hours before. . . . He was dreadfully thin. . . ."

"Then he died on the 13th," said Greene.

Marriott nodded.

"That's the very night he came to see you."

Marriott nodded again.

Smith: An Episode in a Lodging-House

"When I was a medical student," began the doctor, half turning towards his circle of listeners in the firelight, "I came across one or two very curious human beings; but there was one fellow I remember particularly, for he caused me the most vivid, and I think the most uncomfortable, emotions I have ever known.

"For many months I knew Smith only by name as the occupant of the floor above me. Obviously his name meant nothing to me. Moreover I was busy with lectures, reading, cliniques and the like, and had little leisure to devise plans for scraping acquaintance with any of the other lodgers in the house. Then chance brought us curiously together, and this fellow Smith left a deep impression upon me as the result of our first meeting. At the time the strength of this first impression seemed quite inexplicable to me, but looking back at the episode now from a stand-point of greater knowledge I judge the fact to have been that he stirred my curiosity to an unusual degree, and at the same time awakened my sense of horror—whatever that may be in a medical student—about as deeply and permanently as these two emotions were capable of being stirred at all in the particular system and set of nerves called *Me*.

"How he knew that I was interested in the study of languages was something I could never explain, but one day, quite unannounced, he came quietly into my room in the evening and asked me point-blank if I knew enough Hebrew to help him in the pronunciation of certain words.

"He caught me along the line of least resistance, and I was greatly flattered to be able to give him the desired information; but it was only when he had thanked me and was gone that I realised I had been in the presence of an unusual individuality. For the life of me I could not quite seize and label the peculiarities of what I felt to be a very striking personality, but it was borne in upon me that he was a man apart from his fellows, a mind that followed a line leading away from ordinary human intercourse and human interests, and into regions that left in his atmosphere something remote, rarefied, chilling.

"The moment he was gone I became conscious of two things—an intense curiosity to know more about this man and what his real interests were, and secondly, the fact that my skin was crawling and that my hair had a tendency to rise."

The doctor paused a moment here to puff hard at his pipe, which, however, had gone out beyond recall without the assistance of a match; and in the deep silence, which testified to the genuine interest of his listeners, someone poked the fire up into a little blaze, and one or two others glanced over their shoulders into the dark distances of the big hall.

"On looking back," he went on, watching the momentary flames in the grate, "I see a short, thick-set man of perhaps forty-five, with immense shoulders and small, slender hands. The contrast was noticeable, for I remember thinking that such a giant frame and such slim finger bones hardly belonged together. His head, too, was large and very long, the head of an idealist beyond all question, yet with an unusually strong development of the jaw and chin. Here again was a singular contradiction, though I am better able now to appreciate its full meaning, with a greater experience in judging the values of physiognomy. For this meant, of course, an enthusiastic idealism balanced and kept in check by will and judgment—elements usually deficient in dreamers and visionaries.

"At any rate, here was a being with probably a very wide range of possibilities, a machine with a pendulum that most likely had an unusual length of swing.

"The man's hair was exceedingly fine, and the lines about his nose and mouth were cut as with a delicate steel instrument in wax. His eyes I have left to the last. They were large and quite changeable, not in colour only, but in character, size, and shape. Occasionally they seemed the eyes of someone else, if you can understand what I mean, and at the same time, in their shifting shades of blue, green, and a nameless sort of dark grey, there was a sinister light in them that lent to the whole face an aspect almost alarming. Moreover, they were the most luminous optics I think I have ever seen in any human being.

"There, then, at the risk of a wearisome description, is Smith as I saw him for the first time that winter's evening in my shabby student's rooms in Edinburgh. And yet the real part of him, of course, I have left untouched, for it is both indescribable and un-get-at-able. I have spoken already of an atmosphere of warning and aloofness he carried about with him. It is impossible further to analyse the series of little shocks his presence always communicated to my being; but there was that about him which made me instantly on the *qui vive* in his presence, every nerve alert, every sense strained and on the watch. I do not mean that he deliberately suggested danger, but rather that he brought forces in his wake which automatically warned the nervous centres of my system to be on their guard and alert.

"Since the days of my first acquaintance with this man I have lived through other experiences and have seen much I cannot pretend to explain or understand; but, so far in my life, I have only once come across a human being who suggested a disagreeable familiarity with unholy things, and who made me feel uncanny and 'creepy' in his presence; and that unenviable individual was Mr. Smith.

"What his occupation was during the day I never knew. I think he slept until the sun set. No one ever saw him on the stairs, or heard him move in his room during the day. He was a creature of the shadows, who apparently preferred darkness to light. Our landlady either knew nothing, or would say nothing. At any rate she found no fault, and I have since wondered often by what magic this fellow was able to convert a common landlady of a common lodging-house into a discreet and uncommunicative person. This alone was a sign of genius of some sort.

"'He's been here with me for years—long before you come, an' I don't interfere or ask no questions of what doesn't concern me, as long as people pays their rent,' was the only remark on the subject that I ever succeeded in winning from that quarter, and it certainly told me nothing nor gave me any encouragement to ask for further information.

"Examinations, however, and the general excitement of a medical student's life for a time put Mr. Smith completely out of my head. For a long period he did not call upon me again, and for my part, I felt no courage to return his unsolicited visit.

"Just then, however, there came a change in the fortunes of those who controlled my very limited income, and I was obliged to give up my ground-floor and move aloft to more modest chambers on the top of the house. Here I was directly over Smith, and had to pass his door to reach my own.

"It so happened that about this time I was frequently called out at all hours of the night for the maternity cases which a fourth-year student takes at a certain period of his studies, and on returning from one of these visits at about two o'clock in the morning I was surprised to hear the sound of voices as I passed his door. A peculiar sweet odour, too, not unlike the smell of incense, penetrated into the passage.

"I went upstairs very quietly, wondering what was going on there at this hour of the morning. To my knowledge Smith never had visitors. For a moment I hesitated outside the door with one foot on the stairs. All my interest in this strange man revived, and my curiosity rose to a point not far from action. At last I might learn something of the habits of this lover of the night and the darkness.

"The sound of voices was plainly audible, Smith's predominating so much that I never could catch more than points of sound from the other, penetrating now and then the steady stream of his voice. Not a single word reached me, at least, not a word that I could understand, though the voice was loud and distinct, and it was only afterwards that I realised he must have been speaking in a foreign language.

"The sound of footsteps, too, was equally distinct. Two persons were moving about the room, passing and re-passing the door, one of them a light, agile person, and the other ponderous and somewhat awkward. Smith's voice went on incessantly with its odd, monotonous droning, now loud, now soft, as he crossed and re-crossed the floor. The other person was also on the move, but in a different and less regular fashion, for I heard rapid steps that seemed to end sometimes in stumbling, and quick sudden movements that brought up with a violent lurching against the wall or furniture.

"As I listened to Smith's voice, moreover, I began to feel afraid. There was something in the sound that made me feel intuitively he was in a tight place, and an impulse stirred faintly in me—very faintly, I admit—to knock at the door and inquire if he needed help.

"But long before the impulse could translate itself into an act, or even before it had been properly weighed and considered by the mind, I heard a voice close beside me in the air, a sort of hushed whisper which I am certain was Smith speaking, though the sound did not seem to have come to me through the door. It was close in my very ear, as though he stood beside me, and it gave me such a start, that I clutched the banisters to save myself from stepping backwards and making a clatter on the stairs.

"'There is nothing you can do to help me,' it said distinctly, 'and you will be much safer in your own room.'

"I am ashamed to this day of the pace at which I covered the flight of stairs in the darkness to the top floor, and of the shaking hand with which I lit my candles and bolted the door. But, there it is, just as it happened.

"This midnight episode, so odd and yet so trivial in itself, fired me with more curiosity than ever about my fellow-lodger. It also made me connect him in my mind with a sense of fear and distrust. I never saw him, yet I was often, and uncomfortably, aware of his presence in the upper regions of that gloomy lodging-house. Smith and his secret mode of life and mysterious pursuits, somehow contrived to awaken in my being a line of reflection that disturbed my comfortable condition of ignorance. I never saw him, as I have said, and exchanged no sort of communication with him, yet it seemed to me that his mind was in contact with mine, and some of the strange forces of his atmosphere filtered through into my being and disturbed my equilibrium. Those upper floors became haunted for me after dark, and, though outwardly our lives never came into contact, I became unwillingly involved in certain pursuits on which his mind was centred. I felt that he was somehow making use of me against my will, and by methods which passed my comprehension.

"I was at that time, moreover, in the heavy, unquestioning state of materialism which is common to medical students when they begin to understand something of the human anatomy and nervous system, and jump at once to the conclusion that they control the universe and hold in their forceps the last word of life and death. I 'knew it all,' and regarded a belief in anything beyond matter as the wanderings of weak, or at best, untrained minds. And this condition of mind, of course, added to the strength of this upsetting fear which emanated from the floor below and began slowly to take possession of me.

"Though I kept no notes of the subsequent events in this matter, they made too deep an impression for me ever to forget the sequence in which they occurred. Without difficulty I can recall the next step in the adventure with Smith, for adventure it rapidly grew to be."

The doctor stopped a moment and laid his pipe on the table behind him before continuing. The fire had burned low, and no one stirred to poke it. The silence in the great hall was so deep that when the speaker's pipe touched the table the sound woke audible echoes at the far end among the shadows.

"One evening, while I was reading, the door of my room opened and Smith came in. He made no attempt at ceremony. It was after ten o'clock and I was tired, but the presence of the man immediately galvanised me into activity. My attempts at ordinary politeness he thrust on one side at once, and began asking me to vocalise, and then pronounce for him, certain Hebrew words; and when this was done he abruptly inquired if I was not the fortunate possessor of a very rare Rabbinical Treatise, which he named.

"How he knew that I possessed this book puzzled me exceedingly; but I was still more surprised to see him cross the room and take it out of my book-shelf almost before I had had time to answer in the affirmative. Evidently he knew exactly where it was kept. This excited my curiosity beyond all bounds, and I immediately began asking him questions; and though, out of sheer respect for the man, I put them very delicately to him, and almost by way of mere conversation, he had only one reply for the lot. He would look up at me from the pages of the book with an expression of complete comprehension on his extraordinary features, would bow his head a little and say very gravely—

"'That, of course, is a perfectly proper question,'—which was absolutely all I could ever get out of him.

"On this particular occasion he stayed with me perhaps ten or fifteen minutes. Then he went quickly downstairs to his room with my Hebrew Treatise in his hand, and I heard him close and bolt his door.

"But a few moments later, before I had time to settle down to my book again, or to recover from the surprise his visit had caused me, I heard the door open, and there stood Smith once again beside my chair. He made no excuse for his second interruption, but bent his head down to the level of my reading lamp and peered across the flame straight into my eyes.

"'I hope,' he whispered, 'I hope you are never disturbed at night?'

"'Eh?' I stammered, 'disturbed at night? Oh no, thanks, at least, not that I know of—'

"'I'm glad,' he replied gravely, appearing not to notice my confusion and surprise at his question. 'But, remember, should it ever be the case, please let me know at once.'

"And he was gone down the stairs and into his room again.

"For some minutes I sat reflecting upon his strange behaviour. He was not mad, I argued, but was the victim of some harmless delusion that had gradually grown upon him as a result of his solitary mode of life; and from the books he used, I judged that it had something to do with mediæval magic, or some system of ancient Hebrew mysticism. The words he asked me to pronounce for him were probably 'Words of Power,' which, when uttered with the vehemence of a strong will behind them, were supposed to produce physical results, or set up vibrations in one's own inner being that had the effect of a partial lifting of the veil.

"I sat thinking about the man, and his way of living, and the probable effects in the long-run of his dangerous experiments, and I can recall perfectly well the sensation of disappointment that crept over me when I realised that I had labelled his particular form of aberration, and that my curiosity would therefore no longer be excited.

"For some time I had been sitting alone with these reflections—it may have been ten minutes or it may have been half an hour—when I was aroused from my reverie by the knowledge that someone was again in the room standing close beside my chair. My first thought was that Smith had come back again in his swift, unaccountable manner, but almost at the same moment I realised that this could not be the case at all. For the door faced my position, and it certainly had not been opened again.

"Yet, someone was in the room, moving cautiously to and fro, watching me, almost touching me. I was as sure of it as I was of myself, and though at the moment I do not think I was actually afraid, I am bound to admit that a certain weakness came over me and that I felt that strange disinclination for action which is probably the beginning of the horrible paralysis of real terror. I should have been glad to hide myself, if that had been possible, to cower into a corner, or behind a door, or anywhere so that I could not be watched and observed.

"But, overcoming my nervousness with an effort of the will, I got up quickly out of my chair and held the reading lamp aloft so that it shone into all the corners like a searchlight.

"The room was utterly empty! It was utterly empty, at least, to the eye, but to the nerves, and especially to that combination of sense perception which is made up by all the senses acting together, and by no one in particular, there was a person standing there at my very elbow.

"I say 'person,' for I can think of no appropriate word. For, if it *was* a human being, I can only affirm that I had the overwhelming conviction that it was *not*, but that it was some form of life wholly unknown to me both as to its essence and its nature. A sensation of gigantic force and power came with it, and I remember vividly to this day my terror on realising that I was close to an invisible being who could crush me as easily as I could crush a fly, and who could see my every movement while itself remaining invisible.

"To this terror was added the certain knowledge that the 'being' kept in my proximity for a definite purpose. And that this purpose had some direct bearing upon my well-being, indeed upon my life, I was equally convinced; for I became aware of a sensation of growing lassitude as though the vitality were being steadily drained out of my body. My heart began to beat irregularly at first, then faintly. I was conscious, even within a few minutes, of a general drooping of the powers of life in the whole system, an ebbing away of self-control, and a distinct approach of drowsiness and torpor.

"The power to move, or to think out any mode of resistance, was fast leaving me, when there rose, in the distance as it were, a tremendous commotion. A door opened with a clatter, and I heard the peremptory and commanding tones of a human voice calling aloud in a language I could not comprehend. It was Smith, my fellow-lodger, calling up the stairs; and his voice had not sounded for more than a few seconds, when I felt something withdrawn from my presence, from my person, indeed from my very skin. It seemed as if there was a rushing of air and some large creature swept by me at about the level of my shoulders. Instantly the pressure on my heart was relieved, and the atmosphere seemed to resume its normal condition.

"Smith's door closed quietly downstairs, as I put the lamp down with trembling hands. What had happened I do not know; only, I was alone again and my strength was returning as rapidly as it had left me.

"I went across the room and examined myself in the glass. The skin was very pale, and the eyes dull. My temperature, I found, was a little below normal and my pulse faint and irregular. But these smaller signs of disturbance were as nothing compared with the feeling I had—though no outward signs bore testimony to the fact—that I had narrowly escaped a real and ghastly catastrophe. I felt shaken, somehow, shaken to the very roots of my being."

The doctor rose from his chair and crossed over to the dying fire, so that no one could see the expression on his face as he stood with his back to the grate, and continued his weird tale.

"It would be wearisome," he went on in a lower voice, looking over our heads as though he still saw the dingy top floor of that haunted Edinburgh lodging-house; "it would be tedious for me at this length of time to analyse my feelings, or attempt to reproduce for you the thorough examination to which I endeavoured then to subject my whole being, intellectual, emotional, and physical. I need only mention the dominant emotion with which this curious episode left me—the indignant anger against myself that I could ever have lost my self-control enough to come under the sway of so gross and absurd a delusion. This protest, however, I remember making with all the emphasis possible. And I also remember noting that it brought me very little satisfaction, for it was the protest of my reason only, when all the rest of my being was up in arms against its conclusions.

"My dealings with the 'delusion,' however, were not yet over for the night; for very early next morning, somewhere about three o'clock, I was awakened by a curiously stealthy noise in the room, and the next minute there followed a crash as if all my books had been swept bodily from their shelf on to the floor.

"But this time I was not frightened. Cursing the disturbance with all the resounding and harmless words I could accumulate, I jumped out of bed and lit the candle in a second, and in the first dazzle of the flaring match—but before the wick had time to catch—I was certain I *saw* a dark grey shadow, of ungainly shape, and with something more or less like a human head, drive rapidly past the side of the wall farthest from me and disappear into the gloom by the angle of the door.

"I waited one single second to be sure the candle was alight, and then dashed after it, but before I had gone two steps, my foot stumbled against something hard piled up on the carpet and I only just saved myself from falling headlong. I picked myself up and found that all the books from what I called my 'language shelf' were strewn across the floor. The room, meanwhile, as a minute's search revealed, was quite empty. I looked in every corner and behind every stick of furniture, and a student's bedroom on a top floor, costing twelve shillings a week, did not hold many available hiding-places, as you may imagine.

"The crash, however, was explained. Some very practical and physical force had thrown the books from their resting-place. That, at least, was beyond all doubt. And as I replaced them on the shelf and noted that not one was missing, I busied myself mentally with the sore problem of how the agent of this little practical joke had gained access to my room, and then escaped again. *For my door was locked and bolted.*

"Smith's odd question as to whether I was disturbed in the night, and his warning injunction to let him know at once if such were the case, now of course returned to affect me as I stood there in the early morning, cold and shivering on the carpet; but I realised at the same moment how impossible it would be for me to admit that a more than usually vivid nightmare could have any connection with himself. I would rather stand a hundred of these mysterious visitations than consult such a man as to their possible cause.

"A knock at the door interrupted my reflections, and I gave a start that sent the candle grease flying.

"'Let me in,' came in Smith's voice.

"I unlocked the door. He came in fully dressed. His face wore a curious pallor. It seemed to me to be under the skin and to shine through and almost make it luminous. His eyes were exceedingly bright.

"I was wondering what in the world to say to him, or how he would explain his visit at such an hour, when he closed the door behind him and came close up to me—uncomfortably close.

"'You should have called me at once,' he said in his whispering voice, fixing his great eyes on my face.

"I stammered something about an awful dream, but he ignored my remark utterly, and I caught his eye wandering next—if any movement of those optics can be described as 'wandering'—to the book-shelf. I watched him, unable to move my gaze from his person. The man fascinated me horribly for some reason. Why, in the devil's name, was he up and dressed at three in the morning? How did he know anything had happened unusual in my room? Then his whisper began again.

"'It's your amazing vitality that causes you this annoyance,' he said, shifting his eyes back to mine.

"I gasped. Something in his voice or manner turned my blood into ice.

"'That's the real attraction,' he went on. 'But if this continues one of us will have to leave, you know.'

"I positively could not find a word to say in reply. The channels of speech dried up within me. I simply stared and wondered what he would say next. I watched him in a sort of dream, and as far as I can remember, he asked me to promise to call him sooner another time, and then began to walk round the room, uttering strange sounds, and making signs with his arms and hands until he reached the door. Then he was gone in a second, and I had closed and locked the door behind him.

"After this, the Smith adventure drew rapidly to a climax. It was a week or two later, and I was coming home between two and three in the morning from a maternity case, certain features of which for the time being had very much taken possession of my mind, so much so, indeed, that I passed Smith's door without giving him a single thought.

"The gas jet on the landing was still burning, but so low that it made little impression on the waves of deep shadow that lay across the stairs. Overhead, the faintest possible gleam of grey showed that the morning was not far away. A few stars shone down through the sky-light. The house was still as the grave, and the only sound to break the silence was the rushing of the wind round the walls and over the roof. But this was a fitful sound, suddenly rising and as suddenly falling away again, and it only served to intensify the silence.

"I had already reached my own landing when I gave a violent start. It was automatic, almost a reflex action in fact, for it was only when I caught myself fumbling at the door handle and thinking where I could conceal myself quickest that I realised a voice had sounded close beside me in the air. It was the same voice I had heard before, and it seemed to me to be calling for help. And yet the very same minute I pushed on into the room, determined to disregard it, and seeking to persuade myself it was the creaking of the boards under my weight or the rushing noise of the wind that had deceived me.

"But hardly had I reached the table where the candles stood when the sound was unmistakably repeated: 'Help! help!' And this time it was accompanied by what I can only describe as a vivid tactile hallucination. I was touched: the *skin* of my arm was clutched by fingers.

"Some compelling force sent me headlong downstairs as if the haunting forces of the whole world were at my heels. At Smith's door I paused. The force of his previous warning injunction to seek his aid without delay acted suddenly and I leant my whole weight against the panels, little dreaming that I should be called upon to give help rather than to receive it.

"The door yielded at once, and I burst into a room that was so full of a choking vapour, moving in slow clouds, that at first I could distinguish nothing at all but a set of what seemed to be huge shadows passing in and out of the mist. Then, gradually, I perceived that a red lamp on the mantelpiece gave all the light there was, and that the room which I now entered for the first time was almost empty of furniture.

"The carpet was rolled back and piled in a heap in the corner, and upon the white boards of the floor I noticed a large circle drawn in black of some material that emitted a faint glowing light and was apparently smoking. Inside this circle, as well as at regular intervals outside it, were curious-looking designs, also traced in the same black, smoking substance. These, too, seemed to emit a feeble light of their own.

"My first impression on entering the room had been that it was full of—*people*, I was going to say; but that hardly expresses my meaning. *Beings*, they certainly were, but it was borne in upon me beyond the possibility of doubt, that they were not human beings. That I had caught a momentary glimpse of living, intelligent entities I can never doubt, but I am equally convinced, though I cannot prove it, that these entities were from some other scheme of evolution altogether, and had nothing to do with the ordinary human life, either incarnate or discarnate.

"But, whatever they were, the visible appearance of them was exceedingly fleeting. I no longer saw anything, though I still felt convinced of their immediate presence. They were, moreover, of the same order of life as the visitant in my bedroom of a few nights before, and their proximity to my atmosphere in numbers, instead of singly as before, conveyed to my mind something that was quite terrible and overwhelming. I fell into a violent trembling, and the perspiration poured from my face in streams.

"They were in constant motion about me. They stood close to my side; moved behind me; brushed past my shoulder; stirred the hair on my forehead; and circled round me without ever actually touching me, yet always pressing closer and closer. Especially in the air just over my head there seemed ceaseless movement, and it was accompanied by a confused noise of whispering and sighing that threatened every moment to become articulate in words. To my intense relief, however, I heard no distinct words, and the noise continued more like the rising and falling of the wind than anything else I can imagine.

"But the characteristic of these 'Beings' that impressed me most strongly at the time, and of which I have carried away the most permanent recollection, was that each one of them possessed what seemed to be a *vibrating centre* which impelled it with tremendous force and caused a rapid whirling motion of the atmosphere as it passed me. The air was full of these little vortices of whirring, rotating force, and whenever one of them pressed me too closely I felt as if the nerves in that particular portion of my body had been literally drawn out, absolutely depleted of vitality, and then immediately replaced—but replaced dead, flabby, useless.

"Then, suddenly, for the first time my eyes fell upon Smith. He was crouching against the wall on my right, in an attitude that was obviously defensive, and it was plain he was in extremities. The terror on his face was pitiable, but at the same time there was another expression about the tightly clenched teeth and mouth which showed that he had not lost all control of himself. He wore the most resolute expression I have ever seen on a human countenance, and, though for the moment at a fearful disadvantage, he looked like a man who had confidence in himself, and, in spite of the working of fear, was waiting his opportunity.

"For my part, I was face to face with a situation so utterly beyond my knowledge and comprehension, that I felt as helpless as a child, and as useless.

"'Help me back—quick—into that circle,' I heard him half cry, half whisper to me across the moving vapours.

"My only value appears to have been that I was not afraid to act. Knowing nothing of the forces I was dealing with I had no idea of the deadly perils risked, and I sprang forward and caught him by the arms. He threw all his weight in my direction, and by our combined efforts his body left the wall and lurched across the floor towards the circle.

"Instantly there descended upon us, out of the empty air of that smoke-laden room, a force which I can only compare to the pushing, driving power of a great wind pent up within a narrow space. It was almost explosive in its effect, and it seemed to operate upon all parts of my body equally. It fell upon us with a rushing noise that filled my ears and made me think for a moment the very walls and roof of the building had been torn asunder. Under its first blow we staggered back against the wall, and I understood plainly that its purpose was to prevent us getting back into the circle in the middle of the floor.

"Pouring with perspiration, and breathless, with every muscle strained to the very utmost, we at length managed to get to the edge of the circle, and at this moment, so great was the opposing force, that I felt myself actually torn from Smith's arms, lifted from my feet, and twirled round in the direction of the windows as if the wheel of some great machine had caught my clothes and was tearing me to destruction in its revolution.

"But, even as I fell, bruised and breathless, against the wall, I saw Smith firmly upon his feet in the circle and slowly rising again to an upright position. My eyes never left his figure once in the next few minutes.

"He drew himself up to his full height. His great shoulders squared themselves. His head was thrown back a little, and as I looked I saw the expression on his face change swiftly from fear to one of absolute command. He looked steadily round the room and then his voice began to *vibrate*. At first in a low tone, it gradually rose till it assumed the same volume and intensity I had heard that night when he called up the stairs into my room.

"It was a curiously increasing sound, more like the swelling of an instrument than a human voice; and as it grew in power and filled the room, I became aware that a great change was being effected slowly and surely. The confusion of noise and rushings of air fell into the roll of long, steady vibrations not unlike those caused by the deeper pedals of an organ. The movements in the air became less violent, then grew decidedly weaker, and finally ceased altogether. The whisperings and sighings became fainter and fainter, till at last I could not hear them at all; and, strangest of all, the light emitted by the circle, as well as by the designs round it, increased to a steady glow, casting their radiance upwards with the weirdest possible effect upon his features. Slowly, by the power of his voice, behind which lay undoubtedly a genuine knowledge of the occult manipulation of sound, this man dominated the forces that had escaped from their proper sphere, until at length the room was reduced to silence and perfect order again.

"Judging by the immense relief which also communicated itself to my nerves I then felt that the crisis was over and Smith was wholly master of the situation.

"But hardly had I begun to congratulate myself upon this result, and to gather my scattered senses about me, when, uttering a loud cry, I saw him leap out of the circle and fling himself into the air—as it seemed to me, into the empty air. Then, even while holding my breath for dread of the crash he was bound to come upon the floor, I saw him strike with a dull thud against a solid body in mid-air, and the next instant he was wrestling with some ponderous thing that was absolutely invisible to me, and the room shook with the struggle.

"To and fro *they* swayed, sometimes lurching in one direction, sometimes in another, and always in horrible proximity to myself, as I leaned trembling against the wall and watched the encounter.

"It lasted at most but a short minute or two, ending as suddenly as it had begun. Smith, with an unexpected movement, threw up his arms with a cry of relief. At the same instant there was a wild, tearing shriek in the air beside me and something rushed past us with a noise like the passage of a flock of big birds. Both windows rattled as if they would break away from their sashes. Then a sense of emptiness and peace suddenly came over the room, and I knew that all was over.

"Smith, his face exceedingly white, but otherwise strangely composed, turned to me at once.

"'God!—if you hadn't come—You deflected the stream; broke it up—' he whispered. 'You saved me.'"

The doctor made a long pause. Presently he felt for his pipe in the darkness, groping over the table behind us with both hands. No one spoke for a bit, but all dreaded the sudden glare that would come when he struck the match. The fire was nearly out and the great hall was pitch dark.

But the story-teller did not strike that match. He was merely gaining time for some hidden reason of his own. And presently he went on with his tale in a more subdued voice.

"I quite forget," he said, "how I got back to my own room. I only know that I lay with two lighted candles for the rest of the night, and the first thing I did in the morning was to let the landlady know I was leaving her house at the end of the week.

"Smith still has my Rabbinical Treatise. At least he did not return it to me at the time, and I have never seen him since to ask for it."

The Listener

Sept. 4.—I have hunted all over London for rooms suited to my income—£120 a year—and have at last found them. Two rooms, without modern conveniences, it is true, and in an old, ramshackle building, but within a stone's throw of P— Place and in an eminently respectable street. The rent is only £ 25 a year. I had begun to despair when at last I found them by chance. The chance was a mere chance, and unworthy of record. I had to sign a lease for a year, and I did so willingly. The furniture from our old place in Hampshire, which has been stored so long, will just suit them.

Oct. 1.—Here I am in my two rooms, in the centre of London, and not far from the offices of the periodicals, where occasionally I dispose of an article or two. The building is at the end of a *cul-de-sac*. The alley is well paved and clean, and lined chiefly with the backs of sedate and institutional-looking buildings. There is a stable in it. My own house is dignified with the title of "Chambers". I feel as if one day the honor must prove too much for it, and it will swell with pride—and fall asunder. It is very old. The floor of my sitting-room has valleys and low hills on it, and the top of the door slants away from the ceiling with a glorious disregard of what is usual. They must have quarrelled—fifty years ago—and have been going apart ever since.

Oct. 2.—My landlady is old and thin, with a faded, dusty face. She is uncommunicative. The few words she utters seem to cost her pain. Probably her lungs are half choked with dust. She keeps my rooms as free from this commodity as possible, and has the assistance of a strong girl who brings up the breakfast and lights the fire. As I have said already, she is not communicative. In reply to pleasant efforts on my part she informed me briefly that I was the only occupant of the house at present. My rooms had not been occupied for some years. There had been other gentlemen upstairs, but they had left.

She never looks straight at me when she speaks, but fixes her dim eyes on my middle waistcoat button, till I get nervous and begin to think it isn't on straight, or is the wrong sort of button altogether.

Oct. 8.—My week's book is nicely kept, and so far is reasonable. Milk and sugar 7d., bread 6d., butter 8d., marmalade 6d., eggs 1s. 8d., laundress 2s. 9d., oil 6d., attendance 5s.; total 12s. 2d.

The landlady has a son who, she told me, is "somethink on a homnibus". He comes occasionally to see her. I think he drinks, for he talks very loud, regardless of the hour of the day or night, and tumbles about over the furniture downstairs.

All the morning I sit indoors writing—articles; verses for the comic papers; a novel I've been "at" for three years, and concerning which I have dreams; a children's book, in which the imagination has free rein; and another book which is to last as long as myself, since it is an honest record of my soul's advance or retreat in the struggle of life. Besides these, I keep a book of poems which I use as a safety valve, and concerning which I have no dreams whatsoever. Between the lot I am always occupied. In the afternoons I generally try to take a walk for my health's sake, through Regent's Park, into Kensington Gardens, or farther afield to Hampstead Heath.

Oct. 10.—Everything went wrong to-day. I have two eggs for breakfast. This morning one of them was bad. I rang the bell for Emily. When she came in I was reading the paper, and, without looking up, I said, "Egg's bad." "Oh, is it, sir?" she said; "I'll get another one," and went out, taking the egg with her. I waited my breakfast for her return, which was in five minutes. She put the new egg on the table and went away. But, when I looked down, I saw that she had taken away the good egg and left the bad one—all green and yellow—in the slop basin. I rang again.

"You've taken the wrong egg," I said.

"Oh!" she exclaimed; "I thought the one I took down didn't smell so *very* bad." In due time she returned with the good egg, and I resumed my breakfast with two eggs, but less appetite. It was all very trivial, to be sure, but so stupid that I felt annoyed. The character of that egg influenced everything I did. I wrote a bad article, and tore it up. I got a bad headache. I used bad words—to myself. Everything was bad, so I "chucked" work and went for a long walk.

I dined at a cheap chop-house on my way back, and reached home about nine o'clock.

Rain was just beginning to fall as I came in, and the wind was rising. It promised an ugly night. The alley looked dismal and dreary, and the hall of the house, as I passed through it, felt chilly as a tomb. It was the first stormy night I had experienced in my new quarters. The draughts were awful. They came criss-cross, met in the middle of the room, and formed eddies and whirlpools and cold silent currents that almost lifted the hair of my head. I stuffed up the sashes of the windows with neckties and odd socks, and sat over the smoky fire to keep warm. First I tried to write, but found it too cold. My hand turned to ice on the paper.

What tricks the wind did play with the old place! It came rushing up the forsaken alley with a sound like the feet of a hurrying crowd of people who stopped suddenly at the door. I felt as if a lot of curious folk had arranged themselves just outside and were staring up at my windows.

Then they took to their heels again and fled whispering and laughing down the lane, only, however, to return with the next gust of wind and repeat their impertinence. On the other side of my room a single square window opens into a sort of shaft, or well, that measures about six feet across to the back wall of another house. Down this funnel the wind dropped, and puffed and shouted. Such noises I never heard before. Between these two entertainments I sat over the fire in a great-coat, listening to the deep booming in the chimney. It was like being in a ship at sea, and I almost looked for the floor to rise in undulations and rock to and fro.

Oct. 12.—I wish I were not quite so lonely—and so poor. And yet I love both my loneliness and my poverty. The former makes me appreciate the companionship of the wind and rain, while the latter preserves my liver and prevents me wasting time in dancing attendance upon women. Poor, ill-dressed men are not acceptable "attendants".

My parents are dead, and my only sister is—no, not dead exactly, but married to a very rich man. They travel most of the time, he to find his health, she to lose herself. Through sheer neglect on her part she has long passed out of my life. The door closed when, after an absolute silence of five years, she sent me a cheque for £50 at Christmas. It was signed by her husband! I returned it to her in a thousand pieces and in an unstamped envelope. So at least I had the satisfaction of knowing that it cost her something! She wrote back with a broad quill pen that covered a whole page with three lines, "You are evidently as cracked as ever, and rude and ungrateful into the bargain." It had always been my special terror lest the insanity of my father's family should leap across the generations and appear in me. This thought haunted me, and she knew it. So after this little exchange of civilities the door slammed, never to open again. I heard the crash it made, and, with it, the falling from the walls of my heart of many little bits of china with their own peculiar value—rare china, some of it, that only needed dusting. The same walls, too, carried mirrors in which I used sometimes to see reflected the misty lawns of childhood, the daisy chains, the wind-torn blossoms scattered through the orchard by warm rains, the robbers' cave in the long walk, and the hidden store of apples in the hayloft. She was my inseparable companion then—but, when the door slammed, the mirrors cracked across their entire length, and the visions they held vanished for ever. Now I am quite alone. At forty one cannot begin all over again to build up careful friendships, and all others are comparatively worthless.

Oct. 14.—My bedroom is 10 by 10. It is below the level of the front room, and a step leads down into it. Both rooms are very quiet on calm nights, for there is no traffic down this forsaken alley-way. In spite of the occasional larks of the wind, it is a most sheltered strip. At its upper end, below my windows, all the cats of the neighbourhood congregate as soon as darkness gathers. They lie undisturbed on the long ledge of a blind window of the opposite building, for after the postman has come and gone at 9.30, no footsteps ever dare to interrupt their sinister conclave, no step but my own, or sometimes the unsteady footfall of the son who "is somethink on a homnibus".

Oct. 15.—I dined at an "A.B.C." shop on poached eggs and coffee, and then went for a stroll round the outer edge of Regent's Park. It was ten o'clock when I got home.1 counted no less than thirteen cats, all of a dark color, crouching under the lee side of the alley walls. It was a cold night, and the stars shone like points of ice in a blue-black sky. The cats turned their heads and stared at me in silence as I passed. An odd sensation of shyness took possession of me under the glare of so many pairs of unblinking eyes. As I fumbled with the latch-key they jumped noiselessly down and pressed against my legs, as if anxious to be let in. But I slammed the door in their faces and ran quickly upstairs. The front room, as I entered to grope for the matches, felt as cold as a stone vault, and the air held an unusual dampness.

Oct. 17.—For several days I have been working on a ponderous article that allows no play for the fancy. My imagination requires a judicious rein; I am afraid to let it loose, for it carries me sometimes into appalling places beyond the stars and beneath the world. No one realises the danger more than I do. But what a foolish thins to write here—for there is no one to know, no one to realize! My mind of late has held unusual thoughts, thoughts I have never had before, about medicines and drugs and the treatment of strange illnesses. I cannot imagine their source. At no time in my life have I dwelt upon such ideas now constantly throng my brain. I have had no exercise lately, for the weather has been shocking; and all my afternoons have been spent in the reading-room of the British Museum, where I have a reader's ticket.

I have made an unpleasant discovery: there are rats in the house. At night from my bed I have heard them scampering across the hills and valleys of the front room, and my sleep has been a good deal disturbed in consequence.

Oct. 19.—The landlady, I find, has a little boy with her, probably her son's child. In fine weather he plays in the alley, and draws a wooden cart over the cobbles. One of the wheels is off, and it makes a most distracting noise. After putting up with it as long as possible, I found it was getting on my nerves, and I could not write. So I rang the bell. Emily answered it.

"Emily, will you ask the little fellow to make less noise? It's impossible to work."

The girl went downstairs, and soon afterwards the child was called in by the kitchen door. I felt rather a brute for spoiling his play. In a few minutes, however, the noise began again, and I felt that he was the brute. He dragged the broken toy with a string over the stones till the rattling noise jarred every nerve in my body. It became unbearable, and I rang the bell a second time.

"That noise *must* be put a stop to!" I said to the girl, with decision.

"Yes, sir," she grinned, "I know; but one of the wheels is hoff. The men in the stable offered to mend it for 'im, but he wouldn't let them. He says he likes it that way."

"I can't help what he likes. The noise must stop. I can't write."

"Yes, sir; I'll tell Mrs. Monson."

The noise stopped for the day then.

Oct. 23.—Every day for the past week that cart has rattled over the stones, till I have come to think of it as a huge carrier's van with four wheels and two horses; and every morning I have been obliged to ring the bell and have it stopped. The last time Mrs. Monson herself came up, and said she was sorry I had been annoyed; the sounds should not occur again. With rare discursiveness she went on to ask if I was comfortable, and how I liked the rooms. I replied cautiously. I mentioned the rats. She said they were mice. I spoke of the draughts. She said, "Yes, it were a draughty 'ouse." I referred to the cats, and she said they had been as long as she could remember. By way of conclusion, she informed me that the house was over two hundred years old, and that the last gentleman who had occupied my rooms was a painter who "'ad real Jimmy Bueys and Raffles 'anging all hover the walls". It took me some moments to discern that Cimabue and Raphael were in the woman's mind.

Oct. 24.—Last night the son who is "somethink on a homnibus" came in. He had evidently been drinking, for I heard loud and angry voices below in the kitchen long after I had gone to bed. Once, too, I caught the singular words rising up to me through the floor, "Burning from top to bottom is the only thing that'll ever make this 'ouse right."

I knocked on the floor, and the voices ceased suddenly, though later I again heard their clamour in my dreams.

These rooms are very quiet, almost too quiet sometimes. On windless nights they are silent as the grave, and the house might be miles in the country. The roar of London's traffic reaches me only in heavy, distant vibrations. It holds an ominous note sometimes, like that of an approaching army, or an immense tidal-wave very far away thundering in the night.

Oct. 27.—Mrs. Monson, though admirably silent, is a foolish, fussy woman. She does such stupid things. In dusting the room she puts all my things in the wrong places. The ash-trays, which should be on the writing-table, she sets in a silly row on the mantelpiece. The pen-tray, which should be beside the inkstand, she hides away cleverly among the books on my reading-desk. My gloves she arranges daily in idiotic array upon a half-filled bookshelf, and I always have to rearrange them on the low table by the door. She places my armchair at impossible angles between the fire and the light, and the tablecloth—the one with Trinity Hall stains—she puts on the table in such a fashion that when I look at it I feel as if my tie and all my clothes were on crooked and awry. She exasperates me. Her very silence and meekness are irritating. Sometimes I feel inclined to throw the inkstand at her, just to bring an expression into her watery eyes and a squeak from those colorless lips. Dear me! What violent expressions I am making use of! How very foolish of me! And yet it almost seems as if the words were not my own, but had been spoken into my ear—I mean, I never make use of such terms naturally.

Oct. 30.—I have been here a month. The place does not agree with me, I think. My headaches are more frequent and violent, and my nerves are a perpetual source of discomfort and annoyance.

I have conceived a great dislike for Mrs. Monson, a feeling I am certain she reciprocates.

Somehow, the impression comes frequently to me that there are goings on in this house of which I know nothing, and which she is careful to hide from me.

Last night her son slept in the house, and this morning as I was standing at the window I saw him go out. He glanced up and caught my eye. It was a loutish figure and a singularly repulsive face that I saw, and he gave me the benefit of a very unpleasant leer. At least, so I imagined.

Evidently I am getting absurdly sensitive to trifles, and I suppose it is my disordered nerves making themselves felt. In the British Museum this afternoon I noticed several people at the readers' table staring at me and watching every movement I made. Whenever I looked up from my books I found their eyes upon me. It seemed to me unnecessary and unpleasant, and I left earlier than was my custom. When I reached the door I threw back a last look into the room, and saw every head at the table turned in my direction. It annoyed me very much, and yet I know it is foolish to take note of such things. When I am well they pass me by. I must get more regular exercise. Of late I have had next to none.

Nov. 2.—The utter stillness of this house is beginning to oppress me. I wish there were other fellows living upstairs. No footsteps ever sound overhead, and no tread ever passes my door to go up the next flight of stairs. I am beginning to feel some curiosity to go up myself and see what the upper rooms are like. I feel lonely here and isolated, swept into a deserted corner of the world and forgotten. . . . Once I actually caught myself gazing into the long, cracked mirrors, trying to sec the sunlight dancing beneath the trees in the orchard. But only deep shadows seemed to congregate there now, and I soon desisted.

It has been very dark all day, and no wind stirring. The fogs have begun. I had to use a reading-lamp all this morning. There was no cart to be heard to-day. I actually missed it. This morning, in the gloom and silence, I think I could almost have welcomed it. After all, the sound is a very human one, and this empty house at the end of the alley holds other noises that are not quite so satisfactory.

I have never once seen a policeman in the lane, and the postmen always hurry out with no evidence of a desire to loiter.

10 p.m.—As I write this I hear no sound but the deep murmur of the distant traffic and the low sighing of the wind. The two sounds melt into one another. Now and again a cat raises its shrill, uncanny cry upon the darkness. The cats are always there under my windows when the darkness falls. The wind is dropping into the funnel with a noise like the sudden sweeping of immense distant wings. It is a dreary night. I feel lost and forgotten.

Nov. 3.—From my windows I can see arrivals. When anyone comes to the door I can just see the hat and shoulders and the hand on the bell. Only two fellows have been to see me since I came here two months ago. Both of them I saw from the window before they came tip, and heard their voices asking if I was in. Neither of them ever came back.

I have finished the ponderous article. On reading it through, however, I was dissatisfied with it, and drew my pencil through almost every page. There were strange expressions and ideas in it that 1 could not explain, and viewed with amazement, not to say alarm. They did not sound like my *very own*, and I could not remember having written them. Can it be that my memory is beginning to be affected?

My pens are never to be found. That stupid old woman puts them in a different place each day. I must give her due credit for finding so many new hiding places; such ingenuity is wonderful. I have told her repeatedly, but she always says, "I'll speak to Emily, sir." Emily always says, "I'll tell Mrs. Monson, sir." Their foolishness makes me irritable and scatters all my thoughts. I should like to stick the lost pens into them and turn them out, blind-eyed, to be scratched and mauled by those thousand hungry cats. Whew! What a ghastly thought! Where in the world did it come from? Such an idea is no more my own than it is the policeman's. Yet I felt I *had* to write it. It was like a voice singing in my head, and my pen wouldn't stop till the last word was finished. What ridiculous nonsense! I must and will restrain myself. I must take more regular exercise; my nerves and liver plague me horribly.

Nov. 4.—I attended a curious lecture in the French quarter on "Death", but the room was so hot and I was so weary that I fell asleep. The only part I heard, however, touched my imagination vividly. Speaking of suicides, the lecturer said that self-murder was no escape from the miseries of the present, but only a preparation of greater sorrow for the future. Suicides, he declared, cannot shirk their responsibilities so easily. They must return to take up life exactly where they laid it so violently down, but with the added pain and punishment of their weakness. Many of them wander the earth in unspeakable misery till they can *reclothe* themselves in the body of someone else— generally a lunatic, or weak-minded person, who cannot resist the hideous obsession. This is their only means of escape. Surely a weird and horrible idea! I wish I had slept all the time and not heard it at all. My mind is morbid enough without such ghastly fancies. Such mischievous propaganda should be stopped by the police. I'll write to the *Times* and suggest it. Good idea!

I walked home through Greek Street, Soho, and imagined that a hundred years had slipped back into place and De Quincey was still there, haunting the night with invocations to his "just, subtle, and mighty" drug. His vast dreams seemed to hover not very far away. Once started in my brain, the pictures refused to go away; and I saw him sleeping in that cold, tenantless mansion with the strange little waif who was afraid of its ghosts, both together in the shadows under a single horseman's cloak; or wandering in the companionship of the spectral Anne; or, later still, on his way to the eternal rendezvous at the foot of Great Titchfield Street, the rendezvous she never was able to keep. What an unutterable gloom, what an untold horror of sorrow and suffering comes over me as I try to realise something of what that man—boy he then was—must have taken into his lonely heart.

As I came up the alley I saw a light in the top window, and a head and shoulders thrown in an exaggerated shadow upon the blind. I wondered what the son could be doing up there at such an hour.

Nov. 5.—This morning, while writing, someone came up the creaking stairs and knocked cautiously at my door. Thinking it was the landlady, I said, "Come in!" The knock was repeated, and I cried louder, "Come in, come in!" But no one turned the handle, and I continued my writing with a vexed "Well, stay out, then!" under my breath. Went on writing? I tried to, but my thoughts had suddenly dried up at their source. I could not set down a single word. It was a dark, yellow-fog morning, and there was little enough inspiration in the air as it was, but that stupid woman standing just outside my door waiting to be told again to come in roused a spirit of vexation that filled my head to the exclusion of all else. At last I jumped up and opened the door myself.

"What do you want, and why in the world don't you come in?" I cried out. But the words dropped into empty air. There was no one there. The fog poured up the dingy staircase in deep yellow coils, but there was no sign of a human being anywhere.

I slammed the door, with imprecations upon the house and its noises, and went back to my work. A few minutes later Emily came in with a letter.

"Were you or Mrs. Monson outside a few minutes ago knocking at my door?"

"No, sir."

"Are you sure?

"Mrs. Monson's gone to market, and there's no one but me and the child in the 'ole 'ouse, and I've been washing the dishes for the last hour, sir."

I fancied the girl's face turned a shade paler. She fidgeted towards the door with a glance over her shoulder.

"Wait, Emily," I said, and then told her what I had heard. She stared stupidly at me, though her eyes shifted now and then over the articles in the room.

"Who was it? "I asked when I had come to the end. "Mrs. Monson says it's holy mice," she said, as if repeating a learned lesson.

"Mice!" I exclaimed; "it's nothing of the sort. Someone was feeling about outside my door.

Who was it? Is the son in the house?"

Her whole manner changed suddenly, and she became earnest instead of evasive. She seemed anxious to tell the truth.

"Oh no, sir; there's no one in the house at all but you and me and the child, and there couldn't 'ave been nobody at your door. As for them knocks—" She stopped abruptly, as though she had said too much.

"Well, what about the knocks?" I said more gently.

"Of course," she stammered, "the knocks isn't mice, nor the

footsteps neither, but then—"

Again she came to a full halt.

"Anything wrong with the house?"

"Lor', no, sir; the drains is splendid!"

"I don't mean drains, girl. I mean, did anything—anything bad ever happen here?"

She flushed up to the roots of her hair, and then turned suddenly pale again. She was obviously in considerable distress, and there was something she was anxious, yet afraid to tell— some forbidden thing she was not allowed to mention.

"I don't mind what it was, only I should like to know," I said encouragingly.

Raising her frightened eyes to my face, she began to blurt out something about "that which 'appened once to a gentleman that lived hupstairs", when a shrill voice calling her name sounded below.

"Emily, Emily!" It was the returning landlady, and the girl tumbled downstairs as if pulled backwards by a rope, leaving me full of conjectures as to what in the world could have happened to a gentleman *upstairs* that could in so curious a manner affect my ears *downstairs*.

Nov. 10.—I have done capital work; have finished the ponderous article and had it accepted for the Review, and another one ordered. I feel well and cheerful, and have had regular exercise and good sleep; no headaches, no nerves, no liver! Those pills the chemist recommended are wonderful. I can watch the child playing with his cart and feel no annoyance; sometimes I almost feel inclined to join him. Even the grey-faced landlady rouses pity in me; I am sorry for her: so worn, so weary, so oddly put together, just like the building. She looks as if she had once suffered some shock of terror, and was momentarily dreading another. When I spoke to her to-day very gently about not putting the pens in the ash-tray and the gloves on the hook-shelf she raised her faint eyes to mine for the first time, and said with the ghost of a smile, "I'll try and re-member, sir." I felt inclined to pat her on the back and say, "Come, cheer up and be jolly. Life's not so bad after all." Oh! I am much better. There's nothing like open air and success and good sleep. They build up as if by magic the portions of the heart eaten down by despair and unsatisfied yearnings. Even to the cats I feel friendly. When I came in at eleven o'clock to-night they followed me to the door in a stream, and I stooped down to stroke the one nearest to me. Bah! The brute hissed and spat, and struck at me with her paws. The claw caught my hand and drew blood in a thin line. The others danced sideways into the darkness, screeching, as though I had done them an injury. I believe these cats really hate me. Perhaps they are only waiting to be reinforced. Then they will attack me. Ha, ha! In spite of the momentary annoyance, this fancy sent me laughing upstairs to my room.

The fire was out, and the room seemed unusually cold. As I groped my way over to the mantelpiece to find the matches I realised all at once that there was another person standing beside me in the darkness. I could, of course, see nothing, but my fingers, feeling along the ledge, came into forcible contact with something that was at once withdrawn. It was cold and moist. I could have sworn it was somebody's hand. My flesh began to creep instantly.

"Who's that?" I exclaimed in a loud voice.

My voice dropped into the silence like a pebble into a deep well. There was no answer, but at the same moment I heard someone moving away from me across the room in the direction of the door. It was a confused sort of footstep, and the sound of garments brushing the furniture on the way. The same second my hand stumbled upon the match-box, and I struck a light. I expected to see Mrs. Monson, or Emily, or perhaps the son who is something on an omnibus. But the flare of the gas-jet illumined an empty room; there was not a sign of a person anywhere. I felt the hair stir upon my head, and instinctively I backed tip against the wall, lest something should approach me from behind. I was distinctly alarmed. But the next minute I recovered myself. The door was open on to the landing, and I crossed the room, not without some inward trepidation, and went out. The light from the room fell upon the stairs, but there was no one to be seen anywhere, nor was there any sound on the creaking wooden staircase to indicate a departing creature.

I was in the act of turning to go in again when a sound overhead caught my ear. It was a very faint sound, not unlike the sigh of wind; yet it could not have been the wind, for the night was still as the grave. Though it was not repeated, I resolved to go upstairs and see for myself what it all meant. Two senses had been affected—touch and hearing— and I could not believe that I had been deceived. So, with a lighted candle, I went stealthily forth on my unpleasant journey into the upper regions of this queer little old house.

On the first landing there was only one door, and it was locked. On the second there was also only one door, but when I turned the handle it opened. There came forth to meet me the chill musty air that is characteristic of a long unoccupied room. With it there came an indescribable odor. I use the adjective advisedly. Though very faint, diluted as it were, it was nevertheless an odor that made my gorge rise. I had never smelt anything like it before, and I cannot describe it.

The room was small and square, close under the roof, with a sloping ceiling and two tiny windows. It was cold as the grave, without a shred of carpet or a stick of furniture. The icy atmosphere and the nameless odor combined to make the room abominable to me, and, after lingering a moment to see that it contained no cupboards or corners into which a person might have crept for concealment, I made haste to shut the door, and went downstairs again to bed.

Evidently I had been deceived after all as to the noise.

In the night I had a foolish but very vivid dream. I dreamed that the landlady and another person, dark and not properly visible, entered my room on all fours, followed by a horde of immense cats. They attacked me as I lay in bed, and murdered me, and then dragged my body upstairs and deposited it on the floor of that cold little square room under the roof.

Nov. 11.—Since my talk with Emily—the unfinished talk—I have hardly once set eyes on her. Mrs. Monson now attends wholly to my wants. As usual, she does everything exactly as I don't like it done. It is all too utterly trivial to mention, but it is exceedingly irritating. Like small doses of morphine often repeated, she has finally a cumulative effect.

Nov. 12.—This morning I woke early, and came into the front room to get a book, meaning to read in bed till it was time to get tip. Emily was laying the fire.

"Good morning!" I said cheerfully. "Mind you make a good fire. It's very cold."

The girl turned and showed me a startled face. It was not Emily at all!

"Where's Emily?" I exclaimed.

"You mean the girl as was 'ere before me?"

"Has Emily left?"

"I came on the 6th," she replied sullenly, "and she'd gone then." I got my book and went back to bed. Emily must have been sent away almost immediately after our conversation. This reflection kept coming between me and the printed page. I was glad when it was time to get up.

Such prompt energy, such merciless decision, seemed to argue something of importance—to somebody.

Nov. 13.—The wound inflicted by the cat's claw has swollen, and causes me annoyance and some pain. It throbs and itches. I'm afraid my blood must be in poor condition, or it would have healed by now. I opened it with a penknife soaked in an antiseptic solution, and cleansed it thoroughly. I have heard unpleasant stories of the results of wounds inflicted by cats.

Nov. 14.—In spite of the curious effect this house certainly exercises upon my nerves, I like it. It is lonely and deserted in the very heart of London, but it is also for that reason quiet to work in. I wonder why it is so cheap. Some people might he suspicious, but I did not even ask the reason. No answer is better than a lie. If only I could remove the cats from the outside and the rats from the inside. I feel that I shall grow accustomed more and more to its peculiarities, and shall die here. Ah, that expression reads queerly and gives a wrong impression: I meant live and die here. I shall renew the lease from year to year till one of us crumbles to pieces. From present indications the building will be the first to go.

Nov. 16.—It is abominable the way my nerves go up and down with me—and rather discouraging. This morning I woke to find my clothes scattered about the room, and a cane chair overturned beside the bed. My coat and waistcoat looked just as if they had been tried on by someone in the night. I had horribly vivid dreams, too, in which someone covering his face with his hands kept coming close up to me, crying out as if in pain. "Where can I find covering? Oh, who will clothe me?" How silly, and yet it frightened me a little. It was so dreadfully real. It is now over a year since I last walked in my sleep and woke up with such a shock on the cold pavement of Earl's Court Road, where I then lived. I thought I was cured, but evidently not. This discovery has rather a disquieting effect upon me. To-night I shall resort to the old trick of tying my toe to the bed-post.

Nov. 17.—Last night I was again troubled by most oppressive dreams. Someone seemed to be moving in the night up and down my room, sometimes passing into the front room, and then returning to stand beside the bed and stare intently down upon me. I was being watched by this person all night long. I never actually awoke, though I was often very near it. I suppose it was a nightmare from indigestion, for this morning I have one of my old vile headaches. Yet all my clothes lay about the floor when I awoke, where they had evidently been flung (had I so tossed them?) during the dark hours, and my trousers trailed over the step into the front room.

Worse than this, though—I fancied I noticed about the room in the morning that strange, fetid odor. Though very faint, its mere suggestion is foul and nauseating. 'What in the world can it be, I wonder? . . . In future I shall lock my door.

Nov. 26.—I have accomplished a lot of good work during this past week, and have also managed to get regular exercise. I have felt well and in an equable state of mind. Only two things have occurred to disturb my equanimity. The first is trivial in itself, and no doubt to be easily explained. The upper window where I saw the light on the night of November 4, with the shadow of a large head and shoulders upon the blind, is one of the windows in the square room under the roof. In reality it has *no blind at all!*

Here is the other thing. I was coming home last night in a fresh fall of snow about eleven o'clock, my umbrella low down over my head. Half-way up the alley, where the snow was wholly untrodden, I saw a man's legs in front of me. The umbrella hid the rest of his figure, but on raising it I saw that he was tall and broad and was walking, as I was, towards the door of my house. He could not have been four feet ahead of me. I had thought the alley was empty when I entered it, but might of course have been mistaken very easily.

A sudden gust of wind compelled me to lower the umbrella, and when I raised it again, not half a minute later, there was no longer any man to be seen. With a few more steps I reached the door. It was closed as usual. I then noticed with a sudden sensation of dismay that the surface of the freshly fallen snow was *unbroken.* My own foot-marks were the only ones to be seen anywhere, and though I retraced my way to tile point where I had first seen the man, I could find no slightest impression of any other boots. Feeling creepy and uncomfortable, I went upstairs, and was glad to get into bed.

Nov. 28.—With the fastening of my bedroom door the disturbances ceased. I am convinced that I walked in my sleep. Probably I untied my toe and then tied it up again. The fancied security of the locked door would alone have been enough to restore sleep to my troubled spirit and enable me to rest quietly.

Last night, however, the annoyance was suddenly renewed another and more aggressive form. I woke in the darkness with the impression that someone was standing outside my bedroom door *listening.* As I became more awake the impression grew into positive knowledge.

Though there was no appreciable sound of moving or breathing, I was so convinced of the propinquity of a listener that I crept out of bed and approached the door. As I did so there came faintly from the next room the unmistakable sound of someone retreating stealthily across the floor. Yet, as I heard it, it was neither the tread of a man nor a regular footstep, but rather, it seemed to me, a confused sort of crawling, almost as of someone on his hands and knees.

I unlocked the door in less than a second, and passed quickly into the front room, and I could feel, as by the subtlest imaginable vibrations upon my nerves, that the spot I was standing in had just that instant been vacated! The Listener had moved; he was now behind the other door, standing in the passage. Yet this door was also closed. I moved swiftly, and as silently as possible, across the floor, and turned the handle. A cold rush of air met me from the passage and sent shiver after shiver down my back. There was no one in the doorway; there was no one on the little landing; there was no one moving down the staircase. Yet I had been so quick that this midnight Listener could not be very far away, and I felt that if I persevered I should eventually come face to face with him. And the courage that came so opportunely to overcome my nervousness and horror seemed born of the unwelcome conviction that it was somehow necessary for my safety as well as my sanity that I should find this intruder and force his secret from him. For was it not the intent action of his mind upon my own, in concentrated listening, that had awakened me with such a vivid realization of his presence?

Advancing across the narrow landing, I peered down into the well of the little house. There was nothing to be seen; no one was moving in the darkness. How cold the oilcloth was to my bare feet.

I cannot say what it was that suddenly drew my eyes upwards. I only know that, without apparent reason, I looked up and saw a person about half-way up the next turn of the stairs, leaning forward over the balustrade and staring straight into my face. It was a man. He appeared to be clinging to the rail rather than standing on the stairs. The gloom made it impossible to see much beyond the general outline, but the head and shoulders were seemingly enormous, and stood sharply silhouetted against the skylight in the roof immediately above. The idea flashed into my brain in a moment that I was looking into the visage of something monstrous. The huge skull, the mane-like hair, the wide-humped shoulders, suggested, in a way I did not pause to analyze, that which was scarcely human; and for some seconds, fascinated by horror, I returned the gaze and stared into the dark, inscrutable countenance above me, without knowing exactly where I was or what I was doing.

Then I realised in quite a new way that I was face to face with the secret midnight Listener, and I steeled myself as best I could for what was about to come.

The source of the rash courage that came to me at this awful moment will ever be to me an inexplicable mystery. Though shivering with fear, and my forehead wet with an unholy dew, I resolved to advance. Twenty questions leaped to my lips: What are you? What do you want?

Why do you listen and watch? Why do you come into my room? But none of them found articulate utterance.

I began forthwith to climb the stairs, and with the first signs of my advance he drew himself back into the shadows and began to move. He retreated as swiftly as I advanced. I heard the sound of his crawling motion a few steps ahead of me, ever maintaining the same distance. When I reached the landing he was half-way up the next flight, and when I was half-way up the next flight he had already arrived at the top landing. I then heard him open the door of the little square room under the roof and go in. Immediately, though the door did not close after him, the sound of his moving entirely ceased.

At this moment I longed for a light, or a stick, or any weapon whatsoever; but I had none of these things, and it was impossible to go back. So I marched steadily up the rest of the stairs, and in less than a minute found myself standing in the gloom face to face with the door through which this creature had just entered.

For a moment I hesitated. The door was about half-way open, and the Listener was standing evidently in his favourite attitude just behind it—listening. To search through that dark room for him seemed hopeless; to enter the same small space where he was seemed horrible. The very idea filled me with loathing, and I almost decided to turn back.

It is strange at such times how trivial things impinge on the consciousness with a shock as of something important and immense. Something—it may have been a beetle or a mouse—scuttled over the bare boards behind me. The door moved a quarter of an inch, closing. My decision came back with a sudden rush, as it were, and thrusting out a foot, I kicked the door so that it swung sharply back to its full extent, and permitted me to walk forward slowly into the aperture of profound blackness beyond. What a queer soft sound my bare feet made on the boards! how the blood sang and buzzed in my head!

I was inside. The darkness closed over me, hiding even the windows. I began to grope my way round the walls in a thorough search; but in order to prevent all possibility of the other's escape, I first of all *closed the door.*

There we were, we two, shut in together between four walls, within a few feet of one another.

But with what, with whom, was I thus momentarily imprisoned? A new light flashed suddenly over the affair with a swift, illuminating brilliance—and I knew I was a fool, an utter fool! I was wide awake at last, and the horror was evaporating. My cursed nerves again; a dream, a nightmare, and the old result—walking in my sleep. The figure was a dream-figure. Many a time before had the actors in my dreams stood before me for some moments after I was awake. . . .

There was a chance match in my pajamas' pocket, and I struck it on the wall. The room was utterly empty. It held not even a shadow. I went quickly down to bed, cursing my wretched nerves and my foolish, vivid dreams. But as soon as ever I was asleep again, the same uncouth figure of a man crept back to my bedside, and bending over me with his immense head close to my ear, whispered repeatedly in my dreams, "I want your body; I want its covering. I'm waiting for it, and listening always." Words scarcely less foolish than the dream.

But I wonder what that queer odor was up in the square room. I noticed it again, and stronger than ever before, and it seemed to be also in my bedroom when I woke this morning.

Nov. 29.—Slowly, as moonbeams rise over a misty sea in June, the thought is entering my mind that my nerves and somnambulistic dreams do not adequately account for the influence this house exercises upon me. It holds me as with a fine, invisible net. I cannot escape if I would. It draws me, and it means to keep me.

Nov. 30.—The post this morning brought me a letter from Aden, forwarded from my old rooms in Earl's Court. It was from Chapter, my former Trinity chum, who is on his way home from the East, and asks for my address. I sent it to him at the hotel he mentioned, "to await arrival".

As I have already said, my windows command a view of the alley, and I can see an arrival without difficulty. This morning, while I was busy writing, the sound of footsteps coming up the alley filled me with a sense of vague alarm that I could in no way account for. I went over to the window, and saw a man standing below waiting for the door to be opened. His shoulders were broad, his top-hat glossy, and his overcoat fitted beautifully round the collar. All this I could see, but no more. Presently the door was opened, and the shock to my nerves was unmistakable when I heard a man's voice ask, "Is Mr. — still here?" mentioning my name. I could not catch the answer, but it could only have been in the affirmative, for the man entered the hall and the door shut to behind him. But I waited in vain for the sound of his steps on the stairs. There was no sound of any kind. It seemed to me so strange that I opened my door and looked out. No one was anywhere to be seen. I walked across the narrow landing, and looked through the window that commands the whole length of the alley. There was no sign of a human being, coming or going. The lane was deserted. Then I deliberately walked downstairs into the kitchen, and asked the grey-faced landlady if a gentleman had just that minute called for me.

The answer, given with an odd, weary sort of smile, was "No!"

Dec. 1.—I feel genuinely alarmed and uneasy over the state of my nerves. Dreams are dreams, but never before have I had dreams in broad daylight.

I am looking forward very much to Chapter's arrival. He is a capital fellow, vigorous, healthy, with no nerves, and even less imagination; and he has £2,000 a year into the bargain. Periodically he makes me offers—the last was to travel round the world with him as secretary, which was a delicate way of paying my expenses and giving me some pocket-money—offers, however, which I invariably decline. I prefer to keep his friendship. Women could not come between us; money might—therefore I give it no opportunity. Chapter always laughed at what he called my "fancies", being himself possessed only of that thin-blooded quality of imagination which is ever associated with the prosaic-minded man. Yet, if taunted with this obvious lack, his wrath is deeply stirred. His psychology is that of the crass materialist— always a rather funny article. It will afford me genuine relief, none the less, to hear the cold judgment his mind will have to pass upon the story of this house as I shall have it to tell.

Dec. 2.—The strangest part of it all I have not referred to in this brief diary. Truth to tell, I have been afraid to set it down in black and white. I have kept it in the background of my thoughts, preventing it as far as possible from taking shape. In spite of my efforts, however, it has continued to grow stronger.

Now that I come to face the issue squarely it is harder to express than I imagined. Like a half-remembered melody that trips in the head but vanishes the moment you try to sing it, these thoughts form a group in the background of my mind, *behind* my mind, as it were, and refuse to come forward. They are crouching ready to spring, but the actual leap never takes place.

In these rooms, except when my mind is strongly concentrated on my own work, I find myself suddenly dealing in thoughts and ideas that are not my own! New, strange conceptions, wholly foreign to my temperament, are for ever cropping up in my head. What precisely they are is of no particular importance. The point is that they are entirely apart from the channel in which my thoughts have hitherto been accustomed to flow. Especially they come when my mind is at rest, unoccupied; when I'm dreaming over the fire, or sitting with a book which fails to hold my attention. Then these thoughts which are not mine spring into life and make me feel exceedingly uncomfortable. Sometimes they are so strong that I almost feel as if someone were in the room beside me, thinking aloud.

Evidently my nerves and liver are shockingly out of order. I must work harder and take more vigorous exercise. The horrid thoughts never come when my mind is much occupied. But they are always there—waiting and as it were *alive.*

What I have attempted to describe above came first upon me gradually after I had been some days in the house, and then grew steadily in strength. The other strange thing has come to me only twice in all these weeks. It *appals me.* It is the consciousness of the propinquity of some deadly and loathsome disease. It comes over me like a wave of fever heat, and then passes off, leaving me cold and trembling. The air seems for a few seconds to become tainted. So penetrating and convincing is the thought of this sickness, that on both occasions my brain has turned momentarily dizzy, and through my mind, like flames of white heat, have flashed the ominous names of all the dangerous illnesses I know. I can no more explain these visitations than I can fly, yet I know there is no dreaming about the clammy skin and palpitating heart which they always leave as witnesses of their brief visit.

Most strongly of all was I aware of this nearness of a mortal sickness when, on the night of the 28th, I went upstairs in pursuit of the listening figure. When we were shut in together in that little square room under the roof, I felt that I was face to face with the actual essence of this invisible and malignant disease. Such a feeling never entered my heart before, and I pray to God it never may again.

There! Now I have confessed. I have given some expression at least to the feelings that so far I have been afraid to see in my own writing. For—since I can no longer deceive myself—the experiences of that night (28th) were no more a dream than my daily breakfast is a dream; and the trivial entry in this diary by which I sought to explain away an occurrence that caused me unutterable horror was due solely to my desire not to acknowledge in words what I really felt and believed to be true. The increase that would have accrued to my horror by so doing might have been more than I could stand.

Dec. 3.—I wish Chapter would come. My facts are all ready marshaled, and I can see his cool, grey eyes fixed incredulously on my face as I relate them: the knocking at my door, the well-dressed caller, the light in the upper window and the shadow upon the blind, the man who preceded me in the snow, the scattering of my clothes at night, Emily's arrested confession, the landlady's suspicious reticence, the midnight listener on the stairs, and those awful subsequent words in my sleep; and above all, and hardest to tell, the presence of the abominable sickness, and the stream of thoughts and ideas that are not my own.

I can see Chapter's face, and I can almost hear his deliberate words, "You've been at the tea again, and underfeeding, I expect, as usual. Better see my nerve doctor, and then come with me to the south of France." For this fellow, who knows nothing of disordered liver or high-strung nerves, goes regularly to a great nerve specialist with the periodical belief that his nervous system is beginning to decay.

Dec. 5.—Ever since the incident of the Listener, I have kept a night-light burning in my bedroom, and my sleep has been undisturbed. Last night, however, I was subjected to a far worse annoyance. I woke suddenly, and saw a man in front of the dressing-table regarding himself in the mirror. The door was locked, as usual. I knew at once it was the Listener, and the blood turned to ice in my veins. Such a wave of horror and dread swept over me that it seemed to turn me rigid in the bed, and I could neither move nor speak. I noted, however, that the odor I so abhorred was strong in the room.

The man seemed to be tall and broad. He was stooping forward over the mirror. His back was turned to me, but in the glass I saw the reflection of a huge head and face illumined fitfully by the flicker of the night-light. The spectral grey of very early morning stealing in round the edges of the curtains lent an additional horror to the picture, for it fell upon hair that was tawny and mane-like, hanging loosely about a face whose swollen, rugose features bore the once seen never forgotten leonine expression of— I dare not write down that awful word. But, byway of corroborative proof, I saw in the faint mingling of the two lights that there were several bronze-colored blotches on the cheeks which the man was evidently examining with great care in the glass. The lips were pale and very thick and large. One hand I could not see, but the other rested on the ivory back of my hair-brush. Its muscles were strangely contracted, the fingers thin to emaciation, the back of the hand closely puckered up. It was like a big grey spider crouching to spring, or the claw of a great bird.

The full realization that I was alone in the room with this nameless creature, almost within arm's reach of him, overcame me to such a degree that, when he suddenly turned and regarded me with small beady eyes, wholly out of proportion to the grandeur of their massive setting, I sat bolt upright in bed, uttered a loud cry, and then fell back in a dead swoon of terror upon the bed.

Dec. 5.—. . . When I came to this morning, the first thing I noticed was that my clothes were strewn all over the floor. . . . I find it difficult to put my thoughts together, and have sudden accesses of violent trembling. I determined that I would go at once to Chapter's hotel and find out when he is expected. I cannot refer to what happened in the night; it is too awful, and I have to keep my thoughts rigorously away from it. I feel light-headed and queer, couldn't eat any breakfast, and have twice vomited with blood. While dressing to go out, a hansom rattled up noisily over the cobbles, and a minute later the door opened, and to my great joy in walked the very subject of my thoughts.

The sight of his strong face and quiet eyes had an immediate effect upon me, and I grew calmer again. His very handshake was a sort of tonic. But, as I listened eagerly to the deep tones of his reassuring voice, and the visions of the night-time paled a little, I began to realise how very hard it was going to be to tell him my wild intangible tale. Some men radiate an animal vigour that destroys the delicate woof of a vision and effectually prevents its reconstruction. Chapter was one of these men.

We talked of incidents that had filled the interval since we last met, and he told me something of his travels. He talked and I listened. But, so full was I of the horrid thing I had to tell, that I made a poor listener. I was for ever watching my opportunity to leap in and explode it all under his nose.

Before very long, however, it was borne in upon me that he too was merely talking for time. He too held something of importance in the background of his mind, something too weighty to let fall till the right moment presented itself. So that during the whole of the first half-hour we were both waiting for the psychological moment in which properly to release our respective bombs; and the intensity of our minds' action set up opposing forces that merely sufficed to hold one another in check—and nothing more. As soon as I realised this, therefore, I resolved to yield. I renounced for the time my purpose of telling my story, and had the satisfaction of seeing that his mind, released from the restraint of my own, at once began to make preparations for the discharge of its momentous burden. The talk grew less and less magnetic; the interest waned; the descriptions of his travels became less alive. There were pauses between his sentences. Presently he repeated himself. His words clothed no living thoughts. The pauses grew longer. Then the interest dwindled altogether and went out like a candle in the wind. His voice ceased, and he looked up squarely into my face with serious and anxious eyes.

The psychological moment had come at last!

"I say—" he began, and then stopped short.

I made an unconscious gesture of encouragement, but said no word. I dreaded the impending disclosure exceedingly. A dark shadow seemed to precede it.

"I say," he blurted out at last, "what in the world made you ever come to this place—to these rooms, I mean?"

"They're cheap, for one thing," I began, "and central and—"

"They're too cheap," he interrupted. "Didn't you ask what made 'em so cheap?"

"It never occurred to me at the time."

There was a pause in which he avoided my eyes.

"For God's sake, go on, man, and tell it!" I cried, for the suspense was getting more than I could stand in my nervous condition.

"This was where Blount lived so long," he said quietly, "and where he—died. You know, in the old days I often used to come here and see him, and do what I could to alleviate his—" He stuck fast again.

"Well!" I said with a great effort. "Please go on— faster."

"But," Chapter went on, turning his face to the window with a perceptible shiver, "he finally got so terrible I simply couldn't stand it, though I always thought I could stand anything. It got on my nerves and made me dream, and haunted me day and night."

I stared at him, and said nothing. I had never heard of Blount in my life, and didn't know what he was talking about. But, all the same, I was trembling, and my mouth had become strangely dry.

"This is the first time I've been back here since," he said almost in a whisper, "and, 'pon my word, it gives me the creeps. I swear it isn't fit for a man to live in. I never saw you look so bad, old man."

"I've got it for a year," I jerked out, with a forced laugh; "signed the lease and all. I thought it was rather a bargain."

Chapter shuddered, and buttoned his overcoat up to his neck. Then he spoke in a low voice, looking occasionally behind him as though he thought someone was listening. I too could have sworn someone else was in the room with us.

"He did it himself, you know, and no one blamed him a bit; his sufferings were awful. For the last two years he used to wear a veil when he went out, and even then it was always in a closed carriage. Even the attendant who had nursed him for so long was at length obliged to leave. The extremities of both the lower limbs were gone, dropped off, and he moved about the ground on all fours with a sort of crawling motion. The odor, too, was——"

I was obliged to interrupt him here. I could hear no more details of that sort. My skin was moist, I felt hot and cold by turns, for at last I was beginning to understand.

"Poor devil," Chapter went on; "I used to keep my eyes closed as much as possible. He always begged to be allowed to take his veil off, and asked if I minded very much. I used to stand by the open window. He never touched me, though. He rented the whole house. Nothing would induce him to leave it."

"Did he occupy—these very rooms?"

"No. He had the little room on the top floor, the square one just under the roof. He preferred it because it was dark. These rooms were too near the ground, and he was afraid people might see him through the windows. A crowd had been known to follow him up to the very door, and then stand below the windows in the hope of catching a glimpse of his face."

"But there were hospitals."

"He wouldn't go near one, and they didn't like to force him. You know, they say it's *not* contagious, so there was nothing to prevent his staying here if he wanted to. He spent all his time reading medical books, about drugs and so on. His head and face were something appalling, just like a lion's."

I held up my hand to arrest further description.

"He was a burden to the world, and he knew it. One night I suppose he realised it too keenly to wish to live. He had the free use of drugs—and in the morning he was found dead on the floor. Two years ago, that was, and they said then he had still several years to live."

"Then, in Heaven's name!" I cried, unable to bear the suspense any longer, "tell me what it was he had, and be quick about it."

"I thought you knew!" he exclaimed, with genuine surprise. "I thought you knew!"

He leaned forward and our eyes met. In a scarcely audible whisper
I caught the words his lips seemed almost afraid to utter:
"He was a leper!"

Max Hensig

Besides the departmental men on the New York *Vulture*, there
were about twenty reporters for general duty, and Williams had worked
his way up till he stood easily among the first half-dozen; for, in
addition to being accurate and painstaking, he was able to bring to his
reports of common things that touch of imagination and humor which
just lifted them out of the rut of mere faithful recording. Moreover, the
city editor (*anglice* news editor) appreciated his powers, and always
tried to give him assignments that did himself and the paper credit, and
he was justified now in expecting to be relieved of the hack jobs that
were usually allotted to new men.

He was therefore puzzled and a little disappointed one morning as
he saw his inferiors summoned one after another to the news desk to
receive the best assignments of the day, and when at length his turn
came, and the city editor asked him to cover "the Hensig story", he
gave a little start of vexation that almost betrayed him into asking what
the devil "the Hensig story" was. For it is the duty of every morning
newspaper man—in New York at least—to have made himself familiar
with all the news of the day before he shows himself at the office, and
though Williams had already done this, he could not recall either the
name or the story.

"You can run to a hundred or a hundred and fifty, Mr. Williams.
Cover the trial thoroughly, and get good interviews with Hensig and the
lawyers. There'll be no night assignment for you till the case is over."

Williams was going to ask if there were any private "tips" from the
District Attorney's office, but the editor was already speaking with
Weekes, who wrote the daily "weather story", and he went back slowly
to his desk, angry and disappointed, to read up the Hensig case and lay
his plans for the day accordingly. At any rate, he reflected, it looked
like "a soft job", and as there was to be no second assignment for him
that night, he would get off by eight o'clock, and be able to dine and
sleep for once like a civilised man. And that was something.

It took him some time, however, to discover that the Hensig case
was only a murder story. And this increased his disgust. It was tucked
away in the corners of most of the papers, and little importance was
attached to it. A murder trial is not first-class news unless there are very
special features connected with it, and Williams had already covered
scores of them. There was a heavy sameness about them that made it
difficult to report them interestingly, and as a rule they were left to the
tender mercies of the "flimsy" men—the Press Associations—and no

paper sent a special man unless the case was distinctly out of the usual. Moreover, a hundred and fifty meant a column and a half, and Williams, not being a space man, earned the same money whether he wrote a stickful or a page; so that he felt doubly aggrieved, and walked out into the sunny open spaces opposite Newspaper Row heaving a deep sigh and cursing the boredom of his trade.

Max Hensig, he found, was a German doctor accused of murdering his second wife by injecting arsenic. The woman had been buried several weeks when the suspicious relatives got the body exhumed, and a quantity of the poison had been found in her. Williams recalled something about the arrest, now he came to think of it; but he felt no special interest in it, for ordinary murder trials were no longer his legitimate work, and he scorned them. At first, of course, they had thrilled him horribly, and some of his interviews with the prisoners, especially just before execution, had deeply impressed his imagination and kept him awake o' nights. Even now he could not enter the gloomy Tombs Prison, or cross the Bridge of Sighs leading from it to the courts, without experiencing a real sensation, for its huge Egyptian columns and massive walls closed round him like death; and the first time he walked down Murderers' Row, and came in view of the cell doors, his throat was dry, and he had almost turned and run out of the building.

The first time, too, that he covered the trial of a Negro and listened to the man's hysterical speech before sentence was pronounced, he was absorbed with interest, and his heart leaped. The wild appeals to the Deity, the long invented words, the ghastly pallor under the black skin, the rolling eyes, and the torrential sentences all seemed to him to be something tremendous to describe for his sensational sheet; and the stickfull that was eventually printed—written by the flimsy man too—had given him quite a new standard of the relative value of news and of the quality of the satiated public palate. He had reported the trials of a Chinaman, stolid as wood; of an Italian who had been too quick with his knife; and of a farm girl who had done both her parents to death in their beds, entering their room stark naked, so that no stains should betray her; and at the beginning these things haunted him for days.

But that was all months ago, when he first came to New York. Since then his work had been steadily in the criminal courts, and he had grown a second skin. An execution in the electric chair at Sing Sing could still unnerve him somewhat, but mere murder no longer thrilled or excited him, and he could be thoroughly depended on to write a good "murder story"—an account that his paper could print without blue pencil.

Accordingly he entered the Tombs Prison with nothing stronger than the feeling of vague oppression that gloomy structure always stirred in him, and certainly with no particular emotion connected with the prisoner he was about to interview; and when he reached the second iron door, where a warder peered at him through a small grating, he heard a voice behind him, and turned to find the Chronicle man at his heels.

"Hullo, Senator! What good trail are you following down here?" he cried, for the other got no small assignments, and never had less than a column on the Chronicle front page at space rates.

"Same as you, I guess—Hensig," was the reply.

"But there's no space in Hensig," said Williams with surprise. "Are you back on salary again?"

"Not much," laughed the Senator—no one knew his real name, but he was always called Senator. "But Hensig's good for two hundred easy. There's a whole list of murders behind him, we hear, and this is the first time he's been caught."

"Poison?"

The Senator nodded in reply, turning to ask the warder some question about another case, and Williams waited for him in the corridor, impatiently rather, for he loathed the musty prison odor. He watched the Senator as he talked, and was distinctly glad he had come. They were good friends: he had helped Williams when he first joined the small army of newspaper men and was not much welcomed, being an Englishman. Common origin and good-heartedness mixed themselves delightfully in his face, and he always made Williams think of a friendly, honest cart-horse— stolid, strong, with big and simple emotions.

"Get a hustle on, Senator," he said at length impatiently. The two reporters followed the warder down the flagged corridor, past a row of dark cells, each with its occupant, until the man, swinging his keys in the direction indicated, stopped and pointed:

"Here's your gentleman," he said, and then moved on down the corridor, leaving them staring through the bars at a tail, slim young man, pacing to and fro. He had flaxen hair and very bright blue eyes; his skin was white, and his face wore so open and innocent an expression that one would have said he could not twist a kitten's tail without wincing.

From the *Chronicle* and *Vulture*," explained Williams, by way of introduction, and the talk at once began in the usual way.

The man in the cell ceased his restless pacing up and down, and stopped opposite the bars to examine them. He stared straight into Williams's eyes for a moment, and the reporter noted a very different expression from the one he had first seen. It actually made him shift his position and stand a little to one side. But the movement was wholly instinctive. He could not have explained why he did it.

"Guess you vish me to say I did it, and then egsplain to you *how* I did it," the young doctor said coolly, with a marked German accent.

"But I haf no copy to gif you shust now. You see at the trial it is nothing but spite—and shealosy of another woman. I lofed my vife. I vould not haf gilled her for anything in the vorld—"

"Oh, of course, of course, Dr. Hensig," broke in the Senator, who was more experienced in the ways of difficult interviewing. "We quite understand that. But, you know, in New York the newspapers try a man as much as the courts, and we thought you might like to make a statement to the public which we should be very glad to print for you. It may help your case—"

"Nothing can help my case in this tamned country where shustice is to he pought mit tollars!" cried the prisoner, with a sudden anger and an expression of face still further belying the first one; "nothing except a lot of money. But I tell you now two things you may write for your public: One is, no motive can be shown for the murder, because I lofed Zinka and vished her to live alvays. And the other is" He stopped a moment and stared steadily at Williams making shorthand notes—"that with my knowledge—my egceptional knowledge—of poisons and pacteriology I could have done it in a dozen ways without pumping arsenic into her body. That is a fool's way of killing. It is clumsy and childish and sure of discofery! See?"

He turned away, as though to signify that the interview was over, and sat down on his wooden bench.

"Seems to have taken a fancy to you," laughed the Senator, as they went off to get further interviews with the lawyers. "He never looked at me once."

"He's got a bad face—the face of a devil. I don't feel complimented," said Williams shortly.

"I'd hate to be in his power."

"Same here," returned the other. "Let's go into Silver Dollars and wash the dirty taste out."

So, after the custom of reporters, they made their way up the Bowery and went into a saloon that had gained a certain degree of fame because the Tammany owner had let a silver dollar into each stone of the floor. Here they washed away most of the "dirty taste" left by the Tombs atmosphere and Hensig, and then went on to Steve Brodie's, another saloon a little higher up the same street.

"There'll be others there," said the Senator, meaning drinks as well as reporters, and Williams, still thinking over their interview, silently agreed.

Brodie was a character; there was always something lively going on in his place. He had the reputation of having once jumped from the Brooklyn Bridge and reached the water alive. No one could actually deny it, and no one could p rove that it really happened: and anyhow, he had enough imagination and personality to make the myth live and to sell much bad liquor on the strength of it. The walls of his saloon were plastered with lurid oil-paintings of the bridge, the height enormously magnified, and Steve's body in midair, an expression of a happy puppy on his face.

Here, as expected, they found "Whitey" Fife, of the *Recorder*, and Galusha Owen, of the *World*. "Whitey", as his nickname implied, was an albino, and clever. He wrote the daily "weather story" for his paper, and the way he spun a column out of rain, wind, and temperature was the envy of everyone except the Weather Clerk, who objected to being described as "Farmer Dunne, cleaning his rat-tail file", and to having his dignified office referred to in the public press as "a down-country farm". But the public liked it, and laughed, and "Whitey" was never really spiteful.

Owen, too, when sober, was a good man who had long passed the rubicon of hack assignments. Yet both these men were also on the Hensig story. And Williams, who had already taken an instinctive dislike to the case, was sorry to see this, for it meant frequent interviewing and the possession, more or less, of his mind and imagination. Clearly, he would have much to do with this German doctor. Already, even at this stage, he began to hate him.

The four reporters spent an hour drinking and talking. They fell at length to discussing the last time they had chanced to meet on the same assignment—a private lunatic asylum owned by an incompetent quack without a license, and where most of the inmates, not mad in the first instance, and all heavily paid for by relatives who wished them out of the way, had gone mad from ill-treatment. The place had been surrounded before dawn by the Board of Health officers, and the quasi-doctor arrested as he opened his front door. It was a splendid newspaper "story", of course.

"My space bill ran to sixty dollars a day for nearly a week," said Whitey Fife thickly, and the others laughed, because Whitey wrote most of his stuff by cribbing it from the evening papers.

"A dead cinch," said Galusha Owen, his dirty flannel collar poking up through his long hair almost to his ears. "I 'faked' the whole of the second day without going down there at all."

He pledged Whitey for the tenth time that morning, and the albino leered happily across the table at him, and passed him a thick compliment before emptying his glass.

"Hensig's going to be good, too," broke in the Senator, ordering a round of gin-fizzes, and Williams gave a little start of annoyance to hear the name brought up again. "He'll make good stuff at the trial. I never saw a cooler hand. You should've heard him talk about poisons and bacteriology, and boasting he could kill in a dozen ways without fear of being caught. I guess he was telling the truth right enough!"

"That so?" cried Galusha and Whitey in the same breath, not having done a stroke of work so far on the case.

"Run down to the Tombsh angetaninerview," added Whitey, turning with a sudden burst of enthusiasm to his companion. His white eyebrows and pink eyes fairly shone against the purple of his tipsy face.

"No, no," cried the Senator; "don't spoil a good story. You're both as full as ticks. I'll match with Williams which of us goes. Hensig knows us already, and we'll all 'give up' in this story right along. No 'beats'."

So they decided to divide news till the case was finished, and to keep no exclusive items to themselves; and Williams, having lost the toss, swallowed his gin-fizz and went back to the Tombs to get a further talk with the prisoner on his knowledge of expert poisoning and bacteriology.

Meanwhile his thoughts were very busy elsewhere. He had taken no part in the noisy conversation in the barroom, because something lay at the back of his mind, bothering him, and claiming attention with great persistence. Something was at work in his deeper consciousness, something that had impressed him with a vague sense of unpleasantness and nascent fear, reaching below that second skin he had grown.

And, as he walked slowly through the malodorous slum streets that lay between the Bowery and the Tombs, dodging the pullers-in outside the Jew clothing stores, and nibbling at a bag of pea-nuts be caught up off an Italian push-cart *en route*, this "something" rose a little higher out of its obscurity, and began to play with the roots of the ideas floating higgledy-piggledy on the surface of his mind. He thought he knew what it was, but could not make quite sure. From the roots of his thoughts it rose a little higher, so that he clearly felt it as something disagreeable. Then, with a sudden rush, it came to the surface, and poked its face before him so that he fully recognised it.

The blond visage of Dr. Max Hensig rose before him, cool, smiling, and implacable.

Somehow, he had expected it would prove to be Hensig— this unpleasant thought that was troubling him. He was not really surprised to have labeled it, because the man's personality had made an unwelcome impression upon him at the very start. He stopped nervously in the Street, and looked round. He did not expect to see anything out of the way, or to find that he was being followed. It was not that exactly. The act of turning was merely the outward expression of a sudden inner discomfort, and a man with better nerves, or nerves more under control, would not have turned at all.

But what caused this tremor of the nerves? Williams probed and searched within himself. It came, he felt, from some part of his inner being he did not understand; there had been an intrusion, an incongruous intrusion, into the stream of his normal consciousness. Messages from this region always gave him pause; and in this particular case he saw no reason why he should think specially of Dr. Hensig with alarm—this light-haired stripling with blue eyes and drooping moustache. The faces of other murderers had haunted him once or twice because they were more than ordinarily bad, or because their case possessed unusual features of horror. But there was nothing so very much out of the way about Hensig—at least, if there was, the reporter could not seize and analyze it. There seemed no adequate reason to explain his emotion. Certainly, it had nothing to do with the fact that he was merely a murderer, for that stirred no thrill in him at all, except a kind of pity, and a wonder how the man would meet his execution. It must, he argued, be something to do with the *personality* of the man, apart from any particular deed or characteristic.

Puzzled, and still a little nervous, he stood in the road, hesitating. In front of him the dark walls of the Tombs rose in massive steps of granite. Overhead white summer clouds sailed across a deep blue sky; the wind sang cheerfully among the wires and chimney-pots, making him think of fields and trees; and down the Street surged the usual cosmopolitan New York crowd of laughing Italians, surly Negroes, Hebrews chattering Yiddish, tough-looking hooligans with that fighting lurch of the shoulders peculiar to New York roughs, Chinamen, taking little steps like boys— and every other sort of nondescript imaginable. It was early June, and there were faint odors of the sea and of sea-beaches in the air. Williams caught himself shivering a little with delight at the sight of the sky and scent of the wind.

Then he looked back at the great prison, rightly named the Tombs, and the sudden change of thought from the fields to the cells, from life to death, somehow landed him straight into the discovery of what caused this attack of nervousness:

Hensig was no ordinary murderer! That was it. There was something quite out of the ordinary about him. The man was a horror, pure and simple, standing apart from normal humanity. The knowledge of this rushed over him like a revelation, bringing unalterable conviction in its train.

Something of it had reached him in that first brief interview, but without explaining itself sufficiently to be recognised, and since then it had been working in his system, like a poison, and was now causing a disturbance, not having been assimilated. A quicker temperament would have labeled it long before.

Now, Williams knew well that he drank too much, and had more than a passing acquaintance with drugs; his nerves were shaky at the best of times. His life on the newspapers afforded no opportunity of cultivating pleasant social relations, but brought him all the time into contact with the seamy side of life—the criminal, the abnormal, the unwholesome in human nature. He knew, too, that strange thoughts, *idées fixes* and what not, grew readily in such a soil as this, and, not wanting these, he had formed a habit—peculiar to himself—of deliberately sweeping his mind clean once a week of all that had haunted, obsessed, or teased him, of the horrible or unclean, during his work; and his eighth day, his holiday, he invariably spent in the woods, walking, building fires, cooking a meal in the open, and getting all the country air and the exercise he possibly could. He had in this way kept his mind free from many unpleasant pictures that might otherwise have lodged there abidingly, and the habit of thus cleansing his imagination had proved more than once of real value to him.

So now he laughed to himself, and turned on those whizzing brooms of his, trying to forget these first impressions of Hensig, and simply going in, as he did a hundred other times, to get an ordinary interview with an ordinary prisoner. This habit, being nothing more nor less than the practice of suggestion, was more successful sometimes than others. This time—since fear is less susceptible to suggestion than other emotions—it was less so.

Williams got his interview, and came away fairly creeping with horror. Hensig was all that he had felt, and more besides. He belonged, the reporter felt convinced, to that rare type of deliberate murderer, cold-blooded and calculating, who kills for a song, delights in killing, and gives its whole intellect to the consideration of each detail, glorying in evading detection and revelling in the notoriety of the trial, if caught. At first he had answered reluctantly, but as Williams plied his questions intelligently, the young doctor warmed up and became enthusiastic with a sort of cold intellectual enthusiasm, till at last he held forth like a lecturer, pacing his cell, gesticulating, explaining with admirable exposition how easy murder could be to a man who knew his business.

And *he* did know his business! No man, in these days of inquests and post-mortem examination, would inject poisons that might be found weeks afterwards in the viscera of the victim. No man who knew his business!

"What is more easy," he said, holding the bars with his long white fingers and gazing into the reporter's eyes, "than to take a disease germ ['cherm' he pronounced it] of typhus, plague, or any cherm you blease, and make so virulent a culture that no medicine in the world could counteract it; a really powerful microbe—and then scratch the skin of your victim with a pin? And who could drace it to you, or acctise you of murder?"

Williams, as he watched and heard, was glad the bars were between them; but, even so, something invisible seemed to pass from the prisoner's atmosphere and lay an icy finger on his heart. He had come into contact with every possible kind of crime and criminal, and had interviewed scores of men who, for jealousy, greed, passion or other comprehensible emotion, had killed and paid the penalty of

killing. He understood that. Any man with strong passions was a
potential killer. But never before bad he met a man who in cold blood,
deliberately, under no emotion greater than boredom, would destroy a
human life and then boast of his ability to do it. Yet this, he felt sure,
was what Hensig had done, and what his vile words shadowed forth
and betrayed. Here was something outside humanity, something
terrible, monstrous; and it made him shudder. This young doctor, he
felt, was a fiend incarnate, a man who thought less of human life than
the lives of flies in summer, and who would kill with as steady a hand
and cool a brain as though he were performing a common operation in
the hospital.

Thus the reporter left the prison gates with a vivid impression in
his mind, though exactly how his conclusion was reached was more
than he could tell. This time the mental brooms failed to act. The horror
of it remained.

On the way out into the street he ran against Policeman Dowling of
the ninth precinct, with whom he had been fast friends since the day he
wrote a glowing account of Dowling's capture of a "greengoods-man",
when Dowling had been so drunk that he nearly lost his prisoner
altogether. The policeman had never forgotten the good turn; it had
promoted him to plain clothes; and he was always ready to give the
reporter any news he had.

"Know of anything good to-day?" he asked by way of habit.

"Bet your bottom dollar I do," replied the coarse-faced Irish
policeman; "one of the best, too.

I've got Hensig!"

Dowling spoke with pride and affection. He was mighty pleased,
too, because his name would be in the paper every day for a week or
more, and a big case helped the chances of promotion.

Williams cursed inwardly. Apparently there was no escape from
this man Hensig.

"Not much of a case, is it?" he asked.

"It's a jim dandy, that's what it is," replied the other, a little
offended. "Hensig may miss the Chair because the evidence is weak,
but he's the worst I've ever met. Why, he'd poison you as soon as spit
in your eye, and if he's got a heart at all he keeps it on ice."

"What makes you think that?"

"Oh, they talk pretty freely to us sometimes," the policeman said,
with a significant wink.

"Can't be used against them at the trial, and it kind o' relieves their
mind, I guess. But I'd just as soon not have heard most of what that guy
told me—see? Come in," he added, looking round cautiously; "I'll set
'em up and tell you a bit."

Williams entered the side-door of a saloon with him, but not too
willingly.

"A glarss of Scotch for the Englishman," ordered the officer facetiously, "and I'll take a horse's collar with a dash of peach bitters in it—just what you'd notice, no more." He flung down a half-dollar, and the bar-tender winked and pushed it back to him across the counter.

"What's yours, Mike?" he asked him.

"I'll take a cigar," said the bar-tender, pocketing the proffered dime and putting a cheap cigar in his waistcoat pocket, and then moving off to allow the two men elbowroom to talk in.

They talked in low voices with heads close together for fifteen minutes, and then the reporter set up another round of drinks. The bar-tender took his money. Then they talked a bit longer, Williams rather white about the gills and the policeman very much in earnest.

"The boys are waiting for me up at Brodie's," said Williams at length. "I must be off."

"That's so," said Dowling, straightening up. "We'll just liquor up again to show there's no ill-feeling. And mind you see mc every morning before the case is called. Trial begins to-morrow."

They swallowed their drinks, and again the bar-tender took a ten-cent piece and pocketed a cheap cigar.

"Don't print what I've told you, and don't give it up to the other reporters," said Dowling as they separated. "And if you want confirmation jest take the cars and run down to Amityville, Long Island, and you'll find what I've said is O.K. every time."

Williams went back to Steve Brodie's, his thoughts whizzing about him like bees in a swarm. What he had heard increased tenfold his horror of the man. Of course, Dowling may have lied or exaggerated, but he thought not. It was probably all true, and the newspaper offices knew something about it when they sent good men to cover the case. Williams wished to Heaven he had nothing to do with the thing; but meanwhile he could not write what he had heard, and all the other reporters wanted was the result of his interview. That was good for half a column, even expurgated.

He found the Senator in the middle of a story to Galusha, while Whitey Fife was knocking cocktail glasses off the edge of the table and catching them just before they reached the floor, pretending they were Steve Brodie jumping from the Brooklyn Bridge. He had promised to set up the drinks for the whole bar if he missed, and just as Williams entered a glass smashed to atoms on the stones, and a roar of laughter went up from the room. Five or six men moved up to the bar and took their liquor, Williams included, and soon after Whitey and Galusha went off to get some lunch and sober up, having first arranged to meet Williams later in the evening and get the "story" from him.

"Get much?" asked the Senator.

"More than I care about," replied the other, and then told his friend the story.

The Senator listened with intense interest, making occasional notes from time to time, and asking a few questions. Then, when Williams had finished, he said quietly:

"I guess Dowling's right. Let's jump on a car and go down to Amityville, and see what they think about him down there."

Amityville was a scattered village some twenty miles away on Long Island, where Dr. Hensig had lived and practised for the last year or two, and where Mrs. Hensig No. 2 had come to her suspicious death. The neighbours would be sure to have plenty to say, and though it might not prove of great value, it would be certainly interesting. So the two reporters went down there, and interviewed anyone and everyone they could find, from the man in the drug-store to the parson and the undertaker, and the stories they heard would fill a book.

"Good stuff," said the Senator, as they journeyed back to New York on the steamer, "but nothing we can use, I guess." His face was very grave, and he seemed troubled in his mind.

"Nothing the District Attorney can use either at the trial," observed Williams.

"It's simply a devil—not a man at all," the other continued, as if talking to himself. "Utterly unmoral! I swear I'll make MacSweater put me to another job."

For the stories they had heard showed Dr. Hensig as a man who openly boasted that he could kill without detection; that no enemy of his lived long; that, as a doctor, he had, or ought to have, the right over life and death; and that if a person was a nuisance, or a trouble to him, there was no reason he should not put them away, provided he did it without rousing suspicion. Of course he had not shouted these views aloud in the market-place, but he had let people know that he held them, and held them seriously. They had fallen from him in conversation, in unguarded moments, and were clearly the natural expression of his mind and views. And many people in the village evidently had no doubt that he had put them into practice more than once.

"There's nothing to give up to Whitey or Galusha, though," said the Senator decisively, "and there's hardly anything we can use in our story."

"I don't think I should care to use it anyhow," Williams said, with rather a forced laugh.

The Senator looked round sharply by way of question.

"Hensig *may be acquitted and get out*," added Williams.

"Same here. I guess you're dead right," he said slowly, and then added more cheerfully, "Let's go and have dinner in Chinatown, and write our copy together."

So they went down Pell Street, and turned up some dark wooden stairs into a Chinese restaurant, smelling strongly of opium and of cooking not Western. Here at a little table on the sanded floor they ordered chou chop suey and chou om dong in brown bowls, and washed it down with frequent doses of the fiery white whisky, and then moved into a corner and began to cover their paper with pencil writing for the consumption of the great American public in the morning.

"There's not much to choose between Hensig and *that*," said the Senator, as one of the degraded white women who frequent Chinatown entered the room and sat down at an empty table to order whisky. For, with four thousand Chinamen in the quarter, there is not a single Chinese woman.

"All the difference in the world," replied Williams, following his glance across the smoky room. "She's been decent once, and may be again some day, but that damned doctor has never been anything but what he is—a soulless, intellectual devil. He doesn't belong to humanity at all. I've got a horrid idea that—"

"How do you spell 'bacteriology', two *r*'s or one?" asked the Senator, going on with his scrawly writing of a story that would be read with interest by thousands next day.

"Two *r*'s and one *k*," laughed the other. And they wrote on for another hour, and then went to turn it into their respective offices in Park Row.

The trial of Max Hensig lasted two weeks, for his relations supplied money, and he got good lawyers and all manner of delays. From a newspaper point of view it fell utterly flat, and before the end of the fourth day most of the papers had shunted their big men on to other jobs more worthy of their powers.

From Williams's point of view, however, it did not fall flat, and he was kept on it till the end. A reporter, of course, has no right to indulge in editorial remarks, especially when a case is still *sub judice*, but in New York journalism and the dignity of the law have a standard all their own, and into his daily reports there crept the distinct flavour of his own conclusions. Now that new men, with whom he had no agreement to "give up", were covering the story for the other papers, he felt free to use any special knowledge in his possession, and a good deal of what he had heard at Amityville and from officer Dowling somehow managed to creep into his writing. Something of the horror and loathing he felt for this doctor also betrayed itself, more by inference than actual statement, and no one who read his daily column could come to any other conclusion than that Hensig was a calculating, cool-headed murderer of the most dangerous type.

This was a little awkward for the reporter, because it was his duty every morning to interview the prisoner in his cell, and get his views on the conduct of the case in general and on his chances of escaping the Chair in particular.

Yet Hensig showed no embarrassment. All the newspapers were supplied to him, and he evidently read every word that Williams wrote. He must have known what the reporter thought about him, at least so far as his guilt or innocence was concerned, but he expressed no opinion as to the fairness of the articles, and talked freely of his chances of ultimate escape. The very way in which he glorified in being the central figure of a matter that bulked so large in the public eye seemed to the reporter an additional proof of the man's perversity. His vanity was immense. He made most careful toilets, appearing every day in a clean shirt and a new tie, and never wearing the same suit on two consecutive days. He noted the descriptions of his personal appearance in the Press, and was quite offended if his clothes and bearing in court were not referred to in detail. And he was unusually delighted and pleased when any of the papers stated that he looked smart and self-possessed, or showed great self-control—which some of them did.

"They make a hero of me," he said one morning when Williams went to see him as usual before court opened, "and if I go to the Chair—which I tink I not do, you know—you shall see something fine. Berhaps they electrocute a corpse only!"

And then, with dreadful callousness, he began to chaff the reporter about the tone of his articles—for the first time.

"I only report what is said and done in court," stammered Williams, horribly uncomfortable, "and I am always ready to write anything you care to say—"

"I haf no fault to find," answered Hensig, his cold blue eyes fixed on the reporter's face through the bars, "none at all. You tink I haf killed, and you show it in all your sendences. Haf you ever seen a man in the Chair, I ask you?"

Williams was obliged to say he had.

"*Ach was*! You haf indeed!" said the doctor coolly.

"It's instantaneous, though," the other added quickly, "and must be quite painless" This was not exactly what he thought, but what else could he say to the poor devil who might presently be strapped down into it with that horrid band across his shaved head!

Hensig laughed, and turned away to walk up and down the narrow cell. Suddenly he made a quick movement and sprang like a panther close up to the bars, pressing his face between them with an expression that was entirely new. Williams started back a pace in spite of himself.

"There are worse ways of dying than that," he said in a low voice, with a diabolical look in his eyes: "slower ways that are bainful much more. I shall get oudt. I shall not be conficted. I shall get oudt, and then perhaps I come and tell you apout them."

The hatred in his voice and expression was unmistakable, but almost at once the face changed back to the cold pallor it usually wore, and the extraordinary doctor was laughing again and quietly discussing his lawyers and their good or bad points.

After all, then, that skin of indifference was only assumed, and the man really resented bitterly the tone of his articles. He liked the publicity, but was furious with Williams for having come to a conclusion and for letting that conclusion show through his reports.

The reporter was relieved to get out into the fresh air. He walked briskly up the stone steps to the court-room, still haunted by the memory of that odious white face pressing between the bars and the dreadful look in the eyes that had come and gone so swiftly. And what did those words mean exactly? Had he heard them right? Were they a threat?

"There are slower and more painful ways of dying, and if I get out I shall perhaps come and tell you about them."

The work of reporting the evidence helped to chase the disagreeable vision, and the compliments of the city editor on the excellence of his "story", with its suggestion of a possible increase of salary, gave his mind quite a different turn; yet always at the back of his consciousness there remained the vague, unpleasant memory that he had roused the bitter hatred of this man, and, as he thought, of a man who was a veritable monster.

There may have been something hypnotic, a little perhaps, in this obsessing and haunting idea of the man's steely wickedness, intellectual and horribly skilful, moving freely through life with something like a god's power and with a list of unproved and unprovable murders behind him. Certainly it impressed his imagination with very vivid force, and he could not think of this doctor, young, with unusual knowledge and out-of-the-way skill, yet utterly unmoral, free to work his will on men and women who displeased him, and almost safe from detection—he could not think of it all without a shudder and a crawling of the skin. He was exceedingly glad when the last day of the trial was reached and he no longer was obliged to seek the daily interview in the cell, or to sit all day in the crowded court watching the detestable white face of the prisoner in the dock and listening to the web of evidence closing round him, but just failing to hold him tight enough for the Chair. For Hensig was acquitted, though the jury sat up all night to come to a decision, and the final interview Williams had with the man immediately before his release into the street was the pleasantest and yet the most disagreeable of all.

"I knew I get oudt all right," said Hensig with a slight laugh, but without showing the real relief he must have felt. "No one peliefed me guilty but my vife's family and yourself, Mr. *Vulture* reporter. I read efery day your repordts. You chumped to a conglusion too quickly, I tink"

"Oh, we write what we're told to write—"

"Berhaps some day you write anozzer story, or berhaps you read the story someone else write of your own trial. Then you understand better what you make me feel."

Williams hurried on to ask the doctor for his opinion of the conduct of the trial, and then inquired what his plans were for the future. The answer to the question caused him genuine relief.

"Ach! I return of course to Chermany," he said. "People here are now afraid of me a liddle. The newspapers haf killed me instead of the Chair. Goot-bye, *Mr. Vulture* reporter, goot-bye!"

And Williams wrote out his last interview with as great a relief, probably, as Hensig felt when he heard the foreman of the jury utter the words "Not guilty"; but the line that gave him most pleasure was the one announcing the intended departure of the acquitted man for Germany.

The New York public want sensational reading in their daily life, and they get it, for the newspaper that refused to furnish it would fail in a week, and New York newspaper proprietors do not pose as philanthropists. Horror succeeds horror, and the public interest is never for one instant allowed to faint by the way.

Like any other reporter who betrayed the smallest powers of description, Williams realised this fact with his very first week on the *Vulture*. His daily work became simply a series of sensational reports of sensational happenings; be lived in a perpetual whirl of exciting arrests, murder trials, cases of blackmail, divorce, forgery, arson, corruption, and every other kind of wickedness imaginable. Each case thrilled him a little less than the preceding one; excess of sensation bad simply numbed him; he became, not callous, but irresponsive, and had long since reached the stage when excitement ceases to betray judgment, as with inexperienced reporters it was apt to do.

The Hensig case, however, for a long time lived in his imagination and haunted him. The bald facts were buried in the police files at Mulberry Street headquarters and in the newspaper office "morgues", while the public, thrilled daily by fresh horrors, forgot the very existence of the evil doctor a couple of days after the acquittal of the central figure.

But for Williams it was otherwise. The personality of the heartless and calculating murderer—the intellectual poisoner, as he called him—had made a deep impression on his imaginations and for many weeks his memory kept him alive as a moving and actual horror in his life. The words he had heard him titter, with their covert threats and ill-concealed animosity, helped, no doubt, to vivify the recollection and to explain why Hensig stayed in his thoughts and haunted his dreams with a persistence that reminded him of his very earliest cases on the paper.

With time, however, even Hensig began to fade away into the confused background of piled up memories of prisoners and prison scenes, and at length the memory became so deeply buried that it no longer troubled him at all.

The summer passed, and Williams came back from his hard-earned holiday of two weeks in the Maine backwoods. New York was at its best, and the thousands who had been forced to stay and face its torrid summer heats were beginning to revive tinder the spell of the brilliant autumn days. Cool sea breezes swept over its burnt streets from the Lower Bay, and across the splendid flood of the Hudson River the woods on the Palisades of New Jersey had turned to crimson and gold. The air was electric, sharp, sparkling, and the life of the city began to pulse anew with its restless and impetuous energy. Bronzed faces from sea and mountains thronged the streets, health and light-heartedness showed in every eye, for autumn in New York wields a potent magic not to be denied, and even the East Side slums, where the unfortunates crowd in their squalid thousands, bad the appearance of having been swept and cleansed. Along the water-fronts especially the powers of sea and sun and scented winds combined to work an irresistible fever in the hearts of all who chafed within their prison walls.

And in Williams, perhaps more than in most, there was something that responded vigorously to the influences of hope and cheerfulness everywhere abroad. Fresh with the vigour of his holiday and full of good resolutions for the coming winter he felt released from the evil spell of irregular living, and as he crossed one October morning to Staten Island in the big double-ender ferry-boat, his heart was light, and his eye wandered to the blue waters and the hazy line of woods beyond with feelings of pure gladness and delight.

He was on his way to Quarantine to meet an incoming liner for the *Vulture*. A Jew-baiting member of the German Reichstag was coming to deliver a series of lectures in New York on his favourite subject, and the newspapers who deemed him worthy of notice at all were sending him fair warning that his mission would be tolerated perhaps, but not welcomed. The Jews were good citizens and America a "free country" and his meetings in the Cooper Union Hall would meet with derision certainly, and violence possibly.

The assignment was a pleasant one, and Williams had instructions to poke fun at the officious and interfering German, and advise him to return to Bremen by the next steamer without venturing among flying eggs and dead cats on the platform. He entered fully into the spirit of the job and was telling the Quarantine doctor about it as they steamed down the bay in the little tug to meet the huge liner just anchoring inside Sandy Hook.

The decks of the ship were crowded with passengers watching the arrival of the puffing tug, and just as they drew alongside in the shadow Williams suddenly felt his eyes drawn away from the swinging rope ladder to some point about half-way down the length of the vessel.

There, among the intermediate passengers on the lower deck, he saw a face staring at him with fixed intentness. The eyes were bright blue, and the skin, in that row of bronzed passengers, showed remarkably white. At once, and with a violent rush of blood from the heart, he recognised Hensig.

In a moment everything about him changed: the blue waters of the bay turned black, the light seemed to leave the sun, and all the old sensations of fear and loathing came over him again like the memory of some great pain. He shook himself, and clutched the rope ladder to swing up after the Health Officer, angry, and yet genuinely alarmed at the same time, to realise that the return of this man could so affect him. His interview with the Jew-baiter was of the briefest possible description, and he hurried through to catch the Quarantine tug back to Staten Island, instead of steaming up the bay with the great liner into dock, as the other reporters did. He had caught no second glimpse of the hated German, and he even went so far as to harbour a faint hope that he might have been deceived, and that some trick of resemblance in another face had caused a sort of subjective hallucination. At any rate, the days passed into weeks, and October slipped into November, and there was no recurrence of the distressing vision. Perhaps, after all, it was a stranger only; or, if it was Hensig, then he had forgotten all about the reporter, and his return had no connection necessarily with the idea of revenge.

None the less, however, Williams felt uneasy. He told his friend Dowling, the policeman.

"Old news," laughed the Irishman. "Headquarters are keeping an eye on him as a suspect. Berlin wants a man for two murders—goes by the name of Brunner—and from their description we think it's this feller Hensig. Nothing certain yet, but we're on his trail. I'm on his trail," he added proudly, "and don't you forget it! I'll let you know anything when the time comes, but mum's the word just now!"

One night, not long after this meeting, Williams and the Senator were covering a big fire on the West Side docks. They were standing on the outskirts of the crowd watching the immense flames that a shouting wind seemed to carry half-way across the river. The surrounding shipping was brilliantly lit up and the roar was magnificent. The Senator, having come out with none of his own, borrowed his friend's overcoat for a moment to protect him from spray and flying cinders while he went inside the fire lines for the latest information obtainable. It was after midnight, and the main story had been telephoned to the office; all they had now to do was to send in the latest details and corrections to be written up at the news desk.

"I'll wait for you over at the corner!" shouted Williams, in moving off through a scene of indescribable confusion and taking off his fire badge as he went. This conspicuous brass badge, issued to reporters by the Fire Department, gave them the right to pass within the police cordon in the pursuit of information, and at their own risk. Hardly had he unpinned it from his coat when a hand dashed out of the crowd surging up against him and made a determined grab at it. He turned to trace the owner, but at that instant a great lurching of the mob nearly carried him off his feet, and he only just succeeded in seeing the arm withdrawn, having failed of its object, before he was landed with a violent push upon the pavement he had been aiming for.

The incident did not strike him as particularly odd, for in such a crowd there are many who covet the privilege of getting closer to the blaze. He simply laughed and put the badge safely in his pocket, and then stood to watch the dying flames until his friend came to join him with the latest details.

Yet, though time was pressing and the Senator had little enough to do, it was fully half an hour before he came lumbering up through the darkness. Williams recognised him some distance away by the check ulster he wore—his own.

But *was* it the Senator, after all? The figure moved oddly and with a limp, as though injured. A few feet off it stopped and peered at Williams through the darkness.

"That you, Williams?" asked a gruff voice.

"I thought you were someone else for a moment," answered the reporter, relieved to recognise his friend, and moving forward to meet him. "But what's wrong? Are you hurt?"

The Senator looked ghastly in the lurid glow of the fire. His face was white, and there was a little trickle of blood on the forehead.

"Some fellow nearly did for me," he said; "deliberately pushed me clean off the edge of the dock. If I hadn't fallen on to a broken pile and found a boat, I'd have been drowned sure as God made little apples. Think I know who it was, too. *Think*! I mean I *know*, because I saw his damned white face and heard what he said. "Who in the world was it? What did he want?" stammered the other.

The Senator took his arm, and lurched into the saloon behind them for some brandy. As he did so he kept looking over his shoulder.

"Quicker we're off from this dirty neighbourhood, the better," he said.

Then he turned to Williams, looking oddly at him over the glass, and answering his questions.

"Who was it?—why, it was Hensig! And what did he want?—well, he wanted *you*!"

"Me! Hensig!" gasped the other.

"Guess he mistook me for you," went on the Senator, looking behind him at the door. "The crowd was so thick I cut across by the edge of the dock. It was quite dark. There wasn't a soul near me. I was running. Suddenly what I thought was a stump got up in front of me,

and, Gee whiz, man! I tell you it was Hensig, or I'm a drunken
Dutchman. I looked bang into his face. 'Good-pye, Mr. *Vulture*
reporter,' he said, with a damned laugh, and gave me a push that sent
me backwards clean over the edge."

The Senator paused for breath, and to empty his second glass.

"*My* overcoat!" exclaimed Williams faintly.

"Oh, he'd been following you right enough, I guess."

The Senator was not really injured, and the two men walked back
towards Broadway to find a telephone, passing through a region of
dimly-lighted streets known as Little Africa, where the negroes lived,
and where it was safer to keep the middle of the road, thus avoiding
sundry dark alley-ways opening off the side. They talked hard all the
way.

"He's after you, no doubt," repeated the Senator. "I guess he never
forgot your report of his trial. Better keep your eye peeled!" he added
with a laugh.

But Williams didn't feel a bit inclined to laugh, and the thought
that it certainly *was* Hensig he had seen on the steamer, and that he was
following him so closely as to mark his check ulster and make an
attempt on his life, made him feel horribly uncomfortable, to say the
least. To be stalked by such a man was terrible. To realise that he was
marked down by that white-faced, cruel wretch, merciless and
implacable, skilled in the manifold ways of killing by stealth—that
somewhere in the crowds of the great city he was watched and waited
for, hunted, observed: here was an obsession really to torment and
become dangerous. Those light-blue eyes, that keen intelligence, that
mind charged with revenge, had been watching him ever since the trial,
even from across the sea. The idea terrified him. It brought death into
his thoughts for the first time with a vivid sense of nearness and
reality—far greater than anything he had experienced when watching
others die.

That night, in his dingy little room in the East Nineteenth Street
boarding-house, Williams went to bed in a blue funk, and for days
afterwards he went about his business in a continuation of the same
blue funk. It was useless to deny it. He kept his eyes everywhere,
thinking he was being watched and followed. A new face in the office,
at the boarding-house table, or anywhere on his usual beat, made him
jump. His daily work was haunted; his dreams were all nightmares; he
forgot all his good resolutions, and plunged into the old indulgences
that helped him to forget his distress. It took twice as much liquor to
make him jolly, and four times as much to make him reckless.

Not that he really was a drunkard, or cared to drink for its own
sake, but he moved in a thirsty world of reporters, policemen, reckless
and loose-living men and women, whose form of greeting was "What'll
you take?" and method of reproach "Oh, he's sworn off!" Only now he

was more careful how much he took, counting the cocktails and fizzes poured into him during the course of his day's work, and was anxious never to lose control of himself. He must be on the watch. He changed his eating and drinking habits, and altered any habits that could give a clue to the devil on his trail. He even went so far as to change his boardinghouse. His emotion—the emotion of fear—changed everything. It tinged the outer world with gloom, draping it in darker colors, stealing something from the sunlight, reducing enthusiasm, and acting as a heavy drag, as it were, upon all the normal functions of life.

The effect upon his imagination, already diseased by alcohol and drugs, was, of course, exceedingly strong. The doctor's words about developing a germ until it became too powerful to be touched by any medicine, and then letting it into the victim's system by means of a pin-scratch— this possessed him more than anything else. The idea dominated his thoughts; it seemed so clever, so cruel, so devilish. The "accident" at the fire had been, of course, a real accident, conceived on the spur of the moment—the result of a chance meeting and a foolish mistake. Hensig had no need to resort to such clumsy methods. When the right moment came he would adopt a far simpler, *safer* plan.

Finally, he became so obsessed by the idea that Hensig was following him, waiting for his opportunity, that one day he told the news editor the whole story. His nerves were so shaken that he could not do his work properly.

"That's a good story. Make two hundred of it," said the editor at once. "Fake the name, of course. Mustn't mention Hensig, or there'll he a libel suit."

But William was in earnest, and insisted so forcibly that Treherne, though busy as ever, took him aside into his room with the glass door.

"Now, see here, Williams, you're drinking too much," he said; "that's about the size of it. Steady up a bit on the wash, and Hensig's face will disappear." He spoke kindly, but sharply. He was young himself, awfully keen, with much knowledge of human nature and a rare "nose for news". He understood the abilities of his small army of men with intuitive judgment. That they drank was nothing to him, provided they did their work. Everybody in that world drank, and the man who didn't was hooked upon with suspicion.

Williams explained rather savagely that the face was no mere symptom of delirium tremens and the editor spared him another two minutes before rushing out to tackle the crowd of men waiting for him at the news desk.

"That so? You don't say!" he asked, with more interest. "Well, I guess Hensig's simply trying to razzle-dazzle you. You tried to kill him by your reports, and he wants to scare you by way of revenge. But he'll never dare do anything. Throw him a good bluff, and he'll give in like a baby. Everything's pretence in this world. But I rather like the idea of the germs. That's original!"

Williams, a little angry at the other's flippancy, told the story of the Senator's adventure and the changed overcoat.

"May he, may be," replied the hurried editor; "but the Senator drinks Chinese whisky, and a man who does that might imagine anything on God's earth. Take a tip, Williams, from an old hand, and let up a bit on the liquor. Drop cocktails and keep to straight whisky, and never drink on an empty stomach. Above all, *don't mix!*"

He gave him a keen look and was off.

"Next time you see this German," cried Treherne from the door, "go up and ask him for an interview on what it feels like to escape from the Chair—just to show him you don't care a red cent. Talk about having him watched and followed—suspected man—and all that sort of flim-flam. Pretend to warn him. It'll turn the tables and make him digest a bit. See?"

Williams sauntered out into the street to report a meeting of the Rapid Transit Commissioners, and the first person he met as he ran down the office steps was—Max Hensig.

Before he could stop, or swerve aside, they were face to face. His head swam for a moment and he began to tremble. Then some measure of self-possession returned, and he tried instinctively to act on the editor's advice. No other plan was ready, so he drew on the last force that had occupied his mind. It was that—or running.

Hensig, he noticed, looked prosperous; he wore a fur overcoat and cap. His face was whiter than ever, and his blue eyes burned like coals.

"Why! Dr. Hensig, you're back in New York! "he exclaimed. "When did you arrive? I'm glad—I suppose—I mean—er—will you come and have a drink?" he concluded desperately. It was very foolish, but for the life of him he could think of nothing else to say. And the last thing in the world he wished was that his enemy should know that he was afraid.

"I tink not, Mr. *Vulture* reporder, tanks," he answered coolly; "but I sit py and vatch you drink." His self-possession was as perfect, as it always was.

But Williams, more himself now, seized on the refusal and moved on, saying something about having a meeting to go to.

"I walk a liddle way with you, berhaps," Hensig said, following him down the pavement.

It was impossible to prevent him, and they started side by side across City Hall Park towards Broadway. It was after four o'clock: the dusk was falling: the little park was thronged with people walking in all directions, everyone in a terrific hurry as usual. Only Hensig seemed calm and unmoved among that racing, tearing life about them. He carried an atmosphere of ice about with him: it was his voice and manner that produced this impression; his mind was alert, watchful, determined, always sure of itself.

Williams wanted to run. He reviewed swiftly in his mind a dozen ways of getting rid of him quickly, yet knowing well they were all futile. He put his hands in his overcoat pockets—the check ulster—and watched sideways every movement of his companion.

"Living in New York again, aren't you?" he began.

"Not as a doctor any more," was the reply. "I now teach and study. Also I write sciendific hooks a liddle—"

"What about?"

"Cherms," said the other, looking at him and laughing.

"Disease cherms, their culture and development." He put the accent on the "op".

Williams walked more quickly. With a great effort he tried to put Treherne's advice into practice.

"You care to give me an interview any time—on your special subjects?" he asked, as naturally as he could.

"Oh yes; with much bleasure. I lif in Harlem now, if you will call von day—"

"Our office is best," interrupted the reporter. "Paper, desks, library, all handy for use, you know."

"If you're afraid—" began Hensig. Then, without finishing the sentence, he added with a laugh, "I haf no arsenic there. You not tink me any more a pungling boisoner? You haf changed your mind about all dat?"

Williams felt his flesh beginning to creep. How could he speak of such a matter! His own wife, too!

He turned quickly and faced him, standing still for a moment so that the throng of people deflected into two streams past them. He felt it absolutely imperative upon him to say something that should convince the German he was not afraid.

"I suppose you are aware, Dr. Hensig, that the police know you have returned, and that you are being watched probably?" he said in a low voice, forcing himself to meet the odious blue eyes.

"And why not, bray?" he asked imperturbably.

"They may suspect something—"

"Susbected—already again? Ach was!" said the German.

"I only wished to warn you—" stammered Williams, who always found it difficult to remain self-possessed under the other's dreadful stare.

"No boliceman see what I do—or catch me again," he laughed quite horribly. "But I tank you all the same."

Williams turned to catch a Broadway car going at full speed. He could not stand another minute with this man, who affected him so disagreeably.

"I call at the office one day to gif you interview!" Hensig shouted as he dashed off, and the next minute he was swallowed up in the crowd, and Williams, with mixed feelings and a strange inner trembling, went to cover the meeting of the Rapid Transit Board.

But, while he reported the proceedings mechanically, his mind was busy with quite other thoughts. Hensig was at his side the whole time. He felt quite sure, however unlikely it seemed, that there was no fancy in his fears, and that he had judged the German correctly. Hensig hated him, and would put him out of the way if he could. He would do it in such a way that detection would be almost impossible. He would not shoot or poison in the ordinary way, or resort to any clumsy method. He would simply follow, watch, wait his opportunity, and then act with utter callousness and remorseless determination. And Williams already felt pretty certain of the means that would be employed: "*Cherms!*"

This meant proximity. He must watch everyone who came close to him in trains, cars, restaurants—anywhere and everywhere. It could be done in a second: only a slight scratch would be necessary, and the disease would be in his blood with such strength that the chances of recovery would be slight. And what could he do? He could not have Hensig watched or arrested. He had no story to tell to a magistrate, or to the police, for no one would listen to such a tale. And, if he were stricken down by sudden illness, what was more likely than to say he had caught the fever in the ordinary course of his work, since he was always frequenting noisome dens and the haunts of the very poor, the foreign and filthy slums of the East Side, and the hospitals, morgues, and cells of all sorts and conditions of men? No; it was a disagreeable situation, and Williams, young, shaken in nerve, and easily impressionable as he was, could not prevent its obsession of his mind and imagination.

"If I get suddenly ill," he told the Senator, his only friend in the whole city, "and send for you, look carefully for a scratch on my body. Tell Dowling, and tell the doctor the story."

"You think Hensig goes about with a little bottle of plague germs in his vest pockets" laughed the other reporter, ready to scratch you with a pin?"

"Some damned scheme like that, I'm sure."

"Nothing could be proved anyway. He wouldn't keep the evidence in his pocket till he was arrested, would he?"

During the next week or two Williams ran against Hensig twice— accidentally. The first time it happened just outside his own boarding-house—the new one. Hensig had his foot on the stone steps as if just about to come up, but quick as a flash he turned his face away and moved on down the Street. This was about eight o'clock in the evening, and the hall light fell through the opened door upon his face. The second time it was not so clear: the reporter was covering a case in the courts, a case of suspicious death in which a woman was chief prisoner, and he thought he saw the doctor's white visage watching him from among the crowd at the back of the court-room. When he looked a second time, however, the face had disappeared, and there was no sign afterwards of its owner in the lobby or corridor.

That same day he met Dowling in the building; he was promoted now, and was always in plain clothes. The detective drew him aside into a corner. The talk at once turned upon the German.

"We're watching him too," he said. "Nothing you can use yet, but he's changed his name again, and never stops at the same address for more than a week or two. I guess he's Brunner right enough, the man Berlin's looking for. He's a holy terror if ever there was one."

Dowling was happy as a schoolboy to be in touch with such a promising case.

"What's he up to now in particular?" asked the other.

"Something pretty black," said the detective. "But I can't tell you yet awhile. He calls himself Schmidt now, and he's dropped the 'Doctor'. We may take him any day—just waiting for advices from Germany."

Williams told his story of the overcoat adventure with the Senator, and his belief that Hensig was waiting for a suitable opportunity to catch him alone.

"That's dead likely too," said Dowling, and added carelessly, "I guess we'll have to make some kind of a case against him anyway, just to get him out of the way. He's dangerous to be around huntin' on the loose."

So gradual sometimes are the approaches of fear that the processes by which it takes possession of a man's soul are often too insidious to be recognised, much less to be dealt with, until their object has been finally accomplished and the victim has lost the power to act. And by this time the reporter, who had again plunged into excess, felt so nerveless that, if he met Hensig face to face, he could not answer for what he might do. He might assault his tormentor violently—one result of terror—or he might find himself powerless to do anything at all but yield, like a bird fascinated before a snake.

He was always thinking now of the moment when they would meet, and of what would happen; for he was just as certain that they must meet eventually, and that Hensig would try to kill him, as that his next birthday would find him twenty-five years old. That meeting, he well knew, could be delayed only, not prevented, and his changing again to another boarding-house, or moving altogether to a different city, could only postpone the final accounting between them. It was bound to come.

A reporter on a New York newspaper has one day in seven to himself. Williams's day off was Monday, and he was always glad when it came. Sunday was especially arduous for him, because in addition to the unsatisfactory nature of the day's assignments, involving private interviewing which the citizens pretended to resent on their day of rest, he had the task in the evening of reporting a difficult sermon in a Brooklyn church. Having only a column and a half at his disposal, he had to condense as he went along, and the speaker was so rapid, and so fond of lengthy quotations, that the reporter found his shorthand only just equal to the task. It was usually after half-past nine o'clock when he left the church, and there was still the labor of transcribing his notes in the office against time.

The Sunday following the glimpse of his tormentor's face in the court-room he was busily condensing the wearisome periods of the preacher. sitting at a little table immediately under the pulpit, when he glanced up during a brief pause and let his eye wander over the congregation and up to the crowded galleries. Nothing was farther at the moment from his much-occupied brain than the doctor of Amityville, and it was such an unexpected shock to encounter his fixed stare up there among the occupants of the front row, watching him with an evil smile, that his senses temporarily deserted him. The next sentence of the preacher was wholly lost, and his shorthand during the brief remainder of the sermon was quite illegible, he found, when he came to transcribe it at the office.

It was after one o'clock in the morning when he finished, and he went out feeling exhausted and rather shaky. In the all-night drug-store at the corner he indulged accordingly in several more glasses of whisky than usual, and talked a long time with the man who guarded the back room and served liquor to the few who knew the pass-word, since the shop had really no license at all. The true reason for this delay he recognised quite plainly: he was afraid of the journey home along the dark and emptying streets. The lower end of New York is practically deserted after ten o'clock: it has no residences, no theatres, no cafés, and only a few travellers from late ferries share it with reporters, a sprinkling of policemen, and the ubiquitous ne'er-do-wells who haunt the saloon doors. The newspaper world of Park Row was, of course, alive with light and movement, but once outside that narrow zone and the night descended with an effect of general darkness.

Williams thought of spending three dollars on a cab, but dismissed the idea because of its extravagance. Presently Galusha Owens came in—too drunk to be of any use, though, as a companion. Besides, he lived in Harlem, which was miles beyond Nineteenth Street, where Williams had to go. He took another rye whisky—his fourth—and looked cautiously through the colored glass windows into the Street. No one was visible. Then he screwed up his nerves another twist or two, and made a bolt for it, taking the steps in a sort of flying leap— and running full tilt into a man whose figure seemed almost to have risen out of the very pavement.

He gave a cry and raised his fists to strike.

"Where's your hurry?" laughed a familiar voice. "Is the Prince of Wales dead?" It was the Senator, most welcome of all possible appearances.

"Come in and have a horn," said Williams, "and then I'll walk home with you." He was immensely glad to see him, for only a few streets separated their respective boarding-houses.

"But he'd never sit out a long sermon just for the pleasure of watching you," observed the Senator after hearing his friend's excited account.

"That man'll take any trouble in the world to gain his end," said the other with conviction. "He's making a study of all my movements and habits. He's not the sort to take chances when it's a matter of life and death. I'll bet he's not far away at this moment."

"Rats!" exclaimed the Senator, laughing in rather a forced way. "You're getting the jumps with your Hensig and death. Have another rye."

They finished their drinks and went out together, crossing City Hall Park diagonally towards Broadway, and then turning north. They crossed Canal and Grand Streets, deserted and badly lighted. Only a few drunken loiterers passed them. Occasionally a policeman on the corner, always close to the side-door of a saloon, of course, recognised one or other of them and called good night. Otherwise there was no one, and they seemed to have this part of Manhattan Island pretty well to themselves. The presence of the Senator, ever cheery and kind, keeping close to his friend all the way, the effect of the half-dozen whiskies, and the sight of the guardians of the law, combined to raise the reporter's spirits somewhat: and when they reached Fourteenth Street, with its better light and greater traffic, and saw Union Square lying just beyond, close to his own street, he felt a distinct increase of courage and no objection to going on alone.

"Good night!" cried the Senator cheerily. "Get home safe; I turn off here anyway." He hesitated a moment before turning down the street, and then added, "You feel O.K., don't you?"

"You may get double rates for an exclusive bit of news if you come on and see me assaulted," Williams replied, laughing aloud, and then waiting to see the last of his friend.

But the moment the Senator was gone the laughter disappeared. He went on alone, crossing the square among the trees and walking very quickly. Once or twice he turned to see if anybody were following him, and his eyes scanned carefully as he passed every occupant of the park benches where a certain number of homeless loafers always find their night's lodging. But there was nothing apparently to cause him alarm, and in a few minutes more he would be safe in the little back bedroom of his own house. Over the way he saw the lights of Burbacher's saloon, where respectable Germans drank Rhine wine and played chess till all hours. He thought of going in for a night-cap, hesitating for a moment, but finally going on. When he got to the end of the square, however, and saw the dark opening of East Eighteenth Street, he thought after all he would go back and have another drink. He hovered for a moment on the kerbstone and then turned; his will often slipped a cog now in this way.

It was only when he was on his way back that he realised the truth: that his real reason for turning back and avoiding the dark open mouth of the street was because he was afraid of something its shadows might conceal. This dawned upon him quite suddenly. If there had been a light at the corner of the street he would never have turned back at all. And as this passed through his mind, already somewhat fuddled with what he had drunk, he became aware that the figure of a man had slipped forward out of the dark space he had just refused to enter, and was following him down the street. The man was pressing, too, close into the houses, using any protection of shadow or railing that would enable him to move unseen.

But the moment Williams entered the bright section of pavement opposite the wine-room windows he knew that this man had come close up behind him, with a little silent run, and he turned at once to face him. He saw a slim man with dark hair and blue eyes, and recognised him instantly.

"It's very late to be coming home," said the man at once. "I thought I recognised my reporder friend from the Vulhire." These were the actual words, and the voice was meant to be pleasant, but what Williams thought he heard, spoken in tones of ice, was something like, "At last I've caught you! You are in a state of collapse nervously, and you are exhausted. I can do what I please with you." For the face and the voice were those of Hensig the Tormentor, and the dyed hair only served to emphasise rather grotesquely the man's features and make the pallor of the skin greater by contrast.

His first instinct was to turn and run, his second to fly at the man and strike him. A terror beyond death seized him. A pistol held to his head, or a waving bludgeon, he could easily have faced; but this odious creature, slim, limp, and white of face, with his terrible suggestion of cruelty, literally appalled him so that he could think of nothing intelligent to do or to say. This accurate knowledge of his movements, too, added to his distress—this waiting for him at night when he was tired and foolish from excess. At that moment he knew all the sensations of the criminal a few hours before his execution: the bursts of hysterical terror, the inability to realise his position, to hold his thoughts steady, the helplessness of it all. Yet, in the end, the reporter heard his own voice speaking with a rather weak and unnatural kind of tone and accompanied by a gulp of forced laughter—heard himself stammering the ever-ready formula: "I was going to have a drink before turning in—will you join me?"

The invitation, he realised afterwards, was prompted by the one fact that stood forth clearly in his mind at the moment—the thought, namely, that whatever he did or said, he must never let Hensig for one instant imagine that he felt afraid and was so helpless a victim.

Side by side they moved down the street, for Hensig had acquiesced in the suggestion, and Williams already felt dazed by the strong, persistent will of his companion. His thoughts seemed to be flying about somewhere outside his brain, beyond control, scattering wildly. He could think of nothing further to say, and had the smallest diversion furnished the opportunity he would have turned and run for his life through the deserted streets.

"A glass of lager," he heard the German say, "I take berhaps that with you. You know me in spite of—" he added, indicating by a movement the changed color of his hair and moustache. "Also, I gif you now the interview you asked for, if you like."

The reporter agreed feebly, finding nothing adequate to reply. He turned helplessly and looked into his face with something of the sensations a bird may feel when it runs at last straight into the jaws of the reptile that has fascinated it. The fear of weeks settled down upon him, focussing about his heart. It was, of course, an effect of hypnotism, he remembered thinking vaguely through the befuddlement of his drink—this culminating effect of an evil and remorseless personality acting upon one that was diseased and extra receptive. And while he made the suggestion and heard the other's acceptance of it, he knew perfectly well that he was falling in with the plan of the doctor's own making, a plan that would end in an assault upon his person, perhaps a technical assault only—a mere touch—still, an assault that would be at the same time an attempt at murder. The alcohol buzzed in his ears. He felt strangely powerless. He walked steadily to his doom, side by side with his executioner.

Any attempt to analyze the psychology of the situation was utterly beyond him. But, amid the whirl of emotion and the excitement of the whisky, he dimly grasped the importance of *two fundamental things*.

And the first was that, though he was now muddled and frantic, yet a moment would come when his will would be capable of one supreme effort to escape, and that therefore it would be wiser for the present to waste no atom of volition on temporary half-measures. He would play dead dog. The fear that now paralysed him would accumulate till it reached the point of saturation: that would be the time to strike for his life. For just as the coward may reach a stage where he is capable of a sort of frenzied heroism that no ordinarily brave man could compass, so the victim of fear, at a point varying with his balance of imagination and physical vigour, will reach a state where fear leaves him and he becomes numb to its effect from sheer excess of feeling it. It is the point of saturation. He may then turn suddenly calm and act with a judgment and precision that simply bewilder the object of the attack. It is, of course, the inevitable swing of the pendulum, the law of equal action and reaction.

Hazily, tipsily perhaps, Williams was conscious of this potential power deep within him, below the superficial layers of smaller emotions—could he but be *sufficiently terrified to reach it* and bring it to the surface where it must result in action.

And, as a consequence of this foresight of his sober subliminal self, he offered no opposition to the least suggestion of his tormentor, but made up his mind instinctively to agree to all that he proposed. Thus he lost no atom of the force he might eventually call upon, by friction over details which in any case he would yield in the end. And at the same tune he felt intuitively that his utter weakness might even deceive his enemy a little and increase the chances of his single effort to escape when the right moment arrived.

That Williams was able to "imagine" this true psychology, yet wholly unable to analyze it, simply showed that on occasion he could be psychically active. His deeper subliminal self, stirred by the alcohol and the stress of emotion, was guiding him, and would continue to guide him in proportion as he let his fuddled normal self slip into the background without attempt to interfere.

And the second fundamental thing he grasped—due even more than the first to psychic intuition—was the certainty that he could drink more, up to a certain point, with distinct advantage to his power and lucidity—but up to a given point only. After that would come unconsciousness, a single sip too much and he would cross the frontier—a very narrow one. It was as though he knew intuitively that "the drunken consciousness is one bit of the mystic consciousness". At present he was only fuddled and fearful, but additional stimulant would inhibit the effects of the other emotions, give him unbounded confidence, clarify his judgment and increase his capacity to a stage far beyond the normal. Only—he must stop in time.

His chances of escape, therefore, so far as he could understand, depended on these two things: he must drink till he became self-confident and arrived at the abnormally clear-minded stage of drunkenness; and he must wait for the moment when Hensig had so filled him up with fear that he no longer could react to it. Then would be the time to strike. Then his will would be free and have judgment behind it.

These were the two things standing up clearly somewhere behind that great confused turmoil of mingled fear and alcohol.

Thus for the moment, though with scattered forces and rather wildly feeble thoughts, he moved down the street beside the man who hated him and meant to kill him. He had no purpose at all but to agree and to wait. Any attempt he made now could end only in failure.

They talked a little as they went, the German calm, chatting as though he were merely an agreeable acquaintance, but behaving with the obvious knowledge that he held his victim secure, and that his struggles would prove simply rather amusing. He even laughed about his dyed hair, saying by way of explanation that he had done it to please a woman who told him it would make him look younger. Williams knew this was a lie, and that the police had more to do with the change than a woman; but the man's vanity showed through the explanation, and was a vivid little self-revelation.

He objected to entering Burbacher's, saying that he (Burbacher) paid no blackmail to the police, and might be raided for keeping open after hours.

"I know a nice quiet blace on T'ird Avenue. We go there," he said.

Williams, walking unsteadily and shaking inwardly, still groping, too, feebly after a way of escape, turned down the side street with him. He thought of the men he had watched walking down the short corridor from the cell to the "Chair" at Sing Sing, and wondered if they felt as he did. It was like going to his own execution.

"I haf a new disgovery in bacteriology—in cherms," the doctor went on, "and it will make me famous, for it is very imbortant. I gif it you egsclusive for the *Vulture*, as you are a friend." He became technical, and the reporter's mind lost itself among such words as "toxins", "alkaloids", and the like. But he realised clearly enough that Hensig was playing with him and felt absolutely sure of his victim. When he lurched badly, as he did more than once, the German took his arm by way of support, and at the vile touch of the man it was all Williams could do not to scream or strike out blindly.

They turned up Third Avenue and stopped at the side door of a cheap saloon. He noticed the name of Schumacher over the porch, but all lights were out except a feeble glow that came through the glass fanlight. A man pushed his face cautiously round the half-opened door, and after a brief examination let them in with a whispered remark to be quiet. It was the usual formula of the Tammany saloonkeeper, who paid so much a month to the police to be allowed to keep open all night, provided there was no noise or fighting. It was now well after one o'clock in the morning, and the streets were deserted.

The reporter was quite at home in the sort of place they had entered; otherwise the sinister aspect of a drinking "joint" after hours, with its gloom and general air of suspicion, might have caused him some extra alarm. A dozen men, unpleasant of countenance, were standing at the bar, where a single lamp gave just enough light to enable them to see their glasses. The bar-tender gave Hensig a swift glance of recognition as they walked along the sanded floor.

"Come," whispered the German; "we go to the back room. I know the bass-word," he laughed, leading the way.

They walked to the far end of the bar and opened a door into a brightly lit room with about a dozen tables in it, at most of which men sat drinking with highly painted women, talking loudly, quarrelling, singing, and the air thick with smoke. No one took any notice of them as they went down the room to a table in the corner farthest from the door—Hensig chose it; and when the single waiter came up with "Was nehmen die Herren?" and a moment later brought the rye whisky they both asked for, Williams swallowed his own without the "chaser" of soda water, and ordered another on the spot.

"It'sh awfully watered," he said rather thickly to his companion, "and I'm tired."

"Cocaine, under the circumstances, would help you quicker, berhaps!" replied the German with an expression of amusement. Good God! was there nothing about him the man had not found out? He must have been shadowing him for days; it was at least a week since Williams had been to the First Avenue drug store to get the wicked bottle refilled. Had he been on his trail every night when he left the office to go home? This idea of remorseless persistence made him shudder.

"Then we finish quickly if you are tired," the doctor continued, "and to-morrow you can show me your repordt for gorrections if you make any misdakes berhaps. I gif you the address to-night pefore we leave."

The increased ugliness of his speech and accent betrayed his growing excitement. Williams drank his whisky, again without water, and called for yet another, clinking glasses with the murderer opposite, and swallowing half of this last glass, too, while Hensig merely tasted his own, looking straight at him over the performance with his evil eyes.

"I can write shorthand," began the reporter, trying to appear at his ease.

"*Ach*, I know, of course."

There was a mirror behind the table, and he took a quick glance round the room while the other began searching in his coat pocket for the papers he had with him. Williams lost no single detail of his movements, but at the same time managed swiftly to get the "note" of the other occupants of the tables. Degraded and besotted faces he saw, almost without exception, and not one to whom he could appeal for help with any prospect of success. It was a further shock, too, to realise that he preferred the more or less bestial countenances round him to the intellectual and ascetic face opposite. They were at least human, whereas he was something quite outside the pale; and this preference for the low creatures, otherwise loathsome to him, brought his mind by sharp contrast to a new and vivid realisation of the personality before him. He gulped down his drink, and again ordered it to be refilled.

But meanwhile the alcohol was beginning to key him up out of the dazed and negative state into which his first libations and his accumulations of fear had plunged him. His brain became a shade clearer. There was even a faint stirring of the will. He had already drunk enough under normal circumstances to be simply reeling, but to-night the emotion of fear inhibited the effects of the alcohol, keeping him singularly steady. Provided he did not exceed a given point, he could go on drinking till he reached the moment of high power when he could combine all his forces into the single consummate act of cleverly calculated escape. If he missed this psychological moment he would collapse.

A sudden crash made him jump. It was behind him against the other wall. In the mirror he saw that a middle-aged man had lost his balance and fallen off his chair, foolishly intoxicated, and that two women were ostensibly trying to lift him up, but really were going swiftly through his pockets as he lay in a heap on the floor. A big man who had been asleep the whole evening in the corner stopped snoring and woke up to look and laugh, but no one interfered. A man must take care of himself in such a place and with such company, or accept the consequences. The big man composed himself again for sleep, sipping his glass a little first, and the noise of the room continued as before. It was a case of "knock-out drops" in the whisky, put in by the women, however, rather than by the saloon-keeper. Williams remembered thinking he had nothing to fear of that kind. Hensig's method would be far more subtle and clever—*cherms*! A scratch with a pin and a germ!

"I haf zome notes here of my disgovery," he went on, smiling significantly at the interruption, and taking some papers out of an inner pocket. "But they are written in Cherman, so I dranslate for you. You haf paper and benzil?"

The reporter produced the sheaf of office copy paper he always carried about with him, and prepared to write. The rattle of the elevated trains outside and the noisy buzz of drunken conversation inside formed the background against which he heard the German's steely insistent voice going on ceaselessly with the "dranslation and egsplanation". From time to time people left the room, and new customers reeled in. When the clatter of incipient fighting and smashed glasses became too loud, Hensig waited till it was quiet again. He watched every new arrival keenly. They were very few now, for the night had passed into early morning and the room was gradually emptying. The waiter took snatches of sleep in his chair by the door; the big man still snored heavily in the angle of the wall and window. When he was the only one left, the proprietor would certainly close up. He had not ordered a drink for an hour at least. Williams, however, drank on steadily, always aiming at the point when he would be at the top of his power, full of confidence and decision. That moment was undoubtedly coming nearer all the time. Yes, but so was the moment Hensig was waiting for. He, too, felt absolutely confident, encouraging his companion to drink more, and watching his gradual collapse with unmasked glee. He betrayed his gloating quite plainly now: he held his victim too securely to feel anxious; when the big man reeled out they would be alone for a brief minute or two unobserved—and meanwhile he allowed himself to become a little too *careless* from over-confidence. And Williams noted that too.

For slowly the will of the reporter began to assert itself, and with this increase of intelligence he of course appreciated his awful position more keenly, and therefore, *felt more fear*. The two main things he was waiting for were coming perceptibly within reach: to reach the saturation point of terror and the culminating moment of the alcohol. Then, action and escape!

Gradually, thus, as he listened and wrote, he passed from the stage of stupid, negative terror into that of active, positive terror. The alcohol kept driving hotly at those hidden centres of imagination within, which, once touched, begin to reveal: in other words, he became observant, critical, alert. Swiftly the power grew. His lucidity increased till he became almost conscious of the workings of the other man's mind, and it was like sitting opposite a clock whose wheels and needles he could just hear clicking. his eyes seemed to spread their power of vision all over his skin; he could see what was going on without actually looking. In the same way he heard all that passed in the room without turning his head. Every moment he became clearer in mind. He almost touched clairvoyance. The presentiment earlier in the evening that this stage would come was at last being actually fulfilled.

From time to time he sipped his whisky, but more cautiously than at first, for he knew that this keen psychical activity was the forerunner of helpless collapse. Only for a minute or two would he be at the top of his power. The frontier was a dreadfully narrow one, and already he had lost control of his fingers, and was scrawling a shorthand that bore no resemblance to the original system of its inventor.

As the white light of this abnormal perceptiveness increased, the horror of his position became likewise more and more vivid. He knew that he was fighting for his life with a soulless and malefic being who was next door to a devil. The sense of fear was being magnified now with every minute that passed. Presently the power of *perceiving* would pass into *doing*; he would strike the blow for his life, whatever form that blow might take.

Already he was sufficiently master of himself to act—to act in the sense of deceiving. He exaggerated his drunken writing and thickness of speech, his general condition of collapse: and this power of *hearing* the workings of the other man's mind showed him that he was successful. Hensig was a little deceived. He proved this by increased carelessness, and by allowing the expression of his face to become plainly exultant.

Williams's faculties were so concentrated upon the causes operating in the terrible personality opposite to him, that he could spare no part of his brain for the explanations and sentences that came from his lips. He did not hear or understand a hundredth part of what the doctor was saying, but occasionally he caught up the end of a phrase and managed to ask a blundering question out of it; and Hensig, obviously pleased with his increasing obfuscation, always answered at some length, quietly watching with pleasure the reporter's foolish hieroglyphics upon the paper.

The whole thing, of course, was an utter blind. Hensig had no discovery at all. He was talking scientific jargon, knowing full well that those shorthand notes would never be transcribed, and that he himself would be out of harm's way long before his victim's senses had cleared sufficiently to tell him that he was in the grasp of a deadly sickness which no medicines could prevent ending in death.

Williams saw and felt all this clearly. It somehow came to him, rising up in that clear depth of his mind that was stirred by the alcohol, and yet beyond the reach, so far, of its deadly confusion. He understood perfectly well that Hensig was waiting for a moment to act; that he would do nothing violent, but would carry out his murderous intention in such an innocent way that the victim would have no suspicions at the moment, and would only realise later that he had been poisoned and—

Hark! What was that? There was a change. Something had happened. It was like the sound of a gong, and the reporter's fear suddenly doubled. Hensig's scheme had moved forward a step. There was no sound actually, but his senses seemed grouped together into one, and for some reason his perception of the change came by way of audition. Fear brimmed up perilously near the breaking-point. But the moment for action had not quite come yet, and he luckily saved himself by the help of another and contrary emotion. He emptied his glass, spilling half of it purposely over his coat, and burst out laughing in Hensig's face. The vivid picture rose before him of Whitey Fife catching cocktail glasses off the edge of Steve Brodie's table.

The laugh was admirably careless and drunken, but the German was startled and looked up suspiciously. He had not expected this, and through lowered eyelids Williams observed an expression of momentary uncertainty on his features, as though he felt he was not absolutely master of the situation after all, as he imagined.

"Su'nly thought of Whitey Fife knocking Stevebrodie off'sh Brooklyn Bridsh in a co-cock'tail glashh—" Williams explained in a voice hopelessly out of control. "You know Whhhiteyfife, of coursh, don't you ?—ha, ha, ha!"

Nothing could have helped him more in putting Hensig off the scent. His face resumed its expression of certainty and cold purpose. The waiter, wakened by the noise, stirred uneasily in his chair, and the big man in the corner indulged in a gulp that threatened to choke him as he sat with his head sunk upon his chest. But otherwise the empty room became quiet again. The German resumed his confident command of the situation. Williams, he saw, was drunk enough to bring him easily into his net.

None the less, the reporter's perception had not been at fault. There was a change. Hensig *was* about to do something, and his mind was buzzing with preparations.

The victim, now within measuring distance of his supreme moment—the point where terror would release his will, and alcohol would inspire him beyond possibility of error—saw everything as in the clear light of day. Small things led him to the climax: the emptied room; the knowledge that shortly the saloon would close; the grey light of day stealing under the chinks of door and shutter; the increased vileness of the face gleaming at him opposite in the paling gas glare. Ugh! how the air reeked of stale spirits, the fumes of cigar smoke, and the cheap scents of the vanished women. The floor was strewn with sheets of paper, absurdly scrawled over. The table had patches of wet, and cigarette ash lay over everything. His hands and feet were icy, his eyes burning hot. His heart thumped like a soft hammer.

Hensig was speaking in quite a changed voice now. He had been leading up to this point for hours. No one was there to see, even if anything was to be seen—which was unlikely. The big man still snored; the waiter was asleep too. There was silence in the outer room, and between the walls of the inner there was—death.

"Now, Mr. *Vulture* reporder, I *show* you what I mean all this time to egsplain," he was saying in his most metallic voice.

He drew a blank sheet of the reporter's paper towards him across the little table, avoiding carefully the wet splashes.

"Lend me your bencil von moment, please. Yes?"

Williams, simulating almost total collapse, dropped the pencil and shoved it over the polished wood as though the movement was about all he could manage. With his head sunk forward upon his chest he watched stupidly. Hensig began to draw some kind of outline; his touch was firm, and there was a smile on his lips.

"Here, you see, is the human arm," he said, sketching rapidly; "and here are the main nerves, and here the artery. Now, my discovery, as I haf peen egsplaining to you, is simply—" He dropped into a torrent of meaningless scientific phrases, during which the other purposely allowed his hand to lie relaxed upon the table, knowing perfectly well that in a moment Hensig would seize it—for the purposes of illustration.

His terror was so intense that, for the first time this awful night, he was within an ace of action. The point of saturation had been almost reached. Though apparently sodden drunk, his mind was really at the highest degree of clear perception and judgment, and in another moment—the moment Hensig actually began his final assault—the terror would provide the reporter with the extra vigour and decision necessary to strike his one blow. Exactly how he would do it, or what precise form it would take, he had no idea; that could be left to the inspiration of the moment; he only knew that his strength would last just long enough to bring this about, and that then he would collapse in utter intoxication upon the floor.

Hensig dropped the pencil suddenly: it clattered away to a corner of the room, showing it had been propelled with force, not merely allowed to fall, and he made no attempt to pick it up. Williams, to test his intention, made a pretended movement to stoop after it, and the other, as he imagined he would, stopped him in a second.

"I haf another," he said quickly, diving into his inner pocket and producing a long dark pencil. Williams saw in a flash, through his half-closed eyes, that it was sharpened at one end, while the other end was covered by a little protective cap of transparent substance like glass, a third of an inch long. He heard it click as it struck a button of the coat, and also saw that by a very swift motion of the fingers, impossible to be observed by a drunken man, Hensig removed the cap so that the end was free. Something gleamed there for a moment, something like a point of shining metal—the point of a pin.

"Gif me your hand von minute and I drace the nerve up the arm I speak apout," the doctor continued in that steely voice that showed no sign of nervousness, though he was on the edge of murder. "So, I show you much petter vot I mean."

Without a second's hesitation—for the moment for action had not quite come—he lurched forward and stretched his arm clumsily across the table. Hensig seized the fingers in his own and turned the palm uppermost. With his other hand he pointed the pencil at the wrist, and began moving it a little up towards the elbow, pushing the sleeve back for the purpose. His touch was the touch of death. On the point of the black pin, engrafted into the other end of the pencil, Williams knew there clung the germs of some deadly disease, germs unusually powerful from special culture; and that within the next few seconds the pencil would turn and the pin would *accidentally* scratch his wrist and let the virulent poison into his blood.

He knew this, yet at the same time he managed to remain master of himself. For he also realised that at last, just in the nick of time, the moment he had been waiting for all through these terrible hours had actually arrived, and he was ready to act.

And the little unimportant detail that furnished the extra quota of fear necessary to bring him to the point was—*touch*. It was the touch of Hensig's hand that did it, setting every nerve a-quiver to its utmost capacity, filling him with a black horror that reached the limits of sensation.

In that moment Williams regained his self-control and became absolutely sober. Terror removed its paralyzing inhibitions, having led him to the point where numbness succeeds upon excess, and sensation ceases to register in the brain. The emotion of fear was dead, and he was ready to act with all the force of his being—that force, too, raised to a higher power after long repression.

Moreover, he could make no mistake, for at the same time be had reached the culminating effect of the alcohol, and a sort of white light filled his mind, showing him clearly what to do and how to do it. He felt master of himself, confident, capable of anything. He followed blindly that inner guidance he had been dimly conscious of the whole night, and what he did he did instinctively, as it were, without deliberate plan.

He was *waiting for the pencil to turn* so that the pin pointed at his vein. Then, when Hensig was wholly concentrated upon the act of murder, and thus oblivious of all else, he would find his opportunity. For at this supreme moment the German's mind would be focussed on the one thing. He would notice nothing else round him. He would be open to successful attack. But this supreme moment would hardly last more than five seconds at most!

The reporter raised his eyes and stared for the first time steadily into his opponent's eyes, till the room faded out and he saw only the white skin in a blaze of its own light. Thus staring, he caught in himself the full stream of venom, hatred, and revenge that had been pouring at him across the table for so long—caught and held it for one instant, and then returned it into the other's brain with all its original force and the added impetus of his own recovered will behind it.

Hensig felt this, and for a moment seemed to waver; he was surprised out of himself by the sudden change in his victim's attitude. The same instant, availing himself of a diversion caused by the big man in the corner waking noisily and trying to rise, he slowly *turned the pencil round* so that the point of the pin was directed at the hand lying in his. The sleepy waiter was helping the drunken man to cross to the door, and the diversion was all in his favour.

But Williams knew what he was doing. He did not even tremble.

"When that pin scratches me," he said aloud in a firm, sober voice, "it means—death."

The German could not conceal his surprise on hearing the change of voice, but he still felt sure of his victim, and clearly wished to enjoy his revenge thoroughly. After a moment's hesitation he replied, speaking very low:

"You tried, I tink, to get me conficted, and now I punish you, dat is all."

His fingers moved, and the point of the pin descended a little lower. Williams felt the faintest imaginable prick on his skin—or thought he did. The German had lowered his head again to direct the movement of the pin properly. But the moment of Hensig's concentration was also the moment of his own attack. And it had come.

"But the alcohol will counteract it!" he burst out, with a loud and startling laugh that threw the other completely off his guard. The doctor lifted his face in amazement. That same instant the hand that lay so helplessly and tipsily in his turned like a flash of lightning, and, before he knew what had happened, their positions were reversed. Williams held his wrist, pencil and all, in a grasp of iron. And from the reporter's other hand the German received a terrific smashing blow in the face that broke his glasses and dashed him back with a howl of pain against the wall.

There was a brief passage of scramble and wild blows, during which both table and chairs were sent flying, and then Williams was aware that a figure behind him had stretched forth an arm and was holding a bright silvery thing close to Hensig's bleeding face. Another glance showed him that it was a pistol, and that the man holding it was the big drunken man who had apparently slept all night in the corner of the room. Then, in a flash, he recognised him as Dowling's partner—a headquarters detective.

The reporter stepped back, his head swimming again. He was very unsteady on his feet.

"I've been watching your game all the evening," he heard the headquarters man saying as he slipped the handcuffs over the German's unresisting wrists. "We have been on your trail for weeks, and I might jest as soon have taken you when you left the Brooklyn church a few hours ago, only I wanted to see what you were up to—see? You're wanted in Berlin for one or two little dirty tricks, but our advices only came last night. Come along now."

"You'll get nozzing," Hensig replied very quietly, wiping his bloody face with the corner of his sleeve. "See, I have scratched myself!"

The detective took no notice of this remark, not understanding it, probably, but Williams noticed the direction of the eyes, and saw a scratch on his wrist, slightly bleeding. Then he understood that in the struggle the pin had accidentally found another destination than the one intended for it.

But he remembered nothing more after that, for the reaction set in with a rush. The strain of that awful night left him utterly limp, and the accumulated effect of the alcohol, now that all was past, overwhelmed him like a wave, and he sank in a heap upon the floor, unconscious.

* * * * *

The illness that followed was simply "nerves ", and he got over it in a week or two, and returned to his work on the paper. He at once made inquiries, and found that Hensig's arrest had hardly been noticed by the papers. There was no interesting feature about it, and New York was already in the throes of a new horror.

But Dowling, that enterprising Irishman—always with an eye to promotion and the main chance—Dowling had something to say about it.

"No luck, Mr. English," he said ruefully, "no luck at all. It would have been a mighty good story, but it never got in the papers. That damned German, Schmidt, alias Brunner, alias Hensig, died in the prison hospital before we could even get him remanded for further inquiries—"

"What did be die of?" interrupted the reporter quickly.

"Black typhus. I think they call it. But it was terribly swift, and he was dead in four days. The doctor said he'd never known such a case."

"I'm glad he's out of the way," observed Williams.

"Well, yes," Dowling said hesitatingly; "but it was a jim dandy of a story, an' he might have waited a little bit longer jest so as I got something out of it for meself."

The Willows

I

After leaving Vienna, and long before you come to Budapest, the Danube enters a region of singular loneliness and desolation, where its waters spread away on all sides regardless of a main channel, and the country becomes a swamp for miles upon miles, covered by a vast sea of low willow-bushes. On the big maps this deserted area is painted in a fluffy blue, growing fainter in color as it leaves the banks, and across it may be seen in large straggling letters the word *Sümpfe*, meaning marshes.

In high flood this great acreage of sand, shingle-beds, and willow-grown islands is almost topped by the water, but in normal seasons the bushes bend and rustle in the free winds, showing their silver leaves to the sunshine in an ever-moving plain of bewildering beauty. These willows never attain to the dignity of trees; they have no rigid trunks; they remain humble bushes, with rounded tops and soft outline, swaying on slender stems that answer to the least pressure of the wind; supple as grasses, and so continually shifting that they somehow give the impression that the entire plain is moving and *alive*. For the wind sends waves rising and falling over the whole surface, waves of leaves instead of waves of water, green swells like the sea, too, until the branches turn and lift, and then silvery white as their underside turns to the sun.

Happy to slip beyond the control of the stern banks, the Danube here wanders about at will among the intricate network of channels intersecting the islands everywhere with broad avenues down which the waters pour with a shouting sound; making whirlpools, eddies, and foaming rapids; tearing at the sandy banks; carrying away masses of shore and willow-clumps; and forming new islands innumerably which shift daily in size and shape and possess at best an impermanent life, since the flood-time obliterates their very existence.

Properly speaking, this fascinating part of the river's life begins soon after leaving Pressburg, and we, in our Canadian canoe, with gipsy tent and frying-pan on board, reached it on the crest of a rising flood about mid-July. That very same morning, when the sky was reddening before sunrise, we had slipped swiftly through still-sleeping Vienna, leaving it a couple of hours later a mere patch of smoke against the blue hills of the Wienerwald on the horizon; we had breakfasted below Fischeramend under a grove of birch trees roaring in the wind; and had then swept on the tearing current past Orth, Hainburg, Petronell (the old Roman Carnuntum of Marcus Aurelius), and so under the frowning heights of Theben on a spur of the Carpathians, where the March steals in quietly from the left and the frontier is crossed between Austria and Hungary.

Racing along at twelve kilometers an hour soon took us well into Hungary, and the muddy waters—sure sign of flood—sent us aground on many a shingle-bed, and twisted us like a cork in many a sudden belching whirlpool before the towers of Pressburg (Hungarian, Poszóny) showed against the sky; and then the canoe, leaping like a spirited horse, flew at top speed under the grey walls, negotiated safely the sunken chain of the Fliegende Brücke ferry, turned the corner sharply to the left, and plunged on yellow foam into the wilderness of islands, sandbanks, and swamp-land beyond—the land of the willows.

The change came suddenly, as when a series of bioscope pictures snaps down on the streets of a town and shifts without warning into the scenery of lake and forest. We entered the land of desolation on wings, and in less than half an hour there was neither boat nor fishing-hut nor red roof, nor any single sign of human habitation and civilization within sight. The sense of remoteness from the world of humankind, the utter isolation, the fascination of this singular world of willows, winds, and waters, instantly laid its spell upon us both, so that we allowed laughingly to one another that we ought by rights to have held some special kind of passport to admit us, and that we had, somewhat audaciously, come without asking leave into a separate little kingdom of wonder and magic—a kingdom that was reserved for the use of others who had a right to it, with everywhere unwritten warnings to trespassers for those who had the imagination to discover them.

Though still early in the afternoon, the ceaseless buffetings of a most tempestuous wind made us feel weary, and we at once began casting about for a suitable camping-ground for the night. But the bewildering character of the islands made landing difficult; the swirling flood carried us in-shore and then swept us out again; the willow branches tore our hands as we seized them to stop the canoe, and we pulled many a yard of sandy bank into the water before at length we shot with a great sideways blow from the wind into a backwater and managed to beach the bows in a cloud of spray. Then we lay panting and laughing after our exertions on the hot yellow sand, sheltered from the wind, and in the full blaze of a scorching sun, a cloudless blue sky above, and an immense army of dancing, shouting willow bushes, closing in from all sides, shining with spray and clapping their thousand little hands as though to applaud the success of our efforts.

"What a river!" I said to my companion, thinking of all the way we had traveled from the source in the Black Forest, and how he had often been obliged to wade and push in the upper shallows at the beginning of June.

"Won't stand much nonsense now, will it?" he said, pulling the canoe a little farther into safety up the sand, and then composing himself for a nap.

I lay by his side, happy and peaceful in the bath of the elements— water, wind, sand, and the great fire of the sun—thinking of the long journey that lay behind us, and of the great stretch before us to the Black Sea, and how lucky I was to have such a delightful and charming traveling companion as my friend, the Swede.

We had made many similar journeys together, but the Danube, more than any other river I knew, impressed us from the very beginning with its *aliveness*. From its tiny bubbling entry into the world among the pinewood gardens of Donaueschingen, until this moment when it began to play the great river-game of losing itself among the deserted swamps, unobserved, unrestrained, it had seemed to us like following the growth of some living creature. Sleepy at first, but later developing violent desires as it became conscious of its deep soul, it rolled, like some huge fluid being, through all the countries we had passed, holding our little craft on its mighty shoulders, playing roughly with us sometimes, yet always friendly and well-meaning, till at length we had come inevitably to regard it as a Great Personage.

How, indeed, could it be otherwise, since it told us so much of its secret life? At night we heard it singing to the moon as we lay in our tent, uttering that odd sibilant note peculiar to itself and said to be caused by the rapid tearing of the pebbles along its bed, so great is its hurrying speed. We knew, too, the voice of its gurgling whirlpools, suddenly bubbling up on a surface previously quite calm; the roar of its shallows and swift rapids; its constant steady thundering below all mere surface sounds; and that ceaseless tearing of its icy waters at the banks. How it stood up and shouted when the rains fell flat upon its face! And how its laughter roared out when the wind blew up-stream and tried to stop its growing speed! We knew all its sounds and voices, its tumblings and foamings, its unnecessary splashing against the bridges; that self-conscious chatter when there were hills to look on; the affected dignity of its speech when it passed through the little towns, far too important to laugh; and all these faint, sweet whisperings when the sun caught it fairly in some slow curve and poured down upon it till the steam rose.

It was full of tricks, too, in its early life before the great world knew it. There were places in the upper reaches among the Swabian forests, when yet the first whispers of its destiny had not reached it, where it elected to disappear through holes in the ground, to appear again on the other side of the porous limestone hills and start a new river with another name; leaving, too, so little water in its own bed that we had to climb out and wade and push the canoe through miles of shallows.

And a chief pleasure, in those early days of its irresponsible youth, was to lie low, like Brer Fox, just before the little turbulent tributaries came to join it from the Alps, and to refuse to acknowledge them when in, but to run for miles side by side, the dividing line well marked, the very levels different, the Danube utterly declining to recognize the newcomer. Below Passau, however, it gave up this particular trick, for there the Inn comes in with a thundering power impossible to ignore, and so pushes and incommodes the parent river that there is hardly room for them in the long twisting gorge that follows, and the Danube is shoved this way and that against the cliffs, and forced to hurry itself with great waves and much dashing to and fro in order to get through in time. And during the fight our canoe slipped down from its shoulder to its breast, and had the time of its life among the struggling waves. But the Inn taught the old river a lesson, and after Passau it no longer pretended to ignore new arrivals.

This was many days back, of course, and since then we had come to know other aspects of the great creature, and across the Bavarian wheat plain of Straubing she wandered so slowly under the blazing June sun that we could well imagine only the surface inches were water, while below there moved, concealed as by a silken mantle, a whole army of Undines, passing silently and unseen down to the sea, and very leisurely too, lest they be discovered.

Much, too, we forgave her because of her friendliness to the birds and animals that haunted the shores. Cormorants lined the banks in lonely places in rows like short black palings; grey crows crowded the shingle-beds; storks stood fishing in the vistas of shallower water that opened up between the islands, and hawks, swans, and marsh birds of all sorts filled the air with glinting wings and singing, petulant cries. It was impossible to feel annoyed with the river's vagaries after seeing a deer leap with a splash into the water at sunrise and swim past the bows of the canoe; and often we saw fawns peering at us from the underbrush, or looked straight into the brown eyes of a stag as we charged full tilt round a corner and entered another reach of the river. Foxes, too, everywhere haunted the banks, tripping daintily among the driftwood and disappearing so suddenly that it was impossible to see how they managed it.

But now, after leaving Pressburg, everything changed a little, and the Danube became more serious. It ceased trifling. It was half-way to the Black Sea, within seeming distance almost of other, stranger countries where no tricks would be permitted or understood. It became suddenly grown-up, and claimed our respect and even our awe. It broke out into three arms, for one thing, that only met again a hundred kilometers farther down, and for a canoe there were no indications which one was intended to be followed.

"If you take a side channel," said the Hungarian officer we met in the Pressburg shop while buying provisions, "you may find yourselves, when the flood subsides, forty miles from anywhere, high and dry, and you may easily starve. There are no people, no farms, no fishermen. I warn you not to continue. The river, too, is still rising, and this wind will increase."

The rising river did not alarm us in the least, but the matter of being left high and dry by a sudden subsidence of the waters might be serious, and we had consequently laid in an extra stock of provisions. For the rest, the officer's prophecy held true, and the wind, blowing down a perfectly clear sky, increased steadily till it reached the dignity of a westerly gale.

It was earlier than usual when we camped, for the sun was a good hour or two from the horizon, and leaving my friend still asleep on the hot sand, I wandered about in desultory examination of our hotel. The island, I found, was less than an acre in extent, a mere sandy bank standing some two or three feet above the level of the river. The far end, pointing into the sunset, was covered with flying spray which the tremendous wind drove off the crests of the broken waves. It was triangular in shape, with the apex up stream.

I stood there for several minutes, watching the impetuous crimson flood bearing down with a shouting roar, dashing in waves against the bank as though to sweep it bodily away, and then swirling by in two foaming streams on either side. The ground seemed to shake with the shock and rush, while the furious movement of the willow bushes as the wind poured over them increased the curious illusion that the island itself actually moved. Above, for a mile or two, I could see the great river descending upon me; it was like looking up the slope of a sliding hill, white with foam, and leaping up everywhere to show itself to the sun.

The rest of the island was too thickly grown with willows to make walking pleasant, but I made the tour, nevertheless. From the lower end the light, of course, changed, and the river looked dark and angry. Only the backs of the flying waves were visible, streaked with foam, and pushed forcibly by the great puffs of wind that fell upon them from behind. For a short mile it was visible, pouring in and out among the islands, and then disappearing with a huge sweep into the willows, which closed about it like a herd of monstrous antediluvian creatures crowding down to drink. They made me think of gigantic sponge-like growths that sucked the river up into themselves. They caused it to vanish from sight. They herded there together in such overpowering numbers.

Altogether it was an impressive scene, with its utter loneliness, its bizarre suggestion; and as I gazed, long and curiously, a singular emotion began to stir somewhere in the depths of me. Midway in my delight of the wild beauty, there crept, unbidden and unexplained, a curious feeling of disquietude, almost of alarm.

A rising river, perhaps, always suggests something of the ominous; many of the little islands I saw before me would probably have been swept away by the morning; this resistless, thundering flood of water touched the sense of awe. Yet I was aware that my uneasiness lay deeper far than the emotions of awe and wonder. It was not that I felt. Nor had it directly to do with the power of the driving wind—this shouting hurricane that might almost carry up a few acres of willows into the air and scatter them like so much chaff over the landscape. The wind was simply enjoying itself, for nothing rose out of the flat landscape to stop it, and I was conscious of sharing its great game with a kind of pleasurable excitement. Yet this novel emotion had nothing to do with the wind. Indeed, so vague was the sense of distress I experienced, that it was impossible to trace it to its source and deal with it accordingly, though I was aware somehow that it had to do with my realization of our utter insignificance before this unrestrained power of the elements about me. The huge-grown river had something to do with it too—a vague, unpleasant idea that we had somehow trifled with these great elemental forces in whose power we lay helpless every hour of the day and night. For here, indeed, they were gigantically at play together, and the sight appealed to the imagination.

But my emotion, so far as I could understand it, seemed to attach itself more particularly to the willow bushes, to these acres and acres of willows, crowding, so thickly growing there, swarming everywhere the eye could reach, pressing upon the river as though to suffocate it, standing in dense array mile after mile beneath the sky, watching, waiting, listening. And, apart quite from the elements, the willows connected themselves subtly with my malaise, attacking the mind insidiously somehow by reason of their vast numbers, and contriving in some way or other to represent to the imagination a new and mighty power, a power, moreover, not altogether friendly to us.

Great revelations of nature, of course, never fail to impress in one way or another, and I was no stranger to moods of the kind. Mountains overawe and oceans terrify, while the mystery of great forests exercises a spell peculiarly its own. But all these, at one point or another, somewhere link on intimately with human life and human experience. They stir comprehensible, even if alarming, emotions. They tend on the whole to exalt.

With this multitude of willows, however, it was something far different, I felt. Some essence emanated from them that besieged the heart. A sense of awe awakened, true, but of awe touched somewhere by a vague terror. Their serried ranks, growing everywhere darker about me as the shadows deepened, moving furiously yet softly in the wind, woke in me the curious and unwelcome suggestion that we had trespassed here upon the borders of an alien world, a world where we were intruders, a world where we were not wanted or invited to remain—where we ran grave risks perhaps!

The feeling, however, though it refused to yield its meaning entirely to analysis, did not at the time trouble me by passing into menace. Yet it never left me quite, even during the very practical business of putting up the tent in a hurricane of wind and building a fire for the stew-pot. It remained, just enough to bother and perplex, and to rob a most delightful camping-ground of a good portion of its charm. To my companion, however, I said nothing, for he was a man I considered devoid of imagination. In the first place, I could never have explained to him what I meant, and in the second, he would have laughed stupidly at me if I had.

There was a slight depression in the center of the island, and here we pitched the tent. The surrounding willows broke the wind a bit.

"A poor camp," observed the imperturbable Swede when at last the tent stood upright, "no stones and precious little firewood. I'm for moving on early tomorrow—eh? This sand won't hold anything."

But the experience of a collapsing tent at midnight had taught us many devices, and we made the cozy gipsy house as safe as possible, and then set about collecting a store of wood to last till bed-time. Willow bushes drop no branches, and driftwood was our only source of supply. We hunted the shores pretty thoroughly. Everywhere the banks were crumbling as the rising flood tore at them and carried away great portions with a splash and a gurgle.

"The island's much smaller than when we landed," said the accurate Swede. "It won't last long at this rate. We'd better drag the canoe close to the tent, and be ready to start at a moment's notice. *I* shall sleep in my clothes."

He was a little distance off, climbing along the bank, and I heard his rather jolly laugh as he spoke.

"By Jove!" I heard him call, a moment later, and turned to see what had caused his exclamation. But for the moment he was hidden by the willows, and I could not find him.

"What in the world's this?" I heard him cry again, and this time his voice had become serious.

I ran up quickly and joined him on the bank. He was looking over the river, pointing at something in the water.

"Good heavens, it's a man's body!" he cried excitedly. "Look!"

A black thing, turning over and over in the foaming waves, swept rapidly past. It kept disappearing and coming up to the surface again. It was about twenty feet from the shore, and just as it was opposite to where we stood it lurched round and looked straight at us. We saw its eyes reflecting the sunset, and gleaming an odd yellow as the body turned over. Then it gave a swift, gulping plunge, and dived out of sight in a flash.

"An otter, by gad!" we exclaimed in the same breath, laughing.

It *was* an otter, alive, and out on the hunt; yet it had looked exactly like the body of a drowned man turning helplessly in the current. Far below it came to the surface once again, and we saw its black skin, wet and shining in the sunlight.

Then, too, just as we turned back, our arms full of driftwood, another thing happened to recall us to the river bank. This time it really was a man, and what was more, a man in a boat. Now a small boat on the Danube was an unusual sight at any time, but here in this deserted region, and at flood time, it was so unexpected as to constitute a real event. We stood and stared.

Whether it was due to the slanting sunlight, or the refraction from the wonderfully illumined water, I cannot say, but, whatever the cause, I found it difficult to focus my sight properly upon the flying apparition. It seemed, however, to be a man standing upright in a sort of flat-bottomed boat, steering with a long oar, and being carried down the opposite shore at a tremendous pace. He apparently was looking across in our direction, but the distance was too great and the light too uncertain for us to make out very plainly what he was about. It seemed to me that he was gesticulating and making signs at us. His voice came across the water to us shouting something furiously, but the wind drowned it so that no single word was audible. There was something curious about the whole appearance—man, boat, signs, voice—that made an impression on me out of all proportion to its cause. "He's crossing himself!" I cried. "Look, he's making the sign of the Cross!"

"I believe you're right," the Swede said, shading his eyes with his hand and watching the man out of sight. He seemed to be gone in a moment, melting away down there into the sea of willows where the sun caught them in the bend of the river and turned them into a great crimson wall of beauty. Mist, too, had begun to rise, so that the air was hazy.

"But what in the world is he doing at nightfall on this flooded river?" I said, half to myself. "Where is he going at such a time, and what did he mean by his signs and shouting? D'you think he wished to warn us about something?"

"He saw our smoke, and thought we were spirits probably," laughed my companion. "These Hungarians believe in all sorts of rubbish; you remember the shopwoman at Pressburg warning us that no one ever landed here because it belonged to some sort of beings outside man's world! I suppose they believe in fairies and elementals, possibly demons, too. That peasant in the boat saw people on the islands for the first time in his life," he added, after a slight pause, "and it scared him, that's all."

The Swede's tone of voice was not convincing, and his manner lacked something that was usually there. I noted the change instantly while he talked, though without being able to label it precisely.

"If they had enough imagination," I laughed loudly—I remember trying to make as much *noise* as I could—"they might well people a place like this with the old gods of antiquity. The Romans must have haunted all this region more or less with their shrines and sacred groves and elemental deities."

The subject dropped and we returned to our stew-pot, for my friend was not given to imaginative conversation as a rule. Moreover, just then I remember feeling distinctly glad that he was not imaginative; his stolid, practical nature suddenly seemed to me welcome and comforting. It was an admirable temperament, I felt; he could steer down rapids like a red Indian, shoot dangerous bridges and whirlpools better than any white man I ever saw in a canoe. He was a grand fellow for an adventurous trip, a tower of strength when untoward things happened. I looked at his strong face and light curly hair as he staggered along under his pile of driftwood (twice the size of mine!), and I experienced a feeling of relief. Yes, I was distinctly glad just then that the Swede was—what he was, and that he never made remarks that suggested more than they said.

"The river's still rising, though," he added, as if following out some thoughts of his own, and dropping his load with a gasp. "This island will be under water in two days if it goes on."

"I wish the *wind* would go down," I said. "I don't care a fig for the river."

The flood, indeed, had no terrors for us; we could get off at ten minutes' notice, and the more water the better we liked it. It meant an increasing current and the obliteration of the treacherous shingle-beds that so often threatened to tear the bottom out of our canoe.

Contrary to our expectations, the wind did not go down with the sun. It seemed to increase with the darkness, howling overhead and shaking the willows round us like straws. Curious sounds accompanied it sometimes, like the explosion of heavy guns, and it fell upon the water and the island in great flat blows of immense power. It made me think of the sounds a planet must make, could we only hear it, driving along through space.

But the sky kept wholly clear of clouds, and soon after supper the full moon rose up in the east and covered the river and the plain of shouting willows with a light like the day.

We lay on the sandy patch beside the fire, smoking, listening to the noises of the night round us, and talking happily of the journey we had already made, and of our plans ahead. The map lay spread in the door of the tent, but the high wind made it hard to study, and presently we lowered the curtain and extinguished the lantern. The firelight was enough to smoke and see each other's faces by, and the sparks flew about overhead like fireworks. A few yards beyond, the river gurgled and hissed, and from time to time a heavy splash announced the falling away of further portions of the bank.

Our talk, I noticed, had to do with the faraway scenes and incidents of our first camps in the Black Forest, or of other subjects altogether remote from the present setting, for neither of us spoke of the actual moment more than was necessary—almost as though we had agreed tacitly to avoid discussion of the camp and its incidents. Neither the otter nor the boatman, for instance, received the honor of a single mention, though ordinarily these would have furnished discussion for the greater part of the evening. They were, of course, distinct events in such a place.

The scarcity of wood made it a business to keep the fire going, for the wind, that drove the smoke in our faces wherever we sat, helped at the same time to make a forced draught. We took it in turn to make some foraging expeditions into the darkness, and the quantity the Swede brought back always made me feel that he took an absurdly long time finding it; for the fact was I did not care much about being left alone, and yet it always seemed to be my turn to grub about among the bushes or scramble along the slippery banks in the moonlight. The long day's battle with wind and water—such wind and such water!—had tired us both, and an early bed was the obvious program. Yet neither of us made the move for the tent. We lay there, tending the fire, talking in desultory fashion, peering about us into the dense willow bushes, and listening to the thunder of wind and river. The loneliness of the place had entered our very bones, and silence seemed natural, for after a bit the sound of our voices became a trifle unreal and forced; whispering would have been the fitting mode of communication, I felt, and the human voice, always rather absurd amid the roar of the elements, now carried with it something almost illegitimate. It was like talking out loud in church, or in some place where it was not lawful, perhaps not quite *safe*, to be overheard.

The eeriness of this lonely island, set among a million willows, swept by a hurricane, and surrounded by hurrying deep waters, touched us both, I fancy. Untrodden by man, almost unknown to man, it lay there beneath the moon, remote from human influence, on the frontier of another world, an alien world, a world tenanted by willows only and the souls of willows. And we, in our rashness, had dared to invade it, even to make use of it! Something more than the power of its mystery stirred in me as I lay on the sand, feet to fire, and peered up through the leaves at the stars. For the last time I rose to get firewood.

"When this has burnt up," I said firmly, "I shall turn in," and my companion watched me lazily as I moved off into the surrounding shadows.

For an unimaginative man I thought he seemed unusually receptive that night, unusually open to suggestion of things other than sensory. He too was touched by the beauty and loneliness of the place. I was not altogether pleased, I remember, to recognize this slight change in him, and instead of immediately collecting sticks, I made my way to the far point of the island where the moonlight on plain and river could be seen to better advantage. The desire to be alone had come suddenly upon me; my former dread returned in force; there was a vague feeling in me I wished to face and probe to the bottom.

When I reached the point of sand jutting out among the waves, the spell of the place descended upon me with a positive shock. No mere "scenery" could have produced such an effect. There was something more here, something to alarm.

I gazed across the waste of wild waters; I watched the whispering willows; I heard the ceaseless beating of the tireless wind; and, one and all, each in its own way, stirred in me this sensation of a strange distress. But the *willows* especially; for ever they went on chattering and talking among themselves, laughing a little, shrilly crying out, sometimes sighing—but what it was they made so much to-do about belonged to the secret life of the great plain they inhabited. And it was utterly alien to the world I knew, or to that of the wild yet kindly elements. They made me think of a host of beings from another plane of life, another evolution altogether, perhaps, all discussing a mystery known only to themselves. I watched them moving busily together, oddly shaking their big bushy heads, twirling their myriad leaves even when there was no wind. They moved of their own will as though alive, and they touched, by some incalculable method, my own keen sense of the *horrible*.

There they stood in the moonlight, like a vast army surrounding our camp, shaking their innumerable silver spears defiantly, formed all ready for an attack.

The psychology of places, for some imaginations at least, is very vivid; for the wanderer, especially, camps have their "note" either of welcome or rejection. At first it may not always be apparent, because the busy preparations of tent and cooking prevent, but with the first pause—after supper usually—it comes and announces itself. And the note of this willow-camp now became unmistakably plain to me; we were interlopers, trespassers; we were not welcomed. The sense of unfamiliarity grew upon me as I stood there watching. We touched the frontier of a region where our presence was resented. For a night's lodging we might perhaps be tolerated; but for a prolonged and inquisitive stay—No! by all the gods of the trees and wilderness, no! We were the first human influences upon this island, and we were not wanted. *The willows were against us.*

Strange thoughts like these, bizarre fancies, borne I know not whence, found lodgment in my mind as I stood listening. What, I thought, if, after all, these crouching willows proved to be alive; if suddenly they should rise up, like a swarm of living creatures, marshaled by the gods whose territory we had invaded, sweep towards us off the vast swamps, booming overhead in the night—and then *settle down*! As I looked it was so easy to imagine they actually moved, crept nearer, retreated a little, huddled together in masses, hostile, waiting for the great wind that should finally start them a-running. I could have sworn their aspect changed a little, and their ranks deepened and pressed more closely together.

The melancholy shrill cry of a night-bird sounded overhead, and suddenly I nearly lost my balance as the piece of bank I stood upon fell with a great splash into the river, undermined by the flood. I stepped back just in time, and went on hunting for firewood again, half laughing at the odd fancies that crowded so thickly into my mind and cast their spell upon me. I recalled the Swede's remark about moving on next day, and I was just thinking that I fully agreed with him, when I turned with a start and saw the subject of my thoughts standing immediately in front of me. He was quite close. The roar of the elements had covered his approach.

"You've been gone so long," he shouted above the wind, "I thought something must have happened to you."

But there was that in his tone, and a certain look in his face as well, that conveyed to me more than his usual words, and in a flash I understood the real reason for his coming. It was because the spell of the place had entered his soul too, and he did not like being alone.

"River still rising," he cried, pointing to the flood in the moonlight, "and the wind's simply awful."

He always said the same things, but it was the cry for companionship that gave the real importance to his words.

"Lucky," I cried back, "our tent's in the hollow. I think it'll hold all right." I added something about the difficulty of finding wood, in order to explain my absence, but the wind caught my words and flung them across the river, so that he did not hear, but just looked at me through the branches, nodding his head.

"Lucky if we get away without disaster!" he shouted, or words to that effect; and I remember feeling half angry with him for putting the thought into words, for it was exactly what I felt myself. There was disaster impending somewhere, and the sense of presentiment lay unpleasantly upon me.

We went back to the fire and made a final blaze, poking it up with our feet. We took a last look round. But for the wind the heat would have been unpleasant. I put this thought into words, and I remember my friend's reply struck me oddly: that he would rather have the heat, the ordinary July weather, than this "diabolical wind."

Everything was snug for the night; the canoe lying turned over beside the tent, with both yellow paddles beneath her; the provision sack hanging from a willow-stem, and the washed-up dishes removed to a safe distance from the fire, all ready for the morning meal.

We smothered the embers of the fire with sand, and then turned in. The flap of the tent door was up, and I saw the branches and the stars and the white moonlight. The shaking willows and the heavy buffetings of the wind against our taut little house were the last things I remembered as sleep came down and covered all with its soft and delicious forgetfulness.

II

Suddenly I found myself lying awake, peering from my sandy mattress through the door of the tent. I looked at my watch pinned against the canvas, and saw by the bright moonlight that it was past twelve o'clock—the threshold of a new day—and I had therefore slept a couple of hours. The Swede was asleep still beside me; the wind howled as before; something plucked at my heart and made me feel afraid. There was a sense of disturbance in my immediate neighborhood.

I sat up quickly and looked out. The trees were swaying violently to and fro as the gusts smote them, but our little bit of green canvas lay snugly safe in the hollow, for the wind passed over it without meeting enough resistance to make it vicious. The feeling of disquietude did not pass, however, and I crawled quietly out of the tent to see if our belongings were safe. I moved carefully so as not to waken my companion. A curious excitement was on me.

I was half-way out, kneeling on all fours, when my eye first took in that the tops of the bushes opposite, with their moving tracery of leaves, made shapes against the sky. I sat back on my haunches and stared. It was incredible, surely, but there, opposite and slightly above me, were shapes of some indeterminate sort among the willows, and as the branches swayed in the wind they seemed to group themselves about these shapes, forming a series of monstrous outlines that shifted rapidly beneath the moon. Close, about fifty feet in front of me, I saw these things.

My first instinct was to waken my companion, that he too might see them, but something made me hesitate—the sudden realization, probably, that I should not welcome corroboration; and meanwhile I crouched there staring in amazement with smarting eyes. I was wide awake. I remember saying to myself that I was *not* dreaming.

They first became properly visible, these huge figures, just within the tops of the bushes—immense, bronze-colored, moving, and wholly independent of the swaying of the branches. I saw them plainly and noted, now I came to examine them more calmly, that they were very much larger than human, and indeed that something in their appearance proclaimed them to be *not human* at all. Certainly they were not merely the moving tracery of the branches against the moonlight. They shifted independently. They rose upwards in a continuous stream from earth to sky, vanishing utterly as soon as they reached the dark of the sky. They were interlaced one with another, making a great column, and I saw their limbs and huge bodies melting in and out of each other, forming this serpentine line that bent and swayed and twisted spirally with the contortions of the wind-tossed trees. They were nude, fluid shapes, passing up the bushes, *within* the leaves almost—rising up in a living column into the heavens. Their faces I never could see. Unceasingly they poured upwards, swaying in great bending curves, with a hue of dull bronze upon their skins.

I stared, trying to force every atom of vision from my eyes. For a long time I thought they *must* every moment disappear and resolve themselves into the movements of the branches and prove to be an optical illusion. I searched everywhere for a proof of reality, when all the while I understood quite well that the standard of reality had changed. For the longer I looked the more certain I became that these figures were real and living, though perhaps not according to the standards that the camera and the biologist would insist upon.

Far from feeling fear, I was possessed with a sense of awe and wonder such as I have never known. I seemed to be gazing at the personified elemental forces of this haunted and primeval region. Our intrusion had stirred the powers of the place into activity. It was we who were the cause of the disturbance, and my brain filled to bursting with stories and legends of the spirits and deities of places that have been acknowledged and worshipped by men in all ages of the world's history. But, before I could arrive at any possible explanation, something impelled me to go farther out, and I crept forward on the sand and stood upright. I felt the ground still warm under my bare feet; the wind tore at my hair and face; and the sound of the river burst upon my ears with a sudden roar. These things, I knew, were real, and proved that my senses were acting normally. Yet the figures still rose from earth to heaven, silent, majestically, in a great spiral of grace and strength that overwhelmed me at length with a genuine deep emotion of worship. I felt that I must fall down and worship—absolutely worship.

Perhaps in another minute I might have done so, when a gust of wind swept against me with such force that it blew me sideways, and I nearly stumbled and fell. It seemed to shake the dream violently out of me. At least it gave me another point of view somehow. The figures still remained, still ascended into heaven from the heart of the night, but my reason at last began to assert itself. It must be a subjective experience, I argued—none the less real for that, but still subjective. The moonlight and the branches combined to work out these pictures upon the mirror of my imagination, and for some reason I projected them outwards and made them appear objective. I knew this must be the case, of course. I took courage, and began to move forward across the open patches of sand. By Jove, though, was it all hallucination? Was it merely subjective? Did not my reason argue in the old futile way from the little standard of the known?

I only know that great column of figures ascended darkly into the sky for what seemed a very long period of time, and with a very complete measure of reality as most men are accustomed to gauge reality. Then suddenly they were gone!

And, once they were gone and the immediate wonder of their great presence had passed, fear came down upon me with a cold rush. The esoteric meaning of this lonely and haunted region suddenly flamed up within me, and I began to tremble dreadfully. I took a quick look round—a look of horror that came near to panic—calculating vainly ways of escape; and then, realizing how helpless I was to achieve anything really effective, I crept back silently into the tent and lay down again upon my sandy mattress, first lowering the door-curtain to shut out the sight of the willows in the moonlight, and then burying my head as deeply as possible beneath the blankets to deaden the sound of the terrifying wind.

III

As though further to convince me that I had not been dreaming, I remember that it was a long time before I fell again into a troubled and restless sleep; and even then only the upper crust of me slept, and underneath there was something that never quite lost consciousness, but lay alert and on the watch.

But this second time I jumped up with a genuine start of terror. It was neither the wind nor the river that woke me, but the slow approach of something that caused the sleeping portion of me to grow smaller and smaller till at last it vanished altogether, and I found myself sitting bolt upright—listening.

Outside there was a sound of multitudinous little patterings. They had been coming, I was aware, for a long time, and in my sleep they had first become audible. I sat there nervously wide awake as though I had not slept at all. It seemed to me that my breathing came with difficulty, and that there was a great weight upon the surface of my body. In spite of the hot night, I felt clammy with cold and shivered. Something surely was pressing steadily against the sides of the tent and weighing down upon it from above. Was it the body of the wind? Was this the pattering rain, the dripping of the leaves? The spray blown from the river by the wind and gathering in big drops? I thought quickly of a dozen things.

Then suddenly the explanation leaped into my mind: a bough from the poplar, the only large tree on the island, had fallen with the wind. Still half caught by the other branches, it would fall with the next gust and crush us, and meanwhile its leaves brushed and tapped upon the tight canvas surface of the tent. I raised a loose flap and rushed out, calling to the Swede to follow.

But when I got out and stood upright I saw that the tent was free. There was no hanging bough; there was no rain or spray; nothing approached.

A cold, grey light filtered down through the bushes and lay on the faintly gleaming sand. Stars still crowded the sky directly overhead, and the wind howled magnificently, but the fire no longer gave out any glow, and I saw the east reddening in streaks through the trees. Several hours must have passed since I stood there before watching the ascending figures, and the memory of it now came back to me horribly, like an evil dream. Oh, how tired it made me feel, that ceaseless raging wind! Yet, though the deep lassitude of a sleepless night was on me, my nerves were tingling with the activity of an equally tireless apprehension, and all idea of repose was out of the question. The river I saw had risen further. Its thunder filled the air, and a fine spray made itself felt through my thin sleeping shirt.

Yet nowhere did I discover the slightest evidence of anything to cause alarm. This deep, prolonged disturbance in my heart remained wholly unaccounted for.

My companion had not stirred when I called him, and there was no need to waken him now. I looked about me carefully, noting everything; the turned-over canoe; the yellow paddles—two of them, I'm certain; the provision sack and the extra lantern hanging together from the tree; and, crowding everywhere about me, enveloping all, the willows, those endless, shaking willows. A bird uttered its morning cry, and a string of duck passed with whirring flight overhead in the twilight. The sand whirled, dry and stinging, about my bare feet in the wind.

I walked round the tent and then went out a little way into the bush, so that I could see across the river to the farther landscape, and the same profound yet indefinable emotion of distress seized upon me again as I saw the interminable sea of bushes stretching to the horizon, looking ghostly and unreal in the wan light of dawn. I walked softly here and there, still puzzling over that odd sound of infinite pattering, and of that pressure upon the tent that had wakened me. It *must* have been the wind, I reflected—the wind bearing upon the loose, hot sand, driving the dry particles smartly against the taut canvas—the wind dropping heavily upon our fragile roof.

Yet all the time my nervousness and malaise increased appreciably.

I crossed over to the farther shore and noted how the coast-line had altered in the night, and what masses of sand the river had torn away. I dipped my hands and feet into the cool current, and bathed my forehead. Already there was a glow of sunrise in the sky and the exquisite freshness of coming day. On my way back I passed purposely beneath the very bushes where I had seen the column of figures rising into the air, and midway among the clumps I suddenly found myself overtaken by a sense of vast terror. From the shadows a large figure went swiftly by. Someone passed me, as sure as ever man did. . . .

It was a great staggering blow from the wind that helped me forward again, and once out in the more open space, the sense of terror diminished strangely. The winds were about and walking, I remember saying to myself, for the winds often move like great presences under the trees. And altogether the fear that hovered about me was such an unknown and immense kind of fear, so unlike anything I had ever felt before, that it woke a sense of awe and wonder in me that did much to counteract its worst effects; and when I reached a high point in the middle of the island from which I could see the wide stretch of river, crimson in the sunrise, the whole magical beauty of it all was so overpowering that a sort of wild yearning woke in me and almost brought a cry up into the throat.

But this cry found no expression, for as my eyes wandered from the plain beyond to the island round me and noted our little tent half hidden among the willows, a dreadful discovery leaped out at me, compared to which my terror of the walking winds seemed as nothing at all.

For a change, I thought, had somehow come about in the arrangement of the landscape. It was not that my point of vantage gave me a different view, but that an alteration had apparently been effected in the relation of the tent to the willows, and of the willows to the tent. Surely the bushes now crowded much closer—unnecessarily, unpleasantly close. *They had moved nearer.*

Creeping with silent feet over the shifting sands, drawing imperceptibly nearer by soft, unhurried movements, the willows had come closer during the night. But had the wind moved them, or had they moved of themselves? I recalled the sound of infinite small patterings and the pressure upon the tent and upon my own heart that caused me to wake in terror. I swayed for a moment in the wind like a tree, finding it hard to keep my upright position on the sandy hillock. There was a suggestion here of personal agency, of deliberate intention, of aggressive hostility, and it terrified me into a sort of rigidity.

Then the reaction followed quickly. The idea was so bizarre, so absurd, that I felt inclined to laugh. But the laughter came no more readily than the cry, for the knowledge that my mind was so receptive to such dangerous imaginings brought the additional terror that it was through our minds and not through our physical bodies that the attack would come, and was coming.

The wind buffeted me about, and, very quickly it seemed, the sun came up over the horizon, for it was after four o'clock, and I must have stood on that little pinnacle of sand longer than I knew, afraid to come down to close quarters with the willows. I returned quietly, creepily, to the tent, first taking another exhaustive look round and—yes, I confess it—making a few measurements. I paced out on the warm sand the distances between the willows and the tent, making a note of the shortest distance particularly.

I crawled stealthily into my blankets. My companion, to all appearances, still slept soundly, and I was glad that this was so. Provided my experiences were not corroborated, I could find strength somehow to deny them, perhaps. With the daylight I could persuade myself that it was all a subjective hallucination, a fantasy of the night, a projection of the excited imagination.

Nothing further came in to disturb me, and I fell asleep almost at once, utterly exhausted, yet still in dread of hearing again that weird sound of multitudinous pattering, or of feeling the pressure upon my heart that had made it difficult to breathe.

IV

The sun was high in the heavens when my companion woke me from a heavy sleep and announced that the porridge was cooked and there was just time to bathe. The grateful smell of frizzling bacon entered the tent door.

"River still rising," he said, "and several islands out in mid-stream have disappeared altogether. Our own island's much smaller."

"Any wood left?" I asked sleepily.

"The wood and the island will finish tomorrow in a dead heat," he laughed, "but there's enough to last us till then."

I plunged in from the point of the island, which had indeed altered a lot in size and shape during the night, and was swept down in a moment to the landing-place opposite the tent. The water was icy, and the banks flew by like the country from an express train. Bathing under such conditions was an exhilarating operation, and the terror of the night seemed cleansed out of me by a process of evaporation in the brain. The sun was blazing hot; not a cloud showed itself anywhere; the wind, however, had not abated one little jot.

Quite suddenly then the implied meaning of the Swede's words flashed across me, showing that he no longer wished to leave post-haste, and had changed his mind. "Enough to last till tomorrow"—he assumed we should stay on the island another night. It struck me as odd. The night before he was so positive the other way. How had the change come about?

Great crumblings of the banks occurred at breakfast, with heavy splashings and clouds of spray which the wind brought into our frying-pan, and my fellow-traveler talked incessantly about the difficulty the Vienna-Pesth steamers must have to find the channel in flood. But the state of his mind interested and impressed me far more than the state of the river or the difficulties of the steamers. He had changed somehow since the evening before. His manner was different—a trifle excited, a trifle shy, with a sort of suspicion about his voice and gestures. I hardly know how to describe it now in cold blood, but at the time I remember being quite certain of one thing—that he had become frightened!

He ate very little breakfast, and for once omitted to smoke his pipe. He had the map spread open beside him, and kept studying its markings.

"We'd better get off sharp in an hour," I said presently, feeling for an opening that must bring him indirectly to a partial confession at any rate. And his answer puzzled me uncomfortably: "Rather! If they'll let us."

"Who'll let us? The elements?" I asked quickly, with affected indifference.

"The powers of this awful place, whoever they are," he replied, keeping his eyes on the map. "The gods are here, if they are anywhere at all in the world."

"The elements are always the true immortals," I replied, laughing as naturally as I could manage, yet knowing quite well that my face reflected my true feelings when he looked up gravely at me and spoke across the smoke:

"We shall be fortunate if we get away without further disaster."

This was exactly what I had dreaded, and I screwed myself up to the point of the direct question. It was like agreeing to allow the dentist to extract the tooth; it *had* to come anyhow in the long run, and the rest was all pretence.

"Further disaster! Why, what's happened?"

"For one thing—the steering paddle's gone," he said quietly.

"The steering paddle gone!" I repeated, greatly excited, for this was our rudder, and the Danube in flood without a rudder was suicide. "But what—"

"And there's a tear in the bottom of the canoe," he added, with a genuine little tremor in his voice.

I continued staring at him, able only to repeat the words in his face somewhat foolishly. There, in the heat of the sun, and on this burning sand, I was aware of a freezing atmosphere descending round us. I got up to follow him, for he merely nodded his head gravely and led the way towards the tent a few yards on the other side of the fireplace. The canoe still lay there as I had last seen her in the night, ribs uppermost, the paddles, or rather, *the* paddle, on the sand beside her.

"There's only one," he said, stooping to pick it up. "And here's the rent in the base-board."

It was on the tip of my tongue to tell him that I had clearly noticed *two* paddles a few hours before, but a second impulse made me think better of it, and I said nothing. I approached to see.

There was a long, finely made tear in the bottom of the canoe where a little slither of wood had been neatly taken clean out; it looked as if the tooth of a sharp rock or snag had eaten down her length, and investigation showed that the hole went through. Had we launched out in her without observing it we must inevitably have foundered. At first the water would have made the wood swell so as to close the hole, but once out in mid-stream the water must have poured in, and the canoe, never more than two inches above the surface, would have filled and sunk very rapidly.

"There, you see an attempt to prepare a victim for the sacrifice," I heard him saying, more to himself than to me, "two victims rather," he added as he bent over and ran his fingers along the slit.

I began to whistle—a thing I always do unconsciously when utterly nonplussed—and purposely paid no attention to his words. I was determined to consider them foolish.

"It wasn't there last night," he said presently, straightening up from his examination and looking anywhere but at me.

"We must have scratched her in landing, of course," I stopped whistling to say. "The stones are very sharp—"

I stopped abruptly, for at that moment he turned round and met my eye squarely. I knew just as well as he did how impossible my explanation was. There were no stones, to begin with.

"And then there's this to explain too," he added quietly, handing me the paddle and pointing to the blade.

A new and curious emotion spread freezingly over me as I took and examined it. The blade was scraped down all over, beautifully scraped, as though someone had sand-papered it with care, making it so thin that the first vigorous stroke must have snapped it off at the elbow.

"One of us walked in his sleep and did this thing," I said feebly, "or—or it has been filed by the constant stream of sand particles blown against it by the wind, perhaps."

"Ah," said the Swede, turning away, laughing a little, "you can explain everything."

"The same wind that caught the steering paddle and flung it so near the bank that it fell in with the next lump that crumbled," I called out after him, absolutely determined to find an explanation for everything he showed me.

"I see," he shouted back, turning his head to look at me before disappearing among the willow bushes.

Once alone with these perplexing evidences of personal agency, I think my first thoughts took the form of "One of us must have done this thing, and it certainly was not I." But my second thought decided how impossible it was to suppose, under all the circumstances, that either of us had done it. That my companion, the trusted friend of a dozen similar expeditions, could have knowingly had a hand in it, was a suggestion not to be entertained for a moment. Equally absurd seemed the explanation that this imperturbable and densely practical nature had suddenly become insane and was busied with insane purposes.

Yet the fact remained that what disturbed me most, and kept my fear actively alive even in this blaze of sunshine and wild beauty, was the clear certainty that some curious alteration had come about in his *mind*—that he was nervous, timid, suspicious, aware of goings on he did not speak about, watching a series of secret and hitherto unmentionable events—waiting, in a word, for a climax that he expected, and, I thought, expected very soon. This grew up in my mind intuitively—I hardly knew how.

I made a hurried examination of the tent and its surroundings, but the measurements of the night remained the same. There were deep hollows formed in the sand I now noticed for the first time, basin-shaped and of various depths and sizes, varying from that of a tea-cup to a large bowl. The wind, no doubt, was responsible for these miniature craters, just as it was for lifting the paddle and tossing it towards the water. The rent in the canoe was the only thing that seemed quite inexplicable; and, after all, it *was* conceivable that a sharp point had caught it when we landed. The examination I made of the shore did not assist this theory, but all the same I clung to it with that diminishing portion of my intelligence which I called my "reason." An explanation of some kind was an absolute necessity, just as some working explanation of the universe is necessary—however absurd—to the happiness of every individual who seeks to do his duty in the world and face the problems of life. The simile seemed to me at the time an exact parallel.

I at once set the pitch melting, and presently the Swede joined me at the work, though under the best conditions in the world the canoe could not be safe for traveling till the following day. I drew his attention casually to the hollows in the sand.

"Yes," he said, "I know. They're all over the island. But *you* can explain them, no doubt!"

"Wind, of course," I answered without hesitation. "Have you never watched those little whirlwinds in the street that twist and twirl everything into a circle? This sand's loose enough to yield, that's all."

He made no reply, and we worked on in silence for a bit. I watched him surreptitiously all the time, and I had an idea he was watching me. He seemed, too, to be always listening attentively to something I could not hear, or perhaps for something that he expected to hear, for he kept turning about and staring into the bushes, and up into the sky, and out across the water where it was visible through the openings among the willows. Sometimes he even put his hand to his ear and held it there for several minutes. He said nothing to me, however, about it, and I asked no questions. And meanwhile, as he mended that torn canoe with the skill and address of a red Indian, I was glad to notice his absorption in the work, for there was a vague dread in my heart that he would speak of the changed aspect of the willows. And, if he had noticed *that*, my imagination could no longer be held a sufficient explanation of it.

At length, after a long pause, he began to talk.

"Queer thing," he added in a hurried sort of voice, as though he wanted to say something and get it over. "Queer thing. I mean, about that otter last night."

I had expected something so totally different that he caught me with surprise, and I looked up sharply.

"Shows how lonely this place is. Otters are awfully shy things—"

"I don't mean that, of course," he interrupted. "I mean—do you think—did you think it really *was* an otter?"

"What else, in the name of Heaven, what else?"

"You know, I saw it before you did, and at first it seemed—so *much* bigger than an otter."

"The sunset as you looked up-stream magnified it, or something," I replied.

He looked at me absently a moment, as though his mind were busy with other thoughts.

"It had such extraordinary yellow eyes," he went on half to himself.

"That was the sun too," I laughed, a trifle boisterously. "I suppose you'll wonder next if that fellow in the boat—"

I suddenly decided not to finish the sentence. He was in the act again of listening, turning his head to the wind, and something in the expression of his face made me halt. The subject dropped, and we went on with our caulking. Apparently he had not noticed my unfinished sentence. Five minutes later, however, he looked at me across the canoe, the smoking pitch in his hand, his face exceedingly grave.

"I *did* rather wonder, if you want to know," he said slowly, "what that thing in the boat was. I remember thinking at the time it was not a man. The whole business seemed to rise quite suddenly out of the water."

I laughed again boisterously in his face, but this time there was impatience, and a strain of anger too, in my feeling.

"Look here now," I cried, "this place is quite queer enough without going out of our way to imagine things! That boat was an ordinary boat, and the man in it was an ordinary man, and they were both going down-stream as fast as they could lick. And that otter was an otter, so don't let's play the fool about it!"

He looked steadily at me with the same grave expression. He was not in the least annoyed. I took courage from his silence.

"And, for Heaven's sake," I went on, "don't keep pretending you hear things, because it only gives me the jumps, and there's nothing to hear but the river and this cursed old thundering wind."

"You *fool*!" he answered in a low, shocked voice, "you utter fool. That's just the way all victims talk. As if you didn't understand just as well as I do!" he sneered with scorn in his voice, and a sort of resignation. "The best thing you can do is to keep quiet and try to hold your mind as firm as possible. This feeble attempt at self-deception only makes the truth harder when you're forced to meet it."

My little effort was over, and I found nothing more to say, for I knew quite well his words were true, and that *I* was the fool, not *he*. Up to a certain stage in the adventure he kept ahead of me easily, and I think I felt annoyed to be out of it, to be thus proved less psychic, less sensitive than himself to these extraordinary happenings, and half ignorant all the time of what was going on under my very nose. *He knew* from the very beginning, apparently. But at the moment I wholly missed the point of his words about the necessity of there being a victim, and that we ourselves were destined to satisfy the want. I dropped all pretence thenceforward, but thenceforward likewise my fear increased steadily to the climax.

"But you're quite right about one thing," he added, before the subject passed, "and that is that we're wiser not to talk about it, or even to think about it, because what one *thinks* finds expression in words, and what one *says*, happens."

That afternoon, while the canoe dried and hardened, we spent trying to fish, testing the leak, collecting wood, and watching the enormous flood of rising water. Masses of driftwood swept near our shores sometimes, and we fished for them with long willow branches. The island grew perceptibly smaller as the banks were torn away with great gulps and splashes. The weather kept brilliantly fine till about four o'clock, and then for the first time for three days the wind showed signs of abating. Clouds began to gather in the south-west, spreading thence slowly over the sky.

This lessening of the wind came as a great relief, for the incessant roaring, banging, and thundering had irritated our nerves. Yet the silence that came about five o'clock with its sudden cessation was in a manner quite as oppressive. The booming of the river had everything in its own way then; it filled the air with deep murmurs, more musical than the wind noises, but infinitely more monotonous. The wind held many notes, rising, falling always beating out some sort of great elemental tune; whereas the river's song lay between three notes at most—dull pedal notes, that held a lugubrious quality foreign to the wind, and somehow seemed to me, in my then nervous state, to sound wonderfully well the music of doom.

It was extraordinary, too, how the withdrawal suddenly of bright sunlight took everything out of the landscape that made for cheerfulness; and since this particular landscape had already managed to convey the suggestion of something sinister, the change of course was all the more unwelcome and noticeable. For me, I know, the darkening outlook became distinctly more alarming, and I found myself more than once calculating how soon after sunset the full moon would get up in the east, and whether the gathering clouds would greatly interfere with her lighting of the little island.

With this general hush of the wind—though it still indulged in occasional brief gusts—the river seemed to me to grow blacker, the willows to stand more densely together. The latter, too, kept up a sort of independent movement of their own, rustling among themselves when no wind stirred, and shaking oddly from the roots upwards. When common objects in this way become charged with the suggestion of horror, they stimulate the imagination far more than things of unusual appearance; and these bushes, crowding huddled about us, assumed for me in the darkness a bizarre *grotesquerie* of appearance that lent to them somehow the aspect of purposeful and living creatures. Their very ordinariness, I felt, masked what was malignant and hostile to us. The forces of the region drew nearer with the coming of night. They were focusing upon our island, and more particularly upon ourselves. For thus, somehow, in the terms of the imagination, did my really indescribable sensations in this extraordinary place present themselves.

I had slept a good deal in the early afternoon, and had thus recovered somewhat from the exhaustion of a disturbed night, but this only served apparently to render me more susceptible than before to the obsessing spell of the haunting. I fought against it, laughing at my feelings as absurd and childish, with very obvious physiological explanations, yet, in spite of every effort, they gained in strength upon me so that I dreaded the night as a child lost in a forest must dread the approach of darkness.

The canoe we had carefully covered with a waterproof sheet during the day, and the one remaining paddle had been securely tied by the Swede to the base of a tree, lest the wind should rob us of that too. From five o'clock onwards I busied myself with the stew-pot and preparations for dinner, it being my turn to cook that night. We had potatoes, onions, bits of bacon fat to add flavor, and a general thick residue from former stews at the bottom of the pot; with black bread broken up into it the result was most excellent, and it was followed by a stew of plums with sugar and a brew of strong tea with dried milk. A good pile of wood lay close at hand, and the absence of wind made my duties easy. My companion sat lazily watching me, dividing his attentions between cleaning his pipe and giving useless advice—an admitted privilege of the off-duty man. He had been very quiet all the afternoon, engaged in re-caulking the canoe, strengthening the tent ropes, and fishing for driftwood while I slept. No more talk about undesirable things had passed between us, and I think his only remarks had to do with the gradual destruction of the island, which he declared was not fully a third smaller than when we first landed.

The pot had just begun to bubble when I heard his voice calling to me from the bank, where he had wandered away without my noticing. I ran up.

"Come and listen," he said, "and see what you make of it." He held his hand cupwise to his ear, as so often before.

"*Now* do you hear anything?" he asked, watching me curiously.

We stood there, listening attentively together. At first I heard only the deep note of the water and the hissings rising from its turbulent surface. The willows, for once, were motionless and silent. Then a sound began to reach my ears faintly, a peculiar sound—something like the humming of a distant gong. It seemed to come across to us in the darkness from the waste of swamps and willows opposite. It was repeated at regular intervals, but it was certainly neither the sound of a bell nor the hooting of a distant steamer. I can liken it to nothing so much as to the sound of an immense gong, suspended far up in the sky, repeating incessantly its muffled metallic note, soft and musical, as it was repeatedly struck. My heart quickened as I listened.

"I've heard it all day," said my companion. "While you slept this afternoon it came all round the island. I hunted it down, but could never get near enough to see—to localize it correctly. Sometimes it was overhead, and sometimes it seemed under the water. Once or twice, too, I could have sworn it was not outside at all, but *within myself*—you know—the way a sound in the fourth dimension is supposed to come."

I was too much puzzled to pay much attention to his words. I listened carefully, striving to associate it with any known familiar sound I could think of, but without success. It changed in the direction, too, coming nearer, and then sinking utterly away into remote distance. I cannot say that it was ominous in quality, because to me it seemed distinctly musical, yet I must admit it set going a distressing feeling that made me wish I had never heard it.

"The wind blowing in those sand-funnels," I said determined to find an explanation, "or the bushes rubbing together after the storm perhaps."

"It comes off the whole swamp," my friend answered. "It comes from everywhere at once." He ignored my explanations. "It comes from the willow bushes somehow—"

"But now the wind has dropped," I objected. "The willows can hardly make a noise by themselves, can they?"

His answer frightened me, first because I had dreaded it, and secondly, because I knew intuitively it was true.

"It is *because* the wind has dropped we now hear it. It was drowned before. It is the cry, I believe, of the—"

I dashed back to my fire, warned by the sound of bubbling that the stew was in danger, but determined at the same time to escape further conversation. I was resolute, if possible, to avoid the exchanging of views. I dreaded, too, that he would begin about the gods, or the elemental forces, or something else disquieting, and I wanted to keep myself well in hand for what might happen later. There was another night to be faced before we escaped from this distressing place, and there was no knowing yet what it might bring forth.

"Come and cut up bread for the pot," I called to him, vigorously stirring the appetizing mixture. That stew-pot held sanity for us both, and the thought made me laugh.

He came over slowly and took the provision sack from the tree, fumbling in its mysterious depths, and then emptying the entire contents upon the ground-sheet at his feet.

"Hurry up!" I cried; "it's boiling."

The Swede burst out into a roar of laughter that startled me. It was forced laughter, not artificial exactly, but mirthless.

"There's nothing here!" he shouted, holding his sides.

"Bread, I mean."

"It's gone. There is no bread. They've taken it!"

I dropped the long spoon and ran up. Everything the sack had contained lay upon the ground-sheet, but there was no loaf.

The whole dead weight of my growing fear fell upon me and shook me. Then I burst out laughing too. It was the only thing to do: and the sound of my laughter also made me understand his. The strain of psychical pressure caused it—this explosion of unnatural laughter in both of us; it was an effort of repressed forces to seek relief; it was a temporary safety-valve. And with both of us it ceased quite suddenly.

"How criminally stupid of me!" I cried, still determined to be consistent and find an explanation. "I clean forgot to buy a loaf at Pressburg. That chattering woman put everything out of my head, and I must have left it lying on the counter or—"

"The oatmeal, too, is much less than it was this morning," the Swede interrupted.

Why in the world need he draw attention to it? I thought angrily.

"There's enough for tomorrow," I said, stirring vigorously, "and we can get lots more at Komorn or Gran. In twenty-four hours we shall be miles from here."

"I hope so—to God," he muttered, putting the things back into the sack, "unless we're claimed first as victims for the sacrifice," he added with a foolish laugh. He dragged the sack into the tent, for safety's sake, I suppose, and I heard him mumbling to himself, but so indistinctly that it seemed quite natural for me to ignore his words.

Our meal was beyond question a gloomy one, and we ate it almost in silence, avoiding one another's eyes, and keeping the fire bright. Then we washed up and prepared for the night, and, once smoking, our minds unoccupied with any definite duties, the apprehension I had felt all day long became more and more acute. It was not then active fear, I think, but the very vagueness of its origin distressed me far more that if I had been able to ticket and face it squarely. The curious sound I have likened to the note of a gong became now almost incessant, and filled the stillness of the night with a faint, continuous ringing rather than a series of distinct notes. At one time it was behind and at another time in front of us. Sometimes I fancied it came from the bushes on our left, and then again from the clumps on our right. More often it hovered directly overhead like the whirring of wings. It was really everywhere at once, behind, in front, at our sides and over our heads, completely surrounding us. The sound really defies description. But nothing within my knowledge is like that ceaseless muffled humming rising off the deserted world of swamps and willows.

We sat smoking in comparative silence, the strain growing every minute greater. The worst feature of the situation seemed to me that we did not know what to expect, and could therefore make no sort of preparation by way of defense. We could anticipate nothing. My explanations made in the sunshine, moreover, now came to haunt me with their foolish and wholly unsatisfactory nature, and it was more and more clear to us that some kind of plain talk with my companion was inevitable, whether I liked it or not. After all, we had to spend the night together, and to sleep in the same tent side by side. I saw that I could not get along much longer without the support of his mind, and for that, of course, plain talk was imperative. As long as possible, however, I postponed this little climax, and tried to ignore or laugh at the occasional sentences he flung into the emptiness.

Some of these sentences, moreover, were confoundedly disquieting to me, coming as they did to corroborate much that I felt myself: corroboration, too—which made it so much more convincing—from a totally different point of view. He composed such curious sentences, and hurled them at me in such an inconsequential sort of way, as though his main line of thought was secret to himself, and these fragments were mere bits he found it impossible to digest. He got rid of them by uttering them. Speech relieved him. It was like being sick.

"There are things about us, I'm sure, that make for disorder, disintegration, destruction, *our* destruction," he said once, while the fire blazed between us. "We've strayed out of a safe line somewhere."

And, another time, when the gong sounds had come nearer, ringing much louder than before, and directly over our heads, he said as though talking to himself:

"I don't think a gramophone would show any record of that. The sound doesn't come to me by the ears at all. The vibrations reach me in another manner altogether, and seem to be within me, which is precisely how a fourth dimensional sound might be supposed to make itself heard."

I purposely made no reply to this, but I sat up a little closer to the fire and peered about me into the darkness. The clouds were massed all over the sky, and no trace of moonlight came through. Very still, too, everything was, so that the river and the frogs had things all their own way.

"It has that about it," he went on, "which is utterly out of common experience. It is *unknown*. Only one thing describes it really; it is a non-human sound; I mean a sound outside humanity."

Having rid himself of this indigestible morsel, he lay quiet for a time, but he had so admirably expressed my own feeling that it was a relief to have the thought out, and to have confined it by the limitation of words from dangerous wandering to and fro in the mind.

The solitude of that Danube camping-place, can I ever forget it?

The feeling of being utterly alone on an empty planet! My thoughts ran incessantly upon cities and the haunts of men. I would have given my soul, as the saying is, for the "feel" of those Bavarian villages we had passed through by the score; for the normal, human commonplaces: peasants drinking beer, tables beneath the trees, hot sunshine, and a ruined castle on the rocks behind the red-roofed church. Even the tourists would have been welcome.

Yet what I felt of dread was no ordinary ghostly fear. It was infinitely greater, stranger, and seemed to arise from some dim ancestral sense of terror more profoundly disturbing than anything I had known or dreamed of. We had "strayed," as the Swede put it, into some region or some set of conditions where the risks were great, yet unintelligible to us; where the frontiers of some unknown world lay close about us. It was a spot held by the dwellers in some outer space, a sort of peep-hole whence they could spy upon the earth, themselves unseen, a point where the veil between had worn a little thin. As the final result of too long a sojourn here, we should be carried over the border and deprived of what we called "our lives," yet by mental, not physical, processes. In that sense, as he said, we should be the victims of our adventure—a sacrifice.

It took us in different fashion, each according to the measure of his sensitiveness and powers of resistance. I translated it vaguely into a personification of the mightily disturbed elements, investing them with the horror of a deliberate and malefic purpose, resentful of our audacious intrusion into their breeding-place; whereas my friend threw it into the unoriginal form at first of a trespass on some ancient shrine, some place where the old gods still held sway, where the emotional forces of former worshippers still clung, and the ancestral portion of him yielded to the old pagan spell.

At any rate, here was a place unpolluted by men, kept clean by the winds from coarsening human influences, a place where spiritual agencies were within reach and aggressive. Never, before or since, have I been so attacked by indescribable suggestions of a "beyond region," of another scheme of life, another revolution not parallel to the human. And in the end our minds would succumb under the weight of the awful spell, and we should be drawn across the frontier into *their* world.

Small things testified to the amazing influence of the place, and now in the silence round the fire they allowed themselves to be noted by the mind. The very atmosphere had proved itself a magnifying medium to distort every indication: the otter rolling in the current, the hurrying boatman making signs, the shifting willows, one and all had been robbed of its natural character, and revealed in something of its other aspect—as it existed across the border to that other region. And this changed aspect I felt was now not merely to me, but to the race. The whole experience whose verge we touched was unknown to humanity at all. It was a new order of experience, and in the true sense of the word *unearthly*.

"It's the deliberate, calculating purpose that reduces one's courage to zero," the Swede said suddenly, as if he had been actually following my thoughts. "Otherwise imagination might count for much. But the paddle, the canoe, the lessening food—"

"Haven't I explained all that once?" I interrupted viciously.

"You have," he answered dryly; "you have indeed."

He made other remarks too, as usual, about what he called the "plain determination to provide a victim"; but, having now arranged my thoughts better, I recognized that this was simply the cry of his frightened soul against the knowledge that he was being attacked in a vital part, and that he would be somehow taken or destroyed. The situation called for a courage and calmness of reasoning that neither of us could compass, and I have never before been so clearly conscious of two persons in me—the one that explained everything, and the other that laughed at such foolish explanations, yet was horribly afraid.

Meanwhile, in the pitchy night the fire died down and the wood pile grew small. Neither of us moved to replenish the stock, and the darkness consequently came up very close to our faces. A few feet beyond the circle of firelight it was inky black. Occasionally a stray puff of wind set the willows shivering about us, but apart from this not very welcome sound a deep and depressing silence reigned, broken only by the gurgling of the river and the humming in the air overhead.

We both missed, I think, the shouting company of the winds.

At length, at a moment when a stray puff prolonged itself as though the wind were about to rise again, I reached the point for me of saturation, the point where it was absolutely necessary to find relief in plain speech, or else to betray myself by some hysterical extravagance that must have been far worse in its effect upon both of us. I kicked the fire into a blaze, and turned to my companion abruptly. He looked up with a start.

"I can't disguise it any longer," I said; "I don't like this place, and the darkness, and the noises, and the awful feelings I get. There's something here that beats me utterly. I'm in a blue funk, and that's the plain truth. If the other shore was—different, I swear I'd be inclined to swim for it!"

The Swede's face turned very white beneath the deep tan of sun and wind. He stared straight at me and answered quietly, but his voice betrayed his huge excitement by its unnatural calmness. For the moment, at any rate, he was the strong man of the two. He was more phlegmatic, for one thing.

"It's not a physical condition we can escape from by running away," he replied, in the tone of a doctor diagnosing some grave disease; "we must sit tight and wait. There are forces close here that could kill a herd of elephants in a second as easily as you or I could squash a fly. Our only chance is to keep perfectly still. Our insignificance perhaps may save us."

I put a dozen questions into my expression of face, but found no words. It was precisely like listening to an accurate description of a disease whose symptoms had puzzled me.

"I mean that so far, although aware of our disturbing presence, they have not *found* us—not 'located' us, as the Americans say," he went on. "They're blundering about like men hunting for a leak of gas. The paddle and canoe and provisions prove that. I think they *feel* us, but cannot actually see us. We must keep our minds quiet—it's our minds they feel. We must control our thoughts, or it's all up with us."

"Death, you mean?" I stammered, icy with the horror of his suggestion.

"Worse—by far," he said. "Death, according to one's belief, means either annihilation or release from the limitations of the senses, but it involves no change of character. *You* don't suddenly alter just because the body's gone. But this means a radical alteration, a complete change, a horrible loss of oneself by substitution—far worse than death, and not even annihilation. We happen to have camped in a spot where their region touches ours, where the veil between has worn thin"—horrors! he was using my very own phrase, my actual words—"so that they are aware of our being in their neighborhood."

"But *who* are aware?" I asked.

I forgot the shaking of the willows in the windless calm, the humming overhead, everything except that I was waiting for an answer that I dreaded more than I can possibly explain.

He lowered his voice at once to reply, leaning forward a little over the fire, an indefinable change in his face that made me avoid his eyes and look down upon the ground.

"All my life," he said, "I have been strangely, vividly conscious of another region—not far removed from our own world in one sense, yet wholly different in kind—where great things go on unceasingly, where immense and terrible personalities hurry by, intent on vast purposes compared to which earthly affairs, the rise and fall of nations, the destinies of empires, the fate of armies and continents, are all as dust in the balance; vast purposes, I mean, that deal directly with the soul, and not indirectly with mere expressions of the soul—"

"I suggest just now—" I began, seeking to stop him, feeling as though I was face to face with a madman. But he instantly overbore me with his torrent that *had* to come.

"You think," he said, "it is the spirit of the elements, and I thought perhaps it was the old gods. But I tell you now it is—*neither*. These would be comprehensible entities, for they have relations with men, depending upon them for worship or sacrifice, whereas these beings who are now about us have absolutely nothing to do with mankind, and it is mere chance that their space happens just at this spot to touch our own."

The mere conception, which his words somehow made so convincing, as I listened to them there in the dark stillness of that lonely island, set me shaking a little all over. I found it impossible to control my movements.

"And what do you propose?" I began again.

"A sacrifice, a victim, might save us by distracting them until we could get away," he went on, "just as the wolves stop to devour the dogs and give the sleigh another start. But—I see no chance of any other victim now."

I stared blankly at him. The gleam in his eye was dreadful. Presently he continued.

"It's the willows, of course. The willows *mask* the others, but the others are feeling about for us. If we let our minds betray our fear, we're lost, lost utterly." He looked at me with an expression so calm, so determined, so sincere, that I no longer had any doubts as to his sanity. He was as sane as any man ever was. "If we can hold out through the night," he added, "we may get off in the daylight unnoticed, or rather, *undiscovered.*"

"But you really think a sacrifice would—"

That gong-like humming came down very close over our heads as I spoke, but it was my friend's scared face that really stopped my mouth.

"Hush!" he whispered, holding up his hand. "Do not mention them more than you can help. Do not refer to them *by name*. To name is to reveal; it is the inevitable clue, and our only hope lies in ignoring them, in order that they may ignore us."

"Even in thought?" He was extraordinarily agitated.

"Especially in thought. Our thoughts make spirals in their world. We must keep them *out of our minds* at all costs if possible."

I raked the fire together to prevent the darkness having everything its own way. I never longed for the sun as I longed for it then in the awful blackness of that summer night.

"Were you awake all last night?" he went on suddenly.

"I slept badly a little after dawn," I replied evasively, trying to follow his instructions, which I knew instinctively were true, "but the wind, of course—"

"I know. But the wind won't account for all the noises."

"Then you heard it too?"

"The multiplying countless little footsteps I heard," he said, adding, after a moment's hesitation, "and that other sound—"

"You mean above the tent, and the pressing down upon us of something tremendous, gigantic?"

He nodded significantly.

"It was like the beginning of a sort of inner suffocation?" I said.

"Partly, yes. It seemed to me that the weight of the atmosphere had been altered—had increased enormously, so that we should have been crushed."

"And *that*," I went on, determined to have it all out, pointing upwards where the gong-like note hummed ceaselessly, rising and falling like wind. "What do you make of that?"

"It's *their* sound," he whispered gravely. "It's the sound of their world, the humming in their region. The division here is so thin that it leaks through somehow. But, if you listen carefully, you'll find it's not above so much as around us. It's in the willows. It's the willows themselves humming, because here the willows have been made symbols of the forces that are against us."

I could not follow exactly what he meant by this, yet the thought and idea in my mind were beyond question the thought and idea in his. I realized what he realized, only with less power of analysis than his. It was on the tip of my tongue to tell him at last about my hallucination of the ascending figures and the moving bushes, when he suddenly thrust his face again close into mine across the firelight and began to speak in a very earnest whisper. He amazed me by his calmness and pluck, his apparent control of the situation. This man I had for years deemed unimaginative, stolid!

"Now listen," he said. "The only thing for us to do is to go on as though nothing had happened, follow our usual habits, go to bed, and so forth; pretend we feel nothing and notice nothing. It is a question wholly of the mind, and the less we think about them the better our chance of escape. Above all, don't *think*, for what you think happens!"

"All right," I managed to reply, simply breathless with his words and the strangeness of it all; "all right, I'll try, but tell me one more thing first. Tell me what you make of those hollows in the ground all about us, those sand-funnels?"

"No!" he cried, forgetting to whisper in his excitement. "I dare not, simply dare not, put the thought into words. If you have not guessed I am glad. Don't try to. *They* have put it into my mind; try your hardest to prevent their putting it into yours."

He sank his voice again to a whisper before he finished, and I did not press him to explain. There was already just about as much horror in me as I could hold. The conversation came to an end, and we smoked our pipes busily in silence.

Then something happened, something unimportant apparently, as the way is when the nerves are in a very great state of tension, and this small thing for a brief space gave me an entirely different point of view. I chanced to look down at my sand-shoe—the sort we used for the canoe—and something to do with the hole at the toe suddenly recalled to me the London shop where I had bought them, the difficulty the man had in fitting me, and other details of the uninteresting but practical operation. At once, in its train, followed a wholesome view of the modern skeptical world I was accustomed to move in at home. I thought of roast beef, and ale, motor-cars, policemen, brass bands, and a dozen other things that proclaimed the soul of ordinariness or utility. The effect was immediate and astonishing even to myself. Psychologically, I suppose, it was simply a sudden and violent reaction after the strain of living in an atmosphere of things that to the normal consciousness must seem impossible and incredible. But, whatever the cause, it momentarily lifted the spell from my heart, and left me for the short space of a minute feeling free and utterly unafraid. I looked up at my friend opposite.

"You damned old pagan!" I cried, laughing aloud in his face. "You imaginative idiot! You superstitious idolater! You—"

I stopped in the middle, seized anew by the old horror. I tried to smother the sound of my voice as something sacrilegious. The Swede, of course, heard it too—the strange cry overhead in the darkness—and that sudden drop in the air as though something had come nearer.

He had turned ashen white under the tan. He stood bolt upright in front of the fire, stiff as a rod, staring at me.

"After that," he said in a sort of helpless, frantic way, "we must go! We can't stay now; we must strike camp this very instant and go on— down the river."

He was talking, I saw, quite wildly, his words dictated by abject terror—the terror he had resisted so long, but which had caught him at last.

"In the dark?" I exclaimed, shaking with fear after my hysterical outburst, but still realizing our position better than he did. "Sheer madness! The river's in flood, and we've only got a single paddle. Besides, we only go deeper into their country! There's nothing ahead for fifty miles but willows, willows, willows!"

He sat down again in a state of semi-collapse. The positions, by one of those kaleidoscopic changes nature loves, were suddenly reversed, and the control of our forces passed over into my hands. His mind at last had reached the point where it was beginning to weaken.

"What on earth possessed you to do such a thing?" he whispered with the awe of genuine terror in his voice and face.

I crossed round to his side of the fire. I took both his hands in mine, kneeling down beside him and looking straight into his frightened eyes.

"We'll make one more blaze," I said firmly, "and then turn in for the night. At sunrise we'll be off full speed for Komorn. Now, pull yourself together a bit, and remember your own advice about *not thinking fear!*"

He said no more, and I saw that he would agree and obey. In some measure, too, it was a sort of relief to get up and make an excursion into the darkness for more wood. We kept close together, almost touching, groping among the bushes and along the bank. The humming overhead never ceased, but seemed to me to grow louder as we increased our distance from the fire. It was shivery work!

We were grubbing away in the middle of a thickish clump of willows where some driftwood from a former flood had caught high among the branches, when my body was seized in a grip that made me half drop upon the sand. It was the Swede. He had fallen against me, and was clutching me for support. I heard his breath coming and going in short gasps.

"Look! By my soul!" he whispered, and for the first time in my experience I knew what it was to hear tears of terror in a human voice. He was pointing to the fire, some fifty feet away. I followed the direction of his finger, and I swear my heart missed a beat.

There, in front of the dim glow, *something was moving.*

I saw it through a veil that hung before my eyes like the gauze drop-curtain used at the back of a theater—hazily a little. It was neither a human figure nor an animal. To me it gave the strange impression of being as large as several animals grouped together, like horses, two or three, moving slowly. The Swede, too, got a similar result, though expressing it differently, for he thought it was shaped and sized like a clump of willow bushes, rounded at the top, and moving all over upon its surface—"coiling upon itself like smoke," he said afterwards.

"I watched it settle downwards through the bushes," he sobbed at me. "Look, by God! It's coming this way! Oh, oh!"—he gave a kind of whistling cry. *"They've found us."*

I gave one terrified glance, which just enabled me to see that the shadowy form was swinging towards us through the bushes, and then I collapsed backwards with a crash into the branches. These failed, of course, to support my weight, so that with the Swede on top of me we fell in a struggling heap upon the sand. I really hardly knew what was happening. I was conscious only of a sort of enveloping sensation of icy fear that plucked the nerves out of their fleshly covering, twisted them this way and that, and replaced them quivering. My eyes were tightly shut; something in my throat choked me; a feeling that my consciousness was expanding, extending out into space, swiftly gave way to another feeling that I was losing it altogether, and about to die.

An acute spasm of pain passed through me, and I was aware that the Swede had hold of me in such a way that he hurt me abominably. It was the way he caught at me in falling.

But it was the pain, he declared afterwards, that saved me; it caused me to *forget them* and think of something else at the very instant when they were about to find me. It concealed my mind from them at the moment of discovery, yet just in time to evade their terrible seizing of me. He himself, he says, actually swooned at the same moment, and that was what saved him.

I only know that at a later date, how long or short is impossible to say, I found myself scrambling up out of the slippery network of willow branches, and saw my companion standing in front of me holding out a hand to assist me. I stared at him in a dazed way, rubbing the arm he had twisted for me. Nothing came to me to say, somehow.

"I lost consciousness for a moment or two," I heard him say. "That's what saved me. It made me stop thinking about them."

"You nearly broke my arm in two," I said, uttering my only connected thought at the moment. A numbness came over me.

"That's what saved *you!*" he replied. "Between us, we've managed to set them off on a false tack somewhere. The humming has ceased. It's gone—for the moment at any rate!"

A wave of hysterical laughter seized me again, and this time spread to my friend too—great healing gusts of shaking laughter that brought a tremendous sense of relief in their train. We made our way back to the fire and put the wood on so that it blazed at once. Then we saw that the tent had fallen over and lay in a tangled heap upon the ground.

We picked it up, and during the process tripped more than once and caught our feet in sand.

"It's those sand-funnels," exclaimed the Swede, when the tent was up again and the firelight lit up the ground for several yards about us. "And look at the size of them!"

All round the tent and about the fireplace where we had seen the moving shadows there were deep funnel-shaped hollows in the sand, exactly similar to the ones we had already found over the island, only far bigger and deeper, beautifully formed, and wide enough in some instances to admit the whole of my foot and leg.

Neither of us said a word. We both knew that sleep was the safest thing we could do, and to bed we went accordingly without further delay, having first thrown sand on the fire and taken the provision sack and the paddle inside the tent with us. The canoe, too, we propped in such a way at the end of the tent that our feet touched it, and the least motion would disturb and wake us.

In case of emergency, too, we again went to bed in our clothes, ready for a sudden start.

V

It was my firm intention to lie awake all night and watch, but the exhaustion of nerves and body decreed otherwise, and sleep after a while came over me with a welcome blanket of oblivion. The fact that my companion also slept quickened its approach. At first he fidgeted and constantly sat up, asking me if I "heard this" or "heard that." He tossed about on his cork mattress, and said the tent was moving and the river had risen over the point of the island, but each time I went out to look I returned with the report that all was well, and finally he grew calmer and lay still. Then at length his breathing became regular and I heard unmistakable sounds of snoring—the first and only time in my life when snoring has been a welcome and calming influence.

This, I remember, was the last thought in my mind before dozing off.

A difficulty in breathing woke me, and I found the blanket over my face. But something else besides the blanket was pressing upon me, and my first thought was that my companion had rolled off his mattress on to my own in his sleep. I called to him and sat up, and at the same moment it came to me that the tent was *surrounded*. That sound of multitudinous soft pattering was again audible outside, filling the night with horror.

I called again to him, louder than before. He did not answer, but I missed the sound of his snoring, and also noticed that the flap of the tent was down. This was the unpardonable sin. I crawled out in the darkness to hook it back securely, and it was then for the first time I realized positively that the Swede was not here. He had gone.

I dashed out in a mad run, seized by a dreadful agitation, and the moment I was out I plunged into a sort of torrent of humming that surrounded me completely and came out of every quarter of the heavens at once. It was that same familiar humming—gone mad! A swarm of great invisible bees might have been about me in the air. The sound seemed to thicken the very atmosphere, and I felt that my lungs worked with difficulty.

But my friend was in danger, and I could not hesitate.

The dawn was just about to break, and a faint whitish light spread upwards over the clouds from a thin strip of clear horizon. No wind stirred. I could just make out the bushes and river beyond, and the pale sandy patches. In my excitement I ran frantically to and fro about the island, calling him by name, shouting at the top of my voice the first words that came into my head. But the willows smothered my voice, and the humming muffled it, so that the sound only traveled a few feet round me. I plunged among the bushes, tripping headlong, tumbling over roots, and scraping my face as I tore this way and that among the preventing branches.

Then, quite unexpectedly, I came out upon the island's point and saw a dark figure outlined between the water and the sky. It was the Swede. And already he had one foot in the river! A moment more and he would have taken the plunge.

I threw myself upon him, flinging my arms about his waist and dragging him shorewards with all my strength. Of course he struggled furiously, making a noise all the time just like that cursed humming, and using the most outlandish phrases in his anger about "going *inside* to Them," and "taking the way of the water and the wind," and God only knows what more besides, that I tried in vain to recall afterwards, but which turned me sick with horror and amazement as I listened. But in the end I managed to get him into the comparative safety of the tent, and flung him breathless and cursing upon the mattress where I held him until the fit had passed.

I think the suddenness with which it all went and he grew calm, coinciding as it did with the equally abrupt cessation of the humming and pattering outside—I think this was almost the strangest part of the whole business perhaps. For he had just opened his eyes and turned his tired face up to me so that the dawn threw a pale light upon it through the doorway, and said, for all the world just like a frightened child:

"My life, old man—it's my life I owe you. But it's all over now anyhow. They've found a victim in our place!"

Then he dropped back upon his blankets and went to sleep literally under my eyes. He simply collapsed, and began to snore again as healthily as though nothing had happened and he had never tried to offer his own life as a sacrifice by drowning. And when the sunlight woke him three hours later—hours of ceaseless vigil for me—it became so clear to me that he remembered absolutely nothing of what he had attempted to do, that I deemed it wise to hold my peace and ask no dangerous questions.

He woke naturally and easily, as I have said, when the sun was already high in a windless hot sky, and he at once got up and set about the preparation of the fire for breakfast. I followed him anxiously at bathing, but he did not attempt to plunge in, merely dipping his head and making some remark about the extra coldness of the water.

"River's falling at last," he said, "and I'm glad of it."

"The humming has stopped too," I said.

He looked up at me quietly with his normal expression. Evidently he remembered everything except his own attempt at suicide.

"Everything has stopped," he said, "because—"

He hesitated. But I knew some reference to that remark he had made just before he fainted was in his mind, and I was determined to know it.

"Because 'They've found another victim'?" I said, forcing a little laugh.

"Exactly," he answered, "exactly! I feel as positive of it as though—as though—I feel quite safe again, I mean," he finished.

He began to look curiously about him. The sunlight lay in hot patches on the sand. There was no wind. The willows were motionless. He slowly rose to feet.

"Come," he said; "I think if we look, we shall find it."

He started off on a run, and I followed him. He kept to the banks, poking with a stick among the sandy bays and caves and little backwaters, myself always close on his heels.

"Ah!" he exclaimed presently, "ah!"

The tone of his voice somehow brought back to me a vivid sense of the horror of the last twenty-four hours, and I hurried up to join him. He was pointing with his stick at a large black object that lay half in the water and half on the sand. It appeared to be caught by some twisted willow roots so that the river could not sweep it away. A few hours before the spot must have been under water.

"See," he said quietly, "the victim that made our escape possible!"

And when I peered across his shoulder I saw that his stick rested on the body of a man. He turned it over. It was the corpse of a peasant, and the face was hidden in the sand. Clearly the man had been drowned, but a few hours before, and his body must have been swept down upon our island somewhere about the hour of the dawn—*at the very time the fit had passed.*

"We must give it a decent burial, you know."

"I suppose so," I replied. I shuddered a little in spite of myself, for there was something about the appearance of that poor drowned man that turned me cold.

The Swede glanced up sharply at me, an undecipherable expression on his face, and began clambering down the bank. I followed him more leisurely. The current, I noticed, had torn away much of the clothing from the body, so that the neck and part of the chest lay bare.

Halfway down the bank my companion suddenly stopped and held up his hand in warning; but either my foot slipped, or I had gained too much momentum to bring myself quickly to a halt, for I bumped into him and sent him forward with a sort of leap to save himself. We tumbled together on to the hard sand so that our feet splashed into the water. And, before anything could be done, we had collided a little heavily against the corpse.

The Swede uttered a sharp cry. And I sprang back as if I had been shot.

At the moment we touched the body there rose from its surface the loud sound of humming—the sound of several hummings—which passed with a vast commotion as of winged things in the air about us and disappeared upwards into the sky, growing fainter and fainter till they finally ceased in the distance. It was exactly as though we had disturbed some living yet invisible creatures at work.

My companion clutched me, and I think I clutched him, but before either of us had time properly to recover from the unexpected shock, we saw that a movement of the current was turning the corpse round so that it became released from the grip of the willow roots. A moment later it had turned completely over, the dead face uppermost, staring at the sky. It lay on the edge of the main stream. In another moment it would be swept away.

The Swede started to save it, shouting again something I did not catch about a "proper burial"—and then abruptly dropped upon his knees on the sand and covered his eyes with his hands. I was beside him in an instant.

I saw what he had seen.

For just as the body swung round to the current the face and the exposed chest turned full towards us, and showed plainly how the skin and flesh were indented with small hollows, beautifully formed, and exactly similar in shape and kind to the sand-funnels that we had found all over the island.

"Their mark!" I heard my companion mutter under his breath. "Their awful mark!"

And when I turned my eyes again from his ghastly face to the river, the current had done its work, and the body had been swept away into mid-stream and was already beyond our reach and almost out of sight, turning over and over on the waves like an otter.

The Insanity of Jones

(A STUDY IN REINCARNATION)

I

Adventures come to the adventurous, and mysterious things fall in the way of those who, with wonder and imagination, are on the watch for them; but the majority of people go past the doors that are half ajar, thinking them closed, and fail to notice the faint stirrings of the great curtain that hangs ever in the form of appearances between them and the world of causes behind.

For only to the few whose inner senses have been quickened, perchance by some strange suffering in the depths, or by a natural temperament bequeathed from a remote past, comes the knowledge, not too welcome, that this greater world lies ever at their elbow, and that any moment a chance combination of moods and forces may invite them to cross the shifting frontier.

Some, however, are born with this awful certainty in their hearts, and are called to no apprenticeship, and to this select company Jones undoubtedly belonged.

All his life he had realised that his senses brought to him merely a more or less interesting set of sham appearances; that space, as men measure it, was utterly misleading; that time, as the clock ticked it in a succession of minutes, was arbitrary nonsense; and, in fact, that all his sensory perceptions were but a clumsy representation of *real* things behind the curtain—things he was for ever trying to get at, and that sometimes he actually did get at.

He had always been tremblingly aware that he stood on the borderland of another region, a region where time and space were merely forms of thought, where ancient memories lay open to the sight, and where the forces behind each human life stood plainly revealed and he could see the hidden springs at the very heart of the world. Moreover, the fact that he was a clerk in a fire insurance office, and did his work with strict attention, never allowed him to forget for one moment that, just beyond the dingy brick walls where the hundred men scribbled with pointed pens beneath the electric lamps, there existed this glorious region where the important part of himself dwelt and moved and had its being. For in this region he pictured himself playing the part of a spectator to his ordinary workaday life, watching, like a king, the stream of events, but untouched in his own soul by the dirt, the noise, and the vulgar commotion of the outer world.

And this was no poetic dream merely. Jones was not playing prettily with idealism to amuse himself. It was a living, working belief. So convinced was he that the external world was the result of a vast deception practised upon him by the gross senses, that when he stared at a great building like St. Paul's he felt it would not very much surprise him to see it suddenly quiver like a shape of jelly and then melt utterly away, while in its place stood all at once revealed the mass of colour, or the great intricate vibrations, or the splendid sound—the spiritual idea—which it represented in stone.

For something in this way it was that his mind worked.

Yet, to all appearances, and in the satisfaction of all business claims, Jones was normal and un-enterprising. He felt nothing but contempt for the wave of modern psychism. He hardly knew the meaning of such words as "clairvoyance" and "clairaudience." He had never felt the least desire to join the Theosophical Society and to speculate in theories of astral-plane life, or elementals. He attended no meetings of the Psychical Research Society, and knew no anxiety as to whether his "aura" was black or blue; nor was he conscious of the slightest wish to mix in with the revival of cheap occultism which proves so attractive to weak minds of mystical tendencies and unleashed imaginations.

There were certain things he *knew*, but none he cared to argue about; and he shrank instinctively from attempting to put names to the contents of this other region, knowing well that such names could only limit and define things that, according to any standards in use in the ordinary world, were simply un-definable and illusive.

So that, although this was the way his mind worked, there was clearly a very strong leaven of common sense in Jones. In a word, the man the world and the office knew as Jones *was* Jones. The name summed him up and labelled him correctly—John Enderby Jones.

Among the things that he *knew*, and therefore never cared to speak or speculate about, one was that he plainly saw himself as the inheritor of a long series of past lives, the net result of painful evolution, always as himself, of course, but in numerous different bodies each determined by the behaviour of the preceding one. The present John Jones was the last result to date of all the previous thinking, feeling, and doing of John Jones in earlier bodies and in other centuries. He pretended to no details, nor claimed distinguished ancestry, for he realised his past must have been utterly commonplace and insignificant to have produced his present; but he was just as sure he had been at this weary game for ages as that he breathed, and it never occurred to him to argue, to doubt, or to ask questions. And one result of this belief was that his thoughts dwelt upon the past rather than upon the future; that he read much history, and felt specially drawn to certain periods whose spirit he understood instinctively as though he had lived in them; and that he found all religions uninteresting because, almost without exception, they start from the present and speculate ahead as to what men shall become, instead of looking back and speculating why men have got here as they are.

In the insurance office he did his work exceedingly well, but without much personal ambition. Men and women he regarded as the impersonal instruments for inflicting upon him the pain or pleasure he had earned by his past workings, for chance had no place in his scheme of things at all; and while he recognised that the practical world could not get along unless every man did his work thoroughly and conscientiously, he took no interest in the accumulation of fame or money for himself, and simply, therefore, did his plain duty, with indifference as to results.

In common with others who lead a strictly impersonal life, he possessed the quality of utter bravery, and was always ready to face any combination of circumstances, no matter how terrible, because he saw in them the just working-out of past causes he had himself set in motion which could not be dodged or modified. And whereas the majority of people had little meaning for him, either by way of attraction or repulsion, the moment he met some one with whom he felt his past had been *vitally* interwoven his whole inner being leapt up instantly and shouted the fact in his face, and he regulated his life with the utmost skill and caution, like a sentry on watch for an enemy whose feet could already be heard approaching.

Thus, while the great majority of men and women left him uninfluenced—since he regarded them as so many souls merely passing with him along the great stream of evolution—there were, here and there, individuals with whom he recognised that his smallest intercourse was of the gravest importance. These were persons with whom he knew in every fibre of his being he had accounts to settle, pleasant or otherwise, arising out of dealings in past lives; and into his relations with these few, therefore, he concentrated as it were the efforts that most people spread over their intercourse with a far greater number. By what means he picked out these few individuals only those conversant with the startling processes of the subconscious memory may say, but the point was that Jones believed the main purpose, if not quite the entire purpose, of his present incarnation lay in his faithful and thorough settling of these accounts, and that if he sought to evade the least detail of such settling, no matter how unpleasant, he would have lived in vain, and would return to his next incarnation with this added duty to perform. For according to his beliefs there was no Chance, and could be no ultimate shirking, and to avoid a problem was merely to waste time and lose opportunities for development.

And there was one individual with whom Jones had long understood clearly he had a very large account to settle, and towards the accomplishment of which all the main currents of his being seemed to bear him with unswerving purpose. For, when he first entered the insurance office as a junior clerk ten years before, and through a glass door had caught sight of this man seated in an inner room, one of his sudden overwhelming flashes of intuitive memory had burst up into him from the depths, and he had seen, as in a flame of blinding light, a symbolical picture of the future rising out of a dreadful past, and he had, without any act of definite volition, marked down this man for a real account to be settled.

"With *that* man I shall have much to do," he said to himself, as he noted the big face look up and meet his eye through the glass. "There is something I cannot shirk—a vital relation out of the past of both of us."

And he went to his desk trembling a little, and with shaking knees, as though the memory of some terrible pain had suddenly laid its icy hand upon his heart and touched the scar of a great horror. It was a moment of genuine terror when their eyes had met through the glass door, and he was conscious of an inward shrinking and loathing that seized upon him with great violence and convinced him in a single second that the settling of this account would be almost, perhaps, more than he could manage.

The vision passed as swiftly as it came, dropping back again into the submerged region of his consciousness; but he never forgot it, and the whole of his life thereafter became a sort of natural though un-deliberate preparation for the fulfilment of the great duty when the time should be ripe.

In those days—ten years ago—this man was the Assistant Manager, but had since been promoted as Manager to one of the company's local branches; and soon afterwards Jones had likewise found himself transferred to this same branch. A little later, again, the branch at Liverpool, one of the most important, had been in peril owing to mismanagement and defalcation, and the man had gone to take charge of it, and again, by mere chance apparently, Jones had been promoted to the same place. And this pursuit of the Assistant Manager had continued for several years, often, too, in the most curious fashion; and though Jones had never exchanged a single word with him, or been so much as noticed indeed by the great man, the clerk understood perfectly well that these moves in the game were all part of a definite purpose. Never for one moment did he doubt that the Invisibles behind the veil were slowly and surely arranging the details of it all so as to lead up suitably to the climax demanded by justice, a climax in which himself and the Manager would play the leading *rôles*.

"It is inevitable," he said to himself, "and I feel it may be terrible; but when the moment comes I shall be ready, and I pray God that I may face it properly and act like a man."

Moreover, as the years passed, and nothing happened, he felt the horror closing in upon him with steady increase, for the fact was Jones hated and loathed the Manager with an intensity of feeling he had never before experienced towards any human being. He shrank from his presence, and from the glance of his eyes, as though he remembered to have suffered nameless cruelties at his hands; and he slowly began to realise, moreover, that the matter to be settled between them was one of very ancient standing, and that the nature of the settlement was a discharge of accumulated punishment which would probably be very dreadful in the manner of its fulfilment.

When, therefore, the chief cashier one day informed him that the man was to be in London again—this time as General Manager of the head office—and said that he was charged to find a private secretary for him from among the best clerks, and further intimated that the selection had fallen upon himself, Jones accepted the promotion quietly, fatalistically, yet with a degree of inward loathing hardly to be described. For he saw in this merely another move in the evolution of the inevitable Nemesis which he simply dared not seek to frustrate by any personal consideration; and at the same time he was conscious of a certain feeling of relief that the suspense of waiting might soon be mitigated. A secret sense of satisfaction, therefore, accompanied the unpleasant change, and Jones was able to hold himself perfectly well in hand when it was carried into effect and he was formally introduced as private secretary to the General Manager.

Now the Manager was a large, fat man, with a very red face and bags beneath his eyes. Being short-sighted, he wore glasses that seemed to magnify his eyes, which were always a little bloodshot. In hot weather a sort of thin slime covered his cheeks, for he perspired easily. His head was almost entirely bald, and over his turn-down collar his great neck folded in two distinct reddish collops of flesh. His hands were big and his fingers almost massive in thickness.

He was an excellent business man, of sane judgment and firm will, without enough imagination to confuse his course of action by showing him possible alternatives; and his integrity and ability caused him to be held in universal respect by the world of business and finance. In the important regions of a man's character, however, and at heart, he was coarse, brutal almost to savagery, without consideration for others, and as a result often cruelly unjust to his helpless subordinates.

In moments of temper, which were not infrequent, his face turned a dull purple, while the top of his bald head shone by contrast like white marble, and the bags under his eyes swelled till it seemed they would presently explode with a pop. And at these times he presented a distinctly repulsive appearance.

But to a private secretary like Jones, who did his duty regardless of whether his employer was beast or angel, and whose mainspring was principle and not emotion, this made little difference. Within the narrow limits in which any one *could* satisfy such a man, he pleased the General Manager; and more than once his piercing intuitive faculty, amounting almost to clairvoyance, assisted the chief in a fashion that served to bring the two closer together than might otherwise have been the case, and caused the man to respect in his assistant a power of which he possessed not even the germ himself. It was a curious relationship that grew up between the two, and the cashier, who enjoyed the credit of having made the selection, profited by it indirectly as much as any one else.

So for some time the work of the office continued normally and very prosperously. John Enderby Jones received a good salary, and in the outward appearance of the two chief characters in this history there was little change noticeable, except that the Manager grew fatter and redder, and the secretary observed that his own hair was beginning to show rather greyish at the temples.

There were, however, two changes in progress, and they both had to do with Jones, and are important to mention.

One was that he began to dream evilly. In the region of deep sleep, where the possibility of significant dreaming first develops itself, he was tormented more and more with vivid scenes and pictures in which a tall thin man, dark and sinister of countenance, and with bad eyes, was closely associated with himself. Only the setting was that of a past age, with costumes of centuries gone by, and the scenes had to do with dreadful cruelties that could not belong to modern life as he knew it.

The other change was also significant, but is not so easy to describe, for he had in fact become aware that some new portion of himself, hitherto un-awakened, had stirred slowly into life out of the very depths of his consciousness. This new part of himself amounted almost to another personality, and he never observed its least manifestation without a strange thrill at his heart.

For he understood that it had begun to *watch* the Manager!

II

It was the habit of Jones, since he was compelled to work among conditions that were utterly distasteful, to withdraw his mind wholly from business once the day was over. During office hours he kept the strictest possible watch upon himself, and turned the key on all inner dreams, lest any sudden uprush from the deeps should interfere with his duty. But, once the working day was over, the gates flew open, and he began to enjoy himself.

He read no modern books on the subjects that interested him, and, as already said, he followed no course of training, nor belonged to any society that dabbled with half-told mysteries; but, once released from the office desk in the Manager's room, he simply and naturally entered the other region, because he was an old inhabitant, a rightful denizen, and because he belonged there. It was, in fact, really a case of dual personality; and a carefully drawn agreement existed between Jones-of-the-fire-insurance-office and Jones-of-the-mysteries, by the terms of which, under heavy penalties, neither region claimed him out of hours.

For the moment he reached his rooms under the roof in Bloomsbury, and had changed his city coat to another, the iron doors of the office clanged far behind him, and in front, before his very eyes, rolled up the beautiful gates of ivory, and he entered into the places of flowers and singing and wonderful veiled forms. Sometimes he quite lost touch with the outer world, forgetting to eat his dinner or go to bed, and lay in a state of trance, his consciousness working far out of the body. And on other occasions he walked the streets on air, half-way between the two regions, unable to distinguish between incarnate and discarnate forms, and not very far, probably, beyond the strata where poets, saints, and the greatest artists have moved and thought and found their inspiration. But this was only when some insistent bodily claim prevented his full release, and more often than not he was entirely independent of his physical portion and free of the real region, without let or hindrance.

One evening he reached home utterly exhausted after the burden of the day's work. The Manager had been more than usually brutal, unjust, ill-tempered, and Jones had been almost persuaded out of his settled policy of contempt into answering back. Everything seemed to have gone amiss, and the man's coarse, underbred nature had been in the ascendant all day long: he had thumped the desk with his great fists, abused, found fault unreasonably, uttered outrageous things, and behaved generally as he actually was—beneath the thin veneer of acquired business varnish. He had done and said everything to wound all that was woundable in an ordinary secretary, and though Jones fortunately dwelt in a region from which he looked down upon such a man as he might look down on the blundering of a savage animal, the strain had nevertheless told severely upon him, and he reached home wondering for the first time in his life whether there was perhaps a point beyond which he would be unable to restrain himself any longer.

For something out of the usual had happened. At the close of a passage of great stress between the two, every nerve in the secretary's body tingling from undeserved abuse, the Manager had suddenly turned full upon him, in the corner of the private room where the safes stood, in such a way that the glare of his red eyes, magnified by the glasses, looked straight into his own. And at this very second that other personality in Jones—the one that was ever *watching*—rose up swiftly from the deeps within and held a mirror to his face.

A moment of flame and vision rushed over him, and for one single second—one merciless second of clear sight—he saw the Manager as the tall dark man of his evil dreams, and the knowledge that he had suffered at his hands some awful injury in the past crashed through his mind like the report of a cannon.

It all flashed upon him and was gone, changing him from fire to ice, and then back again to fire; and he left the office with the certain conviction in his heart that the time for his final settlement with the man, the time for the inevitable retribution, was at last drawing very near.

According to his invariable custom, however, he succeeded in putting the memory of all this unpleasantness out of his mind with the changing of his office coat, and after dozing a little in his leather chair before the fire, he started out as usual for dinner in the Soho French restaurant, and began to dream himself away into the region of flowers and singing, and to commune with the Invisibles that were the very sources of his real life and being.

For it was in this way that his mind worked, and the habits of years had crystallised into rigid lines along which it was now necessary and inevitable for him to act.

At the door of the little restaurant he stopped short, a half-remembered appointment in his mind. He had made an engagement with some one, but where, or with whom, had entirely slipped his memory. He thought it was for dinner, or else to meet just after dinner, and for a second it came back to him that it had something to do with the office, but, whatever it was, he was quite unable to recall it, and a reference to his pocket engagement book showed only a blank page. Evidently he had even omitted to enter it; and after standing a moment vainly trying to recall either the time, place, or person, he went in and sat down.

But though the details had escaped him, his subconscious memory seemed to know all about it, for he experienced a sudden sinking of the heart, accompanied by a sense of foreboding anticipation, and felt that beneath his exhaustion there lay a centre of tremendous excitement. The emotion caused by the engagement was at work, and would presently cause the actual details of the appointment to reappear.

Inside the restaurant the feeling increased, instead of passing: some one was waiting for him somewhere—some one whom he had definitely arranged to meet. He was expected by a person that very night and just about that very time. But by whom? Where? A curious inner trembling came over him, and he made a strong effort to hold himself in hand and to be ready for anything that might come.

And then suddenly came the knowledge that the place of appointment was this very restaurant, and, further, that the person he had promised to meet was already here, waiting somewhere quite close beside him.

He looked up nervously and began to examine the faces round him. The majority of the diners were Frenchmen, chattering loudly with much gesticulation and laughter; and there was a fair sprinkling of clerks like himself who came because the prices were low and the food good, but there was no single face that he recognised until his glance fell upon the occupant of the corner seat opposite, generally filled by himself.

"There's the man who's waiting for me!" thought Jones instantly.

He knew it at once. The man, he saw, was sitting well back into the corner, with a thick overcoat buttoned tightly up to the chin. His skin was very white, and a heavy black beard grew far up over his cheeks. At first the secretary took him for a stranger, but when he looked up and their eyes met, a sense of familiarity flashed across him, and for a second or two Jones imagined he was staring at a man he had known years before. For, barring the beard, it was the face of an elderly clerk who had occupied the next desk to his own when he first entered the service of the insurance company, and had shown him the most painstaking kindness and sympathy in the early difficulties of his work. But a moment later the illusion passed, for he remembered that Thorpe had been dead at least five years. The similarity of the eyes was obviously a mere suggestive trick of memory.

The two men stared at one another for several seconds, and then Jones began to act *instinctively*, and because he had to. He crossed over and took the vacant seat at the other's table, facing him; for he felt it was somehow imperative to explain why he was late, and how it was he had almost forgotten the engagement altogether.

No honest excuse, however, came to his assistance, though his mind had begun to work furiously.

"Yes, you *are* late," said the man quietly, before he could find a single word to utter. "But it doesn't matter. Also, you had forgotten the appointment, but that makes no difference either."

"I knew—that there was an engagement," Jones stammered, passing his hand over his forehead; "but somehow—"

"You will recall it presently," continued the other in a gentle voice, and smiling a little. "It was in deep sleep last night we arranged this, and the unpleasant occurrences of to-day have for the moment obliterated it."

A faint memory stirred within him as the man spoke, and a grove of trees with moving forms hovered before his eyes and then vanished again, while for an instant the stranger seemed to be capable of self-distortion and to have assumed vast proportions, with wonderful flaming eyes.

"Oh!" he gasped. "It was there—in the other region?"

"Of course," said the other, with a smile that illumined his whole face. "You will remember presently, all in good time, and meanwhile you have no cause to feel afraid."

There was a wonderful soothing quality in the man's voice, like the whispering of a great wind, and the clerk felt calmer at once. They sat a little while longer, but he could not remember that they talked much or ate anything. He only recalled afterwards that the head waiter came up and whispered something in his ear, and that he glanced round and saw the other people were looking at him curiously, some of them laughing, and that his companion then got up and led the way out of the restaurant.

They walked hurriedly through the streets, neither of them speaking; and Jones was so intent upon getting back the whole history of the affair from the region of deep sleep, that he barely noticed the way they took. Yet it was clear he knew where they were bound for just as well as his companion, for he crossed the streets often ahead of him, diving down alleys without hesitation, and the other followed always without correction.

The pavements were very full, and the usual night crowds of London were surging to and fro in the glare of the shop lights, but somehow no one impeded their rapid movements, and they seemed to pass through the people as if they were smoke. And, as they went, the pedestrians and traffic grew less and less, and they soon passed the Mansion House and the deserted space in front of the Royal Exchange, and so on down Fenchurch Street and within sight of the Tower of London, rising dim and shadowy in the smoky air.

Jones remembered all this perfectly well, and thought it was his intense preoccupation that made the distance seem so short. But it was when the Tower was left behind and they turned northwards that he began to notice how altered everything was, and saw that they were in a neighbourhood where houses were suddenly scarce, and lanes and fields beginning, and that their only light was the stars overhead. And, as the deeper consciousness more and more asserted itself to the exclusion of the surface happenings of his mere body during the day, the sense of exhaustion vanished, and he realised that he was moving somewhere in the region of causes behind the veil, beyond the gross deceptions of the senses, and released from the clumsy spell of space and time.

Without great surprise, therefore, he turned and saw that his companion had altered, had shed his overcoat and black hat, and was moving beside him absolutely *without sound*. For a brief second he saw him, tall as a tree, extending through space like a great shadow, misty and wavering of outline, followed by a sound like wings in the darkness; but, when he stopped, fear clutching at his heart, the other resumed his former proportions, and Jones could plainly see his normal outline against the green field behind.

Then the secretary saw him fumbling at his neck, and at the same moment the black beard came away from the face in his hand.

"Then you *are* Thorpe!" he gasped, yet somehow without overwhelming surprise.

They stood facing one another in the lonely lane, trees meeting overhead and hiding the stars, and a sound of mournful sighing among the branches.

"I am Thorpe," was the answer in a voice that almost seemed part of the wind. "And I have come out of our far past to help you, for my debt to you is large, and in this life I had but small opportunity to repay."

Jones thought quickly of the man's kindness to him in the office, and a great wave of feeling surged through him as he began to remember dimly the friend by whose side he had already climbed, perhaps through vast ages of his soul's evolution.

"To help me *now*?" he whispered.

"You will understand me when you enter into your real memory and recall how great a debt I have to pay for old faithful kindnesses of long ago," sighed the other in a voice like falling wind.

"Between us, though, there can be no question of *debt*," Jones heard himself saying, and remembered the reply that floated to him on the air and the smile that lightened for a moment the stern eyes facing him.

"Not of debt, indeed, but of privilege."

Jones felt his heart leap out towards this man, this old friend, tried by centuries and still faithful. He made a movement to seize his hand. But the other shifted like a thing of mist, and for a moment the clerk's head swam and his eyes seemed to fail.

"Then you are *dead*?" he said under his breath with a slight shiver.

"Five years ago I left the body you knew," replied Thorpe. "I tried to help you then instinctively, not fully recognising you. But now I can accomplish far more."

With an awful sense of foreboding and dread in his heart, the secretary was beginning to understand.

"It has to do with—with—?"

"Your past dealings with the Manager," came the answer, as the wind rose louder among the branches overhead and carried off the remainder of the sentence into the air.

Jones's memory, which was just beginning to stir among the deepest layers of all, shut down suddenly with a snap, and he followed his companion over fields and down sweet-smelling lanes where the air was fragrant and cool, till they came to a large house, standing gaunt and lonely in the shadows at the edge of a wood. It was wrapped in utter stillness, with windows heavily draped in black, and the clerk, as he looked, felt such an overpowering wave of sadness invade him that his eyes began to burn and smart, and he was conscious of a desire to shed tears.

The key made a harsh noise as it turned in the lock, and when the door swung open into a lofty hall they heard a confused sound of rustling and whispering, as of a great throng of people pressing forward to meet them. The air seemed full of swaying movement, and Jones was certain he saw hands held aloft and dim faces claiming recognition, while in his heart, already oppressed by the approaching burden of vast accumulated memories, he was aware of the *uncoiling of something that had been asleep for ages.*

As they advanced he heard the doors close with a muffled thunder behind them, and saw that the shadows seemed to retreat and shrink away towards the interior of the house, carrying the hands and faces with them. He heard the wind singing round the walls and over the roof, and its wailing voice mingled with the sound of deep, collective breathing that filled the house like the murmur of a sea; and as they walked up the broad staircase and through the vaulted rooms, where pillars rose like the stems of trees, he knew that the building was crowded, row upon row, with the thronging memories of his own long past.

"This is the *House of the Past*," whispered Thorpe beside him, as they moved silently from room to room; "the house of *your* past. It is full from cellar to roof with the memories of what you have done, thought, and felt from the earliest stages of your evolution until now.

"The house climbs up almost to the clouds, and stretches back into the heart of the wood you saw outside, but the remoter halls are filled with the ghosts of ages ago too many to count, and even if we were able to waken them you could not remember them now. Some day, though, they will come and claim you, and you must know them, and answer their questions, for they can never rest till they have exhausted themselves again through you, and justice has been perfectly worked out.

"But now follow me closely, and you shall see the particular memory for which I am permitted to be your guide, so that you may know and understand a great force in your present life, and may use the sword of justice, or rise to the level of a great forgiveness, according to your degree of power."

Icy thrills ran through the trembling clerk, and as he walked slowly beside his companion he heard from the vaults below, as well as from more distant regions of the vast building, the stirring and sighing of the serried ranks of sleepers, sounding in the still air like a chord swept from unseen strings stretched somewhere among the very foundations of the house.

Stealthily, picking their way among the great pillars, they moved up the sweeping staircase and through several dark corridors and halls, and presently stopped outside a small door in an archway where the shadows were very deep.

"Remain close by my side, and remember to utter no cry," whispered the voice of his guide, and as the clerk turned to reply he saw his face was stern to whiteness and even shone a little in the darkness.

The room they entered seemed at first to be pitchy black, but gradually the secretary perceived a faint reddish glow against the farther end, and thought he saw figures moving silently to and fro.

"Now watch!" whispered Thorpe, as they pressed close to the wall near the door and waited. "But remember to keep absolute silence. It is a torture scene."

Jones felt utterly afraid, and would have turned to fly if he dared, for an indescribable terror seized him and his knees shook; but some power that made escape impossible held him remorselessly there, and with eyes glued on the spots of light he crouched against the wall and waited.

The figures began to move more swiftly, each in its own dim light that shed no radiance beyond itself, and he heard a soft clanking of chains and the voice of a man groaning in pain. Then came the sound of a door closing, and thereafter Jones saw but one figure, the figure of an old man, naked entirely, and fastened with chains to an iron framework on the floor. His memory gave a sudden leap of fear as he looked, for the features and white beard were familiar, and he recalled them as though of yesterday.

The other figures had disappeared, and the old man became the centre of the terrible picture. Slowly, with ghastly groans, as the heat below him increased into a steady glow, the aged body rose in a curve of agony, resting on the iron frame only where the chains held wrists and ankles fast. Cries and gasps filled the air, and Jones felt exactly as though they came from his own throat, and as if the chains were burning into his own wrists and ankles, and the heat scorching the skin and flesh upon his own back. He began to writhe and twist himself.

"Spain!" whispered the voice at his side, "and four hundred years ago."

"And the purpose?" gasped the perspiring clerk, though he knew quite well what the answer must be.

"To extort the name of a friend, to his death and betrayal," came the reply through the darkness.

A sliding panel opened with a little rattle in the wall immediately above the rack, and a face, framed in the same red glow, appeared and looked down upon the dying victim. Jones was only just able to choke a scream, for he recognised the tall dark man of his dreams. With horrible, gloating eyes he gazed down upon the writhing form of the old man, and his lips moved as in speaking, though no words were actually audible.

"He asks again for the name," explained the other, as the clerk struggled with the intense hatred and loathing that threatened every moment to result in screams and action. His ankles and wrists pained him so that he could scarcely keep still, but a merciless power held him to the scene.

He saw the old man, with a fierce cry, raise his tortured head and spit up into the face at the panel, and then the shutter slid back again, and a moment later the increased glow beneath the body, accompanied by awful writhing, told of the application of further heat. There came the odour of burning flesh; the white beard curled and burned to a crisp; the body fell back limp upon the red-hot iron, and then shot up again in fresh agony; cry after cry, the most awful in the world, rang out with deadened sound between the four walls; and again the panel slid back creaking, and revealed the dreadful face of the torturer.

Again the name was asked for, and again it was refused; and this time, after the closing of the panel, a door opened, and the tall thin man with the evil face came slowly into the chamber. His features were savage with rage and disappointment, and in the dull red glow that fell upon them he looked like a very prince of devils. In his hand he held a pointed iron at white heat.

"Now the murder!" came from Thorpe in a whisper that sounded as if it was outside the building and far away.

Jones knew quite well what was coming, but was unable even to close his eyes. He felt all the fearful pains himself just as though he were actually the sufferer; but now, as he stared, he felt something more besides; and when the tall man deliberately approached the rack and plunged the heated iron first into one eye and then into the other, he heard the faint fizzing of it, and felt his own eyes burst in frightful pain from his head. At the same moment, unable longer to control himself, he uttered a wild shriek and dashed forward to seize the torturer and tear him to a thousand pieces. Instantly, in a flash, the entire scene vanished; darkness rushed in to fill the room, and he felt himself lifted off his feet by some force like a great wind and borne swiftly away into space.

When he recovered his senses he was standing just outside the house and the figure of Thorpe was beside him in the gloom. The great doors were in the act of closing behind him, but before they shut he fancied he caught a glimpse of an immense veiled figure standing upon the threshold, with flaming eyes, and in his hand a bright weapon like a shining sword of fire.

"Come quickly now—all is over!" Thorpe whispered.

"And the dark man—?" gasped the clerk, as he moved swiftly by the other's side.

"In this present life is the Manager of the company."

"And the victim?"

"Was yourself!"

"And the friend he—*I* refused to betray?"

"I was that friend," answered Thorpe, his voice with every moment sounding more and more like the cry of the wind. "You gave your life in agony to save mine."

"And again, in this life, we have all three been together?"

"Yes. Such forces are not soon or easily exhausted, and justice is not satisfied till all have reaped what they sowed."

Jones had an odd feeling that he was slipping away into some other state of consciousness. Thorpe began to seem unreal. Presently he would be unable to ask more questions. He felt utterly sick and faint with it all, and his strength was ebbing.

"Oh, quick!" he cried, "now tell me more. Why did I see this? What must I do?"

The wind swept across the field on their right and entered the wood beyond with a great roar, and the air round him seemed filled with voices and the rushing of hurried movement.

"To the ends of justice," answered the other, as though speaking out of the centre of the wind and from a distance, "which sometimes is entrusted to the hands of those who suffered and were strong. One wrong cannot be put right by another wrong, but your life has been so worthy that the opportunity is given to—"

The voice grew fainter and fainter, already it was far overhead with the rushing wind.

"You may punish or—" Here Jones lost sight of Thorpe's figure altogether, for he seemed to have vanished and melted away into the wood behind him. His voice sounded far across the trees, very weak, and ever rising.

"Or if you can rise to the level of a great forgiveness—"

The voice became inaudible. . . . The wind came crying out of the wood again.

Jones shivered and stared about him. He shook himself violently and rubbed his eyes. The room was dark, the fire was out; he felt cold and stiff. He got up out of his armchair, still trembling, and lit the gas. Outside the wind was howling, and when he looked at his watch he saw that it was very late and he must go to bed.

He had not even changed his office coat; he must have fallen asleep in the chair as soon as he came in, and he had slept for several hours. Certainly he had eaten no dinner, for he felt ravenous.

III

Next day, and for several weeks thereafter, the business of the office went on as usual, and Jones did his work well and behaved outwardly with perfect propriety. No more visions troubled him, and his relations with the Manager became, if anything, somewhat smoother and easier.

True, the man *looked* a little different, because the clerk kept seeing him with his inner and outer eye promiscuously, so that one moment he was broad and red-faced, and the next he was tall, thin, and dark, enveloped, as it were, in a sort of black atmosphere tinged with red. While at times a confusion of the two sights took place, and Jones saw the two faces mingled in a composite countenance that was very horrible indeed to contemplate. But, beyond this occasional change in the outward appearance of the Manager, there was nothing that the secretary noticed as the result of his vision, and business went on more or less as before, and perhaps even with a little less friction.

But in the rooms under the roof in Bloomsbury it was different, for there it was perfectly clear to Jones that Thorpe had come to take up his abode with him. He never saw him, but he knew all the time he was there. Every night on returning from his work he was greeted by the well-known whisper, "Be ready when I give the sign!" and often in the night he woke up suddenly out of deep sleep and was aware that Thorpe had that minute moved away from his bed and was standing waiting and watching somewhere in the darkness of the room. Often he followed him down the stairs, though the dim gas jet on the landings never revealed his outline; and sometimes he did not come into the room at all, but hovered outside the window, peering through the dirty panes, or sending his whisper into the chamber in the whistling of the wind.

For Thorpe had come to stay, and Jones knew that he would not get rid of him until he had fulfilled the ends of justice and accomplished the purpose for which he was waiting.

Meanwhile, as the days passed, he went through a tremendous

struggle with himself, and came to the perfectly honest decision that the "level of a great forgiveness" was impossible for him, and that he must therefore accept the alternative and use the secret knowledge placed in his hands—and execute justice. And once this decision was arrived at, he noticed that Thorpe no longer left him alone during the day as before, but now accompanied him to the office and stayed more or less at his side all through business hours as well. His whisper made itself heard in the streets and in the train, and even in the Manager's room where he worked; sometimes warning, sometimes urging, but never for a moment suggesting the abandonment of the main purpose, and more than once so plainly audible that the clerk felt certain others must have heard it as well as himself.

The obsession was complete. He felt he was always under Thorpe's eye day and night, and he knew he must acquit himself like a man when the moment came, or prove a failure in his own sight as well in the sight of the other.

And now that his mind was made up, nothing could prevent the carrying out of the sentence. He bought a pistol, and spent his Saturday afternoons practising at a target in lonely places along the Essex shore, marking out in the sand the exact measurements of the Manager's room. Sundays he occupied in like fashion, putting up at an inn overnight for the purpose, spending the money that usually went into the savings bank on travelling expenses and cartridges. Everything was done very thoroughly, for there must be no possibility of failure; and at the end of several weeks he had become so expert with his six-shooter that at a distance of 25 feet, which was the greatest length of the Manager's room, he could pick the inside out of a halfpenny nine times out of a dozen, and leave a clean, unbroken rim.

There was not the slightest desire to delay. He had thought the matter over from every point of view his mind could reach, and his purpose was inflexible. Indeed, he felt proud to think that he had been chosen as the instrument of justice in the infliction of so well-deserved and so terrible a punishment. Vengeance may have had some part in his decision, but he could not help that, for he still felt at times the hot chains burning his wrists and ankles with fierce agony through to the bone. He remembered the hideous pain of his slowly roasting back, and the point when he thought death must intervene to end his suffering, but instead new powers of endurance had surged up in him, and awful further stretches of pain had opened up, and unconsciousness seemed farther off than ever. Then at last the hot irons in his eyes. . . . It all came back to him, and caused him to break out in icy perspiration at the mere thought of it . . . the vile face at the panel . . . the expression of the dark face. . . . His fingers worked. His blood boiled. It was utterly impossible to keep the idea of vengeance altogether out of his mind.

Several times he was temporarily baulked of his prey. Odd things happened to stop him when he was on the point of action. The first day, for instance, the Manager fainted from the heat. Another time when he had decided to do the deed, the Manager did not come down to the office at all. And a third time, when his hand was actually in his hip pocket, he suddenly heard Thorpe's horrid whisper telling him to wait, and turning, he saw that the head cashier had entered the room noiselessly without his noticing it. Thorpe evidently knew what he was about, and did not intend to let the clerk bungle the matter.

He fancied, moreover, that the head cashier was watching him. He was always meeting him in unexpected corners and places, and the cashier never seemed to have an adequate excuse for being there. His movements seemed suddenly of particular interest to others in the office as well, for clerks were always being sent to ask him unnecessary questions, and there was apparently a general design to keep him under a sort of surveillance, so that he was never much alone with the Manager in the private room where they worked. And once the cashier had even gone so far as to suggest that he could take his holiday earlier than usual if he liked, as the work had been very arduous of late and the heat exceedingly trying.

He noticed, too, that he was sometimes followed by a certain individual in the streets, a careless-looking sort of man, who never came face to face with him, or actually ran into him, but who was always in his train or omnibus, and whose eye he often caught observing him over the top of his newspaper, and who on one occasion was even waiting at the door of his lodgings when he came out to dine.

There were other indications too, of various sorts, that led him to think something was at work to defeat his purpose, and that he must act at once before these hostile forces could prevent.

And so the end came very swiftly, and was thoroughly approved by Thorpe.

It was towards the close of July, and one of the hottest days London had ever known, for the City was like an oven, and the particles of dust seemed to burn the throats of the unfortunate toilers in street and office. The portly Manager, who suffered cruelly owing to his size, came down perspiring and gasping with the heat. He carried a light-coloured umbrella to protect his head.

"He'll want something more than that, though!" Jones laughed quietly to himself when he saw him enter.

The pistol was safely in his hip pocket, every one of its six chambers loaded.

The Manager saw the smile on his face, and gave him a long steady look as he sat down to his desk in the corner. A few minutes later he touched the bell for the head cashier—a single ring—and then asked Jones to fetch some papers from another safe in the room upstairs.

A deep inner trembling seized the secretary as he noticed these precautions, for he saw that the hostile forces were at work against him, and yet he felt he could delay no longer and must act that very morning, interference or no interference. However, he went obediently up in the lift to the next floor, and while fumbling with the combination of the safe, known only to himself, the cashier, and the Manager, he again heard Thorpe's horrid whisper just behind him:

"You must do it to-day! You must do it to-day!"

He came down again with the papers, and found the Manager alone. The room was like a furnace, and a wave of dead heated air met him in the face as he went in. The moment he passed the doorway he realised that he had been the subject of conversation between the head cashier and his enemy. They had been discussing him. Perhaps an inkling of his secret had somehow got into their minds. They had been watching him for days past. They had become suspicious.

Clearly, he must act now, or let the opportunity slip by perhaps for ever. He heard Thorpe's voice in his ear, but this time it was no mere whisper, but a plain human voice, speaking out loud.

"Now!" it said. "Do it now!"

The room was empty. Only the Manager and himself were in it.

Jones turned from his desk where he had been standing, and locked the door leading into the main office. He saw the army of clerks scribbling in their shirt-sleeves, for the upper half of the door was of glass. He had perfect control of himself, and his heart was beating steadily.

The Manager, hearing the key turn in the lock, looked up sharply.

"What's that you're doing?" he asked quickly.

"Only locking the door, sir," replied the secretary in a quite even voice.

"Why? Who told you to—?"

"The voice of Justice, sir," replied Jones, looking steadily into the hated face.

The Manager looked black for a moment, and stared angrily across the room at him. Then suddenly his expression changed as he stared, and he tried to smile. It was meant to be a kind smile evidently, but it only succeeded in being frightened.

"That *is* a good idea in this weather," he said lightly, "but it would be much better to lock it on the *outside*, wouldn't it, Mr. Jones?"

"I think not, sir. You might escape me then. Now you can't."

Jones took his pistol out and pointed it at the other's face. Down the barrel he saw the features of the tall dark man, evil and sinister. Then the outline trembled a little and the face of the Manager slipped back into its place. It was white as death, and shining with perspiration.

"You tortured me to death four hundred years ago," said the clerk in the same steady voice, "and now the dispensers of justice have chosen me to punish you."

The Manager's face turned to flame, and then back to chalk again. He made a quick movement towards the telephone bell, stretching out a hand to reach it, but at the same moment Jones pulled the trigger and the wrist was shattered, splashing the wall behind with blood.

"That's *one* place where the chains burnt," he said quietly to himself. His hand was absolutely steady, and he felt that he was a hero.

The Manager was on his feet, with a scream of pain, supporting himself with his right hand on the desk in front of him, but Jones pressed the trigger again, and a bullet flew into the other wrist, so that the big man, deprived of support, fell forward with a crash on to the desk.

"You damned madman!" shrieked the Manager. "Drop that pistol!"

"That's *another* place," was all Jones said, still taking careful aim for another shot.

The big man, screaming and blundering, scrambled beneath the desk, making frantic efforts to hide, but the secretary took a step forward and fired two shots in quick succession into his projecting legs, hitting first one ankle and then the other, and smashing them horribly.

"Two more places where the chains burnt," he said, going a little nearer.

The Manager, still shrieking, tried desperately to squeeze his bulk behind the shelter of the opening beneath the desk, but he was far too large, and his bald head protruded through on the other side. Jones caught him by the scruff of his great neck and dragged him yelping out on to the carpet. He was covered with blood, and flopped helplessly upon his broken wrists.

"Be quick now!" cried the voice of Thorpe.

There was a tremendous commotion and banging at the door, and Jones gripped his pistol tightly. Something seemed to crash through his brain, clearing it for a second, so that he thought he saw beside him a great veiled figure, with drawn sword and flaming eyes, and sternly approving attitude.

"Remember the eyes! Remember the eyes!" hissed Thorpe in the air above him.

Jones felt like a god, with a god's power. Vengeance disappeared from his mind. He was acting impersonally as an instrument in the hands of the Invisibles who dispense justice and balance accounts. He bent down and put the barrel close into the other's face, smiling a little as he saw the childish efforts of the arms to cover his head. Then he pulled the trigger, and a bullet went straight into the right eye, blackening the skin. Moving the pistol two inches the other way, he sent another bullet crashing into the left eye. Then he stood upright over his victim with a deep sigh of satisfaction.

The Manager wriggled convulsively for the space of a single

second, and then lay still in death.

There was not a moment to lose, for the door was already broken in and violent hands were at his neck. Jones put the pistol to his temple and once more pressed the trigger with his finger.

But this time there was no report. Only a little dead click answered the pressure, for the secretary had forgotten that the pistol had only six chambers, and that he had used them all. He threw the useless weapon on to the floor, laughing a little out loud, and turned, without a struggle, to give himself up.

"I *had* to do it," he said quietly, while they tied him. "It was simply my duty! And now I am ready to face the consequences, and Thorpe will be proud of me. For justice has been done and the gods are satisfied."

He made not the slightest resistance, and when the two policemen marched him off through the crowd of shuddering little clerks in the office, he again saw the veiled figure moving majestically in front of him, making slow sweeping circles with the flaming sword, to keep back the host of faces that were thronging in upon him from the Other Region.

Secret Worship

Harris, the silk merchant, was in South Germany on his way home from a business trip when the idea came to him suddenly that he would take the mountain railway from Strassbourg and run down to revisit his old school after an interval of something more than thirty years. And it was to this chance impulse of the junior partner in Harris Brothers of St. Paul's Churchyard that John Silence owed one of the most curious cases of his whole experience, for at that very moment he happened to be tramping these same mountains with a holiday knapsack, and from different points of the compass the two men were actually converging towards the same inn.

Now, deep down in the heart that for thirty years had been concerned chiefly with the profitable buying and selling of silk, this school had left the imprint of its peculiar influence, and, though perhaps unknown to Harris, had strongly colored the whole of his subsequent existence. It belonged to the deeply religious life of a small Protestant community (which it is unnecessary to specify), and his father had sent him there at the age of fifteen, partly because he would learn the German requisite for the conduct of the silk business, and partly because the discipline was strict, and discipline was what his soul and body needed just then more than anything else.

The life, indeed, had proved exceedingly severe, and young Harris benefited accordingly; for though corporal punishment was unknown, there was a system of mental and spiritual correction which somehow made the soul stand proudly erect to receive it, while it struck at the very root of the fault and taught the boy that his character was being cleaned and strengthened, and that he was not merely being tortured in a kind of personal revenge.

That was over thirty years ago, when he was a dreamy and impressionable youth of fifteen; and now, as the train climbed slowly up the winding mountain gorges, his mind travelled back somewhat lovingly over the intervening period, and forgotten details rose vividly again before him out of the shadows. The life there had been very wonderful, it seemed to him, in that remote mountain village, protected from the tumults of the world by the love and worship of the devout Brotherhood that ministered to the needs of some hundred boys from every country in Europe. Sharply the scenes came back to him. He smelt again the long stone corridors, the hot pinewood rooms, where the sultry hours of summer study were passed with bees droning through open windows in the sunshine, and German characters struggling in the mind with dreams of English lawns—and then the sudden awful cry of the master in German—

"Harris, stand up! You sleep!"

And he recalled the dreadful standing motionless for an hour, book in hand, while the knees felt like wax and the head grew heavier than a cannon-ball.

The very smell of the cooking came back to him—the daily *Sauerkraut*, the watery chocolate on Sundays, the flavor of the stringy meat served twice a week at *Mittagessen*; and he smiled to think again of the half-rations that was the punishment for speaking English. The very odor of the milk-bowls,—the hot sweet aroma that rose from the soaking peasant-bread at the six-o'clock breakfast,—came back to him pungently, and he saw the huge *Speisesaal* with the hundred boys in their school uniform, all eating sleepily in silence, gulping down the coarse bread and scalding milk in terror of the bell that would presently cut them short—and, at the far end where the masters sat, he saw the narrow slit windows with the vistas of enticing field and forest beyond.

And this, in turn, made him think of the great barnlike room on the top floor where all slept together in wooden cots, and he heard in memory the clamour of the cruel bell that woke them on winter mornings at five o'clock and summoned them to the stone-flagged *Waschkammer*, where boys and masters alike, after scanty and icy washing, dressed in complete silence.

From this his mind passed swiftly, with vivid picture-thoughts, to other things, and with a passing shiver he remembered how the loneliness of never being alone had eaten into him, and how everything—work, meals, sleep, walks, leisure—was done with his "division" of twenty other boys and under the eyes of at least two masters. The only solitude possible was by asking for half an hour's practice in the cell-like music rooms, and Harris smiled to himself as he recalled the zeal of his violin studies.

Then, as the train puffed laboriously through the great pine forests that cover these mountains with a giant carpet of velvet, he found the pleasanter layers of memory giving up their dead, and he recalled with admiration the kindness of the masters, whom all addressed as Brother, and marveled afresh at their devotion in burying themselves for years in such a place, only to leave it, in most cases, for the still rougher life of missionaries in the wild places of the world.

He thought once more of the still, religious atmosphere that hung over the little forest community like a veil, barring the distressful world; of the picturesque ceremonies at Easter, Christmas, and New Year; of the numerous feast-days and charming little festivals. The *Beschehr-Fest*, in particular, came back to him,—the feast of gifts at Christmas,—when the entire community paired off and gave presents, many of which had taken weeks to make or the savings of many days to purchase. And then he saw the midnight ceremony in the church at New Year, with the shining face of the *Prediger* in the pulpit,—the village preacher who, on the last night of the old year, saw in the empty gallery beyond the organ loft the faces of all who were to die in the ensuing twelve months, and who at last recognised himself among them, and, in the very middle of his sermon, passed into a state of rapt ecstasy and burst into a torrent of praise.

Thickly the memories crowded upon him. The picture of the small village dreaming its unselfish life on the mountain-tops, clean, wholesome, simple, searching vigorously for its God, and training hundreds of boys in the grand way, rose up in his mind with all the power of an obsession. He felt once more the old mystical enthusiasm, deeper than the sea and more wonderful than the stars; he heard again the winds sighing from leagues of forest over the red roofs in the moonlight; he heard the Brothers' voices talking of the things beyond this life as though they had actually experienced them in the body; and, as he sat in the jolting train, a spirit of unutterable longing passed over his seared and tired soul, stirring in the depths of him a sea of emotions that he thought had long since frozen into immobility.

And the contrast pained him,—the idealistic dreamer then, the man of business now,—so that a spirit of unworldly peace and beauty known only to the soul in meditation laid its feathered finger upon his heart, moving strangely the surface of the waters.

Harris shivered a little and looked out of the window of his empty carriage. The train had long passed Hornberg, and far below the streams tumbled in white foam down the limestone rocks. In front of him, dome upon dome of wooded mountain stood against the sky. It was October, and the air was cool and sharp, woodsmoke and damp moss exquisitely mingled in it with the subtle odors of the pines.

Overhead, between the tips of the highest firs, he saw the first stars peeping, and the sky was a clean, pale amethyst that seemed exactly the color all these memories clothed themselves with in his mind.

He leaned back in his corner and sighed. He was a heavy man, and he had not known sentiment for years; he was a big man, and it took much to move him, literally and figuratively; he was a man in whom the dreams of God that haunt the soul in youth, though overlaid by the scum that gathers in the fight for money, had not, as with the majority, utterly died the death.

He came back into this little neglected pocket of the years, where so much fine gold had collected and lain undisturbed, with all his semi-spiritual emotions aquiver; and, as he watched the mountain-tops come nearer, and smelt the forgotten odors of his boyhood, something melted on the surface of his soul and left him sensitive to a degree he had not known since, thirty years before, he had lived here with his dreams, his conflicts, and his youthful suffering.

A thrill ran through him as the train stopped with a jolt at a tiny station and he saw the name in large black lettering on the grey stone building, and below it, the number of meters it stood above the level of the sea.

"The highest point on the line!" he exclaimed. "How well I remember it—Sommerau—Summer Meadow. The very next station is mine!"

And, as the train ran downhill with brakes on and steam shut off, he put his head out of the window and one by one saw the old familiar landmarks in the dusk. They stared at him like dead faces in a dream. Queer, sharp feelings, half poignant, half sweet, stirred in his heart.

"There's the hot, white road we walked along so often with the two Brüder always at our heels," he thought; "and there, by Jove, is the turn through the forest to '*Die Galgen*,' the stone gallows where they hanged the witches in olden days!"

He smiled a little as the train slid past.

"And there's the copse where the Lilies of the Valley powdered the ground in spring; and, I swear,"—he put his head out with a sudden impulse—"if that's not the very clearing where Calame, the French boy, chased the swallow-tail with me, and Bruder Pagel gave us half-rations for leaving the road without permission, and for shouting in our mother tongues!" And he laughed again as the memories came back with a rush, flooding his mind with vivid detail.

The train stopped, and he stood on the grey gravel platform like a man in a dream. It seemed half a century since he last waited there with corded wooden boxes, and got into the train for Strassbourg and home after the two years' exile. Time dropped from him like an old garment and he felt a boy again. Only, things looked so much smaller than his memory of them; shrunk and dwindled they looked, and the distances seemed on a curiously smaller scale.

He made his way across the road to the little Gasthaus, and, as he went, faces and figures of former schoolfellows,—German, Swiss, Italian, French, Russian,—slipped out of the shadowy woods and silently accompanied him. They flitted by his side, raising their eyes questioningly, sadly, to his. But their names he had forgotten. Some of the Brothers, too, came with them, and most of these he remembered by name—Bruder Röst, Bruder Pagel, Bruder Schliemann, and the bearded face of the old preacher who had seen himself in the haunted gallery of those about to die—Bruder Gysin. The dark forest lay all about him like a sea that any moment might rush with velvet waves upon the scene and sweep all the faces away. The air was cool and wonderfully fragrant, but with every perfumed breath came also a pallid memory. . . .

Yet, in spite of the underlying sadness inseparable from such an experience, it was all very interesting, and held a pleasure peculiarly its own, so that Harris engaged his room and ordered supper feeling well pleased with himself, and intending to walk up to the old school that very evening. It stood in the centre of the community's village, some four miles distant through the forest, and he now recollected for the first time that this little Protestant settlement dwelt isolated in a section of the country that was otherwise Catholic. Crucifixes and shrines surrounded the clearing like the sentries of a beleaguering army. Once beyond the square of the village, with its few acres of field and orchard, the forest crowded up in solid phalanxes, and beyond the rim of trees began the country that was ruled by the priests of another faith. He vaguely remembered, too, that the Catholics had showed sometimes a certain hostility towards the little Protestant oasis that flourished so quietly and benignly in their midst. He had quite forgotten this. How trumpery it all seemed now with his wide experience of life and his knowledge of other countries and the great outside world. It was like stepping back, not thirty years, but three hundred.

There were only two others besides himself at supper. One of them, a bearded, middle-aged man in tweeds, sat by himself at the far end, and Harris kept out of his way because he was English. He feared he might be in business, possibly even in the silk business, and that he would perhaps talk on the subject. The other traveller, however, was a Catholic priest. He was a little man who ate his salad with a knife, yet so gently that it was almost inoffensive, and it was the sight of "the cloth" that recalled his memory of the old antagonism. Harris mentioned by way of conversation the object of his sentimental journey, and the priest looked up sharply at him with raised eyebrows and an expression of surprise and suspicion that somehow piqued him. He ascribed it to his difference of belief.

"Yes," went on the silk merchant, pleased to talk of what his mind was so full, "and it was a curious experience for an English boy to be dropped down into a school of a hundred foreigners. I well remember the loneliness and intolerable *Heimweh* of it at first." His German was very fluent.

The priest opposite looked up from his cold veal and potato salad and smiled. It was a nice face. He explained quietly that he did not belong here, but was making a tour of the parishes of Wurttemberg and Baden.

"It was a strict life," added Harris. "We English, I remember, used to call it *Gefängnisleben*—prison life!"

The face of the other, for some unaccountable reason, darkened. After a slight pause, and more by way of politeness than because he wished to continue the subject, he said quietly—

"It was a flourishing school in those days, of course. Afterwards, I have heard—" He shrugged his shoulders slightly, and the odd look—it almost seemed a look of alarm—came back into his eyes. The sentence remained unfinished.

Something in the tone of the man seemed to his listener uncalled for—in a sense reproachful, singular. Harris bridled in spite of himself.

"It has changed?" he asked. "I can hardly believe—"

"You have not heard, then?" observed the priest gently, making a gesture as though to cross himself, yet not actually completing it. "You have not heard what happened there before it was abandoned—?"

It was very childish, of course, and perhaps he was overtired and overwrought in some way, but the words and manner of the little priest seemed to him so offensive—so disproportionately offensive—that he hardly noticed the concluding sentence. He recalled the old bitterness and the old antagonism, and for a moment he almost lost his temper.

"Nonsense," he interrupted with a forced laugh, "*Unsinn!* You must forgive me, sir, for contradicting you. But I was a pupil there myself. I was at school there. There was no place like it. I cannot believe that anything serious could have happened to—to take away its character. The devotion of the Brothers would be difficult to equal anywhere—"

He broke off suddenly, realizing that his voice had been raised unduly and that the man at the far end of the table might understand German; and at the same moment he looked up and saw that this individual's eyes were fixed upon his face intently. They were peculiarly bright. Also they were rather wonderful eyes, and the way they met his own served in some way he could not understand to convey both a reproach and a warning. The whole face of the stranger, indeed, made a vivid impression upon him, for it was a face, he now noticed for the first time, in whose presence one would not willingly have said or done anything unworthy. Harris could not explain to himself how it was he had not become conscious sooner of its presence.

But he could have bitten off his tongue for having so far forgotten himself. The little priest lapsed into silence. Only once he said, looking up and speaking in a low voice that was not intended to be overheard, but that evidently *was* overheard, "You will find it different." Presently he rose and left the table with a polite bow that included both the others.

And, after him, from the far end rose also the figure in the tweed suit, leaving Harris by himself.

He sat on for a bit in the darkening room, sipping his coffee and smoking his fifteen-pfennig cigar, till the girl came in to light the oil lamps. He felt vexed with himself for his lapse from good manners, yet hardly able to account for it. Most likely, he reflected, he had been annoyed because the priest had unintentionally changed the pleasant character of his dream by introducing a jarring note. Later he must seek an opportunity to make amends. At present, however, he was too impatient for his walk to the school, and he took his stick and hat and passed out into the open air.

And, as he crossed before the Gasthaus, he noticed that the priest and the man in the tweed suit were engaged already in such deep conversation that they hardly noticed him as he passed and raised his hat.

He started off briskly, well remembering the way, and hoping to reach the village in time to have a word with one of the Brüder. They might even ask him in for a cup of coffee. He felt sure of his welcome, and the old memories were in full possession once more. The hour of return was a matter of no consequence whatever.

It was then just after seven o'clock, and the October evening was drawing in with chill airs from the recesses of the forest. The road plunged straight from the railway clearing into its depths, and in a very few minutes the trees engulfed him and the clack of his boots fell dead and echoless against the serried stems of a million firs. It was very black; one trunk was hardly distinguishable from another. He walked smartly, swinging his holly stick. Once or twice he passed a peasant on his way to bed, and the guttural "Grüss Got," unheard for so long, emphasized the passage of time, while yet making it seem as nothing. A fresh group of pictures crowded his mind. Again the figures of former schoolfellows flitted out of the forest and kept pace by his side, whispering of the doings of long ago. One reverie stepped hard upon the heels of another. Every turn in the road, every clearing of the forest, he knew, and each in turn brought forgotten associations to life. He enjoyed himself thoroughly.

He marched on and on. There was powdered gold in the sky till the moon rose, and then a wind of faint silver spread silently between the earth and stars. He saw the tips of the fir trees shimmer, and heard them whisper as the breeze turned their needles towards the light. The mountain air was indescribably sweet. The road shone like the foam of a river through the gloom. White moths flitted here and there like silent thoughts across his path, and a hundred smells greeted him from the forest caverns across the years.

Then, when he least expected it, the trees fell away abruptly on both sides, and he stood on the edge of the village clearing.

He walked faster. There lay the familiar outlines of the houses, sheeted with silver; there stood the trees in the little central square with the fountain and small green lawns; there loomed the shape of the church next to the Gasthof der Brüdergemeinde; and just beyond, dimly rising into the sky, he saw with a sudden thrill the mass of the huge school building, blocked castlelike with deep shadows in the moonlight, standing square and formidable to face him after the silences of more than a quarter of a century.

He passed quickly down the deserted village street and stopped close beneath its shadow, staring up at the walls that had once held him prisoner for two years—two unbroken years of discipline and homesickness. Memories and emotions surged through his mind; for the most vivid sensations of his youth had focused about this spot, and it was here he had first begun to live and learn values. Not a single footstep broke the silence, though lights glimmered here and there through cottage windows; but when he looked up at the high walls of the school, draped now in shadow, he easily imagined that well-known faces crowded to the windows to greet him—closed windows that really reflected only moonlight and the gleam of stars.

This, then, was the old school building, standing foursquare to the world, with its shuttered windows, its lofty, tiled roof, and the spiked lightning-conductors pointing like black and taloned fingers from the corners. For a long time he stood and stared. Then, presently, he came to himself again, and realised to his joy that a light still shone in the windows of the *Bruderstube*.

He turned from the road and passed through the iron railings; then climbed the twelve stone steps and stood facing the black wooden door with the heavy bars of iron, a door he had once loathed and dreaded with the hatred and passion of an imprisoned soul, but now looked upon tenderly with a sort of boyish delight.

Almost timorously he pulled the rope and listened with a tremor of excitement to the clanging of the bell deep within the building. And the long-forgotten sound brought the past before him with such a vivid sense of reality that he positively shivered. It was like the magic bell in the fairy-tale that rolls back the curtain of Time and summons the figures from the shadows of the dead. He had never felt so sentimental in his life. It was like being young again. And, at the same time, he began to bulk rather large in his own eyes with a certain spurious importance. He was a big man from the world of strife and action. In this little place of peaceful dreams would he, perhaps, not cut something of a figure?

"I'll try once more," he thought after a long pause, seizing the iron bell-rope, and was just about to pull it when a step sounded on the stone passage within, and the huge door slowly swung open.

A tall man with a rather severe cast of countenance stood facing him in silence.

"I must apologize—it is somewhat late," he began a trifle pompously, "but the fact is I am an old pupil. I have only just arrived and really could not restrain myself." His German seemed not quite so fluent as usual. "My interest is so great. I was here in '70."

The other opened the door wider and at once bowed him in with a smile of genuine welcome.

"I am Bruder Kalkmann," he said quietly in a deep voice. "I myself was a master here about that time. It is a great pleasure always to welcome a former pupil." He looked at him very keenly for a few seconds, and then added, "I think, too, it is splendid of you to come—very splendid."

"It is a very great pleasure," Harris replied, delighted with his reception.

The dimly lighted corridor with its flooring of grey stone, and the familiar sound of a German voice echoing through it,—with the peculiar intonation the Brothers always used in speaking,—all combined to lift him bodily, as it were, into the dream-atmosphere of long-forgotten days. He stepped gladly into the building and the door shut with the familiar thunder that completed the reconstruction of the past. He almost felt the old sense of imprisonment, of aching nostalgia, of having lost his liberty.

Harris sighed involuntarily and turned towards his host, who returned his smile faintly and then led the way down the corridor.

"The boys have retired," he explained, "and, as you remember, we keep early hours here. But, at least, you will join us for a little while in the Bruderstube and enjoy a cup of coffee." This was precisely what the silk merchant had hoped, and he accepted with an alacrity that he intended to be tempered by graciousness. "And to-morrow," continued the Bruder, "you must come and spend a whole day with us. You may even find acquaintances, for several pupils of your day have come back here as masters."

For one brief second there passed into the man's eyes a look that made the visitor start. But it vanished as quickly as it came. It was impossible to define. Harris convinced himself it was the effect of a shadow cast by the lamp they had just passed on the wall. He dismissed it from his mind.

"You are very kind, I'm sure," he said politely. "It is perhaps a greater pleasure to me than you can imagine to see the place again.

Ah,"—he stopped short opposite a door with the upper half of glass and peered in—"surely there is one of the music rooms where I used to practise the violin. How it comes back to me after all these years!"

Bruder Kalkmann stopped indulgently, smiling, to allow his guest a moment's inspection.

"You still have the boys' orchestra? I remember I used to play '*zweite Geige*' in it. Bruder Schliemann conducted at the piano. Dear me, I can see him now with his long black hair and—and—" He stopped abruptly. Again the odd, dark look passed over the stern face of his companion. For an instant it seemed curiously familiar.

"We still keep up the pupils' orchestra," he said, "but Bruder Schliemann, I am sorry to say—" he hesitated an instant, and then added, "Bruder Schliemann is dead."

"Indeed, indeed," said Harris quickly. "I am sorry to hear it." He was conscious of a faint feeling of distress, but whether it arose from the news of his old music teacher's death, or—from something else— he could not quite determine. He gazed down the corridor that lost itself among shadows. In the street and village everything had seemed so much smaller than he remembered, but here, inside the school building, everything seemed so much bigger. The corridor was loftier and longer, more spacious and vast, than the mental picture he had preserved. His thoughts wandered dreamily for an instant.

He glanced up and saw the face of the Bruder watching him with a smile of patient indulgence.

"Your memories possess you," he observed gently, and the stern look passed into something almost pitying.

"You are right," returned the man of silk, "they do. This was the most wonderful period of my whole life in a sense. At the time I hated it—" He hesitated, not wishing to hurt the Brother's feelings.

"According to English ideas it seemed strict, of course," the other said persuasively, so that he went on.

"—Yes, partly that; and partly the ceaseless nostalgia, and the solitude which came from never being really alone. In English schools the boys enjoy peculiar freedom, you know."

Bruder Kalkmann, he saw, was listening intently.

"But it produced one result that I have never wholly lost," he continued self-consciously, "and am grateful for."

"*Ach*! *Wie so, denn?*"

"The constant inner pain threw me headlong into your religious life, so that the whole force of my being seemed to project itself towards the search for a deeper satisfaction—a real resting-place for the soul. During my two years here I yearned for God in my boyish way as perhaps I have never yearned for anything since. Moreover, I have never quite lost that sense of peace and inward joy which accompanied the search. I can never quite forget this school and the deep things it taught me."

He paused at the end of his long speech, and a brief silence fell between them. He feared he had said too much, or expressed himself clumsily in the foreign language, and when Bruder Kalkmann laid a hand upon his shoulder, he gave a little involuntary start.

"So that my memories perhaps do possess me rather strongly," he added apologetically; "and this long corridor, these rooms, that barred and gloomy front door, all touch chords that—that—" His German failed him and he glanced at his companion with an explanatory smile and gesture. But the Brother had removed the hand from his shoulder and was standing with his back to him, looking down the passage.

"Naturally, naturally so," he said hastily without turning round. "*Es ist doch selbstverständlich.* We shall all understand."

Then he turned suddenly, and Harris saw that his face had turned most oddly and disagreeably sinister. It may only have been the shadows again playing their tricks with the wretched oil lamps on the wall, for the dark expression passed instantly as they retraced their steps down the corridor, but the Englishman somehow got the impression that he had said something to give offence, something that was not quite to the other's taste. Opposite the door of the *Bruderstube* they stopped. Harris realised that it was late and he had possibly stayed talking too long. He made a tentative effort to leave, but his companion would not hear of it.

"You must have a cup of coffee with us," he said firmly as though he meant it, "and my colleagues will be delighted to see you. Some of them will remember you, perhaps."

The sound of voices came pleasantly through the door, men's voices talking together. Bruder Kalkmann turned the handle and they entered a room ablaze with light and full of people.

"Ah,—but your name?" he whispered, bending down to catch the reply; "you have not told me your name yet."

"Harris," said the Englishman quickly as they went in. He felt nervous as he crossed the threshold, but ascribed the momentary trepidation to the fact that he was breaking the strictest rule of the whole establishment, which forbade a boy under severest penalties to come near this holy of holies where the masters took their brief leisure.

"Ah, yes, of course—Harris," repeated the other as though he remembered it. "Come in, Herr Harris, come in, please. Your visit will be immensely appreciated. It is really very fine, very wonderful of you to have come in this way."

The door closed behind them and, in the sudden light which made his sight swim for a moment, the exaggeration of the language escaped his attention. He heard the voice of Bruder Kalkmann introducing him. He spoke very loud, indeed, unnecessarily,—absurdly loud, Harris thought.

"Brothers," he announced, "it is my pleasure and privilege to introduce to you Herr Harris from England. He has just arrived to make us a little visit, and I have already expressed to him on behalf of us all the satisfaction we feel that he is here. He was, as you remember, a pupil in the year '70."

It was a very formal, a very German introduction, but Harris rather liked it. It made him feel important and he appreciated the tact that made it almost seem as though he had been expected.

The black forms rose and bowed; Harris bowed; Kalkmann bowed. Every one was very polite and very courtly. The room swam with moving figures; the light dazzled him after the gloom of the corridor, there was thick cigar smoke in the atmosphere. He took the chair that was offered to him between two of the Brothers, and sat down, feeling vaguely that his perceptions were not quite as keen and accurate as usual. He felt a trifle dazed perhaps, and the spell of the past came strongly over him, confusing the immediate present and making everything dwindle oddly to the dimensions of long ago. He seemed to pass under the mastery of a great mood that was a composite reproduction of all the moods of his forgotten boyhood.

Then he pulled himself together with a sharp effort and entered into the conversation that had begun again to buzz round him. Moreover, he entered into it with keen pleasure, for the Brothers—there were perhaps a dozen of them in the little room—treated him with a charm of manner that speedily made him feel one of themselves. This, again, was a very subtle delight to him. He felt that he had stepped out of the greedy, vulgar, self-seeking world, the world of silk and markets and profit-making—stepped into the cleaner atmosphere where spiritual ideals were paramount and life was simple and devoted. It all charmed him inexpressibly, so that he realised—yes, in a sense—the degradation of his twenty years' absorption in business. This keen atmosphere under the stars where men thought only of their souls, and of the souls of others, was too rarefied for the world he was now associated with. He found himself making comparisons to his own disadvantage,—comparisons with the mystical little dreamer that had stepped thirty years before from the stern peace of this devout community, and the man of the world that he had since become,—and the contrast made him shiver with a keen regret and something like self-contempt.

He glanced round at the other faces floating towards him through tobacco smoke—this acrid cigar smoke he remembered so well: how keen they were, how strong, placid, touched with the nobility of great aims and unselfish purposes. At one or two he looked particularly. He hardly knew why. They rather fascinated him. There was something so very stern and uncompromising about them, and something, too, oddly, subtly, familiar, that yet just eluded him. But whenever their eyes met his own they held undeniable welcome in them; and some held more—

a kind of perplexed admiration, he thought, something that was between esteem and deference. This note of respect in all the faces was very flattering to his vanity.

Coffee was served presently, made by a black-haired Brother who sat in the corner by the piano and bore a marked resemblance to Bruder Schliemann, the musical director of thirty years ago. Harris exchanged bows with him when he took the cup from his white hands, which he noticed were like the hands of a woman. He lit a cigar, offered to him by his neighbour, with whom he was chatting delightfully, and who, in the glare of the lighted match, reminded him sharply for a moment of Bruder Pagel, his former room-master.

"*Es ist wirklich merkwürdig,*" he said, "how many resemblances I see, or imagine. It is really *very* curious!"

"Yes," replied the other, peering at him over his coffee cup, "the spell of the place is wonderfully strong. I can well understand that the old faces rise before your mind's eye—almost to the exclusion of ourselves perhaps."

They both laughed presently. It was soothing to find his mood understood and appreciated. And they passed on to talk of the mountain village, its isolation, its remoteness from worldly life, its peculiar fitness for meditation and worship, and for spiritual development—of a certain kind.

"And your coming back in this way, Herr Harris, has pleased us all so much," joined in the Bruder on his left. "We esteem you for it most highly. We honor you for it."

Harris made a deprecating gesture. "I fear, for my part, it is only a very selfish pleasure," he said a trifle unctuously.

"Not all would have had the courage," added the one who resembled Bruder Pagel.

"You mean," said Harris, a little puzzled, "the disturbing memories—?"

Bruder Pagel looked at him steadily, with unmistakable admiration and respect. "I mean that most men hold so strongly to life, and can give up so little for their beliefs," he said gravely.

The Englishman felt slightly uncomfortable. These worthy men really made too much of his sentimental journey. Besides, the talk was getting a little out of his depth. He hardly followed it.

"The worldly life still has *some* charms for me," he replied smilingly, as though to indicate that sainthood was not yet quite within his grasp.

"All the more, then, must we honor you for so freely coming," said the Brother on his left; "so unconditionally!"

A pause followed, and the silk merchant felt relieved when the conversation took a more general turn, although he noted that it never travelled very far from the subject of his visit and the wonderful situation of the lonely village for men who wished to develop their spiritual powers and practise the rites of a high worship. Others joined in, complimenting him on his knowledge of the language, making him feel utterly at his ease, yet at the same time a little uncomfortable by the excess of their admiration. After all, it was such a very small thing to do, this sentimental journey.

The time passed along quickly; the coffee was excellent, the cigars soft and of the nutty flavor he loved. At length, fearing to outstay his welcome, he rose reluctantly to take his leave. But the others would not hear of it. It was not often a former pupil returned to visit them in this simple, unaffected way. The night was young. If necessary they could even find him a corner in the great *Schlafzimmer* upstairs. He was easily persuaded to stay a little longer. Somehow he had become the centre of the little party. He felt pleased, flattered, honored.

"And perhaps Bruder Schliemann will play something for us—now."

It was Kalkmann speaking, and Harris started visibly as he heard the name, and saw the black-haired man by the piano turn with a smile. For Schliemann was the name of his old music director, who was dead. Could this be his son? They were so exactly alike.

"If Bruder Meyer has not put his Amati to bed, I will accompany him," said the musician suggestively, looking across at a man whom Harris had not yet noticed, and who, he now saw, was the very image of a former master of that name.

Meyer rose and excused himself with a little bow, and the Englishman quickly observed that he had a peculiar gesture as though his neck had a false join on to the body just below the collar and feared it might break. Meyer of old had this trick of movement. He remembered how the boys used to copy it.

He glanced sharply from face to face, feeling as though some silent, unseen process were changing everything about him. All the faces seemed oddly familiar. Pagel, the Brother he had been talking with, was of course the image of Pagel, his former room-master, and Kalkmann, he now realised for the first time, was the very twin of another master whose name he had quite forgotten, but whom he used to dislike intensely in the old days. And, through the smoke, peering at him from the corners of the room, he saw that all the Brothers about him had the faces he had known and lived with long ago—Röst, Fluheim, Meinert, Rigel, Gysin.

He stared hard, suddenly grown more alert, and everywhere saw, or fancied he saw, strange likenesses, ghostly resemblances,—more, the identical faces of years ago. There was something queer about it all, something not quite right, something that made him feel uneasy. He shook himself, mentally and actually, blowing the smoke from before his eyes with a long breath, and as he did so he noticed to his dismay that every one was fixedly staring. They were watching him.

This brought him to his senses. As an Englishman, and a foreigner, he did not wish to be rude, or to do anything to make himself foolishly conspicuous and spoil the harmony of the evening. He was a guest, and a privileged guest at that. Besides, the music had already begun. Bruder Schliemann's long white fingers were caressing the keys to some purpose.

He subsided into his chair and smoked with half-closed eyes that yet saw everything.

But the shudder had established itself in his being, and, whether he would or not, it kept repeating itself. As a town, far up some inland river, feels the pressure of the distant sea, so he became aware that mighty forces from somewhere beyond his ken were urging themselves up against his soul in this smoky little room. He began to feel exceedingly ill at ease.

And as the music filled the air his mind began to clear. Like a lifted veil there rose up something that had hitherto obscured his vision. The words of the priest at the railway inn flashed across his brain unbidden: "You will find it different." And also, though why he could not tell, he saw mentally the strong, rather wonderful eyes of that other guest at the supper-table, the man who had overheard his conversation, and had later got into earnest talk with the priest. He took out his watch and stole a glance at it. Two hours had slipped by. It was already eleven o'clock.

Schliemann, meanwhile, utterly absorbed in his music, was playing a solemn measure. The piano sang marvelously. The power of a great conviction, the simplicity of great art, the vital spiritual message of a soul that had found itself—all this, and more, were in the chords, and yet somehow the music was what can only be described as impure— atrociously and diabolically impure. And the piece itself, although Harris did not recognise it as anything familiar, was surely the music of a Mass—huge, majestic, somber? It stalked through the smoky room with slow power, like the passage of something that was mighty, yet profoundly intimate, and as it went there stirred into each and every face about him the signature of the enormous forces of which it was the audible symbol. The countenances round him turned sinister, but not idly, negatively sinister: they grew dark with purpose. He suddenly recalled the face of Bruder Kalkmann in the corridor earlier in the evening. The motives of their secret souls rose to the eyes, and mouths, and foreheads, and hung there for all to see like the black banners of an assembly of ill-starred and fallen creatures. Demons—was the horrible word that flashed through his brain like a sheet of fire.

When this sudden discovery leaped out upon him, for a moment he lost his self-control. Without waiting to think and weigh his extraordinary impression, he did a very foolish but a very natural thing.

Feeling himself irresistibly driven by the sudden stress to some kind of action, he sprang to his feet—and screamed! To his own utter amazement he stood up and shrieked aloud!

But no one stirred. No one, apparently, took the slightest notice of his absurdly wild behaviour. It was almost as if no one but himself had heard the scream at all—as though the music had drowned it and swallowed it up—as though after all perhaps he had not really screamed as loudly as he imagined, or had not screamed at all.

Then, as he glanced at the motionless, dark faces before him, something of utter cold passed into his being, touching his very soul. . . . All emotion cooled suddenly, leaving him like a receding tide. He sat down again, ashamed, mortified, angry with himself for behaving like a fool and a boy. And the music, meanwhile, continued to issue from the white and snakelike fingers of Bruder Schliemann, as poisoned wine might issue from the weirdly fashioned necks of antique phials.

And, with the rest of them, Harris drank it in.

Forcing himself to believe that he had been the victim of some kind of illusory perception, he vigorously restrained his feelings. Then the music presently ceased, and every one applauded and began to talk at once, laughing, changing seats, complimenting the player, and behaving naturally and easily as though nothing out of the way had happened. The faces appeared normal once more. The Brothers crowded round their visitor, and he joined in their talk and even heard himself thanking the gifted musician.

But, at the same time, he found himself edging towards the door, nearer and nearer, changing his chair when possible, and joining the groups that stood closest to the way of escape.

"I must thank you all *tausendmal* for my little reception and the great pleasure—the very great honor you have done me," he began in decided tones at length, "but I fear I have trespassed far too long already on your hospitality. Moreover, I have some distance to walk to my inn."

A chorus of voices greeted his words. They would not hear of his going,—at least not without first partaking of refreshment. They produced pumpernickel from one cupboard, and rye-bread and sausage from another, and all began to talk again and eat. More coffee was made, fresh cigars lighted, and Bruder Meyer took out his violin and began to tune it softly.

"There is always a bed upstairs if Herr Harris will accept it," said one.

"And it is difficult to find the way out now, for all the doors are locked," laughed another loudly.

"Let us take our simple pleasures as they come," cried a third. "Bruder Harris will understand how we appreciate the honor of this last visit of his."

They made a dozen excuses. They all laughed, as though the politeness of their words was but formal, and veiled thinly—more and more thinly—a very different meaning.

"And the hour of midnight draws near," added Bruder Kalkmann with a charming smile, but in a voice that sounded to the Englishman like the grating of iron hinges.

Their German seemed to him more and more difficult to understand. He noted that they called him "Bruder" too, classing him as one of themselves.

And then suddenly he had a flash of keener perception, and realised with a creeping of his flesh that he had all along misinterpreted—grossly misinterpreted all they had been saying. They had talked about the beauty of the place, its isolation and remoteness from the world, its peculiar fitness for certain kinds of spiritual development and worship—yet hardly, he now grasped, in the sense in which he had taken the words. They had meant something different. Their spiritual powers, their desire for loneliness, their passion for worship, were not the powers, the solitude, or the worship that *he* meant and understood. He was playing a part in some horrible masquerade; he was among men who cloaked their lives with religion in order to follow their real purposes unseen of men.

What did it all mean? How had he blundered into so equivocal a situation? Had he blundered into it at all? Had he not rather been led into it, deliberately led? His thoughts grew dreadfully confused, and his confidence in himself began to fade. And why, he suddenly thought again, were they so impressed by the mere fact of his coming to revisit his old school? What was it they so admired and wondered at in his simple act? Why did they set such store upon his having the courage to come, to "give himself so freely," "unconditionally" as one of them had expressed it with such a mockery of exaggeration?

Fear stirred in his heart most horribly, and he found no answer to any of his questionings. Only one thing he now understood quite clearly: it was their purpose to keep him here. They did not intend that he should go. And from this moment he realised that they were sinister, formidable and, in some way he had yet to discover, inimical to himself, inimical to his life. And the phrase one of them had used a moment ago—"this *last* visit of his"—rose before his eyes in letters of flame.

Harris was not a man of action, and had never known in all the course of his career what it meant to be in a situation of real danger. He was not necessarily a coward, though, perhaps, a man of untried nerve. He realised at last plainly that he was in a very awkward predicament indeed, and that he had to deal with men who were utterly in earnest. What their intentions were he only vaguely guessed. His mind, indeed, was too confused for definite ratiocination, and he was only able to follow blindly the strongest instincts that moved in him. It never occurred to him that the Brothers might all be mad, or that he himself might have temporarily lost his senses and be suffering under some terrible delusion. In fact, nothing occurred to him—he realised nothing—except that he meant to escape—and the quicker the better. A tremendous revulsion of feeling set in and overpowered him.

Accordingly, without further protest for the moment, he ate his pumpernickel and drank his coffee, talking meanwhile as naturally and pleasantly as he could, and when a suitable interval had passed, he rose to his feet and announced once more that he must now take his leave. He spoke very quietly, but very decidedly. No one hearing him could doubt that he meant what he said. He had got very close to the door by this time.

"I regret," he said, using his best German, and speaking to a hushed room, "that our pleasant evening must come to an end, but it is now time for me to wish you all good-night." And then, as no one said anything, he added, though with a trifle less assurance, "And I thank you all most sincerely for your hospitality."

"On the contrary," replied Kalkmann instantly, rising from his chair and ignoring the hand the Englishman had stretched out to him, "it is we who have to thank you; and we do so most gratefully and sincerely."

And at the same moment at least half a dozen of the Brothers took up their position between himself and the door.

"You are very good to say so," Harris replied as firmly as he could manage, noticing this movement out of the corner of his eye, "but really I had no conception that—my little chance visit could have afforded you so much pleasure." He moved another step nearer the door, but Bruder Schliemann came across the room quickly and stood in front of him. His attitude was uncompromising. A dark and terrible expression had come into his face.

"But it was *not* by chance that you came, Bruder Harris," he said so that all the room could hear; "surely we have not misunderstood your presence here?" He raised his black eyebrows.

"No, no," the Englishman hastened to reply, "I was—I am delighted to be here. I told you what pleasure it gave me to find myself among you. Do not misunderstand me, I beg." His voice faltered a little, and he had difficulty in finding the words. More and more, too, he had difficulty in understanding *their* words.

"Of course," interposed Bruder Kalkmann in his iron bass, "*we* have not misunderstood. You have come back in the spirit of true and unselfish devotion. You offer yourself freely, and we all appreciate it. It is your willingness and nobility that have so completely won our veneration and respect." A faint murmur of applause ran round the room. "What we all delight in—what our great Master will especially delight in—is the value of your spontaneous and voluntary—"

He used a word Harris did not understand. He said "*Opfer*." The bewildered Englishman searched his brain for the translation, and searched in vain. For the life of him he could not remember what it meant. But the word, for all his inability to translate it, touched his soul with ice. It was worse, far worse, than anything he had imagined. He felt like a lost, helpless creature, and all power to fight sank out of him from that moment.

"It is magnificent to be such a willing—" added Schliemann, sidling up to him with a dreadful leer on his face. He made use of the same word—"*Opfer*."

"God! What could it all mean?" "Offer himself!" "True spirit of devotion!" "Willing," "unselfish," "magnificent!" *Opfer, Opfer, Opfer*! What in the name of heaven did it mean, that strange, mysterious word that struck such terror into his heart?

He made a valiant effort to keep his presence of mind and hold his nerves steady. Turning, he saw that Kalkmann's face was a dead white. Kalkmann! He understood that well enough. *Kalkmann* meant "Man of Chalk": he knew that. But what did "*Opfer*" mean? That was the real key to the situation. Words poured through his disordered mind in an endless stream—unusual, rare words he had perhaps heard but once in his life—while "*Opfer*," a word in common use, entirely escaped him. What an extraordinary mockery it all was!

Then Kalkmann, pale as death, but his face hard as iron, spoke a few low words that he did not catch, and the Brothers standing by the walls at once turned the lamps down so that the room became dim. In the half light he could only just discern their faces and movements.

"It is time," he heard Kalkmann's remorseless voice continue just behind him. "The hour of midnight is at hand. Let us prepare. He comes! He comes; Bruder Asmodelius comes!" His voice rose to a chant.

And the sound of that name, for some extraordinary reason, was terrible—utterly terrible; so that Harris shook from head to foot as he heard it. Its utterance filled the air like soft thunder, and a hush came over the whole room. Forces rose all about him, transforming the normal into the horrible, and the spirit of craven fear ran through all his being, bringing him to the verge of collapse.

Asmodelius! *Asmodelius*! The name was appalling. For he understood at last to whom it referred and the meaning that lay between its great syllables. At the same instant, too, he suddenly understood the meaning of that unremembered word. The import of the word "*Opfer*" flashed upon his soul like a message of death.

He thought of making a wild effort to reach the door, but the weakness of his trembling knees, and the row of black figures that stood between, dissuaded him at once. He would have screamed for help, but remembering the emptiness of the vast building, and the loneliness of the situation, he understood that no help could come that way, and he kept his lips closed. He stood still and did nothing. But he knew now what was coming.

Two of the Brothers approached and took him gently by the arm.

"Bruder Asmodelius accepts you," they whispered; "are you ready?"

Then he found his tongue and tried to speak. "But what have I to do with this Bruder Asm—Asmo—?" he stammered, a desperate rush of words crowding vainly behind the halting tongue.

The name refused to pass his lips. He could not pronounce it as they did. He could not pronounce it at all. His sense of helplessness then entered the acute stage, for this inability to speak the name produced a fresh sense of quite horrible confusion in his mind, and he became extraordinarily agitated.

"I came here for a friendly visit," he tried to say with a great effort, but, to his intense dismay, he heard his voice saying something quite different, and actually making use of that very word they had all used: "I came here as a willing *Opfer*," he heard his own voice say, "and *I am quite ready*."

He was lost beyond all recall now! Not alone his mind, but the very muscles of his body had passed out of control. He felt that he was hovering on the confines of a phantom or demon-world,—a world in which the name they had spoken constituted the Master-name, the word of ultimate power.

What followed he heard and saw as in a nightmare.

"In the half light that veils all truth, let us prepare to worship and adore," chanted Schliemann, who had preceded him to the end of the room.

"In the mists that protect our faces before the Black Throne, let us make ready the willing victim," echoed Kalkmann in his great bass.

They raised their faces, listening expectantly, as a roaring sound, like the passing of mighty projectiles, filled the air, far, far away, very wonderful, very forbidding. The walls of the room trembled.

"He comes! He comes! He comes!" chanted the Brothers in chorus.

The sound of roaring died away, and an atmosphere of still and utter cold established itself over all. Then Kalkmann, dark and unutterably stern, turned in the dim light and faced the rest.

"Asmodelius, our *Hauptbruder*, is about us," he cried in a voice that even while it shook was yet a voice of iron; "Asmodelius is about us. Make ready."

There followed a pause in which no one stirred or spoke. A tall Brother approached the Englishman; but Kalkmann held up his hand.

"Let the eyes remain uncovered," he said, "in honor of so freely giving himself." And to his horror Harris then realised for the first time that his hands were already fastened to his sides.

The Brother retreated again silently, and in the pause that followed all the figures about him dropped to their knees, leaving him standing alone, and as they dropped, in voices hushed with mingled reverence and awe, they cried, softly, odiously, appallingly, the name of the Being whom they momentarily expected to appear.

Then, at the end of the room, where the windows seemed to have disappeared so that he saw the stars, there rose into view far up against the night sky, grand and terrible, the outline of a man. A kind of grey glory enveloped it so that it resembled a steel-cased statue, immense, imposing, horrific in its distant splendour; while, at the same time, the face was so spiritually mighty, yet so proudly, so austerely sad, that Harris felt as he stared, that the sight was more than his eyes could meet, and that in another moment the power of vision would fail him altogether, and he must sink into utter nothingness.

So remote and inaccessible hung this figure that it was impossible to gauge anything as to its size, yet at the same time so strangely close, that when the grey radiance from its mightily broken visage, august and mournful, beat down upon his soul, pulsing like some dark star with the powers of spiritual evil, he felt almost as though he were looking into a face no farther removed from him in space than the face of any one of the Brothers who stood by his side.

And then the room filled and trembled with sounds that Harris understood full well were the failing voices of others who had preceded him in a long series down the years. There came first a plain, sharp cry, as of a man in the last anguish, choking for his breath, and yet, with the very final expiration of it, breathing the name of the Worship—of the dark Being who rejoiced to hear it. The cries of the strangled; the short, running gasp of the suffocated; and the smothered gurgling of the tightened throat, all these, and more, echoed back and forth between the walls, the very walls in which he now stood a prisoner, a sacrificial victim. The cries, too, not alone of the broken bodies, but—far worse— of beaten, broken souls. And as the ghastly chorus rose and fell, there came also the faces of the lost and unhappy creatures to whom they belonged, and, against that curtain of pale grey light, he saw float past him in the air, an array of white and piteous human countenances that seemed to beckon and gibber at him as though he were already one of themselves.

Slowly, too, as the voices rose, and the pallid crew sailed past, that giant form of grey descended from the sky and approached the room that contained the worshippers and their prisoner. Hands rose and sank about him in the darkness, and he felt that he was being draped in other garments than his own; a circlet of ice seemed to run about his head, while round the waist, enclosing the fastened arms, he felt a girdle tightly drawn. At last, about his very throat, there ran a soft and silken touch which, better than if there had been full light, and a mirror held to his face, he understood to be the cord of sacrifice—and of death.

At this moment the Brothers, still prostrate upon the floor, began again their mournful, yet impassioned chanting, and as they did so a strange thing happened. For, apparently without moving or altering its position, the huge Figure seemed, at once and suddenly, to be inside the room, almost beside him, and to fill the space around him to the exclusion of all else.

He was now beyond all ordinary sensations of fear, only a drab feeling as of death—the death of the soul—stirred in his heart. His thoughts no longer even beat vainly for escape. The end was near, and he knew it.

The dreadfully chanting voices rose about him in a wave: "We worship! We adore! We offer!" The sounds filled his ears and hammered, almost meaningless, upon his brain.

Then the majestic grey face turned slowly downwards upon him, and his very soul passed outwards and seemed to become absorbed in the sea of those anguished eyes. At the same moment a dozen hands forced him to his knees, and in the air before him he saw the arm of Kalkmann upraised, and felt the pressure about his throat grow strong.

It was in this awful moment, when he had given up all hope, and the help of gods or men seemed beyond question, that a strange thing happened. For before his fading and terrified vision there slid, as in a dream of light,—yet without apparent rhyme or reason—wholly unbidden and unexplained,—the face of that other man at the supper table of the railway inn. And the sight, even mentally, of that strong, wholesome, vigorous English face, inspired him suddenly with a new courage.

It was but a flash of fading vision before he sank into a dark and terrible death, yet, in some inexplicable way, the sight of that face stirred in him unconquerable hope and the certainty of deliverance. It was a face of power, a face, he now realised, of simple goodness such as might have been seen by men of old on the shores of Galilee; a face, by heaven, that could conquer even the devils of outer space.

And, in his despair and abandonment, he called upon it, and called with no uncertain accents. He found his voice in this overwhelming moment to some purpose; though the words he actually used, and whether they were in German or English, he could never remember. Their effect, nevertheless, was instantaneous. The Brothers understood, and that grey Figure of evil understood.

For a second the confusion was terrific. There came a great shattering sound. It seemed that the very earth trembled. But all Harris remembered afterwards was that voices rose about him in the clamour of terrified alarm—

"A man of power is among us! A man of God!"

The vast sound was repeated—the rushing through space as of huge projectiles—and he sank to the floor of the room, unconscious. The entire scene had vanished, vanished like smoke over the roof of a cottage when the wind blows.

And, by his side, sat down a slight un-German figure,—the figure of the stranger at the inn,—the man who had the "rather wonderful eyes."

* * * * *

When Harris came to himself he felt cold. He was lying under the open sky, and the cool air of field and forest was blowing upon his face. He sat up and looked about him. The memory of the late scene was still horribly in his mind, but no vestige of it remained. No walls or ceiling enclosed him; he was no longer in a room at all. There were no lamps turned low, no cigar smoke, no black forms of sinister worshippers, no tremendous grey Figure hovering beyond the windows.

Open space was about him, and he was lying on a pile of bricks and mortar, his clothes soaked with dew, and the kind stars shining brightly overhead. He was lying, bruised and shaken, among the heaped-up débris of a ruined building.

He stood up and stared about him. There, in the shadowy distance, lay the surrounding forest, and here, close at hand, stood the outline of the village buildings. But, underfoot, beyond question, lay nothing but the broken heaps of stones that betokened a building long since crumbled to dust. Then he saw that the stones were blackened, and that great wooden beams, half burnt, half rotten, made lines through the general débris. He stood, then, among the ruins of a burnt and shattered building, the weeds and nettles proving conclusively that it had lain thus for many years.

The moon had already set behind the encircling forest, but the stars that spangled the heavens threw enough light to enable him to make quite sure of what he saw. Harris, the silk merchant, stood among these broken and burnt stones and shivered.

Then he suddenly became aware that out of the gloom a figure had risen and stood beside him. Peering at him, he thought he recognised the face of the stranger at the railway inn.

"Are *you* real?" he asked in a voice he hardly recognised as his own.

"More than real—I'm friendly," replied the stranger; "I followed you up here from the inn."

Harris stood and stared for several minutes without adding anything. His teeth chattered. The least sound made him start; but the simple words in his own language, and the tone in which they were uttered, comforted him inconceivably.

"You're English too, thank God," he said inconsequently. "These German devils—" He broke off and put a hand to his eyes. "But what's become of them all—and the room—and—and—" The hand travelled down to his throat and moved nervously round his neck. He drew a long, long breath of relief. "Did I dream everything—everything?" he said distractedly.

He stared wildly about him, and the stranger moved forward and took his arm. "Come," he said soothingly, yet with a trace of command in the voice, "we will move away from here. The high-road, or even the woods will be more to your taste, for we are standing now on one of the most haunted—and most terribly haunted—spots of the whole world."

He guided his companion's stumbling footsteps over the broken masonry until they reached the path, the nettles stinging their hands, and Harris feeling his way like a man in a dream. Passing through the twisted iron railing they reached the path, and thence made their way to the road, shining white in the night. Once safely out of the ruins, Harris collected himself and turned to look back.

"But, how is it possible?" he exclaimed, his voice still shaking. "How can it be possible? When I came in here I saw the building in the moonlight. They opened the door. I saw the figures and heard the voices and touched, yes touched their very hands, and saw their damned black faces, saw them far more plainly than I see you now." He was deeply bewildered. The glamour was still upon his eyes with a degree of reality stronger than the reality even of normal life. "Was I so utterly deluded?"

Then suddenly the words of the stranger, which he had only half heard or understood, returned to him.

"Haunted?" he asked, looking hard at him; "haunted, did you say?" He paused in the roadway and stared into the darkness where the building of the old school had first appeared to him. But the stranger hurried him forward.

"We shall talk more safely farther on," he said. "I followed you from the inn the moment I realised where you had gone. When I found you it was eleven o'clock—"

"Eleven o'clock," said Harris, remembering with a shudder.

"—I saw you drop. I watched over you till you recovered consciousness of your own accord, and now—now I am here to guide you safely back to the inn. I have broken the spell—the glamour—"

"I owe you a great deal, sir," interrupted Harris again, beginning to understand something of the stranger's kindness, "but I don't understand it all. I feel dazed and shaken." His teeth still chattered, and spells of violent shivering passed over him from head to foot. He found that he was clinging to the other's arm. In this way they passed beyond the deserted and crumbling village and gained the high-road that led homewards through the forest.

"That school building has long been in ruins," said the man at his side presently; "it was burnt down by order of the Elders of the community at least ten years ago. The village has been uninhabited ever since. But the simulacra of certain ghastly events that took place under that roof in past days still continue. And the 'shells' of the chief participants still enact there the dreadful deeds that led to its final destruction, and to the desertion of the whole settlement. They were devil-worshippers!"

Harris listened with beads of perspiration on his forehead that did not come alone from their leisurely pace through the cool night. Although he had seen this man but once before in his life, and had never before exchanged so much as a word with him, he felt a degree of confidence and a subtle sense of safety and well-being in his presence that were the most healing influences he could possibly have wished after the experience he had been through. For all that, he still felt as if he were walking in a dream, and though he heard every word that fell from his companion's lips, it was only the next day that the full import of all he said became fully clear to him. The presence of this quiet stranger, the man with the wonderful eyes which he felt now, rather than saw, applied a soothing anodyne to his shattered spirit that healed him through and through. And this healing influence, distilled from the dark figure at his side, satisfied his first imperative need, so that he almost forgot to realize how strange and opportune it was that the man should be there at all.

It somehow never occurred to him to ask his name, or to feel any undue wonder that one passing tourist should take so much trouble on behalf of another. He just walked by his side, listening to his quiet words, and allowing himself to enjoy the very wonderful experience after his recent ordeal, of being helped, strengthened, blessed. Only once, remembering vaguely something of his reading of years ago, he turned to the man beside him, after some more than usually remarkable words, and heard himself, almost involuntarily it seemed, putting the question: "Then are you a Rosicrucian, sir, perhaps?" But the stranger had ignored the words, or possibly not heard them, for he continued with his talk as though unconscious of any interruption, and Harris became aware that another somewhat unusual picture had taken possession of his mind, as they walked there side by side through the cool reaches of the forest, and that he had found his imagination suddenly charged with the childhood memory of Jacob wrestling with an angel,—wrestling all night with a being of superior quality whose strength eventually became his own.

"It was your abrupt conversation with the priest at supper that first put me upon the track of this remarkable occurrence," he heard the man's quiet voice beside him in the darkness, "and it was from him I learned after you left the story of the devil-worship that became secretly established in the heart of this simple and devout little community."

"Devil-worship! Here—!" Harris stammered, aghast.

"Yes—here;—conducted secretly for years by a group of Brothers before unexplained disappearances in the neighbourhood led to its discovery. For where could they have found a safer place in the whole wide world for their ghastly traffic and perverted powers than here, in the very precincts—under cover of the very shadow of saintliness and holy living?"

"Awful, awful!" whispered the silk merchant, "and when I tell you the words they used to me—"

"I know it all," the stranger said quietly. "I saw and heard everything. My plan first was to wait till the end and then to take steps for their destruction, but in the interest of your personal safety,"—he spoke with the utmost gravity and conviction,—"in the interest of the safety of your soul, I made my presence known when I did, and before the conclusion had been reached—"

"My safety! The danger, then, was real. They were alive and—" Words failed him. He stopped in the road and turned towards his companion, the shining of whose eyes he could just make out in the gloom.

"It was a concourse of the shells of violent men, spiritually developed but evil men, seeking after death—the death of the body—to prolong their vile and unnatural existence. And had they accomplished their object you, in turn, at the death of your body, would have passed into their power and helped to swell their dreadful purposes."

Harris made no reply. He was trying hard to concentrate his mind upon the sweet and common things of life. He even thought of silk and St. Paul's Churchyard and the faces of his partners in business.

"For you came all prepared to be caught," he heard the other's voice like some one talking to him from a distance; "your deeply introspective mood had already reconstructed the past so vividly, so intensely, that you were *en rapport* at once with any forces of those days that chanced still to be lingering. And they swept you up all unresistingly."

Harris tightened his hold upon the stranger's arm as he heard. At the moment he had room for one emotion only. It did not seem to him odd that this stranger should have such intimate knowledge of his mind.

"It is, alas, chiefly the evil emotions that are able to leave their photographs upon surrounding scenes and objects," the other added, "and who ever heard of a place haunted by a noble deed, or of beautiful and lovely ghosts revisiting the glimpses of the moon? It is unfortunate. But the wicked passions of men's hearts alone seem strong enough to leave pictures that persist; the good are ever too lukewarm."

The stranger sighed as he spoke. But Harris, exhausted and shaken as he was to the very core, paced by his side, only half listening. He moved as in a dream still. It was very wonderful to him, this walk home under the stars in the early hours of the October morning, the peaceful forest all about them, mist rising here and there over the small clearings, and the sound of water from a hundred little invisible streams filling in the pauses of the talk. In after life he always looked back to it as something magical and impossible, something that had seemed too beautiful, too curiously beautiful, to have been quite true. And, though at the time he heard and understood but a quarter of what the stranger said, it came back to him afterwards, staying with him till the end of his days, and always with a curious, haunting sense of unreality, as though he had enjoyed a wonderful dream of which he could recall only faint and exquisite portions.

But the horror of the earlier experience was effectually dispelled; and when they reached the railway inn, somewhere about three o'clock in the morning, Harris shook the stranger's hand gratefully, effusively, meeting the look of those rather wonderful eyes with a full heart, and went up to his room, thinking in a hazy, dream-like way of the words with which the stranger had brought their conversation to an end as they left the confines of the forest—

"And if thought and emotion can persist in this way so long after the brain that sent them forth has crumbled into dust, how vitally important it must be to control their very birth in the heart, and guard them with the keenest possible restraint."

But Harris, the silk merchant, slept better than might have been expected, and with a soundness that carried him half-way through the day. And when he came downstairs and learned that the stranger had already taken his departure, he realised with keen regret that he had never once thought of asking his name.

"Yes, he signed the visitors' book," said the girl in reply to his question.

And he turned over the blotted pages and found there, the last entry, in a very delicate and individual handwriting—

"*John Silence, London.*"

Ancient Sorceries

I

There are, it would appear, certain wholly unremarkable persons, with none of the characteristics that invite adventure, who yet once or twice in the course of their smooth lives undergo an experience so strange that the world catches its breath—and looks the other way! And it was cases of this kind, perhaps, more than any other, that fell into the wide-spread net of John Silence, the psychic doctor, and, appealing to his deep humanity, to his patience, and to his great qualities of spiritual sympathy, led often to the revelation of problems of the strangest complexity, and of the profoundest possible human interest.

Matters that seemed almost too curious and fantastic for belief he loved to trace to their hidden sources. To unravel a tangle in the very soul of things—and to release a suffering human soul in the process— was with him a veritable passion. And the knots he untied were, indeed, after passing strange.

The world, of course, asks for some plausible basis to which it can attach credence—something it can, at least, pretend to explain. The adventurous type it can understand: such people carry about with them an adequate explanation of their exciting lives, and their characters obviously drive them into the circumstances which produce the adventures. It expects nothing else from them, and is satisfied. But dull, ordinary folk have no right to out-of-the-way experiences, and the world having been led to expect otherwise, is disappointed with them, not to say shocked. Its complacent judgment has been rudely disturbed.

"Such a thing happened to *that* man!" it cries—"a commonplace person like that! It is too absurd! There must be something wrong!"

Yet there could be no question that something did actually happen to little Arthur Vezin, something of the curious nature he described to Dr. Silence. Outwardly or inwardly, it happened beyond a doubt, and in spite of the jeers of his few friends who heard the tale, and observed wisely that "such a thing might perhaps have come to Iszard, that crack-brained Iszard, or to that odd fish Minski, but it could never have happened to commonplace little Vezin, who was fore-ordained to live and die according to scale."

But, whatever his method of death was, Vezin certainly did not "live according to scale" so far as this particular event in his otherwise uneventful life was concerned; and to hear him recount it, and watch his pale delicate features change, and hear his voice grow softer and more hushed as he proceeded, was to know the conviction that his halting words perhaps failed sometimes to convey. He lived the thing over again each time he told it. His whole personality became muffled in the recital. It subdued him more than ever, so that the tale became a lengthy apology for an experience that he deprecated. He appeared to excuse himself and ask your pardon for having dared to take part in so fantastic an episode. For little Vezin was a timid, gentle, sensitive soul, rarely able to assert himself, tender to man and beast, and almost constitutionally unable to say No, or to claim many things that should rightly have been his. His whole scheme of life seemed utterly remote from anything more exciting than missing a train or losing an umbrella on an omnibus. And when this curious event came upon him he was already more years beyond forty than his friends suspected or he cared to admit.

John Silence, who heard him speak of his experience more than once, said that he sometimes left out certain details and put in others; yet they were all obviously true. The whole scene was unforgettably cinematographed on to his mind. None of the details were imagined or invented. And when he told the story with them all complete, the effect was undeniable. His appealing brown eyes shone, and much of the charming personality, usually so carefully repressed, came forward and revealed itself. His modesty was always there, of course, but in the telling he forgot the present and allowed himself to appear almost vividly as he lived again in the past of his adventure.

He was on the way home when it happened, crossing northern France from some mountain trip or other where he buried himself solitary-wise every summer. He had nothing but an unregistered bag in the rack, and the train was jammed to suffocation, most of the passengers being unredeemed holiday English. He disliked them, not because they were his fellow-countrymen, but because they were noisy and obtrusive, obliterating with their big limbs and tweed clothing all the quieter tints of the day that brought him satisfaction and enabled him to melt into insignificance and forget that he was anybody. These English clashed about him like a brass band, making him feel vaguely that he ought to be more self-assertive and obstreperous, and that he did not claim insistently enough all kinds of things that he didn't want and that were really valueless, such as corner seats, windows up or down, and so forth.

So that he felt uncomfortable in the train, and wished the journey were over and he was back again living with his unmarried sister in Surbiton.

And when the train stopped for ten panting minutes at the little station in northern France, and he got out to stretch his legs on the platform, and saw to his dismay a further batch of the British Isles debouching from another train, it suddenly seemed impossible to him to continue the journey. Even *his* flabby soul revolted, and the idea of staying a night in the little town and going on next day by a slower, emptier train, flashed into his mind. The guard was already shouting "*en voiture*" and the corridor of his compartment was already packed when the thought came to him. And, for once, he acted with decision and rushed to snatch his bag.

Finding the corridor and steps impassable, he tapped at the window (for he had a corner seat) and begged the Frenchman who sat opposite to hand his luggage out to him, explaining in his wretched French that he intended to break the journey there. And this elderly Frenchman, he declared, gave him a look, half of warning, half of reproach, that to his dying day he could never forget; handed the bag through the window of the moving train; and at the same time poured into his ears a long sentence, spoken rapidly and low, of which he was able to comprehend only the last few words: "*à cause du sommeil et à cause des chats.*"

In reply to Dr. Silence, whose singular psychic acuteness at once seized upon this Frenchman as a vital point in the adventure, Vezin admitted that the man had impressed him favourably from the beginning, though without being able to explain why. They had sat facing one another during the four hours of the journey, and though no conversation had passed between them—Vezin was timid about his stuttering French—he confessed that his eyes were being continually drawn to his face, almost, he felt, to rudeness, and that each, by a dozen nameless little politenesses and attentions, had evinced the desire to be kind. The men liked each other and their personalities did not clash, or would not have clashed had they chanced to come to terms of acquaintance. The Frenchman, indeed, seemed to have exercised a silent protective influence over the insignificant little Englishman, and without words or gestures betrayed that he wished him well and would gladly have been of service to him.

"And this sentence that he hurled at you after the bag?" asked John Silence, smiling that peculiarly sympathetic smile that always melted the prejudices of his patient, "were you unable to follow it exactly?"

"It was so quick and low and vehement," explained Vezin, in his small voice, "that I missed practically the whole of it. I only caught the few words at the very end, because he spoke them so clearly, and his face was bent down out of the carriage window so near to mine."

"'*À cause du sommeil et à cause des chats*'?" repeated Dr. Silence, as though half speaking to himself.

"That's it exactly," said Vezin; "which, I take it, means something like 'because of sleep and because of the cats,' doesn't it?"

"Certainly, that's how I should translate it," the doctor observed shortly, evidently not wishing to interrupt more than necessary.

"And the rest of the sentence—all the first part I couldn't understand, I mean—was a warning not to do something—not to stop in the town, or at some particular place in the town, perhaps. That was the impression it made on me."

Then, of course, the train rushed off, and left Vezin standing on the platform alone and rather forlorn.

The little town climbed in straggling fashion up a sharp hill rising out of the plain at the back of the station, and was crowned by the twin towers of the ruined cathedral peeping over the summit. From the station itself it looked uninteresting and modern, but the fact was that the mediaeval position lay out of sight just beyond the crest. And once he reached the top and entered the old streets, he stepped clean out of modern life into a bygone century. The noise and bustle of the crowded train seemed days away. The spirit of this silent hill-town, remote from tourists and motor-cars, dreaming its own quiet life under the autumn sun, rose up and cast its spell upon him. Long before he recognised this spell he acted under it. He walked softly, almost on tiptoe, down the winding narrow streets where the gables all but met over his head, and he entered the doorway of the solitary inn with a deprecating and modest demeanour that was in itself an apology for intruding upon the place and disturbing its dream.

At first, however, Vezin said, he noticed very little of all this. The attempt at analysis came much later. What struck him then was only the delightful contrast of the silence and peace after the dust and noisy rattle of the train. He felt soothed and stroked like a cat.

"Like a cat, you said?" interrupted John Silence, quickly catching him up.

"Yes. At the very start I felt that." He laughed apologetically. "I felt as though the warmth and the stillness and the comfort made me purr. It seemed to be the general mood of the whole place—then."

The inn, a rambling ancient house, the atmosphere of the old coaching days still about it, apparently did not welcome him too warmly. He felt he was only tolerated, he said. But it was cheap and comfortable, and the delicious cup of afternoon tea he ordered at once made him feel really very pleased with himself for leaving the train in this bold, original way. For to him it had seemed bold and original. He felt something of a dog. His room, too, soothed him with its dark panelling and low irregular ceiling, and the long sloping passage that led to it seemed the natural pathway to a real Chamber of Sleep—a little dim cubby hole out of the world where noise could not enter. It looked upon the courtyard at the back. It was all very charming, and made him think of himself as dressed in very soft velvet somehow, and the floors seemed padded, the walls provided with cushions. The sounds of the streets could not penetrate there. It was an atmosphere of absolute rest that surrounded him.

On engaging the two-franc room he had interviewed the only person who seemed to be about that sleepy afternoon, an elderly waiter with Dundreary whiskers and a drowsy courtesy, who had ambled lazily towards him across the stone yard; but on coming downstairs again for a little promenade in the town before dinner he encountered the proprietress herself. She was a large woman whose hands, feet, and features seemed to swim towards him out of a sea of person. They emerged, so to speak. But she had great dark, vivacious eyes that counteracted the bulk of her body, and betrayed the fact that in reality she was both vigorous and alert. When he first caught sight of her she was knitting in a low chair against the sunlight of the wall, and something at once made him see her as a great tabby cat, dozing, yet awake, heavily sleepy, and yet at the same time prepared for instantaneous action. A great mouser on the watch occurred to him.

She took him in with a single comprehensive glance that was polite without being cordial. Her neck, he noticed, was extraordinarily supple in spite of its proportions, for it turned so easily to follow him, and the head it carried bowed so very flexibly.

"But when she looked at me, you know," said Vezin, with that little apologetic smile in his brown eyes, and that faintly deprecating gesture of the shoulders that was characteristic of him, "the odd notion came to me that really she had intended to make quite a different movement, and that with a single bound she could have leaped at me across the width of that stone yard and pounced upon me like some huge cat upon a mouse."

He laughed a little soft laugh, and Dr. Silence made a note in his book without interrupting, while Vezin proceeded in a tone as though he feared he had already told too much and more than we could believe.

"Very soft, yet very active she was, for all her size and mass, and I felt she knew what I was doing even after I had passed and was behind her back. She spoke to me, and her voice was smooth and running. She asked if I had my luggage, and was comfortable in my room, and then added that dinner was at seven o'clock, and that they were very early people in this little country town. Clearly, she intended to convey that late hours were not encouraged."

Evidently, she contrived by voice and manner to give him the impression that here he would be "managed," that everything would be arranged and planned for him, and that he had nothing to do but fall into the groove and obey. No decided action or sharp personal effort would be looked for from him. It was the very reverse of the train. He walked quietly out into the street feeling soothed and peaceful. He realised that he was in a *milieu* that suited him and stroked him the right way. It was so much easier to be obedient. He began to purr again, and to feel that all the town purred with him.

About the streets of that little town he meandered gently, falling deeper and deeper into the spirit of repose that characterised it. With no special aim he wandered up and down, and to and fro. The September sunshine fell slantingly over the roofs. Down winding alleyways, fringed with tumbling gables and open casements, he caught fairylike glimpses of the great plain below, and of the meadows and yellow copses lying like a dream-map in the haze. The spell of the past held very potently here, he felt.

The streets were full of picturesquely garbed men and women, all busy enough, going their respective ways; but no one took any notice of him or turned to stare at his obviously English appearance. He was even able to forget that with his tourist appearance he was a false note in a charming picture, and he melted more and more into the scene, feeling delightfully insignificant and unimportant and unselfconscious. It was like becoming part of a softly colored dream which he did not even realise to be a dream.

On the eastern side the hill fell away more sharply, and the plain below ran off rather suddenly into a sea of gathering shadows in which the little patches of woodland looked like islands and the stubble fields like deep water. Here he strolled along the old ramparts of ancient fortifications that once had been formidable, but now were only vision-like with their charming mingling of broken grey walls and wayward vine and ivy. From the broad coping on which he sat for a moment, level with the rounded tops of clipped plane trees, he saw the esplanade far below lying in shadow. Here and there a yellow sunbeam crept in and lay upon the fallen yellow leaves, and from the height he looked down and saw that the townsfolk were walking to and fro in the cool of the evening. He could just hear the sound of their slow footfalls, and the murmur of their voices floated up to him through the gaps between the trees. The figures looked like shadows as he caught glimpses of their quiet movements far below.

He sat there for some time pondering, bathed in the waves of murmurs and half-lost echoes that rose to his ears, muffled by the leaves of the plane trees. The whole town, and the little hill out of which it grew as naturally as an ancient wood, seemed to him like a being lying there half asleep on the plain and crooning to itself as it dozed.

And, presently, as he sat lazily melting into its dream, a sound of horns and strings and wood instruments rose to his ears, and the town band began to play at the far end of the crowded terrace below to the accompaniment of a very soft, deep-throated drum. Vezin was very sensitive to music, knew about it intelligently, and had even ventured, unknown to his friends, upon the composition of quiet melodies with low-running chords which he played to himself with the soft pedal when no one was about. And this music floating up through the trees from an invisible and doubtless very picturesque band of the townspeople wholly charmed him. He recognised nothing that they played, and it sounded as though they were simply improvising without a conductor. No definitely marked time ran through the pieces, which ended and began oddly after the fashion of wind through an Aeolian harp. It was part of the place and scene, just as the dying sunlight and faintly breathing wind were part of the scene and hour, and the mellow notes of old-fashioned plaintive horns, pierced here and there by the sharper strings, all half smothered by the continuous booming of the deep drum, touched his soul with a curiously potent spell that was almost too engrossing to be quite pleasant.

There was a certain queer sense of bewitchment in it all. The music seemed to him oddly un-artificial. It made him think of trees swept by the wind, of night breezes singing among wires and chimney-stacks, or in the rigging of invisible ships; or—and the simile leaped up in his thoughts with a sudden sharpness of suggestion—a chorus of animals, of wild creatures, somewhere in desolate places of the world, crying and singing as animals will, to the moon. He could fancy he heard the wailing, half-human cries of cats upon the tiles at night, rising and falling with weird intervals of sound, and this music, muffled by distance and the trees, made him think of a queer company of these creatures on some roof far away in the sky, uttering their solemn music to one another and the moon in chorus.

It was, he felt at the time, a singular image to occur to him, yet it expressed his sensation pictorially better than anything else. The instruments played such impossibly odd intervals, and the crescendos and diminuendos were so very suggestive of cat-land on the tiles at night, rising swiftly, dropping without warning to deep notes again, and all in such strange confusion of discords and accords. But, at the same time a plaintive sweetness resulted on the whole, and the discords of these half-broken instruments were so singular that they did not distress his musical soul like fiddles out of tune.

He listened a long time, wholly surrendering himself as his character was, and then strolled homewards in the dusk as the air grew chilly.

"There was nothing to alarm?" put in Dr. Silence briefly.

"Absolutely nothing," said Vezin; "but you know it was all so fantastical and charming that my imagination was profoundly impressed. Perhaps, too," he continued, gently explanatory, "it was this stirring of my imagination that caused other impressions; for, as I walked back, the spell of the place began to steal over me in a dozen ways, though all intelligible ways. But there were other things I could not account for in the least, even then."

"Incidents, you mean?"

"Hardly incidents, I think. A lot of vivid sensations crowded themselves upon my mind and I could trace them to no causes. It was just after sunset and the tumbled old buildings traced magical outlines against an opalescent sky of gold and red. The dusk was running down the twisted streets. All round the hill the plain pressed in like a dim sea, its level rising with the darkness. The spell of this kind of scene, you know, can be very moving, and it was so that night. Yet I felt that what came to me had nothing directly to do with the mystery and wonder of the scene."

"Not merely the subtle transformations of the spirit that come with beauty," put in the doctor, noticing his hesitation.

"Exactly," Vezin went on, duly encouraged and no longer so fearful of our smiles at his expense. "The impressions came from somewhere else. For instance, down the busy main street where men and women were bustling home from work, shopping at stalls and barrows, idly gossiping in groups, and all the rest of it, I saw that I aroused no interest and that no one turned to stare at me as a foreigner and stranger. I was utterly ignored, and my presence among them excited no special interest or attention.

"And then, quite suddenly, it dawned upon me with conviction that all the time this indifference and inattention were merely feigned. Everybody as a matter of fact was watching me closely. Every movement I made was known and observed. Ignoring me was all a pretence—an elaborate pretence."

He paused a moment and looked at us to see if we were smiling, and then continued, reassured—

"It is useless to ask me how I noticed this, because I simply cannot explain it. But the discovery gave me something of a shock. Before I got back to the inn, however, another curious thing rose up strongly in my mind and forced my recognition of it as true. And this, too, I may as well say at once, was equally inexplicable to me. I mean I can only give you the fact, as fact it was to me."

The little man left his chair and stood on the mat before the fire. His diffidence lessened from now onwards, as he lost himself again in the magic of the old adventure. His eyes shone a little already as he talked.

"Well," he went on, his soft voice rising somewhat with his excitement, "I was in a shop when it came to me first—though the idea must have been at work for a long time subconsciously to appear in so complete a form all at once. I was buying socks, I think," he laughed, "and struggling with my dreadful French, when it struck me that the woman in the shop did not care two pins whether I bought anything or not. She was indifferent whether she made a sale or did not make a sale. She was only pretending to sell.

"This sounds a very small and fanciful incident to build upon what follows. But really it was not small. I mean it was the spark that lit the line of powder and ran along to the big blaze in my mind.

"For the whole town, I suddenly realised, was something other than I so far saw it. The real activities and interests of the people were elsewhere and otherwise than appeared. Their true lives lay somewhere out of sight behind the scenes. Their busy-ness was but the outward semblance that masked their actual purposes. They bought and sold, and ate and drank, and walked about the streets, yet all the while the main stream of their existence lay somewhere beyond my ken, underground, in secret places. In the shops and at the stalls they did not care whether I purchased their articles or not; at the inn, they were indifferent to my staying or going; their life lay remote from my own, springing from hidden, mysterious sources, coursing out of sight, unknown. It was all a great elaborate pretence, assumed possibly for my benefit, or possibly for purposes of their own. But the main current of their energies ran elsewhere. I almost felt as an unwelcome foreign substance might be expected to feel when it has found its way into the human system and the whole body organises itself to eject it or to absorb it. The town was doing this very thing to me.

"This bizarre notion presented itself forcibly to my mind as I walked home to the inn, and I began busily to wonder wherein the true life of this town could lie and what were the actual interests and activities of its hidden life.

"And, now that my eyes were partly opened, I noticed other things too that puzzled me, first of which, I think, was the extraordinary silence of the whole place. Positively, the town was muffled. Although the streets were paved with cobbles the people moved about silently, softly, with padded feet, like cats. Nothing made noise. All was hushed, subdued, muted. The very voices were quiet, low-pitched like purring. Nothing clamorous, vehement or emphatic seemed able to live in the drowsy atmosphere of soft dreaming that soothed this little hill-town into its sleep. It was like the woman at the inn—an outward repose screening intense inner activity and purpose.

"Yet there was no sign of lethargy or sluggishness anywhere about it. The people were active and alert. Only a magical and uncanny softness lay over them all like a spell."

Vezin passed his hand across his eyes for a moment as though the memory had become very vivid. His voice had run off into a whisper so that we heard the last part with difficulty. He was telling a true thing obviously, yet something that he both liked and hated telling.

"I went back to the inn," he continued presently in a louder voice, "and dined. I felt a new strange world about me. My old world of reality receded. Here, whether I liked it or no, was something new and incomprehensible. I regretted having left the train so impulsively. An adventure was upon me, and I loathed adventures as foreign to my nature. Moreover, this was the beginning apparently of an adventure somewhere deep within me, in a region I could not check or measure, and a feeling of alarm mingled itself with my wonder—alarm for the stability of what I had for forty years recognised as my 'personality.'

"I went upstairs to bed, my mind teeming with thoughts that were unusual to me, and of rather a haunting description. By way of relief I kept thinking of that nice, prosaic noisy train and all those wholesome, blustering passengers. I almost wished I were with them again. But my dreams took me elsewhere. I dreamed of cats, and soft-moving creatures, and the silence of life in a dim muffled world beyond the senses."

II

Vezin stayed on from day to day, indefinitely, much longer than he had intended. He felt in a kind of dazed, somnolent condition. He did nothing in particular, but the place fascinated him and he could not decide to leave. Decisions were always very difficult for him and he sometimes wondered how he had ever brought himself to the point of leaving the train. It seemed as though some one else must have arranged it for him, and once or twice his thoughts ran to the swarthy Frenchman who had sat opposite. If only he could have understood that long sentence ending so strangely with "*à cause du sommeil et à cause des chats.*" He wondered what it all meant.

Meanwhile the hushed softness of the town held him prisoner and he sought in his muddling, gentle way to find out where the mystery lay, and what it was all about. But his limited French and his constitutional hatred of active investigation made it hard for him to buttonhole anybody and ask questions. He was content to observe, and watch, and remain negative.

The weather held on calm and hazy, and this just suited him. He wandered about the town till he knew every street and alley. The people suffered him to come and go without let or hindrance, though it became clearer to him every day that he was never free himself from observation. The town watched him as a cat watches a mouse. And he got no nearer to finding out what they were all so busy with or where the main stream of their activities lay. This remained hidden. The people were as soft and mysterious as cats.

But that he was continually under observation became more evident from day to day.

For instance, when he strolled to the end of the town and entered a little green public garden beneath the ramparts and seated himself upon one of the empty benches in the sun, he was quite alone—at first. Not another seat was occupied; the little park was empty, the paths deserted. Yet, within ten minutes of his coming, there must have been fully twenty persons scattered about him, some strolling aimlessly along the gravel walks, staring at the flowers, and others seated on the wooden benches enjoying the sun like himself. None of them appeared to take any notice of him; yet he understood quite well they had all come there to watch. They kept him under close observation. In the street they had seemed busy enough, hurrying upon various errands; yet these were suddenly all forgotten and they had nothing to do but loll and laze in the sun, their duties unremembered. Five minutes after he left, the garden was again deserted, the seats vacant. But in the crowded street it was the same thing again; he was never alone. He was ever in their thoughts.

By degrees, too, he began to see how it was he was so cleverly watched, yet without the appearance of it. The people did nothing *directly*. They behaved *obliquely*. He laughed in his mind as the thought thus clothed itself in words, but the phrase exactly described it. They looked at him from angles which naturally should have led their sight in another direction altogether. Their movements were oblique, too, so far as these concerned himself. The straight, direct thing was not their way evidently. They did nothing obviously. If he entered a shop to buy, the woman walked instantly away and busied herself with something at the farther end of the counter, though answering at once when he spoke, showing that she knew he was there and that this was only her way of attending to him. It was the fashion of the cat she followed. Even in the dining-room of the inn, the be-whiskered and courteous waiter, lithe and silent in all his movements, never seemed able to come straight to his table for an order or a dish. He came by zigzags, indirectly, vaguely, so that he appeared to be going to another table altogether, and only turned suddenly at the last moment, and was there beside him.

Vezin smiled curiously to himself as he described how he began to realize these things. Other tourists there were none in the hostel, but he recalled the figures of one or two old men, inhabitants, who took their *déjeuner* and dinner there, and remembered how fantastically they entered the room in similar fashion. First, they paused in the doorway, peering about the room, and then, after a temporary inspection, they came in, as it were, sideways, keeping close to the walls so that he wondered which table they were making for, and at the last minute making almost a little quick run to their particular seats. And again he thought of the ways and methods of cats.

Other small incidents, too, impressed him as all part of this queer, soft town with its muffled, indirect life, for the way some of the people appeared and disappeared with extraordinary swiftness puzzled him exceedingly. It may have been all perfectly natural, he knew, yet he could not make it out how the alleys swallowed them up and shot them forth in a second of time when there were no visible doorways or openings near enough to explain the phenomenon. Once he followed two elderly women who, he felt, had been particularly examining him from across the street—quite near the inn this was—and saw them turn the corner a few feet only in front of him. Yet when he sharply followed on their heels he saw nothing but an utterly deserted alley stretching in front of him with no sign of a living thing. And the only opening through which they could have escaped was a porch some fifty yards away, which not the swiftest human runner could have reached in time.

And in just such sudden fashion people appeared, when he never expected them. Once when he heard a great noise of fighting going on behind a low wall, and hurried up to see what was going on, what should he see but a group of girls and women engaged in vociferous conversation which instantly hushed itself to the normal whispering note of the town when his head appeared over the wall. And even then none of them turned to look at him directly, but slunk off with the most unaccountable rapidity into doors and sheds across the yard. And their voices, he thought, had sounded so like, so strangely like, the angry snarling of fighting animals, almost of cats.

The whole spirit of the town, however, continued to evade him as something elusive, protean, screened from the outer world, and at the same time intensely, genuinely vital; and, since he now formed part of its life, this concealment puzzled and irritated him; more—it began rather to frighten him.

Out of the mists that slowly gathered about his ordinary surface thoughts, there rose again the idea that the inhabitants were waiting for him to declare himself, to take an attitude, to do this, or to do that; and that when he had done so they in their turn would at length make some direct response, accepting or rejecting him. Yet the vital matter concerning which his decision was awaited came no nearer to him.

Once or twice he purposely followed little processions or groups of the citizens in order to find out, if possible, on what purpose they were bent; but they always discovered him in time and dwindled away, each individual going his or her own way. It was always the same: he never could learn what their main interest was. The cathedral was ever empty, the old church of St. Martin, at the other end of the town, deserted. They shopped because they had to, and not because they wished to. The booths stood neglected, the stalls unvisited, the little cafés desolate. Yet the streets were always full, the townsfolk ever on the bustle.

"Can it be," he thought to himself, yet with a deprecating laugh that he should have dared to think anything so odd, "can it be that these people are people of the twilight, that they live only at night their real life, and come out honestly only with the dusk? That during the day they make a sham though brave pretence, and after the sun is down their true life begins? Have they the souls of night-things, and is the whole blessed town in the hands of the cats?"

The fancy somehow electrified him with little shocks of shrinking and dismay. Yet, though he affected to laugh, he knew that he was beginning to feel more than uneasy, and that strange forces were tugging with a thousand invisible cords at the very centre of his being. Something utterly remote from his ordinary life, something that had not waked for years, began faintly to stir in his soul, sending feelers abroad into his brain and heart, shaping queer thoughts and penetrating even into certain of his minor actions. Something exceedingly vital to himself, to his soul, hung in the balance.

And, always when he returned to the inn about the hour of sunset, he saw the figures of the townsfolk stealing through the dusk from their shop doors, moving sentry-wise to and fro at the corners of the streets, yet always vanishing silently like shadows at his near approach. And as the inn invariably closed its doors at ten o'clock he had never yet found the opportunity he rather half-heartedly sought to see for himself what account the town could give of itself at night.

"*—à cause du sommeil et à cause des chats*"—the words now rang in his ears more and more often, though still as yet without any definite meaning.

Moreover, something made him sleep like the dead.

III

It was, I think, on the fifth day—though in this detail his story sometimes varied—that he made a definite discovery which increased his alarm and brought him up to a rather sharp climax. Before that he had already noticed that a change was going forward and certain subtle transformations being brought about in his character which modified several of his minor habits. And he had affected to ignore them. Here, however, was something he could no longer ignore; and it startled him.

At the best of times he was never very positive, always negative rather, compliant and acquiescent; yet, when necessity arose he was capable of reasonably vigorous action and could take a strongish decision. The discovery he now made that brought him up with such a sharp turn was that this power had positively dwindled to nothing. He found it impossible to make up his mind. For, on this fifth day, he realised that he had stayed long enough in the town and that for reasons he could only vaguely define to himself it was wiser *and safer* that he should leave.

And he found that he could not leave!

This is difficult to describe in words, and it was more by gesture and the expression of his face that he conveyed to Dr. Silence the state of impotence he had reached. All this spying and watching, he said, had as it were spun a net about his feet so that he was trapped and powerless to escape; he felt like a fly that had blundered into the intricacies of a great web; he was caught, imprisoned, and could not get away. It was a distressing sensation. A numbness had crept over his will till it had become almost incapable of decision. The mere thought of vigorous action—action towards escape—began to terrify him. All the currents of his life had turned inwards upon himself, striving to bring to the surface something that lay buried almost beyond reach, determined to force his recognition of something he had long forgotten—forgotten years upon years, centuries almost ago. It seemed as though a window deep within his being would presently open and reveal an entirely new world, yet somehow a world that was not unfamiliar. Beyond that, again, he fancied a great curtain hung; and when that too rolled up he would see still farther into this region and at last understand something of the secret life of these extraordinary people.

"Is this why they wait and watch?" he asked himself with rather a shaking heart, "for the time when I shall join them—or refuse to join them? Does the decision rest with me after all, and not with them?"

And it was at this point that the sinister character of the adventure first really declared itself, and he became genuinely alarmed. The stability of his rather fluid little personality was at stake, he felt, and something in his heart turned coward.

Why otherwise should he have suddenly taken to walking stealthily, silently, making as little sound as possible, for ever looking behind him? Why else should he have moved almost on tiptoe about the passages of the practically deserted inn, and when he was abroad have found himself deliberately taking advantage of what cover presented itself? And why, if he was not afraid, should the wisdom of staying indoors after sundown have suddenly occurred to him as eminently desirable? Why, indeed?

And, when John Silence gently pressed him for an explanation of these things, he admitted apologetically that he had none to give.

"It was simply that I feared something might happen to me unless I kept a sharp look-out. I felt afraid. It was instinctive," was all he could say. "I got the impression that the whole town was after me—wanted me for something; and that if it got me I should lose myself, or at least the Self I knew, in some unfamiliar state of consciousness. But I am not a psychologist, you know," he added meekly, "and I cannot define it better than that."

It was while lounging in the courtyard half an hour before the evening meal that Vezin made this discovery, and he at once went upstairs to his quiet room at the end of the winding passage to think it over alone. In the yard it was empty enough, true, but there was always the possibility that the big woman whom he dreaded would come out of some door, with her pretence of knitting, to sit and watch him. This had happened several times, and he could not endure the sight of her. He still remembered his original fancy, bizarre though it was, that she would spring upon him the moment his back was turned and land with one single crushing leap upon his neck. Of course it was nonsense, but then it haunted him, and once an idea begins to do that it ceases to be nonsense. It has clothed itself in reality.

He went upstairs accordingly. It was dusk, and the oil lamps had not yet been lit in the passages. He stumbled over the uneven surface of the ancient flooring, passing the dim outlines of doors along the corridor—doors that he had never once seen opened—rooms that seemed never occupied. He moved, as his habit now was, stealthily and on tiptoe.

Half-way down the last passage to his own chamber there was a sharp turn, and it was just here, while groping round the walls with outstretched hands, that his fingers touched something that was not wall—something that moved. It was soft and warm in texture, indescribably fragrant, and about the height of his shoulder; and he immediately thought of a furry, sweet-smelling kitten. The next minute he knew it was something quite different.

Instead of investigating, however,—his nerves must have been too overwrought for that, he said,—he shrank back as closely as possible against the wall on the other side. The thing, whatever it was, slipped past him with a sound of rustling and, retreating with light footsteps down the passage behind him, was gone. A breath of warm, scented air was wafted to his nostrils.

Vezin caught his breath for an instant and paused, stockstill, half leaning against the wall—and then almost ran down the remaining distance and entered his room with a rush, locking the door hurriedly behind him. Yet it was not fear that made him run: it was excitement, pleasurable excitement. His nerves were tingling, and a delicious glow made itself felt all over his body. In a flash it came to him that this was just what he had felt twenty-five years ago as a boy when he was in love for the first time. Warm currents of life ran all over him and mounted to his brain in a whirl of soft delight. His mood was suddenly become tender, melting, loving.

The room was quite dark, and he collapsed upon the sofa by the window, wondering what had happened to him and what it all meant. But the only thing he understood clearly in that instant was that something in him had swiftly, magically changed: he no longer wished to leave, or to argue with himself about leaving. The encounter in the passage-way had changed all that. The strange perfume of it still hung about him, bemusing his heart and mind. For he knew that it was a girl who had passed him, a girl's face that his fingers had brushed in the darkness, and he felt in some extraordinary way as though he had been actually kissed by her, kissed full upon the lips.

Trembling, he sat upon the sofa by the window and struggled to collect his thoughts. He was utterly unable to understand how the mere passing of a girl in the darkness of a narrow passage-way could communicate so electric a thrill to his whole being that he still shook with the sweetness of it. Yet, there it was! And he found it as useless to deny as to attempt analysis. Some ancient fire had entered his veins, and now ran coursing through his blood; and that he was forty-five instead of twenty did not matter one little jot. Out of all the inner turmoil and confusion emerged the one salient fact that the mere atmosphere, the merest casual touch, of this girl, unseen, unknown in the darkness, had been sufficient to stir dormant fires in the centre of his heart, and rouse his whole being from a state of feeble sluggishness to one of tearing and tumultuous excitement.

After a time, however, the number of Vezin's years began to assert their cumulative power; he grew calmer, and when a knock came at length upon his door and he heard the waiter's voice suggesting that dinner was nearly over, he pulled himself together and slowly made his way downstairs into the dining-room.

Every one looked up as he entered, for he was very late, but he took his customary seat in the far corner and began to eat. The trepidation was still in his nerves, but the fact that he had passed through the courtyard and hall without catching sight of a petticoat served to calm him a little. He ate so fast that he had almost caught up with the current stage of the *table d'hôte*, when a slight commotion in the room drew his attention.

His chair was so placed that the door and the greater portion of the long *salle à manger* were behind him, yet it was not necessary to turn round to know that the same person he had passed in the dark passage had now come into the room. He felt the presence long before he heard or saw any one. Then he became aware that the old men, the only other guests, were rising one by one in their places, and exchanging greetings with some one who passed among them from table to table. And when at length he turned with his heart beating furiously to ascertain for himself, he saw the form of a young girl, lithe and slim, moving down the centre of the room and making straight for his own table in the corner. She moved wonderfully, with sinuous grace, like a young panther, and her approach filled him with such delicious bewilderment that he was utterly unable to tell at first what her face was like, or discover what it was about the whole presentment of the creature that filled him anew with trepidation and delight.

"*Ah, Ma'mselle est de retour!*" he heard the old waiter murmur at his side, and he was just able to take in that she was the daughter of the proprietress, when she was upon him, and he heard her voice. She was addressing him. Something of red lips he saw and laughing white teeth, and stray wisps of fine dark hair about the temples; but all the rest was a dream in which his own emotion rose like a thick cloud before his eyes and prevented his seeing accurately, or knowing exactly what he did. He was aware that she greeted him with a charming little bow; that her beautiful large eyes looked searchingly into his own; that the perfume he had noticed in the dark passage again assailed his nostrils, and that she was bending a little towards him and leaning with one hand on the table at this side. She was quite close to him—that was the chief thing he knew—explaining that she had been asking after the comfort of her mother's guests, and now was introducing herself to the latest arrival—himself.

"M'sieur has already been here a few days," he heard the waiter

Ancient Sorceries

say; and then her own voice, sweet as singing, replied—

"Ah, but M'sieur is not going to leave us just yet, I hope. My mother is too old to look after the comfort of our guests properly, but now I am here I will remedy all that." She laughed deliciously. "M'sieur shall be well looked after."

Vezin, struggling with his emotion and desire to be polite, half rose to acknowledge the pretty speech, and to stammer some sort of reply, but as he did so his hand by chance touched her own that was resting upon the table, and a shock that was for all the world like a shock of electricity, passed from her skin into his body. His soul wavered and shook deep within him. He caught her eyes fixed upon his own with a look of most curious intentness, and the next moment he knew that he had sat down wordless again on his chair, that the girl was already half-way across the room, and that he was trying to eat his salad with a dessert-spoon and a knife.

Longing for her return, and yet dreading it, he gulped down the remainder of his dinner, and then went at once to his bedroom to be alone with his thoughts. This time the passages were lighted, and he suffered no exciting *contretemps*; yet the winding corridor was dim with shadows, and the last portion, from the bend of the walls onwards, seemed longer than he had ever known it. It ran downhill like the pathway on a mountain side, and as he tiptoed softly down it he felt that by rights it ought to have led him clean out of the house into the heart of a great forest. The world was singing with him. Strange fancies filled his brain, and once in the room, with the door securely locked, he did not light the candles, but sat by the open window thinking long, long thoughts that came unbidden in troops to his mind.

IV

This part of the story he told to Dr. Silence, without special coaxing, it is true, yet with much stammering embarrassment. He could not in the least understand, he said, how the girl had managed to affect him so profoundly, and even before he had set eyes upon her. For her mere proximity in the darkness had been sufficient to set him on fire. He knew nothing of enchantments, and for years had been a stranger to anything approaching tender relations with any member of the opposite sex, for he was encased in shyness, and realised his overwhelming defects only too well. Yet this bewitching young creature came to him deliberately. Her manner was unmistakable, and she sought him out on every possible occasion. Chaste and sweet she was undoubtedly, yet frankly inviting; and she won him utterly with the first glance of her shining eyes, even if she had not already done so in the dark merely by the magic of her invisible presence.

"You felt she was altogether wholesome and good!" queried the doctor. "You had no reaction of any sort—for instance, of alarm?"

Vezin looked up sharply with one of his inimitable little apologetic smiles. It was some time before he replied. The mere memory of the adventure had suffused his shy face with blushes, and his brown eyes sought the floor again before he answered.

"I don't think I can quite say that," he explained presently. "I acknowledged certain qualms, sitting up in my room afterwards. A conviction grew upon me that there was something about her—how shall I express it?—well, something unholy. It is not impurity in any sense, physical or mental, that I mean, but something quite indefinable that gave me a vague sensation of the creeps. She drew me, and at the same time repelled me, more than—than—"

He hesitated, blushing furiously, and unable to finish the sentence.

"Nothing like it has ever come to me before or since," he concluded, with lame confusion. "I suppose it was, as you suggested just now, something of an enchantment. At any rate, it was strong enough to make me feel that I would stay in that awful little haunted town for years if only I could see her every day, hear her voice, watch her wonderful movements, and sometimes, perhaps, touch her hand."

"Can you explain to me what you felt was the source of her power?" John Silence asked, looking purposely anywhere but at the narrator.

"I am surprised that *you* should ask me such a question," answered Vezin, with the nearest approach to dignity he could manage. "I think no man can describe to another convincingly wherein lies the magic of the woman who ensnares him. I certainly cannot. I can only say this slip of a girl bewitched me, and the mere knowledge that she was living and sleeping in the same house filled me with an extraordinary sense of delight.

"But there's one thing I can tell you," he went on earnestly, his eyes aglow, "namely, that she seemed to sum up and synthesise in herself all the strange hidden forces that operated so mysteriously in the town and its inhabitants. She had the silken movements of the panther, going smoothly, silently to and fro, and the same indirect, oblique methods as the townsfolk, screening, like them, secret purposes of her own—purposes that I was sure had *me* for their objective. She kept me, to my terror and delight, ceaselessly under observation, yet so carelessly, so consummately, that another man less sensitive, if I may say so"—he made a deprecating gesture—"or less prepared by what had gone before, would never have noticed it at all. She was always still, always reposeful, yet she seemed to be everywhere at once, so that I never could escape from her. I was continually meeting the stare and laughter of her great eyes, in the corners of the rooms, in the passages, calmly looking at me through the windows, or in the busiest parts of the public streets."

Their intimacy, it seems, grew very rapidly after this first encounter which had so violently disturbed the little man's equilibrium. He was naturally very prim, and prim folk live mostly in so small a world that anything violently unusual may shake them clean out of it, and they therefore instinctively distrust originality. But Vezin began to forget his primness after awhile. The girl was always modestly behaved, and as her mother's representative she naturally had to do with the guests in the hotel. It was not out of the way that a spirit of camaraderie should spring up. Besides, she was young, she was charmingly pretty, she was French, and—she obviously liked him.

At the same time, there was something indescribable—a certain indefinable atmosphere of other places, other times—that made him try hard to remain on his guard, and sometimes made him catch his breath with a sudden start. It was all rather like a delirious dream, half delight, half dread, he confided in a whisper to Dr. Silence; and more than once he hardly knew quite what he was doing or saying, as though he were driven forward by impulses he scarcely recognised as his own.

And though the thought of leaving presented itself again and again to his mind, it was each time with less insistence, so that he stayed on from day to day, becoming more and more a part of the sleepy life of this dreamy mediaeval town, losing more and more of his recognisable personality. Soon, he felt, the Curtain within would roll up with an awful rush, and he would find himself suddenly admitted into the secret purposes of the hidden life that lay behind it all. Only, by that time, he would have become transformed into an entirely different being.

And, meanwhile, he noticed various little signs of the intention to make his stay attractive to him: flowers in his bedroom, a more comfortable arm-chair in the corner, and even special little extra dishes on his private table in the dining-room. Conversations, too, with "Mademoiselle Ilsé" became more and more frequent and pleasant, and although they seldom travelled beyond the weather, or the details of the town, the girl, he noticed, was never in a hurry to bring them to an end, and often contrived to interject little odd sentences that he never properly understood, yet felt to be significant.

And it was these stray remarks, full of a meaning that evaded him, that pointed to some hidden purpose of her own and made him feel uneasy. They all had to do, he felt sure, with reasons for his staying on in the town indefinitely.

"And has M'sieur not even yet come to a decision?" she said softly in his ear, sitting beside him in the sunny yard before *déjeuner*, the acquaintance having progressed with significant rapidity. "Because, if it's so difficult, we must all try together to help him!"

The question startled him, following upon his own thoughts. It was spoken with a pretty laugh, and a stray bit of hair across one eye, as she turned and peered at him half roguishly. Possibly he did not quite understand the French of it, for her near presence always confused his small knowledge of the language distressingly. Yet the words, and her manner, and something else that lay behind it all in her mind, frightened him. It gave such point to his feeling that the town was waiting for him to make his mind up on some important matter.

At the same time, her voice, and the fact that she was there so close beside him in her soft dark dress, thrilled him inexpressibly.

"It is true I find it difficult to leave," he stammered, losing his way deliciously in the depths of her eyes, "and especially now that Mademoiselle Ilsé has come."

He was surprised at the success of his sentence, and quite delighted with the little gallantry of it. But at the same time he could have bitten his tongue off for having said it.

"Then after all you like our little town, or you would not be pleased to stay on," she said, ignoring the compliment.

"I am enchanted with it, and enchanted with you," he cried, feeling that his tongue was somehow slipping beyond the control of his brain. And he was on the verge of saying all manner of other things of the wildest description, when the girl sprang lightly up from her chair beside him, and made to go.

"It is *soupe à l'onion* to-day!" she cried, laughing back at him through the sunlight, "and I must go and see about it. Otherwise, you know, M'sieur will not enjoy his dinner, and then, perhaps, he will leave us!"

He watched her cross the courtyard, moving with all the grace and lightness of the feline race, and her simple black dress clothed her, he thought, exactly like the fur of the same supple species. She turned once to laugh at him from the porch with the glass door, and then stopped a moment to speak to her mother, who sat knitting as usual in her corner seat just inside the hall-way.

But how was it, then, that the moment his eye fell upon this ungainly woman, the pair of them appeared suddenly as other than they were? Whence came that transforming dignity and sense of power that enveloped them both as by magic? What was it about that massive woman that made her appear instantly regal, and set her on a throne in some dark and dreadful scenery, wielding a sceptre over the red glare of some tempestuous orgy? And why did this slender stripling of a girl, graceful as a willow, lithe as a young leopard, assume suddenly an air of sinister majesty, and move with flame and smoke about her head, and the darkness of night beneath her feet?

Vezin caught his breath and sat there transfixed. Then, almost simultaneously with its appearance, the queer notion vanished again, and the sunlight of day caught them both, and he heard her laughing to her mother about the *soupe à l'onion*, and saw her glancing back at him over her dear little shoulder with a smile that made him think of a dew-kissed rose bending lightly before summer airs.

And, indeed, the onion soup was particularly excellent that day, because he saw another cover laid at his small table, and, with fluttering heart, heard the waiter murmur by way of explanation that "Ma'mselle Ilsé would honor M'sieur to-day at *déjeuner*, as her custom sometimes is with her mother's guests."

So actually she sat by him all through that delirious meal, talking quietly to him in easy French, seeing that he was well looked after, mixing the salad-dressing, and even helping him with her own hand. And, later in the afternoon, while he was smoking in the courtyard, longing for a sight of her as soon as her duties were done, she came again to his side, and when he rose to meet her, she stood facing him a moment, full of a perplexing sweet shyness before she spoke—

"My mother thinks you ought to know more of the beauties of our little town, and *I* think so too! Would M'sieur like me to be his guide, perhaps? I can show him everything, for our family has lived here for many generations."

She had him by the hand, indeed, before he could find a single word to express his pleasure, and led him, all unresisting, out into the street, yet in such a way that it seemed perfectly natural she should do so, and without the faintest suggestion of boldness or immodesty. Her face glowed with the pleasure and interest of it, and with her short dress and tumbled hair she looked every bit the charming child of seventeen that she was, innocent and playful, proud of her native town, and alive beyond her years to the sense of its ancient beauty.

So they went over the town together, and she showed him what she considered its chief interest: the tumble-down old house where her forebears had lived; the sombre, aristocratic-looking mansion where her mother's family dwelt for centuries, and the ancient market-place where several hundred years before the witches had been burnt by the score. She kept up a lively running stream of talk about it all, of which he understood not a fiftieth part as he trudged along by her side, cursing his forty-five years and feeling all the yearnings of his early manhood revive and jeer at him. And, as she talked, England and Surbiton seemed very far away indeed, almost in another age of the world's history. Her voice touched something immeasurably old in him, something that slept deep. It lulled the surface parts of his consciousness to sleep, allowing what was far more ancient to awaken. Like the town, with its elaborate pretence of modern active life, the upper layers of his being became dulled, soothed, muffled, and what lay underneath began to stir in its sleep. That big Curtain swayed a little to and fro. Presently it might lift altogether. . . .

He began to understand a little better at last. The mood of the town was reproducing itself in him. In proportion as his ordinary external self became muffled, that inner secret life, that was far more real and vital, asserted itself. And this girl was surely the high-priestess of it all, the chief instrument of its accomplishment. New thoughts, with new interpretations, flooded his mind as she walked beside him through the winding streets, while the picturesque old gabled town, softly colored in the sunset, had never appeared to him so wholly wonderful and seductive.

And only one curious incident came to disturb and puzzle him, slight in itself, but utterly inexplicable, bringing white terror into the child's face and a scream to her laughing lips. He had merely pointed to a column of blue smoke that rose from the burning autumn leaves and made a picture against the red roofs, and had then run to the wall and called her to his side to watch the flames shooting here and there through the heap of rubbish. Yet, at the sight of it, as though taken by surprise, her face had altered dreadfully, and she had turned and run like the wind, calling out wild sentences to him as she ran, of which he had not understood a single word, except that the fire apparently frightened her, and she wanted to get quickly away from it, and to get him away too.

Yet five minutes later she was as calm and happy again as though nothing had happened to alarm or waken troubled thoughts in her, and they had both forgotten the incident.

They were leaning over the ruined ramparts together listening to the weird music of the band as he had heard it the first day of his arrival. It moved him again profoundly as it had done before, and somehow he managed to find his tongue and his best French. The girl leaned across the stones close beside him. No one was about. Driven by some remorseless engine within he began to stammer something—he hardly knew what—of his strange admiration for her. Almost at the first word she sprang lightly off the wall and came up smiling in front of him, just touching his knees as he sat there. She was hatless as usual, and the sun caught her hair and one side of her cheek and throat.

"Oh, I'm *so* glad!" she cried, clapping her little hands softly in his face, "so very glad, because that means that if you like me you must also like what I do, and what I belong to."

Already he regretted bitterly having lost control of himself. Something in the phrasing of her sentence chilled him. He knew the fear of embarking upon an unknown and dangerous sea.

"You will take part in our real life, I mean," she added softly, with an indescribable coaxing of manner, as though she noticed his shrinking. "You will come back to us."

Already this slip of a child seemed to dominate him; he felt her power coming over him more and more; something emanated from her that stole over his senses and made him aware that her personality, for all its simple grace, held forces that were stately, imposing, august. He saw her again moving through smoke and flame amid broken and tempestuous scenery, alarmingly strong, her terrible mother by her side. Dimly this shone through her smile and appearance of charming innocence.

"You will, I know," she repeated, holding him with her eyes.

They were quite alone up there on the ramparts, and the sensation that she was overmastering him stirred a wild sensuousness in his blood. The mingled abandon and reserve in her attracted him furiously, and all of him that was man rose up and resisted the creeping influence, at the same time acclaiming it with the full delight of his forgotten youth. An irresistible desire came to him to question her, to summon what still remained to him of his own little personality in an effort to retain the right to his normal self.

The girl had grown quiet again, and was now leaning on the broad wall close beside him, gazing out across the darkening plain, her elbows on the coping, motionless as a figure carved in stone. He took his courage in both hands.

"Tell me, Ilsé," he said, unconsciously imitating her own purring softness of voice, yet aware that he was utterly in earnest, "what is the meaning of this town, and what is this real life you speak of? And why is it that the people watch me from morning to night? Tell me what it all means? And, tell me," he added more quickly with passion in his voice, "what you really are—yourself?"

She turned her head and looked at him through half-closed eyelids, her growing inner excitement betraying itself by the faint color that ran like a shadow across her face.

"It seems to me,"—he faltered oddly under her gaze—"that I have some right to know—"

Suddenly she opened her eyes to the full. "You love me, then?" she asked softly.

"I swear," he cried impetuously, moved as by the force of a rising tide, "I never felt before—I have never known any other girl who—"

"Then you *have* the right to know," she calmly interrupted his confused confession, "for love shares all secrets."

She paused, and a thrill like fire ran swiftly through him. Her words lifted him off the earth, and he felt a radiant happiness, followed almost the same instant in horrible contrast by the thought of death. He became aware that she had turned her eyes upon his own and was speaking again.

"The real life I speak of," she whispered, "is the old, old life within, the life of long ago, the life to which you, too, once belonged, and to which you still belong."

A faint wave of memory troubled the deeps of his soul as her low voice sank into him. What she was saying he knew instinctively to be true, even though he could not as yet understand its full purport. His present life seemed slipping from him as he listened, merging his personality in one that was far older and greater. It was this loss of his present self that brought to him the thought of death.

"You came here," she went on, "with the purpose of seeking it, and the people felt your presence and are waiting to know what you decide, whether you will leave them without having found it, or whether—"

Her eyes remained fixed upon his own, but her face began to change, growing larger and darker with an expression of age.

"It is their thoughts constantly playing about your soul that makes you feel they watch you. They do not watch you with their eyes. The purposes of their inner life are calling to you, seeking to claim you. You were all part of the same life long, long ago, and now they want you back again among them."

Vezin's timid heart sank with dread as he listened; but the girl's eyes held him with a net of joy so that he had no wish to escape. She fascinated him, as it were, clean out of his normal self.

"Alone, however, the people could never have caught and held you," she resumed. "The motive force was not strong enough; it has faded through all these years. But I"—she paused a moment and looked at him with complete confidence in her splendid eyes—"I possess the spell to conquer you and hold you: the spell of old love. I can win you back again and make you live the old life with me, for the force of the ancient tie between us, if I choose to use it, is irresistible. And I do choose to use it. I still want you. And you, dear soul of my dim past"— she pressed closer to him so that her breath passed across his eyes, and her voice positively sang—"I mean to have you, for you love me and are utterly at my mercy."

Vezin heard, and yet did not hear; understood, yet did not understand. He had passed into a condition of exaltation. The world was beneath his feet, made of music and flowers, and he was flying somewhere far above it through the sunshine of pure delight. He was breathless and giddy with the wonder of her words. They intoxicated him. And, still, the terror of it all, the dreadful thought of death, pressed ever behind her sentences. For flames shot through her voice out of black smoke and licked at his soul.

And they communicated with one another, it seemed to him, by a process of swift telepathy, for his French could never have compassed all he said to her. Yet she understood perfectly, and what she said to him was like the recital of verses long since known. And the mingled pain and sweetness of it as he listened were almost more than his little soul could hold.

"Yet I came here wholly by chance—" he heard himself saying.

"No," she cried with passion, "you came here because I called to you. I have called to you for years, and you came with the whole force of the past behind you. You had to come, for I own you, and I claim you."

She rose again and moved closer, looking at him with a certain insolence in the face—the insolence of power.

The sun had set behind the towers of the old cathedral and the darkness rose up from the plain and enveloped them. The music of the band had ceased. The leaves of the plane trees hung motionless, but the chill of the autumn evening rose about them and made Vezin shiver. There was no sound but the sound of their voices and the occasional soft rustle of the girl's dress. He could hear the blood rushing in his ears. He scarcely realised where he was or what he was doing. Some terrible magic of the imagination drew him deeply down into the tombs of his own being, telling him in no unfaltering voice that her words shadowed forth the truth. And this simple little French maid, speaking beside him with so strange authority, he saw curiously alter into quite another being. As he stared into her eyes, the picture in his mind grew and lived, dressing itself vividly to his inner vision with a degree of reality he was compelled to acknowledge. As once before, he saw her tall and stately, moving through wild and broken scenery of forests and mountain caverns, the glare of flames behind her head and clouds of shifting smoke about her feet. Dark leaves encircled her hair, flying loosely in the wind, and her limbs shone through the merest rags of clothing. Others were about her, too, and ardent eyes on all sides cast delirious glances upon her, but her own eyes were always for One only, one whom she held by the hand. For she was leading the dance in some tempestuous orgy to the music of chanting voices, and the dance she led circled about a great and awful Figure on a throne, brooding over the scene through lurid vapours, while innumerable other wild faces and forms crowded furiously about her in the dance. But the one she held by the hand he knew to be himself, and the monstrous shape upon the throne he knew to be her mother.

The vision rose within him, rushing to him down the long years of buried time, crying aloud to him with the voice of memory reawakened. . . . And then the scene faded away and he saw the clear circle of the girl's eyes gazing steadfastly into his own, and she became once more the pretty little daughter of the innkeeper, and he found his voice again.

"And you," he whispered tremblingly—"you child of visions and enchantment, how is it that you so bewitch me that I loved you even before I saw?"

She drew herself up beside him with an air of rare dignity.

"The call of the Past," she said; "and besides," she added proudly, "in the real life I am a princess—"

"A princess!" he cried.

"—and my mother is a queen!"

At this, little Vezin utterly lost his head. Delight tore at his heart and swept him into sheer ecstasy. To hear that sweet singing voice, and to see those adorable little lips utter such things, upset his balance beyond all hope of control. He took her in his arms and covered her unresisting face with kisses.

But even while he did so, and while the hot passion swept him, he felt that she was soft and loathsome, and that her answering kisses stained his very soul. . . . And when, presently, she had freed herself and vanished into the darkness, he stood there, leaning against the wall in a state of collapse, creeping with horror from the touch of her yielding body, and inwardly raging at the weakness that he already dimly realised must prove his undoing.

And from the shadows of the old buildings into which she disappeared there rose in the stillness of the night a singular, long-drawn cry, which at first he took for laughter, but which later he was sure he recognised as the almost human wailing of a cat.

V

For a long time Vezin leant there against the wall, alone with his surging thoughts and emotions. He understood at length that he had done the one thing necessary to call down upon him the whole force of this ancient Past. For in those passionate kisses he had acknowledged the tie of olden days, and had revived it. And the memory of that soft impalpable caress in the darkness of the inn corridor came back to him with a shudder. The girl had first mastered him, and then led him to the one act that was necessary for her purpose. He had been waylaid, after the lapse of centuries—caught, and conquered.

Dimly he realised this, and sought to make plans for his escape. But, for the moment at any rate, he was powerless to manage his thoughts or will, for the sweet, fantastic madness of the whole adventure mounted to his brain like a spell, and he gloried in the feeling that he was utterly enchanted and moving in a world so much larger and wilder than the one he had ever been accustomed to.

The moon, pale and enormous, was just rising over the sea-like plain, when at last he rose to go. Her slanting rays drew all the houses into new perspective, so that their roofs, already glistening with dew, seemed to stretch much higher into the sky than usual, and their gables and quaint old towers lay far away in its purple reaches.

The cathedral appeared unreal in a silver mist. He moved softly, keeping to the shadows; but the streets were all deserted and very silent; the doors were closed, the shutters fastened. Not a soul was astir. The hush of night lay over everything; it was like a town of the dead, a churchyard with gigantic and grotesque tombstones.

Wondering where all the busy life of the day had so utterly disappeared to, he made his way to a back door that entered the inn by means of the stables, thinking thus to reach his room unobserved. He reached the courtyard safely and crossed it by keeping close to the shadow of the wall. He sidled down it, mincing along on tiptoe, just as the old men did when they entered the *salle à manger*. He was horrified to find himself doing this instinctively. A strange impulse came to him, catching him somehow in the centre of his body—an impulse to drop upon all fours and run swiftly and silently. He glanced upwards and the idea came to him to leap up upon his window-sill overhead instead of going round by the stairs. This occurred to him as the easiest, and most natural way. It was like the beginning of some horrible transformation of himself into something else. He was fearfully strung up.

The moon was higher now, and the shadows very dark along the side of the street where he moved. He kept among the deepest of them, and reached the porch with the glass doors.

But here there was light; the inmates, unfortunately, were still about. Hoping to slip across the hall unobserved and reach the stairs, he opened the door carefully and stole in. Then he saw that the hall was not empty. A large dark thing lay against the wall on his left. At first he thought it must be household articles. Then it moved, and he thought it was an immense cat, distorted in some way by the play of light and shadow. Then it rose straight up before him and he saw that it was the proprietress.

What she had been doing in this position he could only venture a dreadful guess, but the moment she stood up and faced him he was aware of some terrible dignity clothing her about that instantly recalled the girl's strange saying that she was a queen. Huge and sinister she stood there under the little oil lamp; alone with him in the empty hall. Awe stirred in his heart, and the roots of some ancient fear. He felt that he must bow to her and make some kind of obeisance. The impulse was fierce and irresistible, as of long habit. He glanced quickly about him. There was no one there. Then he deliberately inclined his head toward her. He bowed.

"*Enfin! M'sieur s'est donc décidé. C'est bien alors. J'en suis contente.*"

Her words came to him sonorously as through a great open space.

Then the great figure came suddenly across the flagged hall at him and seized his trembling hands. Some overpowering force moved with her and caught him.

"*On pourrait faire un p'tit tour ensemble, n'est-ce pas? Nous y allons cette nuit et il faut s'exercer un peu d'avance pour cela. Ilsé, Ilsé, viens donc ici. Viens vite!*"

And she whirled him round in the opening steps of some dance that seemed oddly and horribly familiar. They made no sound on the stones, this strangely assorted couple. It was all soft and stealthy. And presently, when the air seemed to thicken like smoke, and a red glare as of flame shot through it, he was aware that some one else had joined them and that his hand the mother had released was now tightly held by the daughter. Ilsé had come in answer to the call, and he saw her with leaves of vervain twined in her dark hair, clothed in tattered vestiges of some curious garment, beautiful as the night, and horribly, odiously, loathsomely seductive.

"To the Sabbath! to the Sabbath!" they cried. "On to the Witches' Sabbath!"

Up and down that narrow hall they danced, the women on each side of him, to the wildest measure he had ever imagined, yet which he dimly, dreadfully remembered, till the lamp on the wall flickered and went out, and they were left in total darkness. And the devil woke in his heart with a thousand vile suggestions and made him afraid.

Suddenly they released his hands and he heard the voice of the mother cry that it was time, and they must go. Which way they went he did not pause to see. He only realised that he was free, and he blundered through the darkness till he found the stairs and then tore up them to his room as though all hell was at his heels.

He flung himself on the sofa, with his face in his hands, and groaned. Swiftly reviewing a dozen ways of immediate escape, all equally impossible, he finally decided that the only thing to do for the moment was to sit quiet and wait. He must see what was going to happen. At least in the privacy of his own bedroom he would be fairly safe. The door was locked. He crossed over and softly opened the window which gave upon the courtyard and also permitted a partial view of the hall through the glass doors.

As he did so the hum and murmur of a great activity reached his ears from the streets beyond—the sound of footsteps and voices muffled by distance. He leaned out cautiously and listened. The moonlight was clear and strong now, but his own window was in shadow, the silver disc being still behind the house. It came to him irresistibly that the inhabitants of the town, who a little while before had all been invisible behind closed doors, were now issuing forth, busy upon some secret and unholy errand. He listened intently.

At first everything about him was silent, but soon he became aware of movements going on in the house itself. Rustlings and cheepings came to him across that still, moonlit yard. A concourse of living beings sent the hum of their activity into the night. Things were on the move everywhere. A biting, pungent odor rose through the air, coming he knew not whence. Presently his eyes became glued to the windows of the opposite wall where the moonshine fell in a soft blaze. The roof overhead, and behind him, was reflected clearly in the panes of glass, and he saw the outlines of dark bodies moving with long footsteps over the tiles and along the coping. They passed swiftly and silently, shaped like immense cats, in an endless procession across the pictured glass, and then appeared to leap down to a lower level where he lost sight of them. He just caught the soft thudding of their leaps. Sometimes their shadows fell upon the white wall opposite, and then he could not make out whether they were the shadows of human beings or of cats. They seemed to change swiftly from one to the other. The transformation looked horribly real, for they leaped like human beings, yet changed swiftly in the air immediately afterwards, and dropped like animals.

The yard, too, beneath him, was now alive with the creeping movements of dark forms all stealthily drawing towards the porch with the glass doors. They kept so closely to the wall that he could not determine their actual shape, but when he saw that they passed on to the great congregation that was gathering in the hall, he understood that these were the creatures whose leaping shadows he had first seen reflected in the windowpanes opposite. They were coming from all parts of the town, reaching the appointed meeting-place across the roofs and tiles, and springing from level to level till they came to the yard.

Then a new sound caught his ear, and he saw that the windows all about him were being softly opened, and that to each window came a face. A moment later figures began dropping hurriedly down into the yard. And these figures, as they lowered themselves down from the windows, were human, he saw; but once safely in the yard they fell upon all fours and changed in the swiftest possible second into—cats— huge, silent cats. They ran in streams to join the main body in the hall beyond.

So, after all, the rooms in the house had not been empty and unoccupied.

Moreover, what he saw no longer filled him with amazement. For he remembered it all. It was familiar. It had all happened before just so, hundreds of times, and he himself had taken part in it and known the wild madness of it all. The outline of the old building changed, the yard grew larger, and he seemed to be staring down upon it from a much greater height through smoky vapours. And, as he looked, half remembering, the old pains of long ago, fierce and sweet, furiously assailed him, and the blood stirred horribly as he heard the Call of the Dance again in his heart and tasted the ancient magic of Ilsé whirling by his side.

Suddenly he started back. A great lithe cat had leaped softly up from the shadows below on to the sill close to his face, and was staring fixedly at him with the eyes of a human. "Come," it seemed to say, "come with us to the Dance! Change as of old! Transform yourself swiftly and come!" Only too well he understood the creature's soundless call.

It was gone again in a flash with scarcely a sound of its padded feet on the stones, and then others dropped by the score down the side of the house, past his very eyes, all changing as they fell and darting away rapidly, softly, towards the gathering point. And again he felt the dreadful desire to do likewise; to murmur the old incantation, and then drop upon hands and knees and run swiftly for the great flying leap into the air. Oh, how the passion of it rose within him like a flood, twisting his very entrails, sending his heart's desire flaming forth into the night for the old, old Dance of the Sorcerers at the Witches' Sabbath! The whirl of the stars was about him; once more he met the magic of the moon. The power of the wind, rushing from precipice and forest, leaping from cliff to cliff across the valleys, tore him away. . . . He heard the cries of the dancers and their wild laughter, and with this savage girl in his embrace he danced furiously about the dim Throne where sat the Figure with the sceptre of majesty. . . .

Then, suddenly, all became hushed and still, and the fever died down a little in his heart. The calm moonlight flooded a courtyard empty and deserted. They had started. The procession was off into the sky. And he was left behind—alone.

Vezin tiptoed softly across the room and unlocked the door. The murmur from the streets, growing momentarily as he advanced, met his ears. He made his way with the utmost caution down the corridor. At the head of the stairs he paused and listened. Below him, the hall where they had gathered was dark and still, but through opened doors and windows on the far side of the building came the sound of a great throng moving farther and farther into the distance.

He made his way down the creaking wooden stairs, dreading yet longing to meet some straggler who should point the way, but finding no one; across the dark hall, so lately thronged with living, moving things, and out through the opened front doors into the street. He could not believe that he was really left behind, really forgotten, that he had been purposely permitted to escape. It perplexed him.

Nervously he peered about him, and up and down the street; then, seeing nothing, advanced slowly down the pavement.

The whole town, as he went, showed itself empty and deserted, as though a great wind had blown everything alive out of it. The doors and windows of the houses stood open to the night; nothing stirred; moonlight and silence lay over all. The night lay about him like a cloak. The air, soft and cool, caressed his cheek like the touch of a great furry paw. He gained confidence and began to walk quickly, though still keeping to the shadowed side. Nowhere could he discover the faintest sign of the great unholy exodus he knew had just taken place. The moon sailed high over all in a sky cloudless and serene.

Hardly realising where he was going, he crossed the open market-place and so came to the ramparts, whence he knew a pathway descended to the high road and along which he could make good his escape to one of the other little towns that lay to the northward, and so to the railway.

But first he paused and gazed out over the scene at his feet where the great plain lay like a silver map of some dream country. The still beauty of it entered his heart, increasing his sense of bewilderment and unreality. No air stirred, the leaves of the plane trees stood motionless, the near details were defined with the sharpness of day against dark shadows, and in the distance the fields and woods melted away into haze and shimmering mistiness.

But the breath caught in his throat and he stood stockstill as though transfixed when his gaze passed from the horizon and fell upon the near prospect in the depth of the valley at his feet. The whole lower slopes of the hill, that lay hid from the brightness of the moon, were aglow, and through the glare he saw countless moving forms, shifting thick and fast between the openings of the trees; while overhead, like leaves driven by the wind, he discerned flying shapes that hovered darkly one moment against the sky and then settled down with cries and weird singing through the branches into the region that was aflame.

Spellbound, he stood and stared for a time that he could not measure. And then, moved by one of the terrible impulses that seemed to control the whole adventure, he climbed swiftly upon the top of the broad coping, and balanced a moment where the valley gaped at his feet. But in that very instant, as he stood hovering, a sudden movement among the shadows of the houses caught his eye, and he turned to see the outline of a large animal dart swiftly across the open space behind him, and land with a flying leap upon the top of the wall a little lower down. It ran like the wind to his feet and then rose up beside him upon the ramparts. A shiver seemed to run through the moonlight, and his sight trembled for a second. His heart pulsed fearfully. Ilsé stood beside him, peering into his face.

Some dark substance, he saw, stained the girl's face and skin, shining in the moonlight as she stretched her hands towards him; she was dressed in wretched tattered garments that yet became her mightily; rue and vervain twined about her temples; her eyes glittered with unholy light. He only just controlled the wild impulse to take her in his arms and leap with her from their giddy perch into the valley below.

"See!" she cried, pointing with an arm on which the rags fluttered in the rising wind towards the forest aglow in the distance. "See where they await us! The woods are alive! Already the Great Ones are there, and the dance will soon begin! The salve is here! Anoint yourself and come!"

Though a moment before the sky was clear and cloudless, yet even while she spoke the face of the moon grew dark and the wind began to toss in the crests of the plane trees at his feet. Stray gusts brought the sounds of hoarse singing and crying from the lower slopes of the hill, and the pungent odor he had already noticed about the courtyard of the inn rose about him in the air.

"Transform, transform!" she cried again, her voice rising like a song. "Rub well your skin before you fly. Come! Come with me to the Sabbath, to the madness of its furious delight, to the sweet abandonment of its evil worship! See! the Great Ones are there, and the terrible Sacraments prepared. The Throne is occupied. Anoint and come! Anoint and come!"

She grew to the height of a tree beside him, leaping upon the wall with flaming eyes and hair strewn upon the night. He too began to change swiftly. Her hands touched the skin of his face and neck, streaking him with the burning salve that sent the old magic into his blood with the power before which fades all that is good.

A wild roar came up to his ears from the heart of the wood, and the girl, when she heard it, leaped upon the wall in the frenzy of her wicked joy.

"Satan is there!" she screamed, rushing upon him and striving to draw him with her to the edge of the wall. "Satan has come. The Sacraments call us! Come, with your dear apostate soul, and we will worship and dance till the moon dies and the world is forgotten!"

Just saving himself from the dreadful plunge, Vezin struggled to release himself from her grasp, while the passion tore at his reins and all but mastered him. He shrieked aloud, not knowing what he said, and then he shrieked again. It was the old impulses, the old awful habits instinctively finding voice; for though it seemed to him that he merely shrieked nonsense, the words he uttered really had meaning in them, and were intelligible. It was the ancient call. And it was heard below. It was answered.

The wind whistled at the skirts of his coat as the air round him darkened with many flying forms crowding upwards out of the valley. The crying of hoarse voices smote upon his ears, coming closer. Strokes of wind buffeted him, tearing him this way and that along the crumbling top of the stone wall; and Ilsé clung to him with her long shining arms, smooth and bare, holding him fast about the neck. But not Ilsé alone, for a dozen of them surrounded him, dropping out of the air. The pungent odor of the anointed bodies stifled him, exciting him to the old madness of the Sabbath, the dance of the witches and sorcerers doing honor to the personified Evil of the world.

"Anoint and away! Anoint and away!" they cried in wild chorus about him. "To the Dance that never dies! To the sweet and fearful fantasy of evil!"

Another moment and he would have yielded and gone, for his will turned soft and the flood of passionate memory all but overwhelmed him, when—so can a small thing after the whole course of an adventure—he caught his foot upon a loose stone in the edge of the wall, and then fell with a sudden crash on to the ground below. But he fell towards the houses, in the open space of dust and cobblestones, and fortunately not into the gaping depth of the valley on the farther side.

And they, too, came in a tumbling heap about him, like flies upon a piece of food, but as they fell he was released for a moment from the power of their touch, and in that brief instant of freedom there flashed into his mind the sudden intuition that saved him. Before he could regain his feet he saw them scrabbling awkwardly back upon the wall, as though bat-like they could only fly by dropping from a height, and had no hold upon him in the open. Then, seeing them perched there in a row like cats upon a roof, all dark and singularly shapeless, their eyes like lamps, the sudden memory came back to him of Ilsé's terror at the sight of fire.

Quick as a flash he found his matches and lit the dead leaves that lay under the wall.

Dry and withered, they caught fire at once, and the wind carried the flame in a long line down the length of the wall, licking upwards as it ran; and with shrieks and wailings, the crowded row of forms upon the top melted away into the air on the other side, and were gone with a great rush and whirring of their bodies down into the heart of the haunted valley, leaving Vezin breathless and shaken in the middle of the deserted ground.

"Ilsé!" he called feebly; "Ilsé!" for his heart ached to think that she was really gone to the great Dance without him, and that he had lost the opportunity of its fearful joy. Yet at the same time his relief was so great, and he was so dazed and troubled in mind with the whole thing, that he hardly knew what he was saying, and only cried aloud in the fierce storm of his emotion. . . .

The fire under the wall ran its course, and the moonlight came out again, soft and clear, from its temporary eclipse. With one last shuddering look at the ruined ramparts, and a feeling of horrid wonder for the haunted valley beyond, where the shapes still crowded and flew, he turned his face towards the town and slowly made his way in the direction of the hotel.

And as he went, a great wailing of cries, and a sound of howling, followed him from the gleaming forest below, growing fainter and fainter with the bursts of wind as he disappeared between the houses.

VI

"It may seem rather abrupt to you, this sudden tame ending," said Arthur Vezin, glancing with flushed face and timid eyes at Dr. Silence sitting there with his notebook, "but the fact is—er—from that moment my memory seems to have failed rather. I have no distinct recollection of how I got home or what precisely I did.

"It appears I never went back to the inn at all. I only dimly recollect racing down a long white road in the moonlight, past woods and villages, still and deserted, and then the dawn came up, and I saw the towers of a biggish town and so came to a station.

"But, long before that, I remember pausing somewhere on the road and looking back to where the hill-town of my adventure stood up in the moonlight, and thinking how exactly like a great monstrous cat it lay there upon the plain, its huge front paws lying down the two main streets, and the twin and broken towers of the cathedral marking its torn ears against the sky. That picture stays in my mind with the utmost vividness to this day.

"Another thing remains in my mind from that escape—namely, the sudden sharp reminder that I had not paid my bill, and the decision I made, standing there on the dusty highroad, that the small baggage I had left behind would more than settle for my indebtedness.

"For the rest, I can only tell you that I got coffee and bread at a café on the outskirts of this town I had come to, and soon after found my way to the station and caught a train later in the day. That same evening I reached London."

"And how long altogether," asked John Silence quietly, "do you think you stayed in the town of the adventure?"

Vezin looked up sheepishly.

"I was coming to that," he resumed, with apologetic wrigglings of his body. "In London I found that I was a whole week out in my reckoning of time. I had stayed over a week in the town, and it ought to have been September 15th,—instead of which it was only September 10th!"

"So that, in reality, you had only stayed a night or two in the inn?" queried the doctor.

Vezin hesitated before replying. He shuffled upon the mat.

"I must have gained time somewhere," he said at length—"somewhere or somehow. I certainly had a week to my credit. I can't explain it. I can only give you the fact."

"And this happened to you last year, since when you have never been back to the place?"

"Last autumn, yes," murmured Vezin; "and I have never dared to go back. I think I never want to."

"And, tell me," asked Dr. Silence at length, when he saw that the little man had evidently come to the end of his words and had nothing more to say, "had you ever read up the subject of the old witchcraft practices during the Middle Ages, or been at all interested in the subject?"

"Never!" declared Vezin emphatically. "I had never given a thought to such matters so far as I know—"

"Or to the question of reincarnation, perhaps?"

"Never—before my adventure; but I have since," he replied significantly.

There was, however, something still on the man's mind that he wished to relieve himself of by confession, yet could only with difficulty bring himself to mention; and it was only after the sympathetic tactfulness of the doctor had provided numerous openings that he at length availed himself of one of them, and stammered that he would like to show him the marks he still had on his neck where, he said, the girl had touched him with her anointed hands.

He took off his collar after infinite fumbling hesitation, and lowered his shirt a little for the doctor to see. And there, on the surface of the skin, lay a faint reddish line across the shoulder and extending a little way down the back towards the spine. It certainly indicated exactly the position an arm might have taken in the act of embracing. And on the other side of the neck, slightly higher up, was a similar mark, though not quite so clearly defined.

"That was where she held me that night on the ramparts," he whispered, a strange light coming and going in his eyes.

It was some weeks later when I again found occasion to consult John Silence concerning another extraordinary case that had come under my notice, and we fell to discussing Vezin's story. Since hearing it, the doctor had made investigations on his own account, and one of his secretaries had discovered that Vezin's ancestors had actually lived for generations in the very town where the adventure came to him. Two of them, both women, had been tried and convicted as witches, and had been burned alive at the stake. Moreover, it had not been difficult to prove that the very inn where Vezin stayed was built about 1700 upon the spot where the funeral pyres stood and the executions took place. The town was a sort of headquarters for all the sorcerers and witches of the entire region, and after conviction they were burnt there literally by scores.

"It seems strange," continued the doctor, "that Vezin should have remained ignorant of all this; but, on the other hand, it was not the kind of history that successive generations would have been anxious to keep alive, or to repeat to their children. Therefore I am inclined to think he still knows nothing about it.

"The whole adventure seems to have been a very vivid revival of the memories of an earlier life, caused by coming directly into contact with the living forces still intense enough to hang about the place, and, by a most singular chance, too, with the very souls who had taken part with him in the events of that particular life. For the mother and daughter who impressed him so strangely must have been leading actors, with himself, in the scenes and practices of witchcraft which at that period dominated the imaginations of the whole country.

"One has only to read the histories of the times to know that these witches claimed the power of transforming themselves into various animals, both for the purposes of disguise and also to convey themselves swiftly to the scenes of their imaginary orgies. Lycanthropy, or the power to change themselves into wolves, was everywhere believed in, and the ability to transform themselves into cats by rubbing their bodies with a special salve or ointment provided by Satan himself, found equal credence. The witchcraft trials abound in evidences of such universal beliefs."

Dr. Silence quoted chapter and verse from many writers on the subject, and showed how every detail of Vezin's adventure had a basis in the practices of those dark days.

"But that the entire affair took place subjectively in the man's own consciousness, I have no doubt," he went on, in reply to my questions; "for my secretary who has been to the town to investigate, discovered his signature in the visitors' book, and proved by it that he had arrived on September 8th, and left suddenly without paying his bill. He left two days later, and they still were in possession of his dirty brown bag and some tourist clothes. I paid a few francs in settlement of his debt, and have sent his luggage on to him. The daughter was absent from home, but the proprietress, a large woman very much as he described her, told my secretary that he had seemed a very strange, absent-minded kind of gentleman, and after his disappearance she had feared for a long time that he had met with a violent end in the neighbouring forest where he used to roam about alone.

"I should like to have obtained a personal interview with the daughter so as to ascertain how much was subjective and how much actually took place with her as Vezin told it. For her dread of fire and the sight of burning must, of course, have been the intuitive memory of her former painful death at the stake, and have thus explained why he fancied more than once that he saw her through smoke and flame."

"And that mark on his skin, for instance?" I inquired.

"Merely the marks produced by hysterical brooding," he replied, "like the stigmata of the *religieuses*, and the bruises which appear on the bodies of hypnotised subjects who have been told to expect them. This is very common and easily explained. Only it seems curious that these marks should have remained so long in Vezin's case. Usually they disappear quickly."

"Obviously he is still thinking about it all, brooding, and living it all over again," I ventured.

"Probably. And this makes me fear that the end of his trouble is not yet. We shall hear of him again. It is a case, alas! I can do little to alleviate."

Dr. Silence spoke gravely and with sadness in his voice.

"And what do you make of the Frenchman in the train?" I asked further—"the man who warned him against the place, *à cause du sommeil et à cause des chats*? Surely a very singular incident?"

"A very singular incident indeed," he made answer slowly, "and one I can only explain on the basis of a highly improbable coincidence—"

"Namely?"

"That the man was one who had himself stayed in the town and undergone there a similar experience. I should like to find this man and ask him. But the crystal is useless here, for I have no slightest clue to go upon, and I can only conclude that some singular psychic affinity, some force still active in his being out of the same past life, drew him thus to the personality of Vezin, and enabled him to fear what might happen to him, and thus to warn him as he did.

"Yes," he presently continued, half talking to himself, "I suspect in this case that Vezin was swept into the vortex of forces arising out of the intense activities of a past life, and that he lived over again a scene in which he had often played a leading part centuries before. For strong actions set up forces that are so slow to exhaust themselves, they may be said in a sense never to die. In this case they were not vital enough to render the illusion complete, so that the little man found himself caught in a very distressing confusion of the present and the past; yet he was sufficiently sensitive to recognise that it was true, and to fight against the degradation of returning, even in memory, to a former and lower state of development.

"Ah yes!" he continued, crossing the floor to gaze at the darkening sky, and seemingly quite oblivious of my presence, "subliminal up-rushes of memory like this can be exceedingly painful, and sometimes exceedingly dangerous. I only trust that this gentle soul may soon escape from this obsession of a passionate and tempestuous past. But I doubt it, I doubt it."

His voice was hushed with sadness as he spoke, and when he turned back into the room again there was an expression of profound yearning upon his face, the yearning of a soul whose desire to help is sometimes greater than his power.

The Wendigo

I

A considerable number of hunting parties were out that year without finding so much as a fresh trail; for the moose were uncommonly shy, and the various Nimrods returned to the bosoms of their respective families with the best excuses the facts of their imaginations could suggest. Dr. Cathcart, among others, came back without a trophy; but he brought instead the memory of an experience which he declares was worth all the bull moose that had ever been shot. But then Cathcart, of Aberdeen, was interested in other things besides moose—amongst them the vagaries of the human mind. This particular story, however, found no mention in his book on *Collective Hallucination* for the simple reason (so he confided once to a fellow colleague) that he himself played too intimate a part in it to form a competent judgment of the affair as a whole. . . .

Besides himself and his guide, Hank Davis, there was young Simpson, his nephew, a divinity student destined for the "Wee Kirk" (then on his first visit to Canadian backwoods), and the latter's guide, Défago. Joseph Défago was a French "Canuck," who had strayed from his native Province of Quebec years before, and had got caught in Rat Portage when the Canadian Pacific Railway was a-building; a man who, in addition to his unparalleled knowledge of wood-craft and bush-lore, could also sing the old *voyageur* songs and tell a capital hunting yarn into the bargain. He was deeply susceptible, moreover, to that singular spell which the wilderness lays upon certain lonely natures, and he loved the wild solitudes with a kind of romantic passion that amounted almost to an obsession. The life of the backwoods fascinated him—whence, doubtless, his surpassing efficiency in dealing with their mysteries.

On this particular expedition he was Hank's choice. Hank knew him and swore by him. He also swore at him, "jest as a pal might," and since he had a vocabulary of picturesque, if utterly meaningless, oaths, the conversation between the two stalwart and hardy woodsmen was often of a rather lively description. This river of expletives, however, Hank agreed to dam a little out of respect for his old "hunting boss," Dr. Cathcart, whom of course he addressed after the fashion of the country as "Doc," and also because he understood that young Simpson was already a "bit of a parson." He had, however, one objection to Défago, and one only—which was, that the French Canadian sometimes exhibited what Hank described as "the output of a cursed and dismal mind," meaning apparently that he sometimes was true to type, Latin type, and suffered fits of a kind of silent moroseness when nothing could induce him to utter speech. Défago, that is to say, was imaginative and melancholy. And, as a rule, it was too long a spell of "civilization" that induced the attacks, for a few days of the wilderness invariably cured them.

This, then, was the party of four that found themselves in camp the last week in October of that "shy moose year" 'way up in the wilderness north of Rat Portage—a forsaken and desolate country. There was also Punk, an Indian, who had accompanied Dr. Cathcart and Hank on their hunting trips in previous years, and who acted as cook. His duty was merely to stay in camp, catch fish, and prepare venison steaks and coffee at a few minutes' notice. He dressed in the worn-out clothes bequeathed to him by former patrons, and, except for his coarse black hair and dark skin, he looked in these city garments no more like a real redskin than a stage Negro looks like a real African.

For all that, however, Punk had in him still the instincts of his dying race; his taciturn silence and his endurance survived; also his superstition.

The party round the blazing fire that night were despondent, for a week had passed without a single sign of recent moose discovering itself. Défago had sung his song and plunged into a story, but Hank, in bad humor, reminded him so often that "he kep' mussing-up the fac's so, that it was 'most all nothin' but a petred-out lie," that the Frenchman had finally subsided into a sulky silence which nothing seemed likely to break. Dr. Cathcart and his nephew were fairly done after an exhausting day. Punk was washing up the dishes, grunting to himself under the lean-to of branches, where he later also slept. No one troubled to stir the slowly dying fire. Overhead the stars were brilliant in a sky quite wintry, and there was so little wind that ice was already forming stealthily along the shores of the still lake behind them. The silence of the vast listening forest stole forward and enveloped them.

Hank broke in suddenly with his nasal voice.

"I'm in favor of breaking new ground tomorrow, Doc," he observed with energy, looking across at his employer. "We don't stand a dead Dago's chance around here."

"Agreed," said Cathcart, always a man of few words. "Think the idea's good."

"Sure pop, it's good," Hank resumed with confidence. "S'pose, now, you and I strike west, up Garden Lake way for a change! None of us ain't touched that quiet bit o' land yet—"

"I'm with you."

"And you, Défago, take Mr. Simpson along in the small canoe, skip across the lake, portage over into Fifty Island Water, and take a good squint down that thar southern shore. The moose 'yarded' there like hell last year, and for all we know they may be doin' it agin this year jest to spite us."

Défago, keeping his eyes on the fire, said nothing by way of reply. He was still offended, possibly, about his interrupted story.

"No one's been up that way this year, an' I'll lay my bottom dollar on *that*!" Hank added with emphasis, as though he had a reason for knowing. He looked over at his partner sharply. "Better take the little silk tent and stay away a couple o' nights," he concluded, as though the matter were definitely settled. For Hank was recognized as general organizer of the hunt, and in charge of the party.

It was obvious to anyone that Défago did not jump at the plan, but his silence seemed to convey something more than ordinary disapproval, and across his sensitive dark face there passed a curious expression like a flash of firelight—not so quickly, however, that the three men had not time to catch it.

"He funked for some reason, *I* thought," Simpson said afterwards in the tent he shared with his uncle. Dr. Cathcart made no immediate reply, although the look had interested him enough at the time for him to make a mental note of it. The expression had caused him a passing uneasiness he could not quite account for at the moment.

But Hank, of course, had been the first to notice it, and the odd thing was that instead of becoming explosive or angry over the other's reluctance, he at once began to humor him a bit.

"But there ain't no *speshul* reason why no one's been up there this year," he said with a perceptible hush in his tone; "not the reason *you* mean, anyway! Las' year it was the fires that kep' folks out, and this year I guess—I guess it jest happened so, that's all!" His manner was clearly meant to be encouraging.

Joseph Défago raised his eyes a moment, then dropped them again. A breath of wind stole out of the forest and stirred the embers into a passing blaze. Dr. Cathcart again noticed the expression in the guide's face, and again he did not like it. But this time the nature of the look betrayed itself. In those eyes, for an instant, he caught the gleam of a man scared in his very soul. It disquieted him more than he cared to admit.

"Bad Indians up that way?" he asked, with a laugh to ease matters a little, while Simpson, too sleepy to notice this subtle by-play, moved off to bed with a prodigious yawn; "or—or anything wrong with the country?" he added, when his nephew was out of hearing.

Hank met his eye with something less than his usual frankness.

"He's jest skeered," he replied good-humoredly. "Skeered stiff about some ole feery tale! That's all, ain't it, ole pard?" And he gave Défago a friendly kick on the moccasined foot that lay nearest the fire.

Défago looked up quickly, as from an interrupted reverie, a reverie, however, that had not prevented his seeing all that went on about him.

"Skeered—*nuthin'*!" he answered, with a flush of defiance. "There's nuthin' in the Bush that can skeer Joseph Défago, and don't you forget it!" And the natural energy with which he spoke made it impossible to know whether he told the whole truth or only a part of it.

Hank turned towards the doctor. He was just going to add something when he stopped abruptly and looked round. A sound close behind them in the darkness made all three start. It was old Punk, who had moved up from his lean-to while they talked and now stood there just beyond the circle of firelight—listening.

"'Nother time, Doc!" Hank whispered, with a wink, "when the gallery ain't stepped down into the stalls!" And, springing to his feet, he slapped the Indian on the back and cried noisily, "Come up t' the fire an' warm yer dirty red skin a bit." He dragged him towards the blaze and threw more wood on. "That was a mighty good feed you give us an hour or two back," he continued heartily, as though to set the man's thoughts on another scent, "and it ain't Christian to let you stand out there freezin' yer ole soul to hell while we're gettin' all good an' toasted!" Punk moved in and warmed his feet, smiling darkly at the other's volubility which he only half understood, but saying nothing. And presently Dr. Cathcart, seeing that further conversation was impossible, followed his nephew's example and moved off to the tent, leaving the three men smoking over the now blazing fire.

It is not easy to undress in a small tent without waking one's companion, and Cathcart, hardened and warm-blooded as he was in spite of his fifty odd years, did what Hank would have described as "considerable of his twilight" in the open. He noticed, during the process, that Punk had meanwhile gone back to his lean-to, and that Hank and Défago were at it hammer and tongs, or, rather, hammer and anvil, the little French Canadian being the anvil. It was all very like the conventional stage picture of Western melodrama: the fire lighting up their faces with patches of alternate red and black; Défago, in slouch hat and moccasins in the part of the "badlands" villain; Hank, open-faced and hatless, with that reckless fling of his shoulders, the honest and deceived hero; and old Punk, eavesdropping in the background, supplying the atmosphere of mystery. The doctor smiled as he noticed the details; but at the same time something deep within him—he hardly knew what—shrank a little, as though an almost imperceptible breath of warning had touched the surface of his soul and was gone again before he could seize it. Probably it was traceable to that "scared expression" he had seen in the eyes of Défago; "probably"—for this hint of fugitive emotion otherwise escaped his usually so keen analysis. Défago, he was vaguely aware, might cause trouble somehow . . . He was not as steady a guide as Hank, for instance . . . Further than that he could not get . . .

He watched the men a moment longer before diving into the stuffy tent where Simpson already slept soundly. Hank, he saw, was swearing like a mad African in a New York nigger saloon; but it was the swearing of "affection." The ridiculous oaths flew freely now that the cause of their obstruction was asleep. Presently he put his arm almost tenderly upon his comrade's shoulder, and they moved off together into the shadows where their tent stood faintly glimmering. Punk, too, a moment later followed their example and disappeared between his odorous blankets in the opposite direction.

Dr. Cathcart then likewise turned in, weariness and sleep still fighting in his mind with an obscure curiosity to know what it was that had scared Défago about the country up Fifty Island Water way,— wondering, too, why Punk's presence had prevented the completion of what Hank had to say. Then sleep overtook him. He would know tomorrow. Hank would tell him the story while they trudged after the elusive moose.

Deep silence fell about the little camp, planted there so audaciously in the jaws of the wilderness. The lake gleamed like a sheet of black glass beneath the stars. The cold air pricked. In the draughts of night that poured their silent tide from the depths of the forest, with messages from distant ridges and from lakes just beginning to freeze, there lay already the faint, bleak odors of coming winter. White men, with their dull scent, might never have divined them; the fragrance of the wood fire would have concealed from them these almost electrical hints of moss and bark and hardening swamp a hundred miles away. Even Hank and Défago, subtly in league with the soul of the woods as they were, would probably have spread their delicate nostrils in vain. . .

But an hour later, when all slept like the dead, old Punk crept from his blankets and went down to the shore of the lake like a shadow— silently, as only Indian blood can move. He raised his head and looked about him. The thick darkness rendered sight of small avail, but, like the animals, he possessed other senses that darkness could not mute. He listened—then sniffed the air. Motionless as a hemlock stem he stood there. After five minutes again he lifted his head and sniffed, and yet once again. A tingling of the wonderful nerves that betrayed itself by no outer sign, ran through him as he tasted the keen air. Then, merging his figure into the surrounding blackness in a way that only wild men and animals understand, he turned, still moving like a shadow, and went stealthily back to his lean-to and his bed.

And soon after he slept, the change of wind he had divined stirred gently the reflection of the stars within the lake. Rising among the far ridges of the country beyond Fifty Island Water, it came from the direction in which he had stared, and it passed over the sleeping camp with a faint and sighing murmur through the tops of the big trees that was almost too delicate to be audible. With it, down the desert paths of night, though too faint, too high even for the Indian's hair-like nerves, there passed a curious, thin odor, strangely disquieting, an odor of something that seemed unfamiliar—utterly unknown.

The French Canadian and the man of Indian blood each stirred uneasily in his sleep just about this time, though neither of them woke. Then the ghost of that unforgettably strange odor passed away and was lost among the leagues of tenantless forest beyond.

II

In the morning the camp was astir before the sun. There had been a light fall of snow during the night and the air was sharp. Punk had done his duty betimes, for the odors of coffee and fried bacon reached every tent. All were in good spirits.

"Wind's shifted!" cried Hank vigorously, watching Simpson and his guide already loading the small canoe. "It's across the lake—dead right for you fellers. And the snow'll make bully trails! If there's any moose mussing around up thar, they'll not get so much as a tail-end scent of you with the wind as it is. Good luck, Monsieur Défago!" he added, facetiously giving the name its French pronunciation for once, "*bonne chance!*"

Défago returned the good wishes, apparently in the best of spirits, the silent mood gone. Before eight o'clock old Punk had the camp to himself, Cathcart and Hank were far along the trail that led westwards, while the canoe that carried Défago and Simpson, with silk tent and grub for two days, was already a dark speck bobbing on the bosom of the lake, going due east.

The wintry sharpness of the air was tempered now by a sun that topped the wooded ridges and blazed with a luxurious warmth upon the world of lake and forest below; loons flew skimming through the sparkling spray that the wind lifted; divers shook their dripping heads to the sun and popped smartly out of sight again; and as far as eye could reach rose the leagues of endless, crowding Bush, desolate in its lonely sweep and grandeur, un-trodden by foot of man, and stretching its mighty and unbroken carpet right up to the frozen shores of Hudson Bay.

Simpson, who saw it all for the first time as he paddled hard in the bows of the dancing canoe, was enchanted by its austere beauty. His heart drank in the sense of freedom and great spaces just as his lungs drank in the cool and perfumed wind. Behind him in the stern seat, singing fragments of his native chanties, Défago steered the craft of birch bark like a thing of life, answering cheerfully all his companion's questions. Both were gay and light-hearted. On such occasions men lose the superficial, worldly distinctions; they become human beings working together for a common end. Simpson, the employer, and Défago the employed, among these primitive forces, were simply—two men, the "guider" and the "guided." Superior knowledge, of course, assumed control, and the younger man fell without a second thought into the quasi-subordinate position. He never dreamed of objecting when Défago dropped the "Mr.," and addressed him as "Say, Simpson," or "Simpson, boss," which was invariably the case before they reached the farther shore after a stiff paddle of twelve miles against a head wind. He only laughed, and liked it; then ceased to notice it at all.

For this "divinity student" was a young man of parts and character, though as yet, of course, untraveled; and on this trip—the first time he had seen any country but his own and little Switzerland—the huge scale of things somewhat bewildered him. It was one thing, he realized, to hear about primeval forests, but quite another to see them. While to dwell in them and seek acquaintance with their wild life was, again, an initiation that no intelligent man could undergo without a certain shifting of personal values hitherto held for permanent and sacred.

Simpson knew the first faint indication of this emotion when he held the new .303 rifle in his hands and looked along its pair of faultless, gleaming barrels. The three days' journey to their headquarters, by lake and portage, had carried the process a stage farther. And now that he was about to plunge beyond even the fringe of wilderness where they were camped into the virgin heart of uninhabited regions as vast as Europe itself, the true nature of the situation stole upon him with an effect of delight and awe that his imagination was fully capable of appreciating. It was himself and Défago against a multitude—at least, against a Titan!

The bleak splendors of these remote and lonely forests rather overwhelmed him with the sense of his own littleness. That stern quality of the tangled backwoods which can only be described as merciless and terrible, rose out of these far blue woods swimming upon the horizon, and revealed itself. He understood the silent warning. He realized his own utter helplessness. Only Défago, as a symbol of a distant civilization where man was master, stood between him and a pitiless death by exhaustion and starvation.

It was thrilling to him, therefore, to watch Défago turn over the canoe upon the shore, pack the paddles carefully underneath, and then proceed to "blaze" the spruce stems for some distance on either side of an almost invisible trail, with the careless remark thrown in, "Say, Simpson, if anything happens to me, you'll find the canoe all correc' by these marks;—then strike doo west into the sun to hit the home camp agin, see?"

It was the most natural thing in the world to say, and he said it without any noticeable inflexion of the voice, only it happened to express the youth's emotions at the moment with an utterance that was symbolic of the situation and of his own helplessness as a factor in it. He was alone with Défago in a primitive world: that was all. The canoe, another symbol of man's ascendancy, was now to be left behind. Those small yellow patches, made on the trees by the axe, were the only indications of its hiding place.

Meanwhile, shouldering the packs between them, each man carrying his own rifle, they followed the slender trail over rocks and fallen trunks and across half-frozen swamps; skirting numerous lakes that fairly gemmed the forest, their borders fringed with mist; and towards five o'clock found themselves suddenly on the edge of the woods, looking out across a large sheet of water in front of them, dotted with pine-clad islands of all describable shapes and sizes.

"Fifty Island Water," announced Défago wearily, "and the sun jest goin' to dip his bald old head into it!" he added, with unconscious poetry; and immediately they set about pitching camp for the night.

In a very few minutes, under those skilful hands that never made a movement too much or a movement too little, the silk tent stood taut and cozy, the beds of balsam boughs ready laid, and a brisk cooking fire burned with the minimum of smoke. While the young Scotchman cleaned the fish they had caught trolling behind the canoe, Défago "guessed" he would "jest as soon" take a turn through the Bush for indications of moose. "*May* come across a trunk where they bin and rubbed horns," he said, as he moved off, "or feedin' on the last of the maple leaves"—and he was gone.

His small figure melted away like a shadow in the dusk, while Simpson noted with a kind of admiration how easily the forest absorbed him into herself. A few steps, it seemed, and he was no longer visible.

Yet there was little underbrush hereabouts; the trees stood somewhat apart, well spaced; and in the clearings grew silver birch and maple, spear-like and slender, against the immense stems of spruce and hemlock. But for occasional prostrate monsters, and the boulders of grey rock that thrust uncouth shoulders here and there out of the ground, it might well have been a bit of park in the Old Country. Almost, one might have seen in it the hand of man. A little to the right, however, began the great burnt section, miles in extent, proclaiming its real character—*brulé*, as it is called, where the fires of the previous year had raged for weeks, and the blackened stumps now rose gaunt and ugly, bereft of branches, like gigantic match heads stuck into the ground, savage and desolate beyond words. The perfume of charcoal and rain-soaked ashes still hung faintly about it.

The dusk rapidly deepened; the glades grew dark; the crackling of the fire and the wash of little waves along the rocky lake shore were the only sounds audible. The wind had dropped with the sun, and in all that vast world of branches nothing stirred. Any moment, it seemed, the woodland gods, who are to be worshipped in silence and loneliness, might stretch their mighty and terrific outlines among the trees. In front, through doorways pillared by huge straight stems, lay the stretch of Fifty Island Water, a crescent-shaped lake some fifteen miles from tip to tip, and perhaps five miles across where they were camped. A sky of rose and saffron, more clear than any atmosphere Simpson had ever known, still dropped its pale streaming fires across the waves, where the islands—a hundred, surely, rather than fifty—floated like the fairy barques of some enchanted fleet. Fringed with pines, whose crests fingered most delicately the sky, they almost seemed to move upwards as the light faded—about to weigh anchor and navigate the pathways of the heavens instead of the currents of their native and desolate lake.

And strips of colored cloud, like flaunting pennons, signaled their departure to the stars. . . .

The beauty of the scene was strangely uplifting. Simpson smoked the fish and burnt his fingers into the bargain in his efforts to enjoy it and at the same time tend the frying pan and the fire. Yet, ever at the back of his thoughts, lay that other aspect of the wilderness: the indifference to human life, the merciless spirit of desolation which took no note of man. The sense of his utter loneliness, now that even Défago had gone, came close as he looked about him and listened for the sound of his companion's returning footsteps.

There was pleasure in the sensation, yet with it a perfectly comprehensible alarm. And instinctively the thought stirred in him: "What should I—*could* I, do—if anything happened and he did not come back—?"

They enjoyed their well-earned supper, eating untold quantities of fish, and drinking un-milked tea strong enough to kill men who had not covered thirty miles of hard "going," eating little on the way. And when it was over, they smoked and told stories round the blazing fire, laughing, stretching weary limbs, and discussing plans for the morrow. Défago was in excellent spirits, though disappointed at having no signs of moose to report. But it was dark and he had not gone far. The *brulé*, too, was bad. His clothes and hands were smeared with charcoal. Simpson, watching him, realized with renewed vividness their position—alone together in the wilderness.

"Défago," he said presently, "these woods, you know, are a bit too big to feel quite at home in—to feel comfortable in, I mean! . . . Eh?" He merely gave expression to the mood of the moment; he was hardly prepared for the earnestness, the solemnity even, with which the guide took him up.

"You've hit it right, Simpson, boss," he replied, fixing his searching brown eyes on his face, "and that's the truth, sure. There's no end to 'em—no end at all." Then he added in a lowered tone as if to himself, "There's lots found out *that*, and gone plumb to pieces!"

But the man's gravity of manner was not quite to the other's liking; it was a little too suggestive for this scenery and setting; he was sorry he had broached the subject. He remembered suddenly how his uncle had told him that men were sometimes stricken with a strange fever of the wilderness, when the seduction of the uninhabited wastes caught them so fiercely that they went forth, half fascinated, half deluded, to their death. And he had a shrewd idea that his companion held something in sympathy with that queer type. He led the conversation on to other topics, on to Hank and the doctor, for instance, and the natural rivalry as to who should get the first sight of moose.

"If they went doo west," observed Défago carelessly, "there's sixty miles between us now—with ole Punk at halfway house eatin' himself full to bustin' with fish and coffee." They laughed together over the picture. But the casual mention of those sixty miles again made Simpson realize the prodigious scale of this land where they hunted; sixty miles was a mere step; two hundred little more than a step. Stories of lost hunters rose persistently before his memory. The passion and mystery of homeless and wandering men, seduced by the beauty of great forests, swept his soul in a way too vivid to be quite pleasant. He wondered vaguely whether it was the mood of his companion that invited the unwelcome suggestion with such persistence.

"Sing us a song, Défago, if you're not too tired," he asked; "one of those old *voyageur* songs you sang the other night." He handed his tobacco pouch to the guide and then filled his own pipe, while the Canadian, nothing loth, sent his light voice across the lake in one of those plaintive, almost melancholy chanties with which lumbermen and trappers lessen the burden of their labor. There was an appealing and romantic flavor about it, something that recalled the atmosphere of the old pioneer days when Indians and wilderness were leagued together, battles frequent, and the Old Country farther off than it is today. The sound traveled pleasantly over the water, but the forest at their backs seemed to swallow it down with a single gulp that permitted neither echo nor resonance.

It was in the middle of the third verse that Simpson noticed something unusual—something that brought his thoughts back with a rush from faraway scenes. A curious change had come into the man's voice. Even before he knew what it was, uneasiness caught him, and looking up quickly, he saw that Défago, though still singing, was peering about him into the Bush, as though he heard or saw something. His voice grew fainter—dropped to a hush—then ceased altogether. The same instant, with a movement amazingly alert, he started to his feet and stood upright—*sniffing the air*. Like a dog scenting game, he drew the air into his nostrils in short, sharp breaths, turning quickly as he did so in all directions, and finally "pointing" down the lake shore, eastwards. It was a performance unpleasantly suggestive and at the same time singularly dramatic. Simpson's heart fluttered disagreeably as he watched it.

"Lord, man! How you made me jump!" he exclaimed, on his feet beside him the same instant, and peering over his shoulder into the sea of darkness. "What's up? Are you frightened—?"

Even before the question was out of his mouth he knew it was foolish, for any man with a pair of eyes in his head could see that the Canadian had turned white down to his very gills. Not even sunburn and the glare of the fire could hide that.

The student felt himself trembling a little, weakish in the knees. "What's up?" he repeated quickly. "D'you smell moose? Or anything queer, anything—wrong?" He lowered his voice instinctively.

The forest pressed round them with its encircling wall; the nearer tree stems gleamed like bronze in the firelight; beyond that—blackness, and, so far as he could tell, a silence of death. Just behind them a passing puff of wind lifted a single leaf, looked at it, then laid it softly down again without disturbing the rest of the covey. It seemed as if a million invisible causes had combined just to produce that single visible effect. *Other* life pulsed about them—and was gone.

Défago turned abruptly; the livid hue of his face had turned to a dirty grey.

"I never said I heered—or smelt—nuthin'," he said slowly and emphatically, in an oddly altered voice that conveyed somehow a touch of defiance. "I was only—takin' a look round—so to speak. It's always a mistake to be too previous with yer questions." Then he added suddenly with obvious effort, in his more natural voice, "Have you got the matches, Boss Simpson?" and proceeded to light the pipe he had half filled just before he began to sing.

Without speaking another word they sat down again by the fire. Défago changing his side so that he could face the direction the wind came from. For even a tenderfoot could tell that. Défago changed his position in order to hear and smell—all there was to be heard and smelt. And, since he now faced the lake with his back to the trees it was evidently nothing in the forest that had sent so strange and sudden a warning to his marvelously trained nerves.

"Guess now I don't feel like singing any," he explained presently of his own accord. "That song kinder brings back memories that's troublesome to me; I never oughter've begun it. It sets me on t' imagining things, see?"

Clearly the man was still fighting with some profoundly moving emotion. He wished to excuse himself in the eyes of the other. But the explanation, in that it was only a part of the truth, was a lie, and he knew perfectly well that Simpson was not deceived by it. For nothing could explain away the livid terror that had dropped over his face while he stood there sniffing the air. And nothing—no amount of blazing fire, or chatting on ordinary subjects—could make that camp exactly as it had been before. The shadow of an unknown horror, naked if unguessed, that had flashed for an instant in the face and gestures of the guide, had also communicated itself, vaguely and therefore more potently, to his companion. The guide's visible efforts to dissemble the truth only made things worse. Moreover, to add to the younger man's uneasiness, was the difficulty, nay, the impossibility he felt of asking questions, and also his complete ignorance as to the cause . . . Indians, wild animals, forest fires—all these, he knew, were wholly out of the question. His imagination searched vigorously, but in vain. . . .

Yet, somehow or other, after another long spell of smoking, talking and roasting themselves before the great fire, the shadow that had so suddenly invaded their peaceful camp began to lift. Perhaps Défago's efforts, or the return of his quiet and normal attitude accomplished this; perhaps Simpson himself had exaggerated the affair out of all proportion to the truth; or possibly the vigorous air of the wilderness brought its own powers of healing. Whatever the cause, the feeling of immediate horror seemed to have passed away as mysteriously as it had come, for nothing occurred to feed it. Simpson began to feel that he had permitted himself the unreasoning terror of a child. He put it down partly to a certain subconscious excitement that this wild and immense scenery generated in his blood, partly to the spell of solitude, and partly to over-fatigue. That pallor in the guide's face was, of course, uncommonly hard to explain, yet it *might* have been due in some way to an effect of firelight, or his own imagination . . . He gave it the benefit of the doubt; he was Scotch.

When a somewhat unordinary emotion has disappeared, the mind always finds a dozen ways of explaining away its causes . . . Simpson lit a last pipe and tried to laugh to himself. On getting home to Scotland it would make quite a good story. He did not realize that this laughter was a sign that terror still lurked in the recesses of his soul—that, in fact, it was merely one of the conventional signs by which a man, seriously alarmed, tries to persuade himself that he is *not* so.

Défago, however, heard that low laughter and looked up with surprise on his face. The two men stood, side by side, kicking the embers about before going to bed. It was ten o'clock—a late hour for hunters to be still awake.

"What's ticklin' yer?" he asked in his ordinary tone, yet gravely.

"I—I was thinking of our little toy woods at home, just at that moment," stammered Simpson, coming back to what really dominated his mind, and startled by the question, "and comparing them to—to all this," and he swept his arm round to indicate the Bush.

A pause followed in which neither of them said anything.

"All the same I wouldn't laugh about it, if I was you," Défago added, looking over Simpson's shoulder into the shadows. "There's places in there nobody won't never see into—nobody knows what lives in there either."

"Too big—too far off?" The suggestion in the guide's manner was immense and horrible.

Défago nodded. The expression on his face was dark. He, too, felt uneasy. The younger man understood that in a *hinterland* of this size there might well be depths of wood that would never in the life of the world be known or trodden. The thought was not exactly the sort he welcomed. In a loud voice, cheerfully, he suggested that it was time for bed. But the guide lingered, tinkering with the fire, arranging the stones needlessly, doing a dozen things that did not really need doing. Evidently there was something he wanted to say, yet found it difficult to "get at."

"Say, you, Boss Simpson," he began suddenly, as the last shower of sparks went up into the air, "you don't—smell nothing, do you—

nothing pertickler, I mean?" The commonplace question, Simpson realized, veiled a dreadfully serious thought in his mind. A shiver ran down his back.

"Nothing but burning wood," he replied firmly, kicking again at the embers. The sound of his own foot made him start.

"And all the evenin' you ain't smelt—nothing?" persisted the guide, peering at him through the gloom; "nothing extrordiny, and different to anything else you ever smelt before?"

"No, no, man; nothing at all!" he replied aggressively, half angrily.

Défago's face cleared. "That's good!" he exclaimed with evident relief. "That's good to hear."

"Have *you*?" asked Simpson sharply, and the same instant regretted the question.

The Canadian came closer in the darkness. He shook his head. "I guess not," he said, though without overwhelming conviction. "It must've been just that song of mine that did it. It's the song they sing in lumber camps and godforsaken places like that, when they've skeered the Wendigo's somewhere around, doin' a bit of swift travellin'—"

"And what's the Wendigo, pray?" Simpson asked quickly, irritated because again he could not prevent that sudden shiver of the nerves. He knew that he was close upon the man's terror and the cause of it. Yet a rushing passionate curiosity overcame his better judgment, *and* his fear.

Défago turned swiftly and looked at him as though he were suddenly about to shriek. His eyes shone, but his mouth was wide open. Yet all he said, or whispered rather, for his voice sank very low, was— "It's nuthin'—nuthin' but what those lousy fellers believe when they've bin hittin' the bottle too long—a sort of great animal that lives up yonder," he jerked his head northwards, "quick as lightning in its tracks, an' bigger'n anything else in the Bush, an' ain't supposed to be very good to look at—*that's all!*"

"A backwoods superstition—" began Simpson, moving hastily toward the tent in order to shake off the hand of the guide that clutched his arm. "Come, come, hurry up for God's sake, and get the lantern going! It's time we were in bed and asleep if we're going to be up with the sun tomorrow. . . ."

The guide was close on his heels. "I'm coming," he answered out of the darkness, "I'm coming." And after a slight delay he appeared with the lantern and hung it from a nail in the front pole of the tent. The shadows of a hundred trees shifted their places quickly as he did so, and when he stumbled over the rope, diving swiftly inside, the whole tent trembled as though a gust of wind struck it.

The two men lay down, without undressing, upon their beds of soft balsam boughs, cunningly arranged. Inside, all was warm and cozy, but outside the world of crowding trees pressed close about them, marshalling their million shadows, and smothering the little tent that stood there like a wee white shell facing the ocean of tremendous forest.

Between the two lonely figures within, however, there pressed another shadow that was *not* a shadow from the night. It was the Shadow cast by the strange Fear, never wholly exorcised, that had leaped suddenly upon Défago in the middle of his singing. And Simpson, as he lay there, watching the darkness through the open flap of the tent, ready to plunge into the fragrant abyss of sleep, knew first that unique and profound stillness of a primeval forest when no wind stirs . . . and when the night has weight and substance that enters into the soul to bind a veil about it. . . . Then sleep took him. . . .

III

Thus, it seemed to him, at least. Yet it was true that the lap of the water, just beyond the tent door, still beat time with his lessening pulses when he realized that he was lying with his eyes open and that another sound had recently introduced itself with cunning softness between the splash and murmur of the little waves.

And, long before he understood what this sound was, it had stirred in him the centers of pity and alarm. He listened intently, though at first in vain, for the running blood beat all its drums too noisily in his ears. Did it come, he wondered, from the lake, or from the woods? . . .

Then, suddenly, with a rush and a flutter of the heart, he knew that it was close beside him in the tent; and, when he turned over for a better hearing, it focused itself unmistakably not two feet away. It was a sound of weeping; Défago upon his bed of branches was sobbing in the darkness as though his heart would break, the blankets evidently stuffed against his mouth to stifle it.

And his first feeling, before he could think or reflect, was the rush of a poignant and searching tenderness. This intimate, human sound, heard amid the desolation about them, woke pity. It was so incongruous, so pitifully incongruous—and so vain! Tears—in this vast and cruel wilderness: of what avail? He thought of a little child crying in mid-Atlantic. . . . Then, of course, with fuller realization, and the memory of what had gone before, came the descent of the terror upon him, and his blood ran cold.

"Défago," he whispered quickly, "what's the matter?" He tried to make his voice very gentle. "Are you in pain—unhappy—?" There was no reply, but the sounds ceased abruptly. He stretched his hand out and touched him. The body did not stir.

"Are you awake?" for it occurred to him that the man was crying in his sleep. "Are you cold?" He noticed that his feet, which were uncovered, projected beyond the mouth of the tent. He spread an extra fold of his own blankets over them. The guide had slipped down in his bed, and the branches seemed to have been dragged with him. He was afraid to pull the body back again, for fear of waking him.

One or two tentative questions he ventured softly, but though he waited for several minutes there came no reply, nor any sign of movement. Presently he heard his regular and quiet breathing, and putting his hand again gently on the breast, felt the steady rise and fall beneath.

"Let me know if anything's wrong," he whispered, "or if I can do anything. Wake me at once if you feel—queer."

He hardly knew what to say. He lay down again, thinking and wondering what it all meant. Défago, of course, had been crying in his sleep. Some dream or other had afflicted him. Yet never in his life would he forget that pitiful sound of sobbing, and the feeling that the whole awful wilderness of woods listened. . . .

His own mind busied itself for a long time with the recent events, of which *this* took its mysterious place as one, and though his reason successfully argued away all unwelcome suggestions, a sensation of uneasiness remained, resisting ejection, very deep-seated—peculiar beyond ordinary.

IV

But sleep, in the long run, proves greater than all emotions. His thoughts soon wandered again; he lay there, warm as toast, exceedingly weary; the night soothed and comforted, blunting the edges of memory and alarm. Half an hour later he was oblivious of everything in the outer world about him.

Yet sleep, in this case, was his great enemy, concealing all approaches, smothering the warning of his nerves.

As, sometimes, in a nightmare events crowd upon each other's heels with a conviction of dreadfullest reality, yet some inconsistent detail accuses the whole display of incompleteness and disguise, so the events that now followed, though they actually happened, persuaded the mind somehow that the detail which could explain them had been overlooked in the confusion, and that therefore they were but partly true, the rest delusion. At the back of the sleeper's mind something remains awake, ready to let slip the judgment. "All this is not *quite* real; when you wake up you'll understand."

And thus, in a way, it was with Simpson. The events, not wholly inexplicable or incredible in themselves, yet remain for the man who saw and heard them a sequence of separate facts of cold horror, because the little piece that might have made the puzzle clear lay concealed or overlooked.

So far as he can recall, it was a violent movement, running downwards through the tent towards the door, that first woke him and made him aware that his companion was sitting bolt upright beside him—quivering. Hours must have passed, for it was the pale gleam of the dawn that revealed his outline against the canvas. This time the man was not crying; he was quaking like a leaf; the trembling he felt plainly through the blankets down the entire length of his own body. Défago had huddled down against him for protection, shrinking away from something that apparently concealed itself near the door flaps of the little tent.

Simpson thereupon called out in a loud voice some question or other—in the first bewilderment of waking he does not remember exactly what—and the man made no reply. The atmosphere and feeling of true nightmare lay horribly about him, making movement and speech both difficult. At first, indeed, he was not sure where he was—whether in one of the earlier camps, or at home in his bed at Aberdeen. The sense of confusion was very troubling.

And next—almost simultaneous with his waking, it seemed—the profound stillness of the dawn outside was shattered by a most uncommon sound. It came without warning, or audible approach; and it was unspeakably dreadful. It was a voice, Simpson declares, possibly a human voice; hoarse yet plaintive—a soft, roaring voice close outside the tent, overhead rather than upon the ground, of immense volume, while in some strange way most penetratingly and seductively sweet. It rang out, too, in three separate and distinct notes, or cries, that bore in some odd fashion a resemblance, farfetched yet recognizable, to the name of the guide: *"Dé—fa—go!"*

The student admits he is unable to describe it quite intelligently, for it was unlike any sound he had ever heard in his life, and combined a blending of such contrary qualities. "A sort of windy, crying voice," he calls it, "as of something lonely and untamed, wild and of abominable power. . . ."

And, even before it ceased, dropping back into the great gulfs of silence, the guide beside him had sprung to his feet with an answering though unintelligible cry. He blundered against the tent pole with violence, shaking the whole structure, spreading his arms out frantically for more room, and kicking his legs impetuously free of the clinging blankets. For a second, perhaps two, he stood upright by the door, his outline dark against the pallor of the dawn; then, with a furious, rushing speed, before his companion could move a hand to stop him, he shot with a plunge through the flaps of canvas—and was gone. And as he went—so astonishingly fast that the voice could actually be heard dying in the distance—he called aloud in tones of anguished terror that at the same time held something strangely like the frenzied exultation of delight—

"Oh! oh! My feet of fire! My burning feet of fire! Oh! oh! This height and fiery speed!"

And then the distance quickly buried it, and the deep silence of very early morning descended upon the forest as before.

It had all come about with such rapidity that, but for the evidence of the empty bed beside him, Simpson could almost have believed it to have been the memory of a nightmare carried over from sleep. He still felt the warm pressure of that vanished body against his side; there lay the twisted blankets in a heap; the very tent yet trembled with the vehemence of the impetuous departure. The strange words rang in his ears, as though he still heard them in the distance—wild language of a suddenly stricken mind. Moreover, it was not only the senses of sight and hearing that reported uncommon things to his brain, for even while the man cried and ran, he had become aware that a strange perfume, faint yet pungent, pervaded the interior of the tent. And it was at this point, it seems, brought to himself by the consciousness that his nostrils were taking this distressing odor down into his throat, that he found his courage, sprang quickly to his feet—and went out.

The grey light of dawn that dropped, cold and glimmering, between the trees revealed the scene tolerably well. There stood the tent behind him, soaked with dew; the dark ashes of the fire, still warm; the lake, white beneath a coating of mist, the islands rising darkly out of it like objects packed in wool; and patches of snow beyond among the clearer spaces of the Bush—everything cold, still, waiting for the sun. But nowhere a sign of the vanished guide—still, doubtless, flying at frantic speed through the frozen woods. There was not even the sound of disappearing footsteps, nor the echoes of the dying voice. He had gone—utterly.

There was nothing; nothing but the sense of his recent presence, so strongly left behind about the camp; *and*—this penetrating, all-pervading odor.

And even this was now rapidly disappearing in its turn. In spite of his exceeding mental perturbation, Simpson struggled hard to detect its nature, and define it, but the ascertaining of an elusive scent, not recognized subconsciously and at once, is a very subtle operation of the mind. And he failed. It was gone before he could properly seize or name it. Approximate description, even, seems to have been difficult, for it was unlike any smell he knew. Acrid rather, not unlike the odor of a lion, he thinks, yet softer and not wholly unpleasing, with something almost sweet in it that reminded him of the scent of decaying garden leaves, earth, and the myriad, nameless perfumes that make up the odor of a big forest. Yet the "odor of lions" is the phrase with which he usually sums it all up.

Then—it was wholly gone, and he found himself standing by the ashes of the fire in a state of amazement and stupid terror that left him the helpless prey of anything that chose to happen. Had a muskrat poked its pointed muzzle over a rock, or a squirrel scuttled in that instant down the bark of a tree, he would most likely have collapsed without more ado and fainted. For he felt about the whole affair the touch somewhere of a great Outer Horror . . . and his scattered powers had not as yet had time to collect themselves into a definite attitude of fighting self-control.

Nothing did happen, however. A great kiss of wind ran softly through the awakening forest, and a few maple leaves here and there rustled tremblingly to earth. The sky seemed to grow suddenly much lighter. Simpson felt the cool air upon his cheek and uncovered head; realized that he was shivering with the cold; and, making a great effort, realized next that he was alone in the Bush—*and* that he was called upon to take immediate steps to find and succor his vanished companion.

Make an effort, accordingly, he did, though an ill-calculated and futile one. With that wilderness of trees about him, the sheet of water cutting him off behind, and the horror of that wild cry in his blood, he did what any other inexperienced man would have done in similar bewilderment: he ran about, without any sense of direction, like a frantic child, and called loudly without ceasing the name of the guide—

"Défago! Défago! Défago!" he yelled, and the trees gave him back the name as often as he shouted, only a little softened—"Défago! Défago! Défago!"

He followed the trail that lay a short distance across the patches of snow, and then lost it again where the trees grew too thickly for snow to lie. He shouted till he was hoarse, and till the sound of his own voice in all that unanswering and listening world began to frighten him. His confusion increased in direct ratio to the violence of his efforts. His distress became formidably acute, till at length his exertions defeated their own object, and from sheer exhaustion he headed back to the camp again. It remains a wonder that he ever found his way. It was with great difficulty, and only after numberless false clues, that he at last saw the white tent between the trees, and so reached safety.

Exhaustion then applied its own remedy, and he grew calmer. He made the fire and breakfasted. Hot coffee and bacon put a little sense and judgment into him again, and he realized that he had been behaving like a boy. He now made another, and more successful attempt to face the situation collectedly, and, a nature naturally plucky coming to his assistance, he decided that he must first make as thorough a search as possible, failing success in which, he must find his way into the home camp as best he could and bring help.

And this was what he did. Taking food, matches and rifle with him, and a small axe to blaze the trees against his return journey, he set forth. It was eight o'clock when he started, the sun shining over the tops of the trees in a sky without clouds. Pinned to a stake by the fire he left a note in case Défago returned while he was away.

This time, according to a careful plan, he took a new direction, intending to make a wide sweep that must sooner or later cut into indications of the guide's trail; and, before he had gone a quarter of a mile he came across the tracks of a large animal in the snow, and beside it the light and smaller tracks of what were beyond question human feet—the feet of Défago. The relief he at once experienced was natural, though brief; for at first sight he saw in these tracks a simple explanation of the whole matter: these big marks had surely been left by a bull moose that, wind against it, had blundered upon the camp, and uttered its singular cry of warning and alarm the moment its mistake was apparent. Défago, in whom the hunting instinct was developed to the point of uncanny perfection, had scented the brute coming down the wind hours before. His excitement and disappearance were due, of course, to—to his—

Then the impossible explanation at which he grasped faded, as common sense showed him mercilessly that none of this was true. No guide, much less a guide like Défago, could have acted in so irrational a way, going off even without his rifle . . . ! The whole affair demanded a far more complicated elucidation, when he remembered the details of it all—the cry of terror, the amazing language, the grey face of horror when his nostrils first caught the new odor; that muffled sobbing in the darkness, and—for this, too, now came back to him dimly—the man's original aversion for this particular bit of country. . . .

Besides, now that he examined them closer, these were not the tracks of a bull moose at all! Hank had explained to him the outline of a bull's hoofs, of a cow's or calf's, too, for that matter; he had drawn them clearly on a strip of birch bark. And these were wholly different. They were big, round, ample, and with no pointed outline as of sharp hoofs. He wondered for a moment whether bear tracks were like that. There was no other animal he could think of, for caribou did not come so far south at this season, and, even if they did, would leave hoof marks.

They were ominous signs—these mysterious writings left in the snow by the unknown creature that had lured a human being away from safety—and when he coupled them in his imagination with that haunting sound that broke the stillness of the dawn, a momentary dizziness shook his mind, distressing him again beyond belief. He felt the *threatening* aspect of it all. And, stooping down to examine the marks more closely, he caught a faint whiff of that sweet yet pungent odor that made him instantly straighten up again, fighting a sensation almost of nausea.

Then his memory played him another evil trick. He suddenly recalled those uncovered feet projecting beyond the edge of the tent, and the body's appearance of having been dragged towards the opening; the man's shrinking from something by the door when he woke later. The details now beat against his trembling mind with concerted attack. They seemed to gather in those deep spaces of the silent forest about him, where the host of trees stood waiting, listening, watching to see what he would do. The woods were closing round him.

With the persistence of true pluck, however, Simpson went forward, following the tracks as best he could, smothering these ugly emotions that sought to weaken his will. He blazed innumerable trees as he went, ever fearful of being unable to find the way back, and calling aloud at intervals of a few seconds the name of the guide. The dull tapping of the axe upon the massive trunks, and the unnatural accents of his own voice became at length sounds that he even dreaded to make, dreaded to hear. For they drew attention without ceasing to his presence and exact whereabouts, and if it were really the case that something was hunting himself down in the same way that he was hunting down another—

With a strong effort, he crushed the thought out the instant it rose. It was the beginning, he realized, of a bewilderment utterly diabolical in kind that would speedily destroy him.

Although the snow was not continuous, lying merely in shallow flurries over the more open spaces, he found no difficulty in following the tracks for the first few miles. They went straight as a ruled line wherever the trees permitted. The stride soon began to increase in length, till it finally assumed proportions that seemed absolutely impossible for any ordinary animal to have made. Like huge flying leaps they became. One of these he measured, and though he knew that "stretch" of eighteen feet must be somehow wrong, he was at a complete loss to understand why he found no signs on the snow between the extreme points. But what perplexed him even more, making him feel his vision had gone utterly awry, was that Défago's stride increased in the same manner, and finally covered the same incredible distances. It looked as if the great beast had lifted him with it and carried him across these astonishing intervals. Simpson, who was much longer in the limb, found that he could not compass even half the stretch by taking a running jump.

And the sight of these huge tracks, running side by side, silent evidence of a dreadful journey in which terror or madness had urged to impossible results, was profoundly moving. It shocked him in the secret depths of his soul. It was the most horrible thing his eyes had ever looked upon. He began to follow them mechanically, absentmindedly almost, ever peering over his shoulder to see if he, too, were being followed by something with a gigantic tread. . . . And soon it came about that he no longer quite realized what it was they signified—these impressions left upon the snow by something nameless and untamed, always accompanied by the footmarks of the little French Canadian, his guide, his comrade, the man who had shared his tent a few hours before, chatting, laughing, even singing by his side. . . .

V

For a man of his years and inexperience, only a canny Scot, perhaps, grounded in common sense and established in logic, could have preserved even that measure of balance that this youth somehow or other did manage to preserve through the whole adventure. Otherwise, two things he presently noticed, while forging pluckily ahead, must have sent him headlong back to the comparative safety of his tent, instead of only making his hands close more tightly upon the rifle stock, while his heart, trained for the Wee Kirk, sent a wordless prayer winging its way to heaven. Both tracks, he saw, had undergone a change, and this change, so far as it concerned the footsteps of the man, was in some undecipherable manner—appalling.

It was in the bigger tracks he first noticed this, and for a long time he could not quite believe his eyes. Was it the blown leaves that produced odd effects of light and shade, or that the dry snow, drifting like finely ground rice about the edges, cast shadows and high lights? Or was it actually the fact that the great marks had become faintly colored? For round about the deep, plunging holes of the animal there now appeared a mysterious, reddish tinge that was more like an effect of light than of anything that dyed the substance of the snow itself. Every mark had it, and had it increasingly—this indistinct fiery tinge that painted a new touch of ghastliness into the picture.

But when, wholly unable to explain or to credit it, he turned his attention to the other tracks to discover if they, too, bore similar witness, he noticed that these had meanwhile undergone a change that was infinitely worse, and charged with far more horrible suggestion. For, in the last hundred yards or so, he saw that they had grown gradually into the semblance of the parent tread. Imperceptibly the change had come about, yet unmistakably. It was hard to see where the change first began. The result, however, was beyond question. Smaller, neater, more cleanly modeled, they formed now an exact and careful duplicate of the larger tracks beside them. The feet that produced them had, therefore, also changed. And something in his mind reared up with loathing and with terror as he saw it.

Simpson, for the first time, hesitated; then, ashamed of his alarm and indecision, took a few hurried steps ahead; the next instant stopped dead in his tracks. Immediately in front of him all signs of the trail ceased; both tracks came to an abrupt end. On all sides, for a hundred yards and more, he searched in vain for the least indication of their continuance. There was—nothing.

The trees were very thick just there, big trees all of them, spruce, cedar, hemlock; there was no underbrush. He stood, looking about him, all distraught; bereft of any power of judgment. Then he set to work to search again, and again, and yet again, but always with the same result: *nothing*. The feet that printed the surface of the snow thus far had now, apparently, left the ground!

And it was in that moment of distress and confusion that the whip of terror laid its most nicely calculated lash about his heart. It dropped with deadly effect upon the sorest spot of all, completely unnerving him. He had been secretly dreading all the time that it would come— and come it did.

Far overhead, muted by great height and distance, strangely thinned and wailing, he heard the crying voice of Défago, the guide.

The sound dropped upon him out of that still, wintry sky with an effect of dismay and terror unsurpassed. The rifle fell to his feet. He stood motionless an instant, listening as it were with his whole body, then staggered back against the nearest tree for support, disorganized hopelessly in mind and spirit. To him, in that moment, it seemed the most shattering and dislocating experience he had ever known, so that his heart emptied itself of all feeling whatsoever as by a sudden draught.

"Oh! oh! This fiery height! Oh, my feet of fire! My burning feet of fire . . . !" ran in far, beseeching accents of indescribable appeal this voice of anguish down the sky. Once it called—then silence through all the listening wilderness of trees.

And Simpson, scarcely knowing what he did, presently found himself running wildly to and fro, searching, calling, tripping over roots and boulders, and flinging himself in a frenzy of undirected pursuit after the Caller. Behind the screen of memory and emotion with which experience veils events, he plunged, distracted and half-deranged, picking up false lights like a ship at sea, terror in his eyes and heart and soul. For the Panic of the Wilderness had called to him in that far voice—the Power of untamed Distance—the Enticement of the Desolation that destroys. He knew in that moment all the pains of someone hopelessly and irretrievably lost, suffering the lust and travail of a soul in the final Loneliness. A vision of Défago, eternally hunted, driven and pursued across the skiey vastness of those ancient forests fled like a flame across the dark ruin of his thoughts . . .

It seemed ages before he could find anything in the chaos of his disorganized sensations to which he could anchor himself steady for a moment, and think . . .

The cry was not repeated; his own hoarse calling brought no response; the inscrutable forces of the Wild had summoned their victim beyond recall—and held him fast.

Yet he searched and called, it seems, for hours afterwards, for it was late in the afternoon when at length he decided to abandon a useless pursuit and return to his camp on the shores of Fifty Island Water. Even then he went with reluctance, that crying voice still echoing in his ears. With difficulty he found his rifle and the homeward trail. The concentration necessary to follow the badly blazed trees, and a biting hunger that gnawed, helped to keep his mind steady. Otherwise, he admits, the temporary aberration he had suffered might have been prolonged to the point of positive disaster. Gradually the ballast shifted back again, and he regained something that approached his normal equilibrium.

But for all that the journey through the gathering dusk was miserably haunted. He heard innumerable following footsteps; voices that laughed and whispered; and saw figures crouching behind trees and boulders, making signs to one another for a concerted attack the moment he had passed. The creeping murmur of the wind made him start and listen. He went stealthily, trying to hide where possible, and making as little sound as he could. The shadows of the woods, hitherto protective or covering merely, had now become menacing, challenging; and the pageantry in his frightened mind masked a host of possibilities that were all the more ominous for being obscure. The presentiment of a nameless doom lurked ill-concealed behind every detail of what had happened.

It was really admirable how he emerged victor in the end; men of riper powers and experience might have come through the ordeal with less success. He had himself tolerably well in hand, all things considered, and his plan of action proves it. Sleep being absolutely out of the question and traveling an unknown trail in the darkness equally impracticable, he sat up the whole of that night, rifle in hand, before a fire he never for a single moment allowed to die down. The severity of the haunted vigil marked his soul for life; but it was successfully accomplished; and with the very first signs of dawn he set forth upon the long return journey to the home camp to get help. As before, he left a written note to explain his absence, and to indicate where he had left a plentiful *cache* of food and matches—though he had no expectation that any human hands would find them!

How Simpson found his way alone by the lake and forest might well make a story in itself, for to hear him tell it is to *know* the passionate loneliness of soul that a man can feel when the Wilderness holds him in the hollow of its illimitable hand—and laughs. It is also to admire his indomitable pluck.

He claims no skill, declaring that he followed the almost invisible trail mechanically, and without thinking. And this, doubtless, is the truth. He relied upon the guiding of the unconscious mind, which is instinct. Perhaps, too, some sense of orientation, known to animals and primitive men, may have helped as well, for through all that tangled region he succeeded in reaching the exact spot where Défago had hidden the canoe nearly three days before with the remark, "Strike doo west across the lake into the sun to find the camp."

There was not much sun left to guide him, but he used his compass to the best of his ability, embarking in the frail craft for the last twelve miles of his journey with a sensation of immense relief that the forest was at last behind him. And, fortunately, the water was calm; he took his line across the center of the lake instead of coasting round the shores for another twenty miles. Fortunately, too, the other hunters were back. The light of their fires furnished a steering point without which he might have searched all night long for the actual position of the camp.

It was close upon midnight all the same when his canoe grated on the sandy cove, and Hank, Punk and his uncle, disturbed in their sleep by his cries, ran quickly down and helped a very exhausted and broken specimen of Scotch humanity over the rocks toward a dying fire.

VI

The sudden entrance of his prosaic uncle into this world of wizardry and horror that had haunted him without interruption now for two days and two nights, had the immediate effect of giving to the affair an entirely new aspect. The sound of that crisp "Hulloa, my boy! And what's up *now*?" and the grasp of that dry and vigorous hand introduced another standard of judgment. A revulsion of feeling washed through him. He realized that he had let himself "go" rather badly. He even felt vaguely ashamed of himself. The native hard-headedness of his race reclaimed him.

And this doubtless explains why he found it so hard to tell that group round the fire—everything. He told enough, however, for the immediate decision to be arrived at that a relief party must start at the earliest possible moment, and that Simpson, in order to guide it capably, must first have food and, above all, sleep. Dr. Cathcart observing the lad's condition more shrewdly than his patient knew, gave him a very slight injection of morphine. For six hours he slept like the dead.

From the description carefully written out afterwards by this student of divinity, it appears that the account he gave to the astonished group omitted sundry vital and important details. He declares that, with his uncle's wholesome, matter-of-fact countenance staring him in the face, he simply had not the courage to mention them. Thus, all the search party gathered, it would seem, was that Défago had suffered in the night an acute and inexplicable attack of mania, had imagined himself "called" by someone or something, and had plunged into the bush after it without food or rifle, where he must die a horrible and lingering death by cold and starvation unless he could be found and rescued in time. "In time," moreover, meant at once.

In the course of the following day, however—they were off by seven, leaving Punk in charge with instructions to have food and fire always ready—Simpson found it possible to tell his uncle a good deal more of the story's true inwardness, without divining that it was drawn out of him as a matter of fact by a very subtle form of cross examination. By the time they reached the beginning of the trail, where the canoe was laid up against the return journey, he had mentioned how Défago spoke vaguely of "something he called a 'Wendigo'"; how he cried in his sleep; how he imagined an unusual scent about the camp; and had betrayed other symptoms of mental excitement. He also admitted the bewildering effect of "that extraordinary odor" upon himself, "pungent and acrid like the odor of lions." And by the time they were within an easy hour of Fifty Island Water he had let slip the further fact—a foolish avowal of his own hysterical condition, as he felt afterwards—that he had heard the vanished guide call "for help." He omitted the singular phrases used, for he simply could not bring himself to repeat the preposterous language. Also, while describing how the man's footsteps in the snow had gradually assumed an exact miniature likeness of the animal's plunging tracks, he left out the fact that they measured a *wholly* incredible distance. It seemed a question, nicely balanced between individual pride and honesty, what he should reveal and what suppress. He mentioned the fiery tinge in the snow, for instance, yet shrank from telling that body and bed had been partly dragged out of the tent. . . .

With the net result that Dr. Cathcart, adroit psychologist that he fancied himself to be, had assured him clearly enough exactly where his mind, influenced by loneliness, bewilderment and terror, had yielded to the strain and invited delusion. While praising his conduct, he managed at the same time to point out where, when, and how his mind had gone astray. He made his nephew think himself finer than he was by judicious praise, yet more foolish than he was by minimizing the value of the evidence. Like many another materialist, that is, he lied cleverly on the basis of insufficient knowledge, *because* the knowledge supplied seemed to his own particular intelligence inadmissible.

"The spell of these terrible solitudes," he said, "cannot leave any mind untouched, any mind, that is, possessed of the higher imaginative qualities. It has worked upon yours exactly as it worked upon my own when I was your age. The animal that haunted your little camp was undoubtedly a moose, for the 'belling' of a moose may have, sometimes, a very peculiar quality of sound. The colored appearance of the big tracks was obviously a defect of vision in your own eyes produced by excitement. The size and stretch of the tracks we shall prove when we come to them. But the hallucination of an audible voice, of course, is one of the commonest forms of delusion due to mental excitement—an excitement, my dear boy, perfectly excusable, and, let me add, wonderfully controlled by you under the circumstances. For the rest, I am bound to say, you have acted with a splendid courage, for the terror of feeling oneself lost in this wilderness is nothing short of awful, and, had I been in your place, I don't for a moment believe I could have behaved with one quarter of your wisdom and decision. The only thing I find it uncommonly difficult to explain is—that—damned odor."

"It made me feel sick, I assure you," declared his nephew, "positively dizzy!" His uncle's attitude of calm omniscience, merely because he knew more psychological formulae, made him slightly defiant. It was so easy to be wise in the explanation of an experience one has not personally witnessed. "A kind of desolate and terrible odor is the only way I can describe it," he concluded, glancing at the features of the quiet, unemotional man beside him.

"I can only marvel," was the reply, "that under the circumstances it did not seem to you even worse." The dry words, Simpson knew, hovered between the truth, and his uncle's interpretation of "the truth."

And so at last they came to the little camp and found the tent still standing, the remains of the fire, and the piece of paper pinned to a stake beside it—untouched. The *cache*, poorly contrived by inexperienced hands, however, had been discovered and opened—by musk rats, mink and squirrel. The matches lay scattered about the opening, but the food had been taken to the last crumb.

"Well, fellers, he ain't here," exclaimed Hank loudly after his fashion. "And that's as sartain as the coal supply down below! But whar he's got to by this time is 'bout as unsartain as the trade in crowns in t'other place." The presence of a divinity student was no barrier to his language at such a time, though for the reader's sake it may be severely edited. "I propose," he added, "that we start out at once an' hunt for'm like hell!"

The gloom of Défago's probable fate oppressed the whole party with a sense of dreadful gravity the moment they saw the familiar signs of recent occupancy. Especially the tent, with the bed of balsam branches still smoothed and flattened by the pressure of his body, seemed to bring his presence near to them. Simpson, feeling vaguely as if his world were somehow at stake, went about explaining particulars in a hushed tone. He was much calmer now, though overwearied with the strain of his many journeys. His uncle's method of explaining— "explaining away," rather—the details still fresh in his haunted memory helped, too, to put ice upon his emotions.

"And that's the direction he ran off in," he said to his two companions, pointing in the direction where the guide had vanished that morning in the grey dawn. "Straight down there he ran like a deer, in between the birch and the hemlock. . . ."

Hank and Dr. Cathcart exchanged glances.

"And it was about two miles down there, in a straight line," continued the other, speaking with something of the former terror in his voice, "that I followed his trail to the place where—it stopped—dead!"

"And where you heered him callin' an' caught the stench, an' all the rest of the wicked entertainment," cried Hank, with a volubility that betrayed his keen distress.

"And where your excitement overcame you to the point of producing illusions," added Dr. Cathcart under his breath, yet not so low that his nephew did not hear it.

It was early in the afternoon, for they had traveled quickly, and there were still a good two hours of daylight left. Dr. Cathcart and Hank lost no time in beginning the search, but Simpson was too exhausted to accompany them. They would follow the blazed marks on the trees, and where possible, his footsteps. Meanwhile the best thing he could do was to keep a good fire going, and rest.

But after something like three hours' search, the darkness already down, the two men returned to camp with nothing to report. Fresh snow had covered all signs, and though they had followed the blazed trees to the spot where Simpson had turned back, they had not discovered the smallest indication of a human being—or for that matter, of an animal. There were no fresh tracks of any kind; the snow lay undisturbed.

It was difficult to know what was best to do, though in reality there was nothing more they *could* do. They might stay and search for weeks without much chance of success. The fresh snow destroyed their only hope, and they gathered round the fire for supper, a gloomy and despondent party. The facts, indeed, were sad enough, for Défago had a wife at Rat Portage, and his earnings were the family's sole means of support.

Now that the whole truth in all its ugliness was out, it seemed useless to deal in further disguise or pretense. They talked openly of the facts and probabilities. It was not the first time, even in the experience of Dr. Cathcart, that a man had yielded to the singular seduction of the Solitudes and gone out of his mind; Défago, moreover, was predisposed to something of the sort, for he already had a touch of melancholia in his blood, and his fiber was weakened by bouts of drinking that often lasted for weeks at a time. Something on this trip— one might never know precisely what—had sufficed to push him over the line, that was all. And he had gone, gone off into the great wilderness of trees and lakes to die by starvation and exhaustion. The chances against his finding camp again were overwhelming; the delirium that was upon him would also doubtless have increased, and it was quite likely he might do violence to himself and so hasten his cruel fate. Even while they talked, indeed, the end had probably come. On the suggestion of Hank, his old pal, however, they proposed to wait a little longer and devote the whole of the following day, from dawn to darkness, to the most systematic search they could devise. They would divide the territory between them. They discussed their plan in great detail. All that men could do they would do.

And, meanwhile, they talked about the particular form in which the singular Panic of the Wilderness had made its attack upon the mind of the unfortunate guide. Hank, though familiar with the legend in its general outline, obviously did not welcome the turn the conversation had taken. He contributed little, though that little was illuminating. For he admitted that a story ran over all this section of country to the effect that several Indians had "seen the Wendigo" along the shores of Fifty Island Water in the "fall" of last year, and that this was the true reason of Défago's disinclination to hunt there. Hank doubtless felt that he had in a sense helped his old pal to death by over-persuading him. "When an Indian goes crazy," he explained, talking to himself more than to the others, it seemed, "it's always put that he's 'seen the Wendigo.' An' pore old Défaygo was superstitious down to he very heels . . . !"

And then Simpson, feeling the atmosphere more sympathetic, told over again the full story of his astonishing tale; he left out no details this time; he mentioned his own sensations and gripping fears. He only omitted the strange language used.

"But Défago surely had already told you all these details of the Wendigo legend, my dear fellow," insisted the doctor. "I mean, he had talked about it, and thus put into your mind the ideas which your own excitement afterwards developed?"

Whereupon Simpson again repeated the facts. Défago, he declared, had barely mentioned the beast. He, Simpson, knew nothing of the story, and, so far as he remembered, had never even read about it. Even the word was unfamiliar.

Of course he was telling the truth, and Dr. Cathcart was reluctantly compelled to admit the singular character of the whole affair. He did not do this in words so much as in manner, however. He kept his back against a good, stout tree; he poked the fire into a blaze the moment it showed signs of dying down; he was quicker than any of them to notice the least sound in the night about them—a fish jumping in the lake, a twig snapping in the bush, the dropping of occasional fragments of frozen snow from the branches overhead where the heat loosened them. His voice, too, changed a little in quality, becoming a shade less confident, lower also in tone. Fear, to put it plainly, hovered close about that little camp, and though all three would have been glad to speak of other matters, the only thing they seemed able to discuss was this—the source of their fear. They tried other subjects in vain; there was nothing to say about them. Hank was the most honest of the group; he said next to nothing. He never once, however, turned his back to the darkness. His face was always to the forest, and when wood was needed he didn't go farther than was necessary to get it.

VII

A wall of silence wrapped them in, for the snow, though not thick, was sufficient to deaden any noise, and the frost held things pretty tight besides. No sound but their voices and the soft roar of the flames made itself heard. Only, from time to time, something soft as the flutter of a pine moth's wings went past them through the air. No one seemed anxious to go to bed. The hours slipped towards midnight.

"The legend is picturesque enough," observed the doctor after one of the longer pauses, speaking to break it rather than because he had anything to say, "for the Wendigo is simply the Call of the Wild personified, which some natures hear to their own destruction."

"That's about it," Hank said presently. "An' there's no misunderstandin' when you hear it. It calls you by name right 'nough."

Another pause followed. Then Dr. Cathcart came back to the forbidden subject with a rush that made the others jump.

"The allegory *is* significant," he remarked, looking about him into the darkness, "for the Voice, they say, resembles all the minor sounds of the Bush—wind, falling water, cries of the animals, and so forth. And, once the victim hears *that*—he's off for good, of course! His most vulnerable points, moreover, are said to be the feet and the eyes; the feet, you see, for the lust of wandering, and the eyes for the lust of beauty. The poor beggar goes at such a dreadful speed that he bleeds beneath the eyes, and his feet burn."

Dr. Cathcart, as he spoke, continued to peer uneasily into the surrounding gloom. His voice sank to a hushed tone.

"The Wendigo," he added, "is said to burn his feet—owing to the friction, apparently caused by its tremendous velocity—till they drop off, and new ones form exactly like its own."

Simpson listened in horrified amazement; but it was the pallor on Hank's face that fascinated him most. He would willingly have stopped his ears and closed his eyes, had he dared.

"It don't always keep to the ground neither," came in Hank's slow, heavy drawl, "for it goes so high that he thinks the stars have set him all a-fire. An' it'll take great thumpin' jumps sometimes, an' run along the tops of the trees, carrying its partner with it, an' then droppin' him jest as a fish hawk'll drop a pickerel to kill it before eatin'. An' its food, of all the muck in the whole Bush is—moss!" And he laughed a short, unnatural laugh. "It's a moss-eater, is the Wendigo," he added, looking up excitedly into the faces of his companions. "Moss-eater," he repeated, with a string of the most outlandish oaths he could invent.

But Simpson now understood the true purpose of all this talk. What these two men, each strong and "experienced" in his own way, dreaded more than anything else was—silence. They were talking against time. They were also talking against darkness, against the invasion of panic, against the admission reflection might bring that they were in an enemy's country—against anything, in fact, rather than allow their inmost thoughts to assume control. He himself, already initiated by the awful vigil with terror, was beyond both of them in this respect. He had reached the stage where he was immune. But these two, the scoffing, analytical doctor, and the honest, dogged backwoodsman, each sat trembling in the depths of his being.

Thus the hours passed; and thus, with lowered voices and a kind of taut inner resistance of spirit, this little group of humanity sat in the jaws of the wilderness and talked foolishly of the terrible and haunting legend. It was an unequal contest, all things considered, for the wilderness had already the advantage of first attack—and of a hostage. The fate of their comrade hung over them with a steadily increasing weight of oppression that finally became insupportable.

It was Hank, after a pause longer than the preceding ones that no one seemed able to break, who first let loose all this pent-up emotion in very unexpected fashion, by springing suddenly to his feet and letting out the most ear-shattering yell imaginable into the night. He could not contain himself any longer, it seemed. To make it carry even beyond an ordinary cry he interrupted its rhythm by shaking the palm of his hand before his mouth.

"That's for Défago," he said, looking down at the other two with a queer, defiant laugh, "for it's my belief"—the sandwiched oaths may be omitted—"that my ole partner's not far from us at this very minute."

There was a vehemence and recklessness about his performance that made Simpson, too, start to his feet in amazement, and betrayed even the doctor into letting the pipe slip from between his lips. Hank's face was ghastly, but Cathcart's showed a sudden weakness—a loosening of all his faculties, as it were. Then a momentary anger blazed into his eyes, and he too, though with deliberation born of habitual self-control, got upon his feet and faced the excited guide. For this was unpermissible, foolish, dangerous, and he meant to stop it in the bud.

What might have happened in the next minute or two one may speculate about, yet never definitely know, for in the instant of profound silence that followed Hank's roaring voice, and as though in answer to it, something went past through the darkness of the sky overhead at terrific speed—something of necessity very large, for it displaced much air, while down between the trees there fell a faint and windy cry of a human voice, calling in tones of indescribable anguish and appeal—

"Oh, oh! This fiery height! Oh, oh! My feet of fire! My burning feet of fire!"

White to the very edge of his shirt, Hank looked stupidly about him like a child. Dr. Cathcart uttered some kind of unintelligible cry, turning as he did so with an instinctive movement of blind terror towards the protection of the tent, then halting in the act as though frozen. Simpson, alone of the three, retained his presence of mind a little. His own horror was too deep to allow of any immediate reaction. He had heard that cry before.

Turning to his stricken companions, he said almost calmly—

"That's exactly the cry I heard—the very words he used!"

Then, lifting his face to the sky, he cried aloud, "Défago, Défago! Come down here to us! Come down—!"

And before there was time for anybody to take definite action one way or another, there came the sound of something dropping heavily between the trees, striking the branches on the way down, and landing with a dreadful thud upon the frozen earth below. The crash and thunder of it was really terrific.

"That's him, s'help me the good Gawd!" came from Hank in a whispering cry half choked, his hand going automatically toward the hunting knife in his belt. "And he's coming! He's coming!" he added, with an irrational laugh of horror, as the sounds of heavy footsteps crunching over the snow became distinctly audible, approaching through the blackness towards the circle of light.

And while the steps, with their stumbling motion, moved nearer and nearer upon them, the three men stood round that fire, motionless and dumb. Dr. Cathcart had the appearance of a man suddenly withered; even his eyes did not move. Hank, suffering shockingly, seemed on the verge again of violent action; yet did nothing. He, too, was hewn of stone. Like stricken children they seemed. The picture was hideous. And, meanwhile, their owner still invisible, the footsteps came closer, crunching the frozen snow. It was endless—too prolonged to be quite real—this measured and pitiless approach. It was accursed.

VIII

Then at length the darkness, having thus laboriously conceived, brought forth—a figure. It drew forward into the zone of uncertain light where fire and shadows mingled, not ten feet away; then halted, staring at them fixedly. The same instant it started forward again with the spasmodic motion as of a thing moved by wires, and coming up closer to them, full into the glare of the fire, they perceived then that—it was a man; and apparently that this man was—Défago.

Something like a skin of horror almost perceptibly drew down in that moment over every face, and three pairs of eyes shone through it as though they saw across the frontiers of normal vision into the Unknown.

Défago advanced, his tread faltering and uncertain; he made his way straight up to them as a group first, then turned sharply and peered close into the face of Simpson. The sound of a voice issued from his lips—

"Here I am, Boss Simpson. I heered someone calling me." It was a faint, dried up voice, made wheezy and breathless as by immense exertion. "I'm havin' a reg'lar hellfire kind of a trip, I am." And he laughed, thrusting his head forward into the other's face.

But that laugh started the machinery of the group of waxwork figures with the wax-white skins. Hank immediately sprang forward with a stream of oaths so farfetched that Simpson did not recognize them as English at all, but thought he had lapsed into Indian or some other lingo. He only realized that Hank's presence, thrust thus between them, was welcome—uncommonly welcome. Dr. Cathcart, though more calmly and leisurely, advanced behind him, heavily stumbling.

Simpson seems hazy as to what was actually said and done in those next few seconds, for the eyes of that detestable and blasted visage peering at such close quarters into his own utterly bewildered his senses at first. He merely stood still. He said nothing. He had not the trained will of the older men that forced them into action in defiance of all emotional stress. He watched them moving as behind a glass that half destroyed their reality; it was dreamlike; perverted. Yet, through the torrent of Hank's meaningless phrases, he remembers hearing his uncle's tone of authority—hard and forced—saying several things about food and warmth, blankets, whisky and the rest; . . . and, further, that whiffs of that penetrating, unaccustomed odor, vile yet sweetly bewildering, assailed his nostrils during all that followed.

It was no less a person than himself, however—less experienced and adroit than the others though he was—who gave instinctive utterance to the sentence that brought a measure of relief into the ghastly situation by expressing the doubt and thought in each one's heart.

"It *is—You,* isn't it, Défago?" he asked under his breath, horror breaking his speech.

And at once Cathcart burst out with the loud answer before the other had time to move his lips. "Of course it is! Of course it is! Only—can't you see—he's nearly dead with exhaustion, cold and terror! Isn't *that* enough to change a man beyond all recognition?" It was said in order to convince himself as much as to convince the others. The overemphasis alone proved that. And continually, while he spoke and acted, he held a handkerchief to his nose. That odor pervaded the whole camp.

For the "Défago" who sat huddled by the big fire, wrapped in blankets, drinking hot whisky and holding food in wasted hands, was no more like the guide they had last seen alive than the picture of a man of sixty is like a daguerreotype of his early youth in the costume of another generation. Nothing really can describe that ghastly caricature, that parody, masquerading there in the firelight as Défago. From the ruins of the dark and awful memories he still retains, Simpson declares that the face was more animal than human, the features drawn about into wrong proportions, the skin loose and hanging, as though he had been subjected to extraordinary pressures and tensions. It made him think vaguely of those bladder faces blown up by the hawkers on Ludgate Hill, that change their expression as they swell, and as they collapse emit a faint and wailing imitation of a voice. Both face and voice suggested some such abominable resemblance. But Cathcart long afterwards, seeking to describe the indescribable, asserts that thus might have looked a face and body that had been in air so rarified that, the weight of atmosphere being removed, the entire structure threatened to fly asunder and become—*incoherent.* . . .

It was Hank, though all distraught and shaking with a tearing volume of emotion he could neither handle nor understand, who brought things to a head without much ado. He went off to a little distance from the fire, apparently so that the light should not dazzle him too much, and shading his eyes for a moment with both hands, shouted in a loud voice that held anger and affection dreadfully mingled:

"You ain't Défaygo! You ain't Défaygo at all! I don't give a— damn, but that ain't you, my ole pal of twenty years!" He glared upon the huddled figure as though he would destroy him with his eyes. "An' if it is I'll swab the floor of hell with a wad of cotton wool on a toothpick, s'help me the good Gawd!" he added, with a violent fling of horror and disgust.

It was impossible to silence him. He stood there shouting like one possessed, horrible to see, horrible to hear—*because it was the truth.* He repeated himself in fifty different ways, each more outlandish than the last. The woods rang with echoes. At one time it looked as if he meant to fling himself upon "the intruder," for his hand continually jerked towards the long hunting knife in his belt.

But in the end he did nothing, and the whole tempest completed itself very shortly with tears. Hank's voice suddenly broke, he collapsed on the ground, and Cathcart somehow or other persuaded him at last to go into the tent and lie quiet. The remainder of the affair, indeed, was witnessed by him from behind the canvas, his white and terrified face peeping through the crack of the tent door-flap.

Then Dr. Cathcart, closely followed by his nephew who so far had kept his courage better than all of them, went up with a determined air and stood opposite to the figure of Défago huddled over the fire. He looked him squarely in the face and spoke. At first his voice was firm.

"Défago, tell us what's happened—just a little, so that we can know how best to help you?" he asked in a tone of authority, almost of command. And at that point, it *was* command. At once afterwards, however, it changed in quality, for the figure turned up to him a face so piteous, so terrible and so little like humanity, that the doctor shrank back from him as from something spiritually unclean. Simpson, watching close behind him, says he got the impression of a mask that was on the verge of dropping off, and that underneath they would discover something black and diabolical, revealed in utter nakedness. "Out with it, man, out with it!" Cathcart cried, terror running neck and neck with entreaty. "None of us can stand this much longer . . . !" It was the cry of instinct over reason.

And then "Défago," smiling *whitely*, answered in that thin and fading voice that already seemed passing over into a sound of quite another character—

"I seen that great Wendigo thing," he whispered, sniffing the air about him exactly like an animal. "I been with it too—"

Whether the poor devil would have said more, or whether Dr. Cathcart would have continued the impossible cross examination cannot be known, for at that moment the voice of Hank was heard yelling at the top of his voice from behind the canvas that concealed all but his terrified eyes. Such a howling was never heard.

"His feet! Oh, Gawd, his feet! Look at his great changed—feet!"

Défago, shuffling where he sat, had moved in such a way that for the first time his legs were in full light and his feet were visible. Yet Simpson had no time, himself, to see properly what Hank had seen. And Hank has never seen fit to tell. That same instant, with a leap like that of a frightened tiger, Cathcart was upon him, bundling the folds of blanket about his legs with such speed that the young student caught little more than a passing glimpse of something dark and oddly massed where moccasined feet ought to have been, and saw even that but with uncertain vision.

Then, before the doctor had time to do more, or Simpson time to even think a question, much less ask it, Défago was standing upright in front of them, balancing with pain and difficulty, and upon his shapeless and twisted visage an expression so dark and so malicious that it was, in the true sense, monstrous.

"Now *you* seen it too," he wheezed, "you seen my fiery, burning feet! And now—that is, unless you kin save me an' prevent—it's 'bout time for—"

His piteous and beseeching voice was interrupted by a sound that was like the roar of wind coming across the lake. The trees overhead shook their tangled branches. The blazing fire bent its flames as before a blast. And something swept with a terrific, rushing noise about the little camp and seemed to surround it entirely in a single moment of time. Défago shook the clinging blankets from his body, turned towards the woods behind, and with the same stumbling motion that had brought him—was gone: gone, before anyone could move muscle to prevent him, gone with an amazing, blundering swiftness that left no time to act. The darkness positively swallowed him; and less than a dozen seconds later, above the roar of the swaying trees and the shout of the sudden wind, all three men, watching and listening with stricken hearts, heard a cry that seemed to drop down upon them from a great height of sky and distance—

"Oh, oh! This fiery height! Oh, oh! My feet of fire! My burning feet of fire . . . !" then died away, into untold space and silence.

Dr. Cathcart—suddenly master of himself, and therefore of the others—was just able to seize Hank violently by the arm as he tried to dash headlong into the Bush.

"But I want ter know,—you!" shrieked the guide. "I want ter see! That ain't him at all, but some—devil that's shunted into his place . . . !"

Somehow or other—he admits he never quite knew how he accomplished it—he managed to keep him in the tent and pacify him. The doctor, apparently, had reached the stage where reaction had set in and allowed his own innate force to conquer. Certainly he "managed" Hank admirably. It was his nephew, however, hitherto so wonderfully controlled, who gave him most cause for anxiety, for the cumulative strain had now produced a condition of lachrymose hysteria which made it necessary to isolate him upon a bed of boughs and blankets as far removed from Hank as was possible under the circumstances.

And there he lay, as the watches of that haunted night passed over the lonely camp, crying startled sentences, and fragments of sentences, into the folds of his blanket. A quantity of gibberish about speed and height and fire mingled oddly with biblical memories of the classroom. "People with broken faces all on fire are coming at a most awful, awful, pace towards the camp!" he would moan one minute; and the next would sit up and stare into the woods, intently listening, and whisper, "How terrible in the wilderness are—are the feet of them that—" until his uncle came across the change the direction of his thoughts and comfort him.

The hysteria, fortunately, proved but temporary. Sleep cured him, just as it cured Hank.

Till the first signs of daylight came, soon after five o'clock, Dr. Cathcart kept his vigil. His face was the color of chalk, and there were strange flushes beneath the eyes. An appalling terror of the soul battled with his will all through those silent hours. These were some of the outer signs . . .

At dawn he lit the fire himself, made breakfast, and woke the others, and by seven they were well on their way back to the home camp—three perplexed and afflicted men, but each in his own way having reduced his inner turmoil to a condition of more or less systematized order again.

IX

They talked little, and then only of the most wholesome and common things, for their minds were charged with painful thoughts that clamored for explanation, though no one dared refer to them. Hank, being nearest to primitive conditions, was the first to find himself, for he was also less complex. In Dr. Cathcart "civilization" championed his forces against an attack singular enough. To this day, perhaps, he is not *quite* sure of certain things. Anyhow, he took longer to "find himself."

Simpson, the student of divinity, it was who arranged his conclusions probably with the best, though not most scientific, appearance of order. Out there, in the heart of un-reclaimed wilderness, they had surely witnessed something crudely and essentially primitive. Something that had survived somehow the advance of humanity had emerged terrifically, betraying a scale of life still monstrous and immature. He envisaged it rather as a glimpse into prehistoric ages, when superstitions, gigantic and uncouth, still oppressed the hearts of men; when the forces of nature were still untamed, the Powers that may have haunted a primeval universe not yet withdrawn. To this day he thinks of what he termed years later in a sermon "savage and formidable Potencies lurking behind the souls of men, not evil perhaps in themselves, yet instinctively hostile to humanity as it exists."

With his uncle he never discussed the matter in detail, for the barrier between the two types of mind made it difficult. Only once, years later, something led them to the frontier of the subject—of a single detail of the subject, rather—

"Can't you even tell me what—*they* were like?" he asked; and the reply, though conceived in wisdom, was not encouraging, "It is far better you should not try to know, or to find out."

"Well—that odor . . . ?" persisted the nephew. "What do you make of that?"

Dr. Cathcart looked at him and raised his eyebrows.

"Odors," he replied, "are not so easy as sounds and sights of telepathic communication. I make as much, or as little, probably, as you do yourself."

He was not quite so glib as usual with his explanations. That was all.

At the fall of day, cold, exhausted, famished, the party came to the end of the long portage and dragged themselves into a camp that at first glimpse seemed empty. Fire there was none, and no Punk came forward to welcome them. The emotional capacity of all three was too over-spent to recognize either surprise or annoyance; but the cry of spontaneous affection that burst from the lips of Hank, as he rushed ahead of them towards the fire-place, came probably as a warning that the end of the amazing affair was not quite yet. And both Cathcart and his nephew confessed afterwards that when they saw him kneel down in his excitement and embrace something that reclined, gently moving, beside the extinguished ashes, they felt in their very bones that this "something" would prove to be Défago—the true Défago, returned.

And so, indeed, it was.

It is soon told. Exhausted to the point of emaciation, the French Canadian—what was left of him, that is—fumbled among the ashes, trying to make a fire. His body crouched there, the weak fingers obeying feebly the instinctive habit of a lifetime with twigs and matches. But there was no longer any mind to direct the simple operation. The mind had fled beyond recall. And with it, too, had fled memory. Not only recent events, but all previous life was a blank.

This time it was the real man, though incredibly and horribly shrunken. On his face was no expression of any kind whatever—fear, welcome, or recognition. He did not seem to know who it was that embraced him, or who it was that fed, warmed and spoke to him the words of comfort and relief. Forlorn and broken beyond all reach of human aid, the little man did meekly as he was bidden. The "something" that had constituted him "individual" had vanished for ever.

In some ways it was more terribly moving than anything they had yet seen—that idiot smile as he drew wads of coarse moss from his swollen cheeks and told them that he was "a damned moss-eater"; the continued vomiting of even the simplest food; and, worst of all, the piteous and childish voice of complaint in which he told them that his feet pained him—"burn like fire"—which was natural enough when Dr. Cathcart examined them and found that both were dreadfully frozen. Beneath the eyes there were faint indications of recent bleeding.

The details of how he survived the prolonged exposure, of where he had been, or of how he covered the great distance from one camp to the other, including an immense detour of the lake on foot since he had no canoe—all this remains unknown. His memory had vanished completely. And before the end of the winter whose beginning witnessed this strange occurrence, Défago, bereft of mind, memory and soul, had gone with it. He lingered only a few weeks.

And what Punk was able to contribute to the story throws no further light upon it. He was cleaning fish by the lake shore about five o'clock in the evening—an hour, that is, before the search party returned—when he saw this shadow of the guide picking its way weakly into camp. In advance of him, he declares, came the faint whiff of a certain singular odor.

That same instant old Punk started for home. He covered the entire journey of three days as only Indian blood could have covered it. The terror of a whole race drove him. He knew what it all meant. Défago had "seen the Wendigo."

Accessory Before the Fact

At the moorland cross-roads Martin stood examining the sign-post for several minutes in some bewilderment. The names on the four arms were not what he expected, distances were not given, and his map, he concluded with impatience, must be hopelessly out of date. Spreading it against the post, he stooped to study it more closely. The wind blew the corners flapping against his face. The small print was almost indecipherable in the fading light. It appeared, however—as well as he could make out—that two miles back he must have taken the wrong turning.

He remembered that turning. The path had looked inviting; he had hesitated a moment, then followed it, caught by the usual lure of walkers that it "might prove a short cut." The short-cut snare is old as human nature. For some minutes he studied the sign-post and the map alternately. Dusk was falling, and his knapsack had grown heavy. He could not make the two guides tally, however, and a feeling of uncertainty crept over his mind. He felt oddly baffled, frustrated. His thought grew thick. Decision was most difficult. "I'm muddled," he thought; "I must be tired," as at length he chose the most likely arm. "Sooner or later it will bring me to an inn, though not the one I intended." He accepted his walker's luck, and started briskly. The arm read, "Over Litacy Hill" in small, fine letters that danced and shifted every time he looked at them; but the name was not discoverable on the map. It was, however, inviting like the short cut. A similar impulse again directed his choice. Only this time it seemed more insistent, almost urgent.

And he became aware, then, of the exceeding loneliness of the country about him. The road for a hundred yards went straight, then curved like a white river running into space; the deep blue-green of heather lined the banks, spreading upwards through the twilight; and occasional small pines stood solitary here and there, all unexplained. The curious adjective, having made its appearance, haunted him. So many things that afternoon were similarly—unexplained: the short cut, the darkened map, the names on the sign-post, his own erratic impulses, and the growing strange confusion that crept upon his spirit. The entire country-side needed explanation, though perhaps "interpretation" was the truer word. Those little lonely trees had made him see it. Why had he lost his way so easily? Why did he suffer vague impressions to influence his direction? Why was he here—exactly *here*? And why did he go now "over Litacy Hill"?

Then, by a green field that shone like a thought of daylight amid the darkness of the moor, he saw a figure lying in the grass. It was a blot upon the landscape, a mere huddled patch of dirty rags, yet with a certain horrid picturesqueness too; and his mind—though his German was of the schoolroom order—at once picked out the German equivalents as against the English. *Lump* and *Lumpen* flashed across his brain most oddly. They seemed in that moment right, and so expressive, almost like onomatopoeic words, if that were possible of sight. Neither "rags" nor "rascal" would have fitted what he saw. The adequate description was in German.

Here was a clue tossed up by the part of him that did not reason. But it seems he missed it. And the next minute the tramp rose to a sitting posture and asked the time of evening. In German he asked it. And Martin, answering without a second's hesitation, gave it, also in German, *"halb sieben"*—half-past six. The instinctive guess was accurate. A glance at his watch when he looked a moment later proved it. He heard the man say, with the covert insolence of tramps, "T'ank you; much opliged." For Martin had not shown his watch—another intuition subconsciously obeyed.

He quickened his pace along that lonely road, a curious jumble of thoughts and feelings surging through him. He had somehow known the question would come, and come in German. Yet it flustered and dismayed him. Another thing had also flustered and dismayed him. He had expected it in the same queer fashion: it was right. For when the ragged brown thing rose to ask the question, a part of it remained lying on the grass—another brown, dirty thing. There were two tramps. And he saw both faces clearly. Behind the untidy beards, and below the old slouch hats, he caught the look of unpleasant, clever faces that watched him closely while he passed. The eyes followed him. For a second he looked straight into those eyes, so that he could not fail to know them. And he understood, quite horridly, that both faces were too sleek, refined, and cunning for those of ordinary tramps. The men were not really tramps at all. They were disguised.

"How covertly they watched me!" was his thought, as he hurried along the darkening road, aware in dead earnestness now of the loneliness and desolation of the moorland all about him.

Uneasy and distressed, he increased his pace. Midway in thinking what an unnecessarily clanking noise his nailed boots made upon the hard white road, there came upon him with a rush together the company of these things that haunted him as "unexplained." They brought a single definite message: That all this business was not really meant for him at all, and hence his confusion and bewilderment; that he had intruded into someone else's scenery, and was trespassing upon another's map of life. By some wrong inner turning he had interpolated his per-son into a group of foreign forces which operated in the little world of someone else. Unwittingly, somewhere, he had crossed the threshold, and now was fairly in—a trespasser, an eavesdropper, a Peeping Tom. He was listening, peeping; overhearing things he had no right to know, because they were intended for another. Like a ship at sea he was intercepting wireless messages he could not properly interpret, because his Receiver was not accurately tuned to their reception. And more—these messages were warnings!

Then fear dropped upon him like the night. He was caught in a net of delicate, deep forces he could not manage, knowing neither their origin nor purpose. He had walked into some huge psychic trap elaborately planned and baited, yet calculated for another than himself. Something had lured him in, something in the landscape, the time of day, his mood. Owing to some undiscovered weakness in himself he had been easily caught. His fear slipped easily into terror.

What happened next happened with such speed and concentration that it all seemed crammed into a moment. At once and in a heap it happened. It was quite inevitable. Down the white road to meet him a man came swaying from side to side in drunkenness quite obviously feigned—a tramp; and while Martin made room for him to pass, the lurch changed in a second to attack, and the fellow was upon him. The blow was sudden and terrific, yet even while it fell Martin was aware that behind him rushed a second man, who caught his legs from under him and bore him with a thud and crash to the ground. Blows rained then; he saw a gleam of something shining; a sudden deadly nausea plunged him into utter weakness where resistance was impossible. Something of fire entered his throat, and from his mouth poured a thick sweet thing that choked him. The world sank far away into darkness. . . . Yet through all the horror and confusion ran the trail of two clear thoughts: he realised that the first tramp had sneaked at a fast double through the heather and so come down to meet him; and that something heavy was torn from fastenings that clipped it tight and close beneath his clothes against his body. . . .

Abruptly then the darkness lifted, passed utterly away. He found himself peering into the map against the signpost. The wind was flapping the corners against his cheek, and he was poring over names that now he saw quite clear. Upon the arms of the sign-post above were those he had expected to find, and the map recorded them quite faithfully. All was accurate again and as it should be. He read the name of the village he had meant to make—it was plainly visible in the dusk, two miles the distance given. Bewildered, shaken, unable to think of anything, he stuffed the map into his pocket unfolded, and hurried forward like a man who has just wakened from an awful dream that had compressed into a single second all the detailed misery of some prolonged, oppressive nightmare.

He broke into a steady trot that soon became a run; the perspiration poured from him; his legs felt weak, and his breath was difficult to manage. He was only conscious of the overpowering desire to get away as fast as possible from the sign-post at the cross-roads where the dreadful vision had flashed upon him. For Martin, accountant on a holiday, had never dreamed of any world of psychic possibilities. The entire thing was torture. It was worse than a "cooked" balance of the books that some conspiracy of clerks and directors proved at his innocent door. He raced as though the country-side ran crying at his heels. And always still ran with him the incredible conviction that none of this was really meant for himself at all. He had overheard the secrets of another. He had taken the warning for another into himself, and so altered its direction. He had thereby prevented its right delivery. It all shocked him beyond words. It dislocated the machinery of his just and accurate soul. The warning was intended for another, who could not—would not—now receive it.

The physical exertion, however, brought at length a more comfortable reaction and some measure of composure. With the lights in sight, he slowed down and entered the village at a reasonable pace. The inn was reached, a bedroom inspected and engaged, and supper ordered with the solid comfort of a large Bass to satisfy an unholy thirst and complete the restoration of balance. The unusual sensations largely passed away, and the odd feeling that anything in his simple, wholesome world required explanation was no longer present. Still with a vague uneasiness about him, though actual fear quite gone, he went into the bar to smoke an after-supper pipe and chat with the natives, as his pleasure was upon a holiday, and so saw two men leaning upon the counter at the far end with their backs towards him. He saw their faces instantly in the glass, and the pipe nearly slipped from between his teeth. Clean-shaven, sleek, clever faces—and he caught a word or two as they talked over their drinks—German words. Well dressed they were, both men, with nothing about them calling for particular attention; they might have been two tourists holiday-making like himself in tweeds and walking-boots. And they presently paid for their drinks and went out. He never saw them face to face at all; but the sweat broke out afresh all over him, a feverish rush of heat and ice together ran about his body; beyond question he recognised the two tramps, this time not disguised—*not yet* disguised.

He remained in his corner without moving, puffing violently at an extinguished pipe, gripped helplessly by the return of that first vile terror. It came again to him with an absolute clarity of certainty that it was not with himself they had to do, these men, and, further, that he had no right in the world to interfere. He had no *locus standi* at all; it would be immoral. . . even if the opportunity came. And the opportunity, he felt, would come. He had been an eavesdropper, and had come upon private information of a secret kind that he had no right to make use of, even that good might come—even to save life. He sat on in his corner, terrified and silent, waiting for the thing that should happen next.

But night came without explanation. Nothing happened. He slept soundly. There was no other guest at the inn but an elderly man, apparently a tourist like himself. He wore gold-rimmed glasses, and in the morning Martin overheard him asking the landlord what direction he should take for Litacy Hill. His teeth began then to chatter and a weakness came into his knees. "You turn to the left at the cross-roads," Martin broke in before the landlord could reply; "you'll see the sign-post about two miles from here, and after that it's a matter of four miles more." How in the world did he know, flashed horribly through him. "I'm going that way myself," he was saying next; "I'll go with you for a bit—if you don't mind!" The words came out impulsively and ill-considered; of their own accord they came. For his own direction was exactly opposite. *He did not want the man to go alone.* The stranger, however, easily evaded his offer of companionship. He thanked him with the remark that he was starting later in the day. . . . They were standing, all three, beside the horse-trough in front of the inn, when at that very moment a tramp, slouching along the road, looked up and asked the time of day. And it was the man with the gold-rimmed glasses who told him.

"T'ank you; much opliged," the tramp replied, passing on with his slow, slouching gait, while the landlord, a talkative fellow, proceeded to remark upon the number of Germans that lived in England and were ready to swell the Teutonic invasion which he, for his part, deemed imminent.

But Martin heard it not. Before he had gone a mile upon his way he went into the woods to fight his conscience all alone. His feebleness, his cowardice, were surely criminal. Real anguish tortured him. A dozen times he decided to go back upon his steps, and a dozen times the singular authority that whispered he had no right to interfere prevented him. How could he act upon knowledge gained by eavesdropping? How interfere in the private business of another's hidden life merely because he had overheard, as at the telephone, its secret dangers? Some inner confusion prevented straight thinking altogether. The stranger would merely think him mad. He had no "fact" togoupon. . . . He smothered a hundred impulses . . . and finally went on his way with a shaking, troubled heart.

The last two days of his holiday were ruined by doubts and

questions and alarms—all justified later when he read of the murder of a tourist upon Litacy Hill. The man wore gold-rimmed glasses, and carried in a belt about his person a large sum of money. His throat was cut. And the police were hard upon the trail of a mysterious pair of tramps, said to be—Germans.

The Transfer

The child began to cry in the early afternoon—about three o'clock, to be exact. I remember the hour, because I had been listening with secret relief to the sound of the departing carriage. Those wheels fading into the distance down the gravel drive with Mrs. Frene, and her daughter Gladys to whom I was governess, meant for me some hours' welcome rest, and the June day was oppressively hot. Moreover, there was this excitement in the little country household that had told upon us all, but especially upon myself. This excitement, running delicately behind all the events of the morning, was due to some mystery, and the mystery was of course kept concealed from the governess. I had exhausted myself with guessing and keeping on the watch. For some deep and unexplained anxiety possessed me, so that I kept thinking of my sister's dictum that I was really much too sensitive to make a good governess, and that I should have done far better as a professional clairvoyante.

Mr. Frene, senior, "Uncle Frank," was expected for an unusual visit from town about tea-time. That I knew. I also knew that his visit was concerned somehow with the future welfare of little Jamie, Gladys' seven-year-old brother. More than this, indeed, I never knew, and this missing link makes my story in a fashion incoherent—an important bit of the strange puzzle left out. I only gathered that the visit of Uncle Frank was of a condescending nature, that Jamie was told he must be upon his very best behavior to make a good impression, and that Jamie, who had never seen his uncle, dreaded him horribly already in advance. Then, trailing thinly through the dying crunch of the carriage wheels this sultry afternoon, I heard the curious little wail of the child's crying, with the effect, wholly unaccountable, that every nerve in my body shot its bolt electrically, bringing me to my feet with a tingling of unequivocal alarm. Positively, the water ran into my eyes. I recalled his white distress that morning when told that Uncle Frank was motoring down for tea and that he was to be "very nice indeed" to him. It had gone into me like a knife. All through the day, indeed, had run this nightmare quality of terror and vision.

"The man with the 'normous face?" he had asked in a little voice of awe, and then gone speechless from the room in tears that no amount of soothing management could calm. That was all I saw; and what he meant by "the 'normous face" gave me only a sense of vague presentiment. But it came as anticlimax somehow—a sudden revelation of the mystery and excitement that pulsed beneath the quiet of the stifling summer day. I feared for him. For of all that commonplace household I loved Jamie best, though professionally I had nothing to do with him. He was a high-strung, ultra-sensitive child, and it seemed to me that no one understood him, least of all his honest, tender-hearted parents; so that his little wailing voice brought me from my bed to the window in a moment like a call for help.

The haze of June lay over that big garden like a blanket; the wonderful flowers, which were Mr. Frene's delight, hung motionless; the lawns, so soft and thick, cushioned all other sounds; only the limes and huge clumps of guelder roses hummed with bees. Through this muted atmosphere of heat and haze the sound of the child's crying floated faintly to my ears—from a distance. Indeed, I wonder now that I heard it at all, for the next moment I saw him down beyond the garden, standing in his white sailor suit alone, two hundred yards away. He was down by the ugly patch where nothing grew—the Forbidden Corner. A faintness then came over me at once, a faintness as of death, when I saw him *there* of all places—where he never was allowed to go, and where, moreover, he was usually too terrified to go. To see him standing solitary in that singular spot, above all to hear him crying there, bereft me momentarily of the power to act. Then, before I could recover my composure sufficiently to call him in, Mr. Frene came round the corner from the Lower Farm with the dogs, and, seeing his son, performed that office for me. In his loud, good-natured, hearty voice he called him, and Jamie turned and ran as though some spell had broken just in time—ran into the open arms of his fond but uncomprehending father, who carried him indoors on his shoulder, while asking "what all this hubbub was about?" And, at their heels, the tailless sheep-dogs followed, barking loudly, and performing what Jamie called their "Gravel Dance," because they ploughed up the moist, rolled gravel with their feet.

I stepped back swiftly from the window lest I should be seen. Had I witnessed the saving of the child from fire or drowning the relief could hardly have been greater. Only Mr. Frene, I felt sure, would not say and do the right thing quite. He would protect the boy from his own vain imaginings, yet not with the explanation that could really heal. They disappeared behind the rose trees, making for the house. I saw no more till later, when Mr. Frene, senior, arrived.

To describe the ugly patch as "singular" is hard to justify, perhaps, yet some such word is what the entire family sought, though never— oh, never!—used. To Jamie and myself, though equally we never mentioned it, that treeless, flowerless spot was more than singular. It stood at the far end of the magnificent rose garden, a bald, sore place, where the black earth showed uglily in winter, almost like a piece of dangerous bog, and in summer baked and cracked with fissures where green lizards shot their fire in passing. In contrast to the rich luxuriance of death amid life, a center of disease that cried for healing lest it spread. But it never did spread. Behind it stood the thick wood of silver birches and, glimmering beyond, the orchard meadow, where the lambs played.

The gardeners had a very simple explanation of its barrenness— that the water all drained off it owing to the lie of the slopes immediately about it, holding no remnant to keep the soil alive. I cannot say. It was Jamie—Jamie who felt its spell and haunted it, who spent whole hours there, even while afraid, and for whom it was finally labeled "strictly out of bounds" because it stimulated his already big imagination, not wisely but too darkly—it was Jamie who buried ogres there and heard it crying in an earthy voice, swore that it shook its surface sometimes while he watched it, and secretly gave it food in the form of birds or mice or rabbits he found dead upon his wanderings. And it was Jamie who put so extraordinarily into words the *feeling* that the horrid spot had given me from the moment I first saw it.

"It's bad, Miss Gould," he told me.

"But, Jamie, nothing in Nature is bad—exactly; only different from the rest sometimes."

"Miss Gould, if you please, then it's empty. It's not fed. It's dying because it can't get the food it wants."

And when I stared into the little pale face where the eyes shone so dark and wonderful, seeking within myself for the right thing to say to him, he added, with an emphasis and conviction that made me suddenly turn cold: "Miss Gould"—he always used my name like this in all his sentences—"it's hungry, don't you see? But I know what would make it feel all right."

Only the conviction of an earnest child, perhaps, could have made so outrageous a suggestion worth listening to for an instant; but for me, who felt that things an imaginative child believed were important, it came with a vast disquieting shock of reality. Jamie, in this exaggerated way, had caught at the edge of a shocking fact—a hint of dark, undiscovered truth had leaped into that sensitive imagination. Why there lay horror in the words I cannot say, but I think some power of darkness trooped across the suggestion of that sentence at the end, "I know what would make it feel all right." I remember that I shrank from asking explanation. Small groups of other words, veiled fortunately by his silence, gave life to an unspeakable possibility that hitherto had lain at the back of my own consciousness. The way it sprang to life proves, I think, that my mind already contained it. The blood rushed from my heart as I listened. I remember that my knees shook. Jamie's idea was—had been all along—my own as well.

And now, as I lay down on my bed and thought about it all, I understood why the coming of his uncle involved somehow an experience that wrapped terror at its heart. With a sense of nightmare certainty that left me too weak to resist the preposterous idea, too shocked, indeed, to argue or reason it away, this certainty came with its full, black blast of conviction; and the only way I can put it into words, since nightmare horror really is not properly tellable at all, seems this: that there *was* something missing in that dying patch of garden; something lacking that it ever searched for; something, once found and taken, that would turn it rich and living as the rest; more—that there was some living person who could do this for it. Mr. Frene, senior, in a word, "Uncle Frank," was this person who out of his abundant life could supply the lack—unwittingly.

For this connection between the dying, empty patch and the person of this vigorous, wealthy, and successful man had already lodged itself in my subconsciousness before I was aware of it. Clearly it must have lain there all along, though hidden. Jamie's words, his sudden pallor, his vibrating emotion of fearful anticipation had developed the plate, but it was his weeping alone there in the Forbidden Corner that had printed it. The photograph shone framed before me in the air. I hid my eyes. But for the redness—the charm of my face goes to pieces unless my eyes are clear—I could have cried. Jamie's words that morning about the "'normous face" came back upon me like a battering-ram.

Mr. Frene, senior, had been so frequently the subject of conversation in the family since I came, I had so often heard him discussed, and had then read so much about him in the papers—his energy, his philanthropy, his success with everything he laid his hand to—that a picture of the man had grown complete within me. I knew him as he was—within; or, as my sister would have said—clairvoyantly. And the only time I saw him (when I took Gladys to a meeting where he was chairman, and later felt his atmosphere and presence while for a moment he patronizingly spoke with her) had justified the portrait I had drawn. The rest, you may say, was a woman's wild imagining; but I think rather it was that kind of divining intuition which women share with children. If souls could be made visible, I would stake my life upon the truth and accuracy of my portrait.

For this Mr. Frene was a man who drooped alone, but grew vital in a crowd—because he used their vitality. He was a supreme, unconscious artist in the science of taking the fruits of others' work and living—for his own advantage. He vampired, unknowingly no doubt, every one with whom he came in contact; left them exhausted, tired, listless. Others fed him, so that while in a full room he shone, alone by himself and with no life to draw upon he languished and declined. In the man's immediate neighborhood you felt his presence draining you;

he took your ideas, your strength, your very words, and later used them for his own benefit and aggrandizement. Not evilly, of course; the man was good enough; but you felt that he was dangerous owing to the facile way he absorbed into himself all loose vitality that was to be had. His eyes and voice and presence devitalized you. Life, it seemed, not highly organized enough to resist, must shrink from his too near approach and hide away for fear of being appropriated, for fear, that is, of—death.

Jamie, unknowingly, put in the finishing touch to my unconscious portrait. The man carried about with him some silent, compelling trick of drawing out all your reserves—then swiftly pocketing them. At first you would be conscious of taut resistance; this would slowly shade off into weariness; the will would become flaccid; then you either moved away or yielded—agreed to all he said with a sense of weakness pressing ever closer upon the edges of collapse. With a male antagonist it might be different, but even then the effort of resistance would generate force that *he* absorbed and not the other. He never gave out. Some instinct taught him how to protect himself from that. To human beings, I mean, he never gave out. This time it was a very different matter. He had no more chance than a fly before the wheels of a huge— what Jamie used to call—"attraction" engine.

So this was how I saw him—a great human sponge, crammed and soaked with the life, or proceeds of life, absorbed from others—stolen. My idea of a human vampire was satisfied. He went about carrying these accumulations of the life of others. In this sense his "life" was not really his own. For the same reason, I think, it was not so fully under his control as he imagined.

And in another hour this man would be here. I went to the window. My eye wandered to the empty patch, dull black there amid the rich luxuriance of the garden flowers. It struck me as a hideous bit of emptiness yawning to be filled and nourished. The idea of Jamie playing round its bare edge was loathsome. I watched the big summer clouds above, the stillness of the afternoon, the haze. The silence of the overheated garden was oppressive. I had never felt a day so stifling, motionless. It lay there waiting. The household, too, was waiting— waiting for the coming of Mr. Frene from London in his big motor-car.

And I shall never forget the sensation of icy shrinking and distress with which I heard the rumble of the car. He had arrived. Tea was all ready on the lawn beneath the lime trees, and Mrs. Frene and Gladys, back from their drive, were sitting in wicker chairs. Mr. Frene, junior, was in the hall to meet his brother, but Jamie, as I learned afterwards, had shown such hysterical alarm, offered such bold resistance, that it had been deemed wiser to keep him in his room. Perhaps, after all, his presence might not be necessary. The visit clearly had to do with something on the uglier side of life—money, settlements, or what not; I never knew exactly; only that his parents were anxious, and that Uncle Frank had to be propitiated. It does not matter. That has nothing to do with the affair. What has to do with it—or I should not be telling the story—is that Mrs. Frene sent for me to come down "in my nice white dress, if I didn't mind," and that I was terrified, yet pleased, because it meant that a pretty face would be considered a welcome addition to the visitor's landscape. Also, most odd it was, I felt my presence was somehow inevitable, that in some way it was intended that I should witness what I did witness. And the instant I came upon the lawn—I hesitate to set it down, it sounds so foolish, disconnected—I could have sworn, as my eyes met his, that a kind of sudden darkness came, taking the summer brilliance out of everything, and that it was caused by troops of small black horses that raced about us from his person—to attack.

After a first momentary approving glance he took no further notice of me. The tea and talk went smoothly; I helped to pass the plates and cups, filling in pauses with little under-talk to Gladys. Jamie was never mentioned. Outwardly all seemed well, but inwardly everything was awful—skirting the edge of things unspeakable, and so charged with danger that I could not keep my voice from trembling when I spoke.

I watched his hard, bleak face; I noticed how thin he was, and the curious, oily brightness of his steady eyes. They did not glitter, but they drew you with a sort of soft, creamy shine like Eastern eyes. And everything he said or did announced what I may dare to call the *suction* of his presence. His nature achieved this result automatically. He dominated us all, yet so gently that until it was accomplished no one noticed it.

Before five minutes had passed, however, I was aware of one thing only. My mind focussed exclusively upon it, and so vividly that I marveled the others did not scream, or run, or do something violent to prevent it. And it was this; that, separated merely by some dozen yards or so, this man, vibrating with the acquired vitality of others, stood within easy reach of that spot of yawning emptiness, waiting and eager to be filled. Earth scented her prey.

These two active "centers" were within fighting distance; he so thin, so hard, so keen, yet really spreading large with the loose "surround" of others' life he had appropriated, so practiced and triumphant; that other so patient, deep, with so mighty a draw of the whole earth behind it, and—ugh!—so obviously aware that its opportunity at last had come.

I saw it all as plainly as though I watched two great animals prepare for battle, both unconsciously; yet in some inexplicable way I saw it, of course, within me, and not externally. The conflict would be hideously unequal. Each side had already sent out emissaries, how long before I could not tell, for the first evidence *he* gave that something was going wrong with him was when his voice grew suddenly confused, he missed his words, and his lips trembled a moment and turned flabby. The next second his face betrayed that singular and horrid change, growing somehow loose about the bones of the cheek, and larger, so that I remembered Jamie's miserable phrase. The emissaries of the two kingdoms, the human and the vegetable, had met, I make it out, in that very second. For the first time in his long career of battening on others, Mr. Frene found himself pitted against a vaster kingdom than he knew and, so finding, shook inwardly in that little part that was his definite actual self. He felt the huge disaster coming.

"Yes, John," he was saying, in his drawling, self-congratulating voice, "Sir George gave me that car—gave it to me as a present. Wasn't it char—?" and then broke off abruptly, stammered, drew breath, stood up, and looked uneasily about him. For a second there was a gaping pause. It was like the click which starts some huge machinery moving—that instant's pause before it actually starts. The whole thing, indeed, then went with the rapidity of machinery running down and beyond control. I thought of a giant dynamo working silently and invisible.

"What's that?" he cried, in a soft voice charged with alarm. "What's that horrid place? And someone's crying there—who is it?"

He pointed to the empty patch. Then, before anyone could answer, he started across the lawn towards it, going every minute faster. Before anyone could move he stood upon the edge. He leaned over—peering down into it.

It seemed a few hours passed, but really they were seconds, for time is measured by the quality and not the quantity of sensations it contains. I saw it all with merciless, photographic detail, sharply etched amid the general confusion. Each side was intensely active, but only one side, the human, exerted all its force—in resistance. The other merely stretched out a feeler, as it were, from its vast, potential strength; no more was necessary. It was such a soft and easy victory. Oh, it was rather pitiful! There was no bluster or great effort, on one side at least. Close by his side I witnessed it, for I, it seemed, alone had moved and followed him. No one else stirred, though Mrs. Frene clattered noisily with the cups, making some sudden impulsive gesture with her hands, and Gladys, I remember, gave a cry—it was like a little scream—"Oh, mother, it's the heat, isn't it?" Mr. Frene, her father, was speechless, pale as ashes.

But the instant I reached his side, it became clear what had drawn me there thus instinctively. Upon the other side, among the silver birches, stood little Jamie. He was watching. I experienced—for him— one of those moments that shake the heart; a liquid fear ran all over me, the more effective because unintelligible really. Yet I felt that if I could know all, and what lay actually behind, my fear would be more than justified; that the thing *was* awful, full of awe.

And then it happened—a truly wicked sight—like watching a universe in action, yet all contained within a small square foot of space. I think he understood vaguely that if someone could only take his place he might be saved, and that was why, discerning instinctively the easiest substitute within reach, he saw the child and called aloud to him across the empty patch, "James, my boy, come here!"

His voice was like a thin report, but somehow flat and lifeless, as when a rifle misses fire, sharp, yet weak; it had no "crack" in it. It was really supplication. And, with amazement, I heard my own ring out imperious and strong, though I was not conscious of saying it, "Jamie, don't move. Stay where you are!" But Jamie, the little child, obeyed neither of us. Moving up nearer to the edge, he stood there—laughing! I heard that laughter, but could have sworn it did not come from him. The empty, yawning patch gave out that sound.

Mr. Frene turned sideways, throwing up his arms. I saw his hard, bleak face grow somehow wider, spread through the air, and downwards. A similar thing, I saw, was happening at the same time to his entire person, for it drew out into the atmosphere in a stream of movement. The face for a second made me think of those toys of green india rubber that children pull. It grew enormous. But this was an external impression only. What actually happened, I clearly understood, was that all this vitality and life he had transferred from others to himself for years was now in turn being taken from him and transferred—elsewhere.

One moment on the edge he wobbled horribly, then with that queer sideways motion, rapid yet ungainly, he stepped forward into the middle of the patch and fell heavily upon his face. His eyes, as he dropped, faded shockingly, and across the countenance was written plainly what I can only call an expression of destruction. He looked utterly destroyed. I caught a sound—from Jamie?—but this time not of laughter. It was like a gulp; it was deep and muffled and it dipped away into the earth. Again I thought of a troop of small black horses galloping away down a subterranean passage beneath my feet—plunging into the depths—their tramping growing fainter and fainter into buried distance. In my nostrils was a pungent smell of earth.

And then—all passed. I came back into myself. Mr. Frene, junior, was lifting his brother's head from the lawn where he had fallen from the heat, close beside the tea-table. He had never really moved from there. And Jamie, I learned afterwards, had been the whole time asleep upon his bed upstairs, worn out with his crying and unreasoning alarm. Gladys came running out with cold water, sponge and towel, brandy too—all kinds of things. "Mother, it *was* the heat, wasn't it?" I heard her whisper, but I did not catch Mrs. Frene's reply. From her face it struck me that she was bordering on collapse herself. Then the butler followed, and they just picked him up and carried him into the house. He recovered even before the doctor came.

But the queer thing to me is that I was convinced the others all had seen what I saw, only that no one said a word about it; and to this day no one *has* said a word. And that was, perhaps, the most horrid part of all.

From that day to this I have scarcely heard a mention of Mr. Frene, senior. It seemed as if he dropped suddenly out of life. The papers never mentioned him. His activities ceased, as it were. His after-life, at any rate, became singularly ineffective. Certainly he achieved nothing worth public mention. But it may be only that, having left the employ of Mrs. Frene, there was no particular occasion for me to hear anything.

The after-life of that empty patch of garden, however, was quite otherwise. Nothing, so far as I know, was done to it by gardeners, or in the way of draining it or bringing in new earth, but even before I left in the following summer it had changed. It lay untouched, full of great, luscious, driving weeds and creepers, very strong, full—fed, and bursting thick with life.

Sandhills.

The Glamour of the Snow

I

Hibbert, always conscious of two worlds, was in this mountain village conscious of three. It lay on the slopes of the Valais Alps, and he had taken a room in the little post office, where he could be at peace to write his book, yet at the same time enjoy the winter sports and find companionship in the hotels when he wanted it.

The three worlds that met and mingled here seemed to his imaginative temperament very obvious, though it is doubtful if another mind less intuitively equipped would have seen them so well-defined. There was the world of tourist English, civilised, quasi-educated, to which he belonged by birth, at any rate; there was the world of peasants to which he felt himself drawn by sympathy—for he loved and admired their toiling, simple life; and there was this other—which he could only call the world of Nature. To this last, however, in virtue of a vehement poetic imagination, and a tumultuous pagan instinct fed by his very blood, he felt that most of him belonged. The others borrowed from it, as it were, for visits. Here, with the soul of Nature, hid his central life.

Between all three was conflict—potential conflict. On the skating-rink each Sunday the tourists regarded the natives as intruders; in the church the peasants plainly questioned: "Why do you come? We are here to worship; you to stare and whisper!" For neither of these two worlds accepted the other. And neither did Nature accept the tourists, for it took advantage of their least mistakes, and indeed, even of the peasant-world "accepted" only those who were strong and bold enough to invade her savage domain with sufficient skill to protect themselves from several forms of—death.

Now Hibbert was keenly aware of this potential conflict and want of harmony; he felt outside, yet caught by it—torn in the three directions because he was partly of each world, but wholly in only one. There grew in him a constant, subtle effort—or, at least, desire—to unify them and decide positively to which he should belong and live in. The attempt, of course, was largely subconscious. It was the natural instinct of a richly imaginative nature seeking the point of equilibrium, so that the mind could feel at peace and his brain be free to do good work.

Among the guests no one especially claimed his interest. The men were nice but undistinguished—athletic schoolmasters, doctors snatching a holiday, good fellows all; the women, equally various—the clever, the would-be-fast, the dare-to-be-dull, the women "who understood," and the usual pack of jolly dancing girls and "flappers." And Hibbert, with his forty odd years of thick experience behind him, got on well with the lot; he understood them all; they belonged to definite, predigested types that are the same the world over, and that he had met the world over long ago.

But to none of them did he belong. His nature was too "multiple" to subscribe to the set of shibboleths of any one class. And, since all liked him, and felt that somehow he seemed outside of them—spectator, looker-on—all sought to claim him.

In a sense, therefore, the three worlds fought for him: natives, tourists, Nature. . . .

It was thus began the singular conflict for the soul of Hibbert. *In* his own soul, however, it took place. Neither the peasants nor the tourists were conscious that they fought for anything. And Nature, they say, is merely blind and automatic.

The assault upon him of the peasants may be left out of account, for it is obvious that they stood no chance of success. The tourist world, however, made a gallant effort to subdue him to themselves. But the evenings in the hotel, when dancing was not in order, were—English. The provincial imagination was set upon a throne and worshipped heavily through incense of the stupidest conventions possible. Hibbert used to go back early to his room in the post office to work.

"It is a mistake on my part to have *realised* that there is any conflict at all," he thought, as he crunched home over the snow at midnight after one of the dances. "It would have been better to have kept outside it all and done my work. Better," he added, looking back down the silent village street to the church tower, "and—safer."

The adjective slipped from his mind before he was aware of it. He turned with an involuntary start and looked about him. He knew perfectly well what it meant—this thought that had thrust its head up from the instinctive region. He understood, without being able to express it fully, the meaning that betrayed itself in the choice of the adjective. For if he had ignored the existence of this conflict he would at the same time, have remained outside the arena. Whereas now he had entered the lists. Now this battle for his soul must have issue. And he knew that the spell of Nature was greater for him than all other spells in the world combined—greater than love, revelry, pleasure, greater even than study. He had always been afraid to let himself go. His pagan soul dreaded her terrific powers of witchery even while he worshipped.

The little village already slept. The world lay smothered in snow. The châlet roofs shone white beneath the moon, and pitch-black shadows gathered against the walls of the church. His eye rested a moment on the square stone tower with its frosted cross that pointed to the sky: then travelled with a leap of many thousand feet to the enormous mountains that brushed the brilliant stars. Like a forest rose the huge peaks above the slumbering village, measuring the night and heavens. They beckoned him. And something born of the snowy desolation, born of the midnight and the silent grandeur, born of the great listening hollows of the night, something that lay 'twixt terror and wonder, dropped from the vast wintry spaces down into his heart—and called him. Very softly, unrecorded in any word or thought his brain could compass, it laid its spell upon him. Fingers of snow brushed the surface of his heart. The power and quiet majesty of the winter's night appalled him. . . .

Fumbling a moment with the big unwieldy key, he let himself in and went upstairs to bed. Two thoughts went with him—apparently quite ordinary and sensible ones:

"What fools these peasants are to sleep through such a night!"

And the other:

"Those dances tire me. I'll never go again. My work only suffers in the morning." The claims of peasants and tourists upon him seemed thus in a single instant weakened.

The clash of battle troubled half his dreams. Nature had sent her Beauty of the Night and won the first assault. The others, routed and dismayed, fled far away.

II

"Don't go back to your dreary old post office. We're going to have supper in my room—something hot. Come and join us. Hurry up!"

There had been an ice carnival, and the last party, tailing up the snow-slope to the hotel, called him. The Chinese lanterns smoked and sputtered on the wires; the band had long since gone. The cold was bitter and the moon came only momentarily between high, driving clouds. From the shed where the people changed from skates to snow-boots he shouted something to the effect that he was "following"; but no answer came; the moving shadows of those who had called were already merged high up against the village darkness. The voices died away. Doors slammed. Hibbert found himself alone on the deserted rink.

And it was then, quite suddenly, the impulse came to—stay and skate alone. The thought of the stuffy hotel room, and of those noisy people with their obvious jokes and laughter, oppressed him. He felt a longing to be alone with the night; to taste her wonder all by himself there beneath the stars, gliding over the ice. It was not yet midnight, and he could skate for half an hour. That supper party, if they noticed his absence at all, would merely think he had changed his mind and gone to bed.

It was an impulse, yes, and not an unnatural one; yet even at the time it struck him that something more than impulse lay concealed behind it. More than invitation, yet certainly less than command, there was a vague queer feeling that he stayed because he had to, almost as though there was something he had forgotten, overlooked, left undone. Imaginative temperaments are often thus; and impulse is ever weakness. For with such ill-considered opening of the doors to hasty action may come an invasion of other forces at the same time—forces merely waiting their opportunity perhaps!

He caught the fugitive warning even while he dismissed it as absurd, and the next minute he was whirling over the smooth ice in delightful curves and loops beneath the moon. There was no fear of collision. He could take his own speed and space as he willed. The shadows of the towering mountains fell across the rink, and a wind of ice came from the forests, where the snow lay ten feet deep. The hotel lights winked and went out. The village slept. The high wire netting could not keep out the wonder of the winter night that grew about him like a presence. He skated on and on, keen exhilarating pleasure in his tingling blood, and weariness all forgotten.

And then, midway in the delight of rushing movement, he saw a figure gliding behind the wire netting, watching him. With a start that almost made him lose his balance—for the abruptness of the new arrival was so unlooked for—he paused and stared. Although the light was dim he made out that it was the figure of a woman and that she was feeling her way along the netting, trying to get in. Against the white background of the snow-field he watched her rather stealthy efforts as she passed with a silent step over the banked-up snow. She was tall and slim and graceful; he could see that even in the dark. And then, of course, he understood. It was another adventurous skater like himself, stolen down unawares from hotel or châlet, and searching for the opening. At once, making a sign and pointing with one hand, he turned swiftly and skated over to the little entrance on the other side.

But, even before he got there, there was a sound on the ice behind him and, with an exclamation of amazement he could not suppress, he turned to see her swerving up to his side across the width of the rink. She had somehow found another way in.

Hibbert, as a rule, was punctilious, and in these free-and-easy places, perhaps, especially so. If only for his own protection he did not seek to make advances unless some kind of introduction paved the way. But for these two to skate together in the semi-darkness without speech, often of necessity brushing shoulders almost, was too absurd to think of. Accordingly he raised his cap and spoke. His actual words he seems unable to recall, nor what the girl said in reply, except that she answered him in accented English with some commonplace about doing figures at midnight on an empty rink. Quite natural it was, and right. She wore grey clothes of some kind, though not the customary long gloves or sweater, for indeed her hands were bare, and presently when he skated with her, he wondered with something like astonishment at their dry and icy coldness.

And she was delicious to skate with—supple, sure, and light, fast as a man yet with the freedom of a child, sinuous and steady at the same time. Her flexibility made him wonder, and when he asked where she had learned she murmured—he caught the breath against his ear and recalled later that it was singularly cold—that she could hardly tell, for she had been accustomed to the ice ever since she could remember.

But her face he never properly saw. A muffler of white fur buried her neck to the ears, and her cap came over the eyes. He only saw that she was young. Nor could he gather her hotel or châlet, for she pointed vaguely, when he asked her, up the slopes. "Just over there—" she said, quickly taking his hand again. He did not press her; no doubt she wished to hide her escapade. And the touch of her hand thrilled him more than anything he could remember; even through his thick glove he felt the softness of that cold and delicate softness.

The clouds thickened over the mountains. It grew darker. They talked very little, and did not always skate together. Often they separated, curving about in corners by themselves, but always coming together again in the centre of the rink; and when she left him thus

Hibbert was conscious of—yes, of missing her. He found a peculiar satisfaction, almost a fascination, in skating by her side. It was quite an adventure—these two strangers with the ice and snow and night!

Midnight had long since sounded from the old church tower before they parted. She gave the sign, and he skated quickly to the shed, meaning to find a seat and help her take her skates off. Yet when he turned—she had already gone. He saw her slim figure gliding away across the snow . . . and hurrying for the last time round the rink alone he searched in vain for the opening she had twice used in this curious way.

"How very queer!" he thought, referring to the wire netting. "She must have lifted it and wriggled under . . . !"

Wondering how in the world she managed it, what in the world had possessed him to be so free with her, and who in the world she was, he went up the steep slope to the post office and so to bed, her promise to come again another night still ringing delightfully in his ears. And curious were the thoughts and sensations that accompanied him. Most of all, perhaps, was the half suggestion of some dim memory that he had known this girl before, had met her somewhere, more—that she knew him. For in her voice—a low, soft, windy little voice it was, tender and soothing for all its quiet coldness—there lay some faint reminder of two others he had known, both long since gone: the voice of the woman he had loved, and—the voice of his mother.

But this time through his dreams there ran no clash of battle. He was conscious, rather, of something cold and clinging that made him think of sifting snowflakes climbing slowly with entangling touch and thickness round his feet. The snow, coming without noise, each flake so light and tiny none can mark the spot whereon it settles, yet the mass of it able to smother whole villages, wove through the very texture of his mind—cold, bewildering, deadening effort with its clinging network of ten million feathery touches.

III

In the morning Hibbert realised he had done, perhaps, a foolish thing. The brilliant sunshine that drenched the valley made him see this, and the sight of his work-table with its typewriter, books, papers, and the rest, brought additional conviction. To have skated with a girl alone at midnight, no matter how innocently the thing had come about, was unwise—unfair, especially to her. Gossip in these little winter resorts was worse than in a provincial town. He hoped no one had seen them. Luckily the night had been dark. Most likely none had heard the ring of skates.

Deciding that in future he would be more careful, he plunged into work, and sought to dismiss the matter from his mind.

But in his times of leisure the memory returned persistently to haunt him. When he "ski-d," "luged," or danced in the evenings, and especially when he skated on the little rink, he was aware that the eyes of his mind forever sought this strange companion of the night. A hundred times he fancied that he saw her, but always sight deceived him. Her face he might not know, but he could hardly fail to recognise her figure. Yet nowhere among the others did he catch a glimpse of that slim young creature he had skated with alone beneath the clouded stars. He searched in vain. Even his inquiries as to the occupants of the private châlets brought no results. He had lost her. But the queer thing was that he felt as though she were somewhere close; he *knew* she had not really gone. While people came and left with every day, it never once occurred to him that she had left. On the contrary, he felt assured that they would meet again.

This thought he never quite acknowledged. Perhaps it was the wish that fathered it only. And, even when he did meet her, it was a question how he would speak and claim acquaintance, or whether *she* would recognise himself. It might be awkward. He almost came to dread a meeting, though "dread," of course, was far too strong a word to describe an emotion that was half delight, half wondering anticipation.

Meanwhile the season was in full swing. Hibbert felt in perfect health, worked hard, ski-d, skated, luged, and at night danced fairly often—in spite of his decision. This dancing was, however, an act of subconscious surrender; it really meant he hoped to find her among the whirling couples. He was searching for her without quite acknowledging it to himself; and the hotel-world, meanwhile, thinking it had won him over, teased and chaffed him. He made excuses in a similar vein; but all the time he watched and searched and—waited.

For several days the sky held clear and bright and frosty, bitterly cold, everything crisp and sparkling in the sun; but there was no sign of fresh snow, and the ski-ers began to grumble. On the mountains was an icy crust that made "running" dangerous; they wanted the frozen, dry, and powdery snow that makes for speed, renders steering easier and falling less severe. But the keen east wind showed no signs of changing for a whole ten days. Then, suddenly, there came a touch of softer air and the weather-wise began to prophesy.

Hibbert, who was delicately sensitive to the least change in earth or sky, was perhaps the first to feel it. Only he did not prophesy. He knew through every nerve in his body that moisture had crept into the air, was accumulating, and that presently a fall would come. For he responded to the moods of Nature like a fine barometer.

And the knowledge, this time, brought into his heart a strange little wayward emotion that was hard to account for—a feeling of unexplained uneasiness and disquieting joy. For behind it, woven through it rather, ran a faint exhilaration that connected remotely somewhere with that touch of delicious alarm, that tiny anticipating "dread," that so puzzled him when he thought of his next meeting with his skating companion of the night. It lay beyond all words, all telling, this queer relationship between the two; but somehow the girl and snow ran in a pair across his mind.

Perhaps for imaginative writing-men, more than for other workers, the smallest change of mood betrays itself at once. His work at any rate revealed this slight shifting of emotional values in his soul. Not that his writing suffered, but that it altered, subtly as those changes of sky or sea or landscape that come with the passing of afternoon into evening—imperceptibly. A subconscious excitement sought to push outwards and express itself . . . and, knowing the uneven effect such moods produced in his work, he laid his pen aside and took instead to reading that he had to do.

Meanwhile the brilliance passed from the sunshine, the sky grew slowly overcast; by dusk the mountain tops came singularly close and sharp; the distant valley rose into absurdly near perspective. The moisture increased, rapidly approaching saturation point, when it must fall in snow. Hibbert watched and waited.

And in the morning the world lay smothered beneath its fresh white carpet. It snowed heavily till noon, thickly, incessantly, chokingly, a foot or more; then the sky cleared, the sun came out in splendour, the wind shifted back to the east, and frost came down upon the mountains with its keenest and most biting tooth. The drop in the temperature was tremendous, but the ski-ers were jubilant. Next day the "running" would be fast and perfect. Already the mass was settling, and the surface freezing into those moss-like, powdery crystals that make the ski run almost of their own accord with the faint "sishing" as of a bird's wings through the air.

IV

That night there was excitement in the little hotel-world, first because there was a *bal costumé*, but chiefly because the new snow had come. And Hibbert went—felt drawn to go; he did not go in costume, but he wanted to talk about the slopes and ski-ing with the other men, and at the same time. . . .

Ah, there was the truth, the deeper necessity that called. For the singular connection between the stranger and the snow again betrayed itself, utterly beyond explanation as before, but vital and insistent. Some hidden instinct in his pagan soul—heaven knows how he phrased it even to himself, if he phrased it at all—whispered that with the snow the girl would be somewhere about, would emerge from her hiding place, would even look for him.

Absolutely unwarranted it was. He laughed while he stood before the little glass and trimmed his moustache, tried to make his black tie sit straight, and shook down his dinner jacket so that it should lie upon the shoulders without a crease. His brown eyes were very bright. "I look younger than I usually do," he thought. It was unusual, even significant, in a man who had no vanity about his appearance and certainly never questioned his age or tried to look younger than he was. Affairs of the heart, with one tumultuous exception that left no fuel for lesser subsequent fires, had never troubled him. The forces of his soul and mind not called upon for "work" and obvious duties, all went to Nature. The desolate, wild places of the earth were what he loved; night, and the beauty of the stars and snow. And this evening he felt their claims upon him mightily stirring. A rising wildness caught his blood, quickened his pulse, woke longing and passion too. But chiefly snow. The snow whirred softly through his thoughts like white, seductive dreams. . . . For the snow had come; and She, it seemed, had somehow come with it—into his mind.

And yet he stood before that twisted mirror and pulled his tie and coat askew a dozen times, as though it mattered. "What in the world is up with me?" he thought. Then, laughing a little, he turned before leaving the room to put his private papers in order. The green morocco desk that held them he took down from the shelf and laid upon the table. Tied to the lid was the visiting card with his brother's London address "in case of accident." On the way down to the hotel he wondered why he had done this, for though imaginative, he was not the kind of man who dealt in presentiments. Moods with him were strong, but ever held in leash.

"It's almost like a warning," he thought, smiling. He drew his thick coat tightly round the throat as the freezing air bit at him. "Those warnings one reads of in stories sometimes . . . !"

A delicious happiness was in his blood. Over the edge of the hills across the valley rose the moon. He saw her silver sheet the world of snow. Snow covered all. It smothered sound and distance. It smothered houses, streets, and human beings. It smothered—life.

V

In the hall there was light and bustle; people were already arriving from the other hotels and châlets, their costumes hidden beneath many wraps. Groups of men in evening dress stood about smoking, talking "snow" and "ski-ing." The band was tuning up. The claims of the hotel-world clashed about him faintly as of old. At the big glass windows of the verandah, peasants stopped a moment on their way home from the *café* to peer. Hibbert thought laughingly of that conflict he used to imagine. He laughed because it suddenly seemed so unreal. He belonged so utterly to Nature and the mountains, and especially to those desolate slopes where now the snow lay thick and fresh and sweet, that there was no question of a conflict at all. The power of the newly fallen snow had caught him, proving it without effort. Out there, upon those lonely reaches of the moonlit ridges, the snow lay ready— masses and masses of it—cool, soft, inviting. He longed for it. It awaited him. He thought of the intoxicating delight of ski-ing in the moonlight. . . .

Thus, somehow, in vivid flashing vision, he thought of it while he stood there smoking with the other men and talking all the "shop" of ski-ing.

And, ever mysteriously blended with this power of the snow, poured also through his inner being the power of the girl. He could not disabuse his mind of the insinuating presence of the two together. He remembered that queer skating-impulse of ten days ago, the impulse that had let her in. That any mind, even an imaginative one, could pass beneath the sway of such a fancy was strange enough; and Hibbert, while fully aware of the disorder, yet found a curious joy in yielding to it. This insubordinate centre that drew him towards old pagan beliefs had assumed command. With a kind of sensuous pleasure he let himself be conquered.

And snow that night seemed in everybody's thoughts. The dancing couples talked of it; the hotel proprietors congratulated one another; it meant good sport and satisfied their guests; every one was planning trips and expeditions, talking of slopes and telemarks, of flying speed and distance, of drifts and crust and frost. Vitality and enthusiasm pulsed in the very air; all were alert and active, positive, radiating currents of creative life even into the stuffy atmosphere of that crowded ball-room. And the snow had caused it, the snow had brought it; all this discharge of eager sparkling energy was due primarily to the—Snow.

But in the mind of Hibbert, by some swift alchemy of his pagan yearnings, this energy became transmuted. It rarefied itself, gleaming in white and crystal currents of passionate anticipation, which he transferred, as by a species of electrical imagination, into the personality of the girl—the Girl of the Snow. She somewhere was waiting for him, expecting him, calling to him softly from those leagues of moonlit mountain. He remembered the touch of that cool, dry hand; the soft and icy breath against his cheek; the hush and softness of her presence in the way she came and the way she had gone again—like a flurry of snow the wind sent gliding up the slopes. She, like himself, belonged out there. He fancied that he heard her little windy voice come sifting to him through the snowy branches of the trees, calling his name . . . that haunting little voice that dived straight to the centre of his life as once, long years ago, two other voices used to do. . . .

But nowhere among the costumed dancers did he see her slender figure. He danced with one and all, distrait and absent, a stupid partner as each girl discovered, his eyes ever turning towards the door and windows, hoping to catch the luring face, the vision that did not come . . . and at length, hoping even against hope. For the ball-room thinned; groups left one by one, going home to their hotels and châlets; the band tired obviously; people sat drinking lemon-squashes at the little tables, the men mopping their foreheads, everybody ready for bed.

It was close on midnight. As Hibbert passed through the hall to get his overcoat and snow-boots, he saw men in the passage by the "sport-room," greasing their ski against an early start. Knapsack luncheons were being ordered by the kitchen swing doors. He sighed. Lighting a cigarette a friend offered him, he returned a confused reply to some question as to whether he could join their party in the morning. It seemed he did not hear it properly. He passed through the outer vestibule between the double glass doors, and went into the night.

The man who asked the question watched him go, an expression of anxiety momentarily in his eyes.

"Don't think he heard you," said another, laughing. "You've got to shout to Hibbert, his mind's so full of his work."

"He works too hard," suggested the first, "full of queer ideas and dreams."

But Hibbert's silence was not rudeness. He had not caught the invitation, that was all. The call of the hotel-world had faded. He no longer heard it. Another wilder call was sounding in his ears.

For up the street he had seen a little figure moving. Close against the shadows of the baker's shop it glided—white, slim, enticing.

VI

And at once into his mind passed the hush and softness of the snow—yet with it a searching, crying wildness for the heights. He knew by some incalculable, swift instinct she would not meet him in the village street. It was not there, amid crowding houses, she would speak to him. Indeed, already she had disappeared, melted from view up the white vista of the moonlit road. Yonder, he divined, she waited where the highway narrowed abruptly into the mountain path beyond the châlets.

It did not even occur to him to hesitate; mad though it seemed, and was—this sudden craving for the heights with her, at least for open spaces where the snow lay thick and fresh—it was too imperious to be denied. He does not remember going up to his room, putting the sweater over his evening clothes, and getting into the fur gauntlet gloves and the helmet cap of wool. Most certainly he has no recollection of fastening on his ski; he must have done it automatically. Some faculty of normal observation was in abeyance, as it were. His mind was out beyond the village—out with the snowy mountains and the moon.

Henri Défago, putting up the shutters over his *café* windows, saw him pass, and wondered mildly: "*Un monsieur qui fait du ski à cette heure*! *Il est Anglais, donc . . .*!" He shrugged his shoulders, as though a man had the right to choose his own way of death. And Marthe Perotti, the hunchback wife of the shoemaker, looking by chance from her window, caught his figure moving swiftly up the road. She had other thoughts, for she knew and believed the old traditions of the witches and snow-beings that steal the souls of men. She had even heard, 'twas said, the dreaded "synagogue" pass roaring down the street at night, and now, as then, she hid her eyes. "They've called to him . . . and he must go," she murmured, making the sign of the cross.

But no one sought to stop him. Hibbert recalls only a single incident until he found himself beyond the houses, searching for her along the fringe of forest where the moonlight met the snow in a bewildering frieze of fantastic shadows. And the incident was simply this—that he remembered passing the church. Catching the outline of its tower against the stars, he was aware of a faint sense of hesitation. A vague uneasiness came and went—jarred unpleasantly across the flow of his excited feelings, chilling exhilaration. He caught the instant's discord, dismissed it, and—passed on. The seduction of the snow smothered the hint before he realised that it had brushed the skirts of warning.

And then he saw her. She stood there waiting in a little clear space of shining snow, dressed all in white, part of the moonlight and the glistening background, her slender figure just discernible.

"I waited, for I knew you would come," the silvery little voice of windy beauty floated down to him. "You *had* to come."

"I'm ready," he answered, "I knew it too."

The world of Nature caught him to its heart in those few words— the wonder and the glory of the night and snow. Life leaped within him. The passion of his pagan soul exulted, rose in joy, flowed out to her. He neither reflected nor considered, but let himself go like the veriest schoolboy in the wildness of first love.

"Give me your hand," he cried, "I'm coming . . . !"

"A little farther on, a little higher," came her delicious answer. "Here it is too near the village—and the church."

And the words seemed wholly right and natural; he did not dream of questioning them; he understood that, with this little touch of civilisation in sight, the familiarity he suggested was impossible. Once out upon the open mountains, 'mid the freedom of huge slopes and towering peaks, the stars and moon to witness and the wilderness of snow to watch, they could taste an innocence of happy intercourse free from the dead conventions that imprison literal minds.

He urged his pace, yet did not quite overtake her. The girl kept always just a little bit ahead of his best efforts. . . . And soon they left the trees behind and passed on to the enormous slopes of the sea of snow that rolled in mountainous terror and beauty to the stars. The wonder of the white world caught him away. Under the steady moonlight it was more than haunting. It was a living, white, bewildering power that deliciously confused the senses and laid a spell of wild perplexity upon the heart. It was a personality that cloaked, and yet revealed, itself through all this sheeted whiteness of snow. It rose, went with him, fled before, and followed after. Slowly it dropped lithe, gleaming arms about his neck, gathering him in. . . .

Certainly some soft persuasion coaxed his very soul, urging him ever forwards, upwards, on towards the higher icy slopes. Judgment and reason left their throne, it seemed, completely, as in the madness of intoxication. The girl, slim and seductive, kept always just ahead, so that he never quite came up with her. He saw the white enchantment of her face and figure, something that streamed about her neck flying like a wreath of snow in the wind, and heard the alluring accents of her whispering voice that called from time to time: "A little farther on, a little higher. . . . Then we'll run home together!"

Sometimes he saw her hand stretched out to find his own, but each time, just as he came up with her, he saw her still in front, the hand and arm withdrawn. They took a gentle angle of ascent. The toil seemed nothing. In this crystal, wine-like air fatigue vanished. The sishing of the ski through the powdery surface of the snow was the only sound that broke the stillness; this, with his breathing and the rustle of her skirts, was all he heard. Cold moonshine, snow, and silence held the world. The sky was black, and the peaks beyond cut into it like frosted wedges of iron and steel. Far below the valley slept, the village long since hidden out of sight. He felt that he could never tire. . . . The sound of the church clock rose from time to time faintly through the air—more and more distant.

"Give me your hand. It's time now to turn back."

"Just one more slope," she laughed. "That ridge above us. Then we'll make for home." And her low voice mingled pleasantly with the purring of their ski. His own seemed harsh and ugly by comparison.

"But I have never come so high before. It's glorious! This world of silent snow and moonlight—and *you*. You're a child of the snow, I swear. Let me come up—closer—to see your face—and touch your little hand."

Her laughter answered him.

"Come on! A little higher. Here we're quite alone together."

"It's magnificent," he cried. "But why did you hide away so long? I've looked and searched for you in vain ever since we skated—" he was going to say "ten days ago," but the accurate memory of time had gone from him; he was not sure whether it was days or years or minutes. His thoughts of earth were scattered and confused.

"You looked for me in the wrong places," he heard her murmur just above him. "You looked in places where I never go. Hotels and houses kill me. I avoid them." She laughed—a fine, shrill, windy little laugh.

"I loathe them too—"

He stopped. The girl had suddenly come quite close. A breath of ice passed through his very soul. She had touched him.

"But this awful cold!" he cried out, sharply, "this freezing cold that takes me. The wind is rising; it's a wind of ice. Come, let us turn . . . !"

But when he plunged forward to hold her, or at least to look, the girl was gone again. And something in the way she stood there a few feet beyond, and stared down into his eyes so steadfastly in silence, made him shiver. The moonlight was behind her, but in some odd way he could not focus sight upon her face, although so close. The gleam of eyes he caught, but all the rest seemed white and snowy as though he looked beyond her—out into space. . . .

The sound of the church bell came up faintly from the valley far below, and he counted the strokes—five. A sudden, curious weakness seized him as he listened. Deep within it was, deadly yet somehow sweet, and hard to resist. He felt like sinking down upon the snow and lying there. . . . They had been climbing for five hours. . . . It was, of course, the warning of complete exhaustion.

With a great effort he fought and overcame it. It passed away as suddenly as it came.

"We'll turn," he said with a decision he hardly felt. "It will be dawn before we reach the village again. Come at once. It's time for home."

The sense of exhilaration had utterly left him. An emotion that was akin to fear swept coldly through him. But her whispering answer turned it instantly to terror—a terror that gripped him horribly and turned him weak and unresisting.

"Our home is—*here*!" A burst of wild, high laughter, loud and shrill, accompanied the words. It was like a whistling wind. The wind *had* risen, and clouds obscured the moon. "A little higher—where we cannot hear the wicked bells," she cried, and for the first time seized him deliberately by the hand. She moved, was suddenly close against his face. Again she touched him.

And Hibbert tried to turn away in escape, and so trying, found for the first time that the power of the snow—that other power which does not exhilarate but deadens effort—was upon him. The suffocating weakness that it brings to exhausted men, luring them to the sleep of death in her clinging soft embrace, lulling the will and conquering all desire for life—this was awfully upon him. His feet were heavy and entangled. He could not turn or move.

The girl stood in front of him, very near; he felt her chilly breath upon his cheeks; her hair passed blindingly across his eyes; and that icy wind came with her. He saw her whiteness close; again, it seemed, his sight passed through her into space as though she had no face. Her arms were round his neck. She drew him softly downwards to his knees. He sank; he yielded utterly; he obeyed. Her weight was upon him, smothering, delicious. The snow was to his waist. . . . She kissed him softly on the lips, the eyes, all over his face. And then she spoke his name in that voice of love and wonder, the voice that held the accent of two others—both taken over long ago by Death—the voice of his mother, and of the woman he had loved.

He made one more feeble effort to resist. Then, realising even while he struggled that this soft weight about his heart was sweeter than anything life could ever bring, he let his muscles relax, and sank back into the soft oblivion of the covering snow. Her wintry kisses bore him into sleep.

VII

They say that men who know the sleep of exhaustion in the snow find no awakening on the hither side of death. . . . The hours passed and the moon sank down below the white world's rim. Then, suddenly, there came a little crash upon his breast and neck, and Hibbert—woke.

He slowly turned bewildered, heavy eyes upon the desolate mountains, stared dizzily about him, tried to rise. At first his muscles would not act; a numbing, aching pain possessed him. He uttered a long, thin cry for help, and heard its faintness swallowed by the wind. And then he understood vaguely why he was only warm—not dead. For this very wind that took his cry had built up a sheltering mound of driven snow against his body while he slept. Like a curving wave it ran beside him. It was the breaking of its over-toppling edge that caused the crash, and the coldness of the mass against his neck that woke him.

Dawn kissed the eastern sky; pale gleams of gold shot every peak with splendour; but ice was in the air, and the dry and frozen snow blew like powder from the surface of the slopes. He saw the points of his ski projecting just below him. Then he—remembered. It seems he had just strength enough to realise that, could he but rise and stand, he might fly with terrific impetus towards the woods and village far beneath. The ski would carry him. But if he failed and fell . . . !

How he contrived it Hibbert never knew; this fear of death somehow called out his whole available reserve force. He rose slowly, balanced a moment, then, taking the angle of an immense zigzag, started down the awful slopes like an arrow from a bow. And automatically the splendid muscles of the practised ski-er and athlete saved and guided him, for he was hardly conscious of controlling either speed or direction. The snow stung face and eyes like fine steel shot; ridge after ridge flew past; the summits raced across the sky; the valley leaped up with bounds to meet him. He scarcely felt the ground beneath his feet as the huge slopes and distance melted before the lightning speed of that descent from death to life.

He took it in four mile-long zigzags, and it was the turning at each corner that nearly finished him, for then the strain of balancing taxed to the verge of collapse the remnants of his strength.

Slopes that have taken hours to climb can be descended in a short half-hour on ski, but Hibbert had lost all count of time. Quite other thoughts and feelings mastered him in that wild, swift dropping through the air that was like the flight of a bird. For ever close upon his heels came following forms and voices with the whirling snow-dust. He heard that little silvery voice of death and laughter at his back. Shrill and wild, with the whistling of the wind past his ears, he caught its pursuing tones; but in anger now, no longer soft and coaxing. And it was accompanied; she did not follow alone. It seemed a host of these flying figures of the snow chased madly just behind him. He felt them furiously smite his neck and cheeks, snatch at his hands and try to entangle his feet and ski in drifts. His eyes they blinded, and they caught his breath away.

The terror of the heights and snow and winter desolation urged him forward in the maddest race with death a human being ever knew; and so terrific was the speed that before the gold and crimson had left the summits to touch the ice-lips of the lower glaciers, he saw the friendly forest far beneath swing up and welcome him.

And it was then, moving slowly along the edge of the woods, he saw a light. A man was carrying it. A procession of human figures was passing in a dark line laboriously through the snow. And—he heard the sound of chanting.

Instinctively, without a second's hesitation, he changed his course. No longer flying at an angle as before, he pointed his ski straight down the mountain-side. The dreadful steepness did not frighten him. He knew full well it meant a crashing tumble at the bottom, but he also knew it meant a doubling of his speed—with safety at the end. For, though no definite thought passed through his mind, he understood that it was the village *curé* who carried that little gleaming lantern in the dawn, and that he was taking the Host to a châlet on the lower slopes—to some peasant *in extremis*. He remembered her terror of the church and bells. She feared the holy symbols.

There was one last wild cry in his ears as he started, a shriek of the wind before his face, and a rush of stinging snow against closed eyelids—and then he dropped through empty space. Speed took sight from him. It seemed he flew off the surface of the world.

Indistinctly he recalls the murmur of men's voices, the touch of strong arms that lifted him, and the shooting pains as the ski were unfastened from the twisted ankle . . . for when he opened his eyes again to normal life he found himself lying in his bed at the post office with the doctor at his side. But for years to come the story of "mad Hibbert's" ski-ing at night is recounted in that mountain village. He went, it seems, up slopes, and to a height that no man in his senses ever tried before. The tourists were agog about it for the rest of the season, and the very same day two of the bolder men went over the actual ground and photographed the slopes. Later Hibbert saw these photographs. He noticed one curious thing about them—though he did not mention it to any one:

There was only a single track.

The Man Whom the Trees Loved

I

He painted trees as by some special divining instinct of their essential qualities. He understood them. He knew why in an oak forest, for instance, each individual was utterly distinct from its fellows, and why no two beeches in the whole world were alike. People asked him down to paint a favorite lime or silver birch, for he caught the individuality of a tree as some catch the individuality of a horse. How he managed it was something of a puzzle, for he never had painting lessons, his drawing was often wildly inaccurate, and, while his perception of a Tree Personality was true and vivid, his rendering of it might almost approach the ludicrous. Yet the character and personality of that particular tree stood there alive beneath his brush—shining, frowning, dreaming, as the case might be, friendly or hostile, good or evil. It emerged.

There was nothing else in the wide world that he could paint; flowers and landscapes he only muddled away into a smudge; with people he was helpless and hopeless; also with animals. Skies he could sometimes manage, or effects of wind in foliage, but as a rule he left these all severely alone. He kept to trees, wisely following an instinct that was guided by love. It was quite arresting, this way he had of making a tree look almost like a being—alive. It approached the uncanny.

"Yes, Sanderson knows what he's doing when he paints a tree!" thought old David Bittacy, C.B., late of the Woods and Forests. "Why, you can almost hear it rustle. You can smell the thing. You can hear the rain drip through its leaves. You can almost see the branches move. It grows." For in this way somewhat he expressed his satisfaction, half to persuade himself that the twenty guineas were well spent (since his wife thought otherwise), and half to explain this uncanny reality of life that lay in the fine old cedar framed above his study table.

Yet in the general view the mind of Mr. Bittacy was held to be austere, not to say morose. Few divined in him the secretly tenacious love of nature that had been fostered by years spent in the forests and jungles of the eastern world. It was odd for an Englishman, due possibly to that Eurasian ancestor. Surreptitiously, as though half ashamed of it, he had kept alive a sense of beauty that hardly belonged to his type, and was unusual for its vitality. Trees, in particular, nourished it. He, also, understood trees, felt a subtle sense of communion with them, born perhaps of those years he had lived in caring for them, guarding, protecting, nursing, years of solitude among their great shadowy presences. He kept it largely to himself, of course, because he knew the world he lived in. He also kept it from his wife— to some extent. He knew it came between them, knew that she feared it, was opposed. But what he did not know, or realize at any rate, was the extent to which she grasped the power which they wielded over his life. Her fear, he judged, was simply due to those years in India, when for weeks at a time his calling took him away from her into the jungle forests, while she remained at home dreading all manner of evils that might befall him. This, of course, explained her instinctive opposition to the passion for woods that still influenced and clung to him. It was a natural survival of those anxious days of waiting in solitude for his safe return.

For Mrs. Bittacy, daughter of an evangelical clergyman, was a self-sacrificing woman, who in most things found a happy duty in sharing her husband's joys and sorrows to the point of self-obliteration. Only in this matter of the trees she was less successful than in others. It remained a problem difficult of compromise.

He knew, for instance, that what she objected to in this portrait of the cedar on their lawn was really not the price he had given for it, but the unpleasant way in which the transaction emphasized this breach between their common interests—the only one they had, but deep.

Sanderson, the artist, earned little enough money by his strange talent; such checks were few and far between. The owners of fine or interesting trees who cared to have them painted singly were rare indeed, and the "studies" that he made for his own delight he also kept for his own delight. Even were there buyers, he would not sell them. Only a few, and these peculiarly intimate friends, might even see them, for he disliked to hear the undiscerning criticisms of those who did not understand. Not that he minded laughter at his craftsmanship—he admitted it with scorn—but that remarks about the personality of the tree itself could easily wound or anger him. He resented slighting observations concerning them, as though insults offered to personal friends who could not answer for themselves. He was instantly up in arms.

"It really is extraordinary," said a Woman who Understood, "that you can make that cypress seem an individual, when in reality all cypresses are so *exactly* alike."

And though the bit of calculated flattery had come so near to saying the right, true, thing, Sanderson flushed as though she had slighted a friend beneath his very nose. Abruptly he passed in front of her and turned the picture to the wall.

"Almost as queer," he answered rudely, copying her silly emphasis, "as that *you* should have imagined individuality in your husband, Madame, when in reality all men are so *exactly* alike!"

Since the only thing that differentiated her husband from the mob was the money for which she had married him, Sanderson's relations with that particular family terminated on the spot, chance of prospective orders with it. His sensitiveness, perhaps, was morbid. At any rate the way to reach his heart lay through his trees. He might be said to love trees. He certainly drew a splendid inspiration from them, and the source of a man's inspiration, be it music, religion, or a woman, is never a safe thing to criticize.

"I do think, perhaps, it was just a little extravagant, dear," said Mrs. Bittacy, referring to the cedar check, "when we want a lawnmower so badly too. But, as it gives you such pleasure—"

"It reminds me of a certain day, Sophia," replied the old gentleman, looking first proudly at herself, then fondly at the picture, "now long gone by. It reminds me of another tree—that Kentish lawn in the spring, birds singing in the lilacs, and some one in a muslin frock waiting patiently beneath a certain cedar—not the one in the picture, I know, but—"

"I was not waiting," she said indignantly, "I was picking fir-cones for the schoolroom fire—"

"Fir-cones, my dear, do not grow on cedars, and schoolroom fires were not made in June in my young days."

"And anyhow it isn't the same cedar."

"It has made me fond of all cedars for its sake," he answered, "and it reminds me that you are the same young girl still—"

She crossed the room to his side, and together they looked out of the window where, upon the lawn of their Hampshire cottage, a ragged Lebanon stood in a solitary state.

"You're as full of dreams as ever," she said gently, "and I don't regret the check a bit—really. Only it would have been more real if it had been the original tree, wouldn't it?"

"That was blown down years ago. I passed the place last year, and there's not a sign of it left," he replied tenderly. And presently, when he released her from his side, she went up to the wall and carefully dusted

the picture Sanderson had made of the cedar on their present lawn. She
went all round the frame with her tiny handkerchief, standing on tiptoe
to reach the top rim.

"What I like about it," said the old fellow to himself when his wife
had left the room, "is the way he has made it live. All trees have it, of
course, but a cedar taught it to me first—the 'something' trees possess
that make them know I'm there when I stand close and watch. I
suppose I felt it then because I was in love, and love reveals life
everywhere." He glanced a moment at the Lebanon looming gaunt and
somber through the gathering dusk. A curious wistful expression
danced a moment through his eyes. "Yes, Sanderson has seen it as it
is," he murmured, "solemnly dreaming there its dim hidden life against
the Forest edge, and as different from that other tree in Kent as I am
from—from the vicar, say. It's quite a stranger, too. I don't know
anything about it really. That other cedar I loved; this old fellow I
respect. Friendly though—yes, on the whole quite friendly. He's
painted the friendliness right enough. He saw that. I'd like to know that
man better," he added. "I'd like to ask him how he saw so clearly that it
stands there between this cottage and the Forest—yet somehow more in
sympathy with us than with the mass of woods behind—a sort of go-
between. *That* I never noticed before. I see it now—through his eyes. It
stands there like a sentinel—protective rather."

He turned away abruptly to look through the window. He saw the
great encircling mass of gloom that was the Forest, fringing their little
lawn. It pressed up closer in the darkness. The prim garden with its
formal beds of flowers seemed an impertinence almost—some little
colored insect that sought to settle on a sleeping monster—some gaudy
fly that danced impudently down the edge of a great river that could
engulf it with a toss of its smallest wave. That Forest with its thousand
years of growth and its deep spreading being was some such
slumbering monster, yes. Their cottage and garden stood too near its
running lip. When the winds were strong and lifted its shadowy skirts
of black and purple. . . . He loved this feeling of the Forest Personality;
he had always loved it.

"Queer," he reflected, "awfully queer, that trees should bring me
such a sense of dim, vast living! I used to feel it particularly, I
remember, in India; in Canadian woods as well; but never in little
English woods till here. And Sanderson's the only man I ever knew
who felt it too. He's never said so, but there's the proof," and he turned
again to the picture that he loved. A thrill of unaccustomed life ran
through him as he looked. "I wonder; by Jove, I wonder," his thoughts
ran on, "whether a tree—er—in any lawful meaning of the term can
be—alive. I remember some writing fellow telling me long ago that
trees had once been moving things, animal organisms of some sort, that
had stood so long feeding, sleeping, dreaming, or something, in the

same place, that they had lost the power to get away. . . . !"

Fancies flew pell-mell about his mind, and, lighting a cheroot, he dropped into an armchair beside the open window and let them play. Outside the blackbirds whistled in the shrubberies across the lawn. He smelt the earth and trees and flowers, the perfume of mown grass, and the bits of open heath-land far away in the heart of the woods. The summer wind stirred very faintly through the leaves. But the great New Forest hardly raised her sweeping skirts of black and purple shadow.

Mr. Bittacy, however, knew intimately every detail of that wilderness of trees within. He knew all the purple coombs splashed with yellow waves of gorse; sweet with juniper and myrtle, and gleaming with clear and dark-eyed pools that watched the sky. There hawks hovered, circling hour by hour, and the flicker of the peewit's flight with its melancholy, petulant cry, deepened the sense of stillness. He knew the solitary pines, dwarfed, tufted, vigorous, that sang to every lost wind, travelers like the gypsies who pitched their bush-like tents beneath them; he knew the shaggy ponies, with foals like baby centaurs; the chattering jays, the milky call of the cuckoos in the spring, and the boom of the bittern from the lonely marshes. The undergrowth of watching hollies, he knew too, strange and mysterious, with their dark, suggestive beauty, and the yellow shimmer of their pale dropped leaves.

Here all the Forest lived and breathed in safety, secure from mutilation. No terror of the axe could haunt the peace of its vast subconscious life, no terror of devastating Man afflict it with the dread of premature death. It knew itself supreme; it spread and preened itself without concealment. It set no spires to carry warnings, for no wind brought messages of alarm as it bulged outwards to the sun and stars.

But, once its leafy portals left behind, the trees of the countryside were otherwise. The houses threatened them; they knew themselves in danger. The roads were no longer glades of silent turf, but noisy, cruel ways by which men came to attack them. They were civilized, cared for—but cared for in order that some day they might be put to death. Even in the villages, where the solemn and immemorial repose of giant chestnuts aped security, the tossing of a silver birch against their mass, impatient in the littlest wind, brought warning. Dust clogged their leaves. The inner humming of their quiet life became inaudible beneath the scream and shriek of clattering traffic. They longed and prayed to enter the great Peace of the Forest yonder, but they could not move. They knew, moreover, that the Forest with its august, deep splendor despised and pitied them. They were a thing of artificial gardens, and belonged to beds of flowers all forced to grow one way. . . .

"I'd like to know that artist fellow better," was the thought upon which he returned at length to the things of practical life. "I wonder if Sophia would mind him for a bit—?" He rose with the sound of the gong, brushing the ashes from his speckled waistcoat. He pulled the waistcoat down. He was slim and spare in figure, active in his movements. In the dim light, but for that silvery moustache, he might easily have passed for a man of forty. "I'll suggest it to her anyhow," he decided on his way upstairs to dress. His thought really was that Sanderson could probably explain his world of things he had always felt about—trees. A man who could paint the soul of a cedar in that way must know it all.

"Why not?" she gave her verdict later over the bread-and-butter pudding; "unless you think he'd find it dull without companions."

"He would paint all day in the Forest, dear. I'd like to pick his brains a bit, too, if I could manage it."

"You can manage anything, David," was what she answered, for this elderly childless couple used an affectionate politeness long since deemed old-fashioned. The remark, however, displeased her, making her feel uneasy, and she did not notice his rejoinder, smiling his pleasure and content—"Except yourself and our bank account, my dear." This passion of his for trees was of old a bone of contention, though very mild contention. It frightened her. That was the truth. The Bible, her Baedeker for earth and heaven, did not mention it. Her husband, while humoring her, could never alter that instinctive dread she had. He soothed, but never changed her. She liked the woods, perhaps as spots for shade and picnics, but she could not, as he did, love them.

And after dinner, with a lamp beside the open window, he read aloud from *The Times* the evening post had brought, such fragments as he thought might interest her. The custom was invariable, except on Sundays, when, to please his wife, he dozed over Tennyson or Farrar as their mood might be. She knitted while he read, asked gentle questions, told him his voice was a "lovely reading voice," and enjoyed the little discussions that occasions prompted because he always let her with them with "Ah, Sophia, I had never thought of it quite in *that* way before; but now you mention it I must say I think there's something in it. . . ."

For David Bittacy was wise. It was long after marriage, during his months of loneliness spent with trees and forests in India, his wife waiting at home in the Bungalow, that his other, deeper side had developed the strange passion that she could not understand. And after one or two serious attempts to let her share it with him, he had given up and learned to hide it from her. He learned, that is, to speak of it only casually, for since she knew it was there, to keep silence altogether would only increase her pain. So from time to time he skimmed the surface just to let her show him where he was wrong and think she won the day. It remained a debatable land of compromise. He listened with patience to her criticisms, her excursions and alarms, knowing that while it gave her satisfaction, it could not change himself. The thing lay in him too deep and true for change. But, for the sake of peace, some meeting-place was desirable, and he found it thus.

It was her one fault in his eyes, this religious mania carried over from her upbringing, and it did no serious harm. Great emotion could shake it sometimes out of her. She clung to it because her father taught it her and not because she had thought it out for herself. Indeed, like many women, she never really *thought* at all, but merely reflected the images of others' thinking which she had learned to see. So, wise in his knowledge of human nature, old David Bittacy accepted the pain of being obliged to keep a portion of his inner life shut off from the woman he deeply loved. He regarded her little biblical phrases as oddities that still clung to a rather fine, big soul—like horns and little useless things some animals have not yet lost in the course of evolution while they have outgrown their use.

"My dear, what is it? You frightened me!" She asked it suddenly, sitting up so abruptly that her cap dropped sideways almost to her ear. For David Bittacy behind his crackling paper had uttered a sharp exclamation of surprise. He had lowered the sheet and was staring at her over the tops of his gold glasses.

"Listen to this, if you please," he said, a note of eagerness in his voice, "listen to this, my dear Sophia. It's from an address by Francis Darwin before the Royal Society. He is president, you know, and son of the great Darwin. Listen carefully, I beg you. It is *most* significant."

"I *am* listening, David," she said with some astonishment, looking up. She stopped her knitting. For a second she glanced behind her. Something had suddenly changed in the room, and it made her feel wide awake, though before she had been almost dozing. Her husband's voice and manner had introduced this new thing. Her instincts rose in warning. "*Do* read it, dear." He took a deep breath, looking first again over the rims of his glasses to make quite sure of her attention. He had evidently come across something of genuine interest, although herself she often found the passages from these "Addresses" somewhat heavy.

In a deep, emphatic voice he read aloud:

"'It is impossible to know whether or not plants are conscious; but it is consistent with the doctrine of continuity that in all living things there is something psychic, and if we accept this point of view—'"

"*If,*" she interrupted, scenting danger.

He ignored the interruption as a thing of slight value he was accustomed to.

"'If we accept this point of view,'" he continued, "'we must believe that in plants there exists a faint copy of *what we know as consciousness in ourselves.*'"

He laid the paper down and steadily stared at her. Their eyes met.

He had italicized the last phrase.

For a minute or two his wife made no reply or comment. They stared at one another in silence. He waited for the meaning of the words to reach her understanding with full import. Then he turned and read them again in part, while she, released from that curious driving look in his eyes, instinctively again glanced over her shoulder round the room. It was almost as if she felt some one had come in to them unnoticed.

"We must believe that in plants there exists a faint copy of what we know as consciousness in ourselves."

"*If*," she repeated lamely, feeling before the stare of those questioning eyes she must say something, but not yet having gathered her wits together quite.

"*Consciousness*," he rejoined. And then he added gravely: "That, my dear, is the statement of a scientific man of the Twentieth Century."

Mrs. Bittacy sat forward in her chair so that her silk flounces crackled louder than the newspaper. She made a characteristic little sound between sniffling and snorting. She put her shoes closely together, with her hands upon her knees.

"David," she said quietly, "I think these scientific men are simply losing their heads. There is nothing in the Bible that I can remember about any such thing whatsoever."

"Nothing, Sophia, that I can remember either," he answered patiently. Then, after a pause, he added, half to himself perhaps more than to her: "And, now that I come to think about it, it seems that Sanderson once said something to me that was similar.

"Then Mr. Sanderson is a wise and thoughtful man, and a safe man," she quickly took up, "if he said that."

For she thought her husband referred to her remark about the Bible, and not to her judgment of the scientific men. And he did not correct her mistake.

"And plants, you see, dear, are not the same as trees," she drove her advantage home, "not quite, that is."

"I agree," said David quietly; "but both belong to the great vegetable kingdom."

There was a moment's pause before she answered.

"Pah! the vegetable kingdom, indeed!" She tossed her pretty old head. And into the words she put a degree of contempt that, could the vegetable kingdom have heard it, might have made it feel ashamed for covering a third of the world with its wonderful tangled network of roots and branches, delicate shaking leaves, and its millions of spires that caught the sun and wind and rain. Its very right to existence seemed in question.

II

Sanderson accordingly came down, and on the whole his short visit was a success. Why he came at all was a mystery to those who heard of it, for he never paid visits and was certainly not the kind of man to court a customer. There must have been something in Bittacy he liked.

Mrs. Bittacy was glad when he left. He brought no dress-suit for one thing, not even a dinner-jacket, and he wore very low collars with big balloon ties like a Frenchman, and let his hair grow longer than was nice, she felt. Not that these things were important, but that she considered them symptoms of something a little disordered. The ties were unnecessarily flowing.

For all that he was an interesting man, and, in spite of his eccentricities of dress and so forth, a gentleman. "Perhaps," she reflected in her genuinely charitable heart, "he had other uses for the twenty guineas, an invalid sister or an old mother to support!" She had no notion of the cost of brushes, frames, paints, and canvases. Also she forgave him much for the sake of his beautiful eyes and his eager enthusiasm of manner. So many men of thirty were already *blasé*.

Still, when the visit was over, she felt relieved. She said nothing about his coming a second time, and her husband, she was glad to notice, had likewise made no suggestion. For, truth to tell, the way the younger man engrossed the older, keeping him out for hours in the Forest, talking on the lawn in the blazing sun, and in the evenings when the damp of dusk came creeping out from the surrounding woods, all regardless of his age and usual habits, was not quite to her taste. Of course, Mr. Sanderson did not know how easily those attacks of Indian fever came back, but David surely might have told him.

They talked trees from morning to night. It stirred in her the old subconscious trail of dread, a trail that led ever into the darkness of big woods; and such feelings, as her early evangelical training taught her, were temptings. To regard them in any other way was to play with danger.

Her mind, as she watched these two, was charged with curious thoughts of dread she could not understand, yet feared the more on that account. The way they studied that old mangy cedar was a trifle unnecessary, unwise, she felt. It was disregarding the sense of proportion which deity had set upon the world for men's safe guidance.

Even after dinner they smoked their cigars upon the low branches that swept down and touched the lawn, until at length she insisted on their coming in. Cedars, she had somewhere heard, were not safe after sundown; it was not wholesome to be too near them; to sleep beneath them was even dangerous, though what the precise danger was she had forgotten. The upas was the tree she really meant.

At any rate she summoned David in, and Sanderson came presently after him.

For a long time, before deciding on this peremptory step, she had watched them surreptitiously from the drawing-room window—her husband and her guest. The dusk enveloped them with its damp veil of gauze. She saw the glowing tips of their cigars, and heard the drone of voices. Bats flitted overhead, and big, silent moths whirred softly over the rhododendron blossoms. And it came suddenly to her, while she watched, that her husband had somehow altered these last few days—since Mr. Sanderson's arrival in fact. A change had come over him, though what it was she could not say. She hesitated, indeed, to search. That was the instinctive dread operating in her. Provided it passed she would rather not know. Small things, of course, she noticed; small outward signs. He had neglected *The Times* for one thing, left off his speckled waistcoats for another. He was absent-minded sometimes; showed vagueness in practical details where hitherto he showed decision. And—he had begun to talk in his sleep again.

These and a dozen other small peculiarities came suddenly upon her with the rush of a combined attack. They brought with them a faint distress that made her shiver. Momentarily her mind was startled, then confused, as her eyes picked out the shadowy figures in the dusk, the cedar covering them, the Forest close at their backs. And then, before she could think, or seek internal guidance as her habit was, this whisper, muffled and very hurried, ran across her brain: "It's Mr. Sanderson. Call David in at once!"

And she had done so. Her shrill voice crossed the lawn and died away into the Forest, quickly smothered. No echo followed it. The sound fell dead against the rampart of a thousand listening trees.

"The damp is so very penetrating, even in summer," she murmured when they came obediently. She was half surprised at her own audacity, half repentant. They came so meekly at her call. "And my husband is sensitive to fever from the East. No, *please* do not throw away your cigars. We can sit by the open window and enjoy the evening while you smoke_."

She was very talkative for a moment; subconscious excitement was the cause.

"It is so still—so wonderfully still," she went on, as no one spoke, "so peaceful, and the air so very sweet . . . and God is always near to those who need His aid." The words slipped out before she realized quite what she was saying, yet fortunately, in time to lower her voice, for no one heard them. They were, perhaps, an instinctive expression of relief. It flustered her that she could have said the thing at all.

Sanderson brought her shawl and helped to arrange the chairs; she thanked him in her old-fashioned, gentle way, declining the lamps which he had offered to light. "They attract the moths and insects so, I think!"

The three of them sat there in the gloaming. Mr. Bittacy's white moustache and his wife's yellow shawl gleaming at either end of the little horseshoe, Sanderson with his wild black hair and shining eyes midway between them. The painter went on talking softly, continuing evidently the conversation begun with his host beneath the cedar. Mrs. Bittacy, on her guard, listened—uneasily.

"For trees, you see, rather conceal themselves in daylight. They reveal themselves fully only after sunset. I never *know* a tree," he bowed here slightly towards the lady as though to apologize for something he felt she would not quite understand or like, "until I've seen it in the night. Your cedar, for instance," looking towards her husband again so that Mrs. Bittacy caught the gleaming of his turned eyes, "I failed with badly at first, because I did it in the morning. You shall see to-morrow what I mean—that first sketch is upstairs in my portfolio; it's quite another tree to the one you bought. That view"—he leaned forward, lowering his voice—"I caught one morning about two o'clock in very faint moonlight and the stars. I saw the naked being of the thing—"

"You mean that you went out, Mr. Sanderson, at that hour?" the old lady asked with astonishment and mild rebuke. She did not care particularly for his choice of adjectives either.

"I fear it was rather a liberty to take in another's house, perhaps," he answered courteously. "But, having chanced to wake, I saw the tree from my window, and made my way downstairs."

"It's a wonder Boxer didn't bite you; he sleeps loose in the hall," she said.

"On the contrary. The dog came out with me. I hope," he added, "the noise didn't disturb you, though it's rather late to say so. I feel quite guilty." His white teeth showed in the dusk as he smiled. A smell of earth and flowers stole in through the window on a breath of wandering air.

Mrs. Bittacy said nothing at the moment. "We both sleep like tops," put in her husband, laughing. "You're a courageous man, though, Sanderson, and, by Jove, the picture justifies you. Few artists would have taken so much trouble, though I read once that Holman Hunt, Rossetti, or some one of that lot, painted all night in his orchard to get an effect of moonlight that he wanted."

He chattered on. His wife was glad to hear his voice; it made her feel more easy in her mind. But presently the other held the floor again, and her thoughts grew darkened and afraid. Instinctively she feared the influence on her husband. The mystery and wonder that lie in woods, in forests, in great gatherings of trees everywhere, seemed so real and present while he talked.

"The Night transfigures all things in a way," he was saying; "but nothing so searchingly as trees. From behind a veil that sunlight hangs before them in the day they emerge and show themselves. Even buildings do that—in a measure—but trees particularly. In the daytime they sleep; at night they wake, they manifest, turn active—live. You remember," turning politely again in the direction of his hostess, "how clearly Henley understood that?"

"That socialist person, you mean?" asked the lady. Her tone and accent made the substantive sound criminal. It almost hissed, the way she uttered it.

"The poet, yes," replied the artist tactfully, "the friend of Stevenson, you remember, Stevenson who wrote those charming children's verses."

He quoted in a low voice the lines he meant. It was, for once, the time, the place, and the setting all together. The words floated out across the lawn towards the wall of blue darkness where the big Forest swept the little garden with its league-long curve that was like the shore-line of a sea. A wave of distant sound that was like surf accompanied his voice, as though the wind was fain to listen too:

> Not to the staring Day,
> For all the importunate questionings he pursues
> In his big, violent voice,
> Shall those mild things of bulk and multitude,
> The trees—God's sentinels . . .
> Yield of their huge, unutterable selves.
>
> But at the word
> Of the ancient, sacerdotal Night,
> Night of many secrets, whose effect—
> Transfiguring, hierophantic, dread—
> Themselves alone may fully apprehend,
> They tremble and are changed:
> In each the uncouth, individual soul
> Looms forth and glooms
> Essential, and, their bodily presences
> Touched with inordinate significance,
> Wearing the darkness like a livery
> Of some mysterious and tremendous guild,
> They brood—they menace—they appall.

The voice of Mrs. Bittacy presently broke the silence that followed.

"I like that part about God's sentinels," she murmured. There was no sharpness in her tone; it was hushed and quiet. The truth, so musically uttered, muted her shrill objections though it had not lessened her alarm. Her husband made no comment; his cigar, she noticed, had gone out.

"And old trees in particular," continued the artist, as though to himself, "have very definite personalities. You can offend, wound, please them; the moment you stand within their shade you feel whether they come out to you, or whether they withdraw." He turned abruptly towards his host. "You know that singular essay of Prentice Mulford's, no doubt 'God in the Trees'—extravagant perhaps, but yet with a fine true beauty in it? You've never read it, no?" he asked.

But it was Mrs. Bittacy who answered; her husband keeping his curious deep silence.

"I never did!" It fell like a drip of cold water from the face muffled in the yellow shawl; even a child could have supplied the remainder of the unspoken thought.

"Ah," said Sanderson gently, "but there *is* 'God' in the trees, God in a very subtle aspect and sometimes—I have known the trees express it too—that which is *not* God—dark and terrible. Have you ever noticed, too, how clearly trees show what they want—choose their companions, at least? How beeches, for instance, allow no life too near them—birds or squirrels in their boughs, nor any growth beneath? The silence in the beech wood is quite terrifying often! And how pines like bilberry bushes at their feet and sometimes little oaks—all trees making a clear, deliberate choice, and holding firmly to it? Some trees obviously—it's very strange and marked—seem to prefer the human."

The old lady sat up crackling, for this was more than she could permit. Her stiff silk dress emitted little sharp reports.

"We know," she answered, "that He was said to have walked in the garden in the cool of the evening"—the gulp betrayed the effort that it cost her—"but we are nowhere told that He hid in the trees, or anything like that. Trees, after all, we must remember, are only large vegetables."

"True," was the soft answer, "but in everything that grows, has life, that is, there's mystery past all finding out. The wonder that lies hidden in our own souls lies also hidden, I venture to assert, in the stupidity and silence of a mere potato."

The observation was not meant to be amusing. It was *not* amusing. No one laughed. On the contrary, the words conveyed in too literal a sense the feeling that haunted all that conversation. Each one in his own way realized—with beauty, with wonder, with alarm—that the talk had somehow brought the whole vegetable kingdom nearer to that of man. Some link had been established between the two. It was not wise, with that great Forest listening at their very doors, to speak so plainly. The forest edged up closer while they did so.

And Mrs. Bittacy, anxious to interrupt the horrid spell, broke suddenly in upon it with a matter-of-fact suggestion. She did not like her husband's prolonged silence, stillness. He seemed so negative—so changed.

"David," she said, raising her voice, "I think you're feeling the dampness. It's grown chilly. The fever comes so suddenly, you know, and it might be wise to take the tincture. I'll go and get it, dear, at once. It's better." And before he could object she had left the room to bring the homeopathic dose that she believed in, and that, to please her, he swallowed by the tumbler-full from week to week.

And the moment the door closed behind her, Sanderson began again, though now in quite a different tone. Mr. Bittacy sat up in his chair. The two men obviously resumed the conversation—the real conversation interrupted beneath the cedar—and left aside the sham one which was so much dust merely thrown in the old lady's eyes.

"Trees love you, that's the fact," he said earnestly. "Your service to them all these years abroad has made them know you."

"Know me?"

"Made them, yes,"—he paused a moment, then added,—"made them *aware of your presence*; aware of a force outside themselves that deliberately seeks their welfare, don't you see?"

"By Jove, Sanderson—!" This put into plain language actual sensations he had felt, yet had never dared to phrase in words before. "They get into touch with me, as it were?" he ventured, laughing at his own sentence, yet laughing only with his lips.

"Exactly," was the quick, emphatic reply. "They seek to blend with something they feel instinctively to be good for them, helpful to their essential beings, encouraging to their best expression—their life."

"Good Lord, Sir!" Bittacy heard himself saying, "but you're putting my own thoughts into words. D'you know, I've felt something like that for years. As though—" he looked round to make sure his wife was not there, then finished the sentence—"as though the trees were after me!"

"'Amalgamate' seems the best word, perhaps," said Sanderson slowly. "They would draw you to themselves. Good forces, you see, always seek to merge; evil to separate; that's why Good in the end must always win the day—everywhere. The accumulation in the long run becomes overwhelming. Evil tends to separation, dissolution, death. The comradeship of trees, their instinct to run together, is a vital symbol. Trees in a mass are good; alone, you may take it generally, are—well, dangerous. Look at a monkey-puzzler, or better still, a holly. Look at it, watch it, understand it. Did you ever see more plainly an evil thought made visible? They're wicked. Beautiful too, oh yes! There's a strange, miscalculated beauty often in evil—"

"That cedar, then—?"

"Not evil, no; but alien, rather. Cedars grow in forests all together. The poor thing has drifted, that is all."

They were getting rather deep. Sanderson, talking against time, spoke so fast. It was too condensed. Bittacy hardly followed that last bit. His mind floundered among his own less definite, less sorted thoughts, till presently another sentence from the artist startled him into attention again.

"That cedar will protect you here, though, because you both have humanized it by your thinking so lovingly of its presence. The others can't get past it, as it were."

"Protect me!" he exclaimed. "Protect me from their love?"

Sanderson laughed. "We're getting rather mixed," he said; "we're talking of one thing in the terms of another really. But what I mean is—you see—that their love for you, their 'awareness' of your personality and presence involves the idea of winning you—across the border—into themselves—into their world of living. It means, in a way, taking you over."

The ideas the artist started in his mind ran furious wild races to and fro. It was like a maze sprung suddenly into movement. The whirling of the intricate lines bewildered him. They went so fast, leaving but half an explanation of their goal. He followed first one, then another, but a new one always dashed across to intercept before he could get anywhere.

"But India," he said, presently in a lower voice, "India is so far away—from this little English forest. The trees, too, are utterly different for one thing?"

The rustle of skirts warned of Mrs. Bittacy's approach. This was a sentence he could turn round another way in case she came up and pressed for explanation.

"There is communion among trees all the world over," was the strange quick reply. "They always know."

"They always know! You think then—?"

"The winds, you see—the great, swift carriers! They have their ancient rights of way about the world. An easterly wind, for instance, carrying on stage by stage as it were—linking dropped messages and meanings from land to land like the birds—an easterly wind—"

Mrs. Bittacy swept in upon them with the tumbler—

"There, David," she said, "that will ward off any beginnings of attack. Just a spoonful, dear. Oh, oh! not *all*!" for he had swallowed half the contents at a single gulp as usual; "another dose before you go to bed, and the balance in the morning, first thing when you wake."

She turned to her guest, who put the tumbler down for her upon a table at his elbow. She had heard them speak of the east wind. She emphasized the warning she had misinterpreted. The private part of the conversation came to an abrupt end.

"It is the one thing that upsets him more than any other—an east wind," she said, "and I am glad, Mr. Sanderson, to hear you think so too."

III

A deep hush followed, in the middle of which an owl was heard calling its muffled note in the forest. A big moth whirred with a soft collision against one of the windows. Mrs. Bittacy started slightly, but no one spoke. Above the trees the stars were faintly visible. From the distance came the barking of a dog.

Bittacy, relighting his cigar, broke the little spell of silence that had caught all three.

"It's rather a comforting thought," he said, throwing the match out of the window, "that life is about us everywhere, and that there is really no dividing line between what we call organic and inorganic."

"The universe, yes," said Sanderson, "is all one, really. We're puzzled by the gaps we cannot see across, but as a fact, I suppose, there are no gaps at all."

Mrs. Bittacy rustled ominously, holding her peace meanwhile. She feared long words she did not understand. Beelzebub lay hid among too many syllables.

"In trees and plants especially, there dreams an exquisite life that no one yet has proved unconscious."

"Or conscious either, Mr. Sanderson," she neatly interjected. "It's only man that was made after His image, not shrubberies and things. . . ."

Her husband interposed without delay.

"It is not necessary," he explained suavely, "to say that they're alive in the sense that we are alive. At the same time," with an eye to his wife, "I see no harm in holding, dear, that all created things contain some measure of His life Who made them. It's only beautiful to hold that He created nothing dead. We are not pantheists for all that!" he added soothingly.

"Oh, no! Not that, I hope!" The word alarmed her. It was worse than pope. Through her puzzled mind stole a stealthy, dangerous thing . . . like a panther.

"I like to think that even in decay there's life," the painter murmured. "The falling apart of rotten wood breeds sentiency, there's force and motion in the falling of a dying leaf, in the breaking up and crumbling of everything indeed. And take an inert stone: it's crammed with heat and weight and potencies of all sorts. What holds its particles together indeed? We understand it as little as gravity or why a needle always turns to the 'North.' Both things may be a mode of life. . . ."

"You think a compass has a soul, Mr. Sanderson?" exclaimed the lady with a crackling of her silk flounces that conveyed a sense of outrage even more plainly than her tone. The artist smiled to himself in the darkness, but it was Bittacy who hastened to reply.

"Our friend merely suggests that these mysterious agencies," he said quietly, "may be due to some kind of life we cannot understand. Why should water only run downhill? Why should trees grow at right angles to the surface of the ground and towards the sun? Why should the worlds spin for ever on their axes? Why should fire change the form of everything it touches without really destroying them? To say these things follow the law of their being explains nothing. Mr. Sanderson merely suggests—poetically, my dear, of course—that these may be manifestations of life, though life at a different stage to ours."

"The '*breath* of life,' we read, 'He breathed into them.' These things do not breathe." She said it with triumph.

Then Sanderson put in a word. But he spoke rather to himself or to his host than by way of serious rejoinder to the ruffled lady.

"But plants do breathe too, you know," he said. "They breathe, they eat, they digest, they move about, and they adapt themselves to their environment as men and animals do. They have a nervous system too . . . at least a complex system of nuclei which have some of the qualities of nerve cells. They may have memory too. Certainly, they know definite action in response to stimulus. And though this may be physiological, no one has proved that it is only that, and not—psychological."

He did not notice, apparently, the little gasp that was audible behind the yellow shawl. Bittacy cleared his throat, threw his extinguished cigar upon the lawn, crossed and re-crossed his legs.

"And in trees," continued the other, "behind a great forest, for instance," pointing towards the woods, "may stand a rather splendid Entity that manifests through all the thousand individual trees—some huge collective life, quite as minutely and delicately organized as our own. It might merge and blend with ours under certain conditions, so that we could understand it by *being* it, for a time at least. It might even engulf human vitality into the immense whirlpool of its own vast dreaming life. The pull of a big forest on a man can be tremendous and utterly overwhelming."

The mouth of Mrs. Bittacy was heard to close with a snap. Her shawl, and particularly her crackling dress, exhaled the protest that burned within her like a pain. She was too distressed to be overawed, but at the same time too confused 'mid the litter of words and meanings half understood, to find immediate phrases she could use. Whatever the actual meaning of his language might be, however, and whatever subtle dangers lay concealed behind them meanwhile, they certainly wove a kind of gentle spell with the glimmering darkness that held all three delicately enmeshed there by that open window. The odors of dewy lawn, flowers, trees, and earth formed part of it.

"The moods," he continued, "that people waken in us are due to their hidden life affecting our own. Deep calls to sleep. A person, for instance, joins you in an empty room: you both instantly change. The new arrival, though in silence, has caused a change of mood. May not the moods of Nature touch and stir us in virtue of a similar prerogative? The sea, the hills, the desert, wake passion, joy, terror, as the case may be; for a few, perhaps," he glanced significantly at his host so that Mrs. Bittacy again caught the turning of his eyes, "emotions of a curious, flaming splendor that are quite nameless. Well . . . whence come these powers? Surely from nothing that is . . . dead! Does not the influence of a forest, its sway and strange ascendancy over certain minds, betray a direct manifestation of life? It lies otherwise beyond all explanation, this mysterious emanation of big woods. Some natures, of course, deliberately invite it. The authority of a host of trees,"—his voice grew almost solemn as he said the words—"is something not to be denied. One feels it here, I think, particularly."

There was considerable tension in the air as he ceased speaking. Mr. Bittacy had not intended that the talk should go so far. They had drifted. He did not wish to see his wife unhappy or afraid, and he was aware—acutely so—that her feelings were stirred to a point he did not care about. Something in her, as he put it, was "working up" towards explosion.

He sought to generalize the conversation, diluting this accumulated emotion by spreading it.

"The sea is His and He made it," he suggested vaguely, hoping Sanderson would take the hint, "and with the trees it is the same. . . ."

"The whole gigantic vegetable kingdom, yes," the artist took him up, "all at the service of man, for food, for shelter and for a thousand purposes of his daily life. Is it not striking what a lot of the globe they cover . . . exquisitely organized life, yet stationary, always ready to our hand when we want them, never running away? But the taking them, for all that, not so easy. One man shrinks from picking flowers, another from cutting down trees. And, it's curious that most of the forest tales and legends are dark, mysterious, and somewhat ill-omened. The forest-beings are rarely gay and harmless. The forest life was felt as terrible. Tree-worship still survives to-day. Wood-cutters . . . those who take the life of trees . . . you see a race of haunted men. . . ."

He stopped abruptly, a singular catch in his voice. Bittacy felt something even before the sentences were over. His wife, he knew, felt it still more strongly. For it was in the middle of the heavy silence following upon these last remarks, that Mrs. Bittacy, rising with a violent abruptness from her chair, drew the attention of the others to something moving towards them across the lawn. It came silently. In outline it was large and curiously spread. It rose high, too, for the sky above the shrubberies, still pale gold from the sunset, was dimmed by its passage. She declared afterwards that it moved in "looping circles," but what she perhaps meant to convey was "spirals."

She screamed faintly. "It's come at last! And it's you that brought it!"

She turned excitedly, half afraid, half angry, to Sanderson. With a breathless sort of gasp she said it, politeness all forgotten. "I knew it . . . if you went on. I knew it. Oh! Oh!" And she cried again, "Your talking has brought it out!" The terror that shook her voice was rather dreadful.

But the confusion of her vehement words passed unnoticed in the first surprise they caused. For a moment nothing happened.

"What is it you think you see, my dear?" asked her husband, startled. Sanderson said nothing. All three leaned forward, the men still sitting, but Mrs. Bittacy had rushed hurriedly to the window, placing herself of a purpose, as it seemed, between her husband and the lawn. She pointed. Her little hand made a silhouette against the sky, the yellow shawl hanging from the arm like a cloud.

"Beyond the cedar—between it and the lilacs." The voice had lost its shrillness; it was thin and hushed. "There . . . now you see it going round upon itself again—going back, thank God! . . . going back to the Forest." It sank to a whisper, shaking. She repeated, with a great dropping sigh of relief—"Thank God! I thought . . . at first . . . it was coming here . . . to us! . . . David . . . to *you!*"

She stepped back from the window, her movements confused, feeling in the darkness for the support of a chair, and finding her husband's outstretched hand instead. "Hold me, dear, hold me, please . . . tight. Do not let me go." She was in what he called afterwards "a regular state." He drew her firmly down upon her chair again.

"Smoke, Sophie, my dear," he said quickly, trying to make his voice calm and natural. "I see it, yes. It's smoke blowing over from the gardener's cottage. . . ."

"But, David,"—and there was a new horror in her whisper now—"it made a noise. It makes it still. I hear it swishing." Some such word she used—swishing, sishing, rushing, or something of the kind. "David, I'm very frightened. It's something awful! That man has called it out . . . !"

"Hush, hush," whispered her husband. He stroked her trembling hand beside him.

"It is in the wind," said Sanderson, speaking for the first time, very quietly. The expression on his face was not visible in the gloom, but his voice was soft and unafraid. At the sound of it, Mrs. Bittacy started violently again. Bittacy drew his chair a little forward to obstruct her view of him. He felt bewildered himself, a little, hardly knowing quite what to say or do. It was all so very curious and sudden.

But Mrs. Bittacy was badly frightened. It seemed to her that what she saw came from the enveloping forest just beyond their little garden.

It emerged in a sort of secret way, moving towards them as with a purpose, stealthily, difficultly. Then something stopped it. It could not advance beyond the cedar. The cedar—this impression remained with her afterwards too—prevented, kept it back. Like a rising sea the Forest had surged a moment in their direction through the covering darkness, and this visible movement was its first wave. Thus to her mind it seemed . . . like that mysterious turn of the tide that used to frighten and mystify her in childhood on the sands. The outward surge of some enormous Power was what she felt . . . something to which every instinct in her being rose in opposition because it threatened her and hers. In that moment she realized the Personality of the Forest . . . menacing.

In the stumbling movement that she made away from the window and towards the bell she barely caught the sentence Sanderson—or was it her husband?—murmured to himself: "It came because we talked of it; our thinking made it aware of us and brought it out. But the cedar stops it. It cannot cross the lawn, you see. . . ."

All three were standing now, and her husband's voice broke in with authority while his wife's fingers touched the bell.

"My dear, I should *not* say anything to Thompson." The anxiety he felt was manifest in his voice, but his outward composure had returned. "The gardener can go. . . ."

Then Sanderson cut him short. "Allow me," he said quickly. "I'll see if anything's wrong." And before either of them could answer or object, he was gone, leaping out by the open window. They saw his figure vanish with a run across the lawn into the darkness.

A moment later the maid entered, in answer to the bell, and with her came the loud barking of the terrier from the hall.

"The lamps," said her master shortly, and as she softly closed the door behind her, they heard the wind pass with a mournful sound of singing round the outer walls. A rustle of foliage from the distance passed within it.

"You see, the wind *is* rising. It *was* the wind!" He put a comforting arm about her, distressed to feel that she was trembling. But he knew that he was trembling too, though with a kind of odd elation rather than alarm. "And it *was* smoke that you saw coming from Stride's cottage, or from the rubbish heaps he's been burning in the kitchen garden. The noise we heard was the branches rustling in the wind. Why should you be so nervous?"

A thin whispering voice answered him:

"I was afraid for *you*, dear. Something frightened me for *you*. That man makes me feel so uneasy and uncomfortable for his influence upon you. It's very foolish, I know. I think . . . I'm tired; I feel so overwrought and restless." The words poured out in a hurried jumble and she kept turning to the window while she spoke.

"The strain of having a visitor," he said soothingly, "has taxed you. We're so unused to having people in the house. He goes to-morrow." He warmed her cold hands between his own, stroking them tenderly. More, for the life of him, he could not say or do. The joy of a strange, internal excitement made his heart beat faster. He knew not what it was. He knew only, perhaps, whence it came.

She peered close into his face through the gloom, and said a curious thing. "I thought, David, for a moment . . . you seemed . . . different. My nerves are all on edge to-night." She made no further reference to her husband's visitor.

A sound of footsteps from the lawn warned of Sanderson's return, as he answered quickly in a lowered tone—"There's no need to be afraid on my account, dear girl. There's nothing wrong with me. I assure you; I never felt so well and happy in my life."

Thompson came in with the lamps and brightness, and scarcely had she gone again when Sanderson in turn was seen climbing through the window.

"There's nothing," he said lightly, as he closed it behind him. "Somebody's been burning leaves, and the smoke is drifting a little through the trees. The wind," he added, glancing at his host a moment significantly, but in so discreet a way that Mrs. Bittacy did not observe it, "the wind, too, has begun to roar . . . in the Forest . . . further out."

But Mrs. Bittacy noticed about him two things which increased her uneasiness. She noticed the shining of his eyes, because a similar light had suddenly come into her husband's; and she noticed, too, the apparent depth of meaning he put into those simple words that "the wind had begun to roar in the Forest . . . further out." Her mind retained the disagreeable impression that he meant more than he said. In his tone lay quite another implication. It was not actually "wind" he spoke of, and it would not remain "further out" . . . rather, it was coming in. Another impression she got too—still more unwelcome—was that her husband understood his hidden meaning.

IV

"David, dear," she observed gently as soon as they were alone upstairs, "I have a horrible uneasy feeling about that man. I cannot get rid of it." The tremor in her voice caught all his tenderness.

He turned to look at her. "Of what kind, my dear? You're so imaginative sometimes, aren't you?"

"I think," she hesitated, stammering a little, confused, still frightened, "I mean—isn't he a hypnotist, or full of those theofosical ideas, or something of the sort? You know what I mean—"

He was too accustomed to her little confused alarms to explain them away seriously as a rule, or to correct her verbal inaccuracies, but to-night he felt she needed careful, tender treatment. He soothed her as best he could.

"But there's no harm in that, even if he is," he answered quietly. "Those are only new names for very old ideas, you know, dear." There was no trace of impatience in his voice.

"That's what I mean," she replied, the texts he dreaded rising in an unuttered crowd behind the words. "He's one of those things that we are warned would come—one of those Latter-Day things." For her mind still bristled with the bogeys of the Antichrist and Prophecy, and she had only escaped the Number of the Beast, as it were, by the skin of her teeth. The Pope drew most of her fire usually, because she could understand him; the target was plain and she could shoot. But this tree-and-forest business was so vague and horrible. It terrified her. "He makes me think," she went on, "of Principalities and Powers in high places, and of things that walk in the darkness. I did *not* like the way he spoke of trees getting alive in the night, and all that; it made me think of wolves in sheep's clothing. And when I saw that awful thing in the sky above the lawn—"

But he interrupted her at once, for that was something he had decided it was best to leave unmentioned. Certainly it was better not discussed.

"He only meant, I think, Sophie," he put in gravely, yet with a little smile, "that trees may have a measure of conscious life—rather a nice idea on the whole, surely,—something like that bit we read in the *Times* the other night, you remember—and that a big forest may possess a sort of Collective Personality. Remember, he's an artist, and poetical."

"It's dangerous," she said emphatically. "I feel it's playing with fire, unwise, unsafe—"

"Yet all to the glory of God," he urged gently. "We must not shut our ears and eyes to knowledge—of any kind, must we?"

"With you, David, the wish is always farther than the thought," she rejoined. For, like the child who thought that "suffered under Pontius Pilate" was "suffered under a bunch of violets," she heard her proverbs phonetically and reproduced them thus. She hoped to convey her warning in the quotation. "And we must always try the spirits whether they be of God," she added tentatively.

"Certainly, dear, we can always do that," he assented, getting into bed.

But, after a little pause, during which she blew the light out, David Bittacy settling down to sleep with an excitement in his blood that was new and bewilderingly delightful, realized that perhaps he had not said quite enough to comfort her. She was lying awake by his side, still frightened. He put his head up in the darkness.

"Sophie," he said softly, "you must remember, too, that in any case between us and—and all that sort of thing—there is a great gulf fixed, a gulf that cannot be crossed—er—while we are still in the body."

And hearing no reply, he satisfied himself that she was already asleep and happy. But Mrs. Bittacy was not asleep. She heard the sentence, only she said nothing because she felt her thought was better unexpressed. She was afraid to hear the words in the darkness. The Forest outside was listening and might hear them too—the Forest that was "roaring further out."

And the thought was this: That gulf, of course, existed, but Sanderson had somehow bridged it.

It was much later than night when she awoke out of troubled, uneasy dreams and heard a sound that twisted her very nerves with fear. It passed immediately with full waking, for, listen as she might, there was nothing audible but the inarticulate murmur of the night. It was in her dreams she heard it, and the dreams had vanished with it. But the sound was recognizable, for it was that rushing noise that had come across the lawn; only this time closer. Just above her face while she slept had passed this murmur as of rustling branches in the very room, a sound of foliage whispering. "A going in the tops of the mulberry trees," ran through her mind. She had dreamed that she lay beneath a spreading tree somewhere, a tree that whispered with ten thousand soft lips of green; and the dream continued for a moment even after waking.

She sat up in bed and stared about her. The window was open at the top; she saw the stars; the door, she remembered, was locked as usual; the room, of course, was empty. The deep hush of the summer night lay over all, broken only by another sound that now issued from the shadows close beside the bed, a human sound, yet unnatural, a sound that seized the fear with which she had waked and instantly increased it. And, although it was one she recognized as familiar, at first she could not name it. Some seconds certainly passed—and, they were very long ones—before she understood that it was her husband talking in his sleep.

The direction of the voice confused and puzzled her, moreover, for it was not, as she first supposed, beside her. There was distance in it. The next minute, by the light of the sinking candle flame, she saw his white figure standing out in the middle of the room, half-way towards the window. The candle-light slowly grew. She saw him move then nearer to the window, with arms outstretched. His speech was low and mumbled, the words running together too much to be distinguishable.

And she shivered. To her, sleep-talking was uncanny to the point of horror; it was like the talking of the dead, mere parody of a living voice, unnatural.

"David!" she whispered, dreading the sound of her own voice, and half afraid to interrupt him and see his face. She could not bear the sight of the wide-opened eyes. "David, you're walking in your sleep.

Do—come back to bed, dear, *please!*"

Her whisper seemed so dreadfully loud in the still darkness. At the sound of her voice he paused, then turned slowly round to face her. His widely-opened eyes stared into her own without recognition; they looked through her into something beyond; it was as though he knew the direction of the sound, yet cold not see her. They were shining, she noticed, as the eyes of Sanderson had shone several hours ago; and his face was flushed, distraught. Anxiety was written upon every feature. And, instantly, recognizing that the fever was upon him, she forgot her terror temporarily in practical considerations. He came back to bed without waking. She closed his eyelids. Presently he composed himself quietly to sleep, or rather to deeper sleep. She contrived to make him swallow something from the tumbler beside the bed.

Then she rose very quietly to close the window, feeling the night air blow in too fresh and keen. She put the candle where it could not reach him. The sight of the big Baxter Bible beside it comforted her a little, but all through her under-being ran the warnings of a curious alarm. And it was while in the act of fastening the catch with one hand and pulling the string of the blind with the other, that her husband sat up again in bed and spoke in words this time that were distinctly audible. The eyes had opened wide again. He pointed. She stood stock still and listened, her shadow distorted on the blind. He did not come out towards her as at first she feared.

The whispering voice was very clear, horrible, too, beyond all she had ever known.

"They are roaring in the Forest further out . . . and I . . . must go and see." He stared beyond her as he said it, to the woods. "They are needing me. They sent for me. . . ." Then his eyes wandering back again to things within the room, he lay down, his purpose suddenly changed. And that change was horrible as well, more horrible, perhaps, because of its revelation of another detailed world he moved in far away from her.

The singular phrase chilled her blood, for a moment she was utterly terrified. That tone of the somnambulist, differing so slightly yet so distressingly from normal, waking speech, seemed to her somehow wicked. Evil and danger lay waiting thick behind it. She leaned against the window-sill, shaking in every limb. She had an awful feeling for a moment that something was coming in to fetch him.

"Not yet, then," she heard in a much lower voice from the bed, "but later. It will be better so . . . I shall go later. . . ."

The words expressed some fringe of these alarms that had haunted her so long, and that the arrival and presence of Sanderson seemed to have brought to the very edge of a climax she could not even dare to think about. They gave it form; they brought it closer; they sent her thoughts to her Deity in a wild, deep prayer for help and guidance. For here was a direct, unconscious betrayal of a world of inner purposes and claims her husband recognized while he kept them almost wholly to himself.

By the time she reached his side and knew the comfort of his touch, the eyes had closed again, this time of their own accord, and the head lay calmly back upon the pillows. She gently straightened the bed clothes. She watched him for some minutes, shading the candle carefully with one hand. There was a smile of strangest peace upon the face.

Then, blowing out the candle, she knelt down and prayed before getting back into bed. But no sleep came to her. She lay awake all night thinking, wondering, praying, until at length with the chorus of the birds and the glimmer of the dawn upon the green blind, she fell into a slumber of complete exhaustion.

But while she slept the wind continued roaring in the Forest further out. The sound came closer—sometimes very close indeed.

V

With the departure of Sanderson the significance of the curious incidents waned, because the moods that had produced them passed away. Mrs. Bittacy soon afterwards came to regard them as some growth of disproportion that had been very largely, perhaps, in her own mind. It did not strike her that this change was sudden for it came about quite naturally. For one thing her husband never spoke of the matter, and for another she remembered how many things in life that had seemed inexplicable and singular at the time turned out later to have been quite commonplace.

Most of it, certainly, she put down to the presence of the artist and to his wild, suggestive talk. With his welcome removal, the world turned ordinary again and safe. The fever, though it lasted as usual a short time only, had not allowed of her husband's getting up to say good-bye, and she had conveyed his regrets and adieux. In the morning Mr. Sanderson had seemed ordinary enough. In his town hat and gloves, as she saw him go, he seemed tame and un-alarming.

"After all," she thought as she watched the pony-cart bear him off, "he's only an artist!" What she had thought he might be otherwise her slim imagination did not venture to disclose. Her change of feeling was wholesome and refreshing. She felt a little ashamed of her behavior. She gave him a smile—genuine because the relief she felt was genuine—as he bent over her hand and kissed it, but she did not suggest a second visit, and her husband, she noted with satisfaction and relief, had said nothing either.

The little household fell again into the normal and sleepy routine to which it was accustomed. The name of Arthur Sanderson was rarely if ever mentioned. Nor, for her part, did she mention to her husband the incident of his walking in his sleep and the wild words he used. But to forget it was equally impossible. Thus it lay buried deep within her like a center of some unknown disease of which it was a mysterious symptom, waiting to spread at the first favorable opportunity. She prayed against it every night and morning: prayed that she might forget it—that God would keep her husband safe from harm.

For in spite of much surface foolishness that many might have read as weakness, Mrs. Bittacy had balance, sanity, and a fine deep faith. She was greater than she knew. Her love for her husband and her God were somehow one, an achievement only possible to a single-hearted nobility of soul.

There followed a summer of great violence and beauty; of beauty, because the refreshing rains at night prolonged the glory of the spring and spread it all across July, keeping the foliage young and sweet; of violence, because the winds that tore about the south of England brushed the whole country into dancing movement. They swept the woods magnificently, and kept them roaring with a perpetual grand voice. Their deepest notes seemed never to leave the sky. They sang and shouted, and torn leaves raced and fluttered through the air long before their usually appointed time. Many a tree, after days of roaring and dancing, fell exhausted to the ground. The cedar on the lawn gave up two limbs that fell upon successive days, at the same hour too—just before dusk. The wind often makes its most boisterous effort at that time, before it drops with the sun, and these two huge branches lay in dark ruin covering half the lawn. They spread across it and towards the house. They left an ugly gaping space upon the tree, so that the Lebanon looked unfinished, half destroyed, a monster shorn of its old-time comeliness and splendor. Far more of the Forest was now visible than before; it peered through the breach of the broken defenses. They could see from the windows of the house now—especially from the drawing-room and bedroom windows—straight out into the glades and depths beyond.

Mrs. Bittacy's niece and nephew, who were staying on a visit at the time, enjoyed themselves immensely helping the gardeners carry off the fragments. It took two days to do this, for Mr. Bittacy insisted on the branches being moved entire. He would not allow them to be chopped; also, he would not consent to their use as firewood. Under his superintendence the unwieldy masses were dragged to the edge of the garden and arranged upon the frontier line between the Forest and the lawn. The children were delighted with the scheme. They entered into it with enthusiasm. At all costs this defense against the inroads of the Forest must be made secure. They caught their uncle's earnestness, felt even something of a hidden motive that he had; and the visit, usually rather dreaded, became the visit of their lives instead. It was Aunt Sophia this time who seemed discouraging and dull.

"She's got so old and funny," opined Stephen.

But Alice, who felt in the silent displeasure of her aunt some secret thing that alarmed her, said:

"I think she's afraid of the woods. She never comes into them with us, you see."

"All the more reason then for making this wall impreg—all fat and thick and solid," he concluded, unable to manage the longer word. "Then nothing—simply *nothing*—can get through. Can't it, Uncle David?"

And Mr. Bittacy, jacket discarded and working in his speckled waistcoat, went puffing to their aid, arranging the massive limb of the cedar like a hedge.

"Come on," he said, "whatever happens, you know, we must finish before it's dark. Already the wind is roaring in the Forest further out." And Alice caught the phrase and instantly echoed it. "Stevie," she cried below her breath, "look sharp, you lazy lump. Didn't you hear what Uncle David said? It'll come in and catch us before we've done!"

They worked like Trojans, and, sitting beneath the wisteria tree that climbed the southern wall of the cottage, Mrs. Bittacy with her knitting watched them, calling from time to time insignificant messages of counsel and advice. The messages passed, of course, unheeded. Mostly, indeed, they were unheard, for the workers were too absorbed. She warned her husband not to get too hot, Alice not to tear her dress, Stephen not to strain his back with pulling. Her mind hovered between the homeopathic medicine-chest upstairs and her anxiety to see the business finished.

For this breaking up of the cedar had stirred again her slumbering alarms. It revived memories of the visit of Mr. Sanderson that had been sinking into oblivion; she recalled his queer and odious way of talking, and many things she hoped forgotten drew their heads up from that subconscious region to which all forgetting is impossible. They looked at her and nodded. They were full of life; they had no intention of being pushed aside and buried permanently. "Now look!" they whispered, "didn't we tell you so?" They had been merely waiting the right moment to assert their presence. And all her former vague distress crept over her. Anxiety, uneasiness returned. That dreadful sinking of the heart came too.

This incident of the cedar's breaking up was actually so unimportant, and yet her husband's attitude towards it made it so significant. There was nothing that he said in particular, or did, or left undone that frightened, her, but his general air of earnestness seemed so unwarranted. She felt that he deemed the thing important. He was so exercised about it. This evidence of sudden concern and interest, buried all the summer from her sight and knowledge, she realized now had been buried purposely, he had kept it intentionally concealed. Deeply submerged in him there ran this tide of other thoughts, desires, hopes. What were they? Whither did they lead? The accident to the tree betrayed it most unpleasantly, and, doubtless, more than he was aware.

She watched his grave and serious face as he worked there with the children, and as she watched she felt afraid. It vexed her that the children worked so eagerly. They unconsciously supported him. The thing she feared she would not even name. But it was waiting.

Moreover, as far as her puzzled mind could deal with a dread so vague and incoherent, the collapse of the cedar somehow brought it nearer. The fact that, all so ill-explained and formless, the thing yet lay in her consciousness, out of reach but moving and alive, filled her with a kind of puzzled, dreadful wonder. Its presence was so very real, its power so gripping, its partial concealment so abominable. Then, out of the dim confusion, she grasped one thought and saw it stand quite clear before her eyes. She found difficulty in clothing it in words, but its meaning perhaps was this: That cedar stood in their life for something friendly; its downfall meant disaster; a sense of some protective influence about the cottage, and about her husband in particular, was thereby weakened.

"Why do you fear the big winds so?" he had asked her several days before, after a particularly boisterous day; and the answer she gave surprised her while she gave it. One of those heads poked up unconsciously, and let slip the truth.

"Because, David, I feel they—bring the Forest with them," she faltered. "They blow something from the trees—into the mind—into the house."

He looked at her keenly for a moment.

"That must be why I love them then," he answered. "They blow the souls of the trees about the sky like clouds."

The conversation dropped. She had never heard him talk in quite that way before.

And another time, when he had coaxed her to go with him down one of the nearer glades, she asked why he took the small hand-axe with him, and what he wanted it for.

"To cut the ivy that clings to the trunks and takes their life away," he said.

"But can't the verdurers do that?" she asked. "That's what they're paid for, isn't it?"

Whereupon he explained that ivy was a parasite the trees knew not how to fight alone, and that the verdurers were careless and did not do it thoroughly. They gave a chop here and there, leaving the tree to do the rest for itself if it could.

"Besides, I like to do it for them. I love to help them and protect," he added, the foliage rustling all about his quiet words as they went.

And these stray remarks, as his attitude towards the broken cedar, betrayed this curious, subtle change that was going forward to his personality. Slowly and surely all the summer it had increased.

It was growing—the thought startled her horribly—just as a tree grows, the outer evidence from day to day so slight as to be unnoticeable, yet the rising tide so deep and irresistible. The alteration spread all through and over him, was in both mind and actions, sometimes almost in his face as well. Occasionally, thus, it stood up straight outside himself and frightened her. His life was somehow becoming linked so intimately with trees, and with all that trees signified. His interests became more and more their interests, his activity combined with theirs, his thoughts and feelings theirs, his purpose, hope, desire, his fate—

His fate! The darkness of some vague, enormous terror dropped its shadow on her when she thought of it. Some instinct in her heart she dreaded infinitely more than death—for death meant sweet translation for his soul—came gradually to associate the thought of him with the thought of trees, in particular with these Forest trees. Sometimes, before she could face the thing, argue it away, or pray it into silence, she found the thought of him running swiftly through her mind like a thought of the Forest itself, the two most intimately linked and joined together, each a part and complement of the other, one being.

The idea was too dim for her to see it face to face. Its mere possibility dissolved the instant she focused it to get the truth behind it. It was too utterly elusive, made, protæan. Under the attack of even a minute's concentration the very meaning of it vanished, melted away. The idea lay really behind any words that she could ever find, beyond the touch of definite thought.

Her mind was unable to grapple with it. But, while it vanished, the trail of its approach and disappearance flickered a moment before her shaking vision. The horror certainly remained.

Reduced to the simple human statement that her temperament sought instinctively, it stood perhaps at this: Her husband loved her, and he loved the trees as well; but the trees came first, claimed parts of him she did not know. *She* loved her God and him. *He* loved the trees and her.

Thus, in guise of some faint, distressing compromise, the matter shaped itself for her perplexed mind in the terms of conflict. A silent, hidden battle raged, but as yet raged far away. The breaking of the cedar was a visible outward fragment of a distant and mysterious encounter that was coming daily closer to them both. The wind, instead of roaring in the Forest further out, now came nearer, booming in fitful gusts about its edge and frontiers.

Meanwhile the summer dimmed. The autumn winds went sighing

through the woods, leaves turned to golden red, and the evenings were drawing in with cozy shadows before the first sign of anything seriously untoward made its appearance. It came then with a flat, decided kind of violence that indicated mature preparation beforehand. It was not impulsive nor ill-considered. In a fashion it seemed expected, and indeed inevitable. For within a fortnight of their annual change to the little village of Seillans above St. Raphael—a change so regular for the past ten years that it was not even discussed between them—David Bittacy abruptly refused to go.

Thompson had laid the tea-table, prepared the spirit lamp beneath the urn, pulled down the blinds in that swift and silent way she had, and left the room. The lamps were still unlit. The fire-light shone on the chintz armchairs, and Boxer lay asleep on the black horse-hair rug. Upon the walls the gilt picture frames gleamed faintly, the pictures themselves indistinguishable. Mrs. Bittacy had warmed the teapot and was in the act of pouring the water in to heat the cups when her husband, looking up from his chair across the hearth, made the abrupt announcement:

"My dear," he said, as though following a train of thought of which she only heard this final phrase, "it's really quite impossible for me to go."

And so abrupt, inconsequent, it sounded that she at first misunderstood. She thought he meant to go out into the garden or the woods. But her heart leaped all the same. The tone of his voice was ominous.

"Of course not," she answered, "it would be *most* unwise. Why should you—?" She referred to the mist that always spread on autumn nights upon the lawn, but before she finished the sentence she knew that *he* referred to something else. And her heart then gave its second horrible leap.

"David! You mean abroad?" she gasped.

"I mean abroad, dear, yes."

It reminded her of the tone he used when saying good-bye years ago, before one of those jungle expeditions she dreaded. His voice then was so serious, so final. It was serious and final now. For several moments she could think of nothing to say. She busied herself with the teapot. She had filled one cup with hot water till it overflowed, and she emptied it slowly into the slop-basin, trying with all her might not to let him see the trembling of her hand. The firelight and the dimness of the room both helped her. But in any case he would hardly have noticed it. His thoughts were far away. . . .

VI

Mrs. Bittacy had never liked their present home. She preferred a flat, more open country that left approaches clear. She liked to see things coming. This cottage on the very edge of the old hunting grounds of William the Conqueror had never satisfied her ideal of a safe and pleasant place to settle down in. The sea-coast, with treeless downs behind and a clear horizon in front, as at Eastbourne, say, was her ideal of a proper home.

It was curious, this instinctive aversion she felt to being shut in— by trees especially; a kind of claustrophobia almost; probably due, as has been said, to the days in India when the trees took her husband off and surrounded him with dangers. In those weeks of solitude the feeling had matured. She had fought it in her fashion, but never conquered it. Apparently routed, it had a way of creeping back in other forms. In this particular case, yielding to his strong desire, she thought the battle won, but the terror of the trees came back before the first month had passed. They laughed in her face.

She never lost knowledge of the fact that the leagues of forest lay about their cottage like a mighty wall, a crowding, watching, listening presence that shut them in from freedom and escape. Far from morbid naturally, she did her best to deny the thought, and so simple and un-artificial was her type of mind that for weeks together she would wholly lose it. Then, suddenly it would return upon her with a rush of bleak reality. It was not only in her mind; it existed apart from any mere mood; a separate fear that walked alone; it came and went, yet when it went—went only to watch her from another point of view. It was in abeyance—hidden round the corner.

The Forest never let her go completely. It was ever ready to encroach. All the branches, she sometimes fancied, stretched one way—towards their tiny cottage and garden, as though it sought to draw them in and merge them in itself. Its great, deep-breathing soul resented the mockery, the insolence, the irritation of the prim garden at its very gates. It would absorb and smother them if it could. And every wind that blew its thundering message over the huge sounding-board of the million, shaking trees conveyed the purpose that it had. They had angered its great soul. At its heart was this deep, incessant roaring.

All this she never framed in words, the subtleties of language lay far beyond her reach. But instinctively she felt it; and more besides. It troubled her profoundly. Chiefly, moreover, for her husband. Merely for herself, the nightmare might have left her cold. It was David's peculiar interest in the trees that gave the special invitation. Jealousy, then, in its most subtle aspect came to strengthen this aversion and dislike, for it came in a form that no reasonable wife could possibly object to. Her husband's passion, she reflected, was natural and inborn. It had decided his vocation, fed his ambition, nourished his dreams, desires, hopes. All his best years of active life had been spent in the care and guardianship of trees. He knew them, understood their secret life and nature, "managed" them intuitively as other men "managed" dogs and horses. He could not live for long away from them without a strange, acute nostalgia that stole his peace of mind and consequently his strength of body. A forest made him happy and at peace; it nursed and fed and soothed his deepest moods. Trees influenced the sources of his life, lowered or raised the very heart-beat in him. Cut off from them he languished as a lover of the sea can droop inland, or a mountaineer may pine in the flat monotony of the plains.

This she could understand, in a fashion at least, and make allowances for. She had yielded gently, even sweetly, to his choice of their English home; for in the little island there is nothing that suggests the woods of wilder countries so nearly as the New Forest. It has the genuine air and mystery, the depth and splendor, the loneliness, and here and there the strong, untamable quality of old-time forests as Bittacy of the Department knew them.

In a single detail only had he yielded to her wishes. He consented to a cottage on the edge, instead of in the heart of it. And for a dozen years now they had dwelt in peace and happiness at the lips of this great spreading thing that covered so many leagues with its tangle of swamps and moors and splendid ancient trees.

Only with the last two years or so—with his own increasing age, and physical decline perhaps—had come this marked growth of passionate interest in the welfare of the Forest. She had watched it grow, at first had laughed at it, then talked sympathetically so far as sincerity permitted, then had argued mildly, and finally come to realize that its treatment lay altogether beyond her powers, and so had come to fear it with all her heart.

The six weeks they annually spent away from their English home, each regarded very differently, of course. For her husband it meant a painful exile that did his health no good; he yearned for his trees—the sight and sound and smell of them; but for herself it meant release from a haunting dread—escape. To renounce those six weeks by the sea on the sunny, shining coast of France, was almost more than this little woman, even with her unselfishness, could face.

After the first shock of the announcement, she reflected as deeply as her nature permitted, prayed, wept in secret—and made up her mind. Duty, she felt clearly, pointed to renouncement. The discipline would certainly be severe—she did not dream at the moment how severe!— but this fine, consistent little Christian saw it plain; she accepted it, too, without any sighing of the martyr, though the courage she showed was of the martyr order. Her husband should never know the cost. In all but this one passion his unselfishness was ever as great as her own. The love she had borne him all these years, like the love she bore her anthropomorphic deity, was deep and real. She loved to suffer for them both. Besides, the way her husband had put it to her was singular. It did not take the form of a mere selfish predilection. Something higher than two wills in conflict seeking compromise was in it from the beginning.

"I feel, Sophia, it would be really more than I could manage," he said slowly, gazing into the fire over the tops of his stretched-out muddy boots. "My duty and my happiness lie here with the Forest and with you. My life is deeply rooted in this place. Something I can't define connects my inner being with these trees, and separation would make me ill—might even kill me. My hold on life would weaken; here is my source of supply. I cannot explain it better than that." He looked up steadily into her face across the table so that she saw the gravity of his expression and the shining of his steady eyes.

"David, you feel it as strongly as that!" she said, forgetting the tea things altogether.

"Yes," he replied, "I do. And it's not of the body only, I feel it in my soul."

The reality of what he hinted at crept into that shadow-covered room like an actual Presence and stood beside them. It came not by the windows or the door, but it filled the entire space between the walls and ceiling. It took the heat from the fire before her face. She felt suddenly cold, confused a little, frightened. She almost felt the rush of foliage in the wind. It stood between them.

"There are things—some things," she faltered, "we are not intended to know, I think." The words expressed her general attitude to life, not alone to this particular incident.

And after a pause of several minutes, disregarding the criticism as though he had not heard it—"I cannot explain it better than that, you see," his grave voice answered. "There *is* this deep, tremendous link,— some secret power they emanate that keeps me well and happy and— alive. If you cannot understand, I feel at least you may be able to— forgive." His tone grew tender, gentle, soft. "My selfishness, I know, must seem quite unforgivable. I cannot help it somehow; these trees, this ancient Forest, both seem knitted into all that makes me live, and if I go—"

There was a little sound of collapse in his voice. He stopped abruptly, and sank back in his chair. And, at that, a distinct lump came up into her throat which she had great difficulty in managing while she went over and put her arms about him.

"My dear," she murmured, "God will direct. We will accept His guidance. He has always shown the way before."

"My selfishness afflicts me—" he began, but she would not let him finish.

"David, He will direct. Nothing shall harm you. You've never once been selfish, and I cannot bear to hear you say such things. The way will open that is best for you—for both of us." She kissed him, she would not let him speak; her heart was in her throat, and she felt for him far more than for herself.

And then he had suggested that she should go alone perhaps for a shorter time, and stay in her brother's villa with the children, Alice and Stephen. It was always open to her as she well knew.

"You need the change," he said, when the lamps had been lit and the servant had gone out again; "you need it as much as I dread it. I could manage somehow until you returned, and should feel happier that way if you went. I cannot leave this Forest that I love so well. I even feel, Sophie dear"—he sat up straight and faced her as he half whispered it—"that I can *never* leave it again. My life and happiness lie here together."

And even while scorning the idea that she could leave him alone with the Influence of the Forest all about him to have its unimpeded way, she felt the pangs of that subtle jealousy bite keen and close. He loved the Forest better than herself, for he placed it first. Behind the words, moreover, hid the unuttered thought that made her so uneasy. The terror Sanderson had brought revived and shook its wings before her very eyes. For the whole conversation, of which this was a fragment, conveyed the unutterable implication that while he could not spare the trees, they equally could not spare him. The vividness with which he managed to conceal and yet betray the fact brought a profound distress that crossed the border between presentiment and warning into positive alarm.

He clearly felt that the trees would miss him—the trees he tended, guarded, watched over, loved.

"David, I shall stay here with you. I think you need me really,—don't you?" Eagerly, with a touch of heart-felt passion, the words poured out.

"Now more than ever, dear. God bless you for you sweet unselfishness. And your sacrifice," he added, "is all the greater because you cannot understand the thing that makes it necessary for me to stay."

"Perhaps in the spring instead—" she said, with a tremor in the voice.

"In the spring—perhaps," he answered gently, almost beneath his breath. "For they will not need me then. All the world can love them in the spring. It's in the winter that they're lonely and neglected. I wish to stay with them particularly then. I even feel I ought to—and I must."

And in this way, without further speech, the decision was made. Mrs. Bittacy, at least, asked no more questions. Yet she could not bring herself to show more sympathy than was necessary. She felt, for one thing, that if she did, it might lead him to speak freely, and to tell her things she could not possibly bear to know. And she dared not take the risk of that.

VII

This was at the end of summer, but the autumn followed close. The conversation really marked the threshold between the two seasons, and marked at the same time the line between her husband's negative and aggressive state. She almost felt she had done wrong to yield; he grew so bold, concealment all discarded. He went, that is, quite openly to the woods, forgetting all his duties, all his former occupations. He even sought to coax her to go with him. The hidden thing blazed out without disguise. And, while she trembled at his energy, she admired the virile passion he displayed. Her jealousy had long ago retired before her fear, accepting the second place. Her one desire now was to protect. The wife turned wholly mother.

He said so little, but—he hated to come in. From morning to night he wandered in the Forest; often he went out after dinner; his mind was charged with trees—their foliage, growth, development; their wonder, beauty, strength; their loneliness in isolation, their power in a herded mass. He knew the effect of every wind upon them; the danger from the boisterous north, the glory from the west, the eastern dryness, and the soft, moist tenderness that a south wind left upon their thinning boughs. He spoke all day of their sensations: how they drank the fading sunshine, dreamed in the moonlight, thrilled to the kiss of stars. The dew could bring them half the passion of the night, but frost sent them plunging beneath the ground to dwell with hopes of a later coming softness in their roots. They nursed the life they carried—insects, larvae, chrysalis—and when the skies above them melted, he spoke of them standing "motionless in an ecstasy of rain," or in the noon of sunshine "self-poised upon their prodigy of shade."

And once in the middle of the night she woke at the sound of his voice, and heard him—wide awake, not talking in his sleep—but talking towards the window where the shadow of the cedar fell at noon:

O art thou sighing for Lebanon
In the long breeze that streams to thy delicious East?
Sighing for Lebanon,
Dark cedar;

and, when, half charmed, half terrified, she turned and called to him by name, he merely said—

"My dear, I felt the loneliness—suddenly realized it—the alien desolation of that tree, set here upon our little lawn in England when all her Eastern brothers call her in sleep." And the answer seemed so queer, so "un-evangelical," that she waited in silence till he slept again. The poetry passed her by. It seemed unnecessary and out of place. It made her ache with suspicion, fear, jealousy.

The fear, however, seemed somehow all lapped up and banished soon afterwards by her unwilling admiration of the rushing splendor of her husband's state. Her anxiety, at any rate, shifted from the religious to the medical. She thought he might be losing his steadiness of mind a little. How often in her prayers she offered thanks for the guidance that had made her stay with him to help and watch is impossible to say. It certainly was twice a day.

She even went so far once, when Mr. Mortimer, the vicar, called, and brought with him a more or less distinguished doctor—as to tell the professional man privately some symptoms of her husband's queerness. And his answer that there was "nothing he could prescribe for" added not a little to her sense of unholy bewilderment. No doubt Sir James had never been "consulted" under such unorthodox conditions before. His sense of what was becoming naturally overrode his acquired instincts as a skilled instrument that might help the race.

"No fever, you think?" she asked insistently with hurry, determined to get something from him.

"Nothing that *I* can deal with, as I told you, Madam," replied the offended allopathic Knight.

Evidently he did not care about being invited to examine patients in this surreptitious way before a teapot on the lawn, chance of a fee most problematical. He liked to see a tongue and feel a thumping pulse; to know the pedigree and bank account of his questioner as well. It was most unusual, in abominable taste besides. Of course it was. But the drowning woman seized the only straw she could.

For now the aggressive attitude of her husband overcame her to the point where she found it difficult even to question him. Yet in the house he was so kind and gentle, doing all he could to make her sacrifice as easy as possible.

"David, you really *are* unwise to go out now. The night is damp and very chilly. The ground is soaked in dew. You'll catch your death of cold."

His face lightened. "Won't you come with me, dear,—just for once? I'm only going to the corner of the hollies to see the beech that stands so lonely by itself."

She had been out with him in the short dark afternoon, and they had passed that evil group of hollies where the gypsies camped. Nothing else would grow there, but the hollies thrive upon the stony soil.

"David, the beech is all right and safe." She had learned his phraseology a little, made clever out of due season by her love.

"There's no wind to-night."

"But it's rising," he answered, "rising in the east. I heard it in the bare and hungry larches. They need the sun and dew, and always cry out when the wind's upon them from the east."

She sent a short unspoken prayer most swiftly to her deity as she heard him say it. For every time now, when he spoke in this familiar, intimate way of the life of the trees, she felt a sheet of cold fasten tight against her very skin and flesh. She shivered. How *could* he possibly know such things?

Yet, in all else, and in the relations of his daily life, he was sane and reasonable, loving, kind and tender. It was only on the subject of the trees he seemed unhinged and queer. Most curiously it seemed that, since the collapse of the cedar they both loved, though in different fashion, his departure from the normal had increased. Why else did he watch them as a man might watch a sickly child? Why did he hunger especially in the dusk to catch their "mood of night" as he called it? Why think so carefully upon them when the frost was threatening or the wind appeared to rise?

As she put it so frequently now herself—How could he possibly *know* such things?

He went. As she closed the front door after him she heard the distant roaring in the Forest.

And then it suddenly struck her: How could she know them too?

It dropped upon her like a blow that she felt at once all over, upon body, heart and mind. The discovery rushed out from its ambush to overwhelm. The truth of it, making all arguing futile, numbed her faculties. But though at first it deadened her, she soon revived, and her being rose into aggressive opposition. A wild yet calculated courage like that which animates the leaders of splendid forlorn hopes flamed in her little person—flamed grandly, and invincible. While knowing herself insignificant and weak, she knew at the same time that power at her back which moves the worlds. The faith that filled her was the weapon in her hands, and the right by which she claimed it; but the spirit of utter, selfless sacrifice that characterized her life was the means by which she mastered its immediate use. For a kind of white and faultless intuition guided her to the attack. Behind her stood her Bible and her God.

How so magnificent a divination came to her at all may well be a matter for astonishment, though some clue of explanation lies, perhaps, in the very simpleness of her nature. At any rate, she saw quite clearly certain things; saw them in moments only—after prayer, in the still silence of the night, or when left alone those long hours in the house with her knitting and her thoughts—and the guidance which then flashed into her remained, even after the manner of its coming was forgotten.

They came to her, these things she saw, formless, wordless; she could not put them into any kind of language; but by the very fact of being uncaught in sentences they retained their original clear vigor.

Hours of patient waiting brought the first, and the others followed easily afterwards, by degrees, on subsequent days, a little and a little. Her husband had been gone since early morning, and had taken his luncheon with him. She was sitting by the tea things, the cups and teapot warmed, the muffins in the fender keeping hot, all ready for his return, when she realized quite abruptly that this thing which took him off, which kept him out so many hours day after day, this thing that was against her own little will and instincts—was enormous as the sea. It was no mere prettiness of single Trees, but something massed and mountainous. About her rose the wall of its huge opposition to the sky, its scale gigantic, its power utterly prodigious. What she knew of it hitherto as green and delicate forms waving and rustling in the winds was but, as it were the spray of foam that broke into sight upon the nearer edge of viewless depths far, far away. The trees, indeed, were sentinels set visibly about the limits of a camp that itself remained invisible. The awful hum and murmur of the main body in the distance passed into that still room about her with the firelight and hissing kettle. Out yonder—in the Forest further out—the thing that was ever roaring at the center was dreadfully increasing.

The sense of definite battle, too—battle between herself and the Forest for his soul—came with it. Its presentiment was as clear as though Thompson had come into the room and quietly told her that the cottage was surrounded. "Please, ma'am, there are trees come up about the house," she might have suddenly announced. And equally might have heard her own answer: "It's all right, Thompson. The main body is still far away."

Immediately upon its heels, then, came another truth, with a close reality that shocked her. She saw that jealousy was not confined to the human and animal world alone, but ran though all creation. The Vegetable Kingdom knew it too. So-called inanimate nature shared it with the rest. Trees felt it. This Forest just beyond the window—standing there in the silence of the autumn evening across the little lawn—this Forest understood it equally. The remorseless, branching power that sought to keep exclusively for itself the thing it loved and needed, spread like a running desire through all its million leaves and stems and roots. In humans, of course, it was consciously directed; in animals it acted with frank instinctiveness; but in trees this jealousy rose in some blind tide of impersonal and unconscious wrath that would sweep opposition from its path as the wind sweeps powdered snow from the surface of the ice. Their number was a host with endless reinforcements, and once it realized its passion was returned the power increased. . . . Her husband loved the trees. . . . They had become aware of it. . . . They would take him from her in the end. . . .

Then, while she heard his footsteps in the hall and the closing of the front door, she saw a third thing clearly;—realized the widening of the gap between herself and him. This other love had made it. All these weeks of the summer when she felt so close to him, now especially when she had made the biggest sacrifice of her life to stay by his side and help him, he had been slowly, surely—drawing away. The estrangement was here and now—a fact accomplished. It had been all this time maturing; there yawned this broad deep space between them. Across the empty distance she saw the change in merciless perspective. It revealed his face and figure, dearly-loved, once fondly worshipped, far on the other side in shadowy distance, small, the back turned from her, and moving while she watched—moving away from her.

They had their tea in silence then. She asked no questions, he volunteered no information of his day. The heart was big within her, and the terrible loneliness of age spread through her like a rising icy mist. She watched him, filling all his wants. His hair was untidy and his boots were caked with blackish mud. He moved with a restless, swaying motion that somehow blanched her cheek and sent a miserable shivering down her back. It reminded her of trees. His eyes were very bright.

He brought in with him an odor of the earth and forest that seemed to choke her and make it difficult to breathe; and—what she noticed with a climax of almost uncontrollable alarm—upon his face beneath the lamplight shone traces of a mild, faint glory that made her think of moonlight falling upon a wood through speckled shadows. It was his new-found happiness that shone there, a happiness uncaused by her and in which she had no part.

In his coat was a spray of faded yellow beech leaves. "I brought this from the Forest to you," he said, with all the air that belonged to his little acts of devotion long ago. And she took the spray of leaves mechanically with a smile and a murmured "thank you, dear," as though he had unknowingly put into her hands the weapon for her own destruction and she had accepted it.

And when the tea was over and he left the room, he did not go to his study, or to change his clothes. She heard the front door softly shut behind him as he again went out towards the Forest.

A moment later she was in her room upstairs, kneeling beside the bed—the side she slept on—and praying wildly through a flood of tears that God would save and keep him to her. Wind brushed the window panes behind her while she knelt.

VIII

One sunny November morning, when the strain had reached a
pitch that made repression almost unmanageable, she came to an
impulsive decision, and obeyed it. Her husband had again gone out
with luncheon for the day. She took adventure in her hands and
followed him. The power of seeing-clear was strong upon her, forcing
her up to some unnatural level of understanding. To stay indoors and
wait inactive for his return seemed suddenly impossible. She meant to
know what he knew, feel what he felt, put herself in his place. She
would dare the fascination of the Forest—share it with him. It was
greatly daring; but it would give her greater understanding how to help
and save him and therefore greater Power. She went upstairs a moment
first to pray.

In a thick, warm skirt, and wearing heavy boots—those walking
boots she used with him upon the mountains about Seillans—she left
the cottage by the back way and turned towards the Forest. She could
not actually follow him, for he had started off an hour before and she
knew not exactly his direction. What was so urgent in her was the wish
to be with him in the woods, to walk beneath leafless branches just as
he did: to be there when he was there, even though not together. For it
had come to her that she might thus share with him for once this
horrible mighty life and breathing of the trees he loved. In winter, he
had said, they needed him particularly, and winter now was coming.
Her love *must* bring her something of what he felt himself—the huge
attraction, the suction and the pull of all the trees. Thus, in some
vicarious fashion, she might share, though unknown to himself, this
very thing that was taking him away from her. She might thus even
lessen its attack upon himself.

The impulse came to her clairvoyantly, and she obeyed without a
sign of hesitation. Deeper comprehension would come to her of the
whole awful puzzle. And come it did, yet not in the way she imagined
and expected.

The air was very still, the sky a cold pale blue, but cloudless. The
entire Forest stood silent, at attention. It knew perfectly well that she
had come. It knew the moment when she entered; watched and
followed her; and behind her something dropped without a sound and
shut her in. Her feet upon the glades of mossy grass fell silently, as the
oaks and beeches shifted past in rows and took up their positions at her
back. It was not pleasant, this way they grew so dense behind her the
instant she had passed. She realized that they gathered in an ever-
growing army, massed, herded, trooped, between her and the cottage,
shutting off escape. They let her pass so easily, but to get out again she
would know them differently—thick, crowded, branches all drawn and

hostile. Already their increasing numbers bewildered her. In front, they looked so sparse and scattered, with open spaces where the sunshine fell; but when she turned it seemed they stood so close together, a serried army, darkening the sunlight. They blocked the day, collected all the shadows, stood with their leafless and forbidding rampart like the night. They swallowed down into themselves the very glade by which she came. For when she glanced behind her—rarely—the way she had come was shadowy and lost.

Yet the morning sparkled overhead, and a glance of excitement ran quivering through the entire day. It was what she always knew as "children's weather," so clear and harmless, without a sign of danger, nothing ominous to threaten or alarm. Steadfast in her purpose, looking back as little as she dared, Sophia Bittacy marched slowly and deliberately into the heart of the silent woods, deeper, ever deeper.

And then, abruptly, in an open space where the sunshine fell unhindered, she stopped. It was one of the breathing places of the forest. Dead, withered bracken lay in patches of unsightly grey. There were bits of heather too. All round the trees stood looking on—oak, beech, holly, ash, pine, larch, with here and there small groups of juniper. On the lips of this breathing space of the woods she stopped to rest, disobeying her instinct for the first time. For the other instinct in her was to go on. She did not really want to rest.

This was the little act that brought it to her—the wireless message from a vast Emitter.

"I've been stopped," she thought to herself with a horrid qualm.

She looked about her in this quiet, ancient place. Nothing stirred. There was no life nor sign of life; no birds sang; no rabbits scuttled off at her approach. The stillness was bewildering, and gravity hung down upon it like a heavy curtain. It hushed the heart in her. Could this be part of what her husband felt—this sense of thick entanglement with stems, boughs, roots, and foliage?

"This has always been as it is now," she thought, yet not knowing why she thought it. "Ever since the Forest grew it has been still and secret here. It has never changed." The curtain of silence drew closer while she said it, thickening round her. "For a thousand years—I'm here with a thousand years. And behind this place stand all the forests of the world!"

So foreign to her temperament were such thoughts, and so alien to all she had been taught to look for in Nature, that she strove against them. She made an effort to oppose. But they clung and haunted just the same; they refused to be dispersed. The curtain hung dense and heavy as though its texture thickened. The air with difficulty came through.

And then she thought that curtain stirred. There was movement somewhere. That obscure dim thing which ever broods behind the visible appearances of trees came nearer to her. She caught her breath and stared about her, listening intently. The trees, perhaps because she saw them more in detail now, it seemed to her had changed. A vague, faint alteration spread over them, at first so slight she scarcely would admit it, then growing steadily, though still obscurely, outwards. "They tremble and are changed," flashed through her mind the horrid line that Sanderson had quoted. Yet the change was graceful for all the uncouthness attendant upon the size of so vast a movement. They had turned in her direction. That was it. *They saw her.*

In this way the change expressed itself in her groping, terrified thought. Till now it had been otherwise: she had looked at them from her own point of view; now they looked at her from theirs. They stared her in the face and eyes; they stared at her all over. In some unkind, resentful, hostile way, they watched her. Hitherto in life she had watched them variously, in superficial ways, reading into them what her own mind suggested. Now they read into her the things they actually *were*, and not merely another's interpretations of them.

They seemed in their motionless silence there instinct with life, a life, moreover, that breathed about her a species of terrible soft enchantment that bewitched. It branched all through her, climbing to the brain. The Forest held her with its huge and giant fascination. In this secluded breathing spot that the centuries had left untouched, she had stepped close against the hidden pulse of the whole collective mass of them. They were aware of her and had turned to gaze with their myriad, vast sight upon the intruder. They shouted at her in the silence. For she wanted to look back at them, but it was like staring at a crowd, and her glance merely shifted from one tree to another, hurriedly, finding in none the one she sought. They saw her so easily, each and all. The rows that stood behind her also stared. But she could not return the gaze. Her husband, she realized, could. And their steady stare shocked her as though in some sense she knew that she was naked. They saw so much of her: she saw of them—so little.

Her efforts to return their gaze were pitiful. The constant shifting increased her bewilderment. Conscious of this awful and enormous sight all over her, she let her eyes first rest upon the ground, and then she closed them altogether. She kept the lids as tight together as ever they would go.

But the sight of the trees came even into that inner darkness behind the fastened lids, for there was no escaping it. Outside, in the light, she still knew that the leaves of the hollies glittered smoothly, that the dead foliage of the oaks hung crisp in the air about her, that the needles of the little junipers were pointing all one way. The spread perception of the Forest was focused on herself, and no mere shutting of the eyes could hide its scattered yet concentrated stare—the all-inclusive vision of great woods.

There was no wind, yet here and there a single leaf hanging by its dried-up stalk shook all alone with great rapidity—rattling. It was the sentry drawing attention to her presence. And then, again, as once long weeks before, she felt their Being as a tide about her. The tide had turned. That memory of her childhood sands came back, when the nurse said, "The tide has turned now; we must go in," and she saw the mass of piled-up waters, green and heaped to the horizon, and realized that it was slowly coming in. The gigantic mass of it, too vast for hurry, loaded with massive purpose, she used to feel, was moving towards herself. The fluid body of the sea was creeping along beneath the sky to the very spot upon the yellow sands where she stood and played. The sight and thought of it had always overwhelmed her with a sense of awe—as though her puny self were the object of the whole sea's advance. "The tide has turned; we had better now go in."

This was happening now about her—the same thing was happening in the woods—slow, sure, and steady, and its motion as little discernible as the sea's. The tide had turned. The small human presence that had ventured among its green and mountainous depths, moreover, was its objective.

That all was clear within her while she sat and waited with tight-shut lids. But the next moment she opened her eyes with a sudden realization of something more. The presence that it sought was after all not hers. It was the presence of some one other than herself. And then she understood. Her eyes had opened with a click, it seemed, but the sound, in reality, was outside herself.

Across the clearing where the sunshine lay so calm and still, she saw the figure of her husband moving among the trees—a man, like a tree, walking.

With hands behind his back, and head uplifted, he moved quite slowly, as though absorbed in his own thoughts. Hardly fifty paces separated them, but he had no inkling of her presence there so near. With mind intent and senses all turned inwards, he marched past her like a figure in a dream, and like a figure in a dream she saw him go. Love, yearning, pity rose in a storm within her, but as in nightmare she found no words or movement possible. She sat and watched him go— go from her—go into the deeper reaches of the green enveloping woods. Desire to save, to bid him stop and turn, ran in a passion through her being, but there was nothing she could do. She saw him go away from her, go of his own accord and willingly beyond her; she saw the branches drop about his steps and hid him. His figure faded out among the speckled shade and sunlight. The trees covered him. The tide just took him, all unresisting and content to go. Upon the bosom of the green soft sea he floated away beyond her reach of vision. Her eyes could follow him no longer. He was gone.

And then for the first time she realized, even at that distance, that the look upon his face was one of peace and happiness—rapt, and caught away in joy, a look of youth. That expression now he never showed to her. But she *had* known it. Years ago, in the early days of their married life, she had seen it on his face. Now it no longer obeyed the summons of her presence and her love. The woods alone could call it forth; it answered to the trees; the Forest had taken every part of him—from her—his very heart and soul. . . .

Her sight that had plunged inwards to the fields of faded memory now came back to outer things again. She looked about her, and her love, returning empty-handed and unsatisfied, left her open to the invading of the bleakest terror she had ever known. That such things could be real and happen found her helpless utterly. Terror invaded the quietest corners of her heart, that had never yet known quailing. She could not—for moments at any rate—reach either her Bible or her God. Desolate in an empty world of fear she sat with eyes too dry and hot for tears, yet with a coldness as of ice upon her very flesh. She stared, unseeing, about her. That horror which stalks in the stillness of the noonday, when the glare of an artificial sunshine lights up the motionless trees, moved all about her. In front and behind she was aware of it. Beyond this stealthy silence, just within the edge of it, the things of another world were passing. But she could not know them. Her husband knew them, knew their beauty and their awe, yes, but for her they were out of reach. She might not share with him the very least of them. It seemed that behind and through the glare of this wintry noonday in the heart of the woods there brooded another universe of life and passion, for her all unexpressed. The silence veiled it, the stillness hid it; but he moved with it all and understood. His love interpreted it.

She rose to her feet, tottered feebly, and collapsed again upon the moss. Yet for herself she felt no terror; no little personal fear could touch her whose anguish and deep longing streamed all out to him whom she so bravely loved. In this time of utter self-forgetfulness, when she realized that the battle was hopeless, thinking she had lost even her God, she found Him again quite close beside her like a little Presence in this terrible heart of the hostile Forest. But at first she did not recognize that He was there; she did not know Him in that strangely unacceptable guise. For He stood so very close, so very intimate, so very sweet and comforting, and yet so hard to understand—as Resignation.

Once more she struggled to her feet, and this time turned successfully and slowly made her way along the mossy glade by which she came. And at first she marveled, though only for a moment, at the ease with which she found the path. For a moment only, because almost at once she saw the truth. The trees were glad that she should go. They helped her on her way. The Forest did not want her.

The tide was coming in, indeed, yet not for her.

And so, in another of those flashes of clear-vision that of late had lifted life above the normal level, she saw and understood the whole terrible thing complete.

Till now, though unexpressed in thought or language, her fear had been that the woods her husband loved would somehow take him from her—to merge his life in theirs—even to kill him on some mysterious way. This time she saw her deep mistake, and so seeing, let in upon herself the fuller agony of horror. For their jealousy was not the petty jealousy of animals or humans. They wanted him because they loved him, but they did *not* want him dead. Full charged with his splendid life and enthusiasm they wanted him. They wanted him—alive.

It was she who stood in their way, and it was she whom they intended to remove.

This was what brought the sense of abject helplessness. She stood upon the sands against an entire ocean slowly rolling in against her. For, as all the forces of a human being combine unconsciously to eject a grain of sand that has crept beneath the skin to cause discomfort, so the entire mass of what Sanderson had called the Collective Consciousness of the Forest strove to eject this human atom that stood across the path of its desire. Loving her husband, she had crept beneath its skin. It was her they would eject and take away; it was her they would destroy, not him. Him, whom they loved and needed, they would keep alive. They meant to take him living. She reached the house in safety, though she never remembered how she found her way. It was made all simple for her. The branches almost urged her out.

But behind her, as she left the shadowed precincts, she felt as though some towering Angel of the Woods let fall across the threshold the flaming sword of a countless multitude of leaves that formed behind her a barrier, green, shimmering, and impassable. Into the Forest she never walked again.

And she went about her daily duties with a calm and quietness that was a perpetual astonishment even to herself, for it hardly seemed of this world at all. She talked to her husband when he came in for tea— after dark. Resignation brings a curious large courage—when there is nothing more to lose. The soul takes risks, and dares. Is it a curious short-cut sometimes to the heights?

"David, I went into the Forest, too, this morning, soon after you I went. I saw you there."

"Wasn't it wonderful?" he answered simply, inclining his head a little. There was no surprise or annoyance in his look; a mild and gentle *ennui* rather. He asked no real question. She thought of some garden tree the wind attacks too suddenly, bending it over when it does not want to bend—the mild unwillingness with which it yields. She often saw him this way now, in the terms of trees.

"It was very wonderful indeed, dear, yes," she replied low, her voice not faltering though indistinct. "But for me it was too—too strange and big."

The passion of tears lay just below the quiet voice all un-betrayed. Somehow she kept them back.

There was a pause, and then he added:

"I find it more and more so every day." His voice passed through the lamp-lit room like a murmur of the wind in branches. The look of youth and happiness she had caught upon his face out there had wholly gone, and an expression of weariness was in its place, as of a man distressed vaguely at finding himself in uncongenial surroundings where he is slightly ill at ease. It was the house he hated—coming back to rooms and walls and furniture. The ceilings and closed windows confined him. Yet, in it, no suggestion that he found *her* irksome. Her presence seemed of no account at all; indeed, he hardly noticed her. For whole long periods he lost her, did not know that she was there. He had no need of her. He lived alone. Each lived alone.

The outward signs by which she recognized that the awful battle was against her and the terms of surrender accepted were pathetic. She put the medicine-chest away upon the shelf; she gave the orders for his pocket-luncheon before he asked; she went to bed alone and early, leaving the front door unlocked, with milk and bread and butter in the hall beside the lamp—all concessions that she felt impelled to make. For more and more, unless the weather was too violent, he went out after dinner even, staying for hours in the woods. But she never slept until she heard the front door close below, and knew soon afterwards his careful step come creeping up the stairs and into the room so softly. Until she heard his regular deep breathing close beside her, she lay awake. All strength or desire to resist had gone for good. The thing against her was too huge and powerful. Capitulation was complete, a fact accomplished. She dated it from the day she followed him to the Forest.

Moreover, the time for evacuation—her own evacuation—seemed approaching. It came stealthily ever nearer, surely and slowly as the rising tide she used to dread. At the high-water mark she stood waiting calmly—waiting to be swept away. Across the lawn all those terrible days of early winter the encircling Forest watched it come, guiding its silent swell and currents towards her feet. Only she never once gave up her Bible or her praying. This complete resignation, moreover, had somehow brought to her a strange great understanding, and if she could not share her husband's horrible abandonment to powers outside himself, she could, and did, in some half-groping way grasp at shadowy meanings that might make such abandonment—possible, yes, but more than merely possible—in some extraordinary sense not evil.

Hitherto she had divided the beyond-world into two sharp halves— spirits good or spirits evil. But thoughts came to her now, on soft and very tentative feet, like the footsteps of the gods which are on wool, that besides these definite classes, there might be other Powers as well, belonging definitely to neither one nor other. Her thought stopped dead at that. But the big idea found lodgment in her little mind, and, owing to the largeness of her heart, remained there un-ejected. It even brought a certain solace with it.

The failure—or unwillingness, as she preferred to state it—of her God to interfere and help, that also she came in a measure to understand. For here, she found it more and more possible to imagine, was perhaps no positive evil at work, but only something that usually stands away from humankind, something alien and not commonly recognized. There *was* a gulf fixed between the two, and Mr. Sanderson *had* bridged it, by his talk, his explanations, his attitude of mind. Through these her husband had found the way into it. His temperament and natural passion for the woods had prepared the soul in him, and the moment he saw the way to go he took it—the line of least resistance. Life was, of course, open to all, and her husband had the right to choose it where he would. He had chosen it—away from her, away from other men, but not necessarily away from God. This was an enormous concession that she skirted, never really faced; it was too revolutionary to face. But its possibility peeped into her bewildered mind. It might delay his progress, or it might advance it. Who could know? And why should God, who ordered all things with such magnificent detail, from the pathway of a sun to the falling of a sparrow, object to his free choice, or interfere to hinder him and stop?

She came to realize resignation, that is, in another aspect. It gave her comfort, if not peace. She fought against all belittling of her God. It was, perhaps, enough that He—knew.

"You are not alone, dear in the trees out there?" she ventured one night, as he crept on tiptoe into the room not far from midnight. "God is with you?"

"Magnificently," was the immediate answer, given with enthusiasm, "for He is everywhere. And I only wish that you—"

But she stuffed the clothes against her ears. That invitation on his lips was more than she could bear to hear. It seemed like asking her to hurry to her own execution. She buried her face among the sheets and blankets, shaking all over like a leaf.

IX

And so the thought that she was the one to go remained and grew. It was, perhaps, the first sign of that weakening of the mind which indicated the singular manner of her going. For it was her mental opposition, the trees felt, that stood in their way. Once that was overcome, obliterated, her physical presence did not matter. She would be harmless.

Having accepted defeat, because she had come to feel that his obsession was not actually evil, she accepted at the same time the conditions of an atrocious loneliness. She stood now from her husband farther than from the moon. They had no visitors. Callers were few and far between, and less encouraged than before. The empty dark of winter was before them. Among the neighbors was none in whom, without disloyalty to her husband, she could confide. Mr. Mortimer, had he been single, might have helped her in this desert of solitude that preyed upon her mind, but his wife was there the obstacle; for Mrs. Mortimer wore sandals, believed that nuts were the complete food of man, and indulged in other idiosyncrasies that classed her inevitably among the "latter signs" which Mrs. Bittacy had been taught to dread as dangerous. She stood most desolately alone.

Solitude, therefore, in which the mind unhindered feeds upon its own delusions, was the assignable cause of her gradual mental disruption and collapse.

With the definite arrival of the colder weather her husband gave up his rambles after dark; evenings were spent together over the fire; he read *The Times*; they even talked about their postponed visit abroad in the coming spring. No restlessness was on him at the change; he seemed content and easy in his mind; spoke little of the trees and woods; enjoyed far better health than if there had been change of scene, and to herself was tender, kind, solicitous over trifles, as in the distant days of their first honeymoon.

But this deep calm could not deceive her; it meant, she fully understood, that he felt sure of himself, sure of her, and sure of the trees as well. It all lay buried in the depths of him, too secure and deep, too intimately established in his central being to permit of those surface fluctuations which betray disharmony within. His life was hid with trees. Even the fever, so dreaded in the damp of winter, left him free. She now knew why: the fever was due to their efforts to obtain him, his efforts to respond and go—physical results of a fierce unrest he had never understood till Sanderson came with his wicked explanations. Now it was otherwise. The bridge was made. And—he had gone.

And she, brave, loyal, and consistent soul, found herself utterly alone, even trying to make his passage easy. It seemed that she stood at the bottom of some huge ravine that opened in her mind, the walls whereof instead of rock were trees that reached enormous to the sky, engulfing her. God alone knew that she was there. He watched, permitted, even perhaps approved. At any rate—He knew.

During those quiet evenings in the house, moreover, while they sat over the fire listening to the roaming winds about the house, her husband knew continual access to the world his alien love had furnished for him. Never for a single instant was he cut off from it. She gazed at the newspaper spread before his face and knees, saw the smoke of his cheroot curl up above the edge, noticed the little hole in his evening socks, and listened to the paragraphs he read aloud as of old. But this was all a veil he spread about himself of purpose. Behind it—he escaped. It was the conjurer's trick to divert the sight to unimportant details while the essential thing went forward unobserved. He managed wonderfully; she loved him for the pains he took to spare her distress; but all the while she knew that the body lolling in that armchair before her eyes contained the merest fragment of his actual self. It was little better than a corpse. It was an empty shell. The essential soul of him was out yonder with the Forest—farther out near that ever-roaring heart of it.

And, with the dark, the Forest came up boldly and pressed against the very walls and windows, peering in upon them, joining hands above the slates and chimneys. The winds were always walking on the lawn and gravel paths; steps came and went and came again; some one seemed always talking in the woods, some one was in the building too. She passed them on the stairs, or running soft and muffled, very large and gentle, down the passages and landings after dusk, as though loose fragments of the Day had broken off and stayed there caught among the shadows, trying to get out. They blundered silently all about the house. They waited till she passed, then made a run for it. And her husband always knew. She saw him more than once deliberately avoid them— because *she* was there. More than once, too, she saw him stand and listen when he thought she was not near, then heard herself the long bounding stride of their approach across the silent garden. Already *he* had heard them in the windy distance of the night, far, far away. They sped, she well knew, along that glade of mossy turf by which she last came out; it cushioned their tread exactly as it had cushioned her own.

It seemed to her the trees were always in the house with him, and in their very bedroom. He welcomed them, unaware that she also knew, and trembled.

One night in their bedroom it caught her unawares. She woke out of deep sleep and it came upon her before she could gather her forces for control.

The day had been wildly boisterous, but now the wind had dropped, only its rags went fluttering through the night. The rays of the full moon fell in a shower between the branches. Overhead still raced the scud and wrack, shaped like hurrying monsters; but below the earth was quiet. Still and dripping stood the hosts of trees. Their trunks gleamed wet and sparkling where the moon caught them. There was a strong smell of mould and fallen leaves. The air was sharp—heavy with odor.

And she knew all this the instant that she woke; for it seemed to her that she had been elsewhere—following her husband—as though she had been *out!* There was no dream at all, merely the definite, haunting certainty. It dived away, lost, buried in the night. She sat upright in bed. She had come back.

The room shone pale in the moonlight reflected through the windows, for the blinds were up, and she saw her husband's form beside her, motionless in deep sleep. But what caught her unawares was the horrid thing that by this fact of sudden, unexpected waking she had surprised these other things in the room, beside the very bed, gathered close about him while he slept. It was their dreadful boldness—herself of no account as it were—that terrified her into screaming before she could collect her powers to prevent. She screamed before she realized what she did—a long, high shriek of terror that filled the room, yet made so little actual sound. For wet and shimmering presences stood grouped all round that bed. She saw their outline underneath the ceiling, the green, spread bulk of them, their vague extension over walls and furniture. They shifted to and fro, massed yet translucent, mild yet thick, moving and turning within themselves to a hushed noise of multitudinous soft rustling. In their sound was something very sweet and sinning that fell into her with a spell of horrible enchantment. They were so mild, each one alone, yet so terrific in their combination. Cold seized her. The sheets against her body had turned to ice.

She screamed a second time, though the sound hardly issued from her throat. The spell sank deeper, reaching to the heart; for it softened all the currents of her blood and took life from her in a stream— towards themselves. Resistance in that moment seemed impossible.

Her husband then stirred in his sleep, and woke. And, instantly, the forms drew up, erect, and gathered themselves in some amazing way together. They lessened in extent—then scattered through the air like an effect of light when shadows seek to smother it. It was tremendous, yet most exquisite. A sheet of pale-green shadow that yet had form and substance filled the room. There was a rush of silent movement, as the Presences drew past her through the air,—and they were gone.

But, clearest of all, she saw the manner of their going; for she recognized in their tumult of escape by the window open at the top, the same wide "looping circles"—spirals as it seemed—that she had seen upon the lawn those weeks ago when Sanderson had talked. The room once more was empty.

In the collapse that followed, she heard her husband's voice, as though coming from some great distance. Her own replies she heard as well. Both were so strange and unlike their normal speech, the very words unnatural.

"What is it, dear? Why do you wake me *now?*" And his voice whispered it with a sighing sound, like wind in pine boughs.

"A moment since something went past me through the air of the room. Back to the night outside it went." Her voice, too, held the same note as of wind entangled among too many leaves.

"My dear, it *was* the wind."

"But it called, David. It was calling *you*—by name!"

"The air of the branches, dear, was what you heard. Now, sleep again, I beg you, sleep."

"It had a crowd of eyes all through and over it—before and behind—" Her voice grew louder. But his own in reply sank lower, far away, and oddly hushed.

"The moonlight, dear, upon the sea of twigs and boughs in the rain, was what you saw."

"But it frightened me. I've lost my God—and you—I'm cold as death!"

"My dear, it is the cold of the early morning hours. The whole world sleeps. Now sleep again yourself."

He whispered close to her ear. She felt his hand stroking her. His voice was soft and very soothing. But only a part of him was there; only a part of him was speaking; it was a half-emptied body that lay beside her and uttered these strange sentences, even forcing her own singular choice of words. The horrible, dim enchantment of the trees was close about them in the room—gnarled, ancient, lonely trees of winter, whispering round the human life they loved.

"And let me sleep again," she heard him murmur as he settled down among the clothes, "sleep back into that deep, delicious peace from which you called me . . ."

His dreamy, happy tone, and that look of youth and joy she discerned upon his features even in the filtered moonlight, touched her again as with the spell of those shining, mild green presences. It sank down into her. She felt sleep grope for her. On the threshold of slumber one of those strange vagrant voices that loss of consciousness lets loose cried faintly in her heart—

"There is joy in the Forest over one sinner that—"

Then sleep took her before she had time to realize even that she was vilely parodying one of her most precious texts, and that the irreverence was ghastly.

And though she quickly slept again, her sleep was not as usual, dreamless. It was not woods and trees she dreamed of, but a small and curious dream that kept coming again and again upon her; that she stood upon a wee, bare rock in the sea, and that the tide was rising. The water first came to her feet, then to her knees, then to her waist. Each time the dream returned, the tide seemed higher. Once it rose to her neck, once even to her mouth, covering her lips for a moment so that she could not breathe. She did not wake between the dreams; a period of drab and dreamless slumber intervened. But, finally, the water rose above her eyes and face, completely covering her head.

And then came explanation—the sort of explanation dreams bring. She understood. For, beneath the water, she had seen the world of seaweed rising from the bottom of the sea like a forest of dense green-long, sinuous stems, immense thick branches, millions of feelers spreading through the darkened watery depths the power of their ocean foliage. The Vegetable Kingdom was even in the sea. It was everywhere. Earth, air, and water helped it, way of escape there was none.

And even underneath the sea she heard that terrible sound of roaring—was it surf or wind or voices?—further out, yet coming steadily towards her.

And so, in the loneliness of that drab English winter, the mind of Mrs. Bittacy, preying upon itself, and fed by constant dread, went lost in disproportion. Dreariness filled the weeks with dismal, sunless skies and a clinging moisture that knew no wholesome tonic of keen frosts. Alone with her thoughts, both her husband and her God withdrawn into distance, she counted the days to Spring. She groped her way, stumbling down the long dark tunnel. Through the arch at the far end lay a brilliant picture of the violet sea sparkling on the coast of France. There lay safety and escape for both of them, could she but hold on. Behind her the trees blocked up the other entrance. She never once looked back.

She drooped. Vitality passed from her, drawn out and away as by some steady suction. Immense and incessant was this sensation of her powers draining off. The taps were all turned on. Her personality, as it were, streamed steadily away, coaxed outwards by this Power that never wearied and seemed inexhaustible. It won her as the full moon wins the tide. She waned; she faded; she obeyed.

At first she watched the process, and recognized exactly what was going on. Her physical life, and that balance of mind which depends on physical well-being, were being slowly undermined. She saw that clearly. Only the soul, dwelling like a star apart from these and independent of them, lay safe somewhere—with her distant God. That she knew—tranquilly. The spiritual love that linked her to her husband was safe from all attack. Later, in His good time, they would merge together again because of it. But meanwhile, all of her that had kinship with the earth was slowly going. This separation was being remorselessly accomplished. Every part of her the trees could touch was being steadily drained from her. She was being—removed.

After a time, however, even this power of realization went, so that she no longer "watched the process" or knew exactly what was going on. The one satisfaction she had known—the feeling that it was sweet to suffer for his sake—went with it. She stood utterly alone with this terror of the trees . . . mid the ruins of her broken and disordered mind.

She slept badly; woke in the morning with hot and tired eyes; her head ached dully; she grew confused in thought and lost the clues of daily life in the most feeble fashion. At the same time she lost sight, too, of that brilliant picture at the exit of the tunnel; it faded away into a tiny semicircle of pale light, the violet sea and the sunshine the merest point of white, remote as a star and equally inaccessible. She knew now that she could never reach it. And through the darkness that stretched behind, the power of the trees came close and caught her, twining about her feet and arms, climbing to her very lips. She woke at night, finding it difficult to breathe. There seemed wet leaves pressing against her mouth, and soft green tendrils clinging to her neck. Her feet were heavy, half rooted, as it were, in deep, thick earth. Huge creepers stretched along the whole of that black tunnel, feeling about her person for points where they might fasten well, as ivy or the giant parasites of the Vegetable Kingdom settle down on the trees themselves to sap their life and kill them.

Slowly and surely the morbid growth possessed her life and held her. She feared those very winds that ran about the wintry forest. They were in league with it. They helped it everywhere.

"Why don't you sleep, dear?" It was her husband now who played the *rôle* of nurse, tending her little wants with an honest care that at least aped the services of love. He was so utterly unconscious of the raging battle he had caused. "What is it keeps you so wide awake and restless?"

"The winds," she whispered in the dark. For hours she had been watching the tossing of the trees through the blindless windows. "They go walking and talking everywhere to-night, keeping me awake. And all the time they call so loudly to you."

And his strange whispered answer appalled her for a moment until the meaning of it faded and left her in a dark confusion of the mind that was now becoming almost permanent.

"The trees excite them in the night. The winds are the great swift carriers. Go with them, dear—and not against. You'll find sleep that way if you do."

"The storm is rising," she began, hardly knowing what she said.

"All the more then—go with them. Don't resist. They'll take you to the trees, that's all."

Resist! The word touched on the button of some text that once had helped her.

"Resist the devil and he will flee from you," she heard her whispered answer, and the same second had buried her face beneath the clothes in a flood of hysterical weeping.

But her husband did not seem disturbed. Perhaps he did not hear it, for the wind ran just then against the windows with a booming shout, and the roaring of the Forest farther out came behind the blow, surging into the room. Perhaps, too, he was already asleep again. She slowly regained a sort of dull composure. Her face emerged from the tangle of sheets and blankets. With a growing terror over her—she listened. The storm was rising. It came with a sudden and impetuous rush that made all further sleep for her impossible.

Alone in a shaking world, it seemed, she lay and listened. That storm interpreted for her mind the climax. The Forest bellowed out its victory to the winds; the winds in turn proclaimed it to the Night. The whole world knew of her complete defeat, her loss, her little human pain. This was the roar and shout of victory that she listened to.

For, unmistakably, the trees were shouting in the dark. These were sounds, too, like the flapping of great sails, a thousand at a time, and sometimes reports that resembled more than anything else the distant booming of enormous drums. The trees stood up—the whole beleaguering host of them stood up—and with the uproar of their million branches drummed the thundering message out across the night. It seemed as if they had all broken loose. Their roots swept trailing over field and hedge and roof. They tossed their bushy heads beneath the clouds with a wild, delighted shuffling of great boughs. With trunks upright they raced leaping through the sky. There was upheaval and adventure in the awful sound they made, and their cry was like the cry of a sea that has broken through its gates and poured loose upon the world. . . .

Through it all her husband slept peacefully as though he heard it not. It was, as she well knew, the sleep of the semi-dead. For he was out with all that clamoring turmoil. The part of him that she had lost was there. The form that slept so calmly at her side was but the shell, half emptied. . . .

And when the winter's morning stole upon the scene at length, with a pale, washed sunshine that followed the departing tempest, the first thing she saw, as she crept to the window and looked out, was the ruined cedar lying on the lawn. Only the gaunt and crippled trunk of it remained. The single giant bough that had been left to it lay dark upon the grass, sucked endways towards the Forest by a great wind eddy. It lay there like a mass of drift-wood from a wreck, left by the ebbing of a high spring-tide upon the sands—remnant of some friendly, splendid vessel that once sheltered men.

And in the distance she heard the roaring of the Forest further out.

Her husband's voice was in it.

Ancient Lights

From Southwater, where he left the train, the road led due west.
That he knew; for the rest he trusted to luck, being one of those born
walkers who dislike asking the way. He had that instinct, and as a rule
it served him well. "A mile or so due west along the sandy road till you
come to a stile on the right; then across the fields. You'll see the red
house straight before you." He glanced at the post-card's instructions
once again, and once again he tried to decipher the scratched-out
sentence—without success. It had been so elaborately inked over that
no word was legible. Inked-out sentences in a letter were always
enticing. He wondered what it was that had to be so very carefully
obliterated.

The afternoon was boisterous, with a tearing, shouting wind that
blew from the sea, across the Sussex weald. Massive clouds with
rounded, piled-up edges, cannoned across gaping spaces of blue sky.
Far away the line of Downs swept the horizon, like an arriving wave.
Chanc-tonbury Ring rode their crest—a scudding ship, hull down
before the wind. He took his hat off and walked rapidly, breathing great
draughts of air with delight and exhilaration. The road was deserted; no
horsemen, bicycles, or motors; not even a tradesman's cart; no single
walker. But anyhow he would never have asked the way. Keeping a
sharp eye for the stile, he pounded along, while the wind tossed the
cloak against his face, and made waves across the blue puddles in the
yellow road. The trees showed their under leaves of white. The bracken
and the high new grass bent all one way. Great life was in the day, high
spirits and dancing every-where. And for a Croydon surveyor's clerk
just out of an office this was like a holiday at the sea.

It was a day for high adventure, and his heart rose up to meet the
mood of Nature. His umbrella with the silver ring ought to have been a
sword, and his brown shoes should have been top-boots with spurs
upon the heels. Where hid the enchanted Castle and the princess with
the hair of sunny gold? His horse . . .

The stile came suddenly into view and nipped adventure in the
bud. Everyday clothes took him prisoner again. He was a surveyor's
clerk, middle-aged, earning three pounds a week, coming from
Croydon to see about a client's proposed alterations in a wood—
something to ensure a better view from the dining-room window.
Across the fields, perhaps a mile away, he saw the red house gleaming
in the sunshine; and resting on the stile a moment to get his breath he
noticed a copse of oak and hornbeam on the right. "Aha," he told
himself "so that must be the wood he wants to cut down to improve the
view? I'll 'ave a look at it." There were boards up, of course, but there

was an inviting little path as well. "I'm not a trespasser," he said; "it's part of my business, this is." He scrambled awkwardly over the gate and entered the copse. A little round would bring him to the field again.

But the moment he passed among the trees the wind ceased shouting and a stillness dropped upon the world. So dense was the growth that the sunshine only came through in isolated patches. The air was close. He mopped his forehead and put his green felt hat on, but a low branch knocked it off again at once, and as he stooped an elastic twig swung back and stung his face. There were flowers along both edges of the little path; glades opened on either side; ferns curved about in damper corners, and the smell of earth and foliage was rich and sweet. It was cooler here. What an enchanting little wood, he thought, turning down a small green glade where the sunshine flickered like silver wings. How it danced and fluttered and moved about! He put a dark blue flower in his buttonhole. Again his hat, caught by an oak branch as he rose, was knocked from his head, falling across his eyes. And this time he did not put it on again. Swinging his umbrella, he walked on with uncovered head, whistling rather loudly as he went. But the thickness of the trees hardly encouraged whistling, and something of his gaiety and high spirits seemed to leave him. He suddenly found himself treading circumspectly and with caution. The stillness in the wood was so peculiar.

There was a rustle among the ferns and leaves and something shot across the path ten yards ahead, stopped abruptly an instant with head cocked sideways to stare, then dived again beneath the underbrush with the speed of a shadow. He started like a frightened child, laughing the next second that a mere pheasant could have made him jump. In the distance he heard wheels upon the road, and wondered why the sound was pleasant. "Good old butcher's cart," he said to himself—then realised that he was going in the wrong direction and had somehow got turned round. For the road should be behind him, not in front.

And he hurriedly took another narrow glade that lost itself in greenness to the right. "That's my direction, of course," he said; "the trees has mixed me up a bit, it seems"—then found himself abruptly by the gate he had first climbed over. He had merely made a circle. Surprise became almost discomfiture then. And a man, dressed like a gamekeeper in browny green, leaned against the gate, hitting his legs with a switch. "I'm making for Mr. Lumley's farm," explained the walker. "This is his wood, I believe—" then stopped dead, because it was no man at all, but merely an effect of light and shade and foliage. He stepped back to reconstruct the singular illusion, but the wind shook the branches roughly here on the edge of the wood and the foliage refused to recon-struct the figure. The leaves all rustled strangely. And just then the sun went behind a cloud, making the whole wood look otherwise. Yet how the mind could be thus doubly deceived was indeed remarkable, for it almost seemed to him the man had answered, spoken—or was this the shuffling noise the branches made ?—and had pointed with his switch to the notice-board upon the nearest tree. The words rang on in his head, but of course he had imagined them: "No, it's not his wood. It's ours." And some village wit, moreover, had changed the lettering on the weather-beaten board, for it read quite plainly, "Trespassers will be persecuted."

And while the astonished clerk read the words and chuckled, he said to himself, thinking what a tale he'd have to tell his wife and children later—"The blooming wood has tried to chuck me out. But I'll go in again. Why, it's only a matter of a square acre at most. I'm bound to reach the fields on the other side if I keep straight on." He remembered his position in the office. He had a certain dignity to maintain.

The cloud passed from below the sun, and light splashed suddenly in all manner of unlikely places. The man went straight on. He felt a touch of puzzling con-fusion somewhere; this way the copse had of shifting from sunshine into shadow doubtless troubled sight a little. To his relief at last, a new glade opened through the trees and disclosed the fields with a glimpse of the red house in the distance at the far end. But a little wicket gate that stood across the path had first to be climbed, and as he scrambled heavily over—for it would not open—he got the astonishing feeling that it slid off sideways beneath his weight, and towards the wood. Like the moving staircases at Harrod's and Earl's Court, it began to glide off with him. It was quite horrible. He made a violent effort to get down before it carried him into the trees, but his feet became entangled with the bars and umbrella, so that he fell heavily upon the farther side, arms spread across the grass and nettles, boots clutched between the first and second bars. He lay there a moment like a man crucified upside down, and while he struggled to get disentangled—feet, bars, and umbrella formed a regular net—he saw the little man in browny green go past him with extreme rapidity through the wood. The man was laughing. He passed across the glade some fifty yards away, and he was not alone this time. A companion like himself went with him. The clerk, now upon his feet again, watched them disappear into the gloom of green beyond. "They're tramps, not gamekeepers," he said to himself, half mortified, half angry. But his heart was thumping dreadfully, and he dared not utter all his thought.

He examined the wicket gate, convinced it was a trick gate somehow—then went hurriedly on again, disturbed beyond belief to see that the glade no longer opened into fields, but curved away to the right. What in the world had happened to him? His sight was so utterly at fault. Again the sun flamed out abruptly and lit the floor of the wood with pools of silver, and at the same moment a violent gust of wind passed shouting overhead. Drops fell clattering everywhere upon the leaves, making a sharp pattering as of many footsteps. The whole copse shuddered and went moving.

"Rain, by George," thought the clerk, and feeling for his umbrella, discovered he had lost it. He turned back to the gate and found it lying on the farther side. To his amazement he saw the fields at the far end of the glade, the red house, too, ashine in the sunset. He laughed then, for, of course, in his struggle with the gate, he had somehow got turned round—had fallen back instead of forwards. Climbing over, this time quite easily, he retraced his steps. The silver band, he saw, had been torn from the umbrella. No doubt his foot, a nail, or something had caught in it and ripped it off. The clerk began to run; he felt extraordinarily dismayed.

But, while he ran, the entire wood ran with him, round him, to and fro, trees shifting like living things, leaves folding and unfolding, trunks darting backwards and forwards, and branches disclosing enormous empty spaces, then closing up again before he could look into them. There were footsteps everywhere, and laughing, crying voices, and crowds of figures gathering just behind his back till the glade, he knew, was thick with moving life. The wind in his ears, of course, produced the voices and the laughter, while sun and clouds, plunging the copse alternately in shadow and bright dazzling light, created the figures. But he did not like it, and went as fast as ever his sturdy legs could take him. He was frightened now. This was no story for his wife and children. He ran like the wind. But his feet made no sound upon the soft mossy turf.

Then, to his horror, he saw that the glade grew narrow, nettles and weeds stood thick across it, it dwindled down into a tiny path, and twenty yards ahead it stopped finally and melted off among the trees. What the trick gate had failed to achieve, this twisting glade accomplished easily—carried him in bodily among the dense and crowding trees.

There was only one thing to do—turn sharply and dash back again, run headlong into the life that followed at his back, followed so closely too that now it almost touched him, pushing him in. And with reckless courage this was what he did. It seemed a fearful thing to do. He turned with a sort of violent spring, head down and shoulders forward, hands stretched before his face. He made the plunge; like a hunted creature he charged full tilt the other way, meeting the wind now in his face.

Good Lord! The glade behind him had closed up as well; there was no longer any path at all. Turning round and round, like an animal at bay, he searched for an opening, a way of escape, searched frantically, breath-lessly, terrified now in his bones. But foliage surrounded him, branches blocked the way; the trees stood close and still, unshaken by a breath of wind; and the sun dipped that moment behind a great black cloud. The entire wood turned dark and silent. It watched him.

Perhaps it was this final touch of sudden blackness that made him act so foolishly, as though he had really lost his head. At any rate, without pausing to think, he dashed headlong in among the trees again. There was a sensation of being stiflingly surrounded and entangled, and that he must break out at all costs—out and away into the open of the blessed fields and air. He did this ill-considered thing, and apparently charged straight into an oak that deliber-ately moved into his path to stop him. He saw it shift across a good full yard, and being a measuring man, accustomed to theodolite and chain, he ought to know. He fell, saw stars, and felt a thousand tiny fingers tugging and pulling at his hands and neck and ankles. The stinging nettles, no doubt, were responsible for this. He thought of it later. At the moment it felt diabolically calculated.

But another remarkable illusion was not so easily explained. For all in a moment, it seemed, the entire wood went sliding past him with a thick deep rustling of leaves and laughter, myriad footsteps, and tiny little active, energetic shapes; two men in browny green gave him a mighty hoist—and he opened his eyes to find himself lying in the meadow beside the stile where first his incredible adventure had begun. The wood stood in its usual place and stared down upon him in the sunlight. There was the red house in the distance as before. Above him grinned the weather-beaten notice-board: "Tres-passers will be prosecuted."

Disheveled in mind and body, and a good deal shaken in his official soul, the clerk walked slowly across the fields. But on the way he glanced once more at the post-card of instructions, and saw with dull amazement that the inked-out sentence was quite legible after all beneath the scratches made across it: "There *is* a short cut through the wood—the wood I want cut down—if you care to take it." Only "care" was so badly written, it looked more like another word; the "c" was uncommonly like "d."

"That's the copse that spoils my view of the Downs, you see," his client explained to him later, pointing across the fields, and referring to the ordnance map beside him. "I want it cut down and a path made so and so." His finger indicated direction on the map. "The Fairy Wood— it's still called, and it's far older than this house. Come now, if you're ready, Mr. Thomas, we might go out and have a look at it . . ."

Sand

I

As Felix Henriot came through the streets that January night the fog was stifling, but when he reached his little flat upon the top floor there came a sound of wind. Wind was stirring about the world. It blew against his windows, but at first so faintly that he hardly noticed it. Then, with an abrupt rise and fall like a wailing voice that sought to claim attention, it called him. He peered through the window into the blurred darkness, listening.

There is no cry in the world like that of the homeless wind. A vague excitement, scarcely to be analysed, ran through his blood. The curtain of fog waved momentarily aside. Henriot fancied a star peeped down at him.

"It will change things a bit—at last," he sighed, settling back into his chair. "It will bring movement!"

Already something in himself had changed. A restlessness, as of that wandering wind, woke in his heart—the desire to be off and away. Other things could rouse this wildness too: falling water, the singing of a bird, an odour of wood-fire, a glimpse of winding road. But the cry of wind, always searching, questioning, travelling the world's great routes, remained ever the master-touch. High longing took his mood in hand. Mid seven millions he felt suddenly—lonely.

"I will arise and go now, for always night and day
I hear lake water lapping with low sounds by the shore;
While I stand on the roadway, or on the pavements gray,
I hear it in the deep heart's core."

He murmured the words over softly to himself. The emotion that produced Innisfree passed strongly through him. He too would be over the hills and far away. He craved movement, change, adventure—somewhere far from shops and crowds and motor-'busses. For a week the fog had stifled London. This wind brought life.

Where should he go? Desire was long; his purse was short.

He glanced at his books, letters, newspapers. They had no interest now. Instead he listened. The panorama of other journeys rolled in colour through the little room, flying on one another's heels. Henriot enjoyed this remembered essence of his travels more than the travels themselves. The crying wind brought so many voices, all of them seductive:

There was a soft crashing of waves upon the Black Sea shores, where the huge Caucasus beckoned in the sky beyond; a rustling in the umbrella pines and cactus at Marseilles, whence magic steamers start about the world like flying dreams. He heard the plash of fountains upon Mount Ida's slopes, and the whisper of the tamarisk on Marathon. It was dawn once more upon the Ionian Sea, and he smelt the perfume of the Cyclades. Blue-veiled islands melted in the sunshine, and across the dewy lawns of Tempe, moistened by the spray of many waterfalls, he saw—Great Heavens above!—the dancing of white forms . . . or was it only mist the sunshine painted against Pelion?. . . "Methought, among the lawns together, we wandered underneath the young grey dawn. And multitudes of dense white fleecy clouds shepherded by the slow, unwilling wind . . ."

And then, into his stuffy room, slipped the singing perfume of a wall-flower on a ruined tower, and with it the sweetness of hot ivy. He heard the "yellow bees in the ivy bloom." Wind whipped over the open hills—this very wind that laboured drearily through the London fog.

And—he was caught. The darkness melted from the city. The fog whisked off into an azure sky. The roar of traffic turned into booming of the sea. There was a whistling among cordage, and the floor swayed to and fro. He saw a sailor touch his cap and pocket the two-franc piece. The syren hooted—ominous sound that had started him on many a journey of adventure—and the roar of London became mere insignificant clatter of a child's toy carriages.

He loved that syren's call; there was something deep and pitiless in it. It drew the wanderers forth from cities everywhere: "Leave your known world behind you, and come with me for better or for worse! The anchor is up; it is too late to change. Only—beware! You shall know curious things—and alone!"

Henriot stirred uneasily in his chair. He turned with sudden energy to the shelf of guide-books, maps and time-tables—possessions he most valued in the whole room. He was a happy-go-lucky, adventure-loving soul, careless of common standards, athirst ever for the new and strange.

"That's the best of having a cheap flat," he laughed, "and no ties in the world. I can turn the key and disappear. No one cares or knows—no one but the thieving caretaker. And he's long ago found out that there's nothing here worth taking!"

There followed then no lengthy indecision. Preparation was even shorter still. He was always ready for a move, and his sojourn in cities was but breathing-space while he gathered pennies for further wanderings. An enormous kit-bag—sack-shaped, very worn and dirty—emerged speedily from the bottom of a cupboard in the wall. It was of limitless capacity. The key and padlock rattled in its depths. Cigarette ashes covered everything while he stuffed it full of ancient, indescribable garments. And his voice, singing of those "yellow bees in the ivy bloom," mingled with the crying of the rising wind about his windows. His restlessness had disappeared by magic.

This time, however, there could be no haunted Pelion, nor shady groves of Tempe, for he lived in sophisticated times when money markets regulated movement sternly. Travelling was only for the rich; mere wanderers must pig it. He remembered instead an opportune invitation to the Desert. "Objective" invitation, his genial hosts had called it, knowing his hatred of convention. And Helouan danced into letters of brilliance upon the inner map of his mind. For Egypt had ever held his spirit in thrall, though as yet he had tried in vain to touch the great buried soul of her. The excavators, the Egyptologists, the archaeologists most of all, plastered her grey ancient face with labels like hotel advertisements on travellers' portmanteaux. They told where she had come from last, but nothing of what she dreamed and thought and loved. The heart of Egypt lay beneath the sand, and the trifling robbery of little details that poked forth from tombs and temples brought no true revelation of her stupendous spiritual splendour. Henriot, in his youth, had searched and dived among what material he could find, believing once—or half believing—that the ceremonial of that ancient system veiled a weight of symbol that was reflected from genuine supersensual knowledge. The rituals, now taken literally, and so pityingly explained away, had once been genuine pathways of approach. But never yet, and least of all in his previous visits to Egypt itself, had he discovered one single person, worthy of speech, who caught at his idea. "Curious," they said, then turned away—to go on digging in the sand. Sand smothered her world to-day. Excavators discovered skeletons. Museums everywhere stored them—grinning, literal relics that told nothing.

But now, while he packed and sang, these hopes of enthusiastic younger days stirred again—because the emotion that gave them birth was real and true in him. Through the morning mists upon the Nile an old pyramid bowed hugely at him across London roofs: "Come," he heard its awful whisper beneath the ceiling, "I have things to show you, and to tell." He saw the flock of them sailing the Desert like weird grey solemn ships that make no earthly port. And he imagined them as one: multiple expressions of some single unearthly portent they adumbrated in mighty form—dead symbols of some spiritual conception long vanished from the world.

"I mustn't dream like this," he laughed, "or I shall get absent-minded and pack fire-tongs instead of boots. It looks like a jumble sale already!" And he stood on a heap of things to wedge them down still tighter.

But the pictures would not cease. He saw the kites circling high in the blue air. A couple of white vultures flapped lazily away over shining miles. Felucca sails, like giant wings emerging from the ground, curved towards him from the Nile. The palm-trees dropped long shadows over Memphis. He felt the delicious, drenching heat, and the Khamasin, that over-wind from Nubia, brushed his very cheeks. In the little gardens the mish-mish was in bloom. . . . He smelt the Desert . . . grey sepulchre of cancelled cycles. . . . The stillness of her interminable reaches dropped down upon old London. . . .

The magic of the sand stole round him in its silent-footed tempest.

And while he struggled with that strange, capacious sack, the piles of clothing ran into shapes of gleaming Bedouin faces; London garments settled down with the mournful sound of camels' feet, half dropping wind, half water flowing underground—sound that old Time has brought over into modern life and left a moment for our wonder and perhaps our tears.

He rose at length with the excitement of some deep enchantment in his eyes. The thought of Egypt plunged ever so deeply into him, carrying him into depths where he found it difficult to breathe, so strangely far away it seemed, yet indefinably familiar. He lost his way. A touch of fear came with it.

"A sack like that is the wonder of the world," he laughed again, kicking the unwieldy, sausage-shaped monster into a corner of the room, and sitting down to write the thrilling labels: "Felix Henriot, Alexandria *via* Marseilles." But his pen blotted the letters; there was sand in it. He rewrote the words. Then he remembered a dozen things he had left out. Impatiently, yet with confusion somewhere, he stuffed them in. They ran away into shifting heaps; they disappeared; they emerged suddenly again. It was like packing hot, dry, flowing sand. From the pockets of a coat—he had worn it last summer down Dorset way—out trickled sand. There was sand in his mind and thoughts.

And his dreams that night were full of winds, the old sad winds of Egypt, and of moving, sifting sand. Arabs and Afreets danced amazingly together across dunes he could never reach. For he could not follow fast enough. Something infinitely older than these ever caught his feet and held him back. A million tiny fingers stung and pricked him. Something flung a veil before his eyes. Once it touched him—his face and hands and neck. "Stay here with us," he heard a host of muffled voices crying, but their sound was smothered, buried, rising through the ground. A myriad throats were choked. Till, at last, with a violent effort he turned and seized it. And then the thing he grasped at slipped between his fingers and ran easily away. It had a grey and yellow face, and it moved through all its parts. It flowed as water flows, and yet was solid. It was centuries old.

He cried out to it. "Who are you? What is your name? I surely know you . . . but I have forgotten . . . ?"

And it stopped, turning from far away its great uncovered countenance of nameless colouring. He caught a voice. It rolled and boomed and whispered like the wind. And then he woke, with a curious

shaking in his heart, and a little touch of chilly perspiration on the skin.
But the voice seemed in the room still—close beside him:
"I am the Sand," he heard, before it died away.

And next he realised that the glitter of Paris lay behind him, and a
steamer was taking him with much unnecessary motion across a
sparkling sea towards Alexandria. Gladly he saw the Riviera fade
below the horizon, with its hard bright sunshine, treacherous winds, and
its smear of rich, conventional English. All restlessness now had left
him. True vagabond still at forty, he only felt the unrest and discomfort
of life when caught in the network of routine and rigid streets, no
chance of breaking loose. He was off again at last, money scarce
enough indeed, but the joy of wandering expressing itself in happy
emotions of release. Every warning of calculation was stifled. He
thought of the American woman who walked out of her Long Island
house one summer's day to look at a passing sail—and was gone eight
years before she walked in again. Eight years of roving travel! He had
always felt respect and admiration for that woman.

For Felix Henriot, with his admixture of foreign blood, was
philosopher as well as vagabond, a strong poetic and religious strain
sometimes breaking out through fissures in his complex nature. He had
seen much life; had read many books. The passionate desire of youth to
solve the world's big riddles had given place to a resignation filled to
the brim with wonder. Anything *might* be true. Nothing surprised him.
The most outlandish beliefs, for all he knew, might fringe truth
somewhere. He had escaped that cheap cynicism with which
disappointed men soothe their vanity when they realise that an
intelligible explanation of the universe lies beyond their powers. He no
longer expected final answers.

For him, even the smallest journeys held the spice of some
adventure; all minutes were loaded with enticing potentialities. And
they shaped for themselves somehow a dramatic form. "It's like a
story," his friends said when he told his travels. It always was a story.

But the adventure that lay waiting for him where the silent streets
of little Helouan kiss the great Desert's lips, was of a different kind to
any Henriot had yet encountered. Looking back, he has often asked
himself, "How in the world can I accept it?"

And, perhaps, he never yet has accepted it. It was sand that brought
it. For the Desert, the stupendous thing that mothers little Helouan,
produced it.

II

He slipped through Cairo with the same relief that he left the Riviera, resenting its social vulgarity so close to the imperial aristocracy of the Desert; he settled down into the peace of soft and silent little Helouan. The hotel in which he had a room on the top floor had been formerly a Khedivial Palace. It had the air of a palace still. He felt himself in a country-house, with lofty ceilings, cool and airy corridors, spacious halls. Soft-footed Arabs attended to his wants; white walls let in light and air without a sign of heat; there was a feeling of a large, spread tent pitched on the very sand; and the wind that stirred the oleanders in the shady gardens also crept in to rustle the palm leaves of his favourite corner seat. Through the large windows where once the Khedive held high court, the sunshine blazed upon vistaed leagues of Desert.

And from his bedroom windows he watched the sun dip into gold and crimson behind the swelling Libyan sands. This side of the pyramids he saw the Nile meander among palm groves and tilled fields. Across his balcony railings the Egyptian stars trooped down beside his very bed, shaping old constellations for his dreams; while, to the south, he looked out upon the vast untamable Body of the sands that carpeted the world for thousands of miles towards Upper Egypt, Nubia, and the dread Sahara itself. He wondered again why people thought it necessary to go so far afield to know the Desert. Here, within half an hour of Cairo, it lay breathing solemnly at his very doors.

For little Helouan, caught thus between the shoulders of the Libyan and Arabian Deserts, is utterly sand-haunted. The Desert lies all round it like a sea. Henriot felt he never could escape from it, as he moved about the island whose coasts are washed with sand. Down each broad and shining street the two end houses framed a vista of its dim immensity—glimpses of shimmering blue, or flame-touched purple. There were stretches of deep sea-green as well, far off upon its bosom. The streets were open channels of approach, and the eye ran down them as along the tube of a telescope laid to catch incredible distance out of space. Through them the Desert reached in with long, thin feelers towards the village. Its Being flooded into Helouan, and over it. Past walls and houses, churches and hotels, the sea of Desert pressed in silently with its myriad soft feet of sand. It poured in everywhere, through crack and slit and crannie. These were reminders of possession and ownership. And every passing wind that lifted eddies of dust at the street corners were messages from the quiet, powerful Thing that permitted Helouan to lie and dream so peacefully in the sunshine. Mere artificial oasis, its existence was temporary, held on lease, just for ninety-nine centuries or so.

This sea idea became insistent. For, in certain lights, and especially in the brief, bewildering dusk, the Desert rose—swaying towards the small white houses. The waves of it ran for fifty miles without a break. It was too deep for foam or surface agitation, yet it knew the swell of tides. And underneath flowed resolute currents, linking distance to the centre. These many deserts were really one. A storm, just retreated, had tossed Helouan upon the shore and left it there to dry; but any morning he would wake to find it had been carried off again into the depths. Some fragment, at least, would disappear. The grim Mokattam Hills were rollers that ever threatened to topple down and submerge the sandy bar that men called Helouan.

Being soundless, and devoid of perfume, the Desert's message reached him through two senses only—sight and touch; chiefly, of course, the former. Its invasion was concentrated through the eyes. And vision, thus uncorrected, went what pace it pleased. The Desert played with him. Sand stole into his being—through the eyes.

And so obsessing was this majesty of its close presence, that Henriot sometimes wondered how people dared their little social activities within its very sight and hearing; how they played golf and tennis upon reclaimed edges of its face, picnicked so blithely hard upon its frontiers, and danced at night while this stern, unfathomable Thing lay breathing just beyond the trumpery walls that kept it out. The challenge of their shallow admiration seemed presumptuous, almost provocative. Their pursuit of pleasure suggested insolent indifference. They ran fool-hardy hazards, he felt; for there was no worship in their vulgar hearts. With a mental shudder, sometimes he watched the cheap tourist horde go laughing, chattering past within view of its ancient, half-closed eyes. It was like defying deity.

For, to his stirred imagination the sublimity of the Desert dwarfed humanity. These people had been wiser to choose another place for the flaunting of their tawdry insignificance. Any minute this Wilderness, "huddled in grey annihilation," might awake and notice them . . . !

In his own hotel were several "smart," so-called "Society" people who emphasised the protest in him to the point of definite contempt. Overdressed, the latest worldly novel under their arms, they strutted the narrow pavements of their tiny world, immensely pleased with themselves. Their vacuous minds expressed themselves in the slang of their exclusive circle—value being the element excluded. The pettiness of their outlook hardly distressed him—he was too familiar with it at home—but their essential vulgarity, their innate ugliness, seemed more than usually offensive in the grandeur of its present setting. Into the mighty sands they took the latest London scandal, gabbling it over even among the Tombs and Temples. And "it was to laugh," the pains they spent wondering whom they might condescend to know, never dreaming that they themselves were not worth knowing. Against the background of the noble Desert their titles seemed the cap and bells of clowns.

And Henriot, knowing some of them personally, could not always escape their insipid company. Yet he was the gainer. They little guessed how their commonness heightened contrast, set mercilessly thus beside the strange, eternal beauty of the sand.

Occasionally the protest in his soul betrayed itself in words, which of course they did not understand. "He is so clever, isn't he?" And then, having relieved his feelings, he would comfort himself characteristically:

"The Desert has not noticed them. The Sand is not aware of their existence. How should the sea take note of rubbish that lies above its tide-line?"

For Henriot drew near to its great shifting altars in an attitude of worship. The wilderness made him kneel in heart. Its shining reaches led to the oldest Temple in the world, and every journey that he made was like a sacrament. For him the Desert was a consecrated place. It was sacred.

And his tactful hosts, knowing his peculiarities, left their house open to him when he cared to come—they lived upon the northern edge of the oasis—and he was as free as though he were absolutely alone. He blessed them; he rejoiced that he had come. Little Helouan accepted him. The Desert knew that he was there.

From his corner of the big dining-room he could see the other guests, but his roving eye always returned to the figure of a solitary man who sat at an adjoining table, and whose personality stirred his interest. While affecting to look elsewhere, he studied him as closely as might be. There was something about the stranger that touched his curiosity—a certain air of expectation that he wore. But it was more than that: it was anticipation, apprehension in it somewhere. The man was nervous, uneasy. His restless way of suddenly looking about him proved it. Henriot tried every one else in the room as well; but, though his thought settled on others too, he always came back to the figure of this solitary being opposite, who ate his dinner as if afraid of being seen, and glanced up sometimes as if fearful of being watched. Henriot's curiosity, before he knew it, became suspicion. There was mystery here. The table, he noticed, was laid for two.

"Is he an actor, a priest of some strange religion, an enquiry agent, or just—a crank?" was the thought that first occurred to him. And the question suggested itself without amusement. The impression of subterfuge and caution he conveyed left his observer unsatisfied.

The face was clean shaven, dark, and strong; thick hair, straight yet bushy, was slightly unkempt; it was streaked with grey; and an unexpected mobility when he smiled ran over the features that he seemed to hold rigid by deliberate effort. The man was cut to no quite common measure. Henriot jumped to an intuitive conclusion: "He's not here for pleasure or merely sight-seeing. Something serious has brought him out to Egypt." For the face combined too ill-assorted qualities: an obstinate tenacity that might even mean brutality, and was certainly repulsive, yet, with it, an undecipherable dreaminess betrayed by lines of the mouth, but above all in the very light blue eyes, so rarely raised. Those eyes, he felt, had looked upon unusual things; "dreaminess" was not an adequate description; "searching" conveyed it better. The true source of the queer impression remained elusive. And hence, perhaps, the incongruous marriage in the face—mobility laid upon a matter-of-fact foundation underneath. The face showed conflict.

And Henriot, watching him, felt decidedly intrigued. "I'd like to know that man, and all about him." His name, he learned later, was Richard Vance; from Birmingham; a business man. But it was not the Birmingham he wished to know; it was the—other: cause of the elusive, dreamy searching. Though facing one another at so short a distance, their eyes, however, did not meet. And this, Henriot well knew, was a sure sign that he himself was also under observation. Richard Vance, from Birmingham, was equally taking careful note of Felix Henriot, from London.

Thus, he could wait his time. They would come together later. An opportunity would certainly present itself. The first links in a curious chain had already caught; soon the chain would tighten, pull as though by chance, and bring their lives into one and the same circle. Wondering in particular for what kind of a companion the second cover was laid, Henriot felt certain that their eventual coming together was inevitable. He possessed this kind of divination from first impressions, and not uncommonly it proved correct.

Following instinct, therefore, he took no steps towards acquaintance, and for several days, owing to the fact that he dined frequently with his hosts, he saw nothing more of Richard Vance, the business man from Birmingham. Then, one night, coming home late from his friend's house, he had passed along the great corridor, and was actually a step or so into his bedroom, when a drawling voice sounded close behind him. It was an unpleasant sound. It was very near him too—

"I beg your pardon, but have you, by any chance, such a thing as a compass you could lend me?"

The voice was so close that he started. Vance stood within touching distance of his body. He had stolen up like a ghostly Arab, must have followed him, too, some little distance, for further down the passage the light of an open door—he had passed it on his way—showed where he came from.

"Eh? I beg your pardon? A—compass, did you say?" He felt

disconcerted for a moment. How short the man was, now that he saw him standing. Broad and powerful too. Henriot looked down upon his thick head of hair. The personality and voice repelled him. Possibly his face, caught unawares, betrayed this.

"Forgive my startling you," said the other apologetically, while the softer expression danced in for a moment and disorganised the rigid set of the face. "The soft carpet, you know. I'm afraid you didn't hear my tread. I wondered"—he smiled again slightly at the nature of the request—"if—by any chance—you had a pocket compass you could lend me?"

"Ah, a compass, yes! Please don't apologise. I believe I have one—if you'll wait a moment. Come in, won't you? I'll have a look."

The other thanked him but waited in the passage. Henriot, it so happened, had a compass, and produced it after a moment's search.

"I am greatly indebted to you—if I may return it in the morning. You will forgive my disturbing you at such an hour. My own is broken, and I wanted—er—to find the true north."

Henriot stammered some reply, and the man was gone. It was all over in a minute. He locked his door and sat down in his chair to think. The little incident had upset him, though for the life of him he could not imagine why. It ought by rights to have been almost ludicrous, yet instead it was the exact reverse—half threatening. Why should not a man want a compass? But, again, why should he? And at midnight? The voice, the eyes, the near presence—what did they bring that set his nerves thus asking unusual questions? This strange impression that something grave was happening, something unearthly—how was it born exactly? The man's proximity came like a shock. It had made him start. He brought—thus the idea came unbidden to his mind— something with him that galvanised him quite absurdly, as fear does, or delight, or great wonder. There was a music in his voice too—a certain—well, he could only call it lilt, that reminded him of plainsong, intoning, chanting. Drawling was *not* the word at all.

He tried to dismiss it as imagination, but it would not be dismissed. The disturbance in himself was caused by something not imaginary, but real. And then, for the first time, he discovered that the man had brought a faint, elusive suggestion of perfume with him, an aromatic odour, that made him think of priests and churches. The ghost of it still lingered in the air. Ah, here then was the origin of the notion that his voice had chanted: it was surely the suggestion of incense. But incense, intoning, a compass to find the true north—at midnight in a Desert hotel!

A touch of uneasiness ran through the curiosity and excitement that he felt.

And he undressed for bed. "Confound my old imagination," he thought, "what tricks it plays me! It'll keep me awake!"

But the questions, once started in his mind, continued. He must find explanation of one kind or another before he could lie down and sleep, and he found it at length in—the stars. The man was an astronomer of sorts; possibly an astrologer into the bargain! Why not? The stars were wonderful above Helouan. Was there not an observatory on the Mokattam Hills, too, where tourists could use the telescopes on privileged days? He had it at last. He even stole out on to his balcony to see if the stranger perhaps was looking through some wonderful apparatus at the heavens. Their rooms were on the same side. But the shuttered windows revealed no stooping figure with eyes glued to a telescope. The stars blinked in their many thousands down upon the silent desert. The night held neither sound nor movement. There was a cool breeze blowing across the Nile from the Lybian Sands. It nipped; and he stepped back quickly into the room again. Drawing the mosquito curtains carefully about the bed, he put the light out and turned over to sleep.

And sleep came quickly, contrary to his expectations, though it was a light and surface sleep. That last glimpse of the darkened Desert lying beneath the Egyptian stars had touched him with some hand of awful power that ousted the first, lesser excitement. It calmed and soothed him in one sense, yet in another, a sense he could not understand, it caught him in a net of deep, deep feelings whose mesh, while infinitely delicate, was utterly stupendous. His nerves this deeper emotion left alone: it reached instead to something infinite in him that mere nerves could neither deal with nor interpret. The soul awoke and whispered in him while his body slept.

And the little, foolish dreams that ran to and fro across this veil of surface sleep brought oddly tangled pictures of things quite tiny and at the same time of others that were mighty beyond words. With these two counters Nightmare played. They interwove. There was the figure of this dark-faced man with the compass, measuring the sky to find the true north, and there were hints of giant Presences that hovered just outside some curious outline that he traced upon the ground, copied in some nightmare fashion from the heavens. The excitement caused by his visitor's singular request mingled with the profounder sensations his final look at the stars and Desert stirred. The two were somehow inter-related.

Some hours later, before this surface sleep passed into genuine slumber, Henriot woke—with an appalling feeling that the Desert had come creeping into his room and now stared down upon him where he lay in bed. The wind was crying audibly about the walls outside. A faint, sharp tapping came against the window panes.

He sprang instantly out of bed, not yet awake enough to feel actual alarm, yet with the nightmare touch still close enough to cause a sort of feverish, loose bewilderment. He switched the lights on. A moment

finds here what one brings." He knew the delightful experience of talking fluently on subjects he was at home in, and to some one who understood. The feeling at first that to this woman he could not say mere anythings, slipped into its opposite—that he could say everything. Strangers ten minutes ago, they were at once in deep and intimate talk together. He found his ideas readily followed, agreed with up to a point—the point which permits discussion to start from a basis of general accord towards speculation. In the excitement of ideas he neglected the uncomfortable note that had stirred his caution, forgot the warning too. Her mind, moreover, seemed known to him; he was often aware of what she was going to say before he actually heard it; the current of her thoughts struck a familiar gait, and more than once he experienced vividly again the odd sensation that it all had happened before. The very sentences and phrases with which she pointed the turns of her unusual ideas were never wholly unexpected.

For her ideas were decidedly unusual, in the sense that she accepted without question speculations not commonly deemed worth consideration at all, indeed not ordinarily even known. Henriot knew them, because he had read in many fields. It was the strength of her belief that fascinated him. She offered no apologies. She knew. And while he talked, she listening with folded arms and her black eyes fixed upon his own, Richard Vance watched with vigilant eyes and listened too, ceaselessly alert. Vance joined in little enough, however, gave no opinions, his attitude one of general acquiescence. Twice, when pauses of slackening interest made it possible, Henriot fancied he surprised another quality in this negative attitude. Interpreting it each time differently, he yet dismissed both interpretations with a smile. His imagination leaped so absurdly to violent conclusions. They were not tenable: Vance was neither her keeper, nor was he in some fashion a detective. Yet in his manner was sometimes this suggestion of the detective order. He watched with such deep attention, and he concealed it so clumsily with an affectation of careless indifference.

There is nothing more dangerous than that impulsive intimacy strangers sometimes adopt when an atmosphere of mutual sympathy takes them by surprise, for it is akin to the false frankness friends affect when telling "candidly" one another's faults. The mood is invariably regretted later. Henriot, however, yielded to it now with something like abandon. The pleasure of talking with this woman was so unexpected, and so keen.

For Lady Statham believed apparently in some Egypt of her dreams. Her interest was neither historical, archaeological, nor political. It was religious—yet hardly of this earth at all. The conversation turned upon the knowledge of the ancient Egyptians from an unearthly point of view, and even while he talked he was vaguely aware that it was *her* mind talking through his own. She drew out his ideas and made him say them. But this he was properly aware of only afterwards—that she had cleverly, mercilessly pumped him of all he had ever known or read upon the subject. Moreover, what Vance watched so intently was himself, and the reactions in himself this remarkable woman produced. That also he realised later.

His first impression that these two belonged to what may be called the "crank" order was justified by the conversation. But, at least, it was interesting crankiness, and the belief behind it made it even fascinating. Long before the end he surprised in her a more vital form of his own attitude that anything *may* be true, since knowledge has never yet found final answers to any of the biggest questions.

He understood, from sentences dropped early in the talk, that she was among those few "superstitious" folk who think that the old Egyptians came closer to reading the eternal riddles of the world than any others, and that their knowledge was a remnant of that ancient Wisdom Religion which existed in the superb, dark civilization of the sunken Atlantis, lost continent that once joined Africa to Mexico. Eighty thousand years ago the dim sands of Poseidonis, great island adjoining the main continent which itself had vanished a vast period before, sank down beneath the waves, and the entire known world to-day was descended from its survivors. Hence the significant fact that all religions and "mythological" systems begin with a story of a flood—some cataclysmic upheaval that destroyed the world. Egypt itself was colonised by a group of Atlantean priests who brought their curious, deep knowledge with them. They had foreseen the cataclysm.

Lady Statham talked well, bringing into her great dream this strong, insistent quality of belief and fact. She knew, from Plato to Donelly, all that the minds of men have ever speculated upon the gorgeous legend. The evidence for such a sunken continent—Henriot had skimmed it too in years gone by—she made bewilderingly complete. He had heard Baconians demolish Shakespeare with an array of evidence equally overwhelming. It catches the imagination though not the mind. Yet out of her facts, as she presented them, grew a strange likelihood. The force of this woman's personality, and her calm and quiet way of believing all she talked about, took her listener to some extent—further than ever before, certainly—into the great dream after her. And the dream, to say the least, was a picturesque one, laden with wonderful possibilities. For as she talked the spirit of old Egypt moved up, staring down upon him out of eyes lidded so curiously level. Hitherto all had prated to him of the Arabs, their ancient faith and customs, and the splendour of the Bedouins, those Princes of the Desert. But what he sought, barely confessed in words even to himself, was something older far than this. And this strange, dark woman brought it close. Deeps in his soul, long slumbering, awoke. He heard forgotten questions.

Only in this brief way could he attempt to sum up the storm she roused in him.

She carried him far beyond mere outline, however, though afterwards he recalled the details with difficulty. So much more was suggested than actually expressed. She contrived to make the general modern scepticism an evidence of cheap mentality. It was so easy; the depth it affects to conceal, mere emptiness. "We have tried all things, and found all wanting"—the mind, as measuring instrument, merely confessed inadequate. Various shrewd judgments of this kind increased his respect, although her acceptance went so far beyond his own. And, while the label of credulity refused to stick to her, her sense of imaginative wonder enabled her to escape that dreadful compromise, a man's mind in a woman's temperament. She fascinated him.

The spiritual worship of the ancient Egyptians, she held, was a symbolical explanation of things generally alluded to as the secrets of life and death; their knowledge was a remnant of the wisdom of Atlantis. Material relics, equally misunderstood, still stood to-day at Karnac, Stonehenge, and in the mysterious writings on buried Mexican temples and cities, so significantly akin to the hieroglyphics upon the Egyptian tombs.

"The one misinterpreted as literally as the other," she suggested, "yet both fragments of an advanced knowledge that found its grave in the sea. The Wisdom of that old spiritual system has vanished from the world, only a degraded literalism left of its undecipherable language. The jewel has been lost, and the casket is filled with sand, sand, sand."

How keenly her black eyes searched his own as she said it, and how oddly she made the little word resound. The syllable drew out almost into chanting. Echoes answered from the depths within him, carrying it on and on across some desert of forgotten belief. Veils of sand flew everywhere about his mind. Curtains lifted. Whole hills of sand went shifting into level surfaces whence gardens of dim outline emerged to meet the sunlight.

"But the sand may be removed." It was her nephew, speaking almost for the first time, and the interruption had an odd effect, introducing a sharply practical element. For the tone expressed, so far as he dared express it, disapproval. It was a baited observation, an invitation to opinion.

"We are not sand-diggers, Mr. Henriot," put in Lady Statham, before he decided to respond. "Our object is quite another one; and I believe—I have a feeling," she added almost questioningly, "that you might be interested enough to help us perhaps."

He only wondered the direct attack had not come sooner. Its bluntness hardly surprised him. He felt himself leap forward to accept it. A sudden subsidence had freed his feet.

Then the warning operated suddenly—for an instant. Henriot *was* interested; more, he was half seduced; but, as yet, he did not mean to be included in their purposes, whatever these might be. That shrinking dread came back a moment, and was gone again before he could question it. His eyes looked full at Lady Statham. "What is it that you know?" they asked her. "Tell me the things we once knew together, you and I. These words are merely trifling. And why does another man now stand in my place? For the sands heaped upon my memory are shifting, and it is *you* who are moving them away."

His soul whispered it; his voice said quite another thing, although the words he used seemed oddly chosen:

"There is much in the ideas of ancient Egypt that has attracted me ever since I can remember, though I have never caught up with anything definite enough to follow. There was majesty somewhere in their conceptions—a large, calm majesty of spiritual dominion, one might call it perhaps. I *am* interested."

Her face remained expressionless as she listened, but there was grave conviction in the eyes that held him like a spell. He saw through them into dim, faint pictures whose background was always sand. He forgot that he was speaking with a woman, a woman who half an hour ago had been a stranger to him. He followed these faded mental pictures, though he never caught them up. . . . It was like his dream in London.

Lady Statham was talking—he had not noticed the means by which she effected the abrupt transition—of familiar beliefs of old Egypt; of the Ka, or Double, by whose existence the survival of the soul was possible, even its return into manifested, physical life; of the astrology, or influence of the heavenly bodies upon all sublunar activities; of terrific forms of other life, known to the ancient worship of Atlantis, great Potencies that might be invoked by ritual and ceremonial, and of their lesser influence as recognised in certain lower forms, hence treated with veneration as the "Sacred Animal" branch of this dim religion. And she spoke lightly of the modern learning which so glibly imagined it was the animals themselves that were looked upon as "gods"—the bull, the bird, the crocodile, the cat. "It's there they all go so absurdly wrong," she said, "taking the symbol for the power symbolised. Yet natural enough. The mind to-day wears blinkers, studies only the details seen directly before it. Had none of us experienced love, we should think the first lover mad. Few to-day know the Powers *they* knew, hence deny them. If the world were deaf it would stand with mockery before a hearing group swayed by an orchestra, pitying both listeners and performers. It would deem our admiration of a great swinging bell mere foolish worship of form and movement. Similarly, with high Powers that once expressed themselves in common forms—where best they could—being themselves bodiless. The learned men classify the forms with painstaking detail. But deity has gone out of life. The Powers symbolised are no longer experienced."

"These Powers, you suggest, then—their Kas, as it were—may still—"

But she waved aside the interruption. "They are satisfied, as the common people were, with a degraded literalism," she went on. "Nut was the Heavens, who spread herself across the earth in the form of a woman; Shu, the vastness of space; the ibis typified Thoth, and Hathor was the Patron of the Western Hills; Khonsu, the moon, was personified, as was the deity of the Nile. But the high priest of Ra, the sun, you notice, remained ever the Great One of Visions."

The High Priest, the Great One of Visions!—How wonderfully again she made the sentence sing. She put splendour into it. The pictures shifted suddenly closer in his mind. He saw the grandeur of Memphis and Heliopolis rise against the stars and shake the sand of ages from their stern old temples.

"You think it possible, then, to get into touch with these High Powers you speak of, Powers once manifested in common forms?"

Henriot asked the question with a degree of conviction and solemnity that surprised himself. The scenery changed about him as he listened. The spacious halls of this former khedivial Palace melted into Desert spaces. He smelt the open wilderness, the sand that haunted Helouan. The soft-footed Arab servants moved across the hall in their white sheets like eddies of dust the wind stirred from the Libyan dunes. And over these two strangers close beside him stole a queer, indefinite alteration. Moods and emotions, nameless as unknown stars, rose through his soul, trailing dark mists of memory from unfathomable distances.

Lady Statham answered him indirectly. He found himself wishing that those steady eyes would sometimes close.

"Love is known only by feeling it," she said, her voice deepening a little. "Behind the form you feel the person loved. The process is an evocation, pure and simple. An arduous ceremonial, involving worship and devotional preparation, is the means. It is a difficult ritual—the only one acknowledged by the world as still effectual. Ritual is the passage way of the soul into the Infinite."

He might have said the words himself. The thought lay in him while she uttered it. Evocation everywhere in life was as true as assimilation. Nevertheless, he stared his companion full in the eyes with a touch of almost rude amazement. But no further questions prompted themselves; or, rather, he declined to ask them. He recalled, somehow uneasily, that in ceremonial the points of the compass have significance, standing for forces and activities that sleep there until invoked, and a passing light fell upon that curious midnight request in the corridor upstairs. These two were on the track of undesirable experiments, he thought. . . . They wished to include him too.

"You go at night sometimes into the Desert?" he heard himself saying. It was impulsive and miscalculated. His feeling that it would be wise to change the conversation resulted in giving it fresh impetus instead.

"We saw you there—in the Wadi Hof," put in Vance, suddenly breaking his long silence; "you too sleep out, then? It means, you know, the Valley of Fear."

"We wondered—" It was Lady Statham's voice, and she leaned forward eagerly as she said it, then abruptly left the sentence incomplete. Henriot started; a sense of momentary acute discomfort again ran over him. The same second she continued, though obviously changing the phrase—"we wondered how you spent your day there, during the heat. But you paint, don't you? You draw, I mean?"

The commonplace question, he realised in every fibre of his being, meant something *they* deemed significant. Was it his talent for drawing that they sought to use him for? Even as he answered with a simple affirmative, he had a flash of intuition that might be fanciful, yet that might be true: that this extraordinary pair were intent upon some ceremony of evocation that should summon into actual physical expression some Power—some type of life—known long ago to ancient worship, and that they even sought to fix its bodily outline with the pencil—his pencil.

A gateway of incredible adventure opened at his feet. He balanced on the edge of knowing unutterable things. Here was a clue that might lead him towards the hidden Egypt he had ever craved to know. An awful hand was beckoning. The sands were shifting. He saw the million eyes of the Desert watching him from beneath the level lids of centuries. Speck by speck, and grain by grain, the sand that smothered memory lifted the countless wrappings that embalmed it.

And he was willing, yet afraid. Why in the world did he hesitate and shrink? Why was it that the presence of this silent, watching personality in the chair beside him kept caution still alive, with warning close behind? The pictures in his mind were gorgeously coloured. It was Richard Vance who somehow streaked them through with black. A thing of darkness, born of this man's unassertive presence, flitted ever across the scenery, marring its grandeur with something evil, petty, dreadful. He held a horrible thought alive. His mind was thinking venal purposes.

In Henriot himself imagination had grown curiously heated, fed by what had been suggested rather than actually said. Ideas of immensity crowded his brain, yet never assumed definite shape. They were familiar, even as this strange woman was familiar. Once, long ago, he had known them well; had even practised them beneath these bright Egyptian stars. Whence came this prodigious glad excitement in his heart, this sense of mighty Powers coaxed down to influence the very details of daily life? Behind them, for all their vagueness, lay an archetypal splendour, fraught with forgotten meanings. He had always been aware of it in this mysterious land, but it had ever hitherto eluded him. It hovered everywhere. He had felt it brooding behind the towering Colossi at Thebes, in the skeletons of wasted temples, in the uncouth comeliness of the Sphinx, and in the crude terror of the Pyramids even. Over the whole of Egypt hung its invisible wings. These were but isolated fragments of the Body that might express it. And the Desert remained its cleanest, truest symbol. Sand knew it closest. Sand might even give it bodily form and outline.

But, while it escaped description in his mind, as equally it eluded visualisation in his soul, he felt that it combined with its vastness something infinitely small as well. Of such wee particles is the giant Desert born. . . .

Henriot started nervously in his chair, convicted once more of unconscionable staring; and at the same moment a group of hotel people, returning from a dance, passed through the hall and nodded him good-night. The scent of the women reached him; and with it the sound of their voices discussing personalities just left behind. A London atmosphere came with them. He caught trivial phrases, uttered in a drawling tone, and followed by the shrill laughter of a girl. They passed upstairs, discussing their little things, like marionettes upon a tiny stage.

But their passage brought him back to things of modern life, and to some standard of familiar measurement. The pictures that his soul had gazed at so deep within, he realised, were a pictorial transfer caught incompletely from this woman's vivid mind. He had seen the Desert as the grey, enormous Tomb where hovered still the Ka of ancient Egypt. Sand screened her visage with the veil of centuries. But She was there, and She was living. Egypt herself had pitched a temporary camp in him, and then moved on.

There was a momentary break, a sense of abruptness and dislocation. And then he became aware that Lady Statham had been speaking for some time before he caught her actual words, and that a certain change had come into her voice as also into her manner.

V

She was leaning closer to him, her face suddenly glowing and alive. Through the stone figure coursed the fires of a passion that deepened the coal-black eyes and communicated a hint of light—of exaltation—to her whole person. It was incredibly moving. To this deep passion was due the power he had felt. It was her entire life; she lived for it, she would die for it. Her calmness of manner enhanced its effect. Hence the strength of those first impressions that had stormed him. The woman had belief; however wild and strange, it was sacred to her. The secret of her influence was—conviction.

His attitude shifted several points then. The wonder in him passed over into awe. The things she knew were real. They were not merely imaginative speculations.

"I knew I was not wrong in thinking you in sympathy with this line of thought," she was saying in lower voice, steady with earnestness, and as though she had read his mind. "You, too, know, though perhaps you hardly realise that you know. It lies so deep in you that you only get vague feelings of it—intimations of memory. Isn't that the case?"

Henriot gave assent with his eyes; it was the truth.

"What we know instinctively," she continued, "is simply what we are trying to remember. Knowledge is memory." She paused a moment watching his face closely. "At least, you are free from that cheap scepticism which labels these old beliefs as superstition." It was not even a question.

"I—worship real belief—of any kind," he stammered, for her words and the close proximity of her atmosphere caused a strange upheaval in his heart that he could not account for. He faltered in his speech. "It is the most vital quality in life—rarer than deity." He was using her own phrases even. "It is creative. It constructs the world anew—"

"And may reconstruct the old."

She said it, lifting her face above him a little, so that her eyes looked down into his own. It grew big and somehow masculine. It was the face of a priest, spiritual power in it. Where, oh where in the echoing Past had he known this woman's soul? He saw her in another setting, a forest of columns dim about her, towering above giant aisles. Again he felt the Desert had come close. Into this tent-like hall of the hotel came the sifting of tiny sand. It heaped softly about the very furniture against his feet, blocking the exits of door and window. It shrouded the little present. The wind that brought it stirred a veil that had hung for ages motionless. . . .

She had been saying many things that he had missed while his mind went searching. "There were types of life the Atlantean system knew it might revive—life un-manifested to-day in any bodily form," was the sentence he caught with his return to the actual present.

"A type of life?" he whispered, looking about him, as though to see who it was had joined them; "you mean a—soul? Some kind of soul, alien to humanity, or to—to any forms of living thing in the world to-day?" What she had been saying reached him somehow, it seemed, though he had not heard the words themselves. Still hesitating, he was yet so eager to hear. Already he felt she meant to include him in her purposes, and that in the end he must go willingly. So strong was her persuasion on his mind.

And he felt as if he knew vaguely what was coming. Before she answered his curious question—prompting it indeed—rose in his mind that strange idea of the Group-Soul: the theory that big souls cannot express themselves in a single individual, but need an entire group for their full manifestation.

He listened intently. The reflection that this sudden intimacy was unnatural, he rejected, for many conversations were really gathered into one. Long watching and preparation on both sides had cleared the way for the ripening of acquaintance into confidence—how long he dimly wondered? But if this conception of the Group-Soul was not new, the suggestion Lady Statham developed out of it was both new and startling—and yet always so curiously familiar. Its value for him lay, not in far-fetched evidence that supported it, but in the deep belief which made it a vital asset in an honest inner life.

"An individual," she said quietly, "one soul expressed completely in a single person, I mean, is exceedingly rare. Not often is a physical instrument found perfect enough to provide it with adequate expression. In the lower ranges of humanity—certainly in animal and insect life—one soul is shared by many. Behind a tribe of savages stands one Savage. A flock of birds is a single Bird, scattered through the consciousness of all. They wheel in mid-air, they migrate, they obey the deep intelligence called instinct—all as one. The life of any one lion is the life of all—the lion group-soul that manifests itself in the entire genus. An ant-heap is a single Ant; through the bees spreads the consciousness of a single Bee."

Henriot knew what she was working up to. In his eagerness to hasten disclosure he interrupted—

"And there may be types of life that have no corresponding bodily expression at all, then?" he asked as though the question were forced out of him. "They exist as Powers—un-manifested on the earth to-day?"

"Powers," she answered, watching him closely with unswerving stare, "that need a group to provide their body—their physical expression—if they came back."

"Came back!" he repeated below his breath.

But she heard him. "They once had expression. Egypt, Atlantis knew them—spiritual Powers that never visit the world to-day."

"Bodies," he whispered softly, "actual bodies?"

"Their sphere of action, you see, would be their body. And it might be physical outline. So potent a descent of spiritual life would select materials for its body where it could find them. Our conventional notion of a body—what is it? A single outline moving altogether in one direction. For little human souls, or fragments, this is sufficient. But for vaster types of soul an entire host would be required."

"A church?" he ventured. "Some Body of belief, you surely mean?"

She bowed her head a moment in assent. She was determined he should seize her meaning fully.

"A wave of spiritual awakening—a descent of spiritual life upon a nation," she answered slowly, "forms itself a church, and the body of true believers are its sphere of action. They are literally its bodily expression. Each individual believer is a corpuscle in that Body. The Power has provided itself with a vehicle of manifestation. Otherwise we could not know it. And the more real the belief of each individual, the more perfect the expression of the spiritual life behind them all. A Group-soul walks the earth. Moreover, a nation naturally devout could attract a type of soul unknown to a nation that denies all faith. Faith brings back the gods. . . . But to-day belief is dead, and Deity has left the world."

She talked on and on, developing this main idea that in days of older faiths there were deific types of life upon the earth, evoked by worship and beneficial to humanity. They had long ago withdrawn because the worship which brought them down had died the death. The world had grown pettier. These vast centres of Spiritual Power found no "Body" in which they now could express themselves or manifest. . . . Her thoughts and phrases poured over him like sand. It was always sand he felt—burying the Present and uncovering the Past. . . .

He tried to steady his mind upon familiar objects, but wherever he looked Sand stared him in the face. Outside these trivial walls the Desert lay listening. It lay waiting too. Vance himself had dropped out of recognition. He belonged to the world of things to-day. But this woman and himself stood thousands of years away, beneath the columns of a Temple in the sands. And the sands were moving. His feet went shifting with them . . . running down vistas of ageless memory that woke terror by their sheer immensity of distance. . . .

Like a muffled voice that called to him through many veils and wrappings, he heard her describe the stupendous Powers that evocation might coax down again among the world of men.

"To what useful end?" he asked at length, amazed at his own temerity, and because he knew instinctively the answer in advance. It rose through these layers of coiling memory in his soul.

"The extension of spiritual knowledge and the widening of life," she answered. "The link with the 'unearthly kingdom' wherein this ancient system went forever searching, would be re-established. Complete rehabilitation might follow. Portions—little portions of these Powers—expressed themselves naturally once in certain animal types, instinctive life that did not deny or reject them. The worship of sacred animals was the relic of a once gigantic system of evocation—not of monsters," and she smiled sadly, "but of Powers that were willing and ready to descend when worship summoned them."

Again, beneath his breath, Henriot heard himself murmur—his own voice startled him as he whispered it: "Actual bodily shape and outline?"

"Material for bodies is everywhere," she answered, equally low; "dust to which we all return; sand, if you prefer it, fine, fine sand. Life moulds it easily enough, when that life is potent."

A certain confusion spread slowly through his mind as he heard her. He lit a cigarette and smoked some minutes in silence. Lady Statham and her nephew waited for him to speak. At length, after some inner battling and hesitation, he put the question that he knew they waited for. It was impossible to resist any longer.

"It would be interesting to know the method," he said, "and to revive, perhaps, by experiment—"

Before he could complete his thought, she took him up:

"There are some who claim to know it," she said gravely—her eyes a moment masterful. "A clue, thus followed, might lead to the entire reconstruction I spoke of."

"And the method?" he repeated faintly.

"Evoke the Power by ceremonial evocation—the ritual is obtainable—and note the form it assumes. Then establish it. This shape or outline once secured, could then be made permanent—a mould for its return at will—its natural physical expression here on earth."

"Idol!" he exclaimed.

"Image," she replied at once. "Life, before we can know it, must have a body. Our souls, in order to manifest here, need a material vehicle."

"And—to obtain this form or outline?" he began; "to fix it, rather?"

"Would be required the clever pencil of a fearless looker-on—some one not engaged in the actual evocation. This form, accurately made permanent in solid matter, say in stone, would provide a channel always open. Experiment, properly speaking, might then begin. The cisterns of Power behind would be accessible."

"An amazing proposition!" Henriot exclaimed. What surprised him was that he felt no desire to laugh, and little even to doubt.

"Yet known to every religion that ever deserved the name," put in Vance like a voice from a distance. Blackness came somehow with his interruption—a touch of darkness. He spoke eagerly.

To all the talk that followed, and there was much of it, Henriot listened with but half an ear. This one idea stormed through him with an uproar that killed attention. Judgment was held utterly in abeyance. He carried away from it some vague suggestion that this woman had hinted at previous lives she half remembered, and that every year she came to Egypt, haunting the sands and temples in the effort to recover lost clues. And he recalled afterwards that she said, "This all came to me as a child, just as though it was something half remembered." There was the further suggestion that he himself was not unknown to her; that they, too, had met before. But this, compared to the grave certainty of the rest, was merest fantasy that did not hold his attention. He answered, hardly knowing what he said. His preoccupation with other thoughts deep down was so intense, that he was probably barely polite, uttering empty phrases, with his mind elsewhere. His one desire was to escape and be alone, and it was with genuine relief that he presently excused himself and went upstairs to bed. The halls, he noticed, were empty; an Arab servant waited to put the lights out. He walked up, for the lift had long ceased running.

And the magic of old Egypt stalked beside him. The studies that had fascinated his mind in earlier youth returned with the power that had subdued his mind in boyhood. The cult of Osiris woke in his blood again; Horus and Nephthys stirred in their long-forgotten centres. There revived in him, too long buried, the awful glamour of those liturgal rites and vast body of observances, those spells and formulae of incantation of the oldest known recension that years ago had captured his imagination and belief—the Book of the Dead. Trumpet voices called to his heart again across the desert of some dim past. There were forms of life—impulses from the Creative Power which is the Universe—other than the soul of man. They could be known. A spiritual exaltation, roused by the words and presence of this singular woman, shouted to him as he went.

Then, as he closed his bedroom door, carefully locking it, there stood beside him—Vance. The forgotten figure of Vance came up close—the watching eyes, the simulated interest, the feigned belief, the detective mental attitude, these broke through the grandiose panorama, bringing darkness. Vance, strong personality that hid behind assumed nonentity for some purpose of his own, intruded with sudden violence, demanding an explanation of his presence.

And, with an equal suddenness, explanation offered itself then and there. It came unsought, its horror of certainty utterly unjustified; and it came in this unexpected fashion:

Behind the interest and acquiescence of the man ran—fear: but behind the vivid fear ran another thing that Henriot now perceived was vile. For the first time in his life, Henriot knew it at close quarters, actual, ready to operate. Though familiar enough in daily life to be of common occurrence, Henriot had never realised it as he did now, so close and terrible. In the same way he had never realised that he would die—vanish from the busy world of men and women, forgotten as though he had never existed, an eddy of wind-blown dust. And in the man named Richard Vance this thing was close upon blossom. Henriot could not name it to himself. Even in thought it appalled him.

He undressed hurriedly, almost with the child's idea of finding safety between the sheets. His mind undressed itself as well. The business of the day laid itself automatically aside; the will sank down; desire grew inactive. Henriot was exhausted. But, in that stage towards slumber when thinking stops, and only fugitive pictures pass across the mind in shadowy dance, his brain ceased shouting its mechanical explanations, and his soul unveiled a peering eye. Great limbs of memory, smothered by the activities of the Present, stirred their stiffened lengths through the sands of long ago—sands this woman had begun to excavate from some far-off pre-existence they had surely known together. Vagueness and certainty ran hand in hand. Details were unrecoverable, but the emotions in which they were embedded moved.

He turned restlessly in his bed, striving to seize the amazing clues and follow them. But deliberate effort hid them instantly again; they retired instantly into the subconsciousness. With the brain of this body he now occupied they had nothing to do. The brain stored memories of each life only. This ancient script was graven in his soul. Subconsciousness alone could interpret and reveal. And it was his subconscious memory that Lady Statham had been so busily excavating.

Dimly it stirred and moved about the depths within him, never clearly seen, indefinite, felt as a yearning after unrecoverable knowledge. Against the darker background of Vance's fear and sinister purpose—both of this present life, and recent—he saw the grandeur of this woman's impossible dream, and *knew*, beyond argument or reason, that it was true. Judgment and will asleep, he left the impossibility aside, and took the grandeur. The Belief of Lady Statham was not credulity and superstition; it was Memory. Still to this day, over the sands of Egypt, hovered immense spiritual potencies, so vast that they could only know physical expression in a group—in many. Their sphere of bodily manifestation must be a host, each individual unit in that host a corpuscle in the whole.

The wind, rising from the Lybian wastes across the Nile, swept up against the exposed side of the hotel, and made his windows rattle—the old, sad winds of Egypt. Henriot got out of bed to fasten the outside shutters. He stood a moment and watched the moon floating down behind the Sakkara Pyramids. The Pleiades and Orion's Belt hung brilliantly; the Great Bear was close to the horizon. In the sky above the Desert swung ten thousand stars. No sounds rose from the streets of Helouan. The tide of sand was coming slowly in.

And a flock of enormous thoughts swooped past him from fields of this unbelievable, lost memory. The Desert, pale in the moon, was coextensive with the night, too huge for comfort or understanding, yet charged to the brim with infinite peace. Behind its majesty of silence lay whispers of a vanished language that once could call with power upon mighty spiritual Agencies. Its skirts were folded now, but, slowly across the leagues of sand, they began to stir and rearrange themselves. He grew suddenly aware of this enveloping shroud of sand—as the raw material of bodily expression: Form.

The sand was in his imagination and his mind. Shaking loosely the folds of its gigantic skirts, it rose; it moved a little towards him. He saw the eternal countenance of the Desert watching him—immobile and unchanging behind these shifting veils the winds laid so carefully over it. Egypt, the ancient Egypt, turned in her vast sarcophagus of Desert, wakening from her sleep of ages at the Belief of approaching worshippers.

Only in this insignificant manner could he express a letter of the terrific language that crowded to seek expression through his soul. . . . He closed the shutters and carefully fastened them. He turned to go back to bed, curiously trembling. Then, as he did so, the whole singular delusion caught him with a shock that held him motionless. Up rose the stupendous apparition of the entire Desert and stood behind him on that balcony. Swift as thought, in silence, the Desert stood on end against his very face. It towered across the sky, hiding Orion and the moon; it dipped below the horizons. The whole grey sheet of it rose up before his eyes and stood. Through its unfolding skirts ran ten thousand eddies of swirling sand as the creases of its grave-clothes smoothed themselves out in moonlight. And a bleak, scarred countenance, huge as a planet, gazed down into his own. . . .

Through his dreamless sleep that night two things lay active and awake . . . in the subconscious part that knows no slumber. They were incongruous. One was evil, small and human; the other unearthly and sublime. For the memory of the fear that haunted Vance, and the sinister cause of it, pricked at him all night long. But behind, beyond this common, intelligible emotion, lay the crowding wonder that caught his soul with glory:

The Sand was stirring, the Desert was awake. Ready to mate with them in material form, brooded close the Ka of that colossal Entity that once expressed itself through the myriad life of ancient Egypt.

VI

Next day, and for several days following, Henriot kept out of the path of Lady Statham and her nephew. The acquaintanceship had grown too rapidly to be quite comfortable. It was easy to pretend that he took people at their face value, but it was a pose; one liked to know something of antecedents. It was otherwise difficult to "place" them. And Henriot, for the life of him, could not "place" these two. His

Subconsciousness brought explanation when it came—but the Subconsciousness is only temporarily active. When it retired he floundered without a rudder, in confusion.

With the flood of morning sunshine the value of much she had said evaporated. Her presence alone had supplied the key to the cipher. But while the indigestible portions he rejected, there remained a good deal he had already assimilated. The discomfort remained; and with it the grave, unholy reality of it all. It was something more than theory. Results would follow—if he joined them. He would witness curious things.

The force with which it drew him brought hesitation. It operated in him like a shock that numbs at first by its abrupt arrival, and needs time to realise in the right proportions to the rest of life. These right proportions, however, did not come readily, and his emotions ranged between sceptical laughter and complete acceptance. The one detail he felt certain of was this dreadful thing he had divined in Vance. Trying hard to disbelieve it, he found he could not. It was true. Though without a shred of real evidence to support it, the horror of it remained. He knew it in his very bones.

And this, perhaps, was what drove him to seek the comforting companionship of folk he understood and felt at home with. He told his host and hostess about the strangers, though omitting the actual conversation because they would merely smile in blank miscomprehension. But the moment he described the strong black eyes beneath the level eyelids, his hostess turned with a start, her interest deeply roused: "Why, it's that awful Statham woman," she exclaimed, "that must be Lady Statham, and the man she calls her nephew."

"Sounds like it, certainly," her husband added. "Felix, you'd better clear out. They'll bewitch you too."

And Henriot bridled, yet wondering why he did so. He drew into his shell a little, giving the merest sketch of what had happened. But he listened closely while these two practical old friends supplied him with information in the gossiping way that human nature loves. No doubt there was much embroidery, and more perversion, exaggeration too, but the account evidently rested upon some basis of solid foundation for all that. Smoke and fire go together always.

"He is her nephew right enough," Mansfield corrected his wife, before proceeding to his own man's form of elaboration; "no question about that, I believe. He's her favourite nephew, and she's as rich as a pig. He follows her out here every year, waiting for her empty shoes. But they are an unsavoury couple. I've met 'em in various parts, all over Egypt, but they always come back to Helouan in the end. And the stories about them are simply legion. You remember—" he turned hesitatingly to his wife—"some people, I heard," he changed his sentence, "were made quite ill by her."

"I'm sure Felix ought to know, yes," his wife boldly took him up, "my niece, Fanny, had the most extraordinary experience." She turned to Henriot. "Her room was next to Lady Statham in some hotel or other at Assouan or Edfu, and one night she woke and heard a kind of mysterious chanting or intoning next her. Hotel doors are so dreadfully thin. There was a funny smell too, like incense of something sickly, and a man's voice kept chiming in. It went on for hours, while she lay terrified in bed—"

"Frightened, you say?" asked Henriot.

"Out of her skin, yes; she said it was so uncanny—made her feel icy. She wanted to ring the bell, but was afraid to leave her bed. The room was full of—of things, yet she could see nothing. She *felt* them, you see. And after a bit the sound of this sing-song voice so got on her nerves, it half dazed her—a kind of enchantment—she felt choked and suffocated. And then—" It was her turn to hesitate.

"Tell it all," her husband said, quite gravely too.

"Well—something came in. At least, she describes it oddly, rather; she said it made the door bulge inwards from the next room, but not the door alone; the walls bulged or swayed as if a huge thing pressed against them from the other side. And at the same moment her windows—she had two big balconies, and the venetian shutters were fastened—both her windows *darkened*—though it was two in the morning and pitch dark outside. She said it was all *one* thing—trying to get in; just as water, you see, would rush in through every hole and opening it could find, and all at once. And in spite of her terror—that's the odd part of it—she says she felt a kind of splendour in her—a sort of elation."

"She saw nothing?"

"She says she doesn't remember. Her senses left her, I believe—though she won't admit it."

"Fainted for a minute, probably," said Mansfield.

"So there it is," his wife concluded, after a silence. "And that's true. It happened to my niece, didn't it, John?"

Stories and legendary accounts of strange things that the presence of these two brought poured out then. They were obviously somewhat mixed, one account borrowing picturesque details from another, and all in disproportion, as when people tell stories in a language they are little familiar with. But, listening with avidity, yet also with uneasiness, somehow, Henriot put two and two together. Truth stood behind them somewhere. These two held traffic with the powers that ancient Egypt knew.

"Tell Felix, dear, about the time you met the nephew—horrid creature—in the Valley of the Kings," he heard his wife say presently. And Mansfield told it plainly enough, evidently glad to get it done, though.

"It was some years ago now, and I didn't know who he was then, or anything about him. I don't know much more now—except that he's a dangerous sort of charlatan-devil, *I* think. But I came across him one night up there by Thebes in the Valley of the Kings—you know, where they buried all their Johnnies with so much magnificence and processions and masses, and all the rest. It's the most astounding, the most haunted place you ever saw, gloomy, silent, full of gorgeous lights and shadows that seem alive—terribly impressive; it makes you creep and shudder. You feel old Egypt watching you."

"Get on, dear," said his wife.

"Well, I was coming home late on a blasted lazy donkey, dog-tired into the bargain, when my donkey boy suddenly ran for his life and left me alone. It was after sunset. The sand was red and shining, and the big cliffs sort of fiery. And my donkey stuck its four feet in the ground and wouldn't budge. Then, about fifty yards away, I saw a fellow— European apparently—doing something—Heaven knows what, for I can't describe it—among the boulders that lie all over the ground there. Ceremony, I suppose you'd call it. I was so interested that at first I watched. Then I saw he wasn't alone. There were a lot of moving things round him, towering big things, that came and went like shadows. That twilight is fearfully bewildering; perspective changes, and distance gets all confused. It's fearfully hard to see properly. I only remember that I got off my donkey and went up closer, and when I was within a dozen yards of him—well, it sounds such rot, you know, but I swear the things suddenly rushed off and left him there alone. They went with a roaring noise like wind; shadowy but tremendously big, they were, and they vanished up against the fiery precipices as though they slipped bang into the stone itself. The only thing I can think of to describe 'em is—well, those sand-storms the Khamasin raises—the hot winds, you know."

"They probably *were* sand," his wife suggested, burning to tell another story of her own.

"Possibly, only there wasn't a breath of wind, and it was hot as blazes—and—I had such extraordinary sensations—never felt anything like it before—wild and exhilarated—drunk, I tell you, drunk."

"You saw them?" asked Henriot. "You made out their shape at all, or outline?"

"Sphinx," he replied at once, "for all the world like sphinxes. You know the kind of face and head these limestone strata in the Desert take—great visages with square Egyptian head-dresses where the driven sand has eaten away the softer stuff beneath? You see it everywhere—enormous idols they seem, with faces and eyes and lips awfully like the sphinx—well, that's the nearest I can get to it." He puffed his pipe hard. But there was no sign of levity in him. He told the actual truth as far as in him lay, yet half ashamed of what he told. And a good deal he left out, too.

"She's got a face of the same sort, that Statham horror," his wife said with a shiver. "Reduce the size, and paint in awful black eyes, and you've got her exactly—a living idol." And all three laughed, yet a laughter without merriment in it.

"And you spoke to the man?"

"I did," the Englishman answered, "though I confess I'm a bit ashamed of the way I spoke. Fact is, I was excited, thunderingly excited, and felt a kind of anger. I wanted to kick the beggar for practising such bally rubbish, and in such a place too. Yet all the time—well, well, I believe it was sheer funk now," he laughed; "for I felt uncommonly queer out there in the dusk, alone with—with that kind of business; and I was angry with myself for feeling it. Anyhow, I went up—I'd lost my donkey boy as well, remember—and slated him like a dog. I can't remember what I said exactly—only that he stood and stared at me in silence. That made it worse—seemed twice as real then. The beggar said no single word the whole time. He signed to me with one hand to clear out. And then, suddenly out of nothing—she— that woman—appeared and stood beside him. I never saw her come. She must have been behind some boulder or other, for she simply rose out of the ground. She stood there and stared at me too—bang in the face. She was turned towards the sunset—what was left of it in the west—and her black eyes shone like—ugh! I can't describe it—it was shocking."

"She spoke?"

"She said five words—and her voice—it'll make you laugh—it was metallic like a gong: 'You are in danger here.' That's all she said. I simply turned and cleared out as fast as ever I could. But I had to go on foot. My donkey had followed its boy long before. I tell you—smile as you may—my blood was all curdled for an hour afterwards."

Then he explained that he felt some kind of explanation or apology was due, since the couple lodged in his own hotel, and how he approached the man in the smoking-room after dinner. A conversation resulted—the man was quite intelligent after all—of which only one sentence had remained in his mind.

"Perhaps you can explain it, Felix. I wrote it down, as well as I could remember. The rest confused me beyond words or memory; though I must confess it did not seem—well, not utter rot exactly. It was about astrology and rituals and the worship of the old Egyptians, and I don't know what else besides. Only, he made it intelligible and almost sensible, if only I could have got the hang of the thing enough to remember it. You know," he added, as though believing in spite of himself, "there *is* a lot of that wonderful old Egyptian religious business still hanging about in the atmosphere of this place, say what you like."

"But this sentence?" Henriot asked. And the other went off to get a note-book where he had written it down.

"He was jawing, you see," he continued when he came back, Henriot and his wife having kept silence meanwhile, "about direction being of importance in religious ceremonies, West and North symbolising certain powers, or something of the kind, why people turn to the East and all that sort of thing, and speaking of the whole Universe as if it had living forces tucked away in it that expressed themselves somehow when roused up. That's how I remember it anyhow. And then he said this thing—in answer to some fool question probably that I put." And he read out of the note-book:

"'You were in danger because you came through the Gateway of the West, and the Powers from the Gateway of the East were at that moment rising, and therefore in direct opposition to you.'"

Then came the following, apparently a simile offered by way of explanation. Mansfield read it in a shamefaced tone, evidently prepared for laughter:

"'Whether I strike you on the back or in the face determines what kind of answering force I rouse in you. Direction is significant.' And he said it was the period called the Night of Power—time when the Desert encroaches and spirits are close."

And tossing the book aside, he lit his pipe again and waited a moment to hear what might be said. "Can you explain such gibberish?" he asked at length, as neither of his listeners spoke. But Henriot said he couldn't. And the wife then took up her own tale of stories that had grown about this singular couple.

These were less detailed, and therefore less impressive, but all contributed something towards the atmosphere of reality that framed the entire picture. They belonged to the type one hears at every dinner party in Egypt—stories of the vengeance mummies seem to take on those who robbed them, desecrating their peace of centuries; of a woman wearing a necklace of scarabs taken from a princess's tomb, who felt hands about her throat to strangle her; of little Ka figures, Pasht goddesses, amulets and the rest, that brought curious disaster to those who kept them. They are many and various, astonishingly circumstantial often, and vouched for by persons the reverse of credulous. The modern superstition that haunts the desert gullies with Afreets has nothing in common with them. They rest upon a basis of indubitable experience; and they remain—inexplicable. And about the personalities of Lady Statham and her nephew they crowded like flies attracted by a dish of fruit. The Arabs, too, were afraid of her. She had difficulty in getting guides and dragomen.

"My dear chap," concluded Mansfield, "take my advice and have nothing to do with 'em. There *is* a lot of queer business knocking about in this old country, and people like that know ways of reviving it somehow. It's upset you already; you looked scared, I thought, the moment you came in." They laughed, but the Englishman was in earnest. "I tell you what," he added, "we'll go off for a bit of shooting together. The fields along the Delta are packed with birds now: they're home early this year on their way to the North. What d'ye say, eh?"

But Henriot did not care about the quail shooting. He felt more inclined to be alone and think things out by himself. He had come to his friends for comfort, and instead they had made him uneasy and excited. His interest had suddenly doubled. Though half afraid, he longed to know what these two were up to—to follow the adventure to the bitter end. He disregarded the warning of his host as well as the premonition in his own heart. The sand had caught his feet.

There were moments when he laughed in utter disbelief, but these were optimistic moods that did not last. He always returned to the feeling that truth lurked somewhere in the whole strange business, and that if he joined forces with them, as they seemed to wish, he would witness—well, he hardly knew what—but it enticed him as danger does the reckless man, or death the suicide. The sand had caught his mind.

He decided to offer himself to all they wanted—his pencil too. He would see—a shiver ran through him at the thought—what they saw, and know some eddy of that vanished tide of power and splendour the ancient Egyptian priesthood knew, and that perhaps was even common experience in the far-off days of dim Atlantis. The sand had caught his imagination too. He was utterly sand-haunted.

VII

And so he took pains, though without making definite suggestion, to place himself in the way of this woman and her nephew—only to find that his hints were disregarded. They left him alone, if they did not actually avoid him. Moreover, he rarely came across them now. Only at night, or in the queer dusk hours, he caught glimpses of them moving hurriedly off from the hotel, and always desertwards. And their disregard, well calculated, enflamed his desire to the point when he almost decided to propose himself. Quite suddenly, then, the idea flashed through him—how do they come, these odd revelations, when the mind lies receptive like a plate sensitised by anticipation?—that they were waiting for a certain date, and, with the notion, came Mansfield's remark about "the Night of Power," believed in by the old Egyptian Calendar as a time when the super-sensuous world moves close against the minds of men with all its troop of possibilities. And the thought, once lodged in its corner of imagination, grew strong. He looked it up. Ten days from now, he found, Leyel-el-Sud would be upon him, with a moon, too, at the full. And this strange hint of guidance he accepted. In his present mood, as he admitted, smiling to himself, he could accept anything. It was part of it, it belonged to the adventure. But, even while he persuaded himself that it was play, the solemn reality of what lay ahead increased amazingly, sketched darkly in his very soul.

These intervening days he spent as best he could—impatiently, a prey to quite opposite emotions. In the blazing sunshine he thought of it and laughed; but at night he lay often sleepless, calculating chances of escape. He never did escape, however. The Desert that watched little Helouan with great, un-winking eyes watched also every turn and twist he made. Like this oasis, he basked in the sun of older time, and dreamed beneath forgotten moons. The sand at last had crept into his inmost heart. It sifted over him.

Seeking a reaction from normal, everyday things, he made tourist trips; yet, while recognising the comedy in his attitude, he never could lose sight of the grandeur that banked it up so hauntingly. These two contrary emotions grafted themselves on all he did and saw. He crossed the Nile at Bedrashein, and went again to the Tomb-World of Sakkara; but through all the chatter of veiled and helmeted tourists, the *bandar-log* of our modern Jungle, ran this dark under-stream of awe their monkey methods could not turn aside. One world lay upon another, but this modern layer was a shallow crust that, like the phenomenon of the "desert-film," a mere angle of falling light could instantly obliterate. Beneath the sand, deep down, he passed along the Street of Tombs, as he had often passed before, moved then merely by historical curiosity and admiration, but now by emotions for which he found no name. He saw the enormous sarcophagi of granite in their gloomy chambers where the sacred bulls once lay, swathed and embalmed like human beings, and, in the flickering candle light, the mood of ancient rites surged round him, menacing his doubts and laughter. The least human whisper in these subterraneans, dug out first four thousand years ago, revived ominous Powers that stalked beside him, forbidding and premonitive. He gazed at the spots where Mariette, unearthing them forty years ago, found fresh as of yesterday the marks of fingers and naked feet—of those who set the sixty-five ton slabs in position. And when he came up again into the sunshine he met the eternal questions of the pyramids, overtopping all his mental horizons. Sand blocked all the avenues of younger emotion, leaving the channels of something in him incalculably older, open and clean swept.

He slipped homewards, uncomfortable and followed, glad to be with a crowd—because he was otherwise alone with more than he could dare to think about. Keeping just ahead of his companions, he crossed the desert edge where the ghost of Memphis walks under rustling palm trees that screen no stone left upon another of all its mile-long populous splendours. For here was a vista his imagination could realise; here he could know the comfort of solid ground his feet could touch. Gigantic Ramases, lying on his back beneath their shade and staring at the sky, similarly helped to steady his swaying thoughts. Imagination could deal with these.

And daily thus he watched the busy world go to and fro to its scale of tips and bargaining, and gladly mingled with it, trying to laugh and study guidebooks, and listen to half-fledged explanations, but always seeing the comedy of his poor attempts. Not all those little donkeys, bells tinkling, beads shining, trotting beneath their comical burdens to the tune of shouting and belabouring, could stem this tide of deeper things the woman had let loose in the subconscious part of him. Everywhere he saw the mysterious camels go slouching through the sand, gurgling the water in their skinny, extended throats. Centuries passed between the enormous knee-stroke of their stride. And, every night, the sunsets restored the forbidding, graver mood, with their crimson, golden splendour, their strange green shafts of light, then— sudden twilight that brought the Past upon him with an awful leap. Upon the stage then stepped the figures of this pair of human beings, chanting their ancient plainsong of incantation in the moonlit desert, and working their rites of unholy evocation as the priests had worked them centuries before in the sands that now buried Sakkara fathoms deep.

Then one morning he woke with a question in his mind, as though it had been asked of him in sleep and he had waked just before the answer came. "Why do I spend my time sight-seeing, instead of going alone into the Desert as before? What has made me change?"

This latest mood now asked for explanation. And the answer, coming up automatically, startled him. It was so clear and sure—had been lying in the background all along. One word contained it:

Vance.

The sinister intentions of this man, forgotten in the rush of other emotions, asserted themselves again convincingly. The human horror, so easily comprehensible, had been smothered for the time by the hint of unearthly revelations. But it had operated all the time. Now it took the lead. He dreaded to be alone in the Desert with this dark picture in his mind of what Vance meant to bring there to completion. This abomination of a selfish human will returned to fix its terror in him. To be alone in the Desert meant to be alone with the imaginative picture of what Vance—he knew it with such strange certainty—hoped to bring about there.

There was absolutely no evidence to justify the grim suspicion. It seemed indeed far-fetched enough, this connection between the sand and the purpose of an evil-minded, violent man. But Henriot saw it true. He could argue it away in a few minutes—easily. Yet the instant thought ceased, it returned, led up by intuition. It possessed him, filled his mind with horrible possibilities. He feared the Desert as he might have feared the scene of some atrocious crime. And, for the time, this dread of a merely human thing corrected the big seduction of the other—the suggested "super-natural."

Side by side with it, his desire to join himself to the purposes of the woman increased steadily. They kept out of his way apparently; the offer seemed withdrawn; he grew restless, unable to settle to anything for long, and once he asked the porter casually if they were leaving the hotel. Lady Statham had been invisible for days, and Vance was somehow never within speaking distance. He heard with relief that they had not gone—but with dread as well. Keen excitement worked in him underground. He slept badly. Like a schoolboy, he waited for the summons to an important examination that involved portentous issues, and contradictory emotions disturbed his peace of mind abominably.

VIII

But it was not until the end of the week, when Vance approached him with purpose in his eyes and manner, that Henriot knew his fears unfounded, and caught himself trembling with sudden anticipation—because the invitation, so desired yet so dreaded, was actually at hand. Firmly determined to keep caution uppermost, yet he went unresistingly to a secluded corner by the palms where they could talk in privacy. For prudence is of the mind, but desire is of the soul, and while his brain of to-day whispered wariness, voices in his heart of long ago shouted commands that he knew he must obey with joy.

It was evening and the stars were out. Helouan, with her fairy twinkling lights, lay silent against the Desert edge. The sand was at the flood. The period of the Encroaching of the Desert was at hand, and the deeps were all astir with movement. But in the windless air was a great peace. A calm of infinite stillness breathed everywhere. The flow of Time, before it rushed away backwards, stopped somewhere between the dust of stars and Desert. The mystery of sand touched every street with its unutterable softness.

And Vance began without the smallest circumlocution. His voice was low, in keeping with the scene, but the words dropped with a sharp distinctness into the other's heart like grains of sand that pricked the skin before they smothered him. Caution they smothered instantly; resistance too.

"I have a message for you from my aunt," he said, as though he brought an invitation to a picnic. Henriot sat in shadow, but his companion's face was in a patch of light that followed them from the windows of the central hall. There was a shining in the light blue eyes that betrayed the excitement his quiet manner concealed. "We are going—the day after to-morrow—to spend the night in the Desert; she wondered if, perhaps, you would care to join us?"

"For your experiment?" asked Henriot bluntly.

Vance smiled with his lips, holding his eyes steady, though unable to suppress the gleam that flashed in them and was gone so swiftly. There was a hint of shrugging his shoulders.

"It is the Night of Power—in the old Egyptian Calendar, you know," he answered with assumed lightness almost, "the final moment of Leyel-el-Sud, the period of Black Nights when the Desert was held to encroach with—with various possibilities of a supernatural order. She wishes to revive a certain practice of the old Egyptians. There may be curious results. At any rate, the occasion is a picturesque one—better than this cheap imitation of London life." And he indicated the lights, the signs of people in the hall dressed for gaieties and dances, the hotel orchestra that played after dinner.

Henriot at the moment answered nothing, so great was the rush of conflicting emotions that came he knew not whence. Vance went calmly on. He spoke with a simple frankness that was meant to be disarming. Henriot never took his eyes off him. The two men stared steadily at one another.

"She wants to know if you will come and help too—in a certain way only: not in the experiment itself precisely, but by watching merely and—" He hesitated an instant, half lowering his eyes.

"Drawing the picture," Henriot helped him deliberately.

"Drawing what you see, yes," Vance replied, the voice turned graver in spite of himself. "She wants—she hopes to catch the outlines of anything that happens—"

"Comes."

"Exactly. Determine the shape of anything that comes. You may remember your conversation of the other night with her. She is very certain of success."

This was direct enough at any rate. It was as formal as an invitation to a dinner, and as guileless. The thing he thought he wanted lay within his reach. He had merely to say yes. He did say yes; but first he looked about him instinctively, as for guidance. He looked at the stars twinkling high above the distant Libyan Plateau; at the long arms of the Desert, gleaming weirdly white in the moonlight, and reaching towards him down every opening between the houses; at the heavy mass of the Mokattam Hills, guarding the Arabian Wilderness with strange, peaked barriers, their sand-carved ridges dark and still above the Wadi Hof.

These questionings attracted no response. The Desert watched him, but it did not answer. There was only the shrill whistling cry of the lizards, and the sing-song of a white-robed Arab gliding down the sandy street. And through these sounds he heard his own voice answer: "I will come—yes. But how can I help? Tell me what you propose—your plan?"

And the face of Vance, seen plainly in the electric glare, betrayed his satisfaction. The opposing things in the fellow's mind of darkness fought visibly in his eyes and skin. The sordid motive, planning a dreadful act, leaped to his face, and with it a flash of this other yearning that sought unearthly knowledge, perhaps believed it too. No wonder there was conflict written on his features.

Then all expression vanished again; he leaned forward, lowering his voice.

"You remember our conversation about there being types of life too vast to manifest in a single body, and my aunt's belief that these were known to certain of the older religious systems of the world?"

"Perfectly."

"Her experiment, then, is to bring one of these great Powers back—we possess the sympathetic ritual that can rouse some among them to activity—and win it down into the sphere of our minds, our minds heightened, you see, by ceremonial to that stage of clairvoyant vision which can perceive them."

"And then?" They might have been discussing the building of a house, so naturally followed answer upon question. But the whole body of meaning in the old Egyptian symbolism rushed over him with a force that shook his heart. Memory came so marvellously with it.

"If the Power floods down into our minds with sufficient strength for actual form, to note the outline of such form, and from your drawing model it later in permanent substance. Then we should have means of evoking it at will, for we should have its natural Body—the form it built itself, its signature, image, pattern. A starting-point, you see, for more—leading, she hopes, to a complete reconstruction."

"It might take actual shape—assume a bodily form visible to the eye?" repeated Henriot, amazed as before that doubt and laughter did not break through his mind.

"We are on the earth," was the reply, spoken unnecessarily low since no living thing was within earshot, "we are in physical conditions, are we not? Even a human soul we do not recognise unless we see it in a body—parents provide the outline, the signature, the sigil of the returning soul. This," and he tapped himself upon the breast, "is the physical signature of that type of life we call a soul. Unless there is life of a certain strength behind it, no body forms. And, without a body, we are helpless to control or manage it—deal with it in any way. We could not know it, though being possibly *aware* of it."

"To be aware, you mean, is not sufficient?" For he noticed the italics Vance made use of.

"Too vague, of no value for future use," was the reply. "But once obtain the form, and we have the natural symbol of that particular Power. And a symbol is more than image, it is a direct and concentrated expression of the life it typifies—possibly terrific."

"It may be a body, then, this symbol you speak of."

"Accurate vehicle of manifestation; but 'body' seems the simplest word."

Vance answered very slowly and deliberately, as though weighing how much he would tell. His language was admirably evasive. Few perhaps would have detected the profound significance the curious words he next used unquestionably concealed. Henriot's mind rejected them, but his heart accepted. For the ancient soul in him was listening and aware.

"Life, using matter to express itself in bodily shape, first traces a geometrical pattern. From the lowest form in crystals, upwards to more complicated patterns in the higher organisations—there is always first this geometrical pattern as skeleton. For geometry lies at the root of all possible phenomena; and is the mind's interpretation of a living movement towards shape that shall express it." He brought his eyes closer to the other, lowering his voice again. "Hence," he said softly, "the signs in all the old magical systems—skeleton forms into which the Powers evoked descended; outlines those Powers automatically built up when using matter to express themselves. Such signs are material symbols of their bodiless existence. They attract the life they represent and interpret. Obtain the correct, true symbol, and the Power corresponding to it can approach—once roused and made aware. It has, you see, a ready-made mould into which it can come down."

"Once roused and made aware?" repeated Henriot questioningly, while this man went stammering the letters of a language that he himself had used too long ago to recapture fully.

"Because they have left the world. They sleep, un-manifested. Their forms are no longer known to men. No forms exist on earth to-day that could contain them. But they may be awakened," he added darkly. "They are bound to answer to the summons, if such summons be accurately made."

"Evocation?" whispered Henriot, more distressed than he cared to admit.

Vance nodded. Leaning still closer, to his companion's face, he thrust his lips forward, speaking eagerly, earnestly, yet somehow at the same time, horribly: "And we want—my aunt would ask—your draughtsman's skill, or at any rate your memory afterwards, to establish the outline of anything that comes."

He waited for the answer, still keeping his face uncomfortably close.

Henriot drew back a little. But his mind was fully made up now. He had known from the beginning that he would consent, for the desire in him was stronger than all the caution in the world. The Past inexorably drew him into the circle of these other lives, and the little human dread Vance woke in him seemed just then insignificant by comparison. It was merely of To-day.

"You two," he said, trying to bring judgment into it, "engaged in evocation, will be in a state of clairvoyant vision. Granted. But shall I, as an outsider, observing with unexcited mind, see anything, know anything, be aware of anything at all, let alone the drawing of it?"

"Unless," the reply came instantly with decision, "the descent of Power is strong enough to take actual material shape, the experiment is a failure. Anybody can induce subjective vision. Such fantasies have no value though. They are born of an overwrought imagination." And then he added quickly, as though to clinch the matter before caution and hesitation could take effect: "You must watch from the heights above. We shall be in the valley—the Wadi Hof is the place. You must not be too close—"

"Why not too close?" asked Henriot, springing forward like a flash before he could prevent the sudden impulse.

With a quickness equal to his own, Vance answered. There was no faintest sign that he was surprised. His self-control was perfect. Only the glare passed darkly through his eyes and went back again into the sombre soul that bore it.

"For your own safety," he answered low. "The Power, the type of life, she would waken is stupendous. And if roused enough to be attracted by the patterned symbol into which she would decoy it down, it will take actual, physical expression. But how? Where is the Body of Worshippers through whom it can manifest? There is none. It will, therefore, press inanimate matter into the service. The terrific impulse to form itself a means of expression will force all loose matter at hand towards it—sand, stones, all it can compel to yield—everything must rush into the sphere of action in which it operates. Alone, we at the centre, and you, upon the outer fringe, will be safe. Only—you must not come too close."

But Henriot was no longer listening. His soul had turned to ice. For here, in this unguarded moment, the cloven hoof had plainly shown itself. In that suggestion of a particular kind of danger Vance had lifted a corner of the curtain behind which crouched his horrible intention. Vance desired a witness of the extraordinary experiment, but he desired this witness, not merely for the purpose of sketching possible shapes that might present themselves to excited vision. He desired a witness for another reason too. Why had Vance put that idea into his mind, this idea of so peculiar danger? It might well have lost him the very assistance he seemed so anxious to obtain.

Henriot could not fathom it quite. Only one thing was clear to him. He, Henriot, was not the only one in danger.

They talked for long after that—far into the night. The lights went out, and the armed patrol, pacing to and fro outside the iron railings that kept the desert back, eyed them curiously. But the only other thing he gathered of importance was the ledge upon the cliff-top where he was to stand and watch; that he was expected to reach there before sunset and wait till the moon concealed all glimmer in the western sky, and— that the woman, who had been engaged for days in secret preparation of soul and body for the awful rite, would not be visible again until he saw her in the depths of the black valley far below, busy with this man upon audacious, ancient purposes.

IX

An hour before sunset Henriot put his rugs and food upon a donkey, and gave the boy directions where to meet him—a considerable distance from the appointed spot. He went himself on foot. He slipped in the heat along the sandy street, where strings of camels still go slouching, shuffling with their loads from the quarries that built the pyramids, and he felt that little friendly Helouan tried to keep him back. But desire now was far too strong for caution. The desert tide was rising. It easily swept him down the long white street towards the enormous deeps beyond. He felt the pull of a thousand miles before him; and twice a thousand years drove at his back.

Everything still basked in the sunshine. He passed Al Hayat, the stately hotel that dominates the village like a palace built against the sky; and in its pillared colonnades and terraces he saw the throngs of people having late afternoon tea and listening to the music of a regimental band. Men in flannels were playing tennis, parties were climbing off donkeys after long excursions; there was laughter, talking, a babel of many voices. The gaiety called to him; the everyday spirit whispered to stay and join the crowd of lively human beings. Soon there would be merry dinner-parties, dancing, voices of pretty women, sweet white dresses, singing, and the rest. Soft eyes would question and turn dark. He picked out several girls he knew among the palms. But it was all many, oh so many leagues away; centuries lay between him and this modern world. An indescriable loneliness was in his heart. He went searching through the sands of forgotten ages, and wandering among the ruins of a vanished time. He hurried. Already the deeper water caught his breath.

He climbed the steep rise towards the plateau where the Observatory stands, and saw two of the officials whom he knew taking a siesta after their long day's work. He felt that his mind, too, had dived and searched among the heavenly bodies that live in silent, changeless peace remote from the world of men. They recognised him, these two whose eyes also knew tremendous distance close. They beckoned, waving the straws through which they sipped their drinks from tall glasses. Their voices floated down to him as from the star-fields. He saw the sun gleam upon the glasses, and heard the clink of the ice against the sides. The stillness was amazing. He waved an answer, and passed quickly on. He could not stop this sliding current of the years.

The tide moved faster, the draw of piled-up cycles urging it. He emerged upon the plateau, and met the cooler Desert air. His feet went crunching on the "desert-film" that spread its curious dark shiny carpet as far as the eye could reach; it lay everywhere, un-swept and smooth as when the feet of vanished civilizations trod its burning surface, then dipped behind the curtains Time pins against the stars. And here the body of the tide set all one way. There was a greater strength of current, draught and suction. He felt the powerful undertow. Deeper masses drew his feet sideways, and he felt the rushing of the central body of the sand. The sands were moving, from their foundation upwards. He went unresistingly with them.

Turning a moment, he looked back at shining little Helouan in the blaze of evening light. The voices reached him very faintly, merged now in a general murmur. Beyond lay the strip of Delta vivid green, the palms, the roofs of Bedrashein, the blue laughter of the Nile with its flocks of curved felucca sails. Further still, rising above the yellow Libyan horizon, gloomed the vast triangles of a dozen Pyramids, cutting their wedge-shaped clefts out of a sky fast crimsoning through a sea of gold. Seen thus, their dignity imposed upon the entire landscape. They towered darkly, symbolic signatures of the ancient Powers that now watched him taking these little steps across their damaged territory.

He gazed a minute, then went on. He saw the big pale face of the moon in the east. Above the ever-silent Thing these giant symbols once interpreted, she rose, grand, effortless, half-terrible as themselves. And, with her, she lifted up this tide of the Desert that drew his feet across the sand to Wadi Hof. A moment later he dipped below the ridge that buried Helouan and Nile and Pyramids from sight. He entered the ancient waters. Time then, in an instant, flowed back behind his footsteps, obliterating every trace. And with it his mind went too. He stepped across the gulf of centuries, moving into the Past. The Desert lay before him—an open tomb wherein his soul should read presently of things long vanished.

The strange half-lights of sunset began to play their witchery then upon the landscape. A purple glow came down upon the Mokattam Hills. Perspective danced its tricks of false, incredible deception. The soaring kites that were a mile away seemed suddenly close, passing in a moment from the size of gnats to birds with a fabulous stretch of wing. Ridges and cliffs rushed close without a hint of warning, and level places sank into declivities and basins that made him trip and stumble. That indescribable quality of the Desert, which makes timid souls avoid the hour of dusk, emerged; it spread everywhere, undisguised. And the bewilderment it brings is no vain, imagined thing, for it distorts vision utterly, and the effect upon the mind when familiar sight goes floundering is the simplest way in the world of dragging the anchor that grips reality. At the hour of sunset this bewilderment comes upon a man with a disconcerting swiftness. It rose now with all this weird rapidity. Henriot found himself enveloped at a moment's notice.

But, knowing well its effect, he tried to judge it and pass on. The other matters, the object of his journey chief of all, he refused to dwell upon with any imagination. Wisely, his mind, while never losing sight of it, declined to admit the exaggeration that over-elaborate thinking brings. "I'm going to witness an incredible experiment in which two enthusiastic religious dreamers believe firmly," he repeated to himself. "I have agreed to draw—anything I see. There may be truth in it, or they may be merely self-suggested vision due to an artificial exaltation of their minds. I'm interested—perhaps against my better judgment. Yet I'll see the adventure out—because I *must*."

This was the attitude he told himself to take. Whether it was the real one, or merely adopted to warm a cooling courage, he could not tell. The emotions were so complex and warring. His mind, automatically, kept repeating this comforting formula. Deeper than that he could not see to judge. For a man who knew the full content of his thought at such a time would solve some of the oldest psychological problems in the world. Sand had already buried judgment, and with it all attempt to explain the adventure by the standards acceptable to his brain of to-day. He steered subconsciously through a world of dim, huge, half-remembered wonders.

The sun, with that abrupt Egyptian suddenness, was below the horizon now. The pyramid field had swallowed it. Ra, in his golden boat, sailed distant seas beyond the Libyan wilderness. Henriot walked on and on, aware of utter loneliness. He was walking fields of dream, too remote from modern life to recall companionship he once had surely known. How dim it was, how deep and distant, how lost in this sea of an incalculable Past! He walked into the places that are soundless. The soundlessness of ocean, miles below the surface, was about him. He was with One only—this unfathomable, silent thing where nothing breathes or stirs—nothing but sunshine, shadow and the wind-borne sand. Slowly, in front, the moon climbed up the eastern sky, hanging above the silence—silence that ran unbroken across the horizons to where Suez gleamed upon the waters of a sister sea in motion. That moon was glinting now upon the Arabian Mountains by its desolate shores. Southwards stretched the wastes of Upper Egypt a thousand miles to meet the Nubian wilderness. But over all these separate Deserts stirred the soft whisper of the moving sand—deep murmuring message that Life was on the way to unwind Death. The Ka of Egypt, swathed in centuries of sand, hovered beneath the moon towards her ancient tenement.

For the transformation of the Desert now began in earnest. It grew apace. Before he had gone the first two miles of his hour's journey, the twilight caught the rocky hills and twisted them into those monstrous revelations of physiognomies they barely take the trouble to conceal even in the daytime. And, while he well understood the eroding agencies that have produced them, there yet rose in his mind a deeper interpretation lurking just behind their literal meanings. Here, through the motionless surfaces, that nameless thing the Desert ill conceals urged outwards into embryonic form and shape, akin, he almost felt, to those immense deific symbols of Other Life the Egyptians knew and worshipped. Hence, from the Desert, had first come, he felt, the unearthly life they typified in their monstrous figures of granite, evoked in their stately temples, and communed with in the ritual of their Mystery ceremonials.

This "watching" aspect of the Libyan Desert is really natural enough; but it is just the natural, Henriot knew, that brings the deepest revelations. The surface limestones, resisting the erosion, block themselves ominously against the sky, while the softer sand beneath sets them on altared pedestals that define their isolation splendidly. Blunt and unconquerable, these masses now watched him pass between them. The Desert surface formed them, gave them birth. They rose, they saw, they sank down again—waves upon a sea that carried forgotten life up from the depths below. Of forbidding, even menacing type, they somewhere mated with genuine grandeur. Unformed, according to any standard of human or of animal faces, they achieved an air of giant physiognomy which made them terrible. The un-winking stare of eyes—lidless eyes that yet ever succeed in hiding—looked out under well-marked, level eyebrows, suggesting a vision that included the motives and purposes of his very heart. They looked up grandly, understood why he was there, and then—slowly withdrew their mysterious, penetrating gaze.

The strata built them so marvellously up; the heavy, threatening brows; thick lips, curved by the ages into a semblance of cold smiles; jowls drooping into sandy heaps that climbed against the cheeks; protruding jaws, and the suggestion of shoulders just about to lift the entire bodies out of the sandy beds—this host of countenances conveyed a solemnity of expression that seemed everlasting, implacable as Death. Of human signature they bore no trace, nor was comparison possible between their kind and any animal life. They peopled the Desert here. And their smiles, concealed yet just discernible, went broadening with the darkness into a Desert laughter. The silence bore it underground. But Henriot was aware of it. The troop of faces slipped into that single, enormous countenance which is the visage of the Sand. And he saw it everywhere, yet nowhere.

Thus with the darkness grew his imaginative interpretation of the Desert. Yet there was construction in it, a construction, moreover, that was *not* entirely his own. Powers, he felt, were rising, stirring, wakening from sleep. Behind the natural faces that he saw, these other things peered gravely at him as he passed. They used, as it were, materials that lay ready to their hand. Imagination furnished these hints of outline, yet the Powers themselves were real. There *was* this amazing movement of the sand. By no other manner could his mind have conceived of such a thing, nor dreamed of this simple, yet dreadful method of approach.

Approach! that was the word that first stood out and startled him. There was approach; something was drawing nearer. The Desert rose and walked beside him. For not alone these ribs of gleaming limestone contributed towards the elemental visages, but the entire hills, of which they were an outcrop, ran to assist in the formation, and were a necessary part of them. He was watched and stared at from behind, in front, on either side, and even from below. The sand that swept him on, kept even pace with him. It turned luminous too, with a patchwork of glimmering effect that was indescribably weird; lanterns glowed within its substance, and by their light he stumbled on, glad of the Arab boy he would presently meet at the appointed place.

The last torch of the sunset had flickered out, melting into the wilderness, when, suddenly opening at his feet, gaped the deep, wide gully known as Wadi Hof. Its curve swept past him.

This first impression came upon him with a certain violence: that the desolate valley rushed. He saw but a section of its curve and sweep, but through its entire length of several miles the Wadi fled away. The moon whitened it like snow, piling black shadows very close against the cliffs. In the flood of moonlight it went rushing past. It was emptying itself.

For a moment the stream of movement seemed to pause and look up into his face, then instantly went on again upon its swift career. It was like the procession of a river to the sea. The valley emptied itself to make way for what was coming. The approach, moreover, had already begun.

Conscious that he was trembling, he stood and gazed into the depths, seeking to steady his mind by the repetition of the little formula he had used before. He said it half aloud. But, while he did so, his heart whispered quite other things. Thoughts the woman and the man had sown rose up in a flock and fell upon him like a storm of sand. Their impetus drove off all support of ordinary ideas. They shook him where he stood, staring down into this river of strange invisible movement that was hundreds of feet in depth and a quarter of a mile across.

He sought to realise himself as he actually was to-day—mere visitor to Helouan, tempted into this wild adventure with two strangers. But in vain. That seemed a dream, unreal, a transient detail picked out from the enormous Past that now engulfed him, heart and mind and soul. *This* was the reality.

The shapes and faces that the hills of sand built round him were the play of excited fancy only. By sheer force he pinned his thought against this fact: but further he could not get. There were Powers at work; they were being stirred, wakened somewhere into activity. Evocation had already begun. That sense of their approach as he had walked along from Helouan was not imaginary. A descent of some type of life, vanished from the world too long for recollection, was on the way,—so vast that it would manifest itself in a group of forms, a troop, a host, an army. These two were near him somewhere at this very moment, already long at work, their minds driving beyond this little world. The valley was emptying itself—for the descent of life their ritual invited.

And the movement in the sand was likewise true. He recalled the sentences the woman had used. "My body," he reflected, "like the bodies life makes use of everywhere, is mere upright heap of earth and dust and—sand. Here in the Desert is the raw material, the greatest store of it in the world."

And on the heels of it came sharply that other thing: that this descending Life would press into its service all loose matter within its reach—to form that sphere of action which would be in a literal sense its Body.

In the first few seconds, as he stood there, he realised all this, and realised it with an overwhelming conviction it was futile to deny. The fast-emptying valley would later brim with an unaccustomed and terrific life. Yet Death hid there too—a little, ugly, insignificant death. With the name of Vance it flashed upon his mind and vanished, too tiny to be thought about in this torrent of grander messages that shook the depths within his soul. He bowed his head a moment, hardly knowing what he did. He could have waited thus a thousand years it seemed. He was conscious of a wild desire to run away, to hide, to efface himself utterly, his terror, his curiosity, his little wonder, and not be seen of anything. But it was all vain and foolish. The Desert saw him. The Gigantic knew that he was there. No escape was possible any longer. Caught by the sand, he stood amid eternal things. The river of movement swept him too.

These hills, now motionless as statues, would presently glide forward into the cavalcade, sway like vessels, and go past with the procession. At present only the contents, not the frame, of the Wadi moved. An immense soft brush of moonlight swept it empty for what was on the way. . . . But presently the entire Desert would stand up and also go.

Then, making a sideways movement, his feet kicked against something soft and yielding that lay heaped upon the Desert floor, and Henriot discovered the rugs the Arab boy had carefully set down before he made full speed for the friendly lights of Helouan. The sound of his departing footsteps had long since died away. He was alone.

The detail restored to him his consciousness of the immediate present, and, stooping, he gathered up the rugs and overcoat and began to make preparations for the night. But the appointed spot, whence he was to watch, lay upon the summit of the opposite cliffs. He must cross the Wadi bed and climb. Slowly and with labour he made his way down a steep cleft into the depth of the Wadi Hof, sliding and stumbling often, till at length he stood upon the floor of shining moonlight. It was very smooth; windless utterly; still as space; each particle of sand lay in its ancient place asleep. The movement, it seemed, had ceased.

He clambered next up the eastern side, through pitch-black shadows, and within the hour reached the ledge upon the top whence he could see below him, like a silvered map, the sweep of the valley bed. The wind nipped keenly here again, coming over the leagues of cooling sand. Loose boulders of splintered rock, started by his climbing, crashed and boomed into the depths. He banked the rugs behind him, wrapped himself in his overcoat, and lay down to wait. Behind him was a two-foot crumbling wall against which he leaned; in front a drop of several hundred feet through space. He lay upon a platform, therefore, invisible from the Desert at his back. Below, the curving Wadi formed a natural amphitheatre in which each separate boulder fallen from the cliffs, and even the little *silla* shrubs the camels eat, were plainly visible. He noted all the bigger ones among them. He counted them over half aloud.

And the moving stream he had been unaware of when crossing the bed itself, now began again. The Wadi went rushing past before the broom of moonlight. Again, the enormous and the tiny combined in one single strange impression. For, through this conception of great movement, stirred also a roving, delicate touch that his imagination felt as bird-like. Behind the solid mass of the Desert's immobility flashed something swift and light and airy. Bizarre pictures interpreted it to him, like rapid snap-shots of a huge flying panorama: he thought of darting dragon-flies seen at Helouan, of children's little dancing feet, of twinkling butterflies—of birds. Chiefly, yes, of a flock of birds in flight, whose separate units formed a single entity. The idea of the Group-Soul possessed his mind once more. But it came with a sense of more than curiosity or wonder. Veneration lay behind it, a veneration touched with awe. It rose in his deepest thought that here was the first hint of a symbolical representation. A symbol, sacred and inviolable, belonging to some ancient worship that he half remembered in his soul, stirred towards interpretation through all his being.

He lay there waiting, wondering vaguely where his two companions were, yet fear all vanished because he felt attuned to a scale of things too big to mate with definite dread. There was high anticipation in him, but not anxiety. Of himself, as Felix Henriot, indeed, he hardly seemed aware. He was some one else. Or, rather, he was himself at a stage he had known once far, far away in a remote pre-existence. He watched himself from dim summits of a Past, of which no further details were as yet recoverable.

Pencil and sketching-block lay ready to his hand. The moon rose higher, tucking the shadows ever more closely against the precipices. The silver passed into a sheet of snowy whiteness, that made every boulder clearly visible. Solemnity deepened everywhere into awe. The Wadi fled silently down the stream of hours. It was almost empty now. And then, abruptly, he was aware of change. The motion altered somewhere. It moved more quietly; pace slackened; the end of the procession that evacuated the depth and length of it went trailing past and turned the distant bend.

"It's slowing up," he whispered, as sure of it as though he had watched a regiment of soldiers filing by. The wind took off his voice like a flying feather of sound.

And there *was* a change. It had begun. Night and the moon stood still to watch and listen. The wind dropped utterly away. The sand ceased its shifting movement. The Desert everywhere stopped still, and turned.

Some curtain, then, that for centuries had veiled the world, drew softly up, leaving a shaded vista down which the eyes of his soul peered towards long-forgotten pictures. Still buried by the sands too deep for full recovery, he yet perceived dim portions of them—things once honoured and loved passionately. For once they had surely been to him the whole of life, not merely a fragment for cheap wonder to inspect. And they were curiously familiar, even as the person of this woman who now evoked them was familiar. Henriot made no pretence to more definite remembrance; but the haunting certainty rushed over him, deeper than doubt or denial, and with such force that he felt no effort to destroy it. Some lost sweetness of spiritual ambitions, lived for with this passionate devotion, and passionately worshipped as men to-day worship fame and money, revived in him with a tempest of high glory. Centres of memory stirred from an age-long sleep, so that he could have wept at their so complete obliteration hitherto. That such majesty had departed from the world as though it never had existed, was a thought for desolation and for tears. And though the little fragment he was about to witness might be crude in itself and incomplete, yet it was part of a vast system that once explored the richest realms of deity. The reverence in him contained a holiness of the night and of the stars; great, gentle awe lay in it too; for he stood, aflame with anticipation and humility, at the gateway of sacred things.

And this was the mood, no thrill of cheap excitement or alarm to weaken in, in which he first became aware that two spots of darkness he had taken all along for boulders on the snowy valley bed, were actually something very different. They were living figures. They moved. It was not the shadows slowly following the moonlight, but the stir of human beings who all these hours had been motionless as stone. He must have passed them unnoticed within a dozen yards when he crossed the Wadi bed, and a hundred times from this very ledge his eyes had surely rested on them without recognition. Their minds, he knew full well, had not been inactive as their bodies. The important part of the ancient ritual lay, he remembered, in the powers of the evoking mind.

Here, indeed, was no effective nor theatrical approach of the principal figures. It had nothing in common with the cheap external ceremonial of modern days. In forgotten powers of the soul its grandeur lay, potent, splendid, true. Long before he came, perhaps all through the day, these two had laboured with their arduous preparations. They were there, part of the Desert, when hours ago he had crossed the plateau in the twilight. To them—to this woman's potent working of old ceremonial—had been due that singular rush of imagination he had felt. He had interpreted the Desert as alive. Here was the explanation. It *was* alive. Life was on the way. Long latent, her intense desire summoned it back to physical expression; and the effect upon him had steadily increased as he drew nearer to the centre where she would focus its revival and return. Those singular impressions of being watched and accompanied were explained. A priest of this old-world worship performed a genuine evocation; a Great One of Vision revived the cosmic Powers.

Henriot watched the small figures far below him with a sense of dramatic splendour that only this association of far-off Memory could account for. It was their rising now, and the lifting of their arms to form a slow revolving outline, that marked the abrupt cessation of the larger river of movement; for the sweeping of the Wadi sank into sudden stillness, and these two, with motions not unlike some dance of deliberate solemnity, passed slowly through the moonlight to and fro. His attention fixed upon them both. All other movement ceased. They fastened the flow of Time against the Desert's body.

What happened then? How could his mind interpret an experience so long denied that the power of expression, as of comprehension, has ceased to exist? How translate this symbolical representation, small detail though it was, of a transcendent worship entombed for most so utterly beyond recovery? Its splendour could never lodge in minds that conceive Deity perched upon a cloud within telephoning distance of fashionable churches. How should he phrase it even to himself, whose memory drew up pictures from so dim a past that the language fit to frame them lay unreachable and lost?

Henriot did not know. Perhaps he never yet has known. Certainly, at the time, he did not even try to think. His sensations remain his own—untranslatable; and even that instinctive description the mind gropes for automatically, floundered, halted, and stopped dead. Yet there rose within him somewhere, from depths long drowned in slumber, a reviving power by which he saw, divined and recollected— remembered seemed too literal a word—these elements of a worship he once had personally known. He, too, had worshipped thus. His soul had moved amid similar evocations in some aeonian past, whence now the sand was being cleared away. Symbols of stupendous meaning flashed and went their way across the lifting mists. He hardly caught their meaning, so long it was since he had known them; yet they were familiar as the faces seen in dreams, and some hint of their spiritual significance left faint traces in his heart by means of which their grandeur reached towards interpretation. And all were symbols of a cosmic, deific nature; of Powers that only symbols can express— prayer-books and sacraments used in the Wisdom Religion of an older time, but to-day known only in the decrepit, literal shell which is their degradation.

Grandly the figures moved across the valley bed. The powers of the heavenly bodies once more joined them. They moved to the measure of a cosmic dance, whose rhythm was creative. The Universe partnered them.

There was this transfiguration of all common, external things. He realised that appearances were visible letters of a soundless language, a language he once had known. The powers of night and moon and desert sand married with points in the fluid stream of his inmost spiritual being that knew and welcomed them. He understood.

Old Egypt herself stooped down from her uncovered throne. The stars sent messengers. There was commotion in the secret, sandy places of the desert. For the Desert had grown Temple. Columns reared against the sky. There rose, from leagues away, the chanting of the sand.

The temples, where once this came to pass, were gone, their ruin questioned by alien hearts that knew not their spiritual meaning. But here the entire Desert swept in to form a shrine, and the Majesty that once was Egypt stepped grandly back across ages of denial and neglect. The sand was altar, and the stars were altar lights. The moon lit up the vast recesses of the ceiling, and the wind from a thousand miles brought in the perfume of her incense. For with that faith which shifts mountains from their sandy bed, two passionate, believing souls invoked the Ka of Egypt.

And the motions that they made, he saw, were definite harmonious patterns their dark figures traced upon the shining valley floor. Like the points of compasses, with stems invisible, and directed from the sky, their movements marked the outlines of great signatures of power—the sigils of the type of life they would evoke. It would come as a Procession. No individual outline could contain it. It needed for its visible expression—many. The descent of a group-soul, known to the worship of this mighty system, rose from its lair of centuries and moved hugely down upon them. The Ka, answering to the summons, would mate with sand. The Desert was its Body.

Yet it was not this that he had come to fix with block and pencil. Not yet was the moment when his skill might be of use. He waited, watched, and listened, while this river of half-remembered things went past him. The patterns grew beneath his eyes like music. Too intricate and prolonged to remember with accuracy later, he understood that they were forms of that root-geometry which lies behind all manifested life. The mould was being traced in outline. Life would presently inform it. And a singing rose from the maze of lines whose beauty was like the beauty of the constellations.

This sound was very faint at first, but grew steadily in volume. Although no echoes, properly speaking, were possible, these precipices caught stray notes that trooped in from the further sandy reaches. The figures certainly were chanting, but their chanting was not all he heard. Other sounds came to his ears from far away, running past him through the air from every side, and from incredible distances, all flocking down into the Wadi bed to join the parent note that summoned them. The Desert was giving voice. And memory, lifting her hood yet higher, showed more of her grey, mysterious face that searched his soul with questions. Had he so soon forgotten that strange union of form and sound which once was known to the evocative rituals of olden days?

Henriot tried patiently to disentangle this desert-music that their intoning voices woke, from the humming of the blood in his own veins. But he succeeded only in part. Sand was already in the air. There was reverberation, rhythm, measure; there was almost the breaking of the stream into great syllables. But was it due, this strange reverberation, to the countless particles of sand meeting in mid-air about him, or—to larger bodies, whose surfaces caught this friction of the sand and threw it back against his ears? The wind, now rising, brought particles that stung his face and hands, and filled his eyes with a minute fine dust that partially veiled the moonlight. But was not something larger, vaster these particles composed now also on the way?

Movement and sound and flying sand thus merged themselves more and more in a single, whirling torrent. But Henriot sought no commonplace explanation of what he witnessed; and here was the proof that all happened in some vestibule of inner experience where the strain of question and answer had no business. One sitting beside him need not have seen anything at all. His host, for instance, from Helouan, need not have been aware. Night screened it; Helouan, as the whole of modern experience, stood in front of the screen. This thing took place behind it. He crouched motionless, watching in some reconstructed ante-chamber of the soul's pre-existence, while the torrent grew into a veritable tempest.

Yet Night remained unshaken; the veil of moonlight did not quiver; the stars dropped their slender golden pillars unobstructed. Calmness reigned everywhere as before. The stupendous representation passed on behind it all.

But the dignity of the little human movements that he watched had become now indescribable. The gestures of the arms and bodies invested themselves with consummate grandeur, as these two strode into the caverns behind manifested life and drew forth symbols that represented vanished Powers. The sound of their chanting voices broke in cadenced fragments against the shores of language. The words Henriot never actually caught, if words they were; yet he understood their purport—these Names of Power to which the type of returning life gave answer as they approached. He remembered fumbling for his drawing materials, with such violence, however, that the pencil snapped in two between his fingers as he touched it. For now, even here, upon the outer fringe of the ceremonial ground, there was a stir of forces that set the very muscles working in him before he had become aware of it. . . .

Then came the moment when his heart leaped against his ribs with a sudden violence that was almost pain, standing a second later still as death. The lines upon the valley floor ceased their maze-like dance. All movement stopped. Sound died away. In the midst of this profound and dreadful silence the sigils lay empty there below him. They waited to be in-formed. For the moment of entrance had come at last. Life was close.

And he understood why this return of life had all along suggested a Procession and could be no mere momentary flash of vision. From such appalling distance did it sweep down towards the present.

Upon this network, then, of splendid lines, at length held rigid, the entire Desert reared itself with walls of curtained sand, that dwarfed the cliffs, the shouldering hills, the very sky. The Desert stood on end. As once before he had dreamed it from his balcony windows, it rose upright, towering, and close against his face. It built sudden ramparts to the stars that chambered the thing he witnessed behind walls no centuries could ever bring down crumbling into dust.

He himself, in some curious fashion, lay just outside, viewing it apart. As from a pinnacle, he peered within—peered down with straining eyes into the vast picture-gallery Memory threw abruptly open. And the picture spaced its noble outline thus against the very stars. He gazed between columns, that supported the sky itself, like pillars of sand that swept across the field of vanished years. Sand poured and streamed aside, laying bare the Past.

For down the enormous vista into which he gazed, as into an avenue running a million miles towards a tiny point, he saw this moving Thing that came towards him, shaking loose the countless veils of sand the ages had swathed about it. The Ka of buried Egypt wakened out of sleep. She had heard the potent summons of her old, time-honoured ritual. She came. She stretched forth an arm towards the worshippers who evoked her. Out of the Desert, out of the leagues of sand, out of the immeasurable wilderness which was her mummied Form and Body, she rose and came. And this fragment of her he would actually see—this little portion that was obedient to the stammered and broken ceremonial. The partial revelation he would witness—yet so vast, even this little bit of it, that it came as a Procession and a host.

For a moment there was nothing. And then the voice of the woman rose in a resounding cry that filled the Wadi to its furthest precipices, before it died away again to silence. That a human voice could produce such volume, accent, depth, seemed half incredible. The walls of towering sand swallowed it instantly. But the Procession of life, needing a group, a host, an army for its physical expression, reached at that moment the nearer end of the huge avenue. It touched the Present; it entered the world of men.

X

The entire range of Henriot's experience, read, imagined, dreamed, then fainted into unreality before the sheer wonder of what he saw. In the brief interval it takes to snap the fingers the climax was thus so hurriedly upon him. And, through it all, he was clearly aware of the pair of little human figures, man and woman, standing erect and commanding at the centre—knew, too, that she directed and controlled, while he in some secondary fashion supported her—and ever watched. But both were dim, dropped somewhere into a lesser scale. It was the knowledge of their presence, however, that alone enabled him to keep his powers in hand at all. But for these two *human* beings there within possible reach, he must have closed his eyes and swooned.

For a tempest that seemed to toss loose stars about the sky swept round about him, pouring up the pillared avenue in front of the procession. A blast of giant energy, of liberty, came through. Forwards and backwards, circling spirally about him like a whirlwind, came this revival of Life that sought to dip itself once more in matter and in form. It came to the accurate out-line of its form they had traced for it. He held his mind steady enough to realise that it was akin to what men call a "descent" of some "spiritual movement" that wakens a body of believers into faith—a race, an entire nation; only that he experienced it in this brief, concentrated form before it has scattered down into ten thousand hearts. Here he knew its source and essence, behind the veil.

Crudely, unmanageable as yet, he felt it, rushing loose behind appearances. There was this amazing impact of a twisting, swinging force that stormed down as though it would bend and coil the very ribs of the old stubborn hills. It sought to warm them with the stress of its own irresistible life-stream, to beat them into shape, and make pliable their obstinate resistance. Through all things the impulse poured and spread, like fire at white heat.

Yet nothing visible came as yet, no alteration in the actual landscape, no sign of change in things familiar to his eyes, while impetus thus fought against inertia. He perceived nothing formal. Calm and untouched himself, he lay outside the circle of evocation, watching, waiting, scarcely daring to breathe, yet well aware that any minute the scene would transfer itself from memory that was subjective to matter that was objective.

And then, in a flash, the bridge was built, and the transfer was accomplished. How or where he did not see, he could not tell. It was there before he knew it—there before his normal, earthly sight. He saw it, as he saw the hands he was holding stupidly up to shield his face. For this terrific release of force long held back, long stored up, latent for centuries, came pouring down the empty Wadi bed prepared for its reception. Through stones and sand and boulders it came in an impetuous hurricane of power. The liberation of its life appalled him. All that was free, untied, responded instantly like chaff; loose objects fled towards it; there was a yielding in the hills and precipices; and even in the mass of Desert which provided their foundation. The hinges of the Sand went creaking in the night. It shaped for itself a bodily outline.

Yet, most strangely, nothing definitely moved. How could he express the violent contradiction? For the immobility was apparent only—a sham, a counterfeit; while behind it the essential *being* of these things did rush and shift and alter. He saw the two things side by side: the outer immobility the senses commonly agree upon, *and* this amazing flying-out of their inner, invisible substance towards the vortex of attracting life that sucked them in. For stubborn matter turned docile before the stress of this returning life, taught somewhere to be plastic. It was being moulded into an approach to bodily outline. A mobile elasticity invaded rigid substance. The two officiating human beings, safe at the stationary centre, and himself, just outside the circle of operation, alone remained untouched and unaffected. But a few feet in any direction, for any one of them, meant—instantaneous death. They would be absorbed into the vortex, mere corpuscles pressed into the service of this sphere of action of a mighty Body. . . .

How these perceptions reached him with such conviction, Henriot could never say. He knew it, because he *felt* it. Something fell about him from the sky that already paled towards the dawn. The stars themselves, it seemed, contributed some part of the terrific, flowing impulse that conquered matter and shaped itself this physical expression.

Then, before he was able to fashion any preconceived idea of what visible form this potent life might assume, he was aware of further change. It came at the briefest possible interval after the beginning—this certainty that, to and fro about him, as yet however indeterminate, passed Magnitudes that were stupendous as the desert. There was beauty in them too, though a terrible beauty hardly of this earth at all. A fragment of old Egypt had returned—a little portion of that vast Body of Belief that once was Egypt. Evoked by the worship of one human heart, passionately sincere, the Ka of Egypt stepped back to visit the material it once informed—the Sand.

Yet only a portion came. Henriot clearly realised that. It stretched forth an arm. Finding no mass of worshippers through whom it might express itself completely, it pressed inanimate matter thus into its service.

Here was the beginning the woman had spoken of—little opening clue. Entire reconstruction lay perhaps beyond.

And Henriot next realised that these Magnitudes in which this group-energy sought to clothe itself as visible form, were curiously familiar. It was not a new thing that he would see. Booming softly as they dropped downwards through the sky, with a motion the size of them rendered delusive, they trooped up the Avenue towards the central point that summoned them. He realised the giant flock of them—descent of fearful beauty—outlining a type of life denied to the world for ages, countless as this sand that blew against his skin. Careering over the waste of Desert moved the army of dark Splendours, that dwarfed any organic structure called a body men have ever known. He recognised them, cold in him of death, though the outlines reared higher than the pyramids, and towered up to hide whole groups of stars. Yes, he recognised them in their partial revelation, though he never saw the monstrous host complete. But, one of them, he realised, posing its eternal riddle to the sands, had of old been glimpsed sufficiently to seize its form in stone,—yet poorly seized, as a doll may stand for the dignity of a human being or a child's toy represent an engine that draws trains. . . .

And he knelt there on his narrow ledge, the world of men forgotten. The power that caught him was too great a thing for wonder or for fear; he even felt no awe. Sensation of any kind that can be named or realised left him utterly. He forgot himself. He merely watched. The glory numbed him. Block and pencil, as the reason of his presence there at all, no longer existed. . . .

Yet one small link remained that held him to some kind of consciousness of earthly things: he never lost sight of this—that, being just outside the circle of evocation, he was safe, and that the man and woman, being stationary in its untouched centre, were also safe. But— that a movement of six inches in any direction meant for any one of them instant death.

What was it, then, that suddenly strengthened this solitary link so that the chain tautened and he felt the pull of it? Henriot could not say. He came back with the rush of a descending drop to the realisation— dimly, vaguely, as from great distance—that he was with these two, now at this moment, in the Wadi Hof, and that the cold of dawn was in the air about him. The chill breath of the Desert made him shiver.

But at first, so deeply had his soul been dipped in this fragment of ancient worship, he could remember nothing more. Somewhere lay a little spot of streets and houses; its name escaped him. He had once been there; there were many people, but insignificant people. Who were they? And what had he to do with them? All recent memories had been drowned in the tide that flooded him from an immeasurable Past.

And who were they—these two beings, standing on the white floor of sand below him? For a long time he could not recover their names. Yet he remembered them; and, thus robbed of association that names bring, he saw them for an instant naked, and knew that one of them was evil. One of them was vile. Blackness touched the picture there. The man, his name still out of reach, was sinister, impure and dark at the heart. And for this reason the evocation had been partial only. The admixture of an evil motive was the flaw that marred complete success.

The names then flashed upon him—Lady Statham—Richard Vance.

Vance! With a horrid drop from splendour into something mean and sordid, Henriot felt the pain of it. The motive of the man was so insignificant, his purpose so atrocious. More and more, with the name, came back—his first repugnance, fear, suspicion. And human terror caught him. He shrieked. But, as in nightmare, no sound escaped his lips. He tried to move; a wild desire to interfere, to protect, to prevent, flung him forward—close to the dizzy edge of the gulf below. But his muscles refused obedience to the will. The paralysis of common fear rooted him to the rocks.

But the sudden change of focus instantly destroyed the picture; and so vehement was the fall from glory into meanness, that it dislocated the machinery of clairvoyant vision. The inner perception clouded and grew dark. Outer and inner mingled in violent, inextricable confusion. The wrench seemed almost physical. It happened all at once, retreat and continuation for a moment somehow combined. And, if he did not definitely see the awful thing, at least he was aware that it had come to pass. He knew it as positively as though his eye were glued against a magnifying lens in the stillness of some laboratory. He witnessed it.

The supreme moment of evocation was close. Life, through that awful sandy vortex, whirled and raged. Loose particles showered and pelted, caught by the draught of vehement life that moulded the substance of the Desert into imperial outline—when, suddenly, shot the little evil thing across that marred and blasted it.

Into the whirlpool flew forward a particle of material that was a human being. And the Group-Soul caught and used it.

The actual accomplishment Henriot did not claim to see. He was a witness, but a witness who could give no evidence. Whether the woman was pushed of set intention, or whether some detail of sound and pattern was falsely used to effect the terrible result, he was helpless to determine. He pretends no itemised account. She went. In one second, with appalling swiftness, she disappeared, swallowed out of space and time within that awful maw—one little corpuscle among a million through which the Life, now stalking the Desert wastes, moulded itself a troop-like Body. Sand took her.

There followed emptiness—a hush of unutterable silence, stillness, peace. Movement and sound instantly retired whence they came. The avenues of Memory closed; the Splendours all went down into their sandy tombs. . . .

The moon had sunk into the Libyan wilderness; the eastern sky was red. The dawn drew out that wondrous sweetness of the Desert, which is as sister to the sweetness that the moonlight brings. The Desert settled back to sleep, huge, unfathomable, charged to the brim with life that watches, waits, and yet conceals itself behind the ruins of apparent desolation. And the Wadi, empty at his feet, filled slowly with the gentle little winds that bring the sunrise.

Then, across the pale glimmering of sand, Henriot saw a figure moving. It came quickly towards him, yet unsteadily, and with a hurry that was ugly. Vance was on the way to fetch him. And the horror of the man's approach struck him like a hammer in the face. He closed his eyes, sinking back to hide.

But, before he swooned, there reached him the clatter of the murderer's tread as he began to climb over the splintered rocks, and the faint echo of his voice, calling him by name—falsely and in pretence—for help.

The Man Who Found Out

(A NIGHTMARE)

I

Professor Mark Ebor, the scientist, led a double life, and the only persons who knew it were his assistant, Dr. Laidlaw, and his publishers. But a double life need not always be a bad one, and, as Dr. Laidlaw and the gratified publishers well knew, the parallel lives of this particular man were equally good, and indefinitely produced would certainly have ended in a heaven somewhere that can suitably contain such strangely opposite characteristics as his remarkable personality combined.

For Mark Ebor, F.R.S., etc., etc., was that unique combination hardly ever met with in actual life, a man of science and a mystic.

As the first, his name stood in the gallery of the great, and as the second—but there came the mystery! For under the pseudonym of "Pilgrim" (the author of that brilliant series of books that appealed to so many), his identity was as well concealed as that of the anonymous writer of the weather reports in a daily newspaper. Thousands read the sanguine, optimistic, stimulating little books that issued annually from the pen of "Pilgrim," and thousands bore their daily burdens better for having read; while the Press generally agreed that the author, besides being an incorrigible enthusiast and optimist, was also—a woman; but no one ever succeeded in penetrating the veil of anonymity and discovering that "Pilgrim" and the biologist were one and the same person.

Mark Ebor, as Dr. Laidlaw knew him in his laboratory, was one man; but Mark Ebor, as he sometimes saw him after work was over, with rapt eyes and ecstatic face, discussing the possibilities of "union with God" and the future of the human race, was quite another.

"I have always held, as you know," he was saying one evening as he sat in the little study beyond the laboratory with his assistant and intimate, "that Vision should play a large part in the life of the awakened man—not to be regarded as infallible, of course, but to be observed and made use of as a guide-post to possibilities—"

"I am aware of your peculiar views, sir," the young doctor put in deferentially, yet with a certain impatience.

"For Visions come from a region of the consciousness where observation and experiment are out of the question," pursued the other with enthusiasm, not noticing the interruption, "and, while they should be checked by reason afterwards, they should not be laughed at or ignored. All inspiration, I hold, is of the nature of interior Vision, and

414 *The Man Who Found Out*

all our best knowledge has come—such is my confirmed belief—as a sudden revelation to the brain prepared to receive it—"

"Prepared by hard work first, by concentration, by the closest possible study of ordinary phenomena," Dr. Laidlaw allowed himself to observe.

"Perhaps," sighed the other; "but by a process, none the less, of spiritual illumination. The best match in the world will not light a candle unless the wick be first suitably prepared."

It was Laidlaw's turn to sigh. He knew so well the impossibility of arguing with his chief when he was in the regions of the mystic, but at the same time the respect he felt for his tremendous attainments was so sincere that he always listened with attention and deference, wondering how far the great man would go and to what end this curious combination of logic and "illumination" would eventually lead him.

"Only last night," continued the elder man, a sort of light coming into his rugged features, "the vision came to me again—the one that has haunted me at intervals ever since my youth, and that will not be denied."

Dr. Laidlaw fidgeted in his chair.

"About the Tablets of the Gods, you mean—and that they lie somewhere hidden in the sands," he said patiently. A sudden gleam of interest came into his face as he turned to catch the professor's reply.

"And that I am to be the one to find them, to decipher them, and to give the great knowledge to the world—"

"Who will not believe," laughed Laidlaw shortly, yet interested in spite of his thinly-veiled contempt.

"Because even the keenest minds, in the right sense of the word, are hopelessly—unscientific," replied the other gently, his face positively aglow with the memory of his vision. "Yet what is more likely," he continued after a moment's pause, peering into space with rapt eyes that saw things too wonderful for exact language to describe, "than that there should have been given to man in the first ages of the world some record of the purpose and problem that had been set him to solve? In a word," he cried, fixing his shining eyes upon the face of his perplexed assistant, "that God's messengers in the far-off ages should have given to His creatures some full statement of the secret of the world, of the secret of the soul, of the meaning of life and death—the explanation of our being here, and to what great end we are destined in the ultimate fullness of things?"

Dr. Laidlaw sat speechless. These outbursts of mystical enthusiasm he had witnessed before. With any other man he would not have listened to a single sentence, but to Professor Ebor, man of knowledge and profound investigator, he listened with respect, because he regarded this condition as temporary and pathological, and in some sense a reaction from the intense strain of the prolonged mental concentration of many days.

He smiled, with something between sympathy and resignation as he met the other's rapt gaze.

"But you have said, sir, at other times, that you consider the ultimate secrets to be screened from all possible—"

"The *ultimate* secrets, yes," came the unperturbed reply; "but that there lies buried somewhere an indestructible record of the secret meaning of life, originally known to men in the days of their pristine innocence, I am convinced. And, by this strange vision so often vouchsafed to me, I am equally sure that one day it shall be given to me to announce to a weary world this glorious and terrific message."

And he continued at great length and in glowing language to describe the species of vivid dream that had come to him at intervals since earliest childhood, showing in detail how he discovered these very Tablets of the Gods, and proclaimed their splendid contents—whose precise nature was always, however, withheld from him in the vision—to a patient and suffering humanity.

"The *Scrutator*, sir, well described 'Pilgrim' as the Apostle of Hope," said the young doctor gently, when he had finished; "and now, if that reviewer could hear you speak and realize from what strange depths comes your simple faith—"

The professor held up his hand, and the smile of a little child broke over his face like sunshine in the morning.

"Half the good my books do would be instantly destroyed," he said sadly; "they would say that I wrote with my tongue in my cheek. But wait," he added significantly; "wait till I find these Tablets of the Gods! Wait till I hold the solutions of the old world-problems in my hands! Wait till the light of this new revelation breaks upon confused humanity, and it wakes to find its bravest hopes justified! Ah, then, my dear Laidlaw—"

He broke off suddenly; but the doctor, cleverly guessing the thought in his mind, caught him up immediately.

"Perhaps this very summer," he said, trying hard to make the suggestion keep pace with honesty; "in your explorations in Assyria—your digging in the remote civilization of what was once Chaldea, you may find—what you dream of—"

The professor held up his hand, and the smile of a fine old face.

"Perhaps," he murmured softly, "perhaps!"

And the young doctor, thanking the gods of science that his leader's aberrations were of so harmless a character, went home strong in the certitude of his knowledge of externals, proud that he was able to refer his visions to self-suggestion, and wondering complaisantly whether in his old age he might not after all suffer himself from visitations of the very kind that afflicted his respected chief.

And as he got into bed and thought again of his master's rugged face, and finely shaped head, and the deep lines traced by years of work and self-discipline, he turned over on his pillow and fell asleep with a sigh that was half of wonder, half of regret.

II

It was in February, nine months later, when Dr. Laidlaw made his way to Charing Cross to meet his chief after his long absence of travel and exploration. The vision about the so-called Tablets of the Gods had meanwhile passed almost entirely from his memory.

There were few people in the train, for the stream of traffic was now running the other way, and he had no difficulty in finding the man he had come to meet. The shock of white hair beneath the low-crowned felt hat was alone enough to distinguish him by easily.

"Here I am at last!" exclaimed the professor, somewhat wearily, clasping his friend's hand as he listened to the young doctor's warm greetings and questions. "Here I am—a little older, and *much* dirtier than when you last saw me!" He glanced down laughingly at his travel-stained garments.

"And *much* wiser," said Laidlaw, with a smile, as he bustled about the platform for porters and gave his chief the latest scientific news.

At last they came down to practical considerations.

"And your luggage—where is that? You must have tons of it, I suppose?" said Laidlaw.

"Hardly anything," Professor Ebor answered. "Nothing, in fact, but what you see."

"Nothing but this hand-bag?" laughed the other, thinking he was joking.

"And a small portmanteau in the van," was the quiet reply. "I have no other luggage."

"You have no other luggage?" repeated Laidlaw, turning sharply to see if he were in earnest.

"Why should I need more?" the professor added simply.

Something in the man's face, or voice, or manner—the doctor hardly knew which—suddenly struck him as strange. There was a change in him, a change so profound—so little on the surface, that is—that at first he had not become aware of it. For a moment it was as though an utterly alien personality stood before him in that noisy, bustling throng. Here, in all the homely, friendly turmoil of a Charing Cross crowd, a curious feeling of cold passed over his heart, touching his life with icy finger, so that he actually trembled and felt afraid.

He looked up quickly at his friend, his mind working with startled and unwelcome thoughts.

"Only this?" he repeated, indicating the bag. "But where's all the stuff you went away with? And—have you brought nothing home—no treasures?"

"This is all I have," the other said briefly. The pale smile that went with the words caused the doctor a second indescribable sensation of uneasiness. Something was very wrong, something was very queer; he wondered now that he had not noticed it sooner.

"The rest follows, of course, by slow freight," he added tactfully, and as naturally as possible. "But come, sir, you must be tired and in want of food after your long journey. I'll get a taxi at once, and we can see about the other luggage afterwards."

It seemed to him he hardly knew quite what he was saying; the change in his friend had come upon him so suddenly and now grew upon him more and more distressingly. Yet he could not make out exactly in what it consisted. A terrible suspicion began to take shape in his mind, troubling him dreadfully.

"I am neither very tired, nor in need of food, thank you," the professor said quietly. "And this is all I have. There is no luggage to follow. I have brought home nothing—nothing but what you see."

His words conveyed finality. They got into a taxi, tipped the porter, who had been staring in amazement at the venerable figure of the scientist, and were conveyed slowly and noisily to the house in the north of London where the laboratory was, the scene of their labours of years.

And the whole way Professor Ebor uttered no word, nor did Dr. Laidlaw find the courage to ask a single question.

It was only late that night, before he took his departure, as the two men were standing before the fire in the study—that study where they had discussed so many problems of vital and absorbing interest—that Dr. Laidlaw at last found strength to come to the point with direct questions. The professor had been giving him a superficial and desultory account of his travels, of his journeys by camel, of his encampments among the mountains and in the desert, and of his explorations among the buried temples, and, deeper, into the waste of the pre-historic sands, when suddenly the doctor came to the desired point with a kind of nervous rush, almost like a frightened boy.

"And you found—" he began stammering, looking hard at the other's dreadfully altered face, from which every line of hope and cheerfulness seemed to have been obliterated as a sponge wipes markings from a slate—"you found—"

"I found," replied the other, in a solemn voice, and it was the voice of the mystic rather than the man of science—"I found what I went to seek. The vision never once failed me. It led me straight to the place like a star in the heavens. I found—the Tablets of the Gods."

Dr. Laidlaw caught his breath, and steadied himself on the back of a chair. The words fell like particles of ice upon his heart. For the first time the professor had uttered the well-known phrase without the glow of light and wonder in his face that always accompanied it.

"You have—brought them?" he faltered.

"I have brought them home," said the other, in a voice with a ring like iron; "and I have—deciphered them."

Profound despair, the bloom of outer darkness, the dead sound of a hopeless soul freezing in the utter cold of space seemed to fill in the pauses between the brief sentences. A silence followed, during which Dr. Laidlaw saw nothing but the white face before him alternately fade and return. And it was like the face of a dead man.

"They are, alas, indestructible," he heard the voice continue, with its even, metallic ring.

"Indestructible," Laidlaw repeated mechanically, hardly knowing what he was saying.

Again a silence of several minutes passed, during which, with a creeping cold about his heart, he stood and stared into the eyes of the man he had known and loved so long—aye, and worshipped, too; the man who had first opened his own eyes when they were blind, and had led him to the gates of knowledge, and no little distance along the difficult path beyond; the man who, in another direction, had passed on the strength of his faith into the hearts of thousands by his books.

"I may see them?" he asked at last, in a low voice he hardly recognized as his own. "You will let me know—their message?"

Professor Ebor kept his eyes fixedly upon his assistant's face as he answered, with a smile that was more like the grin of death than a living human smile.

"When I am gone," he whispered; "when I have passed away. Then you shall find them and read the translation I have made. And then, too, in your turn, you must try, with the latest resources of science at your disposal to aid you, to compass their utter destruction." He paused a moment, and his face grew pale as the face of a corpse. "Until that time," he added presently, without looking up, "I must ask you not to refer to the subject again—and to keep my confidence meanwhile— *ab—so—lute—ly.*"

III

A year passed slowly by, and at the end of it Dr. Laidlaw had found it necessary to sever his working connexion with his friend and one-time leader. Professor Ebor was no longer the same man. The light had gone out of his life; the laboratory was closed; he no longer put pen to paper or applied his mind to a single problem. In the short space of a few months he had passed from a hale and hearty man of late middle life to the condition of old age—a man collapsed and on the edge of dissolution. Death, it was plain, lay waiting for him in the shadows of any day—and he knew it.

To describe faithfully the nature of this profound alteration in his character and temperament is not easy, but Dr. Laidlaw summed it up to himself in three words: *Loss of Hope*. The splendid mental powers remained indeed undimmed, but the incentive to use them—to use them for the help of others—had gone. The character still held to its fine and unselfish habits of years, but the far goal to which they had been the leading strings had faded away. The desire for knowledge—knowledge for its own sake—had died, and the passionate hope which hitherto had animated with tireless energy the heart and brain of this splendidly equipped intellect had suffered total eclipse. The central fires had gone out. Nothing was worth doing, thinking, working for. There *was* nothing to work for any longer!

The professor's first step was to recall as many of his books as possible; his second to close his laboratory and stop all research. He gave no explanation, he invited no questions. His whole personality crumbled away, so to speak, till his daily life became a mere mechanical process of clothing the body, feeding the body, keeping it in good health so as to avoid physical discomfort, and, above all, doing nothing that could interfere with sleep. The professor did everything he could to lengthen the hours of sleep, and therefore of forgetfulness.

It was all clear enough to Dr. Laidlaw. A weaker man, he knew, would have sought to lose himself in one form or another of sensual indulgence—sleeping-draughts, drink, the first pleasures that came to hand. Self-destruction would have been the method of a little bolder type; and deliberate evil-doing, poisoning with his awful knowledge all he could, the means of still another kind of man. Mark Ebor was none of these. He held himself under fine control, facing silently and without complaint the terrible facts he honestly believed himself to have been unfortunate enough to discover. Even to his intimate friend and assistant, Dr. Laidlaw, he vouchsafed no word of true explanation or lament. He went straight forward to the end, knowing well that the end was not very far away.

And death came very quietly one day to him, as he was sitting in the arm-chair of the study, directly facing the doors of the laboratory—the doors that no longer opened. Dr. Laidlaw, by happy chance, was with him at the time, and just able to reach his side in response to the sudden painful efforts for breath; just in time, too, to catch the murmured words that fell from the pallid lips like a message from the other side of the grave.

"Read them, if you must; and, if you can—destroy. But"—his voice sank so low that Dr. Laidlaw only just caught the dying syllables—"but—never, never—give them to the world."

And like a grey bundle of dust loosely gathered up in an old garment the professor sank back into his chair and expired.

But this was only the death of the body. His spirit had died two years before.

IV

The estate of the dead man was small and uncomplicated, and Dr. Laidlaw, as sole executor and residuary legatee, had no difficulty in settling it up. A month after the funeral he was sitting alone in his upstairs library, the last sad duties completed, and his mind full of poignant memories and regrets for the loss of a friend he had revered and loved, and to whom his debt was so incalculably great. The last two years, indeed, had been for him terrible. To watch the swift decay of the greatest combination of heart and brain he had ever known, and to realize he was powerless to help, was a source of profound grief to him that would remain to the end of his days.

At the same time an insatiable curiosity possessed him. The study of dementia was, of course, outside his special province as a specialist, but he knew enough of it to understand how small a matter might be the actual cause of how great an illusion, and he had been devoured from the very beginning by a ceaseless and increasing anxiety to know what the professor had found in the sands of "Chaldea," what these precious Tablets of the Gods might be, and particularly—for this was the real cause that had sapped the man's sanity and hope—what the inscription was that he had believed to have deciphered thereon.

The curious feature of it all to his own mind was, that whereas his friend had dreamed of finding a message of glorious hope and comfort, he had apparently found (so far as he had found anything intelligible at all, and not invented the whole thing in his dementia) that the secret of the world, and the meaning of life and death, was of so terrible a nature that it robbed the heart of courage and the soul of hope. What, then, could be the contents of the little brown parcel the professor had bequeathed to him with his pregnant dying sentences?

Actually his hand was trembling as he turned to the writing-table and began slowly to unfasten a small old-fashioned desk on which the small gilt initials "M.E." stood forth as a melancholy memento. He put the key into the lock and half turned it. Then, suddenly, he stopped and looked about him. Was that a sound at the back of the room? It was just as though someone had laughed and then tried to smother the laugh with a cough. A slight shiver ran over him as he stood listening.

"This is absurd," he said aloud; "too absurd for belief—that I should be so nervous! It's the effect of curiosity unduly prolonged." He smiled a little sadly and his eyes wandered to the blue summer sky and the plane trees swaying in the wind below his window. "It's the reaction," he continued. "The curiosity of two years to be quenched in a single moment! The nervous tension, of course, must be considerable."

He turned back to the brown desk and opened it without further delay. His hand was firm now, and he took out the paper parcel that lay inside without a tremor. It was heavy. A moment later there lay on the table before him a couple of weather-worn plaques of grey stone—they looked like stone, although they felt like metal—on which he saw markings of a curious character that might have been the mere tracings of natural forces through the ages, or, equally well, the half-obliterated hieroglyphics cut upon their surface in past centuries by the more or less untutored hand of a common scribe.

He lifted each stone in turn and examined it carefully. It seemed to him that a faint glow of heat passed from the substance into his skin, and he put them down again suddenly, as with a gesture of uneasiness.

"A very clever, or a very imaginative man," he said to himself, "who could squeeze the secrets of life and death from such broken lines as those!"

Then he turned to a yellow envelope lying beside them in the desk, with the single word on the outside in the writing of the professor—the word *Translation*.

"Now," he thought, taking it up with a sudden violence to conceal his nervousness, "now for the great solution. Now to learn the meaning of the worlds, and why mankind was made, and why discipline is worth while, and sacrifice and pain the true law of advancement."

There was the shadow of a sneer in his voice, and yet something in him shivered at the same time. He held the envelope as though weighing it in his hand, his mind pondering many things. Then curiosity won the day, and he suddenly tore it open with the gesture of an actor who tears open a letter on the stage, knowing there is no real writing inside at all.

A page of finely written script in the late scientist's handwriting lay before him. He read it through from beginning to end, missing no word, uttering each syllable distinctly under his breath as he read.

The pallor of his face grew ghastly as he neared the end. He began to shake all over as with ague. His breath came heavily in gasps. He still gripped the sheet of paper, however, and deliberately, as by an intense effort of will, read it through a second time from beginning to end. And this time, as the last syllable dropped from his lips, the whole face of the man flamed with a sudden and terrible anger. His skin became deep, deep red, and he clenched his teeth. With all the strength of his vigorous soul he was struggling to keep control of himself.

For perhaps five minutes he stood there beside the table without stirring a muscle. He might have been carved out of stone. His eyes were shut, and only the heaving of the chest betrayed the fact that he was a living being. Then, with a strange quietness, he lit a match and applied it to the sheet of paper he held in his hand. The ashes fell slowly about him, piece by piece, and he blew them from the window-sill into the air, his eyes following them as they floated away on the summer wind that breathed so warmly over the world.

He turned back slowly into the room. Although his actions and movements were absolutely steady and controlled, it was clear that he was on the edge of violent action. A hurricane might burst upon the still room any moment. His muscles were tense and rigid. Then, suddenly, he whitened, collapsed, and sank backwards into a chair, like a tumbled bundle of inert matter. He had fainted.

In less than half an hour he recovered consciousness and sat up. As before, he made no sound. Not a syllable passed his lips. He rose quietly and looked about the room.

Then he did a curious thing.

Taking a heavy stick from the rack in the corner he approached the mantlepiece, and with a heavy shattering blow he smashed the clock to pieces. The glass fell in shivering atoms.

"Cease your lying voice for ever," he said, in a curiously still, even tone. "There is no such thing as *time!*"

He took the watch from his pocket, swung it round several times by the long gold chain, smashed it into smithereens against the wall with a single blow, and then walked into his laboratory next door, and hung its broken body on the bones of the skeleton in the corner of the room.

"Let one damned mockery hang upon another," he said smiling oddly. "Delusions, both of you, and cruel as false!"

He slowly moved back to the front room. He stopped opposite the bookcase where stood in a row the "Scriptures of the World," choicely bound and exquisitely printed, the late professor's most treasured possession, and next to them several books signed "Pilgrim."

One by one he took them from the shelf and hurled them through the open window.

"A devil's dreams! A devil's foolish dreams!" he cried, with a vicious laugh.

Presently he stopped from sheer exhaustion. He turned his eyes slowly to the wall opposite, where hung a weird array of Eastern swords and daggers, scimitars and spears, the collections of many journeys. He crossed the room and ran his finger along the edge. His mind seemed to waver.

"No," he muttered presently; "not that way. There are easier and better ways than that."

He took his hat and passed downstairs into the street.

V

It was five o'clock, and the June sun lay hot upon the pavement. He felt the metal door-knob burn the palm of his hand.

"Ah, Laidlaw, this is well met," cried a voice at his elbow; "I was in the act of coming to see you. I've a case that will interest you, and besides, I remembered that you flavoured your tea with orange leaves!—and I admit—"

It was Alexis Stephen, the great hypnotic doctor.

"I've had no tea to-day," Laidlaw said, in a dazed manner, after staring for a moment as though the other had struck him in the face. A new idea had entered his mind.

"What's the matter?" asked Dr. Stephen quickly. "Something's wrong with you. It's this sudden heat, or overwork. Come, man, let's go inside."

A sudden light broke upon the face of the younger man, the light of a heaven-sent inspiration. He looked into his friend's face, and told a direct lie.

"Odd," he said, "I myself was just coming to see you. I have something of great importance to test your confidence with. But in your house, please," as Stephen urged him towards his own door—"in *your* house. It's only round the corner, and I—I cannot go back there—to my rooms—till I have told you."

"I'm your patient—for the moment," he added stammeringly as soon as they were seated in the privacy of the hypnotist's sanctum, "and I want—er—"

"My dear Laidlaw," interrupted the other, in that soothing voice of command which had suggested to many a suffering soul that the cure for its pain lay in the powers of its own reawakened will, "I am always at your service, as you know. You have only to tell me what I can do for you, and I will do it." He showed every desire to help him out. His manner was indescribably tactful and direct.

Dr. Laidlaw looked up into his face.

"I surrender my will to you," he said, already calmed by the other's healing presence, "and I want you to treat me hypnotically—and at once. I want you to suggest to me"—his voice became very tense—"that I shall forget—forget till I die—everything that has occurred to me during the last two hours; till I die, mind," he added, with solemn emphasis, "till I die."

He floundered and stammered like a frightened boy. Alexis Stephen looked at him fixedly without speaking.

"And further," Laidlaw continued, "I want you to ask me no questions. I wish to forget for ever something I have recently discovered—something so terrible and yet so obvious that I can hardly understand why it is not patent to every mind in the world—for I have had a moment of absolute *clear vision*—of merciless clairvoyance. But I want no one else in the whole world to know what it is—least of all, old friend, yourself."

He talked in utter confusion, and hardly knew what he was saying. But the pain on his face and the anguish in his voice were an instant passport to the other's heart.

"Nothing is easier," replied Dr. Stephen, after a hesitation so slight that the other probably did not even notice it. "Come into my other room where we shall not be disturbed. I can heal you. Your memory of the last two hours shall be wiped out as though it had never been. You can trust me absolutely."

"I know I can," Laidlaw said simply, as he followed him in.

VI

An hour later they passed back into the front room again. The sun was already behind the houses opposite, and the shadows began to gather.

"I went off easily?" Laidlaw asked.

"You were a little obstinate at first. But though you came in like a lion, you went out like a lamb. I let you sleep a bit afterwards."

Dr. Stephen kept his eyes rather steadily upon his friend's face.

"What were you doing by the fire before you came here?" he asked, pausing, in a casual tone, as he lit a cigarette and handed the case to his patient.

"I? Let me see. Oh, I know; I was worrying my way through poor old Ebor's papers and things. I'm his executor, you know. Then I got weary and came out for a whiff of air." He spoke lightly and with perfect naturalness. Obviously he was telling the truth. "I prefer specimens to papers," he laughed cheerily.

"I know, I know," said Dr. Stephen, holding a lighted match for the cigarette. His face wore an expression of content. The experiment had been a complete success. The memory of the last two hours was wiped out utterly. Laidlaw was already chatting gaily and easily about a dozen other things that interested him. Together they went out into the street, and at his door Dr. Stephen left him with a joke and a wry face that made his friend laugh heartily.

"Don't dine on the professor's old papers by mistake," he cried, as he vanished down the street.

Dr. Laidlaw went up to his study at the top of the house. Half way down he met his housekeeper, Mrs. Fewings. She was flustered and excited, and her face was very red and perspiring.

"There've been burglars here," she cried excitedly, "or something funny! All your things is just any'ow, sir. I found everything all about everywhere!" She was very confused. In this orderly and very precise establishment it was unusual to find a thing out of place.

"Oh, my specimens!" cried the doctor, dashing up the rest of the stairs at top speed. "Have they been touched or—"

He flew to the door of the laboratory. Mrs. Fewings panted up heavily behind him.

"The labatry ain't been touched," she explained, breathlessly, "but they smashed the libry clock and they've 'ung your gold watch, sir, on the skelinton's hands. And the books that weren't no value they flung out er the window just like so much rubbish. They must have been wild drunk, Dr. Laidlaw, sir!"

The young scientist made a hurried examination of the rooms. Nothing of value was missing. He began to wonder what kind of burglars they were. He looked up sharply at Mrs. Fewings standing in the doorway. For a moment he seemed to cast about in his mind for something.

"Odd," he said at length. "I only left here an hour ago and everything was all right then."

"Was it, sir? Yes, sir." She glanced sharply at him. Her room looked out upon the courtyard, and she must have seen the books come crashing down, and also have heard her master leave the house a few minutes later.

"And what's this rubbish the brutes have left?" he cried, taking up two slabs of worn gray stone, on the writing-table. "Bath brick, or something, I do declare."

He looked very sharply again at the confused and troubled housekeeper.

"Throw them on the dust heap, Mrs. Fewings, and—and let me know if anything is missing in the house, and I will notify the police this evening."

When she left the room he went into the laboratory and took his watch off the skeleton's fingers. His face wore a troubled expression, but after a moment's thought it cleared again. His memory was a complete blank.

"I suppose I left it on the writing-table when I went out to take the air," he said. And there was no one present to contradict him.

He crossed to the window and blew carelessly some ashes of burned paper from the sill, and stood watching them as they floated away lazily over the tops of the trees.

The Other Wing

It used to puzzle him that, after dark, someone would look in round the edge of the bedroom door, and withdraw again too rapidly for him to see the face. When the nurse had gone away with the candle this happened: "Good night, Master Tim," she said usually, shading the light with one hand to protect his eyes; "dream of me and I'll dream of you." She went out slowly. The sharp-edged shadow of the door ran across the ceiling like a train. There came a whispered colloquy in the corridor outside, about himself, of course, and—he was alone. He heard her steps going deeper and deeper into the bosom of the old country house; they were audible for a moment on the stone flooring of the hall; and sometimes the dull thump of the baize door into the servants' quarters just reached him, too—then silence. But it was only when the last sound as well as the last sign of her had vanished that the face emerged from its hiding-place and flashed in upon him round the corner. As a rule, too, it came just as he was saying, "Now I'll go to sleep. I won't think any longer. Good night, Master Tim, and happy dreams." He loved to say this to himself; it brought a sense of companionship, as though there were two persons speaking.

The room was on the top of the old house, a big, high-ceilinged room, and his bed against the wall had an iron railing round it; he felt very safe and protected in it. The curtains at the other end of the room were drawn. He lay watching the firelight dancing on the heavy folds, and their pattern, showing a spaniel chasing a long-tailed bird towards a bushy tree, interested and amused him. It was repeated over and over again. He counted the number of dogs, and the number of birds, and the number of trees, but could never make them agree. There was a plan somewhere in that pattern; if only he could discover it, the dogs and birds and trees would "come out right." Hundreds and hundreds of times he had played this game, for the plan in the pattern made it possible to take sides, and the bird and dog were against him. They always won, however; Tim usually fell asleep just when the advantage was on his own side. The curtains hung steadily enough most of the time, but it seemed to him once or twice that they stirred—hiding a dog or bird on purpose to prevent his winning. For instance, he had eleven birds and eleven trees, and, fixing them in his mind by saying, "that's eleven birds and eleven trees, but only ten dogs", his eyes darted back to find the eleventh dog, when—the curtain moved and threw all his calculations into confusion again. The eleventh dog was hidden. He did not quite like the movement; it gave him questionable feelings, rather, for the curtain did not move of itself. Yet, usually, he was too intent upon counting the dogs to feel positive alarm.

Opposite to him was the fireplace, full of red and yellow coals;

and, lying with his head sideways on the pillow, he could see directly in between the bars. When the coals settled with a soft and powdery crash, he turned his eyes from the curtains to the grate, trying to discover exactly which bits had fallen. So long as the glow was there the sound seemed pleasant enough, but sometimes he awoke later in the night, the room huge with darkness, the fire almost out—and the sound was not so pleasant then. It startled him. The coals did not fall of themselves. It seemed that someone poked them cautiously. The shadows were very thick before the bars. As with the curtains, moreover, the morning aspect of the extinguished fire, the ice-cold cinders that made a clinking sound like tin, caused no emotion whatever in his soul.

And it was usually while he lay waiting for sleep, tired both of the curtain and the coal games, on the point, indeed, of saying, "I'll go to sleep now," that the puzzling thing took place. He would be staring drowsily at the dying fire, perhaps counting the stockings and flannel garments that hung along the high fender rail when, suddenly, a person looked in with lightning swiftness through the door and vanished again before he could possibly turn his head to see. The appearance and disappearance were accomplished with amazing rapidity always.

It was a head and shoulders that looked in, and the movement combined the speed, the lightness and the silence of a shadow. Only it was not a shadow. A hand held the edge of the door. The face shot round, saw him, and withdrew like lightning. It was utterly beyond him to imagine anything more quick and clever. It darted. He heard no sound. It went. But—it had seen him, looked him all over, examined him, noted what he was doing with that lightning glance. It wanted to know if he were awake still, or asleep. And though it went off, it still watched him from a distance; it waited somewhere; it knew all about him. *Where* it waited no one could ever guess. It came probably, he felt, from beyond the house, possibly from the roof, but most likely from the garden or the sky. Yet, though strange, it was not terrible. It was a kindly and protective figure, he felt. And when it happened he never called for help, because the occurrence simply took his voice away.

"It comes from the Nightmare Passage," he decided; "but it's *not* a nightmare." It puzzled him.

Sometimes, moreover, it came more than once in a single night. He was pretty sure—not *quite* positive—that it occupied his room as soon as he was properly asleep. It took possession, sitting perhaps before the dying fire, standing upright behind the heavy curtains, or even lying down in the empty bed his brother used when he was home from school. Perhaps it played the curtain game, perhaps it poked the coals; it knew, at any rate, where the eleventh dog had lain concealed. It certainly came in and out; certainly, too, it did not wish to be seen. For, more than once, on waking suddenly in the midnight blackness, Tim knew it was standing close beside his bed and bending over him. He

felt, rather than heard, its presence. It glided quietly away. It moved
with marvellous softness, yet he was positive it moved. He felt the
difference, so to speak: it had been near him, now it was gone. It came
back, too—just as he was falling into sleep again. Its midnight coming
and going, however, stood out sharply different from its first shy,
tentative approach. For in the firelight it came alone; whereas in the
black and silent hours, it had with it—others.

And it was then he made up his mind that its swift and quiet
movements were due to the fact that it had wings. It flew. And the
others that came with it in the darkness were "its little ones." He also
made up his mind that all were friendly, comforting, protective, and
that while positively *not* a Nightmare, it yet came somehow along the
Nightmare Passage before it reached him. "You see, it's like this," he
explained to the nurse: "The big one comes to visit me alone, but it
only brings its little ones when I'm *quite* asleep."

"Then the quicker you get to sleep the better, isn't it, Master Tim?"

He replied: "Rather! I always do. Only I wonder where they come
from!" He spoke, however, as though he had an inkling.

But the nurse was so dull about it that he gave her up and tried his
father. "Of course," replied this busy but affectionate parent, "it's either
nobody at all, or else it's Sleep coming to carry you away to the land of
dreams." He made the statement kindly but somewhat briskly, for he
was worried just then about the extra taxes on his land, and the effort to
fix his mind on Tim's fanciful world was beyond him at the moment.
He lifted the boy on to his knee, kissed and patted him as though he
were a favourite dog, and planted him on the rug again with a flying
sweep. "Run and ask your mother," he added; "she knows all that kind
of thing. Then come back and tell me all about it—another time."

Tim found his mother in an arm-chair before the fire of another
room; she was knitting and reading at the same time—a wonderful
thing the boy could never understand. She raised her head as he came
in, pushed her glasses on to her forehead, and held her arms out. He
told her everything, ending up with what his father said.

"You see, it's *not* Jackman, or Thompson, or anyone like that," he
exclaimed. "It's someone real."

"But nice," she assured him, "someone who comes to take care of
you and see that you're all safe and cosy."

"Oh, yes, I know that. But ——"

"I think your father's right," she added quickly. "It's Sleep, I'm
sure, who pops in round the door like that. Sleep *has* got wings, I've
always heard."

"Then the other thing—the little ones?" he asked. "Are they just
sorts of dozes, you think?"

Mother did not answer for a moment. She turned down the page of
her book, closed it slowly, and put it on the table beside her. More

slowly still she put her knitting away, arranging the wool and needles with some deliberation.

"Perhaps," she said, drawing the boy closer to her and looking into his big eyes of wonder, "they're dreams!"

Tim felt a thrill run through him as she said it. He stepped back a foot or so and clapped his hands softly. "Dreams!" he whispered with enthusiasm and belief; "of course! I never thought of that."

His mother, having proved her sagacity, then made a mistake. She noted her success, but instead of leaving it there, she elaborated and explained. As Tim expressed it she "went on about it." Therefore he did not listen. He followed his train of thought alone. And presently, he interrupted her long sentences with a conclusion of his own:

"Then I know where She hides," he announced with a touch of awe. "Where She lives, I mean." And without waiting to be asked, he imparted the information: "It's in the Other Wing."

"Ah!" said his mother, taken by surprise. "How clever of you, Tim!"—and thus confirmed it.

Thenceforward this was established in his life—that Sleep and her attendant Dreams hid during the daytime in that unused portion of the great Elizabethan mansion called the Other Wing. This other wing was unoccupied, its corridors untrodden, its windows shuttered and its rooms all closed. At various places green baize doors led into it, but no one ever opened them. For many years this part had been shut up; and for the children, properly speaking, it was out of bounds. They never mentioned it as a possible place, at any rate; in hide-and-seek it was not considered, even; there was a hint of the inaccessible about the Other Wing. Shadows, dust, and silence had it to themselves.

But Tim, having ideas of his own about everything, possessed special information about the Other Wing. He believed it *was* inhabited. Who occupied the immense series of empty rooms, who trod the spacious corridors, who passed to and fro behind the shuttered windows, he had not known exactly. He had called these occupants, "they", and the most important among them was "The Ruler." The Ruler of the Other Wing was a kind of deity, powerful, far away, ever present yet never seen.

And about this Ruler he had a wonderful conception for a little boy; he connected her, somehow, with deep thoughts of his own, the deepest of all. When he made up adventures to the moon, to the stars, or to the bottom of the sea, adventures that he lived inside himself, as it were—to reach them he must invariably pass through the chambers of the Other Wing. Those corridors and halls, the Nightmare Passage among them, lay along the route; they were the first stage of the journey. Once the green baize doors swung to behind him and the long dim passage stretched ahead, he was well on his way into the adventure of the moment; the Nightmare Passage once passed, he was safe from capture; but once the shutters of a window had been flung open, he was free of the gigantic world that lay beyond. For then light poured in and he could see his way.

The conception, for a child, was curious. It established a correspondence between the mysterious chambers of the Other Wing and the occupied, but unguessed chambers of his Inner Being. Through these chambers, through these darkened corridors, along a passage, sometimes dangerous, or at least of questionable repute, he must pass to find all adventures that were real. The light—when he pierced far enough to take the shutters down—was discovery. Tim did not actually think, much less say, all this. He was aware of it, however. He felt it. The Other Wing was inside himself as well as through the green baize doors. His inner map of wonder included both of them.

But now, for the first time in his life, he knew who lived there and who the Ruler was. A shutter had fallen of its own accord; light poured in; he made a guess, and Mother had confirmed it. Sleep and her Little Ones, the host of dreams, were the daylight occupants. They stole out when the darkness fell. All adventures in life began and ended by a dream—discoverable by first passing through the Other Wing.

And, having settled this, his one desire now was to travel over the map upon journeys of exploration and discovery. The map inside himself he knew already, but the map of the Other Wing he had not seen. His imagination knew it, he had a clear mental picture of rooms and halls and passages, but his feet had never trod the silent floors where dust and shadows hid the flock of dreams by day. The mighty chambers where Sleep ruled he longed to stand in, to see the Ruler face to face. He made up his mind to get into the Other Wing.

To accomplish this was difficult; but Tim was a determined youngster, and he meant to try; he meant, also, to succeed. He deliberated. At night he could not possibly manage it; in any case, the Ruler and her host all left it after dark to fly about the world; the Wing would be empty, and the emptiness would frighten him. Therefore he must make a daylight visit; and it was a daylight visit he decided on. He deliberated more. There were rules and risks involved: it meant going out of bounds, the danger of being seen, the certainty of being questioned by some idle and inquisitive grown-up: "Where in the world have you been all this time?"—and so forth. These things he thought out carefully, and though he arrived at no solution, he felt satisfied that it would be all right. That is, he recognised the risks. To be thus prepared was half the battle, for nothing then could take him by surprise.

The notion that he might slip in from the garden was soon abandoned; the red bricks showed no openings; there was no door; from the courtyard, also, entrance was impracticable: even on tiptoe he could barely reach the broad window-sills of stone. When playing alone, or walking with the French governess, he examined every outside possibility. None offered. The shutters, supposing he could reach them, were thick and solid.

Meanwhile, when opportunity offered, he stood against the tight red bricks; the towers and gables of the Wing rose overhead; he heard the wind go whispering along the eaves; he imagined tiptoe movements and a sound of wings inside. Sleep and her Little Ones were busily preparing for their journeys after dark; they hid, but they did not sleep; in this unused Wing, vaster alone than any other country house he had ever seen, Sleep taught and trained her flock of feathered Dreams. It was very wonderful. They probably supplied the entire County. But more wonderful still was the thought that the Ruler herself should take the trouble to come to his particular room and personally watch over him all night long. That was amazing. And it flashed across his imaginative inquiring mind: "Perhaps they take me with them! The moment I'm asleep! That's why she comes to see me!"

Yet his chief preoccupation was, how Sleep got out. Through the green baize doors, of course! By a process of elimination he arrived at a conclusion: he, too, must enter through a green baize door and risk detection.

Of late, the lightning visits had ceased. The silent, darting figure had not peeped in and vanished as it used to do. He fell asleep too quickly now, almost before Jackman reached the hall, and long before the fire began to die. Also, the dogs and birds upon the curtains always matched the trees exactly, and he won the curtain game quite easily; there was never a dog or bird too many; the curtain never stirred. It had been thus ever since his talk with Mother and Father. And so he came to make a second discovery: His parents did not really believe in his Figure. She kept away on that account. They doubted her; she hid. Here was still another incentive to go and find her out. He ached for her, she was so kind, she gave herself so much trouble—just for his little self in the big and lonely bedroom. Yet his parents spoke of her as though she were of no account. He longed to see hear, face to face, and tell her that he believed in her and loved her. For he was positive she would like to hear it. She cared. Though he had fallen asleep of late too quickly for him to see her flash in at the door, he had known nicer dreams than in his life before—travelling dreams. And it was she who sent them. More—he was sure she took him out with her.

One evening, in the dusk of a March day, his opportunity came; and only just in time, for his brother, Jack, was expected home from school on the morrow, and with Jack in the other bed, no Figure would ever care to show itself. Also it was Easter, and after Easter, though Tim was not aware of it at the time, he was to say good-bye finally to governesses and become a day-boarder at a preparatory school for

Wellington. The opportunity offered itself so naturally, moreover, that Tim took it without hesitation. It never occurred to him to question, much less to refuse it. The thing was obviously meant to be. For he found himself unexpectedly in front of a green baize door; and the green baize door was—swinging! Somebody, therefore, had just passed through it.

It had come about in this wise. Father, away in Scotland, at Inglemuir, the shooting place, was expected back next morning; Mother had driven over to the church upon some Easter business or other; and the governess had been allowed her holiday at home in France. Tim, therefore, had the run of the house, and in the hour between tea and bed-time he made good use of it. Fully able to defy such second-rate obstacles as nurses and butlers, he explored all manner of forbidden places with ardent thoroughness, arriving finally in the sacred precincts of his father's study. This wonderful room was the very heart and centre of the whole big house; he had been birched here long ago; here, too, his father had told him with a grave yet smiling face: "You've got a new companion, Tim, a little sister; you must be very kind to her." Also, it was the place where all the money was kept. What he called "father's jolly smell" was strong in it—papers, tobacco, books, flavoured by hunting crops and gunpowder.

At first he felt awed, standing motionless just inside the door; but presently, recovering equilibrium, he moved cautiously on tiptoe towards the gigantic desk where important papers were piled in untidy patches. These he did not touch; but beside them his quick eye noted the jagged piece of iron shell his father brought home from his Crimean campaign and now used as a letter-weight. It was difficult to lift, however. He climbed into the comfortable chair and swung round and round. It was a swivel-chair, and he sank down among the cushions in it, staring at the strange things on the great desk before him, as if fascinated. Next he turned away and saw the stick-rack in the corner— this, he knew, he was allowed to touch. He had played with these sticks before. There were twenty, perhaps, all told, with curious carved handles, brought from every corner of the world; many of them cut by his father's own hand in queer and distant places. And, among them, Tim fixed his eye upon a cane with an ivory handle, a slender, polished cane that he had always coveted tremendously. It was the kind he meant to use when he became a man. It bent, it quivered, and when he swished it through the air it trembled like a riding-whip, and made a whistling noise. Yet it was very strong in spite of its elastic qualities. A family treasure, it was also an old-fashioned relic; it had been his great-grandfather's walking stick. Something of another century clung visibly about it still. It had dignity and grace and leisure in its very aspect. And it suddenly occurred to him. "How great-grandpapa must miss it! Wouldn't he just love to have it back again!"

How it happened exactly, Tim did not know, but a few minutes later he found himself walking about the deserted halls and passages of the house with the air of an elderly gentleman of a hundred years ago, proud as a courtier, flourishing the stick like an Eighteenth Century dandy in the Mall. That the cane reached to his shoulder made no difference; he held it accordingly, swaggering on his way. He was off upon an adventure. He dived down through the byways of the Other Wing inside himself, as though the stick transported him to the days of the old gentleman who had used it in another century.

It may seem strange to those who dwell in smaller houses, but in this rambling Elizabethan mansion there were whole sections that, even to Tim, were strange and unfamiliar. In his mind the map of the Other Wing was clearer by far than the geography of the part he travelled daily. He came to passages and dim-lit halls, long corridors of stone beyond the Picture Gallery; narrow, wainscoted connecting-channels with four steps down and a little later two steps up; deserted chambers with arches guarding them—all hung with the soft March twilight and all bewilderingly unrecognized. With a sense of adventure born of naughtiness he went carelessly along, farther and farther into the heart of this unfamiliar country, swinging the cane, one thumb stuck into the arm-pit of his blue serge suit, whistling softly to himself, excited yet keenly on the alert—and suddenly found himself opposite a door that checked all further advance. It was a green baize door. And it was swinging.

He stopped abruptly, facing it. He stared, he gripped his cane more tightly, he held his breath. "The Other Wing!" he gasped in a swallowed whisper.

It was an entrance, but an entrance he had never seen before. He thought he knew every door by heart; but this one was new. He stood motionless for several minutes, watching it; the door had two halves, but one half only was swinging, each swing shorter than the one before; he heard the little puffs of air it made; it settled finally, the last movements very short and rapid; it stopped. And the boy's heart, after similar rapid strokes, stopped also—for a moment.

"Someone's just gone through," he gulped. And even as he said it he knew who the someone was. The conviction just dropped into him. "It's great-grandpapa; he knows I've got his stick. He wants it!" On the heels of this flashed instantly another amazing certainty. "He sleeps in there. He's having dreams. That's what being dead means."

His first impulse, then, took the form of, "I must let Father know; it'll make him burst for joy!" but his second was for himself—to finish his adventure. And it was this, naturally enough, that gained the day. He could tell his father later. His first duty was plainly to go through the door into the Other Wing. He must give the stick back to its owner. He must *hand* it back.

The test of will and character came now. Tim had imagination, and so knew the meaning of fear; but there was nothing craven in him. He could howl and scream and stamp like any other person of his age when the occasion called for such behaviour, but such occasions were due to temper roused by a thwarted will, and the histrionics were half "pretended" to produce a calculated effect. There was no one to thwart his will at present. He also knew how to be afraid of Nothing, to be afraid without ostensible cause that is—which was merely "nerves". He could have "the shudders" with the best of them.

But, when a real thing faced him, Tim's character emerged to meet it. He would clench his hands, brace his muscles, set his teeth—and wish to heaven he was bigger. But he would not flinch. Being imaginative, he lived the worst a dozen times before it happened, yet in the final crash he stood up like a man. He had that highest pluck—the courage of a sensitive temperament. And at this particular juncture, somewhat ticklish for a boy of eight or nine, it did not fail him. He lifted the cane and pushed the swinging door wide open. Then he walked through it—into the Other Wing.

The green baize door swung to behind him; he was even sufficiently master of himself to turn and close it with a steady hand, because he did not care to hear the series of muffled thuds its lessening swings would cause. But he realised clearly his position, knew he was doing a tremendous thing.

Holding the cane between fingers very tightly clenched, he advanced bravely along the corridor that stretched before him. And all fear left him from that moment, replaced, it seemed, by a mild and exquisite surprise. His footsteps made no sound, he walked on air; instead of darkness, or the twilight he expected, a diffused and gentle light that seemed like the silver on the lawn when a half-moon sails a cloudless sky, lay everywhere. He knew his way, moreover, knew exactly where he was and whither he was going. The corridor was as familiar to him as the floor of his own bedroom; he recognised the shape and length of it; it agreed exactly with the map he had constructed long ago. Though he had never, to the best of his knowledge, entered it before, he knew with intimacy its every detail.

And thus the surprise he felt was mild and far from disconcerting. "I'm here again!" was the kind of thought he had. It was *how* he got here that caused the faint surprise, apparently. He no longer swaggered, however, but walked carefully, and half on tiptoe, holding the ivory handle of the cane with a kind of affectionate respect. And as he advanced, the light closed softly up behind him, obliterating the way by which he had come. But this he did not know, because he did not look behind him. He only looked in front, where the corridor stretched its silvery length towards the great chamber where he knew the cane must be surrendered. The person who had preceded him down this ancient corridor, passing through the green baize door just before he reached it, this person, his father's grandfather, now stood in that great chamber, waiting to receive his own. Tim knew it as surely as he knew he breathed. At the far end he even made out the larger patch of silvery light which marked its gaping doorway.

There was another thing he knew as well—that this corridor he moved along between rooms with fast-closed doors, was the Nightmare Corridor; often and often he had traversed it; each room was occupied. "This is the Nightmare Passage," he whispered to himself, "but I know the Ruler—it doesn't matter. None of the Nightmares can get out or do anything." He heard them, none the less, inside, as he passed by; he heard them scratching to get out. The feeling of security made him reckless; he took unnecessary risks; he brushed the panels as he passed. And the love of keen sensation for its own sake, the desire to feel "an awful thrill", tempted him once so sharply that he suddenly raised his stick and poked a fast-shut door with it!

He was not prepared for the result, but he gained the sensation and the thrill. For the door opened with instant swiftness half an inch, a hand emerged, caught the stick and tried to draw it in. Tim sprang back as if he had been struck. He pulled at the ivory handle with all his strength, but his strength was less than nothing. He tried to shout, but his voice had gone. A terror of the moon came over him, for he was unable to loosen his hold of the handle; his fingers had become a part of it. An appalling weakness turned him helpless. He was dragged inch by inch towards the fearful door. The end of the stick was already through the narrow crack. He could not see the hand that pulled, but he knew it was gigantic. He understood now why the world was strange, why horses galloped furiously, and why trains whistled as they raced through stations. All the comedy and terror of nightmare gripped his heart with pincers made of ice. The disproportion was abominable. The final collapse rushed over him when, without a sign of warning, the door slammed silently, and between the jamb and the wall the cane was crushed as flat as if it were a bulrush. So irresistible was the force behind the door that the solid stick just went flat as the stalk of a bulrush.

He looked at it. It *was* a bulrush.

He did not laugh; the absurdity was so distressingly unnatural. The horror of finding a bulrush where he had expected a polished cane— this hideous and appalling detail held the nameless horror of the nightmare. It betrayed him utterly. Why had he not always known really that the stick was not a stick, but a thin and hollow reed . . . ?

Then the cane was safely in his hand, unbroken. He stood looking at it. The Nightmare was in full swing. He heard another door opening behind his back, a door he had not touched. There was just time to see a hand thrusting and waving dreadfully, horribly, at him through the narrow crack—just time to realize that this was another Nightmare acting in atrocious concert with the first, when he saw closely beside him, towering to the ceiling, the protective, kindly Figure that visited his bedroom. In the turning movement he made to meet the attack, he became aware of her. And his terror passed. It was a nightmare terror merely. The infinite horror vanished. Only the comedy remained. He smiled.

He saw her dimly only, she was so vast, but he saw her, the Ruler of the Other Wing at last, and knew that he was safe again. He gazed with a tremendous love and wonder, trying to see her clearly; but the face was hidden far aloft and seemed to melt into the sky beyond the roof. He discerned that she was larger. than the Night, only far, far softer, with wings that folded above him more tenderly even than his mother's arms; that there were points of light like stars among the feathers, and that she was vast enough to cover millions and millions of people all at once. Moreover, she did not fade or go, so far as he could see, but spread herself in such a way that he lost sight of her. She spread over the entire Wing . . .

And Tim remembered that this was all quite natural really. He had often and often been down this corridor before; the Nightmare Corridor was no new experience; it had to be faced as usual. Once knowing what hid inside the rooms, he was bound to tempt them out. They drew, enticed, attracted him; this was their power. It was their special strength that they could suck him helplessly towards them, and that he was obliged to go. He understood exactly why he was tempted to tap with the cane upon their awful doors, but, having done so, he had accepted the challenge and could now continue his journey quietly and safely. The Ruler of the Other Wing had taken him in charge.

A delicious sense of carelessness came on him. There was softness as of water in the solid things about him, nothing that could hurt or bruise. Holding the cane firmly by its ivory handle, he went forward along the corridor, walking as on air.

The end was quickly reached: He stood upon the threshold of the mighty chamber where he knew the owner of the cane was waiting; the long corridor lay behind him, in front he saw the spacious dimensions of a lofty hall that gave him the feeling of being in the Crystal Palace, Euston Station, or St. Paul's. High, narrow windows, cut deeply into the wall, stood in a row upon the other side; an enormous open fireplace of burning logs was on his right; thick tapestries hung from the ceiling to the floor of stone; and in the centre of the chamber was a massive table of dark, shining wood, great chairs with carved stiff backs set here and there beside it. And in the biggest of these throne-like chairs there sat a figure looking at him gravely—the figure of an old, old man.

Yet there was no surprise in the boy's fast-beating heart; there was a thrill of pleasure and excitement only, a feeling of satisfaction. He had known quite well the figure would be there, known also it would look like this exactly. He stepped forward on to the floor of stone without a trace of fear or trembling, holding the precious cane in two hands now before him, as though to present it to its owner. He felt proud and pleased. He had run risks for this.

And the figure rose quietly to meet him, advancing in a stately manner over the hard stone floor. The eyes looked gravely, sweetly down at him, the aquiline nose stood out. Tim knew him perfectly: the knee-breeches of shining satin, the gleaming buckles on the shoes, the neat dark stockings, the lace and ruffles about neck and wrists, the colored waistcoat opening so widely—all the details of the picture over father's mantelpiece, where it hung between two Crimean bayonets, were reproduced in life before his eyes as last. Only the polished cane with the ivory handle was not there.

Tim went three steps nearer to the advancing figure and held out both his hands with the cane laid crosswise on them.

"I've brought it, great-grandpapa," he said, in a faint but clear and steady tone; "here it is."

And the other stooped a little, put out three fingers half concealed by falling lace, and took it by the ivory handle. He made a courtly bow to Tim. He smiled, but though there was pleasure, it was a grave, sad smile. He spoke then: the voice was slow and very deep. There was a delicate softness in it, the suave politeness of an older day.

"Thank you," he said; "I value it. It was given to me by my grandfather. I forgot it when I ——" His voice grew indistinct a little.

"Yes?" said Tim.

"When I—left," the old gentleman repeated.

"Oh," said Tim, thinking how beautiful and kind the gracious figure was.

The old man ran his slender fingers carefully along the cane, feeling the polished surface with satisfaction. He lingered specially over the smoothness of the ivory handle. He was evidently very pleased.

"I was not quite myself—er—at the moment," he went on gently; "my memory failed me somewhat." He sighed, as though an immense relief was in him.

"I forget things, too—sometimes," Tim mentioned sympathetically. He simply loved his great-grandfather. He hoped—for a moment—he would be lifted up and kissed. "I'm *awfully* glad I brought it," he added—"that you've got it again."

The other turned his kind grey eyes upon him; the smile on his face was full of gratitude as he looked down.

"Thank you, my boy. I am truly and deeply indebted to you. You courted danger for my sake. Others have tried before, but the

Nightmare Passage—er ——" He broke off. He tapped the stick firmly on the stone flooring, as thought to test it. Bending a trifle, he put his weight upon it. "Ah!" he exclaimed with a short sigh of relief, "I can now ——"

His voice again grew indistinct; Tim did not catch the words.

"Yes?" he asked again, aware for the first time that a touch of awe was in his heart.

"— get about again," the other continued very low. "Without my cane," he added, the voice failing with each word the old lips uttered, "I could not . . . possibly . . . allow myself . . . to be seen. It was indeed . . . . deplorable . . . unpardonable of me . . . to forget in such a way. Zounds, sir . . . ! I—I . . ."

His voice sank away suddenly into a sound of wind. He straightened up, tapping the iron ferrule of his cane on the stones in a series of loud knocks. Tim felt a strange sensation creep into his legs. The queer words frightened him a little.

The old man took a step towards him. He still smiled, but there was a new meaning in the smile. A sudden earnestness had replaced the courtly, leisurely manner. The next words seemed to blow down upon the boy from above, as though a cold wind brought them from the sky outside.

Yet the words, he knew, were kindly meant, and very sensible. It was only the abrupt change that startled him. Great-grandpapa, after all, was but a man! This distant sound recalled something in him to that outside world from which the cold wind blew.

"My eternal thanks to you," he heard, while the voice and face and figure seemed to withdraw deeper and deeper into the heart of the mighty chamber. "I shall not forget your kindness and your courage. It is a debt I can, fortunately, one day repay . . . . But now you had best return, and with dispatch. For your head and arm lie heavily on the table, the documents are scattered, there is a cushion fallen . . . and my son's son is in the house . . . Farewell! You had best leave me quickly. See! *She* stands behind you, waiting. Go with her! Go now . . . !"

The entire scene had vanished even before the final words were uttered. Tim felt empty space about him. A vast, shadowy Figure bore him through it as with mighty wings. He flew, he rushed, he remembered nothing more—until he heard another voice and felt a heavy hand upon his shoulder.

"Tim, you rascal! What are you doing in my study? And in the dark, like this!"

He looked up into his father's face without a word. He felt dazed. The next minute his father had caught him up and kissed him.

"Ragamuffin! How did you guess I was coming back to-night?" He shook him playfully and kissed his tumbling hair. "And you've been asleep, too, into the bargain. Well—how's everything at home—eh?

Jack's coming back from school to-morrow, you know, and . . ."

Jack came home, indeed, the following day, and when the Easter holidays were over, the governess stayed abroad and Tim went off to adventures of another kind in the preparatory school for Wellington. Life slipped rapidly along with him; he grew into a man; his mother and his father died; Jack followed them within a little space; Tim inherited, married, settled down into his great possessions—and opened up the Other Wing. The dreams of imaginative boyhood all had faded; perhaps he had merely put them away, or perhaps he had forgotten them. At any rate, he never spoke of such things now, and when his Irish wife mentioned her belief that the old country house possessed a family ghost, even declaring that she had met an Eighteenth Century figure of a man in the corridors, "an old, old man who bends down upon a stick"—Tim only laughed and said:

"That's as it ought to be! And if these awful land taxes force us to sell some day, a respectable ghost will increase the market value."

But one night he woke and heard a tapping on the floor. He sat up in bed and listened. There was a chilly feeling down his back. Belief had long since gone out of him; he felt uncannily afraid. The sound came nearer and nearer; there were light footsteps with it. The door opened—it opened a little wider, that is, for it already stood ajar—and there upon the threshold stood a figure that it seemed he knew. He saw the face as with all the vivid sharpness of reality. There was a smile upon it, but a smile of warning and alarm. The arm was raised. Tim saw the slender hand, lace falling down upon the long, thin fingers, and in them, tightly gripped, a polished cane. Shaking the cane twice to and fro in the air, the face thrust forward, spoke certain words, and— vanished. But the words were inaudible; for, though the lips distinctly moved, no sound, apparently, came from them.

And Tim sprang out of bed. The room was full of darkness. He turned the light on. The door, he saw, was shut as usual. He had, of course, been dreaming. But he noticed a curious odor in the air. He sniffed it once or twice—then grasped the truth. It was a smell of burning!

Fortunately, he awoke just in time. . . .

He was acclaimed a hero for his promptitude. After many days, when the damage was repaired, and nerves had settled down once more into the calm routine of country life, he told the story to his wife—the entire story. He told the adventure of his imaginative boyhood with it. She asked to see the old family cane. And it was this request of hers that brought back to memory a detail Tim had entirely forgotten all these years. He remembered it suddenly again—the loss of the cane, the hubbub his father kicked up about it, the endless, futile search. For the stick had never been found, and Tim, who was questioned very closely concerning it, swore with all his might that he had not the smallest notion where it was. Which was, of course, the truth.

THE END